Advance Praise for

America's First Daughter

"A delectable and poignant read. . . . It deftly draws on the volatile atmosphere of Jefferson's time, recounting his daughter's little-known story—a heroine tested to the limit, loaded with grit and determination. All the right chords are struck here. You're going to want to read slow and savor this one. Bravo."

—Steve Berry, *New York Times* bestselling author of
The Jefferson Key

"A triumphant, controversial, and fascinating plunge into the complexities of Revolutionary America, where women held power in subtle ways and men hid dangerous secrets. You'll never look at Jefferson or his legacy the same way again."

—C. W. Gortner, bestselling author of
Mademoiselle Chanel

"Painstakingly researched, beautifully hewn, compulsively readable—this enlightening literary journey takes us from Monticello to Revolutionary Paris to the Jefferson White House, revealing remarkable historical details and dark family secrets, and bringing to life the colorful cast of characters who conceived of our new nation. A must-read."

—Allison Pataki, *New York Times* bestselling author of
The Accidental Empress

"*America's First Daughter* is the story of a generation caught between the past and the future of a nation, and illuminates how the actions of one woman managed to sustain a family in spite of the consequences of both privilege and poverty. Not since *Gone with the Wind* has a single-volume family saga so brilliantly portrayed the triumphs, trials, and sins of a family in the American South."

—Erika Robuck, bestselling author of *Hemingway's Girl* and *The House of Hawthorne*

"Fiction can go boldly where history treads warily. In this compelling, poignant novel, Stephanie Dray and Laura Kamoie open the door into the heart of Martha Jefferson Randolph, the motherless daughter, long-suffering wife, devoted mother, and passionate protector of her famous father's lies, secrets, and silences. A remarkable and insightful achievement."

—Virginia Scharff, author of *The Women Jefferson Loved*

"*America's First Daughter* brings a turbulent era to vivid life. All the conflicts and complexities of the Early Republic are mirrored in Patsy's story. It's breathlessly exciting and heartbreaking by turns—a personal and political page-turner."

—Donna Thorland, author of *The Turncoat*

"I didn't realize how starved I was for a beautifully written American historical until I read *America's First Daughter*. . . . Laced with intricate detailing, plumped with authentic letters, and filled with plenty of fast-paced, harrowing scenes, Dray and Kamoie nailed it!"

—Heather Webb, author of *Rodin's Lover*

America's First Daughter

America's First Daughter

Stephanie Dray & Laura Kamoie

wm

WILLIAM MORROW
An Imprint of HarperCollins*Publishers*

AMERICA'S FIRST DAUGHTER. Copyright © 2016 by Stephanie Dray and Laura Kamoie. All rights reserved. Printed in the United States of America. No part of this book may be used or reproduced in any manner whatsoever without written permission except in the case of brief quotations embodied in critical articles and reviews. For information address HarperCollins Publishers, 195 Broadway, New York, NY 10007.

HarperCollins books may be purchased for educational, business, or sales promotional use. For information please e-mail the Special Markets Department at SPsales@harpercollins.com.

FIRST EDITION

Designed by Diahann Sturge

Library of Congress Cataloging-in-Publication Data has been applied for.

ISBN 978-0-06-234726-8

16 17 18 19 20 OV/RRD 10 9 8

To friendship and perseverance

Note to the Reader

DURING HIS LIFETIME Thomas Jefferson wrote more than eighteen thousand letters. It is through these that we framed this story, and took almost all of his dialogue. Whenever possible, for Jefferson, his daughter, and other historical figures, we quote directly from letters and other primary sources, all of which reflect the biases, prejudices, and political opinions of the time period. However, because the language of the eighteenth century was so stilted and opaque, we've taken the liberty of correcting spelling, grammar, and otherwise editing, abridging, or modernizing the prose in the interest of clarity.

Monticello, 5 April 1823
From Thomas Jefferson to Robert Walsh

*The letters of a person, especially of one whose business
has been chiefly transacted by letters, form the only full
and genuine journal of his life.*

July 5, 1826

SONS OF A REVOLUTION FIGHT FOR LIBERTY. They give blood, flesh, limbs, their very lives. But daughters . . . we sacrifice our eternal souls. This I am sure of, as I stand in the quiet emptiness of my father's private chambers.

I'm here now because my father is dead and buried.

And I'm left to make sense of it all.

My gaze drifts from the alcove bed where Papa drew his last breaths to his private cabinet beyond to the adjustable mahogany drawing desk he brought from Paris so many years before. Light filters down on me from the skylight built into the soaring ceiling and plays off the mirrors to make me feel as an actor upon a stage, playing a secret role.

Even knowing that he'll never return, I hesitate to settle into the red leather swivel armchair upon which my father struggled to write his letters, fewer and fewer every year. His hands, his eyesight, and his endurance all failed him in the end. But never his intellect; *that* he had to the last.

From between the pages of a leather-bound book on his revolving book stand, I find a sketch. A drawing of an obelisk monument and tombstone to be inscribed with what he wished to be remembered for—and not a word more.

THOMAS JEFFERSON
AUTHOR OF THE DECLARATION OF AMERICAN INDEPENDENCE
OF THE STATUTE OF VIRGINIA FOR RELIGIOUS FREEDOM
AND FATHER OF THE UNIVERSITY OF VIRGINIA

I brush my fingertips over the sketch and imagine the coarse granite that will bear these words and stand eternal guardian over Papa's final resting place. Alas, memories are made of more than inscriptions in stone. They're made, too, of the words we leave behind. And my father left so many.

Most of his meticulously ordered, copied, and cataloged letters are stored in wooden cabinets here in his chambers. It will take time to go through them all, but time is all I have now. So I start with the earliest letters, warmed to hold the fading pages in my hands, overcome with pride at seeing his confident script soaring so eloquently across the yellowed paper.

A glass-paned door opens behind me from the direction of the greenhouse where my father's mockingbirds sing, and I swivel in the chair, startled to come face-to-face with my father's lover. Sally Hemings doesn't knock, nor does she apologize for the intrusion. She strides into the space as if she belongs here. And she does. For as much as my father cherished the seclusion of this sanctum sanctorum, almost until his last breath, this was her domain.

But now Thomas Jefferson is gone, and Sally and I have come, at last, to the final reckoning between us. We stand, two aging matriarchs amidst his books, scientific instruments, and a black marbled obelisk clock—the one over his bed that counted down the minutes of his glorious life and now counts down the moments until we will follow him.

Sally, who bears a tawny resemblance to my lovely, petite mother, wears a crisp white apron over the gown she sewed from colorful calico. And she surveys the space much as I did moments ago. Silently, I rise to my feet, towering over her in my dark and somber gown, with hair that has gone from red to reddish brown—the image of my father.

In the reflection of the gilt mirror, we are matched reflections of the ghosts in this room. But it's my father's presence that we both feel now. I suppose some might say she was his beautiful mulatto slave wife and I the plain white wife of his parlor. We both birthed children for him: hers of his bed and his body; mine as a daughter of his bloodline, for his legacy.

He loved us both.

But only his love for me can be remembered.

Standing self-possessed as an ancient priestess, holding a bundle of relics collected from her life with my father, Sally informs me, "I'm taking these." A jeweled shoe buckle Papa wore as the American minister in France. An inkwell that serves, perhaps, as a remembrance of the immortal words he wrote. An old discarded pair of spectacles. Holding them tight, she doesn't say why she wants them. Perhaps it's because it was through those spectacles that he looked at the world and saw her.

I see her, too.

With black glossy hair shot through with only a little gray, the long length pulled back in a chignon at her neck, Sally possesses a beauty that hasn't faded. Is it sadness in her expression for the loss of a great man who left us both alone and in ruin? Or is it defiant triumph?

I cannot know, so my gaze drops to the bundle in her hands and I nod. She's entitled to the spectacles. She's entitled to more than he gave her—more than *I* can give her.

She nods, too, the culmination of a lifetime of conversation between us—sometimes spoken aloud, sometimes in passing glances and measured silences. But now we have nothing left to say. Sally looks one last time at the alcove and my eyes follow the direction of hers, taking note of how his bed sits between his private dressing room and his study—caught between his private and public life, just as he was.

Just as Sally and I have been.

Finally, she shakes her head, as if pulling herself from a memory, and steps toward me. With quick, deft fingers, she unlaces the ribbon at her hip where the key to this room has dangled for nearly forty years. She surrenders it to me, just as my father surrendered to me the fate of everything and everyone that once belonged to him.

Our hands meet in the exchange of the key—her bronzed fingers against my pale, freckled ones—and it feels like a circle closing. We've made this whole journey together, from the time we were innocent children on my father's mountain when this grand house was a mere shadow of itself. I meet her eyes wondering if she knows the sin I'm about to commit and if she would give her blessing, or if she dreads it like I do. But Sally's eyes are like hardened amber in which secrets are preserved but trapped beyond reach.

She doesn't grant permission, nor does she ask it anymore.

She merely walks away.

And I let her go, because she's a part of the story that must remain untold.

I'm then alone again in the quiet of this sacred place where my father's belongings remain exactly as he left them, as if awaiting his return. The silence is suffocating in both its finality and protection, like a cloak that shelters me against a storm, that protects my very nation.

Returning to his desk, I take my seat once more. And I set my mind to the task I and I alone must do.

For my father was the author of our Independence. His pen unleashed one revolution after another by declaring *that all men are created equal, that they are endowed by their creator with certain unalienable rights, that among these are life, liberty, and the pursuit of happiness. That to secure these rights, governments are instituted among men, deriving their just powers from the consent of the governed.*

Deceptively simple words—the greatest words he ever wrote.

Perhaps the greatest words anyone has *ever* written.

Words that inspired men to pledge their lives and fortune to the cause, that inspired women to make countless sacrifices, and that inspired nations to embark upon an experiment of freedom. My father's words gave voice to a movement. His voice was the voice of a nation. A voice that changed the world.

Who am I to censor that voice?

I am a daughter who must see to it that he is remembered exactly the way he wanted to be. I recall the instructions he'd written for his tombstone: *and not a word more.*

Which is why I light the wick of a candle in one of the holders— ingeniously, and somewhat dangerously, fastened to the arms of my father's chair. And with shaking hands, I hold one of his sacred letters above the flame. In so doing, I feel the heat, as if a prelude to hell's fires awaiting me.

But I have defied God before.

My heart is already heavy with sins and secrets and betrayals. I'm stained with the guilt of slavery. I have counted as a necessary sacrifice the blood of patriots. I have denied the truth written upon my own skin in the black and blue ink of bruises. I have vouched for the character of men without honor. I have stayed silent to avoid speaking the truth. What is one more silence when it preserves all we have sacrificed for?

That will be my legacy.

The service I render my country.

For I'm not only my father's daughter, but also a daughter of the nation he founded. And protecting both is what I've always done.

Part One

The Dutiful Daughter

Chapter One

Charlottesville, 29 May 1781
From Thomas Jefferson to the Marquis de Lafayette

I sincerely and anxiously wish you may prevent General Cornwallis from engaging your army till you are sufficiently reinforced and able to engage him on your own terms.

BRITISH! BRITISH!" These words flew with blood and spittle from the gasping mouth of our late-night visitor, a rider who awakened our household with the clatter of horse hooves and the pounding of his fist upon the door. "Leave Monticello now or find yourself in chains."

Still shaking off the fog of sleep, my eight-year-old heart could've kept time with a hummingbird's wings as I stared down from the stairway to where my father greeted our late-night guest wearing only a pair of hastily donned calfskin breeches and a quilted Indian gown of blue. "Are you certain the British are so near?" Papa asked.

Standing in the open doorway, bathed in the light of a slave's lantern, the rider panted for breath. His bloodstained hunting shirt was slashed at the shoulder, leather leggings spattered with mud. And his face . . . oh, his face. It was a grotesque mask of burrs and blood, red and cut open in a dozen places, as if he'd been whipped by every branch in our forest during his frantic ride. "Tarleton and his dragoons are very close, Governor Jefferson," he said, still gasping and wild-eyed. "Neither the militia nor the Marquis de Lafayette and his army will arrive in time to defend us. You must go now or be captured."

My scalp prickled with fear and I clutched the railing tighter. The men of the household—many of them members of the Virginia legislature who recently sought refuge at Monticello—stumbled into the entryway in various states of undress, some shouting in panic. My little sister Polly whimpered, and I put my arm around her shaking shoulders, both of us still in our bed gowns. I softly shushed her so I could hear the conversation below, but I already understood more than the adults thought I did.

How close are the British soldiers? How many? And what will they do if they find us? These questions raced through my mind as more of the plantation's servants spilled into the space, as anxious as we were, though perhaps in a different way. For I'd heard the men say the British promised the slaves freedom.

Sally, my friend and playmate, and a slave girl just my age, tucked herself into the far corner. Her amber eyes were carefully shielded, hiding whether she felt fear or excitement. My mother, however, wore her alarm like a shroud. Though she'd taken the time to dress in frock and mob cap, her skin was pale, her hazel eyes wide with panic. "The British? How near?" Mama asked, the candlestick shaking in her hand.

Only Papa was serene in the face of the coming danger. Looking from the men to Mama, he straightened to his full height—and he was the tallest man I knew, with ginger hair and piercing blue eyes that shone with fierce, quiet power. He held up his hand to silence the room. "Worry not, my friends. The mountains and darkness will delay the British," he said, the certainty of his words calming the panic. He turned to the servants and spoke with a reassuring authority that reminded us all he was master of the plantation. "Martin and Caesar, secure the valuables. Robert, ready a carriage to take my wife and children away after they've had some breakfast—"

"There's no time, sir," the rider dared to argue. "The British are already in Charlottesville. They're coming to burn Monticello."

Burn Monticello? My gaze darted about the brick-walled rooms of our plantation house—cluttered even then, in its first Palladian incarnation, with Papa's cherished artifacts, marble busts and gilt-framed paintings, red silk draperies and a pianoforte, books and buffalo robes. Would all of it go up in a blaze of fire?

My father and mother exchanged a tense glance. Turning to his visitors, Papa said, "Gentlemen, you must forgive my lack of hospitality and reconvene elsewhere. Make haste. My servants are at your disposal."

The room erupted in a flurry of motion. The slaves hurried about hiding the valuables. Metal clanked from the direction of the dining room, the sound of the silver forks, spoons, cups, and candlesticks being stuffed into pillowcases. Mama called Polly and me down to her. We rushed to her side, and she swiftly bundled Polly into her arms, snatching me by the hand and rushing us out into the damp night. My heart galloped as my bare feet scrabbled on the cold ground and I could *feel* my mother's answering pulse pounding as she tugged me with a cold, clammy hand.

Mama had been in poor health since the recent loss of a baby, and she couldn't hide her trembling from Papa as he hurried us to our carriage. "Hush," he said, though she'd not spoken. Pressing his forehead against Mama's, he murmured softly to her and I wished I could hear what he said. All the commotion—heavy feet trampling our flower beds, horses whinnying and jangling in their bridles, and men stuffing papers into saddlebags— obscured whatever words my parents shared. But anyone watching would know that their whispered words were laced with passionate devotion. Then, Papa kissed Mama and released her into the carriage.

"Papa!" I cried. "Aren't you coming with us?"

"Don't fret, Patsy," he said, reaching into the carriage to stroke my cheek and brush away a tendril of ginger hair, just like his. "I'll secure my papers then follow on horseback."

But the rider had warned us to go *now*. The British would capture Papa if he stayed. I wasn't supposed to know that the king had branded my father a traitor nor that the British would hang him if they captured him. But more than once I'd overheard the legislators' fiery speeches ring through Monticello's halls, so fear crawled into my throat. "Come now, Papa. Or they'll catch you. They'll catch you!"

"Never," he replied with a soft, confident smile. If he was afraid, he didn't show it. "My escape route is well planned. I'll take Caractacus. There's no faster horse in Virginia."

The thought of him alone with enemies all around, the thought of us fleeing without him, the terror of never seeing him again— all of these horrid imaginings had my heart pounding so fast it was hard to breathe. I clutched at him. "Surely you won't send us alone."

Papa grasped a large satchel from the hands of a servant and passed it to my mother. "Be my brave girl. You won't be alone," he said, then called over his shoulder to a figure in shadow, and a reedy young man appeared at his side. In the faint light of the rising dawn, William Short, my mother's kinsman and one of the many men who idolized my father, stepped forward.

William. How strange it is to realize now that he was always with us. From the very start. From that first frantic moment when I learned what it truly meant to be the daughter of a revolutionary, William was there, at my side. . . .

In his twenty-second year, William Short boasted of being one of the youngest elected officials in Virginia, but he was no militiaman. He seemed a strange choice to guard us. Even so, Mama gave no protest when Mr. Short alighted our carriage with a sprightly hop, and without further ado, commanded our driver to be off.

"Ha!" the driver shouted at the horses and our carriage lurched forward onto the road leading away from Monticello. Leading away from Papa, who stood tall atop his mountain, unwilling to yet surrender.

~~~~~~

OUR CARRIAGE JUMPED and bumped down the rough road, southward. Thrown together inside, we clasped one another tight, my right hand in Mama's, my left arm hugging Polly. A stunned, scared breathlessness rendered all of us quiet. With her knuckles white around the handle of a satchel of our belongings, Mama lifted her wavering voice to finally ask Mr. Short, "Where will we go?"

"John Coles's place on the Green Mountain," he replied, a wary eye on the road. The certainty in Mr. Short's voice calmed me a little. Mama released a shallow breath, as if the words provided her a bit of ease, as well.

We'd taken supper at Mr. Coles's Enniscorthy estate before. The memory of thick ham steaks and rye bread ought to have made my stomach rumble, for we'd not had breakfast, but the ache in my belly wasn't hunger. To my terrified eyes, the tree branches flying past the carriage window reached for us like the gnarled hands of death. And in the faintest glow of morning, unable to tear my gaze from the blurred view, I gasped at every red flower or rock in a ruddy hue. "Is that a redcoat?" I asked Mr. Short. "Are the dragoons ahead of us on the road?"

Squinting to see, Mr. Short replied, "The dragoons wear green. Worry not, Patsy. We departed in time." He peered over his shoulder at me, the ghost of a smile on his lips, and winked. Ordinarily, that kind reassurance would've lured a returning smile, but I saw the nod he gave to Mama and feared he only told me what I wished to hear.

Another hour passed before we heard the thunder of horse hooves behind us. When we did, Mama gasped and pushed me and Polly down to the carriage floor. While my sister cleaved tight to my chest, I saw the glint of a pistol in Mr. Short's hand.

"Stay silent, whatever comes," he said, his voice thin and shaky.

Still, Mr. Short's arm was steady as he pulled himself up to the window of the carriage, ready to fire upon our enemies. Blood rushing past my ears, I waited for the blast.

Instead, the young man blew out a breath. "Mr. Jefferson!"

Relief flooded through me so hard and fast that I bit back a sob. I popped my head up over Mama's shoulder, never happier to hear Caractacus's furious whinny. The stallion's brown coat was slick with sweat and the froth on his lips told us how hard Papa must have ridden him to catch up with us.

"Halt!" Papa cried.

As the carriage slowed and Papa rode up to the window, my mother rose up, shaking with relief. "Pray tell me it's a false report."

"I cannot." Papa sat tall in the saddle like the skilled horseman he was, the leather saddlebags beneath him bulging with papers and the violin he never journeyed without. My eyes scoured over him for any sign he'd come to some harm, but he appeared only a little winded. "British horses have come to Monticello. I rode up Montalto and saw them in my spyglass."

I gasped. Why had he remained behind so long? When everyone else was fleeing in a mad dash, had my father gone up the adjoining mountain to look for the enemy by himself? Whatever he saw convinced him to run. More than that, to worry that we might still be in danger. "I'll ride ahead to scout for enemy soldiers," Papa said.

Mama shook her head. "But—"

"Don't stop for anything," Papa told us. "If you *are* stopped, say you don't know me. Say you're from another state. Say you're passing through to see a kinsman."

Tears stung the backs of my eyes. He was asking us to lie—a thing forbidden by God's laws. To ask it, he must've believed Mama would be safer if she were another man's wife. That I'd be safer if I were someone else's daughter. Perhaps anyone else's daughter.

Mama looked away, as if in agony at the thought of denying him. And my mind rebelled at the very thought.

"Patsy," my father said, reading my mind as he so often did. "You can pretend, can't you?"

His question was more a command. I nodded even while my heart ached. But Papa was relying on us. *Yes. I can pretend.* Not only because he asked it of me, but because, for the first time in my life, I understood that a lie could protect those I loved.

My father rode off, leaving a cloud of dust in his wake. The carriage lurched forward a moment later. When would we reach safety? I didn't remember Enniscorthy being so far. Fear and anticipation made me wonder if we'd *ever* get there, but at long last, morning light filtered through the trees and made a welcoming picture of the big two-story plantation house nestled amongst the mountains.

Enniscorthy.

Climbing from the carriage, my body felt battered and bruised. Mama fussed with my hair beneath my nightcap, but Mr. Coles and his family cared little about our disheveled appearance and quickly ushered us into their home. In the room provided to us, Mama instructed me to wash in a bucket of water while she sponged the dirt from the road off Polly. Then she found clothes for us from her satchel.

By the time she had tugged a white frock dress over my head and tied it with a pretty blue sash, Papa had arrived. He gave us all cheerful kisses atop our heads, as if the British hadn't just chased us from our home. And then we sat down to a meal.

Mama, voice still wavering, thanked the lady of the household again for our food and shelter. With a trembling hand, she fed Polly spoonfuls of porridge, but took for herself only the tiniest bites, washing it down with sips of tea that our host vowed had been honestly smuggled, without tax or duty paid upon it to the British.

Mimicking my mother, I tried to be dainty and nibble at my food, but Papa and Mr. Short gulped down hearty portions of eggs and smoked sausages and bread. The last had been scarce since the start of the war and the prices of food quite high, which made us even more grateful for the hospitality when we were invited to stay. But Papa said we weren't far enough away yet from the reach of the British dragoons.

I dropped my spoon. Weren't we safe yet, having come all this way? Apparently, Papa believed the British were still chasing us through our own countryside like outlaws. And before I could make sense of what was happening, we were off again, with Papa scouting ahead for enemy soldiers and Mr. Short guarding our carriage with his pistol.

I wished I'd eaten more porridge. Hunger squeezed my belly, thirst clawed at my throat, and sweat dampened my hair as our arduous journey continued under the hot summer sun. Dust kicked up under our carriage wheels, and I was grimy with it. But I dared not complain. Not of grime, not of hunger, not of anything else.

For Papa was unshakeable despite the danger. When he circled back to mark our progress, he rode alongside our carriage, pointing out the beautiful natural settings. "We'll remember this as a grand adventure one day," he said. And though Mama's lips tightened at the assertion, I drew strength from Papa's bravery.

But Mama grew paler each time he took us off the main roads, leading us into thick woods where we crossed streams and ramshackle bridges that didn't seem as if they could possibly bear our weight. If our wheels broke through the planks, we were in danger of going down into the water with our carriage, horses and all.

We were afraid to cross, but our terror of what lay behind us was even greater.

Finally, when we reached the dark green rush of Rockfish River, Mama said she could go no farther. Since the death of her infant a few weeks before, she'd been sick in body and heart. Now she appeared ready to swoon. Worried for her, I dampened a kerchief using water from our carved wooden canteen then gently dabbed at her cheeks and forehead. "All will be well, Mama. Just like Papa said."

With a weary smile, she tucked strands of ginger behind my ear. "I know, child."

Finally, we came upon a small cabin in the woods. I peered out of the carriage window as Papa knocked at the door and explained our situation. The owner scowled. "No room for you here, Gov'ner." The man said the last word contemptuously, spitting tobacco juice into the carpet of fallen leaves and pine needles surrounding his shack. "If the king wants you strung up, he'll have you strung up, and I won't risk harboring fugitives."

I gasped, certain Papa would dress down the crude frontiersman for speaking to him this way, but instead, Papa calmly said, "I beg of you only take in my wife and daughters. I won't stay. It's near nightfall and—"

The man abruptly slammed the wooden door in my father's face.

"*Tories,*" Mr. Short muttered like a curse.

Papa said nothing though his jaw was clenched as he mounted Caractacus again. Where could we go now, trapped on this side of the river without shelter? With sunset nearing and a river too treacherous to cross, we'd be forced to sleep the night in these woods where bears prowled and British soldiers might ambush us.

Papa insisted we keep riding, and at length, we came upon a tavern, Joplin's Ordinary. There Papa bought food and supplies, and asked for help fording the river. Mr. Joplin himself offered to guide us to shelter beyond the river, but Papa hesitated, as if the words of the angry frontiersman were still ringing in his ears. "There's no need to risk yourself further, Mr. Joplin."

But Mr. Joplin insisted. "You're of too much consequence to the country to risk your capture, Mr. Jefferson."

As these words echoed in the forest, Papa might've lifted his head with pride. Instead, his eyes fell to the reins in his hands, as if burdened by them. And the words sank into me with an unaccountable weight.

When I think back, perhaps I should remember with bitterness the man who turned us away and who didn't care if the king strung up my papa. But I prefer to remember the way our other neighbors helped us—the dangers they faced for our sake—because it fills me with pride in my countrymen. And because it reminds me that I'm *justified* in honoring them and their cause even through deeds that might otherwise deserve censure.

It was a Virginia militiaman who took us in that night after Mr. Joplin guided us across the river. Gravely, the militiaman told Papa that he worried important state papers and prisoners had fallen into the hands of the British. I tried to listen, but with my mother's warmth and softness beside me on the straw-stuffed mattress, the voices faded to a low hum. And with the faint scent of my mother's lavender water as I buried my nose against her shoulder, I lost the battle against sleep.

The next morning, awakened by the crow of a rooster, I tried to remember where I was. The important thing, I supposed, was that there'd been another dawn, and Papa hadn't yet been caught by the British. We were on the road again before the glow of sunrise, making our way farther into the countryside. And good thing, too, because we would later learn that Tarleton's dragoons were pursuing us, knifing open feather beds, breaking mirrors, and setting fire to homes along the way, hoping to make someone give Papa up.

When we stopped at Mr. Rose's house, slaves hurried out of their cabins to fetch water for our horses. Inside, the smell of warm bread nearly dizzied me and tempted me to forget the danger. *We're safe.* The thought brought more comfort than the food. For who would find us here, hidden in the mountains? Papa must've felt it was safe here, too, because as he cleared his plate he asked if his wife and children might lodge with the Rose family until he returned.

My stomach fell, and I lifted my gaze from the bread I'd been stuffing into my mouth. Mama froze beside me and gripped the edge of the table. Frowning, Mr. Rose said, "You can't be thinking of going back, Mr. Jefferson."

"Lafayette will come to drive the British from Virginia. Until then, we must know where the enemy is," Papa replied, calmly.

But Mr. Rose wasn't reassured by my father's faith in the young French nobleman who was now commanding part of Washington's army. In fact, Mr. Rose pounded the table, making me jump. "If the Virginia militia would only turn out!"

Papa never approved of loud shows of temper, and stared into his cider. "But they haven't. Even the threat of court-martial hasn't worked. I have no military experience, but even I know this: the whole of the British army may be descending upon us and we cannot guess if we'll prevail . . . or if we must sue for peace . . . without knowing our enemy's strength or whereabouts."

"To go back is folly, Thomas," my mother said. We all turned to her in surprise that she'd inserted herself into the men's conversation, contradicted my father, and called him by his given name in mixed company. But the color on her cheeks told me that she was in high temper. "They're hunting you, Thomas. They're *hunting* you."

Papa rested his freckled hand atop hers. "My dearest, the British are rounding up every legislator and patriot in the state. I am but one more."

"No, sir," Mr. Short broke in. "That's not true."

It seemed to me at the time that if there were anyone less likely than my mother to challenge Papa, it would've been my mother's unassuming kinsman, Mr. Short. But, the truth is, William has always argued for what he believed was right. Even when it cost him. Even when it frightened him. Maybe even especially then. And that day, when we were all fugitives together, Mr. Short insisted, "The British want you because you're the author of our independence."

I knew this about my father, of course. About how soldiers were, as we spoke, fighting and bleeding for the ideas my father so ably expressed in the Declaration of Independence. But the pursuit of the British, the willingness of our neighbors to risk themselves, and Mr. Short's vehemence gave me a new understanding of my father's importance. Short leaned forward, intently. "Mr. Jefferson, if the British take you, they'll take Virginia. And if they take Virginia, it will be the end of our revolution."

Hope that this argument would change Father's mind about going back made my heart thunder against my breast. Alas, Mr. Short's words seemed to have the opposite effect intended. Papa squared his shoulders, a determined glint in his eye. "I'm the governor. Or at least, I was until a few days ago. There are others better suited to this emergency, but there can be no revolution without patriots willing to risk themselves."

The bread dropped from my hand to my plate, the remains of it like sawdust in my mouth. Papa's mind was made up. He'd summoned his courage. He'd go back, no matter the risk. . . .

My father's enemies now claim that when his mettle was tested in wartime, he faltered. Their censure forced him to speak of it ever after as an *unfortunate passage* in his conduct. But I was there. I witnessed those days as some of his most courageous moments. And though it was plain to me that my mother wasn't moved by his high-minded sentiments, I was. I was as proud of him as I was terrified for him.

And I knew I'd never want to be *anyone* else's daughter.

WHILE WE AWAITED NEWS that the British had been pushed back or that Papa had been captured, Mama was short-tempered with us and declared we must make ourselves useful at the Rose household. Polly and I were sent off to help the slaves fetch water, churn butter, and sweep the floors. Mama herself was always on her feet, helping to cook breakfast and ease the burden on our kindly hosts. But after a week of this, when she was tending to the laundering of our dirtied clothes, she swayed and fell.

Mr. Short rushed to her side and gently lifted her. Together, we settled her into a rocking chair, where she struggled to recover herself. Given how recently Mama had lost her baby, she was apt to be sad and fragile. And the next day, she was still in that chair, needlework forgotten in her lap, when a rider approached the house.

At the sound of the horse hooves, Mr. Rose readied his musket and Mr. Short crouched by the window, pistol in hand. I froze, clutching a broom, wondering if I could wield it against a Redcoat if one should come through the door.

But then we heard Papa call to us.

Dropping my broom, I ran out to meet him. Though he'd been gone only a week, he looked thin and mangy. His skin was sunburnt and he'd traded his gentleman's clothing for the garb of a frontiersman. Clad in brown leather breeches, a hunting shirt open at the neck, and a black hat that shadowed his eyes, he dismounted Caractacus and grabbed me into his arms, carrying me all the way inside. I clung to him, burying my face in his neck as he entered the house.

From the rocking chair, Mama attempted a smile, but her lower lip wobbled. "Have Lafayette's forces fought back the British? Have we lost Virginia?" And when Papa's mouth thinned into a grim line, she asked, "Is it burned? Is Monticello gone?"

"Only some wine is missing," Papa told us, and relief had me heaving a long breath. But when Papa spoke next, there was ice in his words. "Would that I could say the same of Elk Hill." Elk Hill was one of Papa's other plantations where he grew corn and tobacco and raised livestock. "Elk Hill is left in absolute waste. The British burned the barns and fences, slit the throats of the youngest horses, and took everything. They carried off our crops, our livestock, and our people. At least thirty slaves are gone."

Mama gasped and I knew she worried most for her Hemings slaves. "What of those at Monticello?"

Setting me back down, Papa crossed to the rocker and squeezed Mama's hand. "Some were carried off, but most remain."

"Carried off?" Mr. Short asked with a strange intensity in his boyish gaze. "Or did they flee at the promise of freedom?"

Papa's jaw clenched, as if Mr. Short's question carried with it some note of impertinence. "If Cornwallis took them to give them their freedom, he'd have done right. But I fear he's only consigned them to death from smallpox in his camp."

Mr. Short put his pistol away and bowed his head. "Is the war lost then?"

My gaze flashed to Papa, dread squeezing my stomach.

Papa answered with scarcely disguised bitterness. "The war, I don't know, but my honor is certainly lost. They'll remember me as the governor of Virginia who let plumes of smoke rise over the James River for nearly thirty miles. And there's a nine-year-old girl the British soldiers—" Papa's eyes landed upon me, and because I was nearly nine years old myself, I was desperately curious to know what he'd been about to say. But he didn't finish. "I fear history will never relate the horrors committed by the British army."

"What of the remaining legislators?" Mr. Short asked after a moment. "Surely I'm not the only one who escaped."

"A few were captured. Most are gathering in the Old Trinity Church in Staunton. All things considered, our cause fared well." Despite his words, the etched lines on Papa's face made it clear the losses pained him. "Thanks to Captain Jouett's ride. Had he not warned us . . ."

Mr. Short nodded. "I must join the legislature. I'll carry your messages to them, sir."

I couldn't imagine Mr. Short riding through the woods by himself, even with a pistol in his belt. Papa was the son of a surveyor and knew the land, but Mr. Short was a bookish young man, so gentrified that even in exile, he still wore a lace cravat tight against his throat, as if expecting to pose for a portrait.

The same thought must've occurred to Papa. "It's too dangerous, William."

"Not as dangerous for me as for you," Mr. Short insisted. "Loan me a horse and I'll be out and back again within days."

"We won't be here," Papa replied, grim but resolved. "I'm taking my family into hiding."

And though Mama was still unwell and Polly kicked her little feet in a tantrum, we left that very day. We fled into the Blue Ridge Mountains, to Papa's wilderness property, the one in the shade of poplar trees. In those days, there wasn't a house there, only rude huts for the slaves and a two-room cabin for the overseer. No one came to greet us, for they'd no cause to know we might arrive. Nothing was ready for our comfort. Not even a fire. I thought of the sunny rooms at Monticello and our big warm feather beds, and worried that we might now spend all our days here, in a soot-stained cabin made of rough-hewn logs and a roof that leaked.

What's to become of us now? How long can we hide?

My father was a scientist, a scholar, and a Virginia gentleman, but in the days that followed, he set about repairing fences, thatching roofs, and hunting small game for our supper like a frontiersman. He was wry when presenting my mother with a rabbit for the stew she was trying to boil in our only pot. "Ah, Martha, the circumstances to which I've reduced you . . ."

Yet, Mama was strangely content. "On the eve of our wedding, I rode out with you in the worst winter storm to live in a small chamber of an unfinished house. We called it a Honeymoon Cottage, don't you remember? You were no great man of Virginia then, my dearest. But we were happy."

That's when I first knew my mother had heard enough of revolution and the sacrifice of patriots. Indeed, it seemed to be her singular mission to draw Papa into the delights of simple domestic life. Though the overseer's cabin was no proper home for a gentleman's family, Mama set up housekeeping. She had me down on my knees with her, scrubbing at the floorboards with a stiff brush. We hung quilts and beat dust out of them. And when

Papa had to leave to make his forays into the woods, Mama and I saw to it that there was a candle burning in the one window of the cottage to guide him back to us.

A few weeks later, harvest time for the wheat arrived, and Mama sent me with Papa to oversee the slaves toiling in our fields with sharp sickles. The women cut the stalks, beads of sweat running down their bare brown arms. Meanwhile, the shirtless dark-skinned men gathered the cut wheat into bundles, hauling the golden sheaves into the sun to dry.

I loved nothing more than riding atop majestic Caractacus with Papa, and though we were far away from our mountaintop home, it almost made me feel everything was just the way it should be.

But I knew it wasn't.

"Will the British find us, Papa?" I asked, peering up at him over my shoulder.

His strong arms tightened around me. "This farmstead came to me through your Grandfather Wayles. The British won't think to look here. . . ." he said, trailing off when he heard Mama singing from across the field where she scrubbed linens in a bucket.

Her voice carried sweetly, unaccompanied, until Papa joined in her song. At hearing his tenor, she smiled, and I felt his breath catch, as if she'd never smiled at him before. He loved her, maybe more than ever. And with her eyes on us, Papa used his heels to command his stallion to a proud canter. "Let's show your mother what Caractacus can do."

He urged the stallion into a gallop. The fence was no obstacle for the stallion, who flew up, up, and over with an ease that delighted me. I was still laughing with the thrill of it when we landed on the other side.

Then we heard a rattle. . . .

A coiled snake near its hooves made the stallion snort in fear, rearing up wildly. I held fast to the horse's black mane and my father used his body to keep me from falling. But in protecting me, Papa lost his balance, toppling from the horse. He threw his arm out to break his fall but came down hard upon his hand and howled in pain.

Caractacus trampled a circle and I tried desperately to calm him by digging my knees into his sides. Meanwhile, the overseer of the farm came running to help, several slaves at his back.

"Rattlesnake," Papa gritted out as the serpent slithered away.

The overseer grabbed the horse's reins and called to the closest slave. "Kill it, boy."

The sweat-soaked slave shook his head in fear and refusal as the serpent escaped into the woods.

Outraged, the overseer lifted his lash.

"Stay your whip!" Papa barked, cradling his injured hand against his chest as he slowly rose. "Everyone back to work."

As the slaves dispersed, I could scarcely feel my fingers, so tightly were they wound in the horse's mane. My heart still pounded with fear and thrill. The overseer, by contrast, was overcome with anger. Cheeks and jowls red, he said, "It does no good to be gentle with them, Mr. Jefferson. A firm hand is all the Negro understands."

Papa's voice pulled tight with pain and . . . something else. "What I understand is this: we're two white men, one gentlewoman, and two little girls on a secluded farmstead, hiding from an army promising freedom to the Negro."

My father's gaze darted to the men in our fields with sharp instruments in their hands, and a strange and sickly feeling stole over me. *Is my papa afraid of them? Afraid of his own slaves?* It was the first time I ever wondered such a thing.

Papa's wrist was bent at an ungainly angle. The overseer rode out to fetch a trustworthy doctor while Mama fretted that there might not be one so far from Charlottesville. It was nearly night when the doctor arrived to do his grisly business of resetting Papa's bones. After, Mama wrapped my father's wrist and gave him the last of our brandy for the pain. Upon orders from the physician, Papa was forbidden to ride or go out from our cabin for two weeks. Unless, of course, the British chased us from here.

I remember that in those weeks, Mama and Papa were tender with one another every moment of every day. Our meals were simple. Our days were long. I was forever keeping Polly from mischief. At night, in spite of his painful injury, Papa led us in cheerful song while Polly and I bundled together atop a little nest of quilts.

Kissing us good night, my father gave a sly smile. "Do you girls know how it was that I wooed and won your mother?"

Mama looked up from tucking the blankets around us with a sly smile of her own. "Mr. Jefferson, you're not going to keep our daughters awake with an immodest boast, are you?"

"Indeed, I am. You see, girls, I wooed your mother by making music with her in the parlor—me with my violin and tenor, she with her harpsichord and soprano. And when two other waiting suitors heard the beauty of our song, they left, vanquished, without another word, knowing they had heard the sound of true love."

With that, he kissed my mother's furiously blushing cheek. And, cleaving to one another, our little family, we could almost believe the British would never find us here.

Then one evening we heard the dreaded clatter of a horse's hooves up the path. From the window, I peered out to see it was a horse-drawn wagon. To my relief, William Short rode in the buggy seat—still wearing his now much-dirtied cravat—bearing corn, brandy, and chickens. And that wasn't all. Mr. Short had breathless news. "Tarleton has turned back to join up with Cornwallis, who is being harried by Lafayette. They're retreating, Mr. Jefferson. Thanks to Lafayette, the British are retreating!"

I squinted into the firelight, trying to make sense of Mr. Short's exhilarated glee. Retreating? Then . . . the British wouldn't capture and hang my papa! And whatever British soldiers had done to that nine-year-old girl, they wouldn't do to me. Tears of relief pricked at my eyes while Papa breathed out a long exhale. "What of the legislature?"

"We were able to convene a session." Mr. Short stared into his cup of brandy, as if he were reluctant to tell the rest. "A motion passed accusing you of having failed to defend Virginia. I argued on your behalf, Mr. Jefferson, but I was no match for the machinations of Patrick Henry. There'll be an investigation into your conduct."

My shoulders tensed in indignation. How could anyone question my father's defense of Virginia? No one had been braver! I remembered how he stood so tall, refusing to leave Monticello until everyone else had gone. How he went back to scout for soldiers . . .

Father groaned, as if this news caused him more agony than his injured wrist. "So, my honor *is* gone."

"Only imperiled," Mr. Short swiftly replied. "A thing that can be remedied if you accept an appointment to France. The Marquis de Lafayette sends word that your countrymen wish for you to represent us in Paris."

Renewed hope danced in Papa's eyes. "That *would* be a singular honor."

Paris? I could scarcely conceive of such a place! Would he take us with him?

But Mama's eyes went flat and hard. And when Mr. Short stepped out, tears slipped from beneath her long lashes. "No more, Thomas. I beg you."

He reached for her. "My dearest—"

"*Hear* me," she pleaded. "For this cause, I've endured long absences, followed you to cities far and wide, and sewn linen shirts for soldiers until my fingers bled. I've buried three children and been dragged from my sickbed and sent fleeing in the dead of night. Decline this offer. Retire to the tranquility of private life. Retire, I *beg* of you."

Papa put his hands in her hair, but shook his head. "I'm a gentleman of Virginia. To turn down this offer would give me more mortification than almost any other occurrence in my life. I've said that I'd serve my country even if it took me to hell—"

"Which it *has*," Mama replied, tartly.

And I dared not move or make a sound.

"Martha," he said, a plea for understanding in his voice. "I must defend my honor. That anyone should think me a coward or traitor inflicts a wound on my spirit which will only be cured by the all-healing grave."

The mention of the grave sent my mother's chin jerking up. She touched the locket at her throat, the one that held the hair of her dead babies. "At what cost, your honor?"

Papa flinched, as if he'd taken a blow. Then the fight went out of him. Staring at her fingers on that locket, he seemed to shrink, his shoulders rounding in defeat, and he sucked in a deep breath that sounded like surrender.

And I knew that my mother would have her way.

Brushing her wet cheeks with his thumbs, he murmured, "Leave off your tears, Martha. You have my promise. We'll go home to Monticello. We'll add children to our hearth. I'll retire to my farm, my books, and my family, from which nothing will evermore separate me."

It was a promise. And sometimes I wonder how differently everything might have been if he'd been able to keep it. What a different life we'd have lived. What a different woman I might've become.

What a different nation might have been built . . .

Chapter Two

Monticello, 20 May 1782
From Thomas Jefferson to James Monroe

Mrs. Jefferson has added another daughter to our family. She has been ever since dangerously ill.

I HOLD THIS LETTER IN SHAKING HANDS, the candle casting a golden glow over a bland description of an event that changed us forever. And though I am tempted to burn it because of the sheer pain it gives rise to, I am instead pulled into the memory of the promises that started it all.

Mama's auburn hair curled in fevered sweat against her pale cheek, her hazel eyes shadowed beneath a frilly morning cap. And from the confines of her sickbed, she whispered, "When I escape the unhappy pains of this world, Patsy, you must watch over your father."

She had to whisper it, because Papa would hear no one speak of her dying. Every day he asked if she was recovered enough to walk with him in the gardens. When she couldn't, he sent slaves to fetch flowers for her bedside. In May, it was yellow jonquil, purple hyacinth, orange lilies, and then red hollyhock. But by early autumn the perfume of crimson dwarf roses couldn't disguise the fetid scent of sickness in the room.

Since the birth of the baby Mama had borne after we'd returned from the wilderness, Mama had lingered in bed saying she'd never rise up again. Like Papa, I refused to believe her, but in this moment, she reached for my hand to convince me. My hand had always felt tiny in her palm, but now her hand seemed smaller, fragile.

I turned my head, so she wouldn't see my fear, and glimpsed the small room that opened at the head of her bed where my father spoke with Dr. Gilmer, who treated Mama and asked no more than to borrow some salt and sugar for his pains. Through all the months of my mother's illness, Papa was never farther from her than this.

The men's conversation was hushed and somber until some question forced my father to answer with bitter indignation. "No, I will not leave her. I've retired. My election to the Virginia legislature was without my consent, so let them arrest me and drag me to Richmond if they dare."

Dr. Gilmer took a step back at Papa's quiet ferocity. "I pray it doesn't come to that, Mr. Jefferson."

Still, my father seethed. "Offices of every kind, and given by every power, have been daily and hourly declined from the Declaration of Independence to this moment. No state has the *perpetual* right to the services of its members."

While my father lectured, my mother pulled me close, sighing, as if the scent of my hair were sweeter than her garden flowers. "Patsy, your father will need you all the days of his life. Promise you'll care for him."

I shook my head, blinded by a sudden flood of tears. When one of Papa's musical little mockingbirds died, Polly thought he'd come back again someday. But now, at ten years old, I knew that when my mother died, I wouldn't see her again until we met in heaven.

"Promise me," Mama insisted, eyelids sagging.

I swallowed painfully, once, twice, until finally a whisper ushered forth. "I promise, Mama. I'll care for him always."

The words seemed impossible and carried the weight of the world. And of course, now I know just how essential this promise—this duty—has been to my life.

At the sight of tears spilling over my lashes, Mama's soft hazel eyes went softer. "Don't grieve, Patsy. Don't live with an open wound on your spirit as a motherless child, not as I did. Be happy. That's what I want for you. You're my strong strapping girl, so like your father. You'll care for our little doll Polly, and our baby Lucy, too. Won't you?"

I wondered how I could. Polly was a willful child who never listened and Lucy was just a baby, crying for milk. Still, I couldn't deny my mother. "I'll try, Mama."

"That's my strong girl." She sank deeper into the feather bed, alarming me with the labored rasp of her breath. "Help your father through his sorrow."

I nodded because my throat hurt too much to speak. Mama motioned with a trembling finger toward a book on her night table. The volume was *Tristram Shandy,* one of my father's favorites. It was her habit to copy from the text, words that echoed the sentiments of her heart. With difficulty, she lifted herself against the pillows and insisted that I lay the tray with the book and feathered quill over her knees. When I did, she took the pen and dipped it in the inkwell before copying words in a spidery hand:

Time wastes too fast: every letter I trace tells me with what rapidity life follows my pen. The days and hours of it are flying over our heads like clouds of windy day never to return—more everything presses on—

She stopped there, too weary to go on. I took the quill from her shaking hand just as my father came in. His blue eyes were red-rimmed with exhaustion but he injected a false note of cheer into his voice. "What have we here, my dearest?" One glance at what she'd written and he blanched. "None of this, Martha. You only need rest, my love. You only need rest."

But by the next morning, my mother was plainly fighting a rest of the everlasting kind. She gasped through lips tinged with blue and our house servants drew near, as if straining to hear her last breath. These Hemings slaves had been with Mama since she was a child and some whispered they were kin. Though such things should never be spoken, much less repeated, on a plantation, I'd heard that Nance, Critta, and Sally were all my mother's sisters. That my grandfather Wayles got them upon their enslaved mother, Betty, who now stroked Mama's face as if she were her own daughter.

I didn't know if it was true but I knew better than to ask. What I knew was that in her final hours, my mother wanted the Hemingses near, and I was left to huddle by my Aunt Elizabeth's knees with the heat of the fireplace at my back. I didn't know what else I should do, but stayed silent for fear someone would usher me from the room if they remembered me there.

Papa drew his leather chair close so that he could hold my mother's hand. In a faltering voice, Mama told him everything she wanted done. She gave instructions for matters weighty and mundane. She was letting go of life, giving everything away. Even the little bronze bell she used to ring for servants, she gave to Sally, who pressed a cheek against her mistress's hand.

At last, my mother's gaze fell upon me. *Watch over your father when I am gone*, her eyes said, but I still couldn't believe that she'd go. "The children . . ." Mama wept.

My throat went tight, and I desperately wanted my father to help her—to make matters right, as he always did. But Papa's expression crumbled as if her sobs lashed against his spirit, and I knew with terrible certainty that not all things were in his power. Papa leaned to her, until their foreheads touched, their intimacy unbearably tender.

We ought to have left them alone, but none of us could move. We were, all of us, riveted by my mother's every halting word. She drew back and lifted three shaking fingers, spreading them for my father to see. "Three children we still have together," she said, with great difficulty. "I cannot die happy if I know my daughters must have a stepmother brought in over them."

A sound of anguish escaped my father's throat, as if he couldn't bear the thought of any other woman. There was no hesitation in him when he took my mother's limp hand to make his solemn vow. "Only you, Martha. I swear I'll have no other wife. Only you, my love."

My mother's chest hollowed in a long wheeze and tears squeezed from the corners of her eyes. She was beyond speech, but motioned as if she wished to write. At my mother's gesture, Sally was quick to obey. The slave girl jumped to fetch the tray with the book and the inkwell. Then Sally pressed the quill pen into my mother's unsteady hand. But my mother couldn't hold it. In exacting promises from us, Mama had used all the strength left in her.

Answering the silent plea in her eyes, my father wrapped his hand round her delicate fingers and finished writing the passage she began the day before.

—and every time I kiss thy hand to bid adieu, every absence which follows it, are preludes to that eternal separation which we are shortly to make!

At the sight of his handwriting in bold dark ink, my mother smiled. These were the words she wanted to leave for him. So he folded it and tucked it inside his coat against his heart, where he carried it the rest of his life.

Then my mother closed her eyes and did not open them again. I held my breath as her chest rose, fell, rose, then fell, until she was still. Perfectly still. And the world went quiet.

Her angelic beauty was bathed in the morning sunlight that filtered in from the tall window. Surely she *had* become an angel, I thought as tears blurred my vision and tightened my throat. My mournful cry broke free. The sound was echoed by my father, his eyes wide in a state of insensibility. And *his* cry was like the hollow howl of the grave.

Rushing to his side, my aunt hurried to lead my father from the room before grief unmanned him before his slaves. I was numb watching them go. Then I remembered my promise. I followed, calling, "Papa!"

He didn't look back as my aunt rushed him to the little room where he did his writing. His long limbs became dead weight in my aunt's sturdy arms. She could barely manage him; it was with the greatest difficulty that she tried to heave him into a chair. I ran to him, but my aunt blocked my way, snapping, "Leave him be, Patsy."

Though my mother lay dead behind me, I was beset with the most frantic need to go to my father. To watch over him. To obey my mother in the last thing she ever asked of me. "Papa!"

In answer, his eyes rolled back and he collapsed into the chair.

Then Aunt Elizabeth closed the carved wooden door and I was left completely, utterly alone.

⁓

AT THE HEARTHS OF MONTICELLO, tearful slaves despaired that my mother was gone and my father might never awaken. If asked, they'd have sworn they despaired because they loved my mother and my father, and I believe that even now. But they must've also worried what would become of them if they lost the mistress and master of the plantation in one day. Would they be sold? Separated from one another? Scattered amongst the farms of Virginia and beyond?

Then, I understood none of this. I was too afraid for myself and my sisters, wondering what would become of *us* if we were left orphaned. Long after my aunt ushered us into bed and snuffed out the lanterns, my delicate little Polly cleaved to me and sobbed herself to sleep.

I couldn't sleep, however, until I heard my father rage.

Mama always praised him for his reserved manner and thoughtful nature. But, like me, Papa hid a tempest inside. That's why the violent orchestra of his grief from below the stairs was more soothing to me than the bone-deep drumbeat of my sadness. Papa vented what I couldn't unleash without incurring the ire of my proper aunt, and so I fell asleep to the sound of shattering glass and splintering wood.

It wasn't the noise in the night that eventually awakened me, but the silence. Silence that stole into my room and pressed down cold on my chest, filling me with dread.

It was silent the way Monticello was never silent.

As if the whole plantation was afraid to breathe.

Dread skittered down my spine and brushed away the last tendrils of sleep. Pushing back the bed linens, I disentangled myself from Polly. Then I put my bare feet on the wooden floorboards and felt the early autumn chill on my legs. I glided soundlessly down the stairs, drawn inexorably to Papa's chamber, the only room where the candles still burned bright.

I didn't see him at first. My eyes searched him out amongst the clutter of his spyglass and surveyor's theodolite and the other curiosities we children weren't allowed to touch. Eventually I found him sitting on the floor, amidst the debris of his rage. He was as still as a marble bust. In profile, his strong, sharply curved jaw was clenched tight, and his eyes were fixed downward beneath a sweaty tangle of ginger hair.

I watched him for several heartbeats, and he didn't move. He was a *statue* in the spell of that terrible silence. A spell I was determined to break. "Papa?"

He didn't stir. He didn't look up. He didn't even twitch.

I tried again, this time louder. "Papa!"

He didn't blink. He didn't hear me. He didn't *see* me. It was as if I was a spirit and the two of us stood on either side of an invisible divide. This wasn't like the times my mother would tease him for letting his books swallow his attention until he forgot that he was hungry or thirsty. He wasn't lost in a book, and the bleak look in his eyes was nothing I'd ever witnessed before—or since.

I crept closer, thinking to tug at his linen shirtsleeve.

Then I saw the pistol on the table next to him and froze.

It shouldn't have disturbed me. I'd seen the pistol there before;

I'd watched him polish it many times. But that night, in the candlelight, the notches on the shiny barrel looked like the knuckles of an accusing skeletal finger pointing at my papa. And he stared back at that pistol. He stared and stared at it, as if the pistol had, in the terrible silence, become a wicked thing.

A deadly, avenging thing.

I wanted to shout a warning but the silence had bewitched us both and the cry died dry in my throat. I could say nothing. Yet, some internal force sent me gliding toward him, my feet barely touching the floor. Almost as if I *floated* to his side. My hand reached out and covered the pistol before he could take it.

The smooth walnut grip felt cold and hard beneath my hand. Almost as cold and hard as my father's bleak stare, suddenly fixed on me. I looked into Papa's eyes and what I saw, I dare not trust myself to describe.

All at once, my father shuddered. He took a gulp of air as if he'd been drowning and pulled up suddenly from the water. "Is that my Martha?" he murmured, the spell broken. "My angel?"

"Yes," I said, for Martha was my given name, too. But I think it was my mother he saw in me. Perhaps that was only right, for I knew it was my mother who sent me to him, who made sure I kept my promise to watch over him. Still clutching the pistol, I knelt beside him. "Yes, Papa, I'm here."

Those were the last words we spoke that night, but we sat together for many hours, the pistol like ice in my hands, until the deathly oblivion passed. And I learned that night that the silence was not terrible. The silence was my mother's gift to us. Ours to share. Ours alone.

FROM THAT DAY FORWARD, I stayed at my father's side. Huddled beside the iron-fitted oak chest containing bottles of spirits, I watched Papa walk the rough-hewn wood floors, his buckled shoes clicking with each step. He was on his feet, night and day, pacing incessantly, as if some solution would present itself to undo the tragedy of my mother's death.

He wouldn't touch the trays of food brought to his room, for he had no appetite. My aunts tried to put baby Lucy in his arms, but he wouldn't hold her, for she was the squalling infant that had hastened my mother's death. And when Polly came to the door, my father became unsteady on his feet, as if he might swoon away, for my little sister so closely resembled my mother. It was the same reason, I think, he could not even bear the sight of Sally Hemings; the set of her mouth and shape of her eyes appeared familiar even then and greatly disturbed him.

Papa would have only *me* at his side.

Maybe it was because I was long and lanky like a boy, with ginger hair just like his, that he chose me to be his constant companion. Or maybe he sensed in me more than a daughter. A kindred spirit in the darkness.

Whatever the reason, mourning forged us together like hot metal under a smith's hammer. I was afraid to leave him for fear that if I did, I would be motherless *and* fatherless. I think he feared it, too.

Only I could coax him out of the house to bury my mother beneath the great oak tree in Monticello's graveyard, where my father blinked unseeingly into the afternoon sun and Aunt Elizabeth tried to offer comfort. "Our Martha has found a happier station. She's in heaven, now. Alas, until we join her we all must attend ourselves to *this* life."

My father's frown made it clear he didn't believe a word of it, but he avoided arguments, with silence, whenever possible. Still, he knew he must say something, for my mother's kinsmen had gathered to pay their respects. His voice caught with emotion. "If there *is,* beyond the grave, any concern for this world, then there's one angel who must pity the misery to which life confines me. I'm in a stupor of mind that has rendered me as dead to the world as she whose loss occasioned it."

These words hushed not only the small crowd of stooped

slaves, but also the stern-faced men in powdered wigs and their weepy women in bonnets. The depths of my father's despair seemed to shame them. And him. Papa said nothing more during Mama's funeral, but together, we read the words carved on her tombstone. Not a quote from the Bible, but from Homer's *Iliad*:

NAY IF EVEN IN THE HOUSE OF HADES THE DEAD
FORGET THEIR DEAD, YET WILL I EVEN THERE
BE MINDFUL OF MY DEAR COMRADE.

Below that, a simple accounting of her:

TO THE MEMORY OF MARTHA JEFFERSON,
DAUGHTER OF JOHN WAYLES;
BORN OCTOBER 19TH, 1748, O.S.
INTERMARRIED WITH THOMAS JEFFERSON JANUARY 1ST, 1772
–TORN FROM HIM BY DEATH SEPTEMBER 6TH, 1782
THIS MONUMENT OF HIS LOVE IS INSCRIBED.

The slaves used ropes to lower my mother's coffin into the ground and then shoveled earth over her, rivers of sweat running down their black faces. Then she was gone from us. Truly gone.

One of our neighbors murmured, "Poor Mrs. Jefferson, another victim of the British. Her death is the aftermath of fright . . ."

As if struck guilty by those words, my father stumbled toward her grave. Was it the fault of the British? Had our flight from Monticello and fearful hiding from enemy soldiers stolen my mother's life? And would we have been forced to hide if Papa had not been a revolutionary?

Papa's stricken expression told me that he counted himself to blame.

It was Mr. Short and I who steadied Papa, even when my father tried to push away from our assistance. When Papa found his footing again, he uttered the briefest niceties to my mother's kinsmen, before retreating up the long path to the house, forcing me to chase after him.

Straightaway, he sat down at the table where the pistol still rested, but he didn't touch it. Instead he took up his *Garden Book*. He hadn't made entries since summer. But in the moments after my mother's burial, I watched him write feverishly, scratching ink to paper with each hasty stroke. Curious, I peered over his shoulder, wondering what he was so keen to record, now of all times. . . .

I was shocked by what I saw.

W. Hornsby's Method of Preserving Birds

In painstaking detail, my father wrote . . . a macabre description of how to preserve dead birds in salt and nitre, mortar and pepper.

I clasped a hand to my mouth. *Is this what my aunts did to my mother before setting her to rest in her coffin?*

Mama was delicate; my father used to tease that she had the bones of a bird. I think he would've preserved her for all time, if he could have. He would've used salt and nitre, mortar and pepper, or any other means to keep some part of her with him. But he had only her belongings, her letters, the little scrap of paper still tucked against his heart . . . and her daughters.

Could that ever be enough?

Just then a knock came at the door. My father did not look up from his writing table. Papa continued to scratch notes about dead birds—and I was suddenly vexed that our servants let anyone into the house when Papa was in such a state.

Aunt Elizabeth must have been similarly vexed, for I heard her address our visitor on the other side of the door. "Mr. Short, he cannot receive you. I fear he has lost his wits."

Mortified, I pressed my hot cheek against the cool door and heard Mr. Short chastise my aunt in no uncertain terms. "Never say it! Or you'll inspire every man of Tory sympathies left in the country to crow that the author of the Declaration of Independence has gone mad."

Papa *couldn't* be mad. I wouldn't *let* him go mad. He was writing about birds, but at least he was writing again. Though the sight of my sisters still disturbed him, he was eating again, too. Little nibbles, here and there. And that night, when he collapsed onto his pallet in exhaustion, I stroked Papa's red hair, singing softly a song my mother used to sing to soothe him.

I made sure he was asleep before finding my way to my little sister in our bed. "Courage, Polly," I whispered to soothe her tears, bolstering myself as much as her. "We mustn't cry. We must be of good cheer. Our papa is burdened with such sorrows that we must never burden him with our own."

Chapter Three

WE ROAMED AIMLESSLY on horseback through the dense, mountainous woods that, themselves, seemed to have taken on Papa's sorrow. A misting rain remained after a night's steady showers, and the branches hung heavy. Turning leaves sagged and droplets splashed to the ground, as if the forest grieved with my father. For him. I wiped moisture from my face with a gloved finger, but I was glad for the rain, because I resented the sun as a liar.

No matter how much it shined, there was no light at Monticello.

Since my mother's burial, my father and I had taken many long solitary rides like this, but he got no better. I'd promised myself that I wouldn't let him go mad, but I'd come to understand that my mother was gone forever, and my father was only one step out of the prison of madness her passing created.

On that particular day, Papa's arms rested listlessly around my waist; I wished he'd held me tighter. Not because I feared Caractacus, but because I craved proof that Papa actually saw me, actually knew I was there with him. I missed the warm strength and protection of his embraces.

He was behind me on the broad back of the stallion, but I missed him as if *he* were the one in the grave. The thought made me bite down on the inside of my cheek until the tang of iron spilled onto my tongue. The curious taste, more than the pain, helped me resist the urgent pressure of my tears. My mother bade me not to grieve, and before my Aunt Elizabeth's recent departure she had encouraged me to be strong. As for Papa, it'd been hard enough to coax him out of his confinement. I knew that I mustn't cry.

Caractacus's hooves thudded against the wet ground, and occasionally he gave a low nicker. The trees creaked under the weight of the recent deluge and in the distance, the hammering of a tenacious woodpecker echoed. And yet, it was quiet. That special quiet. My father's quiet and mine.

The memory of how we sang together at Poplar Forest, when we were hiding from the British, swamped me. The contrast was so sharp, I shivered, the dampness of my hair, bodice, and skirts pressing a chill into my skin, as I came to understand that we'd never laugh or sing like that again.

Papa tugged at the reins, directing Caractacus down a diagonal cut between the trees. The horse snorted and blew at the steep decline, but obeyed with a steady hoof. All at once, Papa let out a shuddering breath, the sound that was always the prelude to the wild grief to follow.

Please, no. Not again, I thought, a knot in my belly.

But this moment always came. Every single ride. Nothing I ever did stopped it, or made it end any faster. Papa's chest and arms trembled behind and around me, and his breathing hitched in starts and stops. Then the sob burst out of him and his forehead fell heavily on my shoulder.

Unending moans poured out of him. Their violence pounded against my heart, causing an ache there. He squeezed me until I struggled to breathe. He cried so hard and so much, the desolation of his grief made its way through my rain-soaked frocks to the chilled skin beneath. His words were a mournful jumble, but the hoarse pleading, interspersed with agonized wails, made his lamentation understandable to any living soul.

Even Caractacus, whose ears rotated to the rear. That one small movement was my only proof that someone shared Papa's grief with me, carried the burden of it, too. It made no matter that a horse couldn't speak words of comfort. His very presence, and that turn of his ears, made it possible for me to shoulder my father's outburst.

Suddenly, Papa wrenched his head away and sat back in the saddle. I swayed from the unexpected movement and the sharing of his rage as it washed off of him and through me, hot and acidic. Papa snapped the reins and shouted, "Ha!"

The stallion startled then obeyed. My stomach tossed as Papa pushed the horse into a gallop. A thin branch whipped against my ear. I cried out and pressed my hand against the wound, but Papa didn't slow as the branches lashed at us.

My throat went tight with fear. I wanted to hide my face against the horse's neck, but my father's arms prevented that. So I twisted my fingers around thick chunks of mane and ducked down, eyes shut tight. I prayed a litany that no one heard. And just when I thought we'd ride straight into oblivion, Caractacus swerved with an alarmed whinny.

A second horse answered. Papa pulled up on the reins, bringing us up hard. In fear and confusion, I raised my head too fast, then swooned. Before I knew what had happened, my body slammed to the ground, knocking awareness into me once again. I'd fallen and there'd been no one to catch me. . . .

That was the source of my shock. Unlike the day the rattlesnake made Caractacus rear up, my father hadn't kept from me from falling. He hadn't been able.

A voice sounded from above, calling my name. I rolled onto my back. Gray light filtered down through gloomy trees towering high above. Then a warm hand smoothed my ear where I had been slashed by the branch.

"Patsy, are you injured?" I blinked. It wasn't my father who had dismounted to attend to me; it was William Short. "Patsy, say something. Are you hurt?"

"Yes," I whispered. "I think so."

The young man's green eyes stared down at me. "You're bleeding." He took a kerchief from inside his coat and pressed it into my hand. I accepted the fine linen square and sat up as Mr.

Short glanced over his shoulder. "Mr. Jefferson, have you come to harm?"

Papa didn't answer.

Mr. Short tried again. "Mr. Jefferson, I fear your daughter is concussed."

Papa's blank stare betrayed that he couldn't hear—that he wasn't even with us. Papa was still in the jaws of his grief, caught in the madness I couldn't bear for anyone else to discover. I tried to rise, to go to him, but Mr. Short stopped me with a warm hand upon my arm. "Get your head about you, Patsy. I'll fetch some water." From the saddlebag of his own mount, Mr. Short withdrew a flask and brought it to me. I wiped my mud-smeared hands on one of the few clean spots on my skirt. What a sight I made, and in front of Mr. Short. Mama would've scolded me, but, then, she'd never scold me again for anything. . . .

I took the water. Cool and clean, it eased the constriction of my throat. With sagging shoulders, I held the flask out to him. "I'm sorry. I've muddied the pewter."

Mr. Short smiled. "Pay it no mind. It's but a little dirt. Can you stand?"

I nodded and my gaze flicked to Papa, whose eyes were still blank and distant, his hands twitching on the reins like he was restless to move on. When Mr. Short helped me up from the ground, Papa seemed to remember himself at last. "Come, Patsy," he said, his voice hoarse and strained.

It always sounded that way after one of his secret outbursts, but I think, too, he was ashamed anyone else had seen him this way.

Perhaps Mr. Short was right to say that I was concussed, because when I stepped toward Caractacus, I stumbled. Mr. Short steadied me with his hand at my elbow, then bade me to lean on him. "Mr. Jefferson. If you'll allow me, I'll see your daughter to Monticello."

Papa stared a long minute, his dulled blue eyes moving back and forth between us like we were a puzzle to decipher. Seeing the mud on my dress, as if he'd only just realized that I'd fallen, a flush crept up Papa's neck. "Yes," he finally murmured, his hands lifting the reins. "Yes, of course."

"No!" I cried. The thought of Papa wandering alone filled me with icy dread. In his madness, what would he do?

Mr. Short squeezed my other hand. "Come along, Patsy."

"But, Papa—"

"Go with William," Papa said, his voice cracking. "It's for the best. He can take care of you."

"But you'll be home for supper?" I searched my father's eyes for a promise.

Papa pressed his lips into a thin line and looked away. "I'll be home."

I reached for Caractacus and stroked the stallion, as much to reassure him as myself. "Take care of him," I whispered. The horse nickered and pressed his big, regal face against mine. It was all the reassurance I had that someone, or something, would look after Papa in my stead.

Papa tugged the reins and turned about, forcing Mr. Short to huff out a breath. "Mr. Jefferson? Your daughter—" My father had already wheeled his horse around, but Mr. Short shouted after him, more fiercely. "Mr. Jefferson!"

The young man's tone caught Papa's attention. My father brought the stallion around, almost warily. I remember now that in that moment, William's hand trembled where it rested atop mine, a small show of nerves.

"Mr. Jefferson, it didn't—" Short broke off, swallowing hard on a wavering voice. "This loss didn't happen only to you, sir."

I couldn't appreciate the full measure of these words. Not then. That day, I gasped so forcefully at William's impertinence that I hurt my throat. "Mr. Short!"

Papa blanched but gave a single, tight nod that made my heart feel heavy within my chest. I felt as if that acknowledgment cost him something I couldn't name.

Then he turned Caractacus and kicked him into a trot.

"Papa, I . . ." I didn't think he could hear me. So I shouted, "Papa!"

But he was gone.

Fear drove away concern for manners, and I worried not about offending William Short. I rounded upon him. "How *could* you?"

At my censure, he merely bowed his head. "He lost a wife, but you lost a mother, Patsy. This cannot go on."

So he *knew*.

He knew that Papa had descended into madness. And if he knew, who else did? The heat of shame flooded my face and tears pricked at my eyes at the thought of Papa's political enemies or even our neighbors gossiping. They wouldn't understand. Papa was still the bold hero of the Revolution. Still the great man he'd always been. It was only that Mama's death had laid him low.

Panicked and angered, I no longer felt the cold, the sting of my ear, or the ache in my back. Papa's outbursts were to have been a secret, between Caractacus and me. I was horrified that William Short had witnessed it, too. "You mustn't say a word, Mr. Short. On your honor, you mustn't say anything to anyone."

Mr. Short stiffened as a Virginia gentleman must when honor is mentioned. "Patsy, I admire your father more than any other man. I'd do nothing to damage his reputation. But your aunt shouldn't have left you and your sisters in his care. At the very least, Mr. Jefferson should find it in himself to be firmer in your presence. You're only a child."

"I'm not," I stated.

"You *are* a child, a child who has lost much."

I looked away, sure that if I didn't, I'd find myself sharing things better left unsaid, sharing burdens that were mine alone. I couldn't tell him that I feared Papa was more than mad—that the violence of his emotions might drag him into my mother's grave with her. I bit back these words, for my mother had asked *me* to be my father's solace. No one else.

At my silence, Mr. Short sighed. "Come. I'll take you home."

The word *home* rang between my ears, taunting me with how comforting the very thought of home had been not so very long ago. Even when the British came and we knew not whether Monticello might be burned to the ground, Mama maintained that feeling of home that families provide, even in the worst of situations. *Especially* in the worst of situations. But now that role and responsibility fell to me.

I followed Mr. Short to his horse, an old brown gelding with a white star on his forehead. Mr. Short offered me a hand up onto his mount. I paused before accepting it. William Short had always been kind to us, and I hated the idea that I might do something to change that. But the way he spoke to Papa . . . "You mustn't take such a tone with my father, Mr. Short. You must never do something like that again. We must comfort Papa in his loss."

I held his gaze so he would regard me seriously. Perhaps he did.

"I didn't intend to be provoking, my dear. And I'll try to hold my tongue. But answer me this." His smile was small and sad. "Who comforts you in your loss?"

～

"Done lost his mind," one of the servants said in a harsh whisper. The words froze me outside the cellar kitchen door. "Bringing pox into this house . . . he's gonna kill them babies."

"Maybe it's what he wants, so he can follow them to the grave," another said.

A chorus of agreement from the others sounded out, making my heart fly. Papa had talked about the threat of the pox for days and argued inoculation was the only way to guard against it. But could the slaves' suspicion be based in truth? Could Papa really want to—

"Hush right now!" Mammy Ursula said, as if she knew I was listening.

Forcing my feet to move, I entered the kitchen, finding the group of women gathered in front of the hearth. In many ways, the kitchen was the domain of the slaves, and even before my mother's death, it was the cook's habit to shoo me away when she was busy so that she could gossip with the others. Now, the cook froze by the fire at the sight of me, her wooden spoon clutched in her hand, midair. The other slaves went silent, also stilled.

All of them but Mammy Ursula, the sturdy black laundress and pastry chef whose innate sense of authority was such that the other slaves obeyed her like a queen. With her hair tied tight and regal atop her head in a red-checkered handkerchief, Mammy snapped, "Why are you sneaking about, Miss Patsy?"

I hadn't been sneaking about at all, so despite the nervousness that the slaves' words and Mammy's tone unleashed in my belly, I simply folded my hands over my apron as I remembered my mother doing and met her stern gaze. "Dr. Gilmer is here. Papa wants your help."

Inoculating us was the first decision my father made about anything since the day my mother died over two months before, and it was a decision that came upon him suddenly and with the utmost urgency. Of the slaves carried off by the British, almost all had perished from smallpox and other fevers.

Perhaps it was the stories of how our people had suffered that put my father into a singular fervor that his daughters must be guarded against this illness, no matter how terrifying the treatment. Mammy Ursula had been my nursemaid when I was a babe, so I wanted her to tell me this treatment was a needful thing, and not part of my papa's madness. Instead, Mammy brushed flour from her apron, wiped her dark hands on a cloth, and silently followed me to fetch Polly and the baby.

We found Papa in an agitated state, pacing in front of the clean-linen-covered table where Dr. Gilmer's knives gleamed silver and sharp. In an echo of my wildly beating pulse, a November rainstorm pitter-pattered against the windowpane, and I stole a glance at the menacing little glass vial of noxious pus from a victim of the pox.

With steady hands, Papa tugged up the white linen sleeve of my shift to bare my arm for the physician, and I asked, "Will it hurt?"

Papa stilled, his bleak gaze lifting to my eyes. His lips pursed. "I wish your mother . . ." He shook his head and sighed. "Your mother would know better how to . . . what to . . ."

I hung on the edge of his words for a long moment, then finally looked to Dr. Gilmer. "It will be little more than a scratch, my dear," Dr. Gilmer said as he removed his black frockcoat and placed it over the back of a wooden chair. "When it pains you, you must bravely set the example for your sisters so they won't be frightened when their turn comes."

I glanced at Papa for reassurance, but his expression had gone distant again, his fingers cold as he held fast to my wrist so Dr. Gilmer could bring his knife down on the tender underside of my arm. I hissed as the first slash drew blood, then yelped at the throbbing pain that followed. I clenched my teeth to hold back my cries lest they frighten my little sisters, waiting on the other side of the door, an effort that left me shaking.

Dr. Gilmer buried a thread soaked in the infected fluid between the folds of my rent flesh, then bandaged over it with a linen strip, tying off the ends. "There, there, Patsy. You did very well."

I wiped away a mist of tears and tried to give a brave smile when Ursula came in carrying the baby in one arm and leading Polly with the other. But neither my brave smile nor Ursula's presence did any good when it was Polly's turn. My willful little sister screamed and fought and even tried to *bite* Dr. Gilmer before Mammy wrestled her still.

Papa drifted to the window, pinching the bridge of his nose. He still had his back to Dr. Gilmer when the physician took his leave.

With a worried glance at my father, Ursula hurried to see the physician out. As if Papa had commanded it, she promised to compensate Dr. Gilmer with some of her special bottled cider. I realize now that I wasn't alone in trying to maintain the illusion that Papa was still master of his plantation—and himself.

Because Polly was still crying, I nuzzled her close. "Hush, it's all over. Now we can go out and play."

"No," Papa said without turning. "You and your sisters must be confined for the next few weeks. Then we're leaving Monticello."

My gaze jerked up. "Leaving?"

"I've accepted an appointment to Paris to negotiate the end of the war."

Scarcely anything he could've said would've surprised me more. I remembered his promise to my mother that he'd retire from public life. That he'd retire to his farm, his books, and his family, from which nothing would ever separate him again. Just two months before, hours before my mother's death, he'd angrily refused his election to the Virginia legislature. But now everything had changed, and I was left to wonder if his promises had died with her.

I didn't want to leave. Neither did I want Papa to go without us. "Must you serve, Papa?"

My father gave a curt nod but said no more.

In the days that followed, my sisters and I suffered from nothing more than boredom, cooped up when we would rather have been romping through piles of autumn leaves.

Then the illness came upon us, fast and merciless.

And all Papa's cool reserve melted away. He held the pail for our vomit, wiped the fevered sweats from our brows, and offered hushed, soothing words. Often when I surfaced from delirious dreams, the sound of his violin or his soft, rasping tenor as he sang comforted me back to sleep. Having already taken the treatment, Papa would let no one else care for us, lest we spread the contagion. And he cloistered with us together in the small makeshift infirmary, our world narrowing again to only one another. Our little surviving family of four.

As we shivered in our beds and groaned with aches, we couldn't have asked for a more attentive nurse than our papa.

When any bitterness steals into my heart for the choices I've made in devotion to my father, I remember that even in the depths of his stupor and despair, he found it within himself to protect us the best way he knew how.

At some point in my delirium, I awoke to the soft, mournful strains of his violin. The notes ached with a sweet sadness. Forcing my eyes open, I lifted my head from a sweat-soaked pillow. "Didn't the treatment work, Papa?"

He lowered his instrument. "The science is sound. It asks us to suffer a milder form of the illness to guard against the more virulent attack." He explained more, but the words were beyond my reach and my head ached intolerably. I must've said as much, because he glanced up at the ceiling, closing his eyes. "Patsy, suffering strengthens our constitutions and builds inner fortifications so that we never fall prey to the same agony twice. We must take upon ourselves a smaller evil to defend against the greater evil. We must take upon ourselves a smaller pain in order to survive."

I was too young, then, and too overcome with illness to realize that the agony he spoke of was not smallpox. But his words weren't madness, and they stayed with me long after the fever had passed. Even now they help me understand why my father felt the need to rip us from our home and hasten away with such urgency.

It pained him to leave Monticello.

But what would have survived of him if he'd stayed?

Chapter Four

Ampthill, 26 November 1782
From Thomas Jefferson to Chastellux

Before the catastrophe that closed this summer, my scheme of life had been determined. I'd folded myself in the arms of retirement, and rested all prospects of future happiness on domestic objects. A single event wiped away my plans and left me a blank I had not the spirits to fill. In this state of mind an appointment from Congress required me to cross the Atlantic. My only object now is to hasten over those obstacles which retard my departure.

AFTER THREE MONTHS of searching every brine-scented port in the colonies, Papa couldn't find a ship willing to undertake the perilous winter voyage through waters filled with enemy vessels. And more than a few ship captains muttered darkly at my father's persistence, wondering if he was a man chasing after an icy death.

It shames me still that I cannot say they were wrong.

Indeed, I feared they had exactly the right of it. We'd left Polly and Lucy with Aunt Elizabeth at Eppington, and though I missed my sisters, I was glad they didn't have to witness this latest manifestation of Papa's grief. While my father no longer stared down his pistols in the dead of night, he braved the brigand-infested roads with a recklessness that terrified me.

I wondered if I'd been wrong to keep Papa's secrets. I wondered if I ought to have confessed the full breadth of my fears to Mr. Short the day he came upon us in the woods. But now there was no one to whom I could turn. For Papa kept us always moving from city to city.

Everywhere we found brown and red brick buildings squeezed close together, jostling carriages on snow-covered cobblestone streets, docks burdened with goods waiting to traverse safe seas, and mobs of people. The cities of the new states blurred, one into another, until we returned again to Philadelphia, where bells rang and celebrants gathered around great bonfires blazing orange in the streets in celebration of the news.

Peace with Great Britain had been achieved.

A provisional treaty had been signed, and when I heard, I tugged on Papa's sleeve from my place beside him in the carriage. "Then the war is over?"

"Nearly," was his soft reply.

After so great a struggle, so many harrowing hours and devastating losses, I thought Papa would be overjoyed at our victory. But he received the news with reserve, chagrined to learn that peace was made without need of his negotiations.

I've come to believe that he hoped to regain his honor by ending the revolution he'd helped start. In his guilty grief, he counted my mother as a casualty of that war and felt robbed of his chance to ensure her loss was not in vain. But at the time, I thought the cause of Papa's melancholy was because we wouldn't be going to Paris after all, and he didn't want to go home. Indeed, he seemed to think of every possible excuse to delay, even contriving a visit with our Randolph relations at Tuckahoe.

I wondered if, in this, there was an opportunity. The Randolphs were Papa's people through his mother, and he'd spent his childhood on Tuckahoe Plantation. Some part of me hoped the Randolphs would be able to see behind the cool blue veneer of my father's gaze to the dark abyss I still saw. No one at Monticello had the authority or audacity to question Papa, but I knew Colonel Randolph would have no such qualms.

"You'll be glad to see Colonel Randolph, won't you, Papa?" I asked as the carriage jostled along on the long, narrow drive to Tuckahoe under a foreboding canopy of trees. The drive was so narrow, in fact, that if we veered even a little, our wheels would get stuck in the mud.

"He's a good man," Papa said, which is what he always said about Colonel Randolph, for the two men had been raised together as boys by my grandfather when he was custodian of Tuckahoe.

Yet, even now, I cannot imagine a less likely candidate for my father's friendship than his childhood companion Colonel Randolph. Where Papa projected a calm, composed demeanor, the colonel was a militant man, marching impatiently along the white-painted fence in front of his riverside home, barking out his welcome to Tuckahoe plantation. Where Papa wore a gray homespun frockcoat with wooden buttons, we found Colonel Randolph clad in formal dress, colorful as a Tory in a crimson coat and matching embroidered waistcoat. And whereas Papa was the author of our independence, Colonel Randolph was decidedly conflicted about the revolution. "This damned war," he spat, when my father shared the happy news of a treaty. "The inability to ship tobacco overseas has brought my finances into a very low state. Now, I'll have to pay a fortune on it in customs duties."

"The price of liberty," Papa replied with a tight smile.

Colonel Randolph grunted, waving us into the dark-paneled entryway of his abode. "I fear liberty has impoverished us." It was a boast cloaked in modesty, much like his wooden plantation house itself. At first glance, Tuckahoe looked to be a modest white-painted house with two chimneys, but circling round the drive revealed it was really *two* houses connected by a central block, like the letter H. The rear of the mansion was dedicated to entertaining guests in high style, complete with salons and a great hall, which gave the lie to the idea that the Randolphs were in any way impoverished.

A veritable army of well-dressed house servants carried our luggage up the ornately carved walnut staircase, while I drifted into the parlor, entranced by mirrors and polished rosewood and mahogany—every piece so splendid I was afraid to touch. The only thing to mar its beauty was the damaged paneling over the fireplace, and as I stared at it curiously, Tom Randolph, the eldest of the Randolph children, happened upon me. "The British came searching for your father during the war. When we wouldn't give him up, Tarleton ripped our coat of arms from the wall."

"Your coat of arms?" I asked.

"My ancestors were great lords in England and Scotland," Tom said, showing me a leather-bound book opened to a page of what looked to be heraldry. "My people were amongst the first families of Virginia. Better than yours."

Tom was just an overeager puppy then; if I forget the wolf he became, I can still smile at the memory of the fourteen-year-old boy, tall and lanky, with brown hair and eyes so dark they appeared almost black. Given his imperious pronouncement about his lineage, I felt as if he expected me to curtsy. Instead, I said, "We're kin, Tom. Your people are my people, too."

"But *I'm* also part Indian," he countered, making of his face an amusingly savage scowl. "That's why I'm an excellent horseman. I'm descended of Pocahontas. Are you?"

"I don't think so," I replied, for I was certain Papa would've told me if we had any direct relation to the famous native princess. "But we display buffalo robes at Monticello."

A hint of genuine curiosity shone in Tom's black eyes. "I'd like to see those . . . though savage items are hardly fit to display in a home where girls and women are about."

I bristled with indignation, but this was more attention than a boy of Tom's age had ever paid me, and though I had weightier worries, I didn't want it to go badly. "Papa doesn't agree."

"I'm sure he doesn't. After all, your father thinks nothing of carrying you to Boston and back again, when you should be in the care of a woman to teach you domestic arts."

Red hot anger straightened my spine at these words he must've heard spoken by his parents. Though my journey with Papa had been a terrifying blur of grief and long carriage rides and cobblestone streets, I met his smug gaze and boasted, "Not only Boston. We went to Philadelphia and Baltimore, too, and now I've seen all the states. Have you?"

This proved to be an embarrassing mistake, for Tom quizzed me on all thirteen newly independent states until it became apparent that I was woefully short of the full set. Moreover, my ignorant boast caused Tom to puff up and announce, "Anyway, I've come to tell you that you'll take your supper with the children. I'll be dressing for dinner and sitting at the table with the other men—of course."

He wanted me to feel young and foolish, and I did. But more than that, he made me anxious that Papa and I should be apart even for the length of a supper. Leaving Tom, I found my father dressing for dinner, his manservant adjusting his cravat. When I told Papa what Tom said, he stared into the mirror, muttering, "Patsy, try to get along with Tom. It isn't easy for him as the colonel's *heir apparent*." He said the last words with a hint of contempt, then added, "The Randolphs like to make much of their pedigree, to which I suppose everyone else must ascribe whatever merit they choose."

Thus, banished to the lower-level kitchen where the children ate, I intended to sulk. It didn't quite work out that way when I fell into the company of the Randolph sisters. Judith was my age and Nancy only a little younger, and by the time we'd taken our fill of egg custards and apple tarts and candied cherries, we were fast friends. Their companionship both eased the ache I felt for missing my sisters and worsened it.

Before bed, Mrs. Randolph gathered us round her harpsichord

in the richly appointed great hall, and the men drifted in with their brandy. Puffing on a pipe, Colonel Randolph said to Papa, "It's fortunate your appointment to France came to nothing. You're better off in retirement. No good comes of public service anymore." Ignoring the strained smile of his wife, whose expression seemed to warn him away from such talk, Colonel Randolph continued, "I practically funded Washington's army myself, but I've been criticized by so-called patriots for the liberality with which I treated British soldiers."

Settling into one of the tasseled armchairs, Papa crossed one leg at the knee. "We must endure criticism if we're to honor the spirit of independence."

Colonel Randolph's jowls reddened. "The spirit of independence! Every man who bore arms in this revolution now considers himself on the same footing as his neighbor. I tell you, Jefferson, the spirit of independence has been converted to the abominable idea of *equality*."

Papa, who had declared to the world that *all men are created equal*, was long acquainted with Colonel Randolph's bluster, and merely drank in silence. And in irritation, Mrs. Randolph chirped, "Shall we have Judith play another song?"

Alas, Colonel Randolph wouldn't be silenced. "I won't serve again in the legislature, and you should follow my example, Jefferson."

Papa grimaced, contemplating the crystal goblet in his hand. "What else is left for me but public service when all my private happiness has been so utterly destroyed?"

Colonel Randolph swallowed and Mrs. Randolph fluttered her fan. In the astonished silence, Papa's cheeks reddened. He'd been goaded into expressing his darkest thoughts and his embarrassment pained me like a hot stone in my belly. Some part of me had hoped the Randolphs would see my papa's devastation, that they'd realize he was a man on the edge of something . . . terrible, but their silence was excruciating.

Young Tom had been slumped in his chair, trying to affect an air of manly indifference. But now he perked up, sitting straighter. "I'd like to serve in public office one day, Mr. Jefferson."

I didn't know if Tom blundered forth in self-interest or to ease the tension, but his question gave my father a moment to recover. His mother flashed him an adoring smile of appreciation, and the gratitude *I* felt toward Tom made me forget I'd ever disliked him.

"You'll need an education," Papa suggested. "You'll want to study law—"

"He'll study how to plant tobacco," Colonel Randolph barked. "There's good reason gentlemen are withdrawing from public life, my friend. Retire to Monticello, plant your crops, and enjoy the fruits of your labor. That's my advice to you."

Despite the colonel's provocation, it seemed good advice to me; certainly, it was what Mama had wanted. And, in the days that followed, I hoped Papa would be persuaded by it. But on the day the Randolph sisters coaxed me to play with them and their dollies in the springtime sunshine, Papa saw me laughing and his gaze filled with an even deeper melancholy.

That night he didn't sleep. He paced the floors of his room, then came into mine. I think he knew I'd be awake. Gently brushing my hair from my face beneath my sleeping cap, he asked, "Could you be happy here, Patsy? With the Randolphs?"

The question was mildly spoken, but his eyes had a mad intensity to them. Both sent my heart into a breath-stealing sprint. Was it a rebuke? Did he think I'd forgotten my mother? Did he consider my laughter a dishonor to her memory? My stomach knotted in guilt, and I bunched the quilt in my fists. "No."

"The schoolhouse here," he said softly. "Your grandfather built it. Judith and Nancy are suitable playmates, and Tom might even make a good husband for you one day."

"*No*, Papa," I insisted, my fears rising. "I couldn't be happy here. Not without you."

"You might be—"

"It's not *true*, Papa." Now anger swirled with fear inside me, forcing me to cry, "I can only be happy with you!"

"It's only that circumstances might take me . . . elsewhere for a time." He sighed with a gravity that made me recognize it as a plea. Even if he could hide it from the rest of the world, he couldn't hide from me his longing for death. It was in the spaces and silences between his words that the truth could be found.

I heard it in what he didn't say.

And I determined never to give him an excuse to take his leave of this world. "I'd be *miserable* here, Papa. I find the Randolphs entirely disagreeable. Wherever your duty takes you, it must take me, too."

For the memory of my mother could not be honored, my promises could not be kept, and my own duty could not be met anywhere else.

Only when his shoulders sagged in resignation, and he pressed a tender kiss to my brow, did my heart finally calm within my chest. The next morning, I shied away from Judith and Nancy, instead following Mrs. Randolph past the schoolhouse into her orderly herb garden. There, in the striped linen short gown and straw hat she wore for gardening, she let me help her tend the raspberry and sweet goldenrod she used to brew her liberty tea. "I suppose now that the war is over, we'll drink the real stuff again. But my boy Tom has been kind enough to pretend he's fond of my concoction and I dare say your father likes it, too."

The warm affection in her voice for her son and my father beckoned my trust. Should I tell her that Papa was unwell? Did I dare even hint at what he'd said the night before? Biting my lip, I debated what path was most right in a situation that was so very wrong. Finally, I stayed silent, knowing she wasn't the sort to involve herself in the business of men.

Only someone like Colonel Randolph could make things right. And perhaps he tried, in his own way. When the gentlemen took their ease under an awning on the back lawn overlooking the James River, Papa sketched the gardens into a little leather book and I climbed into his lap, where he encouraged me to nibble at the untouched biscuits on his plate.

That's when Colonel Randolph said, "Jefferson, if you stay longer, we'll organize a horse race to be followed by an evening of dancing. No doubt, every pretty widow and unmarried girl in Virginia will want an invitation."

Papa's pencil stopped midstroke. "No doubt."

Scowling after a gulp of his wife's liberty tea, Colonel Randolph added, "Men like us weren't meant to live alone."

My father stiffened against my back, his whole body rigid and brittle. With awful clarity, I understood that Colonel Randolph was encouraging Papa to take a new wife. *That* was how he thought to help matters. He thought a new wife would keep Papa away from his pistols in the night, which meant that he didn't understand my father's grief at all, nor the promise that Papa had made at my mother's deathbed.

My father quietly closed his sketchbook and excused himself with a litany of bland niceties. The next day, Papa announced our departure. I believed he'd finally realized there was nowhere else for us to go but home.

But I was wrong.

~

Annapolis, 28 November 1783
From Thomas Jefferson to his Dearest Patsy

The conviction that you'd be improved in the situation I've placed you solaces me in parting with you, which my love for you has rendered a difficult thing. Consider the good lady who has taken you under her roof as your mother, as the only person to whom, since the loss with which heaven has been pleased to afflict you, you can now look up.

The acquirements I hope you'll make under the tutors I've provided will render you more worthy of my love, and

if they cannot increase it they'll prevent its diminution.
I've placed my happiness on seeing you good and accom-
plished, and no distress this world can now bring on me
could equal that of your disappointing my hopes.

On a cobblestone street of Philadelphia, sniffling into my
sleeve like a little child, I pleaded, "But, Papa, why can't I stay
with you?"

I couldn't believe what was happening. We'd only been home
long enough to pay a visit to my sisters at Eppington before Papa
informed all of us that he'd been elected to Congress and, this
time, he meant to serve. Now, he meant to leave me in Philadelphia with a Mrs. Hopkinson—a patriotic goodwife supposedly
well known for her pious virtues. Had I convinced Papa not to
leave me with family and friends, only to have him abandon me
with strangers?

I couldn't fathom why Papa would take me by horse and carriage up bumpy roads and by ferry across treacherous rivers only
to part with me here.

In truth, I cannot fathom his reasoning even now.

A wind blew down the alley, howling between the narrow
spaces that separated Mrs. Hopkinson's tall brick home from its
neighbors, rattling the shutters. But my father didn't take it as a
sign of foreboding. Instead, he explained, "Congress is sure to
convene in Philadelphia or nearby, and we need to attend to your
education. I won't be far from you day or night."

In this he turned out to be wrong. Congress wasn't called to
Philadelphia, where, in the Independence Hall, Papa's Declaration had been signed eight Julys before. Instead, because of a
mutiny of Pennsylvania soldiers who hadn't been paid their wages
from the war, Philadelphia was deemed unsafe for the legislators.
So, Congress was called to Annapolis, and three days later, Papa
left for Maryland without me. All I knew, all I could see, was that
I'd been abandoned in a huge, bustling city amongst strangers.

At first, panic left me inconsolable upon my borrowed bed.

Despair rushed in close behind, making me listless and sullen. I was sure that I'd never see my beloved Papa again. At least I'd said my good-byes to Mama before she was taken from us. And she *was* taken; she hadn't left of her own accord.

Not like Papa, who wanted to join her.

My distress was such that I struggled to keep down the victuals Mrs. Hopkinson served at her table. She wasn't an unkind woman, but she urged me to pray for God's solace, and she prayed often. Loudly.

I had a bevy of exotic tutors—the French Mr. Cenas, who taught dancing, the English Mr. Bentley, who taught music, the Swiss Mr. Simitière, who taught art, and a special tutor for the French language, too. But I didn't wish to learn anything. Without my sisters or my papa, I didn't even wish to rise from bed. My stomach pains worsened, but I feared Mrs. Hopkinson didn't believe me, for the only tonic she offered was a morning prayer.

Prayers were not, however, on the schedule Papa wrote out for me. So, I tried to devote myself to my studies—save for drawing, for which I had no capacity. Even Mr. Simitière said so. Fervently and repeatedly. All my efforts ended in my nervous stomach emptying its contents into a bowl I held in filthy hands, smudges of graphite on my fingers and clothes.

Someone must've reported this to Papa, for his next letter from Annapolis upbraided me for slovenliness. *"Let your clothes be clean, whole, and properly put on,"* he wrote. *"For nothing is so disgusting to our sex as the want of cleanliness and delicacy in yours."*

These were the harshest words Papa had ever put to me, and to see the reprimand written so starkly on paper, I gasped and clutched at my stomach, which again tossed with humiliation and upset. Mrs. Hopkinson pulled my trembling body against her sweaty bosom, trying to hush me. "Poor child. Pray for an acquiescent spirit so that you obey your father's commands. Surely you know your papa does God's work, so we must relieve him of temporal worries." Her words echoed Mama's, and everyone in

Philadelphia said that my papa was a great man and that we must put before our own desires a worry for our new country.

But, wickedly, like Colonel Randolph, I no longer cared a fig for it.

Instead, I burned with resentment, angrier with my father than I'd ever been. Papa wanted me to send him my drawings, but he didn't reply when I did. Indeed, it seemed there were a great many things that Papa wished from me while none of my wishes mattered at all. So I wrote Papa only when he wrote to me. And when my drawing teacher couldn't recognize my sketch of Monticello as having any merit, I tore it to bits, prompting Mr. Simitière to quit his post.

Six months passed in Philadelphia.

Christmas. The New Year. Winter. Spring.

It wasn't until May that Papa finally came to fetch me.

I spied through the window the back of a tall man wearing an embroidered blue coat. And, as he made his way to the door, I caught a glimpse of ginger hair beneath his black tricorn hat. I wanted to leap up from my chair and cry "Papa!"

But instead, I waited sullenly while the white-aproned matriarch of the household ushered my father inside. Though I was angry with him for having abandoned me, words could not express my relief at seeing my father again.

While he thanked Mrs. Hopkinson for looking after me, my eyes hung on every detail of his features, looking for any evidence that time had wrought changes. The straight set of his spine and the animation of his blue eyes revealed that he was glad to see me, and it softened the hardest edges of my anger.

"How is my girl?" Papa asked, opening his arms to me. I wanted to run to him, but it had been so long and I had been so scared that I held firm in my seat. When he saw that I would not be so easily wooed, he wryly took from his pocket two tickets to an exhibition of hot air balloons. "I see an inducement is required. Come now, Patsy. Let me show you a glorious thing."

Try as I might, I couldn't resist my papa. In truth, when he put his mind to charm someone, no one could. I rose slowly, but then I flew into his arms and buried my face against his coat. And that very hour, he took me to see the marvelous contraptions that harnessed heat and rendered the balloon lighter than air. That was how I felt, holding my papa's hand again. Watching the colorful balloons rise up, I thought I might float into the heavens. "Tell me we're going home again, Papa. Tell me we won't be apart anymore."

His clear eyes followed the balloons into the sky. "I'm to be an envoy to Paris."

I crashed back down to earth, afraid I'd cry. Right there, in front of the crowd, shaming myself and Papa besides. "No, Papa. Please—"

He gave my hand a small squeeze. "I'm taking you with me. I've learned in these past months that I cannot do without your company. In truth, I am quite lost without it."

Gulping in breaths of relief, I hugged his arm tight. I never wanted to set foot in Mrs. Hopkinson's brick house again. I didn't even want to say good-bye.

Thankfully, Papa sent Jimmy Hemings to fetch my things from the boardinghouse. My father explained that Jimmy was coming with us to Paris to be trained in the art of French cookery so that when we returned to Monticello, we might entertain with the same grace we'd found at Tuckahoe. Those words were a balm to my soul, for they meant that Papa was thinking of a time when we *would* all live together at Monticello again . . . someday. Even if he couldn't bear it now.

The thought made me so glad that not even the jostling three-week trip to Boston, where we traveled to catch our ship, dampened my excitement for this new shared adventure. And in the dawning hours of our nation's eighth birthday, we boarded the *Ceres* and set sail.

Chapter Five

Hartford, 11 October 1784
To Thomas Jefferson from Lafayette

When I heard of your going to France, I lamented I couldn't have the honor to receive you there. My house, my family, and anything that is mine are entirely at your disposal and I beg you will see Madame de Lafayette as you would your brother's wife. Indeed, I'd be very angry with you, if you didn't consider my house as a second home, and Madame de Lafayette is very happy to wait upon Miss Jefferson.

H AS THERE EVER BEEN such a labyrinthine city as Paris? Upon our arrival, we found sooty walls within muddy walls around the city proper and beggars round every corner. But all the soot and mud gave way to beauty when, borne in a fine coach by seven horses, we passed under a bright blue sky onto the wide avenue of the Champs-Élysées.

From there, the whole city fanned out before us in splendor. Stone archways, domes, and pillars all reached for the sun. In truth, the bustling seaports of Philadelphia, Boston, and Baltimore were mere infants in comparison to the ancient majesty of this grand city.

I was giddy at the sight, and I wasn't the only one. Jimmy Hemings removed his cap, thunderstruck. And Papa gasped when the proud Palais-Royal came into view. The palace's expanse of creamy white bricks beyond ironwork gates was nearly too much to take in. I could never have imagined such a place. Overcome, I asked, "This palace belongs to the king?"

The word *king* elicited a frown from my father, but our coachman explained that the gardens were now open to the public—a thing we could plainly see as we turned a corner into the teeming crowds. Every man was ornamented in waistcoat and powdered wig, and the ladies wore their hair as tall as you pleased, strutting about like well-plumed songbirds. Every breeze carried a thousand voices in the melody of the French language.

The breeze also carried the disagreeable smell of so many people crowded close together, but the sweet perfume of the gardens and the ribbons of bright green shrubbery winding in every direction made me forget all else. "Oh, Papa! Is this what heaven looks like?"

"If there be such a place, perhaps it is just so." There was a new light in his eyes. As his gaze slipped over the carved facades of the palace and its surrounding structures, the hard lines of his expression melted away into fascination. I hadn't seen him this engaged with the world since my mother died.

And Paris was very much alive.

Taking it in, Papa sat with his mouth set in an awed half smile. I realized with a jolt that the shadow of grief seemed to have lifted from him. Could I dare to hope this momentous change I sensed was real? Unable to resist, I threaded my fingers through his.

His hand, so often stiff and cold since my mother's death, closed warmly over mine.

We stayed that night at a cheerful little inn. The next morning, Papa was up early to shop for wine and a map of the city, and to look for servants. He hired two men straightaway.

That afternoon, we were paid a visit by one Mr. Adams—a member of our delegation in Paris—and his wife, Abigail. What a relief it was to be in the company of Americans after even a few days of being surrounded by people who spoke only French!

The stout Mr. Adams greeted my father with the warmest friendship.

It was *Mrs.* Adams, however, who commanded our attention. In a gray gown with few ruffles at the sleeves, she rolled into the room like a summer storm. "Oh, poor Mr. Jefferson! I've seen the new house you intend to lease and it's even emptier of furnishings than ours. There is no table better than an oak board, nor even a carpet."

"We'll have to shop for furnishings," Papa allowed.

Mrs. Adams beat back the hotel draperies for dust. "You'll also need table linen, bed linen, china, glass, and plate. Our own house is much larger than we need; forty beds may be made in it. It must be very cold in winter. With a smaller abode, you'll have the advantage."

She wasn't an elegant woman, Mrs. Adams. Nor was she deferential in the way Papa taught me good women must be. I looked to him for signs of disapproval, but when it came to Abigail Adams, he wasn't able to muster it. "I won't need many beds," he said. "There will only be me and my daughter and a few servants. And, of course, my secretary, Mr. Short, when he arrives . . ."

I hadn't heard Mr. Short's name in quite some time. Not since my fall from the horse, when he chastised Papa. The mention now was a pleasant surprise. Almost as pleasant as learning that Mr. Short would be joining us here in Paris.

As I absorbed the happy news, Mrs. Adams turned her gaze to me. "You must be your father's dear Patsy." Then her dark eyes narrowed over a beak of a nose when she saw the stain upon my calico dress. She looked me up and down and when she reached my feet, I wiggled my toes nervously in worn shoes. Mrs. Adams spun to face my father. "Oh, dear. Oh, no. This will never do. Your daughter can't set foot in Paris looking like this."

How provoking! She made me sound like an urchin. My father looked positively mortified, and Mr. Adams grumbled.

Immune to our general discomfort, his wife continued, "For

that matter, Mr. Jefferson, it might be well for you to have some new clothes made, too. We Americans must represent ourselves well, and you've no idea how these Parisians worship fashion. Why, to be out of fashion is more criminal than to be seen in a state of nature . . . to which the Parisians are not averse."

I blushed and so did my papa, but I didn't think it was the mention of Parisians in the state of nature that embarrassed him most. He looked down at his own waistcoat, self-consciously fingering one of the loose fastenings. "Is there no advantage to remaining uncorrupted by sophistication?"

Mrs. Adams smirked but insisted with an innate sense of authority, "You must send immediately for the stay maker, the Mantua maker, the milliner, and even a shoemaker!" In a few hours, merchants of every variety overran our quarters and Mrs. Adams marshaled them this way and that, lecturing my father on the cost. "I could've furnished myself in Boston, twenty or thirty percent cheaper than I've been able to do here. I cannot get a dozen handsome wineglasses under three guineas, nor a pair of small decanters for less than a guinea and a half." When the dressmaker arrived, Papa allowed the garrulous Mrs. Adams to herd me upstairs. "Poor motherless girl. We'll get you in proper order straightaway."

It was a comedy after that, for the dressmaker knew only a little English and neither Mrs. Adams nor I spoke French very well. My apprehension grew when the dressmaker's assistant displayed bolts of cloth for our perusal. Mrs. Adams asked my favorite color, and looking at the samples before me, I hesitated, afraid to give the wrong answer. I'd never been good at keeping my clothes tidy, so I hoped to choose something that might hide the stains.

"The blue silk would suit you," Mrs. Adams said, then seemed to reach into my thoughts and snatch them from the air. "Girls keep their clothes tidier if you let them choose the colors and fabrics they like."

Under her expectant gaze, I tentatively asserted myself. "I *am* fond of the blue, but yellow, too."

Mrs. Adams nodded. "A lovely combination. Perhaps a pale yellow petticoat beneath the blue silk and some yellow bows on the sleeves." With hand motions, Mrs. Adams made the dressmaker understand. Assistants rushed in with a dizzying array of shiny ribbons and frothy lace. Meanwhile, Mrs. Adams looked through my trunks, quite uninvited. "You're nearly twelve?"

I nodded.

"Then you'll need a new wardrobe entirely. We can't get it all done today, but I'll draw up a list." She said I was to have shoes with decorative buckles and bonnets with flowers. I was to have new undergarments and a side-hooped petticoat to give me the illusion of hips in the case of a very formal occasion. I was to have a cape and handkerchiefs and maybe even a chemise gown of pure white muslin like the kind made popular by the French queen. I was to have at least one gown immediately, made of the scraps and bits that the dressmaker sent her assistant to fetch, so that I could go out into proper company while the other dresses were being made.

Standing in the middle of the whirlwind as the seamstress took measurements, I was shy of the attention. But Mrs. Adams encouraged me to stand up straight. "You're going to be tall like your father; there's no help for it. Still, your red hair is lovely and your soulful eyes are sure to be some man's undoing, so never shrink down into yourself."

Her direct manner might have been off-putting but I perceived a compliment. Maybe two. "My thanks, Mrs. Adams . . . but you're sure Papa will consent to the expense for my clothes?"

At this, Mrs. Adams softened. "What a sweet girl you are to worry. The truth is, you'll have to help your father make do. The policy of our country has been, and still is, to be penny-wise and pound-foolish. The nation which degrades their own foreign ministers by obliging them to live in narrow circumstances cannot expect to be held in high esteem. Here in Paris, my dear, *appearances* are indispensable."

I liked that she didn't speak in the falsetto voice some adults do with children. She talked of grown-up concerns as if I was old enough to understand. She was too loquacious to remind me of my own mother, but I felt *mothered* as I hadn't been in years. Though Mrs. Adams offered very firm guidance, she didn't bully me. When the *friseur* came and I declined to have my hair styled in the high plume of fashionable Parisian women, Mrs. Adams said that I should have my own way and I left my copper ringlets down, tied in a simple ribbon.

Eventually the dressmaker's assistant returned with a gown of lilac satin that had been discarded by some other girl. I was virtually sewn into the dress on the spot. When the seamstress was finished, I stroked the fabric, which was soft as peach skin. I'd never owned anything so lovely. Excitement fluttered in my belly that the dresses made for me would be even prettier. In my new gown of draped sleeves, I scarcely recognized myself in the mirror. Indeed, I preened so long that I feared Mrs. Adams would think me vain. But I no longer appeared to be the rustic girl I knew.

Abigail ushered me into the parlor, where we found Papa with a book in his hands, pointing something out to Mr. Adams.

"May I present Miss Martha Jefferson," Abigail said, clearly pleased.

Papa glanced up, his eyes widening. "Why, Miss Jefferson, you have become a miniature lady." He looked to Abigail. "I thank and congratulate you, madam." He pressed his hand to his mouth and shook his head. "Plainly, a woman's touch was just what was needed."

Perhaps not sensing the sadness I heard in his voice, Mrs. Adams clasped her hands and gave a self-satisfied smile. "Indeed."

Their praise made my cheeks heat, but I enjoyed Papa's astonishment so much that I didn't mind the attention. Especially when, after Mrs. Adams left, Papa turned to me once more. "Let me see you," he said. "Spin 'round."

Like a dancer, I held out my arms and twirled, the long skirts swishing around me. And Papa smiled. The first open smile I'd seen in so very long.

I was afraid to pinch myself for fear that I'd wake up in Philadelphia, alone and afraid. But no. I was awake. And I dared to hope that the charms of the Old World had awakened us both from our nightmare of grief and madness, at last.

~

PAPA'S FRENCH FRIENDS who had helped us during the Revolution were also eager to get us settled. In fact, it was the Marquis de Chastellux who arranged for my enrollment at the Abbaye Royale de Panthemont, a convent school where two of the French princesses took their education.

Fearful of being boarded with strangers yet again, I pleaded, "Can't I have tutors? I promise to attend my studies. I want to stay with you, Papa."

I was grown, now. Old enough to help set up his household. If Papa believed, as he said he did, that young girls ought to primarily be trained for domestic tasks, to prepare for a life as wives and mothers, then why did he insist on my learning music, drawing, arithmetic, geography, and Latin? But Papa would not be dissuaded in his plans for my education. Even when my enrollment in the convent was universally criticized by our American friends, who feared royal and papist influences. The abbess swore, however, that though I would be cloistered behind convent walls during the week, I'd be exempt from catechism and the sacraments.

As the day I was to attend the new school dawned, I could scarcely force myself from bed, despite the fact I'd hardly slept all the night before. Papa had to call for me twice, and I was so distraught at our inevitable separation that I didn't even care that my delays earned his ire.

When we finally passed through the gates of the Panthemont, underneath a magnificent clock that faced the street, I clung to my father's arm. In habits, the nuns all looked much the same, rushing about with their charges, girls wearing uniforms of crimson. We were led into a large room filled with beds and writing tables where I was to board with other girls. And though some of the girls were introduced to me as the daughters of English nobility, none would speak anything but French. I thought I was the only American, and when Papa left me for the night, I cried into my pillow hoping no one could hear.

Today, if someone were to ask where I have been happiest in my life—where I found the most companionship and joy and discovered the best in myself—I would name the convent without hesitation. But my first days at the Panthemont were a misery. I lived for the evenings when Papa came to share supper with me. Every night, I thought he'd change his mind and take me home, but he didn't.

I kept quietly to the corners, ignoring the taunts of the older girls. They pointed and laughed at my freckles and my big bony elbows. They mocked my faltering attempts to speak French. And I learned that I wasn't the only American girl after all—there was also Kitty Church, whose mother was from New York, but she seemed to despise me most of all. A kindly abbot encouraged me to play with the other girls in the courtyard during the afternoon, but when I cleaved to him, Kitty teased me that Catholic priests couldn't marry—which made me blush so hotly I could scarcely bear it.

Learning embroidery one day, I was asked by one of the girls, "Is it true that your father owns African slaves?"

The question was softly put, with no hint of malice, but before I could answer, Kitty Church laughed. "Yes, of course it's true. Don't you know that Mr. Jefferson is our slave-holding spokesman for freedom?"

The way Kitty spoke of my father, with such mockery, stung my cheeks with shame. It was a shame deepened by the fact that Kitty's father, like mine, was an American envoy to France. Her family hailed from the North, where slaves were fewer and the abolitionists held much sway. I couldn't help but wonder if she'd learned this scorn for my father from hers, and if her father was a rival to mine.

"Do you own a slave, Patsy?" Kitty singsonged the question. "Do you whip her when she misbehaves?"

This boldness encouraged our classmates, many of whom expressed dismay and made a point to tell me French law freed any slave who set foot in the country. I wondered if my father—or Jimmy Hemings—knew this. And while I fumbled for a reply, mortified and defensive, one of the girls stabbed a needle into her embroidery before berating Kitty Church on my behalf, hurling curses in French.

The savage-tempered girl was raven haired and tiny, and I wondered why she took up for me.

"It isn't how you say it is," I finally argued as the girls outdid one another in imagining horrid abuses. I remembered the day Papa commanded our overseer to stay his hand with the lash; I'd never witnessed slaves being whipped bloody, or flayed open and left to wild animals if they disobeyed. Never had such a thing happened at Monticello!

But the more I tried to defend our plantation, our home, our way of life, the more strident the criticisms became. And the nuns said nothing, for this was a house of pity, and they must've thought my papa a wretched sinner.

I stared down at my crude embroidery, remembering my mother's sewing. Her neat stitches to repair a dress in need of mending. A small embroidered flourish to ornament a bonnet or a tablecloth. In a dark mood, I was lost in that memory until I looked down to see that I'd stabbed my finger with the needle and my blood had seeped into the delicate cloth.

"Come," said the raven-haired French girl. "We'll bandage that."

Before I could protest, she shook her head and pressed her fingers to her lips to hush me. She was delicate and beautiful like my little sister Polly. That's what made me follow her back to the bedroom where she sat beside me until I could face the world again. Her name was Marie de Botidoux, but she couldn't say my name. The closest she came was *Jeffy*. I liked the way it sounded on her tongue. And I was so desperate for a friend I would've let her call me anything at all.

~~~~

THE NEXT AFTERNOON, the nuns made me draw in the parlor, imagining it to be some comfort to me. But I struggled with drawing—as I always had—my lines curving sadly down at each end, my strokes too bold on the paper, smudges on my fingers and clothes. It was in this state that my visitor found me. Deep in melancholy, I looked up slowly, believing that my eyes deceived me.

Could it be William Short, clutching at his hat?

I was so glad to see him that I rushed to embrace him with the exuberance of a Frenchwoman. "Mr. Short! Have you seen my papa?"

He gave a quick bow of his head. "The very reason for my visit, Patsy. Your father suffers of fever. He'll be confined to his house for some days. I know you are apt to worry, so I thought to convey his warmest regards myself."

I was unbearably grateful. He had seen us the day I was thrown from Caractacus, he understood as no one else did. He knew why I worried for Papa. But these were things that couldn't be spoken aloud. My lower lip trembled and he must've seen it, for his eyes softened and he reached for my hand.

"Poor child. If it will comfort you, I'll report to you on your father's health every few days."

The warmth and strength of his hand surprised me as much as steadied me. As his thumb slipped over my knuckle, I blinked up at him, reassured by the amiable smile on his well-bred, handsome face.

For a moment, I couldn't help but study him, the only person who knew even a hint of my struggle with Papa. William Short's countenance appeared more angular, more masculine, less boyish than it had been years before. He carried himself with a new confidence, too, one that made me glad he'd be serving at Papa's side. "Thank you, of course. But . . . can't I go to him, Mr. Short?"

"Don't fret, Patsy. The thing that will best ensure his comfort and well-being is to know that you're well cared for and thriving at your studies. If I can reassure him of this, he'll rest easier."

Alas, I'd presented myself in precisely the way that most vexed Papa. I'd received his new secretary in a slovenly state, smudging his hand with pencil dust. "I'm sorry, Mr. Short. I've dirtied your hand."

He looked down and chuckled at the sight of my blackened fingers, the graphite smearing into the lines of his palm. "So you have." Then mischief lit in his eyes as he reached to playfully smudge my nose with his thumb.

I giggled, which attracted the attention of sour-faced nuns. They scolded me, eyeing my green-eyed, sandy-haired visitor with a mixture of enchantment and disapproval. In French, I told them Mr. Short was a kinsman of my mother and as close to a son as my father had.

One hand pressing to his chest, Mr. Short startled at my diction. "I envy you, Patsy, for your French is so improved. I've been struggling to learn it, but now I have the solution. I'll join the convent and live with you and all these pretty girls so that I may learn it quicker."

His jest *scandalized* the nuns, who blushed and tittered and scowled at him in turn, before showing him out. But then, many women and girls blushed for the handsome Mr. Short. Even Marie—who blushed at nothing.

Indeed, I suspected his visit accounted for my sudden change in social fortune, for the girls made an effort to befriend me after that day. And each time one of them asked an innocent-sounding question about Mr. Short, it forced me to see him not as my family's protector during our flight from the British, and not as my confidant, and not as Papa's secretary, but as a bachelor in a city full of beautiful, forward women.

The thought disconcerted me for reasons I didn't want to understand. At least Mr. Short remained true to his word, delivering regular updates about my father's welfare and providing reassurance that I could devote myself to my studies and my life at the convent.

In that, Marie became my first true friend. We made an odd pair, Marie, who loved all the fine things a lady should love, and me, who longed to run outdoors. I'd been taught never to raise my voice in anger, but she was fierce tempered. Other girls were afraid to provoke her because she repaid them with such abuse as to make their ears bleed. And they were afraid to taunt me, too, because the moment she caught someone mocking my French or the unsophisticated style of my hair, Marie would launch into a tirade so fast and biting I could scarcely follow it.

When Elizabeth and Caroline Tufton, the nieces of the Duke of Dorset, the British ambassador to France, once dared suggest the American experiment would fail, the tongue-lashing Marie gave them for disrespecting me, my father, and the French assistance to the American cause was littered with forbidden insults. Curses like *Casse toi!* and *Je t'emmerde!* and *Meurs, pute!* exploded from her lips like bullets from a musket until both girls cowered, pleading they'd meant nothing by it.

I was so unused to someone rising to my defense that all I could do was gape. But Marie's actions warmed my heart, too, because her friendship was the first thing I'd ever had that was mine alone, untouched by the grief and travails of the past few years. A few days later, the older Tufton sister presented me with a pretty crimson ribbon. I viewed it as a peace offering, just as their country had been forced to a peace treaty with mine. And my acceptance earned me two more steady friends.

But *that* night, I had only Marie. She slid into bed beside me, her gaze daring anyone else to say a word. No one did. When everyone finally settled for sleep, Marie turned and stroked a curl from my cheek. "*Cher Jeffy.* You'll be happy in Paris, you'll see. And if not, I'll teach you to pretend."

————)

"I SHOULD STAY WITH YOU and help Jimmy prepare our Christmas feast," I said to Papa, who'd finally recovered from his illness but was still regaining his strength. "After all, one day I'll have to play hostess for a husband."

"Not for quite some time," Papa said from his armchair, a woolen blanket over his legs. Then he gave a rueful smile. "And let's hope when it comes to marriage, you don't draw a block-head. In this, I put your odds at fourteen to one."

Bad odds, I thought. Could it really be so hard to find a good husband or was my father's long-absent sense of humor returning to him?

Once he felt healthy again, Papa took me to see marionettes and gardens and Yuletide decorations. We visited cafés, billiard halls, shopping complexes, and bookstalls. Once when we strolled the snowy streets, we were treated to a song by a defrocked abbé with a guitar.

With each new outing, Paris enchanted us more and more. Papa declared himself violently smitten by the classical architecture of the Hotel de Salm, and we spent many days watching its construction from a garden terrace across the river. Nearly every American in Paris gathered at our home for a holiday celebration. Another night we went to visit the Adams family and shared a feast of roast goose, and afterward, Nabby Adams taught me to slide on the ice.

Papa came out into the night air to watch us, and it was a merry Christmastide. If only the New Year had been as kind . . .

For at the end of January, the Marquis de Lafayette, returned from his journey to America, came to call. Lafayette was the French general who had saved us from the British, and we hailed him as a military commander second only to General Washington. But on the evening the Marquis came to call upon us, he was a humble gentleman in our doorway, unattended by his aides. In truth, the nobleman cut an impressive figure in white breeches, calfskin gloves, and a martial coat of blue adorned with two rows of gilded buttons. But beneath his powdered wig, he wore the saddest expression I'd ever seen.

What could this man say that occasioned such gravity? When Lafayette finally began to speak, emotion caught in his throat and he nearly wept, begging my father's pardon. He carried a letter to us from the doctor at Eppington. A letter of the most dreadful tidings.

My father went to stone as Lafayette babbled heartfelt condolences, half in French, half in English. The Marquis was shockingly sentimental, even for a Frenchman, and it took me several moments to sift through his emotional speech. I heard the names of my sisters. An illness, born of teething, worms, and whooping cough, had swept through my aunt and uncle's household, striking all the children.

"Your little Polly survived," said Lafayette. "But baby Lucy is gone."

Gone? I pressed a hand to my shuddering chest and struggled to draw in a breath. The pain started as a sting in my heart and burned its way out until I had to choke back a sob. Never once had I imagined my separation from my sisters to be final. Never had I thought our hasty farewell to baby Lucy at Eppington would be the last. I'd written a letter to Aunt Elizabeth just weeks ago with wishes for Lucy she did not live long enough to hear. To learn the sweet girl had been gone for over three months and I hadn't known it, I hadn't felt it, I hadn't sensed the loss.

What a wretched sister I was!

And, poor Polly. Just six years old and she'd already lost her mother and sister to death's grip. And here we were, so far away. The sob finally broke free. My mother bade me to watch over my father, but what of my sisters? I was to watch after them, too, to protect the little family that Mama so loved, and I was stunned by my failure.

Papa made a quick farewell to Lafayette, all but shutting the door in his face. Then he leaned against the wall, shuddering with grief. He thumped his fist on the wood to punctuate each moan and sob. I fell against him, hugging his waist, pressing my face against his rib cage where his heart thudded. His body muffled my wails, and his shirt absorbed my tears. He clutched at me and I clutched at him as if we were wrestling. Perhaps we were.

We were wrestling the pain, thrashing against it, drowning in it, until we were insensible to all else.

And I knew that no one could ever see us like this.

~~~~~

WE MUST HAVE POLLY, I decided. We must have my remaining sister here in France where we could care for her and hold her close. For months, Papa resisted the idea, worrying that the seas were too unsafe for one so young to travel alone. For pirates, privateers, and warships abounded across the Atlantic.

But I couldn't be content without her. There was only one way to honor the losses of my mother and baby sister, and that was to bring our family together again.

Our conversations on the matter were often frustratingly disagreeable, even when I pressed Papa *calmly*—if also frequently—to reunite our family once and for all. Meanwhile, I dared not trouble Papa in any other way for even the smallest thing; I even drew my allowance from the *maître d'hôtel* rather than go to my grieving father.

Our house was in mourning, and our French friends were effusive with their sympathy. Lafayette seemed haunted by having delivered us the news and sent bouquets to brighten the house. The pretty young Duchess de La Rochefoucauld brought sweets for our table and bade me to call her Rosalie. In truth, the very Frenchwomen Mrs. Adams and my father sometimes spoke of so disparagingly for their bold manners were tender and kind to us.

By contrast, some of our American friends and other guests

seemed insensible to our loss. Charles Williamos, a Swiss-born adventurer who often dined with us, said my father should simply remarry and make another baby to heal his broken heart.

At hearing this, Papa excused himself from the table, no doubt to wrestle with his grief in private. But I had not Papa's good manners. Williamos's heartless advice reminded me of Colonel Randolph's suggestion that Papa remarry. Were the affections of these men so shallow they believed a lost life, a lost love, could simply be replaced?

From that moment, I despised Mr. Williamos.

And it must have showed. Mr. Short looked up from the meal, caught a glimpse of the enmity on my face, and said, "Patsy, shouldn't you be abed? Better still, back at the convent?" He dabbed at the corners of his mouth with his napkin and stood up. "I'll carry you there myself."

I shook my head. I couldn't leave Papa when he was so upset. In fact, I wanted to sneak up to my father's room and lie beside him as I did when my mother died. But Mr. Short prevented me. "You're forgotten here in the glumness, Patsy. You'll be better cared for at the convent, and your well-being will weigh less upon your father's mind."

With that, Mr. Short reached for his coat with a stance that brooked no argument.

For a young man of such good humor, there was a hard strength in William Short. And I remembered how, when we were hiding from the British, he went off into the wilderness by himself, against all advice. When he made up his mind, he was as firm in it as my father could be. Maybe even firmer. And so I had no choice but to do as he said.

But I glanced back over my shoulder at Charles Williamos with a promise to myself that I would see the obnoxious man gone from my father's house, somehow. . . .

Chapter Six

Paris, 11 May 1785
From Thomas Jefferson to Francis Eppes

My appointment will keep me somewhat longer. I must have Polly.

DUE TO THE SLOWNESS OF THE POST, we received a letter from Aunt Elizabeth telling us of Lucy's death, seven months after it had been written. Reading the details cut us open all over again. And Papa finally wrote a letter to Uncle Frank commanding him to send Polly to us as soon as he could.

She couldn't arrive soon enough. Knowing that I'd never see baby Lucy again, I longed for Polly. I was fond of Marie and my friends at the convent, but I began to dream of Polly and her angelic blue eyes, which made me sad upon awakening to find myself still without her.

Papa and I were still dispirited the next week when the Adams family came for a farewell dinner. Mr. Adams had been assigned to London, so we'd soon lose them across the narrow channel, which saddened me, too, because they'd been good friends. And Papa confessed their departure would leave him in the dumps.

"Oh, my poor dears," Mrs. Adams exclaimed. "How you must mourn your little Lucy!" But it was hard to remember our sadness when Mrs. Adams swept into the house and expressed a lively opinion about every new thing she saw. She approved of Papa's window coverings, saying they must have set him back his whole salary. She also approved of the pie we served, which delighted me, because I had helped Jimmy crimp the crust before it was put into the oven.

The only thing to spoil the farewell dinner was Charles Williamos, who dined with us again. I watched his fork flick the crust, as if he found it not to his liking. I suppose that was fair, because *he* was not to my liking either, and not merely because he suggested my father take a new wife and make a new baby to replace the dead one.

He was the sort of man who never spoke to me directly, referring to me only when forced as *the girl*. Otherwise, he didn't seem to notice me at all. But I noticed *him* and the shrewd way he directed the dinner conversation, pushing the men to speak of politics in front of the ladies with a relentlessness that bordered on the unmannerly.

I'd have happily listened to Mrs. Adams decry the morals of Frenchwomen, or whispered gossip with her daughter Nabby, but always, Charles Williamos turned the topic to finance. How much could America borrow? How many loans had the envoys secured? And whenever a question was put to him about his own affairs, he answered it with a question of his own.

Since my mother died, I'd come to understand silences better than most. Perhaps that's why I found something strangely suspect in the things Mr. Williamos chose *not* to say.

Later, when I crossed paths with Mr. Short in the hall, I asked, "How did my father come to be in company with Charles Williamos?"

Mr. Short rubbed his cheek in thought. "I can't say I am entirely sure, Patsy, but why do you ask? He's always eager to fetch whatever your father needs. He's made himself a useful friend."

The hollowness in my gut insisted Williamos was no friend at all. "I have no fondness for him."

It was an unladylike thing to say and I wished I could call it back when Mr. Short raised a brow. "Why ever not?" Mr. Short shot a ferocious look in the direction of the dining room, as if he intended to be my champion against some unseen foe. "Has Charles Williamos said something to you?" he asked sharply, eyes narrowed. Then, more darkly, "Has he *done* something untoward?"

Mr. Short's fierceness unleashed a tingle in my hollow belly and helped me voice my suspicions. "It is only that he listens differently than other men at the table. Have you not observed it? He always holds his tongue when he might offer an opinion, and is uninterested in the opinions of others unless they're made with great specificity. He's trying to learn something of us without allowing us to learn anything of him."

Mr. Short appraised me, his gaze running over my face. "You noticed this just sitting at dinner, behaving yourself like a little lady?"

My head bobbed with eager agreement, sensing that it pleased him. "Should I tell Papa?"

He paused a long moment, studying me with an intensity that caused my heart to beat faster. "No. What is there to tell?" He gave a small smile. "You worry too much for your father. Now, go on to bed Patsy, it's getting late."

But in the morning, I knew that I'd have to return to the convent. I'd have no opportunity to protect Papa from those who didn't understand the depths of his sensitivity. To those who felt free to opine about Papa taking a new wife, not knowing—or perhaps, not caring—that he had sworn never to do so.

My father was too trusting; it was always the case.

So, I didn't go to bed. Instead I slipped quietly into the empty room where Charles Williamos slept at night, not knowing what I was looking for. He had few belongings and even fewer that interested me. A scattering of papers on his writing table drew me closer. None of them useful, I thought, but, then . . .

A receipt. A tailoring bill charged to Papa—surely the sort of thing my father's secretary ought to be aware of, if the expense was incurred on my father's behalf. It was nothing, I told myself. Or at least not much. But maybe it was *something*. . . .

I snatched it up and carried it across the hall to where Mr. Short took dictation for my father. And I left Mr. Williamos's paper there, as if it'd merely been mislaid by a servant.

~~~

"CELEBRATIONS ARE IN ORDER, Jefferson," the Marquis de Lafayette exclaimed the next weekend over a glass of wine by the fire. "I'm told it's now official that you're to replace Benjamin Franklin here as minister to France."

"No one can replace Dr. Franklin," Papa replied. "I am only his successor."

It was a modest reply, and Papa was earnest in his admiration for Dr. Franklin, but he couldn't disguise his pride. He'd secured a position of great esteem and importance for our new nation. We were charged here with protecting American citizens, securing documents for travel and letters of introduction. We were to foster goodwill, educate Europeans about our new country, and make reports to America on the happenings overseas.

It was, Papa assured me, great and necessary work. I was very proud, of course. And upon hearing the news, Kitty Church behaved much better toward me. For if her father had been a rival to mine, he was no more.

In celebration, Papa took me to witness the grand procession to Notre Dame in honor of the new prince of France, born to his mother, Queen Marie-Antoinette.

Papa and I bumped and jostled along with the rest of the crowds that lined the roads. Given the harsh words some of the Frenchmen had for their queen, I was surprised they came out in such force to see her. But the moment her carriage rolled into view, the crowd roared and surged with eagerness. Such are the contradictions of monarchy, I supposed.

Even Papa was taken in by the spectacle.

"Look, look!" Papa cried, elbowing a space for me at the front of the crowd.

I clapped my hands in excitement. How beautiful the queen's garments and how regal the king looked at her side! And yet, they were too far away to judge if they looked like their portraits in Philadelphia. "Why do some in the crowd boo the queen, Papa?"

"Because King Louis is too much governed by his queen," Papa replied.

That hardly seemed like a thing *she* ought to be faulted for, but I held my tongue, for we were having a grand time. When the entourage disappeared, Papa and I walked hand in hand to the convent. I was a giddy girl the whole way, and didn't want the feeling to end. "I should like to come out into society with you more often, Papa. Perhaps go with you to concerts and the theater."

Papa smiled and pressed a quick kiss to my cheek. "You're turning into my little lady, aren't you?" The compliment lit me up inside and I stroked my hands over the fine silk of my beautiful green skirt. In truth, I was thirteen, no longer a child, nor even a girl, but, according to the nuns at the convent, *a spring flower on the cusp of blooming.* I'd just experienced my first woman's blood, and I felt all the more like a woman when, with great adult satisfaction, I learned on my next visit home that Mr. Williamos had been sent packing.

Papa would say nothing of why his boon companion had been so unceremoniously ejected from our embassy. So, while he changed out of his formal waistcoat and powdered wig to take an evening brandy, I went to Mr. Short.

I suspected *he* would tell me the truth about such matters, and I was right.

Closeted with an array of ink pots and quill pens scattered upon his desk, my father's secretary explained, "Mr. Williamos was 'sent packing' because he had his tailoring billed to your father's account. What's more, he had the temerity to lay the bill of receipt on my desk!"

I dared a glance up at Mr. Short in the light of a flickering candle. "Did he?"

An eyebrow lifted at my interest. "Indeed. Of course, he accused me of ransacking his belongings to find it. Can you imagine the nerve?"

Mr. Short must've suspected that I was the one who ransacked Mr. Williamos's belongings. But he didn't scold me for my misadventure. Indeed, I saw a hint of admiration in his eyes. That emboldened me to venture, "Surely a tailoring expense isn't the whole reason Mr. Williamos was banished. Papa is very generous with his guests."

Short nodded. "That's true. Your saintly father thinks too well of other men, whereas I'm a sinner with a rather peculiar talent for prying into facts."

I tried valiantly not to imagine what sort of sins Mr. Short may have committed, but my efforts did not prevent a flutter in my belly. "Did you pry into the facts of *this* matter, Mr. Short?"

His smile was thin and conspiratorial. "I made inquiries and got word from a certain Frenchwoman that Charles Williamos is a British spy."

I gasped. A spy!

Pleasure brimmed up inside me at the thought that I had some part in flushing out an enemy, and any guilt I still felt for my sneakiness disappeared on the spot. The rightness of my instincts justified my actions and perhaps saved my father from embarrassment or harm. It was all very well for me to study music and Latin, but I was now decided that it would be much better for our fathers and husbands—for the country itself—if all American women learned to study the manners of people and warn against the bad ones.

It is a belief in which I have never wavered since.

BY LATE SUMMER, all anyone could talk about was Queen Marie-Antoinette. The fascination owed mainly to the accusation that she'd somehow persuaded the Cardinal de Rohan to secretly purchase for her an exquisite diamond necklace. Kitty Church's bold and irreverent opinion was, "The audacious woman wanted an expensive bauble, but didn't dare buy it *openly* while her subjects go hungry. Then, when the bill came due, she couldn't even pay!"

It was patently false, and the nuns ought to have been embarrassed by the cardinal's gullibility to be fooled by a woman impersonating the queen, but many of them seemed to blame the queen anyway. "How can the people believe her guilty?" I asked Papa. "The imposter signed her letter *Marie-Antoinette de France.* Even *I* know that's not how sovereigns sign letters."

Directing the servants as to where to place his favorite mirror in our new embassy, Papa replied, "The people believe it, because the queen of France has a reputation for callous imprudence. It sounds in keeping with her character." He paused, to give me his full attention. "You may take a lesson from this, Patsy. *Reputation* is everything. A soiled reputation in an ordinary person may reduce them to impoverishment, but a soiled reputation in someone like the queen may take down a government."

It was a shocking statement—one that revealed my father's lingering revolutionary sentiments. *Did he think the French would rebel, too?* But he said no more about it.

Because he was now a minister in the Court of Versailles, we were obliged to live in a way the French believed equal to his station lest he be thought ineffectual by the foolish standards of Paris. Foolish standards or no, we were both pleased with our new two-story town-home on the Champs-Élysées. It had more rooms than I dared to count, and in shapes one wouldn't expect. There was a coach house and a stable for the horses. A greenhouse for the plants Papa loved to collect. Even a water closet with a flush toilet!

Of course, we'd need more servants. A coachman, a gardener, and a housekeeper, too. Jimmy Hemings couldn't be expected to do it all. And, in truth, I'd begun to worry for our mulatto slave to be seen in the dining room where he provided ammunition to those who mocked my father as *our slaveholding spokesman for freedom*. But after hearing Mr. Short worry aloud that he wasn't sure how Papa would manage all this on a salary of five hundred guineas per annum, I fretted at the expense of my new gown—lavender silk with a ribbon of lace for my neck in the place of jewels.

Nevertheless, we had a grand time together at a musicale, and afterward, at home, Papa sighed and said, "I miss it."

"What do you miss?"

Absently fingering the watch key in which he kept a braid of my mother's hair, he said, "Music."

His reply ought to have puzzled me, for we had heard more music—and in more variety—since coming to Paris than any time past. But he used to make music with my mother, and he was merely a listener now.

"I should very much like to hear you play your violin, Papa."

He blinked down at me. "It's a lonely instrument without accompaniment."

Till then, I had been a middling student of music. More enthusiastic than talented. But in that moment a desire bloomed inside my chest to sing and play as beautifully as my mother had so that neither of us might ever be so lonely again. "Shall we choose a duet, Papa?"

His lashes swept guardedly down over his blue eyes, as if he meant to refuse and retire early to bed. But then his lips quirked up at one corner and he called for his violin.

We made music that night, and every night I was home from the convent.

And I think Papa forgot his cares.

I think he forgot that Lucy was dead and that Polly still hadn't made the crossing of the sea to be with us, despite Papa's repeated requests. I think he forgot all our unhappiness. And I think I forgot it, too.

At least until the carriage ride home, when he spoiled it all by telling me that he was going to England. "Only for a few weeks, Patsy. You needn't be afraid."

But my memory resurrected our most harrowing days. I lived in dread of British soldiers since the night we had fled Monticello. It was an English king who declared my papa a traitor and tried to capture him. "It's *England*, Papa."

"John Adams reports a civil reception in London," Papa said, to allay my fears. "Besides, I've fought too long against tyrants to let the terrors of monarchy keep my girl awake at night."

This left me with only one suggestion. "Then let me go with you. I'd very much like to see Nabby again."

"You have your schooling," Papa said firmly. "The more you learn, the more I love you. Lose no moment in improving your head, nor any opportunity of exercising your heart in benevolence. Your duty is to attend your studies at the convent. My duty takes me to England."

What of the duty Mama had bestowed upon me to watch over him?

Nevertheless, Papa left me in the care of Mr. Short, who had command of the American embassy while my father was away. I believed it was the increased responsibility that was behind the infrequency of Mr. Short's visits to the convent and not—as my friends whispered behind their hands—that he spent all his free time in the company of notorious women. But their rabid gossip gave me the strangest sinking feeling, so I refused to even acknowledge it.

On the day he came to pay my tuition, Mr. Short reported, "Your father has arrived safely in England. He bids me to look after your happiness."

Tartly, I replied, "I'd be a good deal happier if he'd write me."

Mr. Short straightened his cravat and gave a sympathetic smile as we walked together on the convent grounds. "Perhaps he'll return with a little gift . . . I have it on good authority that he's ordered a special harpsichord for you."

I gasped, imagining the duets Papa and I would play together. My mother played the harpsichord and I wanted to make beautiful music with one, too. "Is that really true?"

My spirits lightened as Mr. Short guided me to a bench and we sat in the cool spring sun. "It is. And maybe he'll return with your sister Polly, too," Mr. Short suggested, perhaps encouraged by the light in my eyes. Hope flooded my heart. Seeing Polly would be even better than a harpsichord! It shocked me to realize that it'd been nearly a year since we wrote instructing Aunt Elizabeth to send Polly to us. Seldom was anything my father commanded left undone, and I began to worry that they were all very ill at Eppington. Too ill to come to us here in France. And I said as much.

"Patsy, if you keep fretting, you'll wither away before your fourteenth birthday and I'd hate to see a fair bloom spoiled before it blossoms."

A thrill rushed through me. Had Mr. Short called me a *fair bloom*? Did he mean anything by it? Certainly not. Still, an odd lightness of being filled my chest until I was nearly giddy. The heat of a blush flustered me. I remembered the gossip about Mr. Short and notorious women, and his words made me bold. Brushing away a tendril of my hair caught by the breeze, I forced my gaze to meet his, which was bright green in the light of the sun. "Mr. Short, what should a friend do if she knew your reputation was in danger?"

He tilted his head. "If my friend was a daughter of the U.S. minister, she should tend to her father's reputation and not mine."

I *had* tended to Papa's reputation; but Papa was better now, his reputation unblemished, his honor as a Virginia gentleman beyond reproach. "Doesn't my father call you his adoptive son? Therefore, by your reasoning, I should tend to your reputation because it reflects upon him."

Mr. Short smirked at my boldness. "Why do you think my reputation is endangered?"

"Rumors say you're overfamiliar with women, especially with

a girl in the village of Saint-Germain, where you first learned French." My brazenness set me to trembling. I clasped my hands to hide it.

"Ah, the Belle of Saint-Germain." He laughed, proving he took no offense.

But I hoped he'd deny it and didn't know how to respond to laughter, nor to the odd disappointment welling in my chest. Finally, I said, "It's gossip. I know it's not true. You're a sprightly dancer. How can you be blamed if licentious Frenchwomen flock to you?"

This only made him laugh harder.

"I've defended your honor," I added hastily, my temper rising with my discomfort. "I've vouched for your good character."

He squinted his green eyes with mischief and mirth. "Oh, never do that. You can never know the heart of a diplomat. Perhaps the gossip about me is true."

My spirits sank, but my spine straightened. "Mr. Short, do you not realize that I'd defend you against disparaging words even if they *were* true?"

My earnestness pierced his bubble of merriment. He sat forward, his amusement dying away. "I'm sorry that such matters should ever concern you, Patsy. Truly. I endeavor to flaunt my affections with such openness that I cannot be suspected of secret lusts or hidden vices. My affections for the Belle of Saint-Germain and for the Duchess de La Rochefoucauld, and any number of Frenchwomen who frequent the salons of Paris, are genuine and transparent. I'll not claim my own actions are innocent, but theirs are blameless."

His admission that he felt affection for these women made my throat go suddenly tight. "Well, I worry," I managed weakly.

Mr. Short smiled. "Your care is ever a comfort. Just be sure you attend to your own happiness, too."

I HOPED PAPA WOULD RETURN from England with my little sister. And failing that, my new harpsichord. Instead, he returned with a startling missive from Polly, who refused to join us in France, writing: *I want to see you and sister Patsy, but you must come to Uncle Eppes's house.*

Polly's willfulness pained me. Never would I have defied Papa's wishes in such a way. And since my sister's letter was written under Aunt Elizabeth's supervision, I couldn't help but think it had my aunt's approval, which left me quite sour toward her.

Poor Papa had been snubbed. By Aunt Elizabeth, by Polly, and by King George, too, in London. But at least there was a little good news from Papa's trip: Nabby Adams was to marry her father's secretary. Upon hearing the news, an unaccountable blush discomfited me. Papa noticed. "Don't fall prey to jealousy, Patsy. There's time enough for you to be a wife."

But time passed too slowly for my taste. I chafed at being treated like a little girl who understood nothing. I wanted to travel and attend lectures in the salons and go to balls. I wanted to be presented in French society like some of the other girls in the convent. Alas, it wasn't until I was nearly *fourteen* that Papa announced he'd take me to the opera in September.

"The opera!" I cried. "I'll need a new dress."

"Yes. You're growing so fast that I cannot keep you in clothes. But this will be a special gown. One ornamented with bows and such fripperies as the most fashionable woman in France might desire. Would that meet with your liking?"

I was so excited I nearly squeaked. The opera was no house party where I'd be swiftly sent to bed when the adult discussions began. This was the *opera*, where the cream of French society gathered to see and be seen. Papa would take me in my new dress, and I knew I must be well rested because the opera started late; I might not even be back to the convent by curfew!

My friends suffered with envy. None of them had ever gone to the opera on the arm of a minister to the Court of Versailles. And I gloried to know I'd have all Papa's attention for myself and imagined how we would ride together in a glittering coach. The girls at the convent told me that I ought to be very careful alighting the carriage in my new gown, so I practiced holding my skirts in one hand and stepping down with the other.

Then I counted the days until the leaves began to fall off the trees.

On the night we were to attend, my friends tittered around me as I dressed. My stays dug into my sides and the shoes pinched my toes—but I looked womanly with my hair tied back and the faintest dusting of powder upon my nose. Marie slipped a little pot of rouge into my hand, but I dared not wear it where the nuns could see.

When the coach arrived to fetch me, I was surprised to find it empty. I'd imagined Papa would hold his hand forth to help me up. No matter, I told myself. Papa would be waiting there for me at the opera, his blue eyes bright and intent upon my face. When the carriage stopped I peeked out to see a beautiful building illuminated by lamps against the coming darkness of night. It was a magical sight, and so I stepped down just as I'd practiced and the coachman escorted me into the carpeted reception hall. I thanked him very properly and smiled at the young men who gazed curiously upon me. But my eyes were all for Papa.

He was easy to find in a crowd because he was so tall. He wore his best blue coat, and his bright white wig was perfectly arranged. As I approached, he was smiling. He looked young and vibrant—his cheeks infused with a healthy pink, as if he'd just returned from riding. He turned, summoning me closer.

Then I saw with sinking spirits that his smile wasn't for me.

Standing with him was a little goldfinch of a woman, colorful and delicate, her tinkling laugh lighting up my father's expression. He'd never looked at me like that; I feared he'd never looked at *anyone* like that. "Allow me to make introductions. Maria Cosway, this is my daughter Patsy."

It was the first time I heard her name, but I heard it a hundred more times by the end of the night. *Maria. Maria. Maria.*

Papa seemed to like the sound of it on his lips.

When and how did they meet? They didn't behave as *old* friends. Yet they spoke affectionately of an outing to see the crown jewels. How could my father have made such a dear friend—dear enough that he felt free to use her given name in public—without my having known about it? And where was her husband? She was a married lady—the ring on her finger revealed as much— and not a widow, I was told, when I asked.

But she didn't behave as if there were any man in her world but my father.

The three of us sat together in our box, but only I seemed to be paying any attention to the performance of *Richard Coeur-de-Lion* and the farcical comedy that followed. Maria laughed during serious moments, while Papa was serious when he ought to have laughed.

And he couldn't take his eyes off her.

Chapter Seven

Paris, 12 October 1786
From Thomas Jefferson to Maria Cosway

Having handed you into your carriage, and seen the wheels in motion, I turned and walked, more dead than alive, solitary and sad. A dialogue took place between my Head and my Heart. We have no rose without its thorn; it is the law of our existence; it is the condition annexed to all our pleasures. True, this condition is pressing cruelly on me at this moment. I feel more fit for death than life. But the pleasures were worth the price I'm paying. Hope is sweeter than despair. In the summer, said the gentleman; but in the spring, said the lady: and I should love her forever, were it only for that!

I SHOULD BURN MY FATHER'S COPY OF THIS LETTER—a love letter, to be certain, written in a fashion only a sensitive heart and brilliant mind like his could've imagined. It unfolds, page after page, in a lengthy debate over whether or not he ought to have loved her.

This letter is a beautiful embarrassment that the world should never see.

But I cannot bring myself to destroy it with all the other evidence of his folly.

In the first place, I'm sure the wretched woman kept the original. And in the second place, I tried to burn it once before. . . .

That autumn, in Paris, somehow the duet of my life with Papa had become a trio. But the music stopped altogether when, in a foolish attempt to impress Maria Cosway by jumping over a fence, Papa badly injured his wrist. The echo of how he'd hurt himself trying to impress my mother all those years ago made me furious.

Mrs. Cosway was now leaving the city—and good riddance to her!—yet, Papa was chancing making a greater fool of himself by insisting on offering a personal farewell. On the dreary October day I returned from the convent to find my father gone, I fretted to Mr. Short, "But the doctor who set his bones said that he shouldn't go anywhere!"

Mr. Short rose from the desk chair where he'd been conducting his work. "Your father insisted, Patsy. I offered my opinion that it wasn't in his best interest to accompany Mrs. Cosway, but he's my employer. I'm not his."

There was something strange in the way he phrased it; something that made me worry Mr. Short also suspected the entanglement between Papa and Mrs. Cosway was improper. So I tried to cast the shameful matter in terms of my father's health. "He's barely sleeping for the pain. Saint-Denis is two hours by carriage each way. He's canceled every other engagement these past weeks, yet, for her . . ." I shook my head, angrily, recalling the migraine that had kept Papa from my birthday dinner and his presentation of the Marquis de Lafayette's bust to the citizens of Paris the next day. In both cases, Mr. Short had appeared in Papa's stead.

"I share your concern, Patsy, but Mr. Jefferson was intent on seeing Mrs. Cosway off on her departure to London."

I wondered if Mr. Short not only suspected but *knew* the danger Maria Cosway presented—to Papa's heart, mind, and reputation. If Mr. Short knew of my father's affair, ought I be glad or horrified? *Horrified*, I decided, and tried to deflect suspicion. "I suppose Papa has such tender sentiments toward his friends that he must see them off personally."

Mr. Short wasn't fooled by my efforts. "You're a good daughter, Patsy. But you must try to remember . . . it's been nearly four years since he lost your mother."

My cheeks warmed. "I never forget it, for now I'm all he has."

A vigorous shake of his head released a lock of sandy hair to shadow his eyes. "No, Patsy. That's not true."

"It *is* true." My chest rose and fell swiftly under the weight of my obligation. I couldn't bear for anything to tempt Papa's melancholy to return. And I was the only one who could protect him from it. "Our kin are far across the sea. Even if they weren't, I'm the only one who understands. . . ." I trailed off, twice as convinced. "I *am* all Papa has."

"Patsy, you're much mistaken," he said with insistence, standing so close that the weight of his presence steadied me. "Mr. Jefferson has me, too. He's a father to me, and ours is a bond of affection that cannot be broken. I honor him. He's the beating pulse of every cause dear to me. He may always rely upon me, and so may you."

The words were a balm to my heart. Mr. Short had repaid my father's patronage with a devotion as clear-eyed as it was ardent. He'd seen my father in strength and weakness, cleaving to his side no matter how his fortunes rose or fell.

Dear Mr. Short.

Knowing that there existed someone else who cared so much for Papa was the greatest relief. And for the first time, I felt *understood*. I believed Mr. Short understood me completely. It was such a revelation that it felt oddly intimate, forcing me to take a step back. "Thank you—"

The jingle and clatter of a carriage sounded from the front of the house. I headed for the stairs, with Mr. Short following, knowing it must be Papa returned from his ill-advised adventure. My father's face was white as a bedsheet, each step costing him a great deal. Mr. Short poured a glass of amber liquor for Papa, who emptied it with a grimace. In a flat voice that invited no discussion, my father said, "Go to bed, Patsy."

I was forever being sent to bed early, but what argument could I make to convince him that I should stay? When Papa was in such a dark mood, he wouldn't hear me. His wrist clearly pained him, but there was something else. Something else terribly wrong. And I knew that it must have something to do with *Maria*.

Acid flooded into my stomach at the realization that Mrs. Cosway had said or done something. Maybe she had quarreled with Papa. I was desperate to know how she returned him to such melancholy, but I dared not ask because I was afraid he'd taken this woman to his heart—a heart he pledged forever to my mother on her deathbed. Having captured that heart, was it possible that Maria had shattered it?

If so, perhaps it was no more than he deserved.

Angry, I pushed up from my chair. "Good night, Papa."

But it wasn't a good night. And my father's mood failed to improve. Indeed, much of the weekend he closed himself in his chamber struggling to write with his uninjured left hand, with which his penmanship was quite poor. Each time I entered to check on him, he scrambled to secure the pages. He didn't fool me, of course. I knew he was writing to her. He was writing a secret letter to a married woman. And I knew that it must be a *shameful* letter if he wouldn't even let Mr. Short write it for him.

What new kind of madness was this?

I feared he had written a love letter—which Maria Cosway might use to embarrass him. Worse, I feared he'd written a plea for her to leave her husband and take up notorious residence as my father's illicit lover. Such scandalous arrangements were not uncommon in France. Indeed, they were common enough for my classmates at the convent to discuss them in excited whispers. But they'd destroy Papa's reputation with our countrymen. And, as Papa had said of the French queen, *reputation is everything.*

Of course, I'd also heard him say that a person ought to give up money, fame, and the earth itself, rather than do an immoral act. *Ask yourself how you'd act if all the world was looking and act accordingly.* This was the advice Papa gave all the men who looked up to him. He said it to his nephews, to Mr. Madison, to Mr. Monroe, and to Mr. Short. He'd also given this advice to me.

But in the matter of Mrs. Cosway, he seemed to have forgotten it.

So it was that I found *myself* doing a dishonorable thing, telling myself that I was doing so in order to protect Papa from his own folly. Having heard my father give instructions that his secret letter should be posted to Maria Cosway, I decided that I must find the letter before Mr. Short had the chance to seal it. Reading Papa's private letters would be wrong, and I knew that, but I could think of no other way.

I dared not sit upon the stiff-backed desk chair for fear it might make the floorboards creak beneath my feet, so I held my skirts tight in one hand while sifting through the stack of letters with the other. My fingers brushed an envelope so thick it formed a packet and my heart dropped. I pulled it from the pile, knowing before I saw the address it was the one I sought.

Dread washed over me as I unfolded the pages.

My hand shaking, I read Papa's secret words.

My heart suddenly beat in my throat.

He characterized himself as *more dead than alive*?

The words pulled me into the past, into the woods surrounding Monticello upon Caractacus's strong back, into our wandering journeys looking for a ship to set sail, into the time when Papa still yearned for the grave. I thought him quite beyond that, quite recovered, but he still claimed, in this extraordinary letter, to feel *more fit for death than life*.

And oh, how furious it made me to read it! It was one thing for Papa to have longed to die of grief for my mother, but to feel that impulse over this . . . this . . . this foreign harlot? Anger and panic tingled up my spine and my gaze flew over Papa's words, some of which leaped up from the parchment as he likened himself to a *gloomy monk, sequestered from the world*. Had the promise he made never to remarry left him to compare himself to a monk? My gaze rushed on. "*The human heart knows no joy which I have not lost, no sorrow of which I have not drank."* The sentiment made my chest tighten, and then I gasped as Papa expressed his wish that Mrs. Cosway never suffer widowhood, but that he, above all men, could offer solace if she did.

It wasn't difficult to see Papa's fantasy through the thin veil of his prose: he wished not only for Mrs. Cosway to be his mistress, but perhaps even for her husband to die so that she might come to live with us at Monticello. Despair rushed through me. This letter was such a betrayal of my mother's memory that I was eager to hurl it into the fire!

Intending to destroy the letter—every scrap of it—I returned my attention to the pile of letters to make sure that I had all the pages. That's when my gaze landed upon my own name within the missive that sat atop the stack. Not in my father's handwriting, but in the hand of *Mr. Short*. It was a scribbled note to a painter of some renown, from whom my father had commissioned a miniature of himself to give as a gift to Maria Cosway.

Mr. Short might have taken it upon himself to cancel such an unwise commission—but instead, he requested the painter make another miniature for me. More astonishingly, Mr. Short asked the painter to pretend the request came from my father. This gesture, at once thoughtful, gallant, and modest, moved me deeply. It also shamed me, for there I was, snooping about in Mr. Short's desk.

I began to wonder how many times Mr. Short had secretly interceded on my behalf. How many men with such responsibilities would take the time to worry after the feelings of a girl? How had I betrayed the trust of such a friend, even if my intentions were good? The full measure of my wickedness sank in, like a stone dropping to the bottom of the sea, when the door creaked open.

Mr. Short caught me where I should not be, still clutching my father's love letter. Given the soft look of reproach in his eyes, he knew just what I'd come here for and why. He came toward me, reaching wordlessly for the letter. "Don't make me wrestle it away from you, Patsy."

I couldn't excuse myself—nor could I lie. Red-faced and miserable in my guilt, I let him take it from me, but pleaded, "Pray throw that letter in the fire!"

He replied with an indulgent chuckle. "I'd never do such a thing. Every shining word that flows from your father's pen is a national treasure."

He was jesting, but I couldn't smile. "You don't know what's in that letter, or how it might embarrass Papa or sully his honor." I hated that I had to speak the words, but it was better than admitting that my father was slipping back into the state of mind that nearly ruined him.

Mr. Short gave a rueful sigh. "I have a rather good idea of what's in this letter. Your father confided that it was a debate between the wishes of his heart and the restraint of his intellect."

Stung that Papa had confided in Mr. Short what he wouldn't confide in me, I said, "Then you know it's better burned. He compared himself to a lonely monk! How can he still be so unhappy when he has your company and mine?"

Mr. Short started to reply, then snapped his mouth shut again before giving a rueful little shake of his head. "Oh, Patsy."

My nostrils flared at his condescension. "Didn't you tell me that my father may rely upon you? Isn't it your duty to keep him from making an error in judgment? Sending this letter would be a grave error!"

"Patsy, it's the very essence of liberty that a person be allowed to err."

And we both knew how *I* had erred in being there like a thief in the night.

Mr. Short met my eyes. "Besides, I'm the last man on earth who may judge another for unwise associations and attachments."

He must've meant the notorious women of whom he and I had once spoken. The Belle of Saint-Germain and the married Rosalie, the Duchess de La Rochefoucauld. But something made me dare to hope that Mr. Short aimed this pointed remark at me. Was he forming an attachment to me and did he think it unwise?

And yet, his apparent reference to those women made my face heat such that it took me a moment to find my voice. "It's for God to judge, but perhaps you can advise Papa against—"

"I've *advised* your father to make a long trip to the south of France."

So he'd counseled my papa to go somewhere he might forget Mrs. Cosway; perhaps it was good counsel. I didn't wish to be left behind in Paris, but I wouldn't be lonely. I had friends at the convent and no harm came to my father when he traveled to London, save for the snubbing at the hands of the English king. . . .

As if to forestall objection, Mr. Short added, "He can use the trip to investigate commercial opportunities that will enable our new nation to meet its financial obligations. It will keep him *busy*."

Yes. Perhaps distraction and duty were exactly what Papa needed right now.

Mr. Short's words were both cloak and candor. And I realized that there was no one else in the world who spoke to me this way. The garrulous Mrs. Adams spoke to me as if I'd become a woman of good sense. Papa shared with me his enthusiasm for science and inventions and architecture and music. Especially music. But only Mr. Short ever spoke to me of politics, spies, and finance. Only Mr. Short seemed to believe I had some *right* to know more about the revolution my family had brought about.

He didn't treat me like a child anymore, and that was for the best, because I very much wanted William Short to know that I hadn't been a child for quite some time.

～◡

THANKFULLY, WHEN PAPA'S WRIST HAD HEALED A BIT, he embarked on the trip to the south of France. As we stood together on the street in front of our embassy waiting for the carriage, I wished I could tell my father to forget Maria Cosway. I wished I could tell him to find joy in discovering the countryside and observing the beauty of nature—instead of the beauty of a married woman.

But I could say none of this without confessing that I'd read his letter. Instead, I let my breaths puff silently into the cold morning air, hoping he could divine my hopes in those little clouds of steam. Hoping he'd sense my love, my longing for him to confide in me where he wished only to confide in others.

Maybe he did. "Patsy, I have a farewell gift that I hope you'll hold close to your heart." He withdrew from the pocket of his embroidered coat a miniature portrait of himself.

I pressed it against my chest. "Oh, it's lovely, Papa. I'll treasure it. Why, it must be one of a kind!" In saying this, I hoped to give him an opening. A chance to confess that it was a duplicate of the one he'd commissioned for Mrs. Cosway. A chance to beg my pardon for remembering me only because of Mr. Short's kindness.

I waited for Papa to say these things, ready to tearfully confess my own sins. Eager for him to embrace me and reassure me that he hadn't forgotten Mama and that he didn't intend to return to Virginia with Mrs. Cosway and make her the new mistress of Monticello. But Papa merely kissed my cheeks. "I'll write to you so often you won't even know I'm absent from Paris."

Then he climbed into the carriage and was gone.

Watching the wheels of Papa's carriage rumble down the street, I backed up the stairs to find Mr. Short waiting there. Still smarting with disappointment, I asked, "So, I suppose you're to be master of the embassy while Papa is away?"

"Custodian anyway." He clasped his hands behind his back, swaying with faux hauteur upon his buckled shoes. "But since you've also been entrusted to my care, I'm uncertain as to which duty will be more trying." He raised a brow, as if to remind me that he knew a part of my nature to which the rest of the world was blind. "If you have any care for the prospects of my career, make certain I'm not forced to account to your father for bad behavior while in my charge."

I *did* have a care for the prospects of Mr. Short's career. I had a very great care. And so, when he next came to the convent to pay my tuition, I quizzed him on France's financial troubles, which, to my ear, sounded like a very grown-up topic indeed.

"The finance minister has called for tax reform," Mr. Short explained as we strolled through the convent's inner courtyard past neatly trimmed shrubbery and an explosion of spring flowers in yellow, red, and pink. "And at least half the city stands insulted by the king's refusal to put the matter before *parlement*."

"I've heard the political quarrel has spilled out into the streets in scuffles," I said, a little ashamed of the thrill in my voice, especially since it wasn't the danger that excited me, but the nearness of Mr. Short. How had I never noticed before how noble a profile he had? And his green eyes . . . how could eyes be so strangely world-weary and enchanting at the same time?

"Men will fight for liberty," Mr. Short was saying, sounding very much like Papa. "But there's always a risk that fighting will descend into lawlessness."

"Then I'm glad our revolution is over in America."

Mr. Short's lips twitched up. "You think our revolution is over and done, Patsy?"

"Have we not wrested our liberty from the British?"

"We've won, at force of arms, the right to draw up a Constitution. Yet, you need look no further than your father's own plantation in Virginia—or indeed, our embassy kitchen—to see that liberty hasn't been secured for *all* men."

My lips parted in astonishment. Mr. Short was unwilling to judge my father for his affair with Mrs. Cosway, but on the matter of slavery, I heard the very certain note of censure. Bristling, I said, "I suppose the Virginia gentlemen of Spring Garden, from whence you hail, don't keep slaves?"

"Not *this* Virginia gentleman," he said, with a determined shake of his head. "I entered this world with a small patrimony. I hope to grow my investments such that my fortune may sustain me. But I will not water it with the infamous traffic in human flesh. The practice compromises our morals and teaches us a habit of despotism."

His vehemence took me entirely unawares. I couldn't imagine this was a conversation of which my father would approve, but the lure of discussing anything with an impassioned Mr. Short proved too much to resist. "Then what—what is to be done about slavery?"

Mr. Short turned us into the bright green hedge maze. "I haven't an answer yet. But I intend to join a society for effecting the abolition of the slave trade."

As we walked, Mr. Short explained to me his vision for a world where slavery was no more and men lived in equality and deference to the law. And for once I didn't curse my long legs, for I had no trouble matching his stride as our shoes fell into rhythm together. I'd always taken him for a pragmatist—a shrewd man if not an entirely virtuous one. But that day I learned he was a man whose ideals were as lofty as my father's.

Perhaps loftier.

When he left me, I raced up to the bedroom so that I could stand at the window overlooking the street to watch him go. Marie came upon me and flounced atop the embroidered-coverlet of the bed, propping herself up on one elbow in bored repose. When she glanced out the window to see the retreating figure of Mr. Short, her mouth formed a little circle of surprise. *"Mon Dieu!* Jeffy, you are smitten."

"Nonsense," I said, not risking a glance at her. "Mr. Short is merely a friend of long acquaintance."

"Then why are you pink to the tips of your freckled ears?"

At last, I decided it would do no good to hide it from her. I spun on my toes in an excited pirouette. "Do you think he fancies me? Whenever he visits, he stays longer than he is obligated to do. He had an artist paint a portrait for me. . . ."

Marie's expression fell. "Oh, poor Jeffy. Has no one told you that your Mr. Short is infatuated with Rosalie, the Duchess de La Rochefoucauld?"

I pretended to dismiss it, waving a hand. "That's a malicious rumor."

She hesitated at my staunch defense, then concluded, "I think it's true that he's infatuated with her, but let's hope it is only rumor that they've become lovers."

Lovers. I was wholly unprepared for the flash of pain that burned just beneath my breastbone at the thought. Mr. Short was a man of twenty-seven who spent his days with the cream of French society . . . of course he took lovers.

With sinking spirits, I decided that I'd been a fool. The reminder made me wonder how I'd ever so much as entertained the notion that he might take an interest in me. How ridiculous to dream, for even a moment, that a mere schoolgirl could compete for his affections with the likes of a duchess, no matter that she was another man's wife. . . .

Wounded, I kept to myself, finding comfort in the scriptures. I reported the political happenings in Paris to Papa by post, hoping to keep him apprised. But he didn't seem pleased by my interest in politics. My letters were all too often met with silence and, in one case, a veiled rebuke that I should attend ancient Latin texts and keep my mind always occupied to guard against the poison of ennui!

How could I care about the translation of Livy with the world in such a state? Moreover, I wouldn't *need* to keep my father apprised of the goings-on in France if he hadn't been away, pining for the plumed and piffling woman who aroused his sinful impulses.

Only you, Martha. That's what he swore to my mother four years before as she gasped her last breaths. I believed him then and so did she. But what I learned about men in Paris—even *American* men in Paris—opened my eyes and bruised my heart. And so I wrote to Papa, bitterly, of the latest news, almost hoping to wound him:

*There was a gentleman, a few days ago, that killed himself
because he thought that his wife did not love him. I believe
that if every husband in Paris were to do as much, there
would be nothing but widows left.*

To that letter, Papa did not reply.

~⁀⁀⁀

IN THE CONVENT'S SALON, clutching his smart tricorn hat and a
nosegay of posies, Mr. Short said, "Patsy, I've had word that you
were ill. I shouldn't have insisted the nuns rouse you from bed,
but when you refused to see me, I feared—"

"It was only a violent headache," I said, pulling my shawl
round myself for warmth, though it was springtime. "The kind
Papa suffers when he's upset."

I didn't tell him of the mysterious pain in my side that had blistered up and caused me such suffering. No doubt elegant duchesses never fell prey to such unsightly maladies. If he was to find
out about my blisters, he'd have to learn it from the bewildered
physician, not from me, so I offered nothing else by way of explanation. Nor could I explain to him the wound on my spirit—
one that'd driven me, in prayer and contemplation, to a religious
epiphany.

What I couldn't tell him, for fear he might tell my papa, was
that I had resolved to take my vows and join the convent.

The idea had first come upon me in a sudden swirl of anger
and resentment . . . and yet, during my illness, it had transformed
itself into a genuine desire. Though I knew my father would despair to hear it, I was more contented at the Abbaye de Panthemont than at any other place I'd ever been. Immersed in its world
of women devoted to each other and the betterment of mankind,
I felt sheltered against the wickedness of Paris. What's more, my
dearest friends were always near to me at the convent, and I felt
more suited to a life of reflection and scholarship than to a mar-

riage or to a plantation to which my father supposed I must one day return.

None of this, of course, could I tell William Short.

At my silence, Mr. Short exhaled a long breath, then drew one of the purgatorial wooden chairs closer. I sat, careful of the shifting of my gown against my side. When he sat, he didn't cross his legs like a man of leisure, but perched on the edge, as if waiting for a verdict at court. "Your father couldn't bear it if anything should happen to you, and under my watch—"

"I'm quite recovered of my infirmity. You needn't worry for your career."

Mr. Short scowled, extending the nosegay to me. "Enjoy these in good health, then."

Taking the posies, a tenderness crept through me that I was forced to steel myself against. "Have you any word of my papa? Of my sister?"

"Your father's return has been delayed, but your sister is en route. I cannot imagine how your Aunt Elizabeth got the girl onto the ship, considering Polly refused to come. Your father is quite bedeviled by the child. She defies him as if he were no more to her than a strange beggar on the streets."

Polly had been scarcely five years old when we left her. Now she was nearly nine. She'd lived half her life with Aunt Elizabeth, and through our neglect, I worried that we had lost her as surely as we'd lost baby Lucy. It was a failure that gave me the greatest pain, and I was determined to live up to the promise I'd made my mother to watch over my little sister. Which I could do right here, in the convent. When Polly came to us in France, Papa said I must teach her to be good, and to tell the truth, for no vice was so mean as the want of truth.

But I'd teach her to be *devoted,* for that seemed to me a much more important virtue. Nuns were devoted. And if I was to be a devoted friend to Mr. Short, I knew that I must overlook the blots on his character as he overlooked mine.

So I determined to think no more about his pretty duchess.

Nuns wouldn't think about his duchess.

I took the posies and inhaled their sweet scent before drawing Mr. Short into conversation. He obliged me, explaining how antislavery sentiment grew hand in hand with constitutionalism in Paris. These talks, in which he showed respect for my opinions, made me think about new things and challenge what I'd been told. Challenge, even, my papa.

And the next day I wrote to my father:

> *It grieves my heart when I think that our fellow creatures should be treated so terribly as they are by many of our country men. Good god have we not enough slaves? I wish with all my soul that the poor negroes were all freed.*

In answer to this sentiment, Papa was also entirely silent.

Chapter Eight

London, 26 June 1787
To Thomas Jefferson from Abigail Adams

I congratulate you upon the safe arrival of your little daughter. She's in fine health and a lovely little girl, but at present everything is strange to her. I told her that I didn't see her sister cry once when she came to Europe. Polly replied that her sister was older and ought to do better, and had her papa with her besides. I showed her your portrait, but she didn't know it. If you could bring Miss Jefferson with you, it would reconcile her little sister to the rest of the journey. The old nurse you expected to have attended her was sick and unable to come. Instead, she has a girl about 15 or 16 with her, one Sally Hemings.

I WAS READY TO FETCH POLLY AT ONCE. But my father bewildered me by sending a French servant to escort Polly from London instead. And I was outraged when Mr. Short let slip the reason why.

Papa had urged Mrs. Cosway to return to Paris. The shameless woman had agreed, and because she was on her way, Papa didn't want to chance the trip to fetch Polly for fear he'd miss his paramour!

Maria. Maria. Maria.

That night, when Papa kissed me good night, I bit down

on the impudence that tempted my tongue. But Mrs. Adams showed none of my reserve in her next letter, in which she tartly informed us:

> *Polly told me this morning that since she had left all her friends in Virginia to come over the ocean to see you, you might have taken the pains to come here for her yourself. I haven't the heart to force her into a carriage against her will and send her from me in a frenzy, as I know will be the case, unless I can reconcile her to going.*

I was glad Abigail Adams's letter shamed Papa.

I took greater solace that Mrs. Adams would reconcile Polly to join us and that I'd soon have my sister with me once more. After all, I knew from experience that people found it extraordinarily difficult to hold out against Mrs. Adams!

Weeks passed before the welcome sound of the hired coach turned from the rue de Berri and into the courtyard of the Hotel de Langeac. Hearing it, I rushed from the salon out to the front steps. As I held my breath, two girls stepped down from the carriage, their eyes wide with wonder and uncertainty.

Oh, dear Polly!

How changed she was. Still petite, with the blue eyes I remembered so well, but now a grown girl that I might've passed on the street without knowing. And yet, when I tried, I could see my mother in miniature.

"Dearest Polly, I am overjoyed to see you," I said, hurrying down the steps.

My little sister turned shy at the sight of me, sucking her lips in as she examined my face. I smiled brightly, holding my arms out to her, but they drooped when I realized that, in fact, she had totally forgotten me.

The pain was an arrow to the heart—as sharp as any wound I've suffered.

Reluctantly, Polly accepted my embrace but then squirmed

away, her gaze swinging over the house's facade. "Everything here is so grand. . . ."

I grasped her hand. "I know. Paris is a wonder. You'll love it here. Come. Papa's eager to see you."

As I guided her to the steps, I glanced over my shoulder at the slave girl. I hadn't seen Sally in many years and she'd changed, too. If I'd ever doubted that Sally was my mother's half-sister, I was convinced the moment she said hello. She had my mother's voice. The soft lilt of her greeting was so familiar. And, in truth, her appearance was strikingly similar to my sister's. Sally was a mulatto of fair complexion, but not so perfectly fair that the French wouldn't suspect she was a slave. And I worried what our French friends would think. I remembered the words spoken against my father's reputation as our *slaveholding spokesman for freedom*. But perhaps Sally's resemblance to Polly would be to our advantage, for it was perfectly common here for lesser relations to take on positions as servants to their wealthier kin.

Like all our Hemings servants, Sally had been raised at the hearth of our family; she'd make a very fit companion in Paris, where she might learn a good trade, just as her brother had been doing with his cooking. When we entered the entrance hall, Jimmy Hemings stood waiting, dressed in his chef's toque and work uniform. He bowed and offered a warm welcome to my sister. And his.

While the Hemings siblings celebrated their own reunion, I led Polly into my father's study, where he leaped to his feet at the sight of us. My little sister stumbled back, still clinging to my hand as my father went down on one knee. "Don't be frightened, child." And when she smiled a little, he asked, "You know me, Polly, don't you?"

She shrugged apologetically. "I think, upon seeing you, I recollect something of you, sir."

It was another barb that dug its way into me. I had dreamed of restoring the happy little family that had laughed and sung in a wilderness cabin while hiding from the British, yet my sister didn't even know us.

By evening, Polly and I started to overcome the deep sense of separation, and I hoped she'd spend the night in my bed, but she wanted to sleep with Sally.

"We had to trick Miss Polly onto the ship," the slave girl explained. "Mrs. Eppes lured her onto the boat for an outing with all their children, then we played with Miss Polly till she was so tuckered out she fell asleep in my arms. When she was asleep, the Eppes family tiptoed off the ship and we set sail. Poor child woke up at sea with no way home but to swim."

Poor Polly. The sudden surge of sympathy redoubled my determination to do my duty by her. And I instructed myself to take no offense at the closeness she seemed to share with Sally.

By week's end, we enrolled Polly in school with me where we finally bonded over our studies. I tutored her in French, not wanting her to experience the teasing I had. I enjoyed teaching her and basked when she complimented me as being a patient and encouraging instructor.

Polly was intelligent—if occasionally too strong-willed—and quick to make friends; she adjusted far more easily than I ever did. She had an independence I admired, even if it caused Papa to fret. Indeed, she took him to task, boldly professing her resentment that he did not go to England to fetch her.

She couldn't know it was because of Mrs. Cosway. I never told Polly how that woman clouded his judgment. No, I held that secret for him with all the others.

～

SHE DIDN'T LOVE HIM. By God, nor *ought* she to have loved him. Why couldn't he see it? Mrs. Cosway returned to Paris at the end of summer without her husband, and I was no longer too naive to understand her liaison with my father was of a passionately carnal nature. Papa rented an apartment in the hermitage of Mont Calvaire on the pretext that he needed privacy from the bustle of our embassy, and it served to excuse his absences when he indulged in clandestine meetings with his mistress.

But Mrs. Cosway was even less faithful to my father than she was to her husband. When unrest fomented in the city, with the king closing all political clubs and dismissing the *parlement,* Papa was forced to attend American interests in the midst of the growing crisis, and Mrs. Cosway pouted and complained of it over dinner one night.

I had to keep my gaze trained on my cutlet of chicken for fear of her seeing the exasperation and disapproval on my face. One day, when Papa was away debating the merits of the newly proposed Constitution for the United States, I told her she might take comfort in his absence with the miniatures he'd given us, but she brooded that he hadn't commissioned them from *her.*

She apparently had a very high opinion of her own artistic talent.

If Mrs. Cosway loved my father, she'd have been his helpmate in this difficult time. If she'd loved him, she'd have been a balm to soothe his agitation. Instead, after only a few weeks, whenever Papa called upon her, she managed not to be at home. Then she called upon Papa at our embassy only when she was sure he'd be out. Because of his bad wrist, he couldn't play the violin for her anymore. And they stopped going to the follies or to the royal gardens or to the opera. She preferred to hold court at the reputedly beautiful Polish princess's salon, while Papa was swamped by a storm of political chaos.

I shielded my little sister from all of it, and the convent was our refuge. And I was comforted by the routine of the place, secretly slipping in to attend mass, for I felt the wont of God. Alas, on Sundays we were often at the Hotel de Langeac, where I worried for the lack of moral examples for Polly, especially when Mrs. Cosway was our guest.

One quiet afternoon, I asked my sister, "Would you like to learn from Jimmy how to make a pudding?"

Cheekily, Polly replied, "Isn't Jimmy our chef? If he knows, why should we learn it?"

"Because Mrs. Adams once told me that every woman ought to know how to make a pudding." The mention of Abigail Adams was the surest way of convincing my little sister, and so Polly trailed behind me into the kitchen, where we found Sally near tears because Jimmy would only speak to her in French.

Pleading amber eyes turned toward me. "Miss Patsy, I'm supposed to take a tray up to your father's chambers, but Jimmy won't tell me in a language I know what's to be on the tray."

"Jimmy, don't be churlish," I said, feeling sympathy for Sally.

But Jimmy insisted, "Sally must learn to speak the language if she's to live in Paris. Perhaps she'll learn it when she's sent away."

This forced Sally *all* the way to tears.

"Hush, don't cry," I said, a hand on her shoulder, shooting a sharp look of rebuke at Jimmy. "Your brother has gotten very much above his station since coming to France. Why, he's become so sullen and secretive Papa jests that he's forgotten how to speak English but doesn't know how to speak French, either. You aren't being sent away, Sally."

Sally stifled her sob in a napkin. "I *am*. I'm being sent to take the pox." This was a surprise to me, though it shouldn't have been. It made sense; my father believed cities like Paris engendered disease. I only wished he'd informed me of his intentions, because it sent Sally into a rare panic. Glaring at her brother, she said, "And I might die of it, so you might never see me again. Then you'll be sorry!"

She meant this to induce Jimmy's guilt for teasing her, but Polly's beautiful blue eyes filled with terrified tears. "Do you mean you're going to die? Like my baby sister Lucy?"

"Of course not," I said, trying to comfort both Polly and the servant girl who shared my little sister's bed at night. "Polly, we took the treatment years ago. So did Jimmy. What's more, it didn't hurt very much." That was at least mostly true. "Why, Polly, you can scarcely remember it, can you?"

Polly shook her head, clinging to Sally's skirts.

"There," I announced. "Do you see? If it was so dreadful, don't you think you'd remember it?" Polly agreed, comforted. Sally seemed to be, too, and Jimmy hugged her before sending her up to my father's rooms with coffee and a pastry.

But that night, Sally crept from my sister's bed to perch at the end of mine. "Miss Patsy," she whispered. "Your father told me I'm likely to get very sick."

"Yes." I remembered what my father said when I took the treatment. "We must take upon ourselves a smaller evil to defend against the greater evil. We must take upon ourselves a smaller pain in order to survive."

Sally nodded, gravely. "But if I pass, I want Polly to have the little bell your mama left me."

I remembered it well. "You still have it?"

"In my bundle," she said of her small satchel of belongings. Moved, I stroked her back between her trembling shoulder blades. "You're not going to die, Sally. And I'll care for you. I've already had the pox, so I can stay with you until you're better." I imagined myself wiping sweat from her brow, brushing her long black hair, and tending to her as gently as Papa once had tended to me.

Alas, that was never a possibility. It wasn't legal to give the treatment within the city limits, so Sally was sent away to a physician's care, where she remained quarantined for the next forty days. Which meant two things. First, that we spent forty days in fright for Sally, not knowing if we'd see her alive again. And second, that Polly finally cleaved to me.

Without Sally between us, Polly climbed into my bed. She let me take her shopping for clothes. She let me style her hair. Together we played a hiding and seeking game in Papa's greenhouse and plucked dried and overripened Indian corn from Papa's garden to make a display for the table. In short, now that I was fifteen, I took upon myself Polly's mothering and cared for her as I promised my own mother I would.

Unfortunately, this only seemed to free Papa to pursue his most dangerous impulses. In spite—or perhaps because—of the way Mrs. Cosway made herself unavailable, Papa couldn't seem to shake her enchantment. When the weather turned cold during Advent, he planned a dinner in Mrs. Cosway's honor. Though he usually preferred small gatherings of friends, for *her,* he invited a large crowd of strangers including exiled Polish and Italian royalty. I hoped at least the crowd would avoid the intimacy of a less grand affair.

Jimmy prepared the feast. He was swiftly becoming an accomplished chef in the French style, whereas I still hadn't mastered pudding, but because I imagined myself to be the hostess of this dinner, he permitted me to chop carrots and onions while he braised beef in a soup of bacon, wine, and brandy. I tried to take note of the amounts of nutmeg and allspice he sprinkled in, but Jimmy worked fast with a pinch here and there, as if he'd committed it to memory. I was obliged to watch a clock for three hours while the concoction boiled away, and while I should've been contemplating a way to ask my father's permission to become a nun, I imagined I was the wife of my father's handsome secretary and that we had a house together just outside of Paris.

It was only a fantasy, for Mr. Short had never expressed interest in taking a bride, and rumors hadn't ceased about his love for a married duchess. But I contented myself with harmless fantasies of domestic bliss, whereas the men in my life were apparently content with nothing but real congress with sinful women.

As I dressed that night, I worried for the scandal Mrs. Cosway might cause, fluttering about my papa like a wounded bird. But when she arrived, Papa bounded toward her to kiss her cheek, whereas she turned her head so the kiss landed upon her ear. At dinner, she took the seat beside him as proffered but slid it closer to a count of some renown, with whom she flirted shamelessly. Though I'd desperately *hoped* Papa would give up this affair, it was painful to watch it unravel before my eyes. Worse, I witnessed the exact moment my father reached to pat her arm, and she recoiled from the sight of the curled fingers of his injured hand, as if she'd only just realized he was twice her age.

Papa looked away, his lips pressing into a tight line. She'd hurt him. And I felt furiously angry at her for doing so. If a woman was to surrender her virtue and risk eternal damnation, she ought to at least do it for good reason. I might have forgiven her if she'd sinned in the cause of love. But the way she recoiled from my father made me certain it was not her heart that led her to sin; it was her vanity. And I've never forgiven her for that. Not for her dalliance with Papa, nor for the way she treated him.

God may forgive her, but I never shall.

The only good to come of her rejection that night was the way it forced Papa to stiffen, as if awakening from a long, fevered dream. Perhaps my father had to suffer this humiliation in order to recover from the fever of Mrs. Cosway. Alas, it seemed that I had to be equally prepared to suffer humiliation when the dinner conversation turned to the Duchess de La Rochefoucauld.

Mr. Short's association with the woman was the cause of several veiled but ribald jests. I pretended at supreme indifference while I surreptitiously fisted my hands into my skirts, agonized by my awareness of the man so close. I stared at the lace that peeked out from under Mr. Short's neatly tailored sleeve, wondering how far apart our knees were spaced beneath the table. Wondering, too, when I'd be humiliated enough by my own infatuation to stop wondering such things . . .

The subject of mockery, Mr. Short only sipped at his wine with an enigmatic smile. There was no blush on his cheeks. Only mine. After a bout of raucous laughter, the Polish princess pointed at Mr. Short and accused, "You're overly fond of French girls!"

He replied, with a sly glance my way. "Oh, I like Virginia girls just as much."

All at once, my burning embarrassment became a different kind of fire and I died a thousand burning deaths of pleasure. Mr. Short's amusing retort meant nothing to these people, who laughed at his defiant wit. But his eyes fastened on mine flirtatiously, and I finally knew with certainty that I hadn't imagined his affection for me after all. . . .

It was real.

The dashing Mr. Short could've had any Frenchwoman in Paris. But he was looking at me in my blue gown with the golden sash. He was looking at *me,* and I felt suddenly as light and warm as the wisps of smoke that floated up from the silver candelabra on the table.

~

THAT NIGHT, long after the guests took their leave, I couldn't stop spinning on my toes. Round and round I went into the bedroom like a whirlwind. Polly peeked up from her goose down pillow in vague alarm. "What's wrong?"

"Nothing at all," I said, falling into bed on a laugh. I was no longer certain I wished to join the convent, because I might soon have, in Mr. Short, a suitor of my very own.

What's more, for the first time I could remember, things were just as they ought to be. My family was together under one roof, domestic tranquility the aim of our existence. Exactly what my mother had always wanted—what I'd always wanted, too.

And a few days later, something even more wonderful happened.

Mrs. Cosway left Paris.

I learned this from Papa, who came in from the wintry cold with frost upon his wig and a crumpled piece of paper in his hand. "I was to have breakfast with her this morning," he bit out. "But I found only a note of farewell."

Papa marched up to his chambers and stayed there. And though my father was always writing, that whole next week, he sent not a single letter. Seeing me fret over this, Mr. Short asked, "Will you never stop wrinkling your forehead with worry for your father, Patsy? He's merely lanced a boil."

Had Mr. Short also believed that Maria Cosway was a plague

on our house? If so, why had he stood by and let her happen? "She might return to Paris."

"He wouldn't see her again if she did. If nothing else, Mrs. Cosway deprived your father of his good-bye, of a closing scene, of a way to make sense of it, categorize it, and put it in final order. He despises nothing so much as that."

He had the right of it, for he knew my father well. Papa might be miserable but would soon be purged of it. What he needed was someone to tend to him so that he could distract himself with work, as he'd always done. Sally had returned from her ordeal in the countryside hale and hearty, not a pock mark on her beauty, so I tasked her with being Papa's chambermaid. It was a cold winter—colder than anyone in Paris could remember—and I instructed Sally to keep the fires blazing at his hearth until Polly and I returned from the convent for Christmastide.

In the meantime, at Jimmy's insistence, Papa hired a special tutor to teach the Hemingses French. I provided Sally with a new wardrobe from my cast-off clothing, so she'd look like a suitable maid to accompany us on social visits. Together, my sister and I took to the city, bedecked in new, elaborate dresses of our own. And Mr. Short sometimes accompanied us, playing the part of gentleman chaperone while stealing little smiles at me whenever I glanced his way. Between this, the gaiety of the holiday, and the passionate political debates on every street corner, it was all a delight.

When Polly and I returned home the Sunday before Christmas, the embassy was alive with the smell of bread. Low candles and crackling fires warmed every room, and I was filled with an undeniable happiness. Polly and I shared tea and buttered rolls, and I showed her the *Cabinet des modes,* a popular fashion leaflet in Paris. "Would you like a gown like this?"

I was eager to dress her just as Mrs. Adams had dressed me upon my own arrival in France. And Polly was so much prettier, just like a little doll. What fun it would be for us, two sisters, to choose fabrics and ribbons and shoes, together. But Polly just shrugged. She was less interested in clothes than in playing out-side, so I tossed the leaflet aside. "Shall we go out and see the snow?"

Polly's face immediately brightened. "Oh, let's!"

We bundled up and went into the courtyard, where we made a game of throwing little balls of snow. To my surprise, Mr. Short joined us in the merriment.

Under threat of slushy snow packed in his gloves, I cried, "You wouldn't dare!"

Mr. Short, cheeks pink from the cold, grinned at me. "*Mademoiselle*, I'm a daring man. The question is whether or not you'll duck away."

Light-headed at his flirtation, I fluttered my eyelashes like a coquette. "I could run."

Packing the snow tighter in his palms, he narrowed his eyes. "If you run from me, Patsy Jefferson, I vow to give chase."

I didn't think we were speaking of the snow game any longer.

Nevertheless, I wanted him to prove it. Giddy, I grabbed my skirts and fled down the pathway. Our garden was nothing next to the snow-covered green majesty of the palace grounds, but that day, ours seemed more beautiful. The cold made my lungs tighten as I ran, laughing. But when Mr. Short chased, I began to feel as if it was each thud of my pounding heart that forced the breath out of me.

In moments, Mr. Short caught me by the coat, spinning me to him. Alas, my heel caught a patch of ice and my foot went out from under me. But I didn't fall. At least, not right away. Mr. Short's arms came around my waist and I crashed against his chest. Then we both lost our footing and, still laughing, fell together into a drift of snow.

With my head cradled upon his shoulder where he lay sprawled, his hat blown away by a gust of snowy wind, I didn't feel the cold. Though the frigid melting water seeped into my woolen dress, I felt only the warmth of Mr. Short's breath on my face. Only the heat banked in his eyes. Only the strange desire that burned in me, to take off my glove and trace his cheek with my bare fingers.

Instead, I let my hand drift near to his, and nearly swooned when he hooked my little finger with his own. We hadn't touched skin to skin, but there was an unmistakable intimacy as his gloved finger linked, tightly but tenderly, with my own. We breathed in perfect harmony, bound so innocently, finger to finger, even as we ached for more.

It was a still and perfect moment. . . .

Which Polly ruined by pelting us with snow.

Declaring herself the victor, she danced over us. Still breathless and exhilarated, we went inside to change into dry clothes. When we came down, Jimmy set out spiced cider, and Mr. Short suggested that we summon Papa to join us. I wondered—perhaps vainly—if Mr. Short meant to speak to my father about a courtship between us. It was with this question in my mind, veritably floating on air, that I went in search of my father.

His sitting room door stood open, and I stepped into the room. "Papa?" Despite the warm glow from the fireplace, the room was empty. A noise sounded from Papa's chamber, the door to which was ajar. Crossing to it, I inhaled to call his name again, but what I saw made the words die in my throat.

Sally stood in the center of the room, her back to me, Papa's coat gripped in her hands. He was smiling softly at her, with an intimacy that stole the breath from me.

After a moment, Papa grasped the jacket from Sally. But, no, he didn't grasp the material, he held her hands where they curled around the stiff collar. He studied her, as if he couldn't quite comprehend the contours of her face.

And my heart thundered against my breastbone.

I was frozen there on the threshold of the room, not quite in, not quite out. I didn't know what was happening, or why every fiber of my body screamed at me to look away. I should have. Or maybe I should have called out to make my presence known.

But I could do neither.

Papa was a tall man, and Sally was small. The way he stared down at her—the girl who looked so much like my mother—it wasn't the stare of an old man, a humiliated lover, or a widower resigned to bachelorhood.

It was the stare of a man who contemplates damnation and salvation.

Slowly, as if even he wasn't conscious of his movement, Papa leaned his face down to Sally's. As his eyes fell closed, her head tilted back and he kissed her.

I could make no sense of the scene unfolding before me. She was a girl my own age. She was my mother's sister, my own aunt. She was his *slave*. And though I knew—of course I knew—that Virginia plantation owners took slaves for mistresses, we'd been so long away from home, I couldn't believe my own eyes.

He *couldn't* be doing this. My mind rejected what I saw clearly until he pursued her lips with more ardor and drew Sally close against his chest. At that embrace, I choked back the cry that worked its way up from my breast, where my heart raced so hard I saw spots.

If Papa saw me . . . *he mustn't see me*. Fingers pressed over my lips, I turned away from the private, heartbreaking moment and flew from the room.

Chapter Nine

I<small>T WAS MY HASTE</small> that made me stumble halfway down the stairs. Only a wild, wrenching grasp at the carved wooden rail saved me from a broken neck. Alas, the heavy fall of my feet echoed up the staircase and drew my father from his rooms.

"Patsy?" he called, peering over the bannister.

I froze, breathless, my belly roiling with shock and anger and revulsion. I ought to have pretended that I didn't hear him say my name. I ought to have hurried on, leaving him with only the sight of my back. I ought never to have looked up at him over my shoulder.

But I *did* look up.

There on the landing my father loomed tall, a tendril of his ginger hair having come loose from its ribbon, his shirt worn without its neck cloth, the stark white linen setting off more vividly the red flush that crept up his throat. Was it shame for his behavior with Sally or . . . ardor?

On the heels of witnessing his behavior, the thought was so excruciatingly horrifying that heat swept over me, leaving me to wish I'd burn away to dust.

"Are you hurt?" Papa asked, hoarsely.

I couldn't reply, my mouth too filled with the bitter taste of bile. Finally, I forced a shake of my head.

He glanced back to the door, then back at me, his hand half-covering his mouth. "Were—were you at my door just now?"

"No," I whispered, as much as I could manage under my suffocating breathlessness. And how dare he ask if I'd been at his door when neither of us could bear the honest answer? Even if Papa didn't know what I'd seen, he knew what he'd done.

He ought to have been downstairs with us, reacquainting himself with the little daughter who still didn't remember him. He ought to have been sipping cider with the young man who fancied me, giving his permission to court. He ought to have been doing a hundred other things. Instead, he was preying upon my dead mother's enslaved half-sister—and the wrongness of it filled my voice with a defiant rage.

"No, I wasn't at your door." I held his gaze, letting him see what he would.

My father paused on the precipice, clearing his throat, absently smearing the corner of his lips with one thumb. "Well—well . . . did you need something?"

As if my needs were at the forefront of his thoughts.

My fingers curled into fists as a lie came to me suddenly, and sullenly. "I was coming up to fetch my prayer book." Surely he knew it was a lie, but I didn't care. If he challenged me, I'd lie again, without even the decency of dropping my eyes. I'd lie because between a father and a daughter, what I'd witnessed was unspeakable. And I'd learned from the man who responded with silence to my letters about politics or adultery or the liberation of slaves. . . .

Papa never spoke on any subject he didn't want to.

Neither would I.

"Are you certain you weren't hurt," Papa finally murmured, " . . . on the stairs?"

Rage burned inside me so hotly I thought it possible that my handprint might be seared upon the railing. I bobbed my head, grasped my skirt, and took two steps down before my father called to me again.

"Patsy?"

I couldn't face him, so I merely stopped, my chest heaving with the effort to restrain myself from taking flight. "*What?*"

A heavy silence descended. One filled with pregnant emotion.

I feared he might be so unwise as to attempt to explain himself, to justify or confess his villainous lapse in judgment, but when he finally spoke, it was only to ask, "What of your prayer book?"

Swallowing hard, I forced words out despite the pain. "I've reconsidered my need of it. I'm not as apt as some people to forget what it says."

~

My heart still in turmoil, I drifted mindlessly back to the parlor, where Polly sipped at her cider, dollies by her feet on the floor. I wanted nothing so much in that moment as to escape my father and his house. To spirit away to the convent and take my little sister with me. But how would I explain myself to Mr. Short?

"Is your father of a mind to join us?" he asked, rising from his chair expectantly, his eyes still dancing with merriment from our games in the snow.

For me, those games now seemed a lifetime ago, our perfect moment sullied. "Papa won't be joining us."

"More cider for us, I suppose," Mr. Short mused, tilting his cup to hide his disappointment.

"Didn't you get Sally?" Polly asked, abandoning her dollies. "I'll fetch her."

"*No*," I said, harshly, grabbing her arm to stop her.

I'd never spoken a harsh word to Polly, much less grabbed her with force. She blinked at me with surprise. "Why not?"

"Papa has need of her." How I nearly choked on those words.

Perhaps Mr. Short heard the catch in my throat, or saw inside me to where a noxious stew of dark and unworthy emotions still boiled. For the merriment in his eyes melted away to concern. "Polly, do you know that Jimmy is working on a wondrous new confection made of egg whites and custard and wine? They're called *snow eggs*. Why don't you help him whip them up?" Polly's eyes widened with delight, so I let her skip away to the kitchen before I thought better of it. And the moment she was gone, Mr.

Short latched on to me with his singular characteristic of prying into facts. "Whatever is the matter?"

"Nothing. I've grown tired and wish to return to the convent."

His brows shot up. "Before the end of Christmastide? Your father hadn't planned for you to return until after the religious observances were at a close... ."

It was his way of reminding me of Papa's antipathy for Catholicism and contempt for Catholic mass and saints' days. Though it was still many years before my father would use a razor to construct his own Bible, cutting out all mentions of miracles and divinity, I already suspected my father observed the holy days only as a matter of form. And the reminder fueled my outrage, making me all the more determined to defy him. "Papa's well contented with his servants. He doesn't need me here. And in matters of faith, mustn't we all follow our own conscience?"

The word *conscience* echoed between us.

Mr. Short glanced to the door and the stairway beyond, in the direction of my father's bedchambers, before rounding his shoulders beneath his dark coat. "Certainly, Mademoiselle Sally can see to your father's comfort, but you're the center of his world, Patsy. Moreover, how would your conscience allow you to leave *me* utterly bereft of your company?"

In spite of his exquisite charm, I winced at his mention of Sally, dying a little at his unwitting implication of how she might see to Papa's comfort, by the way he called her *Mademoiselle*, as if she were a free Frenchwoman.

It was only a wince. It shouldn't have betrayed me. But to William Short, I was capable of betraying myself without a word. "Patsy, sit down before your knees give way." Then, more quietly, without a note of censure, he added, "You're old enough now to know the natural way of it between men and women."

There I suffered my second shock of the evening—the realization that Mr. Short was somehow aware of my father's liaison with his slave girl. Did that mean I'd not witnessed its first incarnation? Could there have been other encounters, other kisses, other. . . .

Sitting down hard upon the chair by the fire, I shook away the knowing of any of it. None of this was anything a lady of character ought allow herself to be aware, nor something a Virginia gentleman like William Short ought to acknowledge. So I exclaimed, "Pray do not speak another word."

But Mr. Short was already more of a Frenchman than a Virginian, and instead of honoring my request, he took the chair beside me and spoke my name very softly. "Patsy. Why not tell me what troubled thoughts are racing under that lace-trimmed cap?"

How soothing he made himself sound, as if he wasn't the same man who had just characterized my father's desire for Sally as *the natural way of it between men and women*. So soothing that the savage whisper of my answer took us both by surprise. "Because you, sir, for whom I've unwisely contrived no small admiration, never find fault in my father's conduct."

Mr. Short gripped the armrest of his chair. "How unjust! I've spoken to your father many times about the evils of slavery and shall continue to do so."

"I'm not speaking of the evils of slavery—"

"But you are, Patsy," he insisted. "Should we object to a man's affection for his slave more than we object to the fact that he holds her in bondage? I've told you before that slavery is a practice that compromises our morals. Perhaps beyond redemption. Whether we claim a slave's labor in the tobacco field or the smoky kitchen or in the pleasures of a candlelit bedchamber, slavery makes it all the same."

"It's *not* the same," I argued, though, unlike Mr. Short, I had no experience in the pleasures of a candlelit bedchamber to guide my convictions. I had only my conscience. And my conscience cried out that this was wrong. I knew it was. So did William Short. Yet apparently he'd do nothing to stop it, even if it meant putting souls, as he said, *beyond redemption*. Was it because Mr. Short had seduced and corrupted the Belle of Saint-Germain and his married duchess, too? Did he feel as if he had no standing to judge my father's illicit conduct when he himself stood guilty of indiscretions?

Mr. Short reached for my hand. His eyes filled with desire, the same desire I'd seen only moments ago on my father's face. . . . "Patsy, it's no sin to—"

"It *is*," I said, pulling away.

Not everything I've felt for Sally Hemings over the years has been noble or unselfish, but that night I perceived a difference between her and the preening, pampered Maria Cosway. With the memory of Sally's tarnished little bell, the one my mother bequeathed her, I felt somehow compelled to defend her. But because I could conceive of no way to influence her circumstance or my own, I was filled with rage not only at my father, but also at William Short—the man who made our helplessness plain.

I wrenched away before he could reach for me again, thinking myself miserably foolish to have ever presumed his flirtation carried with it an honorable intent. Foolish to have ever thought Mr. Short wished to court me—or marry, ever.

"It *is* a sin, Mr. Short," I said, remembering all the teachings my father supposed I didn't hear at the convent. I knew God gave us commandments, the sixth of which forbade adulteries and fornications—even those lusts committed only in the heart. Yet the men of Paris seemed to believe the Lord could not see past the glittering brilliance of Versailles into the darker deeds done in its shadow. Deeds done under the same roof where my innocent little sister played with her dolls.

So it was that with all the righteous indignation that can be mustered by a confused and heartbroken girl of fifteen, I brushed past Mr. Short without a backward glance.

⁓

SALLY HEMINGS WAS AS OPAQUE TO ME as I tried to make myself to the rest of the world. We had that in common. So when she came to brush out Polly's hair that night, she let slip not the slightest hint of anything amiss.

In the days that followed at the Hotel de Langeac, my father's behavior was, in every respect, correct, benevolent, and genteel. Papa was gallant with Polly, spoiling her with gifts on Christmas Day. He contrived to play music with me, ignoring the pain in his wrist, lavishing me with praise and warmly asserting after a particularly well-performed duet that he loved me *infinitely*. He also announced, on the coming of the new year, that he'd begin paying wages to Jimmy—who now insisted upon being called James—both generous and appropriate to his new official station as a *chef de cuisine*, in full command of our kitchen.

Furthermore, Papa bestowed upon Sally a wage of twenty-four livres, plus another twelve as a gift, a sum so wildly excessive for a chambermaid that I could only understand it as a gesture of apology and regret. In truth, this largesse to Sally was all that convinced me I had not imagined the encounter between them. I thought the extravagance must be a farewell to their intimacies. The thought comforted me, and I convinced myself quite easily that it would never happen again.

Ever amiable, Sally's only concern that winter seemed to be a desire to be included in Polly's and my doings, and to see the sights of Paris. Meanwhile, Papa lost himself in assuring the credit of our new nation, and shipping wine, rice, silk, and china to friends who requested it.

Even the intrepid Mr. Short didn't again mention Papa's encounter with Sally.

Nor ours in the snow.

And I was glad of it, because our friendship had cooled considerably since the night he defended my father's indefensible conduct with Sally. And my suspicions of Mr. Short's moral character only increased when, upon having left Sally to sweep up my dressing room after cutting my hair, I returned to ask her some trifle and caught a glimpse of William Short in the doorway, there where he ought not to have been.

His presence there caught me so off guard that I dashed into an empty room so as not to be seen. A moment later, Mr. Short hurried past. As his footsteps retreated down the stairs, I pressed my hand to my heart. What had he been doing in my chamber?

My pulse beating in my ears, the question I'd intended to ask Sally was long forgotten, which was for the best. I didn't want to chance seeing her and witness in her eyes or on her face anything that might confirm my aching suspicions about Mr. Short's actions.

Up until that point, I'd fervently prayed that I'd misjudged Mr. Short—that, in my shock and dismay over my father's conduct, I'd unfairly counted him amongst those men who are unworthy of the kind of affection I bore him—but now I feared that Mr. Short, too, had noticed pretty Sally Hemings.

I won't spare myself by pretending this fear arose only for her sake; her liaison with my father, however brief, taught me an unfortunate habit of jealousy. I'd already compared my unruly red curls to Sally's long, flowing dark mane. Already despaired of my tall stature against her petite frame. Already judged with impatience the plainness of my face, where hers was so beautiful. But I was, at that time, still a good-hearted girl with a mind toward decency.

And in spite of all else, I harbored great affection for Sally.

So it wasn't with *all* self-serving motive that I treated Mr. Short with contempt, turning from him to my new Catholic faith for comfort. My father didn't know of the rosary that I kept beneath my pillow but blamed my moodiness on my friends at the convent. One night before bed, he gave me a kiss on the forehead and the following advice: "Seek out the company of your countrywomen, who are too wise to wrinkle their foreheads with politics and religious superstition like these Frenchwomen do; it is a comparison of Amazons and Angels."

I frowned at him, remembering that he was the one who sent me to the school with all these Frenchwomen, when I hadn't wanted to go. And that the conduct of women seemed to me, in every respect, less objectionable than his.

So while Mr. Short set to work taking dictation as Papa outlined the merits of the Bill of Rights, to be proposed upon adoption of the new Constitution in America, it fell to me to occupy myself with the tender and tranquil amusements of domestic life.

While I mothered Polly, the two men worked tirelessly; so much so that their enterprise spilled out of the study, into the parlor, where my sister and I read our books. That is how I know that Papa worried about the perpetual eligibility of the president for reelection, a thing he feared would make a mockery of liberty. I was there, when, in a tirade, Papa condemned the "degeneracy" of the principles of liberty taking root in America, and Mr. Short slyly chose his moment to convey an invitation for Papa to join the Society of the Friends of the Blacks, of which he, Lafayette, and the Duke de La Rochefoucauld were all members.

My father did pause to consider. But in the end, he said, "Nobody wishes more ardently to see an abolition not only of the trade but of the condition of slavery. But I'm here as a public servant to those who haven't seen fit to give voice against it."

Mr. Short nodded, as if the matter were settled, but I could see plainly in his expression that it was not. There was a dogged stubbornness about William Short—one that would lead him to hold out hope for a cause, long after everyone else knew it to be lost. He was as persistent in matters of the heart as he was in matters of moral principle, though I didn't know it yet. I only knew that I'd judged him to be dishonorable, and yet he stood against slavery, showed loyalty to my father, and had only ever shown me kindness, even when he spoke words that broke my heart.

And so, in the helpless way of a girl who has never learned to guard that heart, I'd fallen most desperately in love with him.

It didn't matter that I was angry. It didn't matter that I believed him a knave. It didn't matter that I'd decided to take my vows.

Try as I might to deny it, my chest felt empty and hollow on the days when we were parted. And that exquisite suffering was replaced with a swelling ache when I came again into his company. Yes, I was a young girl with a secret love. And this tortured predicament was made only more agonizing by my father's decision to tour Europe in March of that year, leaving instructions that Mr. Short was to watch over me and Polly while he was away.

~~~~~~~~~~~~~~~~~~~~~~~~~~~~~~~~

IN PAPA'S ABSENCE, Mr. Short's attention turned to me. He came to the convent within days of my father's departure, ostensibly to ask after Polly's health. Strolling through the courtyard, he said, "I want to be able to assure your father that she's recovered of her illness."

"She was recovered of it before Papa left," I replied, coldly. "But I'll write a letter if he's worried."

"I'll wait, should it please you to have my company while you compose. . . ." There was a thread of hope in his voice, but I knew that my friends at the convent were watching us from the windows above.

So I only shook my head. "I would rather send my letter tonight for you to enclose with your own."

The disappointment that flashed through his eyes pleased me. And he was back again three days later. Then six days after that. Each time, I remained perfectly placid, according him civility but not more than that. Until, at last, he visited on the pretext of delivering to me an allowance. "Your father sent this payment, some for you, some for your tuition, and some to the servants."

It was the mention of the servants that made me say, "I'd like Sally to stay at the convent with us. We'll be glad to have our lady's maid close at hand."

Settling beside me on a bench, and casually crossing his leg at the knee in a way that drew my eyes to the strong and lean muscle of his calf beneath its white silk stocking, Mr. Short replied mildly, "Your father considered sending Sally to stay with you but didn't approve the cost of boarding her at the convent."

"How much can it cost? Perhaps with my allowance and Sally's savings—"

"No. Your father doesn't wish to invite inquiries as to the *special status* of his servants. Such inquiries might not only prove embarrassing to him, but also result in a substantial fine for his failure to register his black servants as per French law."

It surprised me that my father, a great believer in laws, was breaking one. "How large a fine?"

Mr. Short's voice did not waver. "Three thousand livres for Sally and James, each. Six thousand in all. Should their slave status be brought to the attention of the authorities, both of them might be arrested and expelled from the country . . . or, conversely, they might both file a petition for emancipation in the Admiralty Court. Which is certain to be granted, by the way."

There are no slaves in France. That was the official policy.

But the specificity with which Mr. Short imparted the legal procedure was not only a revelation, but also a weapon. He must have struggled over whether or not to make the Hemingses aware of their path to freedom. And now I'd have to struggle with it, too. I remember thinking that if he were any kind of a gentleman, he wouldn't have burdened me with it. Then again, no other man would have guessed it *would* burden me. "How fares your conscience, Miss Patsy?"

The question drew me back to the night of my discovery, back into my confusion and outrage. "I cannot imagine what you mean."

His gaze darkened. "In addition to your other cruelties toward me, are we to now add dishonesty to the mix?"

I gasped. "My cruelties? What injury do you imagine I've done you?"

The squeezing pang of my heart belied my need to ask. I'd seen the shielded flashes of hurt and disappointment in his eyes, the crestfallen expressions, the false cheerfulness at my coldness. I'd never known before it was possible to enjoy being cruel to a man, and I'd *reveled* in it.

His eyes didn't shield the hurt this time but allowed it there plainly for me to see. "You've held yourself so distant from me that the only logical conclusion I can draw is that you *intend* to cause me distress."

I lifted my chin, though my chest throbbed with guilt. "Why, I didn't suspect you'd even notice being held at a distance, Mr. Short. You're known to immerse yourself in your own amusements. Why, not long ago, I saw you pay visit to my dressing chamber at the Hotel de Langeac."

He paled, as he ought to have. But when he recovered from his shock, he said, "Please believe I meant no disrespect or impropriety."

"As I'm sure Sally can attest." This bitter rejoinder escaped my lips before I could stop it, and I regretted it at once.

Especially when Mr. Short only tilted his head in apparent bewilderment. "Sally?" he asked, as if he'd never heard her name. "I waited until she went down for a broom so I wouldn't be seen."

I was now equally bewildered . . . and scandalized. "You don't mean to imply that you came to see *me* in my private chambers, do you?"

Where he'd been pale, color suddenly flooded his cheeks. "Do you take me for a scoundrel?" And when he saw I might answer that question, he hurried forth to say, "I suppose you must. I'm a bit of one, but not in this. At least, it was in no way my intent for you to ever discover. . . ." He shook his head.

I hadn't the faintest idea how to react. "Mr. Short, if you weren't visiting my dressing room to see Sally nor to see me, then why were you there?"

He glanced away. "Ask me again when your father returns."

He meant for that to be the end of the discussion, but because my heart was pounding against my ribs beneath my stays, I feared my unfulfilled curiosity would kill me. "You speak of my cruelty, Mr. Short, yet *you* refuse to answer the simplest question."

"Patsy, leave it be."

Until that moment, I didn't know I had the capacity for coercion, but Mr. Short brought out a great many things in me I didn't know were there. "Since you're so concerned that the matter must wait until my father's return, I'll simply write him about it. . . ."

Mr. Short turned to me with an expression of astonishment at my threat. "And to think everyone who meets you praises you as such a good-natured, happy girl with the charm of a perfect temper. Everyone from Abigail Adams to the nuns at your convent assure your father that you're a girl with the utmost simplicity of character." He gave a rueful laugh. "None of them knows you in the slightest."

I took instant offense. "I behave as Papa wishes me to behave."

"And he knows you least of all. You're his Amazon *disguised* as an angel."

This was another insult, or at least, it should've been. And yet, I sensed in Mr. Short's tone the hint of approval. Nevertheless, I became painfully aware that we were quarreling in an abbey under the eyes of gossipy girls. "Thank you for your visit, Mr. Short. You may assure my father that I won't spend my allowance on fripperies."

It was a dismissal, so he rose, stiffly. Tipped his hat, curtly. But he didn't take his leave. "What a mess of this I've made," he murmured. Then, with one gloved hand, he reached into his coat and pulled from some inner pocket a folded note of linen paper. He placed it gently on the seat beside me, and added, almost timidly, "Mercy, *Mademoiselle*. I beg of you."

My mind raced with all manner of villainy that might've been written upon that paper, but when I opened it, I found no ink at all. Just a blank page, between the folds of which was pressed a glossy curl of ginger. "Is this—is this a clipping of my hair?"

Mr. Short cringed, as if in the greatest mortification. As if he might like to jump the gates and hop out of the convent, escaping into the streets on foot. "You're most unkind to ask. An *angel* would've spared me the humiliation."

Of a sudden, my heart pounded even harder and a flush heated my skin. "Then I vow to pretend I know nothing about it."

He sighed with resignation. "On the day Sally cut your hair, I took this clipping before she could sweep it up. I hope you can forgive my act of petty larceny."

The implications of this confession broke a fissure in my resentment like the sun cracking open a frozen river. Mr. Short hadn't sought out a private moment with Sally. He'd stolen a token of mine! Overcome with a rush of emotion, I pressed a hand to my chest, crushing the front of my crimson frock, and breathed in, as if for the very first time. "Why would you do such a thing?"

He removed his hat and stared at his feet with chagrin. "With our friendship imperiled, I felt the want of a keepsake to remind me of happier times."

My heart insisted it was more than that. I recalled the gold watch key containing a braided lock of my mother's hair that Papa had commissioned. So that he'd never forget her. So that he'd carry her with him always. Mr. Short wanted that kind of connection . . . with me? "Why didn't you simply ask me for such a token?"

"I thought you'd be ill-disposed to such a request. Moreover, I'd never presume without your father's permission. And given that Mr. Jefferson had just confided his intention to leave you and your sister under my protection, any discussion of my feelings for you would have sounded suspect, if not depraved."

Mon Dieu! I thought I might fall into a breathless swoon before I got the words out. "What *are* your feelings for me?"

"Ask me again," Mr. Short said, snatching back the token of hair from my grasp, " . . . when your father returns."

Chapter Ten

WAS THERE EVER A TIME OR PLACE for love better than spring in Paris?

With my father away, William Short and I exchanged witty little notes, discussed books, and railed at the injustice of French commoners paying taxes, while nobles and clergy were exempt. We marveled together at the revolutionary spirit in Paris. Indeed, we knew ourselves to be caught up in a singular moment in history, and hoped the whole world, inspired by my father's ideals, was poised to make itself over anew.

All the while, I kept my vow; I pretended not to know about the lock of hair. At least, I never again made mention of it during Mr. Short's dangerously frequent visits to the convent. Nor did he openly declare his feelings for me. Indeed, during our long walks, we thought ourselves models of restraint, our behavior above the suspicion of even the most censorious nun.

Though we were far too clever together to let restraint, or propriety, or even our confinement get in the way of affection's bloom.

When it rained and we were forced to shelter under the cold, gray arches of the Panthemont, we shared a little bag of chocolate drops. Mr. Short said, "Let's warm ourselves by painting a mental picture of a sun-drenched field. . . ."

I laughed, delighted. "Given my lack of talent for drawing, I fear to take up the imaginary brush. What else do we see but a field?"

"Some trees." He grinned. "Perhaps a church tower in the distance." His grin widened. "A pair of sweethearts picnicking together."

Smiling, too, I closed my eyes to the pitter-patter of rain, allowing myself to imagine sprawling upon a blanket with him in the sun. "Are these sweethearts well suited?"

"Too soon to tell, but they're both enormously fond of chocolate drops, so I have high hopes for them."

That made me laugh. *Dear Mr. Short.* "Is a mutual fondness for chocolate drops a strong basis for affections?"

"It is if you understand how seriously this fellow regards his confections. . . ."

Blinking with guile I asked, "Oh, is he a chocolatier?"

Mr. Short chuckled, his green eyes dancing with mirth. "A country lawyer by training, but he was induced to serve a diplomat in a foreign land. He's very dashing and a sprightly dancer, too."

The desire to twit him was irresistible. "Aha! I've guessed who our sweethearts are. Nabby Adams and her father's secretary, the dashing Colonel Smith."

Mr. Short smirked. "No, but our sweethearts are similarly situated." Then, more peevishly— "You really think Colonel Smith is dashing? He's a dreadfully stiff dancer and whenever the man sings, he's off-key."

"I thought he was your friend!" I exclaimed, warming inside at his displeasure in my complimenting Colonel Smith.

"He *is* my friend. That's why I'm so well acquainted with his faults. I taunt him for his lack of musicality and he taunts me about the elderly Frenchwomen who are taken by my charms."

It wasn't only elderly Frenchwomen who were taken by his charms, but I refused to let the thought dim my enjoyment of our game. "Let's return to the sweethearts in our imaginary painting. Does the fellow enjoy his work?"

"He does, though he's worked for years now, without respite. He arrived desperately eager to see the Continent, but his employer hasn't been able to do without him."

It was a mild, implied complaint that made me laugh, for I believed my papa's resistance had more to do with his fears about young American men being at great risk of corruption in Europe. "To work so hard, without respite, this fellow must be either industrious or ambitious."

"Very ambitious," was Mr. Short's answer. "He'd like to be of both service and consequence to his country."

My heart fluttered anew. How could I not admire such a man? "How brave to make his career so far from home."

"Oh, I wouldn't make too much of his courage. He was so seasick on the way to his post that he now contemplates staying abroad forever rather than face the crossing again."

I smiled at the admission of the shortcoming. "But wouldn't he miss his country?"

Mr. Short contemplated, one finger tapping his lips in a way that drew my gaze there. "He already does, but he's not homesick for some of its peculiar customs. He'd like to return to his native land, secure a comfortable fortune as a planter, and make a home for a suitable wife, but he worries it cannot be done except at the cost of his sacred honor. Do you think that's something his sweetheart could understand?"

I swallowed, trying to make sense of his question. "That depends . . . is his sweetheart a French girl?"

"Virginian."

In spite of my intention to remain coolly, flirtatiously aloof, my breath caught and my lips parted as I met his pointed gaze. "Then she understands."

How ignorant I was. I'd never before given any thought to how difficult it was to prosper in Virginia without slaves. Never contemplated the obstacles of leasing lands to free sharecroppers. Never racked my brain to choose crops requiring only the labor that might keep both a plantation and conscience in good order. The only thing I understood was that Mr. Short was fearful of returning to a way of life in Virginia that he despised.

"And the girl in this picture?" he asked. "What does she dream for her future?"

As tangled as my thoughts had become, the question took me utterly unawares. I had, from the youngest age, been given directives. How to comport myself in a way that honored my father. What to learn to make myself a more pleasing companion. I still heard my mother's reedy voice bidding me to take care of my father all of the days of his life. No one had ever asked me what I wanted. "What can you mean?"

He mischievously stole the last chocolate drop and held it just out of my reach. "What sort of life do you think she'd like to lead? Does she wish to marry or give herself to spinsterhood? Does she see herself the lady of a house in town, visiting with her friends and debating in salons? Does she see herself the mistress of a vast country plantation, brewing beer, slaughtering pigs, haying in its season?"

My father always spoke as if I would, inevitably, return to take up life on a plantation. Except for my now mostly forgotten desire to join the convent, other choices had never before been presented to me. And when faced with this dizzying array, the words that bubbled up from within me were born of raw instinct. "She dreams of a future in which she, too, might be of both service and consequence to her country."

It was an absurd answer. Mr. Short might've laughed in mockery. Or he might've presumed it was a docile, noncommittal reply, rather than the ambitious and prideful one it really was. But knowing I was my father's daughter in this, and everything, he stared with wonder, surrendering to me the last chocolate drop. "Well, then, Miss Jefferson, the sweethearts in this idyllic painting are very well suited indeed."

~~~

THE ONLY THING that clouded our sunny romance was the seemingly endless wait for my father's return. It came in April, when Papa rolled up to the convent with a carriage full of gifts for me and Polly. He was eager to talk about the food, art, and ideas the soils of Germany had given him about the best design for a plow. And though he could no longer play the violin with any real skill, due to his injury, I made enough music for the both of us with my new harpsichord, a thing we both treasured.

Papa's buoyant spirits delighted Polly and reassured me that he'd be receptive to Mr. Short, should he choose to declare himself for me. Waiting for that fateful moment at the convent school, I huddled together with Marie, my only confidante in such matters, and anxiously counted the days before we'd dine together at the Hotel de Langeac. Polly, Papa, me, and Mr. Short. What a pleasant little family of four we'd make!

I was puzzled, then, upon our end-of-week visit, to find Mr. Short not there. My father pulled me into a hug, chiding me gently that I'd not seen fit to pen him but a few lines while he was away. I was ashamed of my neglect, for it was born of my infatuation, and I almost told him as much when asking after Mr. Short.

Papa smiled distractedly over a game board upon which he was playing chess against himself. "He's quite occupied arranging for his travels."

"Travels?" In his role as my father's secretary, Mr. Short was part courier, part negotiator, part translator, and representative—he was Papa's voice wherever Papa couldn't be. He traveled frequently throughout France and sometimes beyond. And yet, I'd have thought I'd first hear of a new mission from Mr. Short himself. More than that, I feared I couldn't bear the waiting if he should decide to postpone his talk with my father until after such a sojourn.

With my heart filled with love that I couldn't express, I was afflicted with the greatest impatience of my life. So much so that I waited up late, going down the stairs on some pretext of needing chamomile tea for an unsettled stomach when I heard Mr. Short come in.

Mr. Short's first, instinctive reaction to the sight of me that night was a smile. But then that smile gave way to sadness. "Whatever are you doing awake at this hour, Patsy?"

My position on the staircase caused me to look down upon him. "I'm told you're to leave Paris."

Setting his hat upon an entryway table, he nodded, gravely. "Yes."

"When?" I forced myself to move down one more step, then another.

"Soon, if all goes as to plan."

"Where will you go?"

"To Rome and other places."

I was unused to his cryptic answers and cringed at the way they turned me into an interrogator. Trying to regain my dignity, I descended the remaining step until only an arm's length separated us. "How wonderful. I know you've wanted to see Rome for yourself. You must be very eager to go . . . but are you in such a rush that you must leave matters behind you unsettled?"

At that, his shoulders sagged. It was only with real effort that he seemed to square them again, and face me directly. "I'm afraid I must."

The acute pain of it was like an arrow. I sucked in air, determined to disguise my anguish. "Do you mean you won't . . . you haven't . . ."

"Miss Jefferson," he began, stiffly. "I've had an illuminating conversation with your father. It began with the topic of domestic contentment and ended on the subject of youth, inexperience, and the need for matured judgment."

Puzzling through his remarks, I wondered if my father had opined on *my* youth and inexperience or Mr. Short's.

Before I could ask, he added, "In light of this conversation, your father has seen fit to release me from my duties. In fact, he's encouraged my oft-wished-for tour of Europe."

His words sounded like the closing of a leather-bound book, and resounded with a hollow thud. There was no question that whatever had passed between my father and Mr. Short would delay our courtship indefinitely, if not make it impossible. And a thousand emotions passed through me at once.

Anger and upset, sadness and fear, panic and a frantic desire to think how I might change these circumstances. Devastation, too, at Mr. Short's apparent resignation. He'd said, in the snow, that he was a daring man, that he wouldn't stop chasing me. But now he wouldn't risk my father's esteem.

Not for me.

And despite our imagined painting, and Mr. Short asking what I wanted, I had no say in the matter at all.

Still, I could make no sense of this. Hadn't Papa said he viewed Mr. Short as his adoptive son? I'd heard him entreat his secretary, on numerous occasions, to buy parcels of land near Monticello, near us. Mr. Short shared my father's views, was a fellow Virginian, was familiar and cherished with great affection. Wouldn't it be natural for Papa to welcome Mr. Short as a suitor for his daughter?

I was young, it was true. But friends my age were already starting to court and marry. Did my father think I was less accomplished, less sensible, less womanly than those French girls? Distress gripped me, making it hard to swallow.

These were all questions I couldn't ask. Mr. Short hadn't declared his feelings for me. And now, if I tried to speak of my *own* feelings, I might drive a wedge between the men I loved best in the world. Mr. Short must've sensed this, because he nodded and softly excused himself to conduct his business.

And for a while, I confided my despair in no one but Marie.

"Poor Jeffy," she said as we whispered in the darkness of our dormitory. "It is only a trip. If Mr. Short feels love for you now, he'll still feel it when he returns."

Yet I worried that whatever he felt for me was already gone. While preparing for his Grand Tour, Mr. Short held himself as distant from me as I once held myself from him, avoiding me at every turn. Long before he left Paris, I felt Mr. Short's absence as a wound to my very core. Worse, I didn't know who to blame. Had Papa discouraged Mr. Short as a potential suitor? Or had Mr. Short toyed with me and given me false hope?

I didn't know. And not knowing was a torment.

One visit home, while I sat staring unseeingly at the artificial flowers I was making as gifts for my friends in the convent, Papa took the seat beside me and handed me a small sack. I blinked up at him. "What is this?" I asked, taking it in hand and working at the little string.

"Something to cheer you," he said, a small smile on his face.

He'd meant it as a kindness. Of course he did. For he had no way of knowing that the chocolate drops that filled the bag would remind me of that day Mr. Short and I had imagined our futures. But remind me they did until I could no longer hold in the torment, or the questions. "Why did you release Mr. Short from his duties, Papa?"

For a long moment, my father didn't answer. "As his mentor," he finally said, "it is my duty to shepherd his career. William wishes to be a diplomat, and that requires that he be well traveled and conversant with places and customs beyond that with which he now has experience." He said this quietly, seriously, as if this was more than a casual answer to a casual question. As if he didn't fully approve. As if he knew why I asked, and thought me quite improper for doing so.

"Will he return to your service when he's completed his travels?" I forced myself to ask around the knot in my throat.

"I hope so. We've talked about his returning to Virginia with me, but each man must make his own destiny. At present, William's is unclear to me." I didn't think I imagined that Papa chose his words very carefully—which confirmed what I already suspected. They'd discussed me, or at least intimated that I might be a part of William's future—a part of his *destiny*—and the result of that discussion had been for Papa to send him away.

And for William to decide to go.

I asked nothing more of my father that night because I was shaking with upset, and I feared I would not be able to speak without my voice quavering. Instead, abandoning the chocolate drops on the side table, I simply walked from the room without another word and sharply closed the door behind me, letting my silence say to my father all that I could not.

But I should have gathered more courage that night. I should have pressed and asked him the more direct questions whirling through my mind. Because Papa never gave me another opening to do so.

My father was always an artful politician, too clever to be drawn into discussions of matters of the heart when his was so guilty. Too crafty to be cornered into a confrontation with his daughter that he wasn't ready to have, especially after I'd asked him about William—and about William's future.

So I was forced to try to win Papa over to reopening the subject. I forced myself to be genial and even-tempered to prove that I was a grown woman with good sense enough to be wooed. Failing that, I hoped my comportment would encourage my father to confide in me any reservations he had about Mr. Short so that I might put his mind at ease. But at the time, my father's praise of Mr. Short was so lavish and his affection so sincere that it left me entirely bewildered.

Meanwhile, there was nothing for me to do but drown my sorrows in tea. British tea, to be precise, taken with the Tufton sisters and our convent friends at the home of the Duke of Dorset. For an ambassador of a country that was so hostile to my own and whose king had ordered his army to hang my Papa, the duke quite generously extended his enormous charm to me. Some of my convent friends jested that the handsome duke was *especially* solicitous of me, but he was known for his solicitations with all sorts of ladies, honorable and notorious. I gave little thought to him at the time, since he was my father's age and prone to talk more about cricket games than matters of importance. Besides, my thoughts were all of William and what objection my father could possibly have to our match.

It wasn't until that summer, when Papa took me to see an opera, that I had my first inkling of the heart of the matter. Squiring me to my seat in gentlemanly fashion, my father asked, almost absently, "Have you had any word from Tom Randolph, Patsy?"

"Cousin Tom? No. Should I have?"

"He'd planned to visit us here in Paris this summer but I haven't heard from him since his last letter. I worry he's been waylaid by brigands."

This was the first I learned of Tom's intention to visit. "I hope no harm has come to him."

"I'd grieve of it," Papa said. "I've set a plan for Tom's education. I want him to study law in France for two years, then embark on a political career. He could be a great man of Virginia. He has the aptitude for it and the Randolph name. Not to mention lands and fortune."

That was my clue. So nakedly obvious I nearly dropped my opera glasses. Mr. Short was a Virginia gentleman with ability and ambition, but he'd divested himself of almost all his landholdings to follow us to Paris. Mr. Short said he had entered the world with a small patrimony, and now, as far as I knew, he relied entirely upon his modest salary. A salary my father perhaps thought *too* modest to provide for a wife. I understood the importance of financial security, but many of Mr. Short's other attributes recommended him. Confusion and sorrow left me unable to reply.

Only one thing seemed clear. Papa disapproved of the man who had claimed my heart. And so he was sending him away.

～

SOME PART OF ME DIDN'T BELIEVE Mr. Short would really leave Paris. Certainly not without a note to explain himself. And some part of me refused to believe it right up until the afternoon when, with guarded eyes, he kissed my gloved hand in farewell, climbed into a carriage, and rolled away.

I stood on the cobblestones, staring after that carriage, half expecting it to stop or even turn back. Only when it was long out of sight and I was shivering against a cool autumn breeze did I finally surrender to reality.

Miserable with longing, I went inside and eased into the chair behind the desk where Mr. Short did his work, reaching for some essence of him in the things he'd left behind. A quill pen. An inkwell. A page of paper.

Nothing more.

Not even a note for me to tear to pieces and throw into the fire.

That night, I sat near a different fire, wondering why it would not warm me and whether or not I was so heartbroken that I would never feel warm again. Seemingly oblivious to my distress, Papa bade us to see how neatly Sally mended a silk stocking. At her master's praise, she bent to show us her work, and I caught a glimpse of a locket round her neck. A silver oval stamped with flowers and tiny hearts hung on a crimson ribbon, delicate and lovely as the girl it adorned.

"It's so pretty, Sally," Polly said, reaching to trace the filigreed locket. "Where did you get it?"

"*C'est un cadeau de mon—mon patron*," Sally said, revealing her near fluency in French. "A gift!" Her glance flicked to my father where he sat reading a book in his stuffed armchair. And though Papa never met her gaze, he smiled.

For a moment, I wondered if there was something in his smile beyond kindness. Sally spent her days lighting fires, dusting books, mending stockings, sewing on buttons, and helping James in the kitchen. But how did she spend her nights? She had a cot in the servants' quarters under her older brother's watchful eye, but no one would question if Papa should call for her at bedtime. And how could she refuse?

What if the locket wasn't just a gift, but . . .

No. As resentful as I was at my papa, he'd been nothing but gentlemanly with Sally since the night I saw him kiss her. Besides, how could I trust myself to see attraction or affection between a man and a woman, when I hadn't even properly understood Mr. Short's feelings for me?

I put it out of my head and dismissed it entirely. I was too miserable with my own troubles to care about the dresses and baubles my father bestowed upon his servants. And to add to my misery, in November we learned Papa had requested a *congé*—a leave of absence that would enable us to return to Virginia.

When I gently questioned the decision, he only said, "When we came to France, I supposed an appointment of five months. We've been here five years. Affairs at home can no longer wait, and political passions here are poised to erupt. I must see you and your sister settled in a more appropriate place."

"You intend to leave us in Virginia?" I asked, horrified. Was it to rid himself of the temptation Sally presented or to keep me away from Mr. Short? I couldn't ask. I didn't dare ask. And what answer could he have given that would've been a balm to my savaged heart?

"It's for the best," was all he said.

And I sat there, staring up at the painted domed ceiling to keep hot tears of helpless anger from escaping the corners of my eyes. Because what *I* thought best didn't matter. It wasn't even deemed proper for me to acknowledge my feelings for William. Not to him, nor to my father, who had not felt the need to consult me. I'd had no say—no sway, even—in his decision to release William, nor in William's decision to go. Or even whether or not I wanted to return to Virginia. And I never would have a say, because in the world outside the convent, men did as they pleased and women were left to simply accept the consequences.

But it seemed to me as if the world outside of the convent was both wicked and unjust, and the only place I could be happy was at the Panthemont, where I thrived in the company of friends and God.

As autumn faded to darkest winter, and not a single letter arrived for me from William Short, the desire to remain at the Panthemont and take my vows grew more and more within me. And once I'd decided upon this course, the only question that remained was how to tell my father.

PAPA HAD DISCOUNTED THE FAITH to which I'd been called as "superstitious and hostile, in every country and every age, to liberty." But I told myself that I didn't care if my spiritual calling made him angry; perhaps I even *hoped* that it would. Still, my desires weren't born of mere petty rebellion. I'd have opportunities to teach in the convent. I could think on great matters and help shape the minds of young girls. It was a vocation, a calling, both earthly and spiritual, to be *of consequence*. And because the desire rose up in me so strongly, I resolved to tell Papa at Christmas.

Why then, having found comfort in God, did I feel consumed by hellfires?

The very night I resolved to tell my father, shivering sent my teeth chattering, and yet, I burned. Outside, the canals were impassible with ice, the Seine River frozen solid, preventing shipments of grain from reaching the city. The other girls huddled together in the convent to keep warm, but a fire consumed me from the inside, and a rash had broken out on my skin.

Marie sent for an abbess. "*Cher Jeffy* has the typhus!"

By morning, Polly was sick, too.

We were both sent from the convent to my father's home, with fear that we wouldn't recover. My recollection is hazy, for I suffered from bouts of delirium. I scarcely knew day from night. I have slight memories of white snow frosting the windows and howling drafts stealing through the blankets under which I tossed and turned. One thing, however, I remember with perfect clarity: it was my father himself who tended us and no one else.

He lodged my sister and me in his own quarters, holding spoonfuls of gruel to our lips, urging us to take sips of wine, wiping our brows, cleaning our messes, and singing us little songs. The illness didn't swiftly pass over us. And while my father's constant attentions helped ease my pain, Polly couldn't be comforted. She *suffered* that bitter winter, through what Papa said was a Siberian degree of cold.

And all the time, he was never far from us. He never uttered a harsh word, no matter how often we called to him for water or cool damp cloths. He was so tender and motherly that I forgot my resentments. Forgot everything but my love for him as we were drawn together again in the fear of losing Polly.

One afternoon, I called to her from my bed and she didn't answer. In terror, I screamed, "Papa! Make her answer. Make her answer me."

In sweat-stained white shirtsleeves that matched his exhausted pallor, my father kissed the damp curls on my sister's brow. "She can't hear you," he whispered, rocking Polly. "The fever has robbed her of hearing."

My little sister wasn't dead but in a stupor, deaf and insensible. At Christmas, Polly could no longer open her eyes. We had no hope she'd live to see the new year.

I half dreamed I saw my mother in our room with angel's wings, but when I woke, I wondered if it was only the white lace curtain at the drafty window. When I asked my father if Mama was watching over us, he lowered his head to his hands and was quiet a long time. "I'd like it to be true . . . you'll never know how I long for her, even still."

The memory of my mother's face had faded for me. Her voice I couldn't remember at all. There'd been in me over the years a slow and gentle farewell. But he'd written on her gravestone that she'd been *torn* from him in death. He may have given up chasing her into the grave, but he was, even all these years later, still bleeding from what he considered a violent parting.

I think it was that desperation that drove him to work harder than any man I ever knew in a cause he deemed greater than himself. And in the midst of my fevered illness, when I had energy only for thoughts and little else, my heart ached in sympathy and sadness.

For I was nearly certain that Polly was to be torn from us, too. That night, I knelt over Polly's bedside and steepled my hands in urgent prayer. *Please save Polly. Save my sister's life and I'll give myself over to you. I'll find the courage to tell my father. Take me as your bride and let her go. Take me and let her live. . . .*

The next morning, Polly opened her eyes. In the days that followed, her rash disappeared, her fever abated, and she answered when we called—her deafness cured. But Polly's mind never entirely recovered. In the months that followed, she suffered from a torpor of intellect. When we returned to the convent school, Polly struggled with her studies. And by springtime, it was manifestly evident that the bright little girl who had charmed Abigail Adams with her cheek and sassed me into exasperation was no more.

Nevertheless, God had answered my prayer. The bargain had been struck. I was bound by my promise to take my vows and didn't despair of it. It'd been almost seven months since Mr. Short left on his tour of the Continent, never writing a line to me in all that time. This painful silence ensured that I didn't see for myself a future as any man's wife, so why shouldn't I welcome the convent as my sanctuary and salvation?

My friends at the Panthemont helped me to practice the words to tell Papa, but no combination of utterances ever seemed to capture everything I felt—and not even putting it to paper made it come out right. Still, I knew I must find a way before my father took us back to Virginia.

The matter was decided for me one Sunday in mid-April, when Polly and I returned to the Hotel de Langeac to find Sally wearing a fashionable new dress in crimson damask that matched the ribbon for her locket. Sally had a trunk full of new clothes, too. Papa had bought her expensive silks and satins, petticoats and stockings, ribbons and heeled shoes—things she'd never have need of were she to return to our plantation in Virginia.

I doubted Sally had asked for any of this largesse. My father had spoiled her, either because he felt responsible for her or infatuated with her. Or perhaps he spoiled her because it eased his conscience for the way he'd once used her. Was it possible that he meant to free her, and leave her here in France when we returned home? Or did he intend to keep Sally Hemings with him, even as he made plans to send me and my sister back to Virginia?

The suspicion made me as sad as it made me angry, and because I was sixteen years old, it finally felt right to tell him my adult inclinations.

Chapter Eleven

Paris, 18 April 1789
To Thomas Jefferson from Patsy

I ask your blessing to take my vows and join the holy order of the convent, where I intend to live out my days with my new sisters.

THIS LETTER AND ALL THE OTHERS I ever sent my father are carefully preserved within these wooden filing presses. My father always said my letters were precious to him; I believe it now as never before. And as I hold this letter above the candle flame—for I cannot let it survive—I remember how my hands shook to write it in the first place, all those years ago.

I'd never feared my father before. I'd feared *for* him, but never before had I dreaded seeing him as I did the day I sent this letter. At the convent, awaiting his reply, time passed so slowly I found myself checking and rechecking the tall case clock that stood sentinel over the library as it counted out the minutes and chimed at the quarter hours.

But Papa didn't send a reply that night.

Part of me knew he wouldn't.

When he rode up in the carriage the next day for our weekly visit, I was afraid to meet his eyes. Thankfully, he gave no evidence that anything was amiss. Instead, he took us to the Palais-Royal, a center of gardens, theaters, shops, and cafés, with gentlemen's clubs open from noon to midnight. I never tired of shopping amongst ladies with frilly parasols, and gentleman being carried in sedan chairs under the colonnade. But on that day, I could barely stand the unspoken tension, waiting for my father to acknowledge the note that I'd sent him.

It wasn't until evening that Papa called me to sit with him, alone, where he sipped at wine by the fire. "Has someone at the convent proselytized to you on the subject of religion?"

"Never," I replied, knowing how much it'd displease him if the answer were otherwise.

He stared down into his wine, which glowed like a garnet in the firelight. "In my role as ambassador, I've been made aware of the plight of an American girl, schooled in a convent just like you. She's somehow been seduced into remaining there as a nun, thereby abandoning her country, her relations, and her religion. And yet, even learning this, never did I think my own daughter was just as vulnerable."

Papa's characterization of a religious epiphany as *seduction* made my belly knot. Worse was his assertion that taking my vows would amount to *abandoning* my family and country. How could I argue for my convictions when the man who opposed me was both beloved and formidable? I tucked my hands between my knees so he wouldn't see them shake. "Would you forbid me to follow the dictates of my conscience?"

He pinched the bridge of his nose, as if the question gave him great pain. "Patsy, you're young and inexperienced. This decision needs more time and consideration. Mature reflection."

His words were unbearably familiar. They sounded like Mr. Short's description of his own conversation with Papa, which also turned on the subject of youth and inexperience. And heat crawled up my neck.

My father and I seldom spoke in open disagreement, only circling about subjects of contention without touching them directly. Yet, this time, I felt as if he allowed me no avenue of retreat. And for once, I said just what I believed. "I'm old enough now to judge my own happiness."

My father took a long drink before returning his glass to the table beside his stuffed chair. He squinted, lines of hurt etching his face. "How can you think to be happy separated by an ocean from your sister and me?"

I'd expected him to be angry; instead, he was wounded. Yet, I bristled, defensively. "I could ask the same of you. Don't you intend to leave us in Virginia and return to France?"

His brows knitted together, as if he'd never considered I might object. "My commission won't keep me in Paris forever. Five years I've served in France, while my own country formed a new government in my absence. I'll stay only as long as duty requires. Very soon I'll retire from public life to Monticello. I've always looked to you to render the evening of my life serene and contented, never realizing you loved me so little."

Guilt formed a lump in my throat that nearly prevented me from speech. Then my words tumbled out all at once. "That isn't true, Papa! Of course I love you. And it isn't that I want to be without you—"

"Then why would you wish to take the veil?" Papa liked to have an iron discipline over himself. He never raised his voice, seldom let emotions rule. But now, to my horror, that self-control cracked and all traces of the seasoned diplomat, the dispassionate philosopher, the objective scientist fell away. Tears sprang to his eyes as he beseeched me. "Have I failed you so *utterly* as a father?"

My heart beat a fast and painful cadence. He *had* failed me. But that wasn't the whole of the story, or even the largest part of it. And at the sight of his anguish, tears welled in my eyes, too. "My dearest Papa, please believe that I'd never leave you, or my country, except for God."

But I did not tell him of my faith.

Instead, breathlessly, I told him of my bargain.

When I finished, he said, "Oh, Patsy. It'd be more pardonable to believe in no god at all than in one who bargains like a pirate for the life of a little girl. That god would be a demon. You mustn't feel bound by such a promise. Not when it would make me so unbearably unhappy." Leaning forward, he grasped my fingers, and it was his gnarled and injured hand that trembled, not mine. "Patsy, I rely on you for the evening of my life, because you know, as no one knows, that the morning of my life was clouded by loss after loss. I have nothing left but you."

The beseeching tone of his words stole my response, but my thoughts raced.

What of Polly?

The question swam silently on the tip of my tongue as he sank to his knees before me, like a penitent, holding my face in his hands. Overwhelming me with his emotion. "My dear girl, nobody in this world can make me happy or miserable as you. You've been my constant companion in my darkest hours. I'd be lost without you. *Lost.*"

His supplication at my feet melted the edges of my anger and left only a desperate need to mend what I'd broken. "I'd never wish to grieve you so, Papa. I only wish to serve God's demand."

Then we were both sobbing, my father's forehead pressed to mine, our tears mingling. "Patsy, a just God would never demand this of you. I know what it is to be truly bound by a vow, for I made one to your mother."

He stopped to pull from his coat pocket the engraved gold watch key in which he'd preserved my mother's hair beneath clear glass. "I swear again, here and now, that I'll never take another wife. I'll always be alone. So if I'm obliged to leave you here, shut up in a convent . . . it would be as much a grief to me as shoveling dirt over your grave. And I'd pray for someone to soon shovel dirt over mine."

I was truly shaken. I'd not seen my father in such a state since the night he stared down his pistols. I remembered our solitary rides. Those days he lay prostrate after my mother's death. Here in Paris, he stood so much taller, a giant amongst men.

I hadn't realized—or perhaps I had forgotten—that he *needed* me, just as my mother said he would. And hadn't I made a vow to her before I made one to God?

Papa's misery put me in doubt of my decision. Had I been seduced? Seduced by my own sadness and heartbreak? Perhaps I *did* need more time to think. More time to decide.

My father had been, for so long, everything to me. My sun, my moon, my stars. No other being—not even William Short— had ever exerted such force in my universe as my father. So it's true that Papa never forbade me from my vocation as a nun, but it is equally true that he didn't think he needed to. Though I remained unsure, Papa clearly considered the matter decided, and the very next day he rode up to the convent gates in a carriage and told Polly and me to gather all our belongings. Then my father paid our tuition in full, closing our account. And we rode away from the Panthemont in silence.

~

"MADEMOISELLE JEFFERSON, would you do me the honor of a dance?" The question was put to me in the opulent gilded ballroom, following a regal bow, by the Marquis de Lafayette. He was, at that time, an elegant man of thirty-one, at the height of his power and his beauty. The heroic soldier, who was no less handsome for the long slope of his forehead beneath his powdered wig, had rescued us from the British when I was but a child. Now he rescued me again by singling me out for attention at my debut, and I couldn't help but wonder if Papa had put him up to it.

In the days after my withdrawal from the convent, Papa undertook what I believed to be a campaign to distract me from my desire to take my vows. He gifted me with a gold watch on a chain. He arranged for riding lessons so that we could ride together as we used to, just the two of us. And he spent three hundred francs on new ball gowns for my coming-out during the social season, jesting that I would be limited to only three balls a week. . . .

Already bewitched by the glow of the many candles burning in glittering crystal chandeliers overhead, my friends giggled and exclaimed in wonder behind their fans. All evening, we'd been gathered against a wall of gilded paintings, watching ladies and lords pass us by in powdered wigs and swishing petticoats. The Tufton sisters wore matching pink brocade and Marie a patterned dark blue silk with lace frothing at her elbows. I towered above my friends in shimmering bronze, my hair styled in a wild halo of red curls, a braid looped behind, all ornamented with ribbons and peacock feathers.

To Lafayette, I curtseyed my gratitude and acceptance. "*Merci.*"

On the dance floor, we circled one another with intricate footwork, touching hands, then retreating. When we came together with the music, the aristocrat said, "I should envy *you* for your graceful dancing, Mademoiselle. Yet, because I'm dancing with you, *I* am the envy of every man on the floor."

I didn't know how to reply to such courtly flattery, except by blushing furiously.

When the music next brought us close, Lafayette insisted, "Send my regards to your father. I see too little of him of late . . . and I hear disturbing rumors that he intends to return to Virginia."

I didn't want to confirm it, in part because I didn't want it to be so myself. Instead, I smiled as if I hadn't heard over the music.

When the dance was done, Lafayette led me back to my friends, saying, "Tell your papa I'll call upon him soon. Mr. Jefferson is still very much needed here in Paris, where his revolution remains undone. In my study, I have a copy of his Declaration of Independence in half a frame. The other half of the frame is empty. One day, with his help, it will house a Declaration of French Rights and they'll stand side by side, like proud brothers. Like France and America. Like your father and me."

Ordinarily, a man's importance can be judged only by the passage of time. But in those years of convulsive political change, we *knew* we walked amongst living legends, and my father was one of them. That's why Lafayette's worshipful words echoed long after our dance, a lingering reminder that my father had never belonged only to me, or to me and my sisters, or even to my mother. . . .

His true mistress had always been the Revolution.

The Republic.

The Enlightenment.

Given that profound calling, and all the people who looked to my father for inspiration, was it really so silly or selfish that I desired a calling of my own? I couldn't help but wonder. And yet, as much as I still thought about my desire to take my vows, I very much enjoyed French society.

As the daughter of a foreign minister, I was welcomed into the highest circles. As an American, I was a curiosity, which garnered me invitations to many balls. I accepted them all, and not only because I loved to dance. I also went because the ballroom reunited me with my bosom friends from the convent. We filled our cards, danced late into the night, and dined past midnight, returning home at unorthodox hours. Marie flirted with gentlemen by dangling her white gloves and taught me to fend them off with a slow wave of my fan. Together, we mastered the subtle language of the ballroom in which entire conversations took place in gestures.

One memorable night, I slowly waved away the attention of several gentleman but touched my right cheek with a closed fan to accept the attentions of the Duke of Dorset. How could I not, given that he was both an ambassador and the uncle of my bosom friends? Besides, every eye was upon him in his bejeweled amber raiment and it would have been churlish to refuse. Guiding me to the dance floor for a minuet, the duke leaned close to whisper, "You are a rare bloom in this garden of forward French flowers. Your simple manners, your enticing reserve, the radiance of your hair—I simply had to have you adorn my arm."

I blushed again, uncertain as to whether this was the practiced flirtation of a diplomat or a rake. Either way I could not take seriously his sweet talk because he was a veritable uncle to me, as he was in fact to the Tufton sisters. "You flatter me overmuch, Your Grace." To which he responded with vehement denials as he whisked me onto the dance floor.

"*Fils de putes!*" Marie cursed, after my dance with the duke was done. "Must you grab the attention of all the most eligible bachelors in France? Will you leave none for the rest of us? The men all stare at you for your height and that red hair. If I did not love you so much, Jeffy, I would rip it from your head."

"I'm merely a freckled American curiosity!" It was true that in a ballroom, I attracted the notice of young men who might have overlooked me on the street. But I don't think it was my height or red hair or even my dancing skills that drew them to me. I think it was because I held myself unattainable.

I'd already foolishly given my heart to a man who abandoned me. I wouldn't make that mistake again. So I remained cordial but cool to the men who asked me to dance, and found myself flattered by admirers and overwhelmed by male attention, bewildered and intrigued.

My most ardent suitor, by far, was the young and energetic Armand Jules Marie Héracle, son of the Duke of Polignac, who, upon making my acquaintance, drew my hand up to kiss as if I were of rank to offer, and said, "*Enchanté . . .*"

The Polignacs were amongst the most powerful families at the court, and my suitor's mother a great favorite of Queen Marie-Antoinette. The *chevalier,* who some afforded the courtesy title of prince, challenged me with an aristocratic bearing. "Do you care to test your American *pionnière* fortitude against my stamina?"

I accepted and we danced a lively cotillion that had me sweating at the back of the neck. When the dance master called the next dance, Polignac said, simply, "Again."

"But that's not permitted," I replied, fanning my flaming cheeks, for we could not dance twice in succession without inviting scandal.

"Then the dance after that," he said with a rakish smile. "I must best the Duke of Dorset, so give me the honor of every other dance, Mademoiselle."

Polignac was brash and pleasant to look at in his sea-green coat with its embroidered gold lapels. Papa would've been appalled by my deference to titled nobility—but I found myself quite unable to refuse the son of a duke. Before the night was through, I'd danced sixteen times, eight of them with him.

We caused a sensation, and I admit to feeling satisfaction at the brazenness of it, even when the ladies Tufton scolded, "Have you set your cap on a Polignac, Patsy?" and "If you aim to be a duchess, at least favor our uncle, so that we can all be family one day!"

Marie hushed the Tufton sisters with a violent whack of her lace fan. "*Tais-toi!*" Then she turned shrewd eyes on me. "*Cher* Jef is just in revolt against her papa. She has half the French court whispering Jefferson's daughter will convert to the true faith. Now the other half will whisper that the daughter of equality's champion aims to marry an aristocrat."

Marie saw in my behavior some spark of hostility, some lack of care for Papa's reputation, and I didn't want to think it was true. "Marry an aristocrat?" No, I had no designs on marriage whatsoever, much less to Polignac or the Duke of Dorset. Besides, neither man was William Short. They were merely pretty distractions . . .

. . . and didn't my father want me distracted?

～⁀

THE START OF THE FRENCH REVOLUTION was orchestrated in my father's parlor. The leading reformers consulted Papa for every scrap of news of America. Our country's independence served as proof men could throw off the chains of tyranny and rule themselves.

Though Polly and I always left the table before the men turned to port and tobacco and more heated political discussions, we heard enough to know that none of them, not Papa nor any of the idealists gathered at our hearth in those early days, feared it would come to armed rebellion.

The king had called for elections and summoned the Estates-General for the first time in more than a century and a half. It was taken as a clarion call to make a new government that gave a voice to the people. We were all excited. When the great day came, we were all awakened before dawn by the peal of bells and booming cannons that sent people into the streets in celebration.

I helped Papa brush the shoulders of his best blue coat while Sally hastily mended the button on his red waistcoat. With white breeches and a dark blue felted hat, he was entirely bedecked in the colors of American and French patriots. Red, white, and blue.

I wanted nothing more than to go along with him to witness the debates from the gallery, but Papa wouldn't have approved even if he had an extra ticket. However, I was able to see the pageantry of the procession in the carriage of the elderly Madame de Tessé, the woman Lafayette called his aunt.

Thousands crowded the streets, swarmed the rooftops of every building along the avenue, clapping and reciting the famous pamphlet, *"What is the Third Estate? The whole people. What has it hitherto been in our form of government? Nothing. What does it want? To become Something."*

Swept up in the excitement, I hummed along with the flutes and trumpets. Soldiers marched in blue coats with gold epaulettes, wearing their proud ranks of insignia. The king marched beneath a canopy covered in fleurs-de-lis. The purple-robed bishops and red-robed cardinals chanted as they made their way to Versailles. The nobles strolled in rank, with gold sashes and feathered hats. Then came the sea of the Third Estate, representatives of the people, obliged to dress in stygian black and slouchy hats to denote their inferior rank.

That's all I saw of the opening day. It was not, however, my last visit to Versailles. So many great personages couldn't be gathered together in one place, even for such serious business, without evening entertainments.

At the next ball, I danced again with the Duke of Dorset and the Duke of Polignac's son, sending a scandalized titter through the politicized crowd, and a ripple of sighs for our precise steps so elegantly made in white-heeled shoes.

My *chevalier* and I stopped only for refreshments near the sideboard table, dodging dripping wax from the candelabras overhead and taking glasses of sweet wine from silver trays. My friends joined us, musing over whether or not we could sneak into the covert card game some aristocratic ladies had arranged in a private room upstairs.

It was, of course, improper for women to play cards in public, or at all, but a certain duchess was an inveterate gambler. "Speaking of dazzling duchesses," murmured my *chevalier*. "Please excuse me, ladies. The lovely Rosalie has arrived and I must pay my respects."

I turned to give my suitor a wave of farewell, but Marie grabbed my arm and pinched it so hard I yelped. "*Mon Dieu,* Jeffy. Don't look up!"

It was too late. I'd already spotted the pretty Duchess de La Rochefoucauld, and there, at her side, was William Short.

Chapter Twelve

OUR EYES LOCKED across the crowded ballroom, never wavering, in spite of the servants passing with silver trays of bubbling pink champagne in crystal glasses.

Without breaking my gaze, William Short whispered a quick word into his companion's bejeweled ear. I hated the sight of his cheek so near to the porcelain skin of her shoulder and plunging décolletage. Then hated more when he left her side to close the distance between us, striding between plumed ladies and men swaggering about with swords on their hips.

Most violently, my heart tried to take flight, leaving me suddenly breathless and light-headed. I'd yearned for our reunion, but now that it was upon me I felt utterly unprepared.

As if sensing my plight, my friends circled to form a phalanx before me in a violent swish of petticoats and lace. Marie, who had the best reason to know the pain Mr. Short's long absence had caused me, didn't bother with subtle gestures. She rudely shook her dance program at him as if shooing away a fly.

"Ladies." Wearing the warmest smile, Mr. Short ignored the flapping page and bowed. "Miss Jefferson . . ."

I just stared.

Eight months he'd been absent. Eight months, without a word. Wars had been fought and won in less time. Certainly, my whole world had changed. Yet, he addressed me as if a mere day had passed since our last visit.

William Short ought not have presumed we were still friends. No, he ought not have presumed.

I finally managed an icy, "Mr. Short. What a surprise."

"May I have a quiet word, Miss Jefferson?"

He scarcely waited for me to nod before herding me away from my coterie. I pulled away, not letting him touch me, not taking his arm, even as I followed him into an empty alcove where gold-tasseled curtains framed a tall, elegant window. I was so dizzied by his presence that the fleurs-de-lis on the blue silk wallpaper danced before my eyes, but I refused to let him see how affected I was.

I crossed my arms, seething. "I had no word you were back in Paris, Mr. Short."

"I just arrived in the past hour, actually, which explains my state of dress." It was then that I realized how out of place he looked in a dark coat and breeches, an outfit more fit for travel than the ballroom. "I feared I might be denied entrance, but fortunately, Rosalie vouched for me."

The gall of mentioning her to me in this moment! My gaze narrowed and my tone chilled even more. "Fortunate, indeed."

Mr. Short winced and shook his head. "I only meant to make clear that I came straightaway, from your father's house."

Accustomed to loss and calamity, I was thrown into instant worry and dropped my arms. "Has something happened to Papa? To Polly?"

He stepped closer. "No. They're both well. But I didn't want to miss seeing you tonight, so I dared not delay in coming here."

I frowned. He wanted me to believe he'd come to the ball to see *me*? I could scarcely credit that. "I'm very curious to know what has happened to make you so suddenly remember my existence."

His hand went to his heart. "I never forgot you, Patsy. Never."

I quite nearly snorted. Men were apt to say sweet nothings. Some men more than others, and Mr. Short was a practiced diplomat. How could I trust anything he said?

It sent a surge of rage through my veins. But rage was a forbidden emotion, so I forced myself to be aloof, to resist his flattery and his handsome face as I'd resisted all the other men in Parisian ballrooms. I waved my fan. "Will you be returning to my father's service at the Hotel de Langeac?"

"Eagerly."

Mon Dieu. When he'd lived at the embassy before, I spent most of my days and nights at the convent. Must we now live together under the same roof? I thought it such an injustice, I could manage only a bland nicety. "Well, then. Welcome back, Mr. Short. My father will be happy for your return."

"Patsy," he said, drawing nearer still. "Please don't retreat behind a polite facade."

An ache of desire opened up inside my chest, an ache my heart said would only be assuaged by giving in to his entreaties. But I still remembered how much worse was the pain of the heartbreak he'd caused. "I cannot imagine what you mean."

"You and your father both do it, but whereas Mr. Jefferson can't help himself, being too vulnerable otherwise, you're resilient enough to say what you think and feel."

How his words provoked me! Certain that I'd make a fool of myself if I didn't flee, I snapped, "Mr. Short, be glad I'm not ill-mannered enough to say what I think and feel. You must excuse me. They're calling the next dance."

Regret and contrition slipped into the cast of his green eyes. "You're angry."

"Ladies are never angry." I was livid.

He blocked my avenue of escape. "Ladies and angels are never angry. But Amazons . . ."

I didn't laugh at his little joke. Instead, I felt penned in, tormented by his use of words that had once meant something between us. *My* words came out as a hiss, leaking past the tight seal of my lips. "You never sent me a letter. Never in all the months you were gone."

"How could I, without offending your father? I asked after you whenever I wrote to him and sent my best wishes. You've no idea the anxiety it put in me to hear that you and your sister were so very ill this winter."

That had been months ago. Whatever anxiety he felt wasn't enough to make him return. Not enough to mean anything. "You can see for yourself that I've recovered."

"Yes." His green eyes traveled with appreciation down my face, over the pale mounds of my bosom, which heaved over the gold satin bows on my gown. Finally, his gaze moved up again, on an intake of breath. "Beautifully . . ."

Heat touched my cheeks. "They're calling the next dance," I reminded him, my own breath shallow. "I've promised another dance to—"

"Polignac?" Mr. Short turned to see the approach of my *chevalier.* "Refuse him."

Outrageous. "What cause do I have to be so rude to a suitor?"

"*Refuse* him," Mr. Short repeated, more emphatically. "Tell him you're tired, tell him you're ill, tell him—I don't care what you tell him, but refuse him."

Gripping my closed fan, I gave an exasperated shake of my head. "Why should I? Why would you even *ask* such a thing of me?"

"Because I hate him," Mr. Short said with uncharacteristic malice. "He's a monarchist. An enemy of liberty. And, more importantly, you just called him your suitor. You've danced with him before?"

Having let loose my temper, it now slipped dangerously out of my control at this apparent show of jealousy. "Yes, I've danced with him before. And other men besides. I'll have you know that I am being pursued by the Duke of Dorset—"

"The British ambassador?" Mr. Short broke in, with a note of abject horror. "Does your father know?"

I had mentioned Dorset more to stoke William's jealousy than because I believed the duke's flirtations to be earnestly intended. But now I wondered if I'd been foolish not to mention it to Papa, given the politics of the situation. "I don't wish to speak of it. Not with you. Besides, why should you mind? You left me feeling quite a fool and I will not be fooled again—"

"Patsy." William's unsettling green eyes pleaded with me from beneath sandy lashes. He shook his head and sighed. "I'm going about this all wrong. Please, I'll beg a thousand pardons if you'll only give me the chance to explain myself."

Before I could answer, I was forced to contend with the expectant gaze of the duke's son. Extending a hand to me that displayed the most elegant lace cuff I'd ever seen, the *chevalier* asked, "Mademoiselle, is this dance not promised to me?"

"Yes, it is . . ." I braved a look at William Short, whose expression barely masked his displeasure at the other man's interruption. Confusion so gripped me that the decision was more instinctual than purposeful. "But I'm afraid I'm feeling dizzy. Will you forgive me for sitting out?"

The *chevalier* narrowed his eyes in concern and glanced between us. "Please, if you're unwell, Mademoiselle, let me see you to—"

Mr. Short stepped between us. "I'll tend her, Polignac."

The two men must've been acquainted because a poisonous look passed between them. In fact, the *chevalier* wouldn't withdraw until I rested my fingertips upon Mr. Short's arm.

"As you wish, Mademoiselle Chefferson," Polignac said, as if he no longer knew quite how to pronounce my name. "Another evening, perhaps."

Given his high color, I doubted very much that there'd be other evenings with the duke's son, as he'd obviously taken my refusal for a snub. I ought to have chased after him and explained myself, but all I wanted was to hear what William Short had to say.

Infuriatingly, he said nothing. Instead he guided me to the grand marble staircase, wrought in iron and tipped with gold. Arm in arm, we descended, together, very slowly, awkwardly passing the Duke of Dorset, who raised a curious brow, making me wonder just what the Tufton sisters had told him of my feelings for William.

Finally, William said, "I never meant to leave you feeling a fool."

A hollowness filled my chest. "Then why did you? Without a word of explanation!"

"Please understand that a year ago, when I begged a hearing of your father on the matter of my feelings for you, he made clear that he still considered you—a mere schoolgirl—too young to be wooed much less wed."

I suspected as much, nevertheless, I swallowed on the word *wed*. "Didn't you try to persuade him otherwise?"

"And risk losing his esteem forever? No, Patsy. Only time would persuade him my intentions were honorable. So I gave us that time by traveling, by trying to convince your father, in my letters, that I want to provide for a wife and a family."

I sniffed, trying to hold firm against the words I'd long yearned to hear. "He said nothing to me of these letters."

"Your father cannot have mistaken my meaning because he wrote with advice on how I might best build a fortune with which to support a wife. Now I've returned to Paris to find everything changed."

"Changed how?"

We stopped on the landing and Mr. Short put his hand on the railing, his gaze searching mine. "The moment I set foot in the Hotel de Langeac tonight, I asked after you. Your father told me that you were no longer in the convent and that he'd let you come out into French society."

Had Papa also confided in him my desire to take my vows as a nun? While I wondered, Mr. Short continued, "That's why I came straightaway to find you. I knew, at long last, I could speak openly. I didn't want to let another hour—not another *second*— tick by without declaring myself."

I swayed on my heeled shoes, quite fearing a swoon. "What is it you wish to declare?"

He looked down, almost shyly. "I've so often planned what I'd say in this moment that it should be ready on my tongue. But poetry has suddenly fled from me . . . how can I find the words?"

I stared, expectantly, wondering if he might dare to take my hand

and kiss it. If he might scandalously twine his fingers with mine. If he might lean close to whisper in my ear. Instead, he reached into his coat and pulled forth the little piece of folded paper, now worn and creased with time, and unfolded it for me to see my hair still pressed within. "Patsy, this token has never left my possession. It's been a reminder, every day. What I want to declare—what I want to offer—is quite beyond abiding friendship."

I gulped, then forgot to breathe. "You kept my hair, all this time?"

"Yes. Near my heart. A year ago, I adored you. But now I adore you even more than before. For you've grown into a graceful and beautiful woman."

How could I believe him? Perhaps I *was* graceful. Shapely, too, with the added allure of an ample bosom and ginger hair. But even then, in the flower of my youth, I knew that I wasn't so much beautiful as appealing, my face a delicate rendering of my father's. Maybe it was the very resemblance to my father that accounted for the beauty Mr. Short saw in me—for I was a feminine reflection of a man he idolized.

But still, I was wary. "There are prettier ladies in Paris."

"Not in my eyes," he insisted, emphatically.

Now he did draw my hand up and clasp it against his chest, where I felt his heart throb beneath the buttons of his waistcoat— evidence that he *did* think me beautiful.

That, in turn, made me *feel* beautiful. It was a heady, intoxicating feeling. A feeling that could rob a girl of all reason.

"Patsy, will you allow me to take you home?"

In that moment, I'd have gone anywhere with him. It didn't matter that I'd left my shawl behind. Or even that when I looked up, I realized that the Duke of Dorset was standing at the top of the stairs and had witnessed the entire exchange. That spring in Paris, defiance was the norm. And a wild defiant liberation had taken hold of me, so I didn't fight it. I simply went with William out into the night, and alighted a carriage back to Paris, quite undone by this turn of fate.

My thoughts were as tumultuous as the jostling ride. I'd built a fortification round my heart, and not only because I'd been hurt. Given my intention to take my vows, I was forced to wonder if Mr. Short was a temptation sent by the devil himself. If so, I was ready to fall into the devil's arms, but I wasn't so unprincipled as to deceive him.

When we disembarked on the Champs-Élysées beneath lamps hung in the trees, I turned to him. "Mr. Short, I'm very much changed since you left. You don't realize the full extent of it. When you learn more, I fear—I fear you must reconsider your declaration."

"That sounds ominously serious. . . ."

"I'm afraid it is." I told him of my bargain with God. Of my admittedly wavering belief that I'd been called to serve as a Bride of Christ, rather than the bride of any man.

When I was finished, he exhaled. "What a relief. I feared you'd given your heart to Polignac. I'm much happier to have God as a rival. More glory in it for me if I win your love, and less shame should I lose."

I gasped at his playful remark. "That's blasphemous."

He winked. "Probably so. I'm a sinner with more faults than you imagine, Patsy. But you're the friend to which my soul is unalterably attached, so I'm prepared to make whatever altera- tions to my character would be conducive to your happiness. Only tell me this. Are my hopes in vain, or can you be induced to love me?"

I loved him already. Had loved him, it seemed, all my life. Loved his loyalty, his ambition, his radical vision for the world. That a man like William Short *wanted* my love filled me with such joy that I could've thrown my arms about his neck, heedless of the eyes upon us, and confessed it on the spot!

But did I not love God just as much?

Even if I hadn't determined to take the veil, I'd been strictly taught that a girl's easy confession of love was indecent and would destroy that love. I couldn't answer him with true candor. Worse, in struggling to think of a reply of sufficient restraint, I uttered words he took for reproach. "Sir, your absence pained me more than I can ever express—"

"You cannot forgive me?" he asked, stiffening.

"I could forgive you anything, but I need time to petition Heaven for guidance."

"You're cruel, Miss Jefferson. I've already spent a year's time waiting for you."

I shook my head. "It's not cruelty but confusion. For in that year's time, I feared you despised me. Now in one night, everything I thought I knew is changed."

"You feel hurried. Yes, I see that now. As do I. For your father tells me he expects permission for his leave of absence in the post any day now, and that you'll set sail for Virginia. I saw the trunks, already packed."

The breath went out of me. I hadn't forgotten my father's *congé*. But I hadn't realized that the need for a decision would steal swiftly upon me. Now, here was Mr. Short, making my choice more complicated. "But I need to understand. If—if I loved you, what then?"

His hands tightened on mine. "Then you'd make me the happiest man who ever lived."

His words radiated warm joy through me, but his answer didn't tell me what I needed to know. "And what of our future . . . ?"

He smiled. "If you could give up all thoughts of the convent, our future depends upon the orders your father is awaiting from America. Your father has asked that in his absence, I be appointed in his place as *chargé d'affaires* with commensurate salary. If I receive such an appointment, then I can present myself to your father as a worthy suitor. Otherwise, I'm afraid he'll consider me a wandering wastrel without employment."

"He would never!"

Mr. Short chuckled mirthlessly. "You think not? I have in my possession a letter from your father lecturing me on the need to build my fortune. The most memorable line reads: *This is not a world in which heaven rains down riches into any open hand.*"

How churlish of Papa, but had I not, from the youngest age, also received letters filled with his lectures? "You mustn't worry, Mr. Short. If my father requested your appointment, then it's sure to come. But until it does, how can I be sure of your intentions in asking for my love?"

I didn't expect him to laugh. "You're Jefferson's daughter, to the bone. You want evidence. Well, give me the chance and I'll give you the proofs you require—both of my love and of the world you should love too much to abandon even for God. I wouldn't have you enter a convent, much less love, in ignorance."

"What do you think me ignorant of?"

With mischief twinkling in his eyes, he stopped, drawing me into a grove of trees. Beyond us, in the ditch, we heard boys playing a ball game in the dim lamplight. Somehow, in the dark, Mr. Short's fingertips found my cheeks, and his mouth stole over mine. This first kiss was soft and tender. As if he feared frightening me. Nevertheless, it *shocked* me. It was like my heart was a loaded cannon he'd held fire to, and it threatened to shoot out of my chest. But I wasn't frightened and I didn't pull away. Instead, it seemed quite the most natural thing to kiss him back, mimicking what he did, glorying in every soft, sweet sensation.

At the feel of my lips teasing softly at his, he groaned and pulled back. "Oh, my heart . . ."

The sweet taste of him still on my lips, our breaths puffing in the night air, I asked, "Have I done something wrong?"

He held my cheeks in his hands. "The error was all mine. I'd beg your pardon if I could bring myself to regret it, but I never want to regret anything with you, so tonight I must content myself with one kiss."

Only one? I wanted to lavish a *thousand* kisses on his face. His lips, his cheeks, his ears. The desire was a sudden hunger, a desperate plea inside me echoing like the cry of peasants for bread. "What if I'm not yet content? Wasn't kissing me meant to be the proof of your intentions?"

"No, Patsy. Kissing you, then stopping before satisfaction, is the proof of my intentions, which I hope you'll see are honorable and directed toward your happiness."

This made no sense to me whatsoever, but I followed as he led me a little farther, to a copse of trees near my father's gate. Then, taking one of the hanging lanterns down, he reached into his boot for a knife—one that I didn't know he carried there. He took it, holding the lamp with one hand and carving the tree with the other. When he finished, he showed me a heart, inside of which he'd carved his own initials. "Like mine, this heart is waiting for you, Patsy. Every morning, I'll come look, and when I see that you've carved your initials here, with mine, I'll have my answer."

~~~

I'D BEEN KISSED! And I wanted to *die* of the delirious pleasure of it, if only I wasn't so delighted to be *alive*. All night, I tossed upon my pillow, touching with my fingertips the place Mr. Short's lips had been. Thinking, all the while, of how much I wanted him to kiss me again.

Though I'd been dreading the arrival of Papa's orders, I was suddenly eager for them, because they'd no doubt name Mr. Short as the *chargé d'affaires*. Then, he'd ask me to marry him.

I was sure of it.

In the morning, I wanted to rush down first thing and declare myself. I wanted to go straight to the kitchen and find James's sharpest knife to carve my initials in that tree and take William Short there to see it. But such an act of imprudence was forestalled by the whole household already at an early breakfast before I could get Sally's help with my laces. And Papa called up that I must hurry because the men needed to be off to Versailles.

When I rushed down, Papa snapped his fingers. "Candlesticks! Yes, that's it, isn't it? There were silver candlesticks on the table. They're missing. Sally, did you take them to polish?"

Sally had been quietly refilling the new silver urn on the

sideboard with hot coffee, and at this question, she overpoured with a quick shake of her head. Hissing as the coffee burned her fingertips, she made haste to clean up the spill. "I wouldn't presume."

Of course she wouldn't. On our plantation, counting and polishing the silver was a task for the mistress. A task my mother claimed as her own. My father frowned, but the mood was quickly dispelled when Mr. Short grinned and set down a gauzy little bag of confections with a pink bow.

"Chocolate drops!" Polly squealed. "For me?"

"Hmm?" My father looked up, having taken a bite of a crumpet browned to his exact specifications the way no one but James could manage.

Mr. Short gave me a private smile that made me blush from head to toe. "The chocolate drops are for Patsy, actually." But by that point, my little sister had already stuffed two in her mouth. " . . . and for you, too, Polly. For both of you, of course."

I didn't mind sharing them, as his thoughtfulness was all the sweetness I needed. Even if he hadn't lain awake all night replaying the kiss and imagining our next, it was still proof that he'd thought of me. And wanted me to know.

He also had a gift for my father. A macaroni machine for the man who was passionate about every sort of invention! With much laughter, Mr. Short demonstrated how the thing could make the long and silly noodles of which we were becoming so fond. How glad I was for us all to be gathered together again under one roof.

My sister, my father, and the man I loved. Could I ever willingly be parted from any of them, even if it was God's desire?

It was a question still on my mind when I returned to the convent.

I went back not to take the veil but to attend in the company of my father a musical performance by the mixed-race prodigy George Bridgetower. Music had long been a special thing between my father and I. The notes, and especially the silences between them, were a language we shared. Our songs were duets; they left no room for other singers. And so I took great pleasure in going, just the two of us.

With gallantry, Papa guided me to my seat saying, "I'll be very interested to see if a boy of only ten years can have such talent as if by way of nature and not learning."

Someone overheard and broke in. "I'm more interested to see if the mulatto boy's talent weighs as evidence against his race's inferiority."

The whole room was alive with such talk as the boy-musician appeared in an exquisite pink suit coat embroidered with satin threads, violin in hand. In that strange moment, it seemed as if the question of slavery rested upon this little boy's shoulders. He tossed his black curls and played to a room filled from velvet curtain to paneled wall. And what shall I say of his music? It was sublime. Technically precise, with stormy flurries that left tears shining in the corners of many eyes.

It left me profoundly affected, too, when, through the din, someone asked Papa, "Given this violinist is of mixed race, how can we know if his talent derives from his African or European ancestry?"

"It doesn't matter," my father replied.

"But if Africans are our natural equals," I dared to ask, "doesn't it make a stronger case for freeing slaves?"

I knew my father didn't care to hear me opine on this subject. More, I feared my father might change the subject, as he did whenever I weighed in on a matter of any controversy. But instead, he replied quietly, "It does not. It's my belief that blacks are more gifted than the whites for tune and time. It's also my belief that the admixture of white blood always improves the black. Any man with eyes can observe differences—"

Perhaps it was the way I recoiled from my father that caused him to stop midsentence, for my heart had dropped to my stomach in shame at his words. And even though everyone else seemed to hang on his every utterance with fawning admiration, the bitter disappointment in my eyes seemed to have shaken him.

Reaching for my hand, he hastened to add, almost apologetically, "And yet, differences shouldn't be used to legitimize the unjust practice of slavery. It makes slavery no less wrong. It's a dangerous premise upon which opponents of slavery ought not rely. Indeed, I tremble for my country when I reflect that God is just and that his justice cannot sleep forever."

I was glad to hear my father reaffirm his opposition to slavery, in spite of our private circumstances. But I was startled, too, by the fact that he'd done it, in part, because I pushed him to. Until this moment, I had rarely dared to question him. But now, I had done more than question him. I had challenged him—perhaps more boldly than even Mr. Short would have done. For I had challenged him in public.

And he had answered that challenge by lending his voice to the cause of justice.

I'd be lost without you. Lost.

That is what Papa had said when he pleaded with me not to shut myself up in this convent. Now I wondered if he had not meant that he needed more than my companionship and care, if my father needed me and William both to challenge him when no one else would. Or could.

Renewed purpose welled inside me until my eyes sought out the crucifix on the wall, a gilded portrait of our Christ in suffering. I stared upon it for a long moment, and the lightness of clarity stole over me. I felt no more guilt for leaving this convent. I'd bargained with God that I'd give myself over to him if he saved my sister, but my father had been sent to France to protect and secure those inalienable rights endowed by our Creator. If Papa himself could be an instrument of God's justice, was it not a moral duty for me and William Short to serve as his helpmates?

Chapter Thirteen

Paris, 9 May 1789
From Thomas Jefferson to John Jay

The revolution of this country has advanced thus far without encountering anything which deserves to be called a difficulty. There've been riots in which there may have been a dozen or twenty lives lost. A few days ago a much more serious riot took place in this city, in which it became necessary for troops to engage with the mob. Neither this nor any other of the riots have had a professed connection with the great national reformation going on. They are such as have happened every year since I've been here.

HOW SANGUINE THIS LETTER READS NOW, with the benefit of hindsight, but we were so hopeful, never anticipating the whirlwind. While men like Lafayette, La Rochefoucauld, Condorcet, and my father shaped the great events unfolding, the storm *I* faced took smaller shape within the Hotel de Langeac. There was, after all, no time for kisses and declarations of love—especially not with Papa and William gone almost daily to Versailles and Lafayette visiting so often for advice, now that he'd been elected to represent the nobles as a representative to the Estates-General.

I took it upon myself to carry the tea service on the day that Lafayette arrived unexpectedly, in a state of great agitation, rambling half in English, half in French, as he was prone to do.

"They will not hear reason!" Lafayette shouted as I poured tea into his cup. "My fellow nobles have only themselves to blame. They want only a sham of democracy, no true national assembly at all." His anger stemmed from his noble constituents instructing him to vote against the common people. "My conscience will not allow me to support the disenfranchisement of ninety-six percent of the nation. Yet, how can I violate the instructions of those who sent me to represent them and still call myself a champion of democracy? I see no choice but to resign."

"Forgive me, my dear friend, if my anxiety for you makes me talk of things I know nothing about," Papa began, using the clever but unassuming manner he often employed to soften the giving of difficult advice. "But if you resign, there will be one less voice of reason in the Estates-General."

"There are *other* voices of reason at Versailles?" asked Mr. Short, sardonically. "I'm told the nobles are quite out of their senses and the commons have amongst them some mad, radical hotheads—"

"My cause is liberty," Lafayette snapped, with all the zeal of his ancestry, which boasted a companion of Joan of Arc. It was on Lafayette's suggestion that the king had called the Estates-General in the first place. Few men were as invested in its outcome. "No matter how mad the agitators in the commons may be, I will die with them rather than betray them."

Mr. Short frowned. "I think it better to compromise and *live* with them rather than die with them. Why not use your voice in your chamber of nobles to bring about a peaceful resolution to this crisis?"

Electrified by the conversation, I poured the next cup slower, not wishing to be dismissed and wondering how serious the threat of violence truly was.

Mr. Short's advice seemed good and sensible.

But perhaps more than any man who ever lived, my father was acutely aware of the interplay between public reputation and political power and the risks that must be taken to acquire both.

"This is your moment of opportunity, Lafayette," Papa said. "Your opportunity to *defy* the instructions of your noble constituents, go over to the people now, and win their hearts forever." Papa's voice rang out with increasing fervor, reminding me of bygone days when I saw my father engaged in our own revolution and inspiring other men to fight for their independence. "If you wait too long, currying favor with both sides, you will lose both. The nobles will only love you so long as you do their dirty work for them. If you do not now declare yourself a man of the people, some other prominent nobleman will do so before you, and he will then have the unprecedented power and influence that ought to be yours. Take at once the honest and manly stand your own principles dictate."

This was Papa at his finest, mixing pragmatism and principle in a way only a handful of men could.

Madison. Adams. Hamilton. And my father.

Lafayette studied Papa and nodded, thoughtfully. "Tell me. How did you feel on that glorious day you took your own honest and manly stand and signed your name to the Declaration of Independence?"

Papa's expression turned wry. "I felt a noose tightening around my neck."

The men barked with dark but well-needed laughter. Then, at length, the conversation turned to brokering a bargain in which taxes would be levied in exchange for a charter of citizens' rights to be signed by the king.

A charter that my father said he would be happy to draft.

He was no unaffected bystander in this struggle. None of us were.

"Miss Patsy!" Sally said, motioning to me from the open door. The alarm in her voice ushered me out of the room. "Someone's robbed us again and they've taken some of your ribbons and rings."

How violated I felt, learning someone had stolen into my bed-chamber, taking little things from me that were not nearly so precious as my peace of mind! Beside my trinkets, the thief—or thieves—made off with food from our larder, some of Papa's favorite Burgundy wines, and some silver to boot.

First the candlesticks, now this.

We might've taken it as a sign of the times, for starving peasants were, every day, streaming into the capital in desperate search of employment or charity. I'd just heard Papa discuss the growing violence but never imagined such a thing would cross our threshold.

That evening, Papa sat at the head of the long dining room table, surrounded by botany books and specimens, and called James and Sally Hemings to account. "James, the thief might be one known to you. Perhaps an acquaintance you met at the taverns?"

With his hands laced behind his back, James's stiffening spine revealed that he bristled at the implication. "No friend breaks into my kitchens and thinks he can leave with stolen goods and an unbloodied nose. But you, sir, have guests in and out of this place day and night."

It was true, of course. We entertained all manner of Americans and Frenchmen here at the Hotel de Langeac, but that didn't make James's challenge any less surprising.

Seated at the table beside my father, I kept my eyes on my lap, wondering if Papa would snap in anger, but he merely cleared his throat. "I'm not accusing you of theft, James. I'm simply prying into the truth of it."

"I'd never lie to you, Mr. Jefferson. Nor to any man." James straightened beneath his white chef's hat, unlacing his hands and letting them hang confidently at his sides. "Lies are for frightened slaves cowering under the whip. And *there are no slaves in France.*"

At this announcement, the room went quiet. I barely bit back a gasp and held my breath until I feared it would explode from my lungs. Sally wobbled as if she might fall.

Papa finally broke the silence, his voice carefully even. "Do you consider yourself a Frenchman, James?"

James eyed my father levelly. "I reckon I should start to. You won't make me go to the Admiralty Court for my freedom, will you?"

Color drained from my father's face, perhaps contemplating the censure he'd face from his revolutionary friends if that came to pass. He couldn't fight the emancipation in court without acute embarrassment; what would Lafayette say?

Papa held up a hand. "That won't be necessary."

James swallowed hard at his apparent victory, as if he'd been nervous to fight for it, or was afraid to believe it. "I'll be happy to serve you here in Paris, Mr. Jefferson, but I want to be free. So when you go back to Virginia, I can't—I *won't*—go back with you."

Papa steepled his fingers beneath his chin. "I see."

Prickles ran over my skin and a thrill warmed my blood as I sat witness to yet another extraordinary conversation, the meaning of the revolutionary fervor swirling around us coming home to me. It was right here, in this man's heart, not asking for his freedom, but taking it.

Not that James did so without trepidation. He swallowed again, obviously finding no pleasure in this confrontation. He had a stubborn sense of pride for a servant, but not all the pride in the world would've made him risk being put out into the streets where thousands were starving. No, he pressed the matter because, like me, he knew his fate was to be decided by our next missive in the post. My father's request for leave had forced James's hand, and having no choice but to play on, his determined gaze flicked to Sally. "My sister will stay with me."

At *that* declaration, I did indeed gasp as my eyes cut to my lady's maid. My father had, until this point, remained calm, but now he scowled with displeasure. He too glanced at Sally, who twitched under our scrutiny like a cornered mouse.

Papa looked to James. "Surely you don't think you can provide for Sally, here in Paris, with the economy of the place in a shambles, with robbers and cutthroats roaming the streets. She needs protection—"

"I can protect her," James replied, taking off his hat and squeezing it in his tawny hands. "Moreover, Sally can sew and launder. She has experience as a chambermaid, and a lady's maid, too. We'll do fine."

Papa didn't look convinced and turned his next question on Sally. "Is that what you want?"

Sally shook her head in misery, as if she didn't know where to look. Into the coaxing eyes of the master who cosseted her but held her in bondage, or into the uncompromising eyes of the brother who meant to liberate her? For a moment, I thought she might take flight.

And when her eyes brimmed with tears, Papa softened his words, as if to a frightened child. "Well, then. Let's not be hasty. The orders haven't come yet, so we can take time to decide what's best."

It was a dismissal. James gave a stiff bow. Sally curtseyed. Then both withdrew, leaving me alone with my father.

In their wake, Papa rubbed his temples. "I face threats of abandonment on all sides."

It felt like a rebuke. Was he still stung by my desire to take the veil? Oh, how, in my distress, I wanted to reassure him that was done now and that all I wanted was to become the wife of Mr. Short and live with both of them forevermore!

But before I could think of even a way to hint at such a thing, Papa said, "It pains me not that he wants his freedom. . . ." I suspected he'd be furious that James had spoken to him in a way that slaves never spoke to their masters. Perhaps he was deeply troubled by the potential loss of their services and hard-pressed to find another chef so well trained to the peculiarities of his palate. But he didn't seem angry. "It's that he could think to leave us and condemn his delicate sister to an uncertain and hardscrabble life in a place so far from home."

Papa was worried. And wounded. Hurt as he'd been, when, on his knees, he'd begged me not to join the nunnery. A possessive man, his distraught expression told me he took the specter of freedom for James and Sally as yet another deeply personal loss. But

I knew it was more than that because I'd heard him speak many times of his honor-bound duty to protect and care for his people.

I debated how to comfort him, especially since I supported James's desire for freedom. Papa and I both believed slavery to be wrong. We both ought to have applauded the man's stand. Yet, beyond the loss of talent and property that James's departure would represent, was the truth that Papa hated little more than to be left behind.

As Mama had done, and Lucy, and as I had nearly done.

But in this, he would simply have to accept it. It would be *good* for him to accept it. So I drew a deep breath and said, "In any other circumstances, I'm sure they'd never leave us. Perhaps Sally and James can remain in France in your employ a bit longer. Mr. Short can watch over them during your leave. We're very fortunate to have Mr. Short for such a constant friend, aren't we?"

"Quite." Papa pulled his tray of leafy specimens closer and retrieved his magnifying glass. One of my father's many scientific acquaintances had requested his opinion on classifying flora he'd found on his estate, and Papa had been poring over Linnaeus's *Philosophia Botanica* all afternoon. After a moment, he frowned and lowered the looking glass.

It was a frown that shot an arrow of worry through me. There had been, since Mr. Short's return, a slight undercurrent of impatience between the two—as if the nature of their relationship had changed. Until this moment, I'd dismissed it as merely the tension of the political moment, but now I was forced to ask, "You *are* happy Mr. Short returned to us, aren't you, Papa?"

"Indeed. William has returned charged like a bee with the honey of wisdom, a blessing to his country and an honor to his friends. I think no one is happier for his return than me, save for his friends in Saint-Germain." In the clearing of his eyes and disappearance of the furrow in his brow, it seemed the change of subject brightened Papa's disposition. If only a little.

But now it was my turn to frown, for I knew of only *one* friend in Saint-Germain. A sweetheart I thought Mr. Short had given up long ago. "He's gone to Saint-Germain tonight?" My heart threatened to creep into my throat in anticipation of the answer.

"Not tonight, no," Papa said, casually, though I sensed some purpose behind his words. "I'd be surprised if he went again to Saint-Germain so soon after his last visit. . . ."

My heart lodged *solidly* in my throat. What could he mean?

Leaning in over his specimens again, Papa added, almost as an aside, "Patsy, we must be good to Mr. Short, for I fear he may soon suffer a great disappointment."

My bewilderment turned to fear. Had Papa guessed at our love? Did he plan to forbid it? Nearly breathless with anxiety, I asked, "What disappointment?"

Papa glanced to his notes. "I've pressed his appointment in my absence as *chargé d'affaires* with my superiors as far as is prudent, but Mr. Short isn't known to them. He may not get the appointment."

I contemplated what that might mean for Mr. Short—and for me. "Will this ruin his future?"

"He may believe so, but it may be his salvation. It would do him good to return to America at the soonest opportunity. Men too long in France acquire a fondness for luxury and a contempt for the simplicity of our own country."

His words left me utterly appalled. "You cannot doubt Mr. Short's patriotism!"

"Of course not." Papa drew his gaze back to me. "I'm merely observing that, in my experience, young men in France get caught up in destructive affairs of the heart. They learn to consider fidelity to the marriage bed as an ungentlemanly practice."

Mon Dieu. Did Papa think Mr. Short a lecher? I burned at the indelicate warning. Indeed, I was too mortified to speak! Did he not recognize the hypocrisy of chiding other men for destructive affairs?

My gaze dropped to fists clenched upon the dining table, and Papa patted my balled-up hand. "If Short doesn't secure the position he desires, we mustn't let him take it too hard, Patsy. An

American too long in Europe loses his knowledge, his morals, his health, his habits, and his happiness. I'd entertained only suspicions of this before, but what I see since coming here proves it."

Having never heard my father speak even indirectly in criticism of Mr. Short before, a hollow pain took up residence in the center of my chest. "You think so ill of him?"

"To the contrary. William has my warmest and most fatherly affection. And I want nothing but the best for *all* my children."

OUR EVENINGS WERE FILLED WITH VISITORS and Papa himself drafting in frantic, coded scribblings for Lafayette a charter of rights that should serve as the new constitution for France. It seemed too fraught a time for carving hearts and initials into trees, especially since I felt keenly the need to question Mr. Short.

Alas, my father kept him too busy. On the day the Third Estate officially declared themselves the *National Assembly,* and the clergy voted by small majority to join them, we heard cries of *"Vive le Roi! Vive le Assemblée Nationale!"*

That was the same day Marie came to call, bringing with her a little black miniature poodle with fluffy balls of fur upon its head and paws and tail. Every Parisian of standing kept at least one dog for a pet, it seemed. Seated in a circle beneath the rising golden sun painted overhead, we tried our hand at embroidering with tambour needles, working to embellish one of my new dresses with pearlescent beads. Truthfully, only Sally had any talent for it, and my mind was on Mr. Short.

"He's asked for my love," I finally confessed.

Polly beamed with excitement. "Have you given it?"

My shoulders fell. "How can I? He's always at Versailles."

Marie set down her needle. "Then we must go to him there."

"You and I, alone?" I asked, wary of such an adventure.

"Bring your sister and Mademoiselle Sally, too. There's room in my carriage. . . ."

Polly groaned. "In this rain? I'd rather drink hot chocolate."

Marie huffed. "To think I came out in this rain just to see you and your sister, you sweet little wretch! The rain is auspicious after such drought. Besides, better for you to be out in fresh air instead of imprisoned in this house."

We were not, of course, prisoners, but I hadn't attended a ball with Marie since the night of Mr. Short's return. In truth, the social scene in Paris had collapsed under the weight of its politics and the official mourning for the poor little dauphin, who died of consumption and left the queen in despair.

Sorely tempted, I asked, "What reason could we possibly give for going to Versailles on our own?"

Marie smiled, mischief in her eyes. "We'll go on the pretense of paying a visit to Madame de Tessé at her château."

Few women were more engaged with the happenings at Versailles than Lafayette's elderly relation. I'd never been allowed to attend her salons, but Papa said she was a Republican of the first feather. And we often drank tea with her, so Papa couldn't possibly raise an objection to my taking her a small harvest of American curiosities from our garden. . . .

Still, as much as I longed to see Mr. Short, I hesitated, and Marie's gaze turned playfully stern. "Come now, *cher* Jeffy. You cannot be timid in matters of love!"

It was decided then. Sally helped me into a gown appropriate for court—jet-black in keeping with mourning customs and in sympathy with the commons, who were still obliged to dress in their dark mark of inferiority. There was no time to don the elegant hedgehog-style wig I'd been saving for such an occasion. Besides, the rain outside would only ruin it and natural hair was now in fashion, so I donned a bonnet, then off we went.

"We'll never find him," I fretted. "Half of Paris is at Versailles. In the throngs of thousands, where will we even look?"

"At your papa's elbow," Sally said as we settled into Marie's carriage. "Your father stands taller above the crowd than anyone excepting perhaps Lafayette."

Marie nodded in agreement, then shrugged. "Besides if we don't find Short, what of it? The king and queen are at their palace at Marly, and I suppose we'll arrive too late for mass, but we'll have a fine day of it in the Hall of Mirrors."

Alas, we had quite underestimated the rain. It drove against the carriage windows in sheets, flooding the streets and sending our wheel into a river of filthy water in a ditch. There was nothing for us to do but abandon it to the coachman, gird ourselves under umbrellas, and run back to the house, with Marie's dog yapping at our heels. In full sprint, blinded by the rain, I reached the corner of rue de Berri and the Champs-Élysées, and crashed into a man standing there.

I looked up into the red and rain-soaked face of Mr. Short.

Puffing for breath, and without even a hat to protect him from the elements, he cried, "Patsy Jefferson, what the devil are you doing?"

WHILE I STRUGGLED WITH MY UMBRELLA against the rising wind, Mr. Short escorted me toward our house, all the while scolding me for rashness in leaving in the first place.

Meanwhile Marie scooped up her bedraggled poodle and said, "*Mon Dieu,* you two are hopeless. Come, Polly. Let's find a roof and leave your sister and Mr. Short to argue like fools in the rain!"

Together with Sally, they dashed up the stairs while Mr. Short caught my elbow and pulled me into the empty carriage house to seek shelter amidst the extra wagon wheels, the scent of horses and liniment oils strong in my nose.

"For shame, Miss Jefferson. Have you *no* understanding of how critical the situation is?"

He was still in high temper with me, and much higher, I thought, than my behavior merited. "Papa says we're in no danger."

Mr. Short slicked rain-soaked hair back from his eyes, letting me look unhurried upon his handsome face for the first time in days. "He doesn't want to frighten you. But yes, there's danger. Today we arrived in Versailles to see placards everywhere, banning the commons from meeting in their hall. The king locked them out of their chambers at threat of bayonet!"

Mr. Short snapped the umbrella from my hand, our fingers brushing, then shook the rain water off it for me before setting it down against a bale of hay. Anger washed off of him and, together with his touch, heated my skin against the rain's chill.

"It's upon some flimsy pretext of needing to redecorate the great hall," he continued. "Better to have said it was in mourning for the dauphin. Either way, with nowhere else to go in the rain, the deputies found shelter in the tennis court."

"But why is this—"

"Think, Patsy," Mr. Short said, giving me a little shake. "There are the people's representatives, huddled together in a tennis court, surrounded by armed soldiers, yet still they insist on their right to govern themselves. They've vowed a sacred oath not to dissolve until a new constitution has been adopted. Never in my life have I seen such brave, patriotic men."

"Not even in America?"

He tilted his head, and some of the anger ebbed from his eyes and brow. "Not even in America. For when your father and the others pledged to each other their lives, fortunes, and sacred honor . . . the king was an ocean away, royal troops with bayonets not *literally* at the door."

Picturing such a scene, it was easy to imagine how passions might become inflamed. The king and his soldiers could slaughter the people's representatives. The reformers might die in a single clash of new principles and ancient tradition. Their bravery became quite clear, and I wondered if they might've even deliberately taken this stand knowing their deaths might come to pass. Would they, in their fervor, speak of my father's authorship of their new constitution?

Finally, a sense of alarm shivered down my spine. "Where is Papa now?"

"On his way. We came in different coaches because we feared unrest in the city might spill over and block the roads. I ran the last bit because I had to see for myself that you were safe. And what do I find but you traipsing toward danger!"

He'd come . . . for me? Hugging myself against the chill of the rain, I shook my head. "I only wanted to find you. I've been wanting to speak to you most desperately. . . ." I trailed off because, given what he'd just told me, my romantic longing sounded suddenly petty even to my own sixteen-year-old ears.

Nevertheless, his expression softened and he stepped closer. "No doubt, you've felt quite abandoned in recent days. What do you wish to speak about so *desperately*?"

My gaze flickered away. "I beg you to forget it, entirely. I see now that it's a trifling matter."

He yanked his soaked neck cloth open from where it had tightened. "Miss Jefferson, is my present state of agitation not enough to convince you that nothing is a trifling matter to me when it concerns you?"

I'd rehearsed what I'd say, how I'd get answers in the most subtle ways. But now that he was waiting so expectantly and standing so close, my heart pounded and I blurted, "You went to Saint-Germain."

He nodded. "Yes. After being gone for eight months, I wanted to look in on—"

"The Belle of Saint-Germain," I interrupted, the heat of jealousy burning my cheeks. "You professed love to me, but you went to see *her*."

The reproach was so plain that he couldn't mistake it. Still, he seemed untroubled. "Indeed. She's a dear friend and I'd not seen her in nearly a year."

His words were entirely reasonable, but I couldn't quell my hurt feelings. "Do you claim your relations with her entirely innocent?"

"They are now."

My mouth fell agape because in making this admission, he'd

skillfully denied me an opportunity to ask more without resorting to indelicacy. Then he made matters worse by meeting my eyes directly. "Ask me, Patsy. Go on. If it troubles you, ask me."

I could do nothing but stammer. "Were you, was she—"

"You don't have to find the polite words. Not with me."

The indecent question burst out of me. "Was she your lover?"

"Yes." He didn't even have the grace to wince. "I've protected her identity because she's married now, and they have together two young sons. But I don't want you turning little mysteries into great obstacles between us, so you may as well know that her name is Lilite Royer."

I didn't care what her name was! Only that she'd known, intimately, the man I loved. That stabbed at a place inside me I wasn't even fully aware existed. Still, this knowledge wasn't enough. I cringed to hear myself interrogate him. "And what of your duchess? They say you're infatuated with her."

His smile disconcerted me. "Along with every other man in Paris. But the beautiful Rosalie is too good and dutiful to betray her marriage bed. Even if she could, it wouldn't be for an infatuation. She'd never have a man who cannot offer his heart . . . and I cannot, for I've given my heart to you. I love you, Patsy."

The whole world stopped. The smell of the carriage house disappeared. The sound of the rain faded. The humidity of the air was no more. The whole world narrowed to the two of us and his declaration. He *loved* me. His answer was delectably sweet, but instead of letting it melt away like chocolate on my tongue, I breathlessly demanded, "Why do you love me, if you do. . . ."

"*If* I love you?" He snorted. "By God, have I taught you to suspect me or is it simply your nature? Of course, that nature is how you won my heart. Ferreting out spies. Stealing letters not meant for your eyes. Prying into facts no other girl would dare. You're like me. Skulking about in the shadow of great moments and great men, doing for them what they cannot do for themselves. Your father doesn't understand what a champion he has in you, but I do. I've said it before; hiding beneath all that flimsy lace beats the heart of an Amazon. And *that* is why I love you."

This answer nearly swept my knees out from under me. "Oh, Mr. Short—"

"William." He cupped my cheek. "Call me William."

The touch of his damp hand, fiery against my cold cheek, made me forget we were quarreling. "William," I whispered, testing it on my tongue for the first time, and tingling with delight. Then I tried it in French. "*Guillaume.*"

His eyes softened as he stroked a damp thumb over my cheekbone. "Patsy, I'll never lie to you, because you cannot love me if you don't know me truly. I'm guilty of indiscretions you've guessed and some you haven't. There have been women before you, but on my honor, if you become my wife, there will be none after."

It felt as if all the air left the close confines of the carriage house. Breathless, I was forced to press a hand over the quick pounding of my heart. *Wife.* He wanted me for his wife. And who was I to judge him harshly for his conduct when mine had never been above reproach?

"Can you love me, Patsy?"

"I already do!" The words burst out of me, and now that I'd been so reckless, I couldn't stop them. "I love you, William. Oh, I love you. I do. I want to carve it on the tree. I want to shout it in the streets!"

"Carve it here." He drew my fingers to his chest, where I felt his heart thump beneath his sodden white shirt. "With a kiss."

Trembling and breathless, I dared to kiss him there, then lifted my lips to his, my fingertips creeping up to the skin he'd bared by removing his neck cloth. He felt hot to the touch, feverish even. And as we kissed, I thought I'd stop for no reason under heaven.

But I was wrong.

We sprang apart the moment we heard the clatter of Papa's coach.

Chapter Fourteen

Paris, 17 June 1789
From Thomas Jefferson to John Jay

A tremendous cloud hovers over France, and the king has neither the courage nor the skill necessary to weather it. Eloquence in a high degree, knowledge and order, are distinguishing traits in his character. He has not discovered that bold, unequivocal virtue is the best handmaid, even to ambition, and would carry him further in the end than the temporizing wavering policy he pursues.

IT WASN'T A TIME FOR LOVE, but revolution. The loss of his army's loyalty forced the king's hand in negotiating with the people, and in Paris, the mood was hopeful. Perhaps that's why I received my first social invitation in nearly a month to attend a dinner hosted by the infamous Georgiana Cavendish, the Duchess of Devonshire. She was a committed *whig* and sympathetic to all the causes we held dear. Papa would never ask me to do something so unladylike as eavesdrop for useful information, but he didn't need to ask.

Instead, he took me to the Palais-Royal past market stalls filled with snuffboxes, bric-a-brac, and jewelry, where he bought me a new ring to replace the one that had been stolen. Planting a kiss atop my head, he said, "Let me pamper you while you're still mine."

Good thing my eyes were fixed on the glass case. For I felt

them widen at his wording and wondered if he knew about the love William and I shared. Had William spoken to him? Maybe even gone as far as declared his intentions?

Emboldened, I found my courage. "Papa, I don't want to go home to Virginia. I'd rather stay with you in Paris as long as your assignment keeps you here."

"What a dutiful daughter you are," he said, sliding the new ring upon my finger, admiring it in the light. "But this is no place for you and your sister. It's too selfish to keep you with me in a city where cutting off heads has become so much à la mode that we're apt to check each morning whether our own heads are still on our shoulders."

How could he say such a thing in the midst of the Palais-Royal, the throbbing heart of Paris? And yet, taking in our surroundings, I noticed unsavory characters. Cutpurses and hungry, bareheaded peasants, and rabble-rousers who read polemic screeds while standing atop café tables. "But there hasn't been violence in a month."

"Yes, but the want of bread greatly endangers the peace. It may yet come to civil war." Papa kept his voice low, for political chatter echoed all around us. And because he was of such renown, often dragged into such conversations even by perfect strangers, we sought a quiet café from which to take coffee.

We never found one. Nor could we find the tender brioche loaves sweetened with sugar and raisins that Polly wanted; it was just as well, for the shortage of flour in France made the indulgence insulting to our sympathies. Instead, we walked home past the tree where William's initials were carved, still waiting for mine. "I'm not afraid, Papa."

"That's because you've always been braver than I am, my dear. Still, my heart can only be content once I know you and your sister are safely settled in Virginia."

I wanted to believe that was the reason he was so determined to take us from France. But I feared there was another reason, and I needed to be clear. It was untoward, but he had to know my choice. "Papa, you must understand that my heart can only be content with Mr. Short."

With scarcely a blink, he said, "I see."

Now that I'd started my confession, the rest rushed out. "There won't be time for a wedding before you return to America, and it'd be unseemly for us to live under one roof without you, once we're betrothed. But I've divined a solution! I've arranged to lodge at the convent. Then Mr. Short and I can be married when you come back."

Now Papa did blink. "William has asked you to wed?"

"Not yet. He wouldn't do so until he was sure of his position because he worries that you don't think him capable of supporting a wife and family—"

"He's not." My father's flat appraisal forced me to utter silence. "He's in no way capable. Our dear William came here with an idea of staying only two years. His loyalty to me has prevented him from making his fortune and his inheritance amounted to nothing even before he gave liberty to the slave that came with it."

How I swelled with pride at my love's actions, even as Papa's words made me wary. "He's very principled."

My father stopped by our gate. "I *think* William means to return to America, where he may buy a farm near to me in Albemarle County; of this I'm not sure, having avoided asking him lest he should mistake curiosity for inclination. But if those are his plans, what happy neighbors we'll be! Then I'll be very happy to give this match my blessing."

My fear melted away and my heart soared with joy. Soared like one of those balloons that Papa had taken me to see, rising up and up and up! I rushed to kiss his cheek in excitement before his words sank in. "Do you mean to say, you won't give your blessing now?"

The light of that Parisian summer day glinted in his blue eyes. "I merely ask that you wait until William has established himself somewhere without the element of danger or poverty. Then, if he proposes marriage, I'll be delighted to welcome into our family a man who is already a son to me, one whose company I find necessary to my happiness."

Papa wanted us to wait, after we'd already waited so long! That I didn't burst into tears on the spot was, I thought, something to be quite proud of. Papa's words had the ring of perfect reason to them, so why did I hear in them such injustice?

When the heart finds its one true desire, any separation and delay is unbearable. And so it was to be a miserable evening, one that I suffered with an ache blooming in my chest. The Duchess of Cavendish commented favorably upon my height just before I was presented to her as "Miss Jefferson, the daughter of His Excellency, Thomas Jefferson, the American minister."

"Ah, yes, I've heard of him," the duchess said. "*We hold these truths to be self-evident, that all men are created equal.*" She made a twirling motion with her fingers. "Et cetera, et cetera."

I curtseyed. "Yes, Your Grace."

"But not the women," she said, frowning. "In France, I'm hoping to meet women dedicated to *égalité* and the right to decide our own fates. Your father wrote all *men* are created equal, but made no mention of the ladies. Haven't you wondered why?"

Yes, I wondered. Because in the spirit of the times, and my own discontent, everything I knew was open to question. . . .

～

GUILT RIDDEN, I confessed to William that our love was no longer secret as we sat admiring our gardens. He lifted my chin with his fingers, the smile he wore revealing that he took my confessions well enough. "It's all right. I suppose your father cannot have been much deceived, given how I dote upon you."

In truth, I thrived upon his doting, as I hoped he knew. "Papa wants to know your plans for the future. He says he hasn't asked if you'll return to Virginia for fear of influencing you."

At this, Mr. Short looked quite taken aback. "I find that painfully curious, since I've already told him my decision."

Confused, I shifted toward him on the bench. "Perhaps I misunderstood him. . . ."

William clutched my hand. "He wants me to set up a law practice in Albemarle County, Patsy, but I intend to pursue foreign service. My appointment as *chargé d'affaires* should make me a candidate to replace your father as minister to France. If not, then I'll seek an appointment to Spain or the Netherlands."

Though William had told me he was an ambitious man, I hadn't grasped just how ambitious. "Then you mean to stay in Europe?"

"For a few years," he said, warming to the subject. "What a fine diplomat's wife you'll make. There's so much of the world you've yet to see, and I dream of showing you. Everywhere on my travels, I wished for you, every treasure diminished before my eyes because it wasn't seen by yours."

Caught up in his enthusiasm, I imagined myself a diplomat's wife, learning new languages, venturing to strange new places, seeing sights few Americans would ever see. What a glamorous adventure we'd have together. "You think I'm suited for such a life?"

"Who better?" he asked with affection and confidence. "You know court etiquette. You've studied diplomacy in your father's own parlor and have learned to make yourself amiable with every sort of person, from peasants to duchesses. I'd count myself blessed to have you for my own."

My heart pounded faster to think it. Then I remembered Papa, and it fell hard, like a stone, into my belly. "But if you stay in Europe, we'd have to leave Papa."

It seems I face threats of abandonment on all sides. . . .

"Oh, President Washington will keep your father quite busy in the coming years. We'll all be back together before he even notices." I didn't like the way William's gaze slid away from mine as he spoke such cavalier words. We'd once shared the burden of my father's madness, protecting him from the world and from himself. Surely William hadn't forgotten.

"Papa relies upon us," I said, searching his eyes for understanding. "He needs us."

William leaned in to place reassuring kisses on my cheeks. "Your father is past those dark days. You've taken care of him since you were a girl. Come with me, now, my love. Let me take care of *you* until the end of our days."

How my heart swelled at his words.

How tempting he was.

How unreasonable and ungrateful I felt for my apprehension.

But I simply couldn't help myself. "How many years before we could join Papa in Virginia?"

William fell silent in a way that troubled me beyond measure. His thumb stroked the back of my hand. Finally, he swallowed and met my eyes. "I cannot make my home in Virginia, Patsy."

It took me a moment to understand his words, and even then, I was left bewildered. The breeze caught my curls, and I brushed them away. "You're a *Virginian*, William. Where else could you make your home?"

He looked at the sky for a long moment. "Somewhere else. Someplace in America where prosperity can be had without slaves. It cannot be done in Virginia."

"That can't be true," I sputtered. "Your practice at the law—"

"Would fail utterly even if I didn't mind the drudgery of it." He bolstered himself with a deep breath. "Perhaps you don't remember Virginia society because you've come of age in France. The gentry will never trust a lawyer who isn't also well established as a Virginia planter."

"Then be a planter," I argued. "Take a small farm, employ only sharecroppers. . . ."

"I'd soon be a very poor, indebted planter, who could, in no way, support the daughter of Thomas Jefferson in the manner to which she has grown accustomed."

"I can grow accustomed to something else!"

He took my face in his hands and smiled. "If anyone could, it would be you, but I'm resolved. I'll never run a slave plantation.

I'll never be a part of that evil. All Virginia is stained with it. My conscience won't allow me to make a home there, and yours shouldn't allow it either."

My confusion gave way to a slow spark of anger that took hold and began to smolder. "And neither should Papa's conscience. That's what you're saying, isn't it?"

Staring hard, he said, "I wouldn't presume to judge your father."

A stinging pressure pricked at the backs of my eyes. "You think he should free all his slaves."

"I think he *cannot* free his slaves without impoverishing himself and his daughters," William replied, his eyes filled with both sadness and understanding. "Without slaves, he'll have nothing. He'll lose it all, right down to the last book. He's shielded you from this, but when your grandfather Wayles died, your father inherited a portion of his debt, more staggering than we ever imagined. Your father has only this year learned the full extent of it, which is why he's eager to return home and deal with his creditors."

My mouth dropped open and I struggled for words. How could that be? For months now, my father had done nothing but lavish gifts upon me. New ball gowns, gold watches, and rings. That was to say nothing of the concerts and horse riding lessons!

This flurry of shopping started when I confessed my desire to join the convent. Had my father been so desperate to keep me with him that he'd driven himself into more dire financial straits? Guilt bit at me. "*Poor Papa!* How can he satisfy the creditors?"

William sighed. "He'll have to sell land or slaves."

A wave of nausea swept over me. "Surely not!"

Owning slaves was an evil, but *selling* them . . .

"Patsy." William forced me to look at him, his voice dropping an octave to meet the severity of his countenance. "When it comes to the evil of slavery, the only choice you'll ever have is in which husband you marry. I want to take you away from plantation life. The government doesn't enrich its ambassadors, but my salary will be enough. We'll scrimp and save enough to make wise investments in stocks and bonds. And that's what we'll live on."

I'd never heard of any man making his fortune this way. Every man of wealth we knew had built his fortune with land. All the Virginia gentry. All our friends in France. William had never sounded more like a wild-eyed radical. It was little wonder Papa thought he couldn't support a family!

He must've seen that I doubted him. "When we return to America, we'll settle somewhere more in keeping with my moral principles. Philadelphia or Boston or New York. If you become my wife, you may have your pick." He gave a small smile. "We'll visit your father in Virginia as often as you like. I'd never keep you from him. But I can never settle near Monticello, as he's pleaded with me to."

His voice was firm. There was no crack or waver in it to give me hope he might change his mind. And I shook my head, at a complete loss. The sun and the birdsong upon the breeze suddenly seemed to mock my predicament. *I would never leave you, or my country, but for God,* I'd said to my father. Was love for William to make a liar of me? "What you're asking!"

He drew my hands to his lips, beseeching me with his eyes. "I'm asking you to make a life with me, not to abandon your duties as a daughter."

Then why did it feel like that's exactly what he was asking me to do?

~

I PASSED THROUGH THE DAYS AND WEEKS that followed in a confused haze, my thoughts preoccupied by my struggle to balance my heart's desire with my lifelong duty. A confusion made worse by the strangest of tea parties, hosted by the Duke of Dorset. Having expected to be one of many guests, I arrived to find the salon bedecked in flowers, empty except for me and the duke. Dressed as if for a ball and not for afternoon tea, he guided me to the table.

"Are the others arriving late?" I asked as I sat. And then I realized there were only two settings.

"I understand that your father will soon take leave to America. But my nieces tell me you might be induced to stay, given the right offer."

"What can you mean?" I asked, my scalp prickling as a servant swept into the room to pour the tea.

In answer, the duke produced a velvet pouch. "I wish to propose an alliance." He dropped the contents of the little bag into his hand, and then held something out to me.

A ring. A diamond ring.

Perspiration dampened the back of my neck. "What kind of alliance is sealed with such an extravagant gift?"

"The kind that would unite your family and mine, and might reunite your people and mine."

The diamond glinted in the candlelight, but I had not the slightest urge to take it. *Mon Dieu,* did he mean to make a proposal of marriage? I could not allow it, and not only because my heart belonged to another. This was highly improper in every way. And setting aside propriety, my father was the voice of American independence. To even entertain such a proposal would be to betray my father's principles.

I had already allowed this to go too far. The duke continued speaking, and I may have replied, but what I remember most is my haste to escape. "Your Grace, I beg you to say no more." I rose clumsily from my chair. "I am beyond grateful for your many kindnesses over the years, and I love your nieces dearly, but I cannot accept more than friendship from you."

The duke's hand sagged and he gave a little incredulous laugh as if he could not quite believe he was being refused. And by an American at that. For long moments, he pressed his case upon me, and I pleaded devotion to my father by way of excuse. Finally, in a resigned voice, he said, "Then take the ring anyway and remember me by it, for it is just a bauble."

Perhaps to him a diamond ring was just a bauble, or perhaps he was salvaging his pride. I was just grateful that he did not seem angry when I finally took my leave.

Without the ring.

By the time I returned home, I was consumed with guilt, wondering if I had misled the duke and somehow disgraced my papa thereby. And I wondered if I should tell my father of the incident. If I should tell *anyone* of the incident. It would mortify Papa and perhaps the entire American embassy. Even if I could bring myself to make such a humiliating confession, it might force a discussion about William's plans for our future. And that was a conversation I wasn't ready to have.

So, that evening, I sat anxiously at the dining room table, nibbling at a spoonful of James's strawberry ice cream.

"Don't you like it?" Sally asked, readying to take my crystal dish. "It's my favorite."

"It's delicious," I said but could barely taste it for the maelstrom in my head and heart.

"Sally, you like ice cream *too* much," Polly said, with a girlish laugh, her spoon clinking as she watched Sally round the table. "You're getting as fat a belly as a pregnant lady. If you aren't careful, everyone will point and say *enceinte*."

"Polly, how unkind!" I scolded, my gaze whipping up. But something about the comment drew my father's eyes to Sally's middle. I looked, too, taking in the slight swell beneath the pink-ribboned belt of her flowing chemise gown. The moment might've passed without suspicion had Sally not spread her fingers over her belly like a fan, and turned her amber gaze to my father in what looked to be heartbreaking desperation.

My sister giggled. But Sally didn't laugh and neither did my father. Instead, they exchanged a stricken, naked look between them that resounded like a thunderclap.

And my father flushed scarlet.

A sound like honeybees buzzed in my ears as the horrific realization slowly made its way past my defenses to assault my reason. *Sally was pregnant.* And Papa wouldn't be sitting there burning with shame unless . . .

No. That couldn't be. It couldn't be *shame* I saw on his countenance. Perhaps it was anger that our lady's maid had been seduced by some villain. Or perhaps jealousy that pretty Sally had given herself to some low-bred delivery boy, or some stranger from the streets, or some visitor.

I looked across the table at my father, searching for the truth, and under my scrutiny, he blanched. The scarlet color in his face drained suddenly away, leaving him in pale, bloodless mortification.

Then I knew he wasn't jealous or angry.

He was *guilty.*

I tore my eyes away to spare us both the agony of acknowledging it. Close on the heels of my shock came a wave of anger and indignation. Here I'd been so tormented about wanting to be with William because it would mean leaving Papa alone. And, yet, Papa hadn't been alone at all!

I clenched my fists beneath the table, which did nothing to still my hammering heart. And before I could compose myself or make any sense of my feelings, Papa shot up from the table, took Sally by the arm, and led her out.

From just outside the dining room, their soft intimate whispers sounded, not meant for our ears. They were lovers having a quarrel, while my sister and I sat there, bewildered, our ice cream forgotten and melting.

"Sally is going to have a baby?" Polly asked.

"Hush." I pressed my lips together and *willed* my little sister to silence.

"But she doesn't have a husband. Will we have to send her to the convent?" We knew girls who had lost their virtue and been sent to the Panthemont in the hopes that the world would forget. Papa had always taught us to treat such girls kindly, and to blame their error upon the wicked men who preyed upon the peculiar vulnerabilities of our sex. But Sally Hemings wasn't a gentlewoman of society with a family reputation to stain.

Unless it was *our* family reputation.

Sally was . . . well, she was a lady's maid and a chambermaid. Who in France—where prostitutes openly roamed the Palais-Royal—would judge her harshly?

However, my father they would gleefully judge.

For even I judged him.

All the same anger and confusion and revulsion I felt the night I came upon them kissing roiled up inside me anew. Was it because Sally was a girl not even my own age, and he a much older man? Unions between older men and young women our age were not so unusual, as the duke's awkward proposal demonstrated. Was it because Sally had the taint of African blood? She didn't seem tainted to me. Was it that Sally was my mother's sister, and looked so much like her? Perhaps. Or was it, as William had once suggested, the evil of slavery that stained the union and corrupted it even here, where Sally was ostensibly free?

It was all these things and more. Deep, bitter resentment rushed through me at the realization that my father indulged his base inclinations while having contrived to separate me from the man I wanted.

I sprang to my feet, as if to flee from the reality of it, but where could I go? Instead, I paced, feeling like I couldn't sit still or I might explode. "Say nothing more about it, Polly."

"But—"

"Nothing at all," I told her, reaching to give her a little shake. "We shouldn't add to Sally's burdens."

Polly stared at me, her blue eyes swimming with confusion. The sister who came to us in France would never have obeyed. She'd have pestered me until her curiosity was satisfied. But in this one matter, we were fortunate Polly's illness had made her into a more pliable creature—or at least one too weary to argue.

But I didn't just want to silence Polly's questions out of consideration for Sally, nor so that I might have a better chance to overhear the conversation playing out just outside the room. I didn't want Polly to speak of it because . . . I didn't want *anyone* to speak of it.

Here I'd been worrying about my father's mortification at my proposal from the British ambassador, when Papa's actions stood to mortify us all.

Just beyond the doorway, Papa reached to tug Sally close. I watched in fascination and horror as his hunger for her became crystal clear. How had I missed it and dismissed it as infatuation all this time? I'd told myself the wages and dresses and locket were some manner of apology for his ungentlemanly behavior.

I'd been such a fool! Perhaps the greatest fool in Paris. A fool not to see the danger in the duke's attentions. A fool not to realize that William Short would never make a home with me and my family in Virginia. And a fool for believing my father was—

How many times did Papa's eyes lock with Sally's across the table without my noticing? How often had they stolen away to . . . to . . .

The memory of the kiss I'd witnessed long ago somehow transformed itself in my mind into two lust-fevered bodies upon my father's bed, tawny limbs tangled with pale, freckled ones. I steadied myself on the back of a chair and shook the vision away.

Then, outside the dining room, Sally pulled free of my father's desperate grasp, daring to turn her back on her master, and strode away, leaving Papa to bury his face in his hands.

That's when I knew. He hadn't just gotten her with child. He had *feelings* for her. Which meant as long as they were together, they'd create the opportunity for people to talk. I could already hear the mockery: *The voice of American liberty, who takes liberties with his enslaved maid.*

What could I possibly do to protect any of us from it?

Truthfully I was so angry, I wasn't sure I cared to try.

Papa went straightaway to bed that night without speaking a single solitary word to anyone. He stayed abed the next morning without soaking his feet in cold water, as was his daily habit. Upon waking, I found the unused basin of water just outside his chambers and Polly said, "He won't take it unless Sally brings it to him, but she won't."

I told myself I didn't care. I told myself to walk past his door and pretend that I didn't hear the silent echo of his suffering over the roar of my anger. But instead I knocked lightly, then turned the ornate knob and found nothing but darkness inside. The drapes were pulled closed, and not even a candle by his bedside lit the room.

Papa's voice came throaty through the blackness. "Go, Patsy. You're letting in the light."

I disobeyed, slipping into his solitary world with him and closing the door behind me. Then, filled with anger at him and shame for him, I dared to challenge Papa as I never had before. "Are you *truly* unwell?"

Silence was my answer. And it stretched on so long that he needn't have replied at all. I understood his silence as humiliation; he'd hoped to carry on with Sally without being found out. *Maybe that's why he'd wanted so desperately to send us back to Virginia,* I thought, resentfully.

"There is a terrible hammering in my head," he finally said in a voice that spoke of true pain. "I cannot begin to describe the agony."

I made my way carefully to his bedside, sidestepping a round wooden table piled high with books. Was his agony caused by the headache or by the thought of losing his lover? Despite my anger, I'd seen the emotion on his face when he learned of Sally's condition. He cared for her, maybe even loved her. If he'd been worried about the idea of her remaining in the chaos of Paris before, how much worse might his fears be now that she carried his child?

Pressing a hand to his forehead, I felt his skin warm and

dry. There was no fever, but he groaned, as if my touch made it worse.

He didn't leave his bed that day, nor could he leave it the next. Instead, he lay writhing on his mattress, put into torment by the slightest bit of light. He ate nothing, read nothing, and wanted to see no one but Sally.

And yet, Sally would not come.

I found her in the kitchen, and all but commanded her to go to him. But Sally stayed put, chopping onions the way her brother had taught us both to do, her eyes watering of it. And when I pressed her, we faced each other as if we were equals for the first time. Dropping her hand to her belly, she said, "I won't go to him until he lets me and the child free."

So it was the explicit grant of freedom she was holding out for. She hadn't dared to demand freedom for herself when James did, but for her child, she'd found the courage to defy my father. To abandon him. To torment him, even, for now there was no question that he was ill.

So ill that I heard him retch on water. It was grief that had made him unable to open his eyes. Grief for how he'd tarnished his honor. An unwillingness to face a world in which he'd be vilified as a seducer of a girl in his charge, and the father of a mixed-race child he might never know if Sally left him to pursue life as a free woman, and I felt his naked fear of what might become of them on their own.

Three days my father lay in bed, shut up, alone, in despair.

Then four. Then five.

He called for me on the sixth.

There, in the near blackness of his room, he twined my fingers with his and said, "Patsy, let me tell you where King Louis went wrong. The king of France wants his people's love so badly that he crushes them in his embrace. He won't let them pursue happiness. He has to be *forced* to every compromise. I've seen enough tyrants in my time to learn from their mistakes, so I won't thwart the rebellion of the young people in my household, even if it means I must lose the love and comfort of those dearest to me. You and William. Sally and James."

With a gasp, I said, "Papa, you can never lose our love!"

No matter what I thought about his conduct with Sally, I loved my father dearly. So dearly that just as I'd hated Maria Cosway for rejecting my father, I now felt a festering resentment for Sally, too. It wasn't the same, of course. This wasn't Sally's fault. But she knew how my father was suffering, and she didn't *need* him to grant her freedom in France. She could take it and he couldn't stop her. So why couldn't she at least offer him a kind word before she left us?

"I will lose you," my father said, with a melancholy sigh. "It's the way of things, I know. I'm going out of life, and you're all coming in."

It horrified me to hear him say that he was *going out of life*. "Let me call for a doctor."

Papa put his finger over my lips as if just the sound of my voice pained him. "I had this headache when your grandmother died. It's a penance that must be endured. It reminds me that I'm past the prime of my life, and I must give way. The earth belongs to the living, and your generation has more life left than mine. Though I'll be lost without you, I won't stand in the way of you and William, even if it means I'll lose what is most precious to me. When William asks for your hand, tell him yes with all your heart if that's your desire."

"Oh, Papa, you'll never lose me," I said, my heart filling with the bittersweet pain of happiness and gratitude, but also sorrow. Because though my father would never lose my love, if I married William, we'd never live together again.

My father must've known it, which made it all the harder for him to let me go. "But Patsy, I would ask this kindness of you. Come back with me to Virginia to settle Polly and say your farewells before returning to France for the wedding."

I nodded, bringing his weak hand to my lips and kissing it, over and over.

But at my kisses Papa turned his face back to the pillow, as if he felt himself unworthy of them. "Would you—would you send Sally to me?"

I knew what it cost him to ask that of me. To ask me to fetch his mistress. The mother of his child. The woman he had plainly fallen in love with.

His *head*. That is what he said ailed him. But it was his *heart*. How many times had I seen this before? The passionate heart he always forced to submit to his surpassing intellect. His heart, like all of France, was in rebellion against its ruler.

And that's why he asked again so sheepishly for her. "Tell her to come to me. Unlike King Louis, I'll treat fairly with her."

He meant to give her up, too, then. Though he felt abandoned and unloved, he meant to give us all the freedom we desired.

And I worried it would destroy him.

Chapter Fifteen

Paris, 17 July 1789
From Thomas Jefferson to Thomas Paine

A more dangerous scene of war I never saw in America than what Paris has presented for five days past.

THE BASTILLE HAD FALLEN and Paris was aflame. Men had been beheaded, their corpses dragged before the mob, and tens of thousands of citizens now marched about with pistols, swords, pikes, pruning hooks, and scythes. The only hope of peace rested upon the shoulders of Lafayette, who had assumed command of the National Guard.

And our tree was gone. The one William had carved. It'd been smashed by cannon fire or hacked to pieces by the hordes of angry citizens in the streets, I knew not which. There I stood at the balcony window, staring down at its fractured stump, mesmerized by the violent destruction of something so dear to me—and the city in which it was born.

"Come away from the windows, Patsy," William urged, his voice strained with worry.

I choked back a sob. "It's all torn apart. Everything is going wrong!"

William dared to fold me into his arms, saying again, "Come away from the window. There is no telling with what violence the king's processional will be met."

I couldn't be made to budge. If there was violence, I would see it. I'd bear witness to it as I'd been witness to everything else. Like all of Paris, I was caught up in the spell of waiting. Waiting for something to happen, not knowing if it would bring liberation or despair.

William's eyes fell upon the ruin of our tree and he held me tighter. "We'll carve another tree."

Turning, I blurted, "I have to go back to Virginia."

"I know you're frightened—"

"I'm not frightened," I said, which wasn't entirely true, but I feared my father's debilitated emotional state even more than the cannon fire we'd heard outside. I couldn't tell William about Sally's pregnancy. Unlike me, he was unlikely to be surprised to learn she'd gotten with child. And Sally's condition would soon be obvious to everyone, so why couldn't I tell him?

It was the shame.

William had once asked if we should object more to a man's affection for his slave than to the fact that he holds her in bondage. But it felt *altogether* objectionable, even though I somehow felt as if my father needed my protection more than ever.

Which is why I bristled to hear William say, "You cannot go back to Virginia with your father, Patsy."

"Papa has asked it of me—it's all he's asked of me."

"He'll never bring you back to France."

I stared at William, half-forgetting to breathe. "Surely, you aren't saying he won't keep his word."

"He'll ask me to return to Virginia to fetch you," William said. "I know he says that he'll finish out his term as minister in Paris, but your father will be offered a position to serve in America as a member of President Washington's cabinet."

This was nothing short of stunning news. "Who told you such a thing?"

"It was in a letter I read from Mr. Madison."

I fumbled for a reply, fumbled to understand what this meant for our future. Or if there was a future for any of us in a city on fire. "Even if Papa is offered such a position, he won't accept it.

He wants to retire from public life. You've heard him say it many times."

"And I wagered a beaver hat that Mr. Jefferson will refuse the appointment. But it's a bet I'm going to lose. I haven't the slightest doubt that your father will accept a cabinet position in the new government no matter what he says to the contrary."

I gasped. "That's twice you've questioned my father's honor." The words came uneasily off my tongue, even though Papa's liaison with Sally had called his honor into question all on its own. And I knew it. "You think he's lying when he says he wants to finish his work here and return to Monticello forevermore?"

"If he's lying, it's only to himself," Mr. Short replied evenly. "Your father will let his friends persuade him, because his mind's already made up. He's the only one who doesn't know it."

Heat came to my cheeks. "I cannot agree."

"Patsy, all the world thinks of your father as a man of cool temper. Some assume that because he dabbles in *everything*, he holds true passion for *nothing*. We know better. The abiding passion of his life is a government that derives its authority from the people. These past few months here, in Paris, working to enlist France in the spirit of revolution—have you ever seen him more himself?"

"No," I whispered, for it was true, even if government was not the *only* thing for which he held a passion. Not since my mother's death had my father been so alive. What part did Sally play in that? And what would happen to him when he accepted that she and the child were both lost to him?

William continued, battering at my weak defenses. "We treat your father like a living monument because he was born to do important work. You're his daughter and he says I'm his adoptive son. But the American Experiment is the child he birthed and will never abandon. So he can wax prosaic about the joys of private domesticity on his mountaintop all day, but in the end, he'll join the president's cabinet. And he won't return to Paris, with or without you."

"You're just impatient for us to be together," I said, desperate to deny it all. Almost as desperate as the people on the streets below, anxious for the answer of their king. "We've waited this long and you don't want to wait any longer. But this is all my father asks of me. To return with him to Virginia and settle Polly there before marrying you."

"And all I'm asking of you is not to go."

I'd loved William all my life, but never had I been angrier with him. As shouts from the crowd rose up to our window, I said, "That's not all you're asking of me. You want me to give up my father, my sister, and my country. You're asking all these things of *me*, but all I'm asking of *you* is to wait for me to return."

It seemed to me to be a perfectly reasonable argument, one that might have persuaded a man in love. Even a man as stubborn as William Short. But his chin jutted out willfully. "I'm thirty years old, Patsy, and what do I have to show for it? No career, no wife, no fortune. I have done everything your father has asked of me save return to Virginia, and still he would keep us apart. Still I am lectured to, by your father, as if I were a boy. And maybe he thinks it right because when he was my age, your father was building Monticello. Already had a wife and child. Had already written *A Summary View of the Rights of British America*—"

"You can't compare yourself to my father!"

His eyes narrowed with . . . something that looked like disappointment, and he shook his head. "All my friends have said you're still too young—"

"What friends say that?" I snapped, anger boiling now.

"That's not important. What's important is that you can be a wife and mother or you can be a devoted daughter all your life. You can't be both. Not when Thomas Jefferson is your father. You have to choose, Patsy."

His words echoed the very debates that I'd been having with myself for weeks. And that horrified me. Because he was saying that I couldn't have them both. "You're asking me to choose you over everything else and blaming my father for it." My voice cracked. "My papa isn't asking me to choose, but *you* are."

William didn't even lower his eyes at my rebuke. "You're right. I am. If you go to Virginia, two months will become six. Six will become a year. We'll never be together. So if you leave France, know that I won't be waiting."

Just then the trumpets blared to announce the king's procession, and we fell silent, watching the street below. Mesmerized by the sight of the surging crowd. Not knowing if it would come to open war, then and there. The people wanted their freedom; they strained for it. Were willing to fight for it in bloody struggle.

But, like a father of the nation, the king had come to Paris to restore order. And between these two forces, between the carriage of the king and his people, was caught the Marquis de Lafayette.

In proud uniform, a cockade of red, white, and blue just like the one I wore pinned to my own gown, he rode at the head of the processional. It required courage and honor in its rawest form to ride as he did, defending the very king whose authority he sought to strip away against an armed mob with whom his heart belonged. And my eyes filled with tears at the thought that Lafayette might falter and be torn to pieces by the crowd.

I didn't brush those tears away as Lafayette's horse passed under our window. And though he rode in a crowd of thousands, he looked up at me. I imagined that our eyes met—that I saw in Lafayette's white-faced grimness an acceptance of his fate so long as he never betrayed his cause.

Then he bowed to me, and I knew I had not imagined it.

He bowed to me, and his honor and courage became my own.

The spark of his *devotion* lit a fire inside me that burned away my doubts.

My hand fell away from William's grasp, and my voice no longer wavered. "I'm going to Virginia with my father, and if you love me, you'll wait for me a little longer."

OUR TRUNKS WERE PACKED and I took a last look at the inventory list of books, busts, pictures, and clocks to be shipped ahead of us. The Hotel de Langeac was strangely bare and quiet. And I kept hoping—hoping desperately—for William. No matter how angry he was at my leaving, surely he'd see us off!

I lingered near the door, jumping up at the sound of every passing carriage in the street. And when a carriage finally pulled inside our gates, I ran out to meet it. It was not William inside that carriage but Marie, her expression bleak. "Has Mr. Short changed his mind?" she asked, coming into the house with a hat box. "Has he agreed to wait for you?"

When I shook my head, she lowered the hat box and her eyes filled with tears as she rained curses down upon William's head. Finally, she asked, "With all the men who pursued you, is there no other offer that might keep you in France?"

No, there was no one for me but William. That morning, a messenger wearing the livery of the Duke of Dorset had presented to me a parting gift—another ring, this one a simple silver band, with a note begging me to accept it as "a feeble proof of my fond remembrance." I had nearly burst into tears on the spot because the duke thought to send me a token of farewell, whereas I had nothing but angry silence from William. But if I told Marie about *that*, then I surely *would* burst into tears, so I only shook my head.

"Then you will not come back." She choked on a sob, utterly undone. "I have not wanted to believe it, but now I cannot bear to part with you, and I cannot stop crying."

"Oh, Marie!" We embraced and held one another tightly, our hearts pounding against one another as we fought off tears.

Finally, Marie murmured, "I shall throw myself into a river without you."

I drew back abruptly. "You must never say anything that, Marie. Never."

She looked abashed, brushing away her tears with her thumbs. "Of course. I am the one who first taught you to pretend at happiness in Paris. Now we must both pretend." She straightened, sniffling into a kerchief. "I've had a hat made for you, because yours are all out of style. They don't indent hats in the front anymore and yours with the rosette is good for nothing. You must wear this one and think of me. And we must promise to write letters."

We promised. We exchanged tokens of remembrance. Then we parted, abruptly, as Marie fled from me in tears. I had not offered her any hope that I would return to France, as I now feared there was none. I think it was the excruciating fear that William might truly let this be the end of it between us that left me so confused to see Sally in the foyer with her own satchel of belongings.

All she owns in the world, I thought. I was moved by her plight, not only because I was fond of her, or even only because she was, in the way of the Hemingses, near kin to me. But also because the truth of our situation was leaking around all the barricades I'd put up against it.

Inside her, she carried my little brother or sister. One I could never acknowledge and might never see born. At least the baby would be born in France—born free. That heartened me, and seeing glimpses of pain and anxiety in her amber eyes, my heart went out to her—the warmth of sympathy and concern a welcome balm from the cold ache of William's absence.

"You won't become destitute," I promised with a small smile, twisting the ring Papa bought me from my finger and pressing it into her hand. "You keep this for a day you need it, but you won't. I'll send a letter to Marie and Madam de Tessé and the Duchess Rosalie to find a place for you as a lady's maid. Until then, why not stay on here at the Hotel de Langeac? Mr. Short won't put you out in the street—"

"James and I are going home with you to Virginia," Sally said, stunning me into silence. "Your papa has made us an offer."

My throat tightened. What offer could he have made them? Though they were his slaves, the Hemingses had the laws of

France on their side, not to mention the laws of God. And I found it hard to imagine my dignified father bargaining with any slave, much less his own.

But then Sally convinced me. "We've been negotiating a treaty."

A treaty. That *did* sound like my father, the minister to France. Recalling the duke's wish to make an alliance with me, I could easily imagine Papa condescending to charm his enslaved lover, giving her the courtesies due an ambassador from a foreign land. "Oh?" I managed, weakly.

She lifted her chin, a hint of pride there. "Your father promises that if James goes back and teaches someone else all he's learned in the kitchens of Paris, he'll go free. And if I go back, your father will keep me and care for me well, till his death. He'll free my babies, too, when they turn twenty-one, upon his solemn oath."

Babies? As if there would be more. As if they meant to carry on indefinitely?

I nearly slapped her. My anger was so volcanic that it burned coherent thought from my mind. I wasn't even sure why I was so angry, only that I was. "You want to be a slave all your life, Sally?" Past my strangled fury I choked out, "You want to be my father's . . . *whore*?"

She brushed the wetness of her eyes away, as if it pained her for me to see her cry. "How am I to leave my family in Virginia, Miss Patsy? Never see my momma again? Knowing your father wants me, how could I refuse? He's good to me, and I hate nothing like disappointing him. It *hurts* to disappoint him."

Who knew the truth of that statement better than I did? And yet I stood there, shaking with a fury at her choice that I couldn't comprehend, biting the insides of my cheeks to keep from howling with it. It was the wrong choice. Could she not see it? "You're giving up your freedom!"

"I know it." Her chest heaved with emotion beneath her pretty blue gown. "But women have to give hard thought to the men we'll wind up with. Make a mistake and get a drunk, a spendthrift, a cruel man. A man who won't keep his word. But your papa gives his word and nobody ever doubts it. You think I'm likely to find some better Frenchman? Or some better man at all? Or any man willing to have a woman carrying another man's baby?"

Sally's shoulders fell, and for just a moment, sympathy pierced my anger. She'd be with child, in a city full of upheaval, with no one to rely upon but her brother.

But then she said, "In marriage, man and woman become one, and that *one* is the husband."

Did she think of herself as my father's *wife*? The very thought of it sent fire through my blood anew and made sense of my rage. It sounded as if she believed that what passed between her and my father was a lifelong sacrament, when it was nothing but sin!

And while I stood there, wondering how to tell her that she'd never replace my mother, she straightened her shoulders and said, "He loves me, Miss Patsy."

I did slap her then.

Sally shrieked and clutched her cheek. But I wasn't moved to pity.

I'd given up William to save my father from dying of a broken heart, thinking that Sally was going to leave him and take his child with her.

Was my whole life in ruin because of this girl?

My rage grew even hotter toward my father. For his words about William's fitness and his melancholy about Sally had brought me to the conclusion that I must give up what I wanted for myself and *do my duty,* and yet all the while Papa was making deals to ensure he'd make no sacrifice at all. Not now. And, very likely, not in the future, not as long as Sally chose to remain at his side. In my mind's eye, I saw him on his knees before me, reaffirming his deathbed promise never to take another wife and pleading that his happiness depended on me—all to keep me from taking my vows.

And now I'd given up *everything* I'd ever dared to want for myself. The convent. My dearest friends. William.

Everything.

The room spun around me, and pressure built inside me that demanded release. I felt less in control of myself than ever before or at any time after. And so I did something that to this day I regret as much as slapping her. I hissed in her tear-streaked face what I knew to be a lie. "Papa doesn't love you. And he never will."

~

I'VE MADE A MISTAKE, I thought, imagining I could see England across the fog-covered waters of the channel.

There was still time to turn back. I could run back to William Short's embrace and beg a thousand pardons for having left him. My father wouldn't stop me. Not when he knew his honor was so tarnished in my eyes.

Indeed, it seemed as if Nature herself *commanded* me to turn back, because the bumpy earth had split the axle of our phaeton and broke the wheels of our carriage to slow us down. Then the most tempestuous weather we'd ever seen trapped us with a storm of wind and squall, the fury of which was an echo of all the turmoil inside me.

But William hadn't tried to stop me from going. He'd never even said good-bye. And so this was an ending, I told myself. Turning away from the view, I knew I wouldn't—*couldn't*—look back. But neither could I go forward, for this storm blew for nine days until the only way Papa could calm my little sister was to promise her a puppy.

Papa said, "Come search out shepherd dogs with me, Patsy."

Why don't you take your lover? I let the silent question show in my sullen eyes. Then, furiously, I grabbed my coat with an insolent stare. Numb with heartbreak, I scarcely felt the chill of the rain or the blow of the wind when we went clambering the cliffs. Though Papa tried to engage me in conversation, I said next to nothing as we walked together for hours, nearly ten miles in all.

It was a fruitless, awkward search. I had too much dignity to pretend there was nothing wrong between us. My father knew what weighed upon my heart and I knew what weighed upon his. And at long last, I decided that if we were going to quarrel, why not do it here in the howling wind?

When we neared the docks, I opened my mouth to reprimand him for his immoral conduct with Sally and for putting a wedge between William and me. But just as I inhaled to speak the words, we heard a crack sharper than thunder.

Hearts hammering, we turned to see a man collapse upon the beach. My father rushed closer, demanding I stay back, but fear carried my feet forward. It was the most ghastly sight I've ever witnessed . . . the body of a man who had, just that moment, shot himself. His pistol had dropped at his feet and he'd fallen backward. The blast completely separated his whole face from the forehead to the chin, pounding it to a bloody pulp. And the center of his head was entirely laid bare . . . red blood, white bone, and blue-gray brain.

Who this dead, mangled man was, or what had caused his anguish, was something I was destined never to know. For my father took me at once in his arms and turned me away from the sight, cradling me against his chest while the rain and hot tears mingled on my cheeks. As I sobbed, my father shielded me from the horror and pulled me from it. When we'd stumbled some distance away, he clutched me tightly. "Oh, Patsy. Would that you had never seen it. Forgive me."

He murmured the sentiment over and over, the tempest hiding the words from everyone except me until I was sure he wasn't speaking only of the dead man. Because despite the dreadful shock of the suicide we'd witnessed, and the reminder of my father's own brush with pistols so long ago, I knew Papa's grief came from someplace much deeper.

His pain made the lingering doubts about the choice I'd made fly away. I couldn't have abandoned my father. Neither for William Short nor for God could I have ever chosen a life away from Papa. The country he'd founded—the land he loved—needed him, and he needed me.

If William had ever truly loved me, this was something he should've known and understood.

~

TWO DAYS BEFORE CHRISTMAS, as we rolled up to the foot of our mountain with carts filled with French treasures, Papa's black field hands and lighter-colored house slaves collected in crowds to greet us. Dressed in their best church clothes, they almost drew the carriage up the mountain by hand. When the door of the carriage was opened, they received their master in their arms and bore him to the house crowding round and kissing his hands—some crying, others laughing.

It seemed impossible to satisfy their anxiety to touch and kiss the very earth that bore him. They lifted him up into the biting air against his wishes, carrying him to the house while James helped me and Polly and Sally down from the carriage. And in spite of being so heavy with child, once Sally got down, she ran into the arms of her mother.

What did Sally's mother think to see her children return from France, when they might've been free? The Hemingses were all too careful to let such emotions play freely on their faces, but I wondered if Sally's mother was secretly furious or proud that her daughter was now the master's mistress.

"Oh, Miss Patsy," Mammy Ursula exclaimed tearfully as she took in my elegant French dress and my pristine traveling gloves. "Look at the lady you've become. We've missed you so very much!"

"I've missed you, too," I said, a sudden tightness in my throat. Standing here again seemed almost a dream, and my heart swelled with affection and ached with guilt for having been gone so long. The lives of Papa's people had been uncertain, at the mercy of those he put over them. They must've wondered if we'd forgotten them. If they'd be ripped away from each other and sold off like farm animals. And because of my father's financial difficulties, we couldn't even promise it wouldn't happen.

"Now, come in and we'll get you settled," Mammy insisted, leading me up the stairs into the house. That's when I realized that the neoclassical double-porticoed plantation manor of my childhood was in shambles. Peeling paint, warped wood, crumbling stairs. Looming over a row of slave cabins in much better repair, the once-lovely mansion looked like it might fall off its pillars.

"*Mon Dieu!*" whispered Polly, who had no memory of the house as it was. I could guess at her thoughts. *This* was Papa's idyllic mountaintop refuge he boasted of so often?

After an absence of six years, perhaps the dilapidated condition of the house was to be expected, but it very much gave the impression that we'd come down in the world. And inside was worse. We stepped past tarps that covered holes stripped down to the brick for renovations barely started and never finished. We'd have no indoor plumbing, as we'd enjoyed at the Hotel de Langeac. The furniture was moth-eaten.

Not much had been made in the way of provisions, either. We lacked for bedding, candles, coffee, and firewood. It was almost Christmas and there was already a bite in the air; how were we to keep warm? Thankfully, I was mostly numb to the cold. A little bit numb to everything, really, since the day I left William Short.

Or, to be more precise, since the day he told me he would not wait for me . . .

Because our journey had been slowed with visits to friends and family along the way, I'd let myself believe that I'd return to Monticello to find a letter from William—a tearful letter reassuring me that all was not ended. Maybe even one that pleaded with me to return to him on the fastest ship I could find.

But there were no letters from William Short waiting at Monticello. Not for me. Not even for my father. William couldn't spare a scrap of paper or a blot of ink for either of us. And all hopes were dashed that the breach between us might ever be mended. I wasn't as practiced at reading William's silences as my father's, but the finality of it came crashing down around me, smashing my heart to pieces.

He wasn't going to forgive me.

He wasn't going to wait for me.

He was done with me forever.

I'd made that choice—an irrevocable choice. How would I ever make peace with it?

Chapter Sixteen

Monticello, 2 April 1790
From Thomas Jefferson to Madam De Corny

My daughter, on her arrival in Virginia, received the ad-
dresses of a young Mr. Randolph, the son of a bosom friend
of mine. Though his talents, dispositions, connections and
fortune would've made him my own first choice, according
to the usage of my country, I scrupulously suppressed my
wishes, so that my daughter might indulge her own senti-
ments freely.

THAT IS NOT, OF COURSE, THE WAY I REMEMBER IT.

"I've invited Tom Randolph to join us at Christmas,"
Papa announced as we took tea in our dilapidated parlor.
One glance provided proof that our house was in no condition
to receive visitors, but I protested because I wanted to be alone
with my secret agonies. More importantly, I couldn't bear visitors
seeing Sally afforded deference by all the slaves at Monticello.

Of course, I said none of this to Papa, who continued, "I intend
to take your cousin Tom under my wing. He excelled in his studies at Edinburgh. With guidance he could be one of the great
men of the next generation. Besides, Patsy, I should think you'd
welcome his company. He's no blockhead, and as the heir pre-
sumptive to Tuckahoe, Tom's the most eligible bachelor amongst
the Virginia gentry."

I couldn't find a reply. Why should I care about the eligibility of the gangly and exceedingly maddening boy who taunted me in my youth? But I knew exactly why Papa thought I should care. After the drama in Paris, William Short had made no proposal of marriage. Whereas I was *heartbroken* at William's silence, my father was *furious* at William's apparent break with us and failure to update him on the revolution, considering that he'd entrusted to his young protégé our American mission in France.

Papa felt betrayed, I think. Perhaps in Tom Randolph, he was seeking a new adoptive son. . . .

"I've invited the Carr brothers, too," Papa said, to put my mind at ease. "Trust me, Patsy, the season will be much merrier in the company of your cousins."

I couldn't begin to see how. But for all of Papa's insistence that he suppressed his feelings, when Tom came riding up our drive on Christmas morn, Papa quite nearly pushed me out the door to greet him.

And I'll say this for Tom. Even from the distance of all these years, staring at the smudged and yellowed letter in my hand, I can still remember the way my breath caught at the sight of him on that horse.

Tom Randolph rode like a demon, his broad shoulders and strong arms exerting expert control over the animal beneath him. He was all athletic grace when he swung down from his saddle in a swirl of black cloak and his boots landed with a splash in the mud. He stood a good deal taller than even my father, so he had to bend his head to acknowledge me. His dark, savage eyes took in my gown and he drawled, "Well, I do declare, Miss Jefferson. You've turned into a Frenchwoman."

Given his unsmiling expression, I couldn't tell if he meant it as a compliment or an insult, and truthfully, I didn't care. With jet-black hair and skin of an olive hue, he'd grown to be, without a doubt, the most handsome man I'd met on any continent. He was beautiful to behold in the way of artwork and more striking in plain riding clothes than a nobleman in satin and lace. I could acknowledge that about him as objective fact, because while his exotic allure roused something in my blood, it stirred nothing in a heart that still longed for William Short.

Moreover, I was too weary to entertain a friendship with any American who didn't embrace the French Revolution. Most of what our countrymen knew about France was defamatory and inflammatory. On several occasions already, Papa had been forced to defend the actions of patriots—as if we ought to blame the French peasants for not cheerfully starving in the streets.

Personally, I couldn't find it in my heart to pity the French royals, who were now rumored to be captives of the revolutionaries. I still recalled our harried flight in the dead of night from British soldiers sent by a king to capture my father. And to my mind, a king who brought troops against his own people was no worthy king at all, if ever there could be such a thing.

So I merely held my head higher so Tom Randolph might get a better look at my red, white, and blue cockade. And I spoke not another word to him during our inelegant supper of chicken and root vegetables.

But he was not to be put off. "Your cockade, Miss Jefferson. Did you wear it in honor of the French revolutionaries who stormed the Bastille?"

As he'd addressed me directly, I replied. "Indeed. The king himself could've seen it if he'd looked up at my window upon entering Paris." The king hadn't looked up, but Lafayette had. And in that moment my life changed, and the French cause became the American cause in my heart.

But that wasn't what interested Tom. "I'm told your French is very elegant. You must be the most well-educated girl in Virginia. You've returned to us a very cultured and accomplished young woman."

It was a simple and unaffected compliment. One that I should've accepted with gracious thanks. But I sensed a flirtation and was still too raw to bear romantic attention with poise. To accept even harmless pleasantries made me feel something akin to nausea. So I answered with a dismissive flick of my fan, as the ladies did in France, to show unavailability and disinterest.

Of course, I should've known better than to try to put off a Randolph with a show of snobbery.

If anything, it made Tom like me better. When he'd known me as a girl, I'd had the stink of a country bumpkin—a lesser relation. Now I was as close to a lady from the Continent as could be found in Virginia. And I suppose Randolph pride demanded that my affections be won over.

"Miss Jefferson," Tom said, rising from the table with great informality. "Would you be so kind as to show me the grounds?"

"There's nothing to show. Everything's covered in snow."

This earned me a frown from my father. But Tom Randolph fastened his black eyes on me with special intensity. "All the better. There's a bleakness to snow that calls to me. A stark white *challenge*."

I had no idea what he could mean, and I meant to refuse him, but my father arched a brow in a way that presaged his displeasure. So I fetched my coat. And I let Tom lead me off into the winter forest, his hands clasped behind his back, as if to keep them from mischief.

As we walked he towered over me, which was remarkable, since I was of a height with most men. "The forest has lost its color," I said, feeling strangely small and delicate in his presence.

"I like the trees this way. Stripped bare." Before I could suspect him of innuendo, his voice lowered, gravely. "They're so exposed now that we can see their great melancholy."

I thought I was the only one who ever considered that trees might suffer melancholy, and the way their branches drooped under the weight of the ice suddenly made my own limbs heavier in sympathy. "But springtime will come, and they'll blossom again."

Tom stopped, taking the unpardonable liberty of grasping my chin. "Yes, but then, they'll hide their true beauty behind a mask of showy flowers and leaves. That's why I prefer them as they are now. You remind me of these trees, Miss Jefferson. You're a veritable Venus with the eyes of a sage."

My gaze narrowed. There was something wrong with Tom Randolph. Something reckless and inappropriate and unguarded. I tried to shield myself from it, asking sarcastically, "What kind of eyes do sages have?"

"Sad ones," Tom replied. "You're very sad."

As a rule, I wasn't sad. I'd been raised to mantle myself always in cheer, and everyone but William Short said I had my father's agreeable disposition. Yet, in that moment, at the vulnerable age of seventeen, stripped bare of all my defenses, I fought back sudden tears. And this man—this stranger, in truth—saw the darkness inside me and found it alluring.

Taking a kerchief from his coat, he said, "You can cry, Patsy."

But I couldn't give him the satisfaction. I couldn't open that well inside me, or I'd never get it closed again.

THE NEXT MORNING, Papa allowed Sally to accompany him into town to pick up some candle snuffers and other supplies at the store where her sister Mary had taken up with the storekeeper, Mr. Bell. Sally and Mary had *both* become mistresses to white men. I wondered if that was to be the natural fate of pretty mulatto girls in Virginia.

Watching Papa help Sally alight the carriage, I regretted having lashed out at her. She'd been wary of me since I struck her, and I wanted to beg her forgiveness but couldn't find the words to do so. Especially not when I felt locked in some manner of battle with her for my father's affections.

Sally was nearing her time now. Her baby would come in a month or so. If she worried that she'd made a mistake, she'd never say. She'd made her choice and I'd made mine, and now we *both* had to reconcile ourselves to it. So I stood at the front window watching Papa and Sally ride off, lost in my thoughts.

Tom came upon me so stealthily that he gave me a start. "I've a gift for you." He presented a book of sheet music and a few lines of poetry scribbled on pretty bark paper. "The music is from my sisters, but the poem is from me."

I cringed because though I'd brought back from Paris some fripperies for his sisters Nancy and Judith, I'd quite forgotten him. "I'm afraid I've no gift for you in return and know little of poetry."

"It's about my late mother," he said, and my heart filled with sorrow to know that the lady who had once taken me into her herb garden to teach me about liberty tea had perished. "Given the loss of your own mother, I thought it might speak to you."

It did, I confess. I'd thought myself quite the most miserable person in the world, but Tom's verse of grief for his mother reminded me that there were worse pains in this world than romantic heartbreak.

Before I could tell him so, Polly raced in, the puppies we'd finally found after that grisly day on the cliffs of England nipping at her heels. "Come on, Patsy," she cried. "You and Tom, come skate with us on the big pond!" Near the end of the trail, she and the Carr brothers ran about, making a little war game with snowballs.

They wanted me to enjoy myself, but Tom didn't seem to mind that I couldn't smile. When I hit a patch of ice that sent me down hard, knocking the wind from my lungs, he lay down beside me, staring up at the clouds.

I remembered William when we fell together in the snow. The way his little finger had clasped mine, and the way I'd felt, so innocently, as if our hearts had touched. And then, that night, I'd seen Papa and Sally. . . .

That was, I think, the very last moment I was an innocent. Now, when my belief in the sweetness and goodness of romantic love was so tarnished, I feared Tom Randolph would whisper sweet things in my ear just as likely to melt away to nothing.

But there was no playfulness or guile in Tom. In truth, he

was as different from William as could be. Instead of whispering sweet words, he pressed his whole body against me in such a reckless manner that I could feel his desire.

Desire. Could a man as handsome as Tom Randolph possibly want me?

There was no mistaking the predatory gleam in his eye. His excitement, his fears, his happiness and pains were always very close to his skin. And now they were close to mine.

Feeling the creep of his fingers into my cloak, I asked, "What are you doing?"

"I want to kiss you," he replied hoarsely. "I want very much to kiss you and beg your leave to do so."

My heartbeat kicked up in offense. "*Tom,* we scarcely know one another."

"To the contrary, we've known each other since we were children. But we're not children anymore. I'm twenty-one and you're seventeen and there's nothing to stop us from doing as nature demands."

As nature demands . . .

I told myself that Tom's sudden interest in me had to do with his admiration for my father. I told myself that by my indifference to him, I'd inadvertently set myself up as the fox to his hound. But I think the truth was that his blood ran hot at the sight of me sad and helpless and mired in the snow. And another truth was that his lustful gaze promised me obliteration. Obliteration of thought, of pain, of doubt.

So when he bent to kiss me, I didn't turn away.

~

"SAY YOU'LL MARRY ME, PATSY." The demand came between panting breaths in the dark of the little schoolhouse at Tuckahoe where Tom and I had stolen away to exchange fevered kisses that made me forget everything.

Only a week had passed since that first, reluctant kiss, and my reluctance hadn't entirely faded. But his kisses appealed to me for a new reason, a darker reason, a *carnal* reason. They made my body burn. It mattered not that I didn't desire the reaction. With his mouth on my skin and his hands skimming over my bodice, I almost felt as if I were possessed.

Tom Randolph kissed with the same demonic ferocity that he rode—his mouth urgent on mine, his grasp rough, his taste like sweet destruction, razing every other thought in my mind, making me forget I had a mind at all.

That's what I wanted more than anything else, so I tried to hush him with another kiss, hoping it would be as annihilating as the last. But he took hold of my coat in his fists as if he might tear it open, and made me look at him in the dim light of the lantern. "I want more than kisses, Patsy. I want you. And I cannot be content until I have you. So say that you'll marry me."

The reality of it all came rushing to me then. The fact that I'd quite scandalously lost my head in the arms of a veritable stranger, in a schoolhouse built by my own grandfather. In the distance, I could hear the music of the wedding party in the main house beyond.

I'd accompanied Tom to see his sister Judith of the Tuckahoe Randolphs sweep down the elegant carved walnut staircase of her father's home and pledge her life to Richard Randolph of Bizarre plantation. The groom and his brothers were all swaggering southern boys who loved pranks and politics and tobacco. They each asked me to dance, which displeased Tom enormously. That I wasn't tripping over myself for his attention, like the other country girls, seemed to fuel in him something akin to fury. Indeed, between bites of a feast that included oysters, lobsters, tarts, and apple pies, I felt the heat of Tom's gaze, urging me to go off with him away from the oppressive house into some secluded place.

But I didn't go until Richard Randolph used the occasion of his wedding to decry the sins of his ancestors, announcing that bringing slaves into the country was a "violation of the inherent, unalienable, and imprescriptible rights of man."

In those words, I heard the echo of William Short.

That's when I stole off with Tom. And so it was that on the very last day of the most eventful year of my life, I spent its waning hours locked in a lustful embrace with a man who terrified me more than a little.

Fortunately, I was no longer naive. I wasn't about to be fooled by reckless words about marriage. Not for a second time. "Tom Randolph, do you think for one moment I'd surrender my virtue for a betrothal?"

Hands still fisted in my coat, he stiffened, as if my words were a mortal affront to his honor. His next words puffed angrily in the cold winter air. "I'm a gentleman of Virginia. I'm not whispering words in the dark to be forgotten in daylight. I'm asking for your hand, Miss Jefferson. You could at least do me the honor of considering my proposal."

I couldn't credit that he meant it. We hadn't discussed books or politics or music. And we hadn't exchanged a single word about love. "But—but this is very sudden. You think we're well suited?"

He nodded, resolutely. "We're of an age. There's a long-standing bond between your family and mine. And the fortune that'll be mine . . . it's not inconsiderable. Your father agrees; he's told me we'd have his blessing to wed."

I cannot overstate the impact of learning that my father had already discussed this match with Tom. Did Papa want me gone, now that Sally was to give him a new child? How it pained me to think that she might replace me as his most constant companion, the one most dear to him. . . .

And as this agony of the spirit ripped through me, Tom Randolph knelt, holding his hand over his heart, as if it might burst out of his chest if his desires weren't satisfied. "I must have you for my wife, Miss Jefferson. I *must* have you. So don't keep me in the misery of suspense, but give me an answer soon."

As I stared down into his brutally beautiful face, his proposal still echoing in the cold air, an unwelcome and unbidden thought came to mind. William Short never went down on his knee for me. He *never* made a formal proposal. Not like this.

Confusion swamped my racing heart and spinning head. Papa approved. Our families would approve. Society would approve. But the last time I'd considered such a thing, I'd ended up with a broken heart. So I wasn't sure how to make the decision.

Indeed, given how little time had passed since we'd returned to Virginia, I could scarcely believe I was being confronted with making it at all.

Chapter Seventeen

S ALLY HEMINGS GAVE BIRTH TO A BOY.

A boy named after my father. A boy who was both my cousin and my brother—and neither. Here on my father's secluded mountain, where Papa's wishes reigned supreme, no one would ever acknowledge Sally's boy as my father's son unless he did. But the Hemingses were as tightly knit a family as ever lived. They all knew, which meant all the slaves knew. And probably some of our nearest neighbors, too.

But it wasn't our only scandal.

Papa's debts were such that he had to sell our mother's favorite plantation—Elk Hill. He'd been forced to sell land. *Land*, which meant everything to a Virginia planter. Everything to him. And I understood that in his perilous financial situation, the only asset I had to contribute was myself.

I'd have to marry, and I'd have to marry well.

Given that my heart was already shattered to pieces, love need be of no consideration in my decision to marry. Sally's words from that day in the foyer at the Hotel de Langeac played back to me. *Women have to give hard thought to the men we'll wind up with. . . .* Her words held a relevance now that I couldn't have known then, and it made me all the more regretful for the way I'd treated her.

So, yes, let my choice of husband be a wealthy man, but also a kind one. A country neighbor and friend. Someone with whom my family shared a history.

If I was to marry, why *not* Tom Randolph?

I could never hope for a man to see me the way William had, but Tom *wanted* me. And that would have to be enough.

I saw no reason to delay.

William and I had parted in September. It was now January of a new year, and he'd still not written to my father or me. William had waited two years before declaring that he'd wait no more. I doubted the young Mr. Randolph would wait that long. And if we didn't marry soon, my father wouldn't be there for the wedding, because William's predictions had proved to be true— President Washington had, indeed, named my father secretary of state. And Papa's friends, like Mr. Madison, convinced him that it was an honor he couldn't refuse.

None of us would return to France. Instead, my father would ride off to the new capital to serve in the president's cabinet before springtime and would send me and Polly to live at Eppington, where we'd learn housewifery from Aunt Elizabeth.

Or . . . I could marry now and be my own mistress. So, I accepted Tom's proposal, and the wedding was planned a few weeks hence.

Tom never smiled at my answer. Instead, standing beneath the pillars of my father's neglected house, he took my hands and crushed them to his chest so I might feel the throbbing pulse beneath my fingers to prove his happiness. "My heart is yours, Patsy. It's racing for you. Galloping with eagerness to make you mine."

I might've hesitated, in that moment, if my own heartbeat hadn't answered in kind. "I'd like to know your plans for our future," I said.

Tom nodded, his gaze serious. "My father is settling on me a plantation near Tuckahoe called Varina, with forty Negroes. Your father is settling on you his best plantation in Bedford and twenty-five Negroes, little and big."

Slaves. My father was giving me slaves.

They wouldn't be mine, of course, not truly. Everything would belong to my husband the moment we wed. Tom would be the slaveholder—not me. And I knew it was considered only right and proper for every genrty bride to be given not only a settlement like this, but also a maid. Usually the girl that had attended her during her youth and courtship. By all the traditions of our country, this was no more than Papa *ought* to have given me, plus Sally Hemings besides. But there was no question that he'd keep her for himself, just as he'd promised.

And I didn't know how I should feel about any of it.

The idealism of France was an ocean away. I'd chosen Virginia and a way of life that William had said was stained with evil. I couldn't pretend I didn't know what I was returning to. But faced now with it, I found myself more troubled than I ever thought I might be.

Tom must've seen the shadow of my conflicted emotions in my expression, but he mistook its cause. "Colonel Randolph intends for us to live at Varina, near Tuckahoe. But you've a right to know that isn't *my* intention. I hope to buy my father's holding at Edgehill and settle closer to Monticello. I'd like a small farm that I can manage myself while pursuing an honorable life of public service. I've no ambition to gobble up lands that can't be farmed without an army of slaves. Such a life would weigh on my conscience more heavily than I could bear. Unlike my new brother-in-law, I don't make wedding toasts to embarrass my hosts about the evils of the institution, but I cannot abide slavery, Miss Jefferson." He frowned, the ferocity in those dark eyes softening until he seemed shamed. "I should've told you this before now. Though I'm violently smitten with you, I should never agree to start a life on a lie. So I consider it entirely pardonable if this revelation changes your mind about marrying me."

For the first time, I kissed Tom Randolph with something more in my heart than carnal desire. I brought my lips to his with an exquisite tenderness and replied, "With all my heart, Tom, you've only made me more certain in my decision."

~

ON A TUESDAY IN MID-FEBRUARY, wearing the bronze silk I wore to my first ball, I pledged my life to Tom Randolph under the watchful eyes of my father and all our country friends.

For music, my father hired the talented mixed-race Scott family to play. But my father's mixed-race mistress and her son could have no place at my wedding. In France, if Sally had been a woman of any social standing, even as notorious courtesan, her presence might be expected. But here we hid her away in the slave cabins to care for her newborn out of sight of the guests.

In truth, I remember very little about my wedding day except for the way my father relinquished my hand to the groom, and I felt in that moment, a nearly unbearable tearing asunder.

More curious, I suppose, is how well I remember the wedding *night*.

Tom descended upon me like a storm, sweeping me up in the violent rapture of our coming together as man and wife. He wanted my love and I think some part of him believed he could squeeze it from me with the power of his hands alone. He was superbly athletic—elastic as steel—and his hands and body crowded out everything but basic animal instinct.

I was the daughter of a rational but passionate philosopher. I'd spent my life contemplating the debate between head and heart. But never before had I contemplated the demands of a ravenous body and the ecstatic escape to be found in surrendering to its appetite.

Tom's lovemaking gave me a pleasure devoid of sentimentality, wrapping a thick gauze of self-delusion over still-bleeding wounds. His tireless passion was an opiate so potent that I became intoxicated on the power I had to arouse. He knew, I think, that though he'd married me, he hadn't mastered me.

So he had to *try* again and again.

Thus, I awakened the next day, exhausted, dewy eyed, and a bit in awe that the impossibly handsome heir to Tuckahoe was, indeed, my husband.

Papa was delighted to see me smile. Polly was less so. While Papa took a measurement of the wall in the entryway to plan where he would display his natural artifacts, Polly said, "Well now that Patsy's wedding is over, it's so very dull here at Monticello."

"Perhaps your new brother will take you riding," Papa suggested, still pondering the space, as if he meant to tear it all out and start again.

My husband, eager to please my father or to win my sister's affection, awkwardly promised he'd race Polly down the mountain and that if she lost, he'd give her a dunking in the pond. I could see that levity didn't come easily to Tom, but I appreciated his effort. So did Polly, who dashed away to get a head start in their race. Then Tom followed.

Left alone with my father, I said, "When *I* complained of boredom at her age you gave me chores and lectured me on the dangers of *ennui*!"

"You think I coddle her," Papa said, his tone light and amused before his expression became grave. "And I do. Because I realize now that I was far too exacting with you, Patsy." He reached for my hand, squeezing it, his throat bobbing with emotion. "After your mother died—what did I know about bringing up children? You taught me more than I taught you, and I thought we'd have more time. If I'd realized how soon I was to lose my precious little girl, I'd have cherished every moment."

"Papa," I said, quite exasperated, an odd pressure behind my eyes. "You haven't lost your precious little girl; she's merely grown up."

"If only that were true," he said, pulling me close. "Having had yourself and dear Polly live with me so long, I'll feel heavily the separation from you. But it consoles me to know that you're happier now." He patted my hand, clearing his throat to give sage advice. "Your new marriage will call for an abundance of little sacrifices. But they'll be greatly overpaid by the affections they'll secure you. The happiness of your life depends now on pleasing a single person. To this, I know all other objects must be secondary, even your love for me."

Hearing sadness in his voice, I rushed to reassure him. "Oh, Papa. I'll make it my study to please my husband and consider all other objects as secondary *except* my love for you."

He smiled, sheepishly, as if it shouldn't please him so much to hear it. "Neither you nor your husband can ever have a more faithful friend than me. Continue to love me as you've done, and render my life a blessing by the prospect that I may see you happy." He kissed my cheek and smoothed it with his fingers. "Be assured of my constant and unchangeable love. Especially now that I must put such a burden on your shoulders. Polly, and Sally, and the little one—I'll sleep easier knowing you're looking after them for me while I'm away."

"Sally?" I asked, more than a little confused.

My father's smile tightened. "I can't leave her to fend for herself. Better for Sally and the baby to stay under your watchful eye until I return. There's no one but you that I trust with such a precious charge."

Though he'd kept Sally from the house during my wedding, I'd seen them exchange looks, both tender and intimate. I'd seen, too, the gleam of pride in his eyes for Sally's newborn boy—the son Papa had always wanted—and I'd feared that he'd take Sally to the capital, where such an arrangement might make him infamous. But now I understood that whether I lived here, or at my husband's new plantation, I was still the guardian of Papa's secrets.

Marriage did not—and would not—end my duty to protect my father.

Just like that, my resentments evaporated. "Oh, Papa," I said, embracing his neck.

He patted my back. "My dear Patsy . . . But no, I suppose we must call you by your given name now. Martha, or, more properly, Mrs. Randolph."

Hearing that name made me marvel anew that I was some man's wife. But a little part of me grieved to think Patsy Jefferson was no more. A thing brought home to me most painfully that afternoon, when a letter finally arrived from William Short.

I found it left open at my father's seat, a sure invitation to read it. And I pored over every line of William's decidedly hurried scrawl, searching for my name. Instead, I found nothing but old news from France about how Lafayette bravely risked his life to save people from the angry mob. A part of me still longed to go back. To witness the struggle in the cause of liberty. But I'd made my choice.

And William Short had made his.

He closed the letter with a simple: *Present my compliments to the young ladies.* So I was just a young lady, now. The same to him as Polly. A daughter of his mentor. Which meant William could be no more than my father's friend. Perhaps it was just as well.

For Patsy Jefferson had loved William Short.

Martha Jefferson Randolph would make herself feel nothing for him at all.

～

"Isn't he adorable?" Polly asked, cuddling Sally's infant son. "As sweet as an angel."

Fortunately, no one at Tuckahoe looked askance at my sister sharing a bed in the dormitory with Sally, who they believed was her lady's maid. And if Colonel Randolph or any of Tom's family guessed the mewling baby was closer kin to us than any other Hemings, they didn't say a word.

Papa had gone off to serve as secretary of state with James Hemings at his side, and Tom intended for us to stay with his family a few weeks before making the traditional round of honeymoon visits to all our friends and country neighbors. But I hoped our stay at Tuckahoe would be brief, because Colonel Randolph reigned over his family like an aging despot.

He cut my husband with casual insults. And the old man's daughters—my new sisters—fared worse. Colonel Randolph spared hardly a glance for his littlest girls and left the older ones quaking in fear of his temper. Especially Nancy, who'd taken on the role of mistress of Tuckahoe for her widowed father. "Keep your pickaninny quiet," Nancy snapped at Sally. "Or my father will rage at the noise."

Seated with Polly on the divan, Sally looked up with only a flicker of indignant anger. In France she'd been an exotic beauty and cosseted mistress. Here in Virginia, she was just a slave again, and it must've been difficult for her to swallow down. Still, she did it, whispering a soft, "Yes, Miss Nancy."

The next day, Nancy glanced nervously at Colonel Randolph's retreating form. "We'll take our tea in the garden when Judith visits. This way we won't call attention to ourselves and give him a reason to scold us."

"I'd rather take tea inside," Polly complained. "Otherwise bees will buzz around our biscuits!"

Nancy huffed. "It's a tea for *ladies*. You'll take your biscuits in the kitchen with your maid."

Though I bristled at Polly being excluded, I wanted desperately to be embraced by my husband's family, so I didn't raise a fuss. Still, I feared what I'd do or say if my father-in-law vented his temper on Polly, so I told her, "Keep out of the colonel's way."

Then I went with Nancy to meet her sister in the drive. When Judith stepped out of her husband's carriage, she cried, "Why Martha! If I'd known you were going to marry my brother, I'd have waited to make it a double-wedding."

Nancy scoffed, leading us to the tea table set up in the garden. "Oh, Judy. As if you could wait." When Judith glared, she added,

"I'm just saying you're too vain to share your day with anyone else!"

"Well, I might have—" Judith broke off, stooping to pull some plants up by the root. "You're a disaster as a housekeeper, Nancy. Just look what you've let happen to Mama's herb garden. It's overrun with weeds!"

Nancy cried, "How am I to know the difference between the herbs and weeds?"

Judith sniffed imperiously. "Well, if you paid attention to the medicinal arts instead of burying your nose in tawdry romance novels . . ."

I took my seat on a lawn chair, disheartened to hear the way my husband's sisters bickered, smiling as though they were just teasing, but with a nasty undercurrent. And I was downright scandalized when Judith pointed to a patch of greenery and said, "If you'd had some clippings of *that,* Patsy, you wouldn't have had to marry my brother in such haste."

My mouth fell quite agape. "I beg your pardon?"

"Gum guaiacum," Judy chirped. "Part of my mother's special recipe for easing colic, but it's also known to bring on a woman's flow. So if you feared you were with child—"

"I *beg* your pardon," I said, again, this time more sharply.

"Oh, don't take offense," Judith cooed. "You're married now, and all the gossip in the world can't undo that."

With a flail of my hand that nearly upset the tea service, I cried, "What gossip?"

Judith put a hand to her hip. "You were scarcely betrothed to my brother a month. It's only natural for everyone to speculate."

"*Judy,*" Nancy said, in harsh reprimand.

"Oh, I'm not judging." Judy lowered onto a seat beside me. "I confess I'm nothing short of pleased at the outcome. I always feared Tom would marry one of those pretty, empty-headed girls who titter behind their fans at the mere sight of him. I never thought he'd take a sensible bride. Why, Patsy, I don't care how you landed my brother, only that you did! Never mind if people start counting back the months from when your first child is born."

My first child. The thought of it nearly stunned me into silence. I knew, of course, it was the duty of a wife to give her husband children. But the reality that I might have a baby growing inside me hadn't struck me until that very moment. Of course, if I *was* with child, there was nothing scandalous about it, and the gossips could count backward all they liked.

~

SALLY'S BABY DIED AT TUCKAHOE.

One spring morning, Sally came to me in a panic, holding her infant against her breast. "He won't suckle and he's coughing something terrible."

We went to Colonel Randolph for help, but he didn't care one whit about a slave girl's baby. He didn't want to send for a doctor, and though there was a cupboard full of dried herbs and medicines, Nancy didn't know what any of them were for.

Only my husband offered any real help. A student of science who had learned medicine at the University of Edinburgh, he put his ear to the little baby's chest. By the fire in the front parlor, cramming his long body into a small rocking chair, he cradled the infant boy, trying to get him to suck at milk from a cloth. But whatever ailed Sally's baby, the poor little boy wasted away fast. And when he stopped breathing, Sally gave a howl that echoed through that big plantation house like wind in a dead winter forest.

I'd never heard her make a sound like that. Never before or since. And in spite of the coolness between us since Paris, I found myself holding her tight in my arms, as if I could keep her from flying apart.

"Poor little baby," Polly sobbed.

Poor little baby, indeed. My poor little cousin, brother, and neither. I was to look after him. Both him and Sally. Papa had entrusted them to me. Now my father's son was gone without ever having become a man, and there was nothing we could ever say to comfort his mother.

Sally Hemings had returned to Virginia, to slavery, to this life—all for the sake of my father and this baby. Now my father was off serving the president and their baby was gone. She'd made choices she could never take back. Choices none of us ever could. And I had to fight off my own tears to stay strong for her and my sister both.

"What's all this carrying on?" Colonel Randolph shouted when he heard our lamentations echoing throughout the halls. When Tom told him, his father snorted with a dismissive flick of his hand. "Put a buck on that girl in a few weeks and she'll breed another."

At those words, my chin snapped up. I gave Colonel Randolph a look that could've set his whole house on fire, hoping to make him ashamed of himself. It didn't mean anything to him to see Sally in pain, but it meant something to us. It meant something to me.

Sensing a brewing rebellion in his parlor, Colonel Randolph snapped, "Do something about your womenfolk, Tom." Then he stalked away.

Choked with tears, Sally asked, "Where will we bury my baby? Can't leave him with strangers."

Trying to take the tiny body from Sally, Nancy Randolph said, "He won't know any different. Why, a little baby like this was only in this world for a few breaths. He won't remember anything in heaven. It'll be as if he was never here at all."

My sister-in-law meant to comfort, but Sally recoiled from Nancy as if she were the devil. It was Tom who had to reason with her. "Sally, your boy won't be buried amongst strangers. When my father passes on, I'll be master of Tuckahoe and Patsy will be mistress here. We'll be buried here and our children, too. With your baby nearby."

That's what it took to make Sally surrender her baby for burial. And I felt a flare of pride in my husband. He wasn't good at laughter and levity—what he did best, he did in the dark—but there was a decency about him.

He said those words to ease the heart of a grieving mother. But when those words got back to Colonel Randolph, they did more damage than I could've imagined.

Maybe it was Nancy who ran telling tales, but it could've been any of the miserable souls in that big old house. Whoever reported the conversation must've made Tom's words sound ugly and entitled, like we were wishing for Colonel Randolph's demise.

That night in the dining room, my father-in-law eyed Tom over a glass of liquor and said, "You and your fancy new convent-educated wife have made yourselves quite at home here at Tuckahoe."

"We're very grateful for your hospitality, sir," Tom replied, stiffly. "Now that the snows are gone, we'll take Miss Polly to Eppington and make our rounds."

Colonel Randolph threw back a gulp of the amber liquid and gestured to a slave to refill his goblet, then he held out his hands, as if in question. "When Mr. Jefferson asked you to call on his relations, did he leave you any horses to take you there or did he expect you to take mine?"

An awkward tension, one that was sadly common at Tuckahoe, settled over the room like the air growing heavy before a storm. Tom swallowed. "I suppose with all the excitement of the wedding, we didn't give it much thought."

Colonel Randolph sneered. "Well, that is a conundrum for you then, isn't it?"

It wasn't about the horses. And to this day, I'd argue that it wasn't even about our sense of presumption. The truth was, that for some reason I could never surmise, nothing Tom or his siblings ever did satisfied or pleased that old man.

"Your new father-in-law is the sort of man who assumes everything will all work out," Colonel Randolph continued. "Sunny disposition, those Jeffersons. But ice water in their veins."

It was an insult. To me, to my father, and to Tom. For a moment, I thought my husband might actually raise a fist to his father; instead, an emotional chill settled between father and son beyond even that which was there before.

Tom was still seething by the time we went to bed. "We're moving to Varina, straightaway."

"Aren't we going visiting at Eppington?" I asked, pouring water into a basin to wash my face and hands.

"Your sister and Sally can stay there, but we're going to Varina to make a home. Better than relying upon the generosity of my father one more day!"

I wondered if Tom had given this plan enough thought. I didn't know if there was time to get crops in the ground at Varina. I didn't even know if there was a habitable home there, and without my sister or a maid, what would I do? Why, the only things James Hemings had taught me to cook were French delicacies. "I'm very much averse to this plan. I thought you intended to buy Edgehill from your father and settle near Monticello?"

"My father's in no mood to sell anything to me right now," Tom snapped. "And I didn't ask your opinion on the matter."

I'd lived too long with Frenchwomen to lower my eyes and apologize for daring to have thoughts on the matter of where I should live. But I didn't want to quarrel. So I used the charms I'd learned in the ballrooms of Paris, and the more natural ones I was only beginning to discover in myself. "Well, if you find it necessary to go to Varina," I began, crawling into bed and reaching for him under the blankets, "I will, of course, comply."

"Yes," he said, gruffly, touching his nose to mine. "You will."

But the touch of my fingers turned the heat of his anger into a different kind of heat, which I found gratifying. Tom was an ardent lover, easily distracted by pleasure. So I forced a wide, sweet smile. "It's my desire and duty, after all, to please you."

The edge of Tom's anger melted away as he glanced at me from beneath lowered lids. "You do, Mrs. Randolph. You please me very well."

Later, spent of seed and rage, he laid his head back on the pillow and spoke softly. Regretfully. "I shouldn't have been harsh with you. It's only . . . I'll always be a boy under his roof, Patsy. That's why we have to go to Varina. Can't stay here another day or it'll come to blows."

It seemed an exaggeration, but I suppose family quarrels never look the same from the outside as they do from within. I was only starting to understand the Randolphs; I wasn't privy to the thousands of injuries they'd done one another, real and imagined. It just seemed to me a silly quarrel over horses between a controlling father and his headstrong son.

Would that it had been.

The next morning, I found Sally staring out the window in the direction of the woods where we put her baby in the ground. An unmarked grave at the edge of the tree line—not far from the Randolph family cemetery—where the ground was carpeted in blue wildflowers.

Softly, I asked, "Should I write to Papa?"

Her eyes still vacant with shock and grief, Sally gave a quick shake of her head. "I'll get word to him through my brothers."

I'm ashamed to say how relieved I was to hear it, because I didn't have the first idea of how to tell my father. That was the way of it in Virginia; for all the things we never said aloud, there were even more we never put to paper.

So when next I wrote Papa, I sent him only reassurances of my love. I wanted to say more, because something felt terribly wrong about *this* silence. But in the end, that's all I wrote.

Chapter Eighteen

New York, 30 May 1790
From Thomas Jefferson to Thomas Mann Randolph Jr.

Your resolution to apply to the study of the law is wise. On my return to Virginia in the fall, I hope some practicable method may be devised for your settling in Albemarle. Nothing could contribute so much to my happiness. You might get into the assembly for that county. Meanwhile, a motion has been made in the Senate to remove the federal government to Philadelphia and the French revolution still goes on well.

MY FATHER WISHED to keep me close to Monticello—and I desired the same—but in marrying Tom, I understood my destiny to be entwined with Tuckahoe. *Tuckahoe* was the family seat. The jewel of the Randolph fortune. And since Tom was the oldest son, tradition held that he'd inherit the place.

It would always have a hold on him.

But the place that had a hold on my little sister was *Eppington*. Polly didn't wait for the carriage Colonel Randolph finally lent us to come to a stop before flinging the door open and leaping out into the arms of Aunt Elizabeth—the only mother my little sister remembered. And watching my aunt's calico housedress billow up as she spun my sister made me forgive her for keeping Polly from us all those years.

But I confess, it made me a little jealous, too. At least until

Aunt Elizabeth grabbed at my hands and I caught a scent of lavender water that she and my mother both used for perfume. "Patsy, you've grown so regal, you make us look like peasants. Your mother would burst to see you now."

Uncle Frank did his best to make my new husband feel welcome, too, pouring him a glass of his best liquor and asking him about his studies at Edinburgh. And I breathed a sigh of relief to be away from the tension at Tuckahoe. Little by little, my reticent husband relaxed into the company of my family until Uncle Frank said, "Mr. Randolph, you must congratulate your father for me on his betrothal."

Tom stared, frozen in surprise, his glass at half tilt. He managed to choke out three words. "My father's *betrothal*?"

Oblivious to Tom's distress, Uncle Frank lifted his own glass for a celebratory toast. "I've yet to set eyes on Gabriella Harvie, but I'm told she's a young lady of great beauty."

It was Aunt Elizabeth who recognized Tom's expression as horrified shock and she tried to silence her husband with a sharp "*Mr. Eppes.*"

But my uncle blundered on in confusion. "Didn't you just ride out from Tuckahoe? Surely your father shared the happy news of his forthcoming remarriage. Everyone else in the countryside has heard by now."

Tom curled slightly inward, as if he'd been run through with a sword and didn't want anyone to see how badly he was bleeding. I reached for him, my own mind reeling, but he pulled from my grasp, excused himself, and begged leave to take Uncle Frank's bottle with him.

Tom strode off to the stables and I followed, half-afraid he'd hop on a horse and ride off. Realizing I was following, he picked up his pace, but so did I.

"My mother is only a year in her grave," Tom said, taking two swallows straight from the bottle. "And my father has set his mind to marry a girl younger than his own daughters."

There was nothing unusual about that; older men of means

took young wives. No, Gabriella Harvie's youth wasn't the trouble; it was that her father was a landed gentleman of Virginia who would expect his daughter and any children she bore to reap the rewards of this marriage at the expense of my husband and his siblings.

Tom took another swallow, his dark eyes burning. "My mother gave him three sons and seven daughters, but now he wants to start a *new* family."

I stepped closer. "Doesn't mean he'll neglect the one he's got."

"Yes he will," Tom hissed. "He'll start fresh and forget us, since we've ever been such a disappointment to him. He's done this to hurt me, I promise you that."

I couldn't imagine anyone wanting to hurt Tom. And, frankly, it seemed impossible that *any son* would ever please that old man. "Colonel Randolph is a widower. Is it possible he's just lonely?" I suggested, trying to be more generous.

It was the wrong thing to say. Tom shrugged away from me and threw himself down on a hay bale. "Patsy, you've only had a taste of how malicious my father can be. You haven't the faintest notion of how miserable he's made me and you wouldn't care if you knew. So go to bed and leave me be."

Something in his eyes frightened me, and left me no room to argue. So I went into the house, fretting the whole while. I *did* care that my husband was miserable. Of course I cared. But I didn't know how to help him.

By the time Tom came to bed that night, he was drunk. He wasn't gentle. But before I could scold him for putting a tear in my nightclothes, he buried his face in my hair, sniffling and sobbing barely coherent apologies. Some part of me was horrified to see him weep like that, a big strong man curled up against me like a boy. But another part opened up to love him just a little.

His loss was altogether too familiar for me not to feel compassion. My mother had died years ago, but Tom's pain was still fresh. So I held him without resentment while he sobbed how much he loved his mother, and how bitterly he resented his father for never having loved her at all. "Patsy, I regret every little neglect I ever made in my affection to my mother. No one will ever love me like she did."

I knew that pain, so I stroked his back, realizing he now feared to lose what little of his *father's* love he'd ever had.

That's what Tom feared.

But as my husband fell asleep on my shoulder, my fears were entirely financial. I married him, in part, because he was the heir to Tuckahoe, as grand a place as there was in Virginia. But I'd seen greater estates fall to ruin in France. How Colonel Randolph's lands would provide for his remaining unmarried daughters was already a matter of concern. As the eldest son, Tom would take the largest share, but how many more ways would the colonel have to divide his holdings if he had more children?

Because my husband's inheritance—and what might be left of it—was a thing of peculiar interest to me now that I suspected I was soon to have a child of my own.

⁓

Colonel Randolph's impending remarriage worked itself like a poison into my husband's blood. My family opposed the idea of setting up housekeeping at Varina, but Tom was now more determined than ever. He'd gone ahead of me to get crops into the ground and expected me to join him soon. And I dreaded it, because it was a hot summer and I was swelling with child and didn't want to live in such proximity to the Randolphs. . . .

"I don't understand it," Aunt Elizabeth said, sitting on the porch, teaching me some tricks of mending while we watched Polly play with the dogs in the summer sun. "You need a maid when you're in this condition, Patsy. Every Virginia gentleman gives one to his daughter on her wedding day. Sally should be tending you. Is your father saving her for your sister?"

Perhaps it was having lived so long in Paris, where slavery had been abolished, or perhaps it was the strong emotions my pregnancy had drawn out of me, but every word of my aunt's inquiry aggravated me. There seemed to be so much wrongness in it that I'd go mad trying to unravel it all. Sally was, after all, almost as much Aunt Elizabeth's sister as Polly was mine. But my aunt never acknowledged the colored part of the family except by calling them that. And because such a thing was never acknowledged in polite company, I'd have to quiet the part of my mind that persisted in thinking about the connection.

As for her question, I knew my father had no intention of giving Sally away. Not to me. Not to anyone. Not ever. He'd made Sally a promise in France, and he was honor-bound to keep it, even now that their child was dead. So I shrugged. "Sally and I wouldn't get on well. . . ."

"Still, your father only gave you field hands," Aunt Elizabeth said, pushing the needle in deep. "You can't trust them in the house. You need someone you know. Someone with intelligence and character."

Someone with lighter skin, she meant. Someone who behaved more like a servant so as to uphold the polite fiction of it all. Someone in the family . . .

Utterly sickened by her implication, I blurted, "Papa intends to free James Hemings. And Mary is now living with Mr. Bell. I think Mr. Bell means to free her, and my father will help arrange that, too. You ought to know my father believes slavery is an injustice."

"Your father and every cultured gentleman in Virginia," Aunt Elizabeth said, not looking very impressed. She pursed her lips. "The world is how it is and no one can change it. Not even your father."

She was wrong, I thought. Papa had already changed it. *France* had changed it. Liberty was spreading across the ocean and the whole world. And what about Mr. Short? He was a Virginia gentleman who had taken a principled stand on the matter, and surely other men would follow suit. My own husband professed to want only a small farmstead he could work himself, but in Virginia, slavery was a way of life, and it would have to be the way of my life. We couldn't get by without the slaves, and my father said they couldn't get by without us.

"Ask your father to give you Mary's daughter, Molly," Aunt Elizabeth said. "She's a girl of almost fourteen now. She knows how a house should run and she's not so pretty as Sally, so your father won't mind parting with her."

That shut me right up. And for more reasons than one.

When I said nothing, my aunt added, "With a child on the way and no proper homestead, you can't get along without a maid. Especially not at Varina, where you'll be the only woman. What with your husband in the field and you by yourself in some old shack, I'd worry about you night and day."

"It's where they say Princess Pocahontas used to live," I said, more hopeful than I had any right to be. "I'm sure it's not so horrible. . . ."

In truth, nothing in my whole life prepared me for what I faced that summer at Varina. I found myself hauling river water up to a ramshackle house, wondering whether or not I'd survive another day. My fingers and ankles were constantly swollen in the heat, and the early stages of my pregnancy made me nauseated and dizzy. Since the slaves were needed in the fields, I spent all day, every day, hauling buckets and firewood by myself. Washing dishes. Scrubbing clothes. Grinding corn. Plucking chickens. Things I'd never done before. Things few plantation mistresses did without the help of servants. Things that made me so tired and filthy I thought I'd never get clean again.

Aunt Elizabeth had been right when she said I badly needed the assistance of a maid. Trapped in an endless cycle of toil and solitude, how I yearned for feminine companionship. Establishing a new plantation left no time for letters or visits with neighbors. And even eating for two, there were nights I'd have happily gone hungry rather than cook something from our near-empty larder over a fire that made the nights hotter and more miserable by far. I couldn't get comfortable on the old bedding or on the wooden floor, and was a meal for mosquitoes either way. Grimy and drenched in sweat, aching from head to toe, I couldn't quite conceive of how I'd come to this.

A year earlier, I'd been drinking bubbling wine from crystal glasses in Paris ballrooms. I'd been decked in silks and satins and brocades, dancing with French and English nobility, taking music lessons, attending concerts, and gambling with duchesses. For the love of God, I could have been a duchess. How did I find myself exiled to this remote farm, tossing and turning, weary to the bone?

If I'd stayed with William Short, accepted his proposed vision for my life—become the wife of a diplomat instead of a planter—

No. Tom was my husband and my place was with him now. I boxed the disloyal thoughts up and locked them away. Especially since every day, under that fiery sun, Tom worked the fields with the slaves, all of them sweating and struggling in the earth. The slaves were obliged to do it at the threat of an overseer's whip, but Tom wanted to learn the work, and I'd never in my life seen any white man work as hard.

Until that summer I'd only known Tom as a schoolboy and then as a gentleman of learning. I didn't know how much of a planter there was in him, and I guess he wasn't too sure either.

In truth, when I wasn't exhausted or sick or otherwise distracted by Varina's countless demands, I was proud of my husband's efforts. But I was equally worried that he was determined to prove something to his father even if it killed him.

And I feared it just might.

Almost every night he came back with his sweat-soaked shirt sucked tight against his broad chest, face sunburned, and his stomach too sick to eat even on those evenings I did manage to have something like a meal ready for him. After a particularly arduous day's labor, Tom retched up his guts outside the house murmuring, "I hate tobacco. Too hard on our people. Too hard on me."

"It's the climate," I replied, hating to see him reduced to this and stroking his handsome face with a wet cloth. A heat rash was spreading all over him, and I could tell it itched something awful. "It's not healthful here."

"It's torture," Tom agreed, peering at me from under his sweat-soaked hair.

That emboldened me, and I knelt to look him in the eyes, swabbing his face with the cool cloth once more. "The air near my father's mountain . . . it's fresher."

"Fresher." Tom nodded, and let his blistered hand come to rest on my lightly swollen belly. The look of defeat in his eyes nearly broke my heart, even as his next words filled me with hope. "Maybe after my father marries the Harvie girl, I'll muster up the courage to ask him to sell us his property at Edgehill."

And because it was as far as I could push him on the matter, I let myself be content. At least until the wedding proper . . .

Gabriella Harvie was a beautiful bride who floated down her father's grand staircase into a hall filled with white flower garlands, wearing a dress of pale blue damask with a tasseled bodice. At eighteen, she had a queenly presence, a charming voice, and—as I would come to learn—no soul at all.

Her long lashes and doe eyes blinded men to the virago that dwelled within, and on her wedding day, the bride smiled so angelically at Colonel Randolph that he seemed thunderstruck by the sight of her. At the time, I hoped she'd bring him such comfort that he'd be kinder to his children. And I myself was in a hopeful mood because I'd availed myself of the amenities of the great house and finally got a good bath.

I felt like a lady again for the first time since moving to Varina.

Once the vows were said and the celebration begun in the great hall, Nancy rushed to me, crying, "Citizen Patsy is going to make me an auntie!" I was glad to see her smile in spite of the awkward circumstance her father's marriage created. Alas, the bride soon swept over to us before I could tell her so.

"My dearest new daughters," Gabriella said.

I laughed, since we were all only a few years apart in age. But

Gabriella laced a cloying arm through Nancy's and announced, "The first thing I'm going to do is paint the parlor white so I'll feel more at home at Tuckahoe. The black walnut walls are so gloomy!"

Nancy stiffened. "My mother chose them."

"All the more reason, then," Gabriella said, her eyes glittering with malice. "It's important for everyone to know there's a new mistress of Tuckahoe."

Was she taking aim at Nancy, who would have to relinquish her mother's keys? Or was it a barb aimed at me, because of Tom's indiscreet remarks when Sally's boy died?

Maybe it was meant for both of us.

The bride batted her lashes. "Patsy, everyone says you're so worldly, so tell Nancy how it works. Perhaps she'll listen when you say that unless she's planning a trip to Paris, she'll never have a better chance to snag herself a wealthy husband than at this wedding. And she can't live at Tuckahoe forever."

From that moment, I knew Gabriella would make life miserable for my husband and his siblings. They must've known it, too, because when it was time for us to leave, Tom's youngest sisters clung to his legs and begged him to take them away with us.

"Now, girls," I said gently. "Do your best to welcome your father's new wife, and make Tuckahoe a place of happiness and contentment for everyone."

But I felt a peculiar uneasiness on the road. And in the carriage, Tom turned to me and said, "I wasn't apt to like her, but I never guessed Gabriella would be such a horrible woman." So alone amongst the men, he hadn't been ensnared by her beauty. And I adored him a little bit for it. Even more when he said, "You cannot imagine how I want to turn around, grab up my sisters, and carry them away with us."

"I don't have to imagine it. I feel it, too."

His head jerked up and he stared. Then, all at once, heedless of who might see us through the carriage windows, he kissed me. He kissed me with such fierceness, such gratitude, such passion . . .

that then and there, I promised myself for the hundredth time that I'd stop comparing him to William Short.

William had been pleasure and principles—in the end, he hadn't understood the inexorable pull of *family*. Tom Randolph understood it, and because he did, a very real tenderness for him took root inside me right along with our babe already growing there. I might never love him; I was half-certain I could *never* fall in love again. But I was starting to feel something for Tom that might be deeper than love, if only I could find a name for it.

I WAS NEVER SO HAPPY to be back at Monticello as I was that autumn, when Papa returned from the capital. Dignity itself wouldn't have stopped me from running into my beloved father's arms, but I was too heavy with child to run.

Seeing me that way put a proud gleam in my father's eye that warmed me from head to toe. But in putting his hand on my belly, that proud gleam faded to sadness, and I wondered if he was thinking of Sally's little boy, dead and buried months ago.

When the news had finally reached him, he'd suffered his most violent headache yet, lasting nearly six weeks in duration, and with no one there to care for him. I wondered now what kind of reunion Papa and Sally might've had if she'd been here with the rest of the servants we'd summoned to welcome my father home. Instead, she was still with Polly at Eppington. I'd been slow to send for her when I learned my father would be coming—a mistake I'd never repeat after seeing Gabriella Harvie installed as mistress of Tuckahoe.

After witnessing the graceless way the new Mrs. Randolph claimed her position, elbowing poor Nancy out of the way, I believed myself to have been a fool for ever raising even the slightest objection to my father's liaison with Sally.

I vowed to change my thinking in the matter. For I understood that the promise my mother exacted from my father not to marry was an act of *maternal,* not wifely, love. Perhaps remembering the remarriages of my grandfather Wayles before he had finally settled upon Elizabeth Hemings as his concubine, my mother had said she couldn't bear to have a stepmother brought in over us.

It was no coincidence, then, that my father took up only with women he could never marry. Beautiful women who meant something to him without having to mean anything to us. Or women like Sally—a slave who could never push me or Polly out of my father's home.

That night, when I sat down to play music with Papa in Monticello's parlor, he grasped my hands and brought them to the light for inspection. "What's this?" he asked of the state of my bruised knuckles and blistered thumbs.

"Just war wounds," I said, remembering how I'd smashed those knuckles between two buckets while hauling water. "I've been fighting a battle against dirt and thirst at Varina."

"Tom isn't doing well for himself there?" he asked, the light of the fire highlighting the red of his hair.

Because I sensed in this some criticism of my husband, I said, "You wouldn't blame him if you knew how little mercy he shows himself in trying to make a profitable farm. He's strong, Papa, but he's working himself near to death."

My father smiled mildly, for he knew better than I did the hard work of plantation life. "No word, yet, on whether Colonel Randolph will sell him Edgehill?"

I shook my head, clenching my teeth to keep from saying something ugly about Colonel Randolph. Just then, Tom came in from some errand, his boots heavy on the floor. "Are you to make music for us, Patsy? I've never heard you sing."

I preferred playing to singing, but Papa rescued me by announcing, "Tom, I regret imposing upon you, but I find myself in need of a favor. I supposed my appointment to France to be the last public office of my life. However, now my duties will keep me at President Washington's side for an indeterminate time. And it pains me to see Monticello in this run-down state, my people still scattered to the winds."

Sally, he meant, and I cursed myself again for not sending for her sooner.

Tom stood just behind me in my chair, his hand on my shoulder while Papa continued. "If you and Patsy would be willing to stay at Monticello through the winter and bring some order here, I'd be forever in your debt."

The truth was that we'd be in *his* debt. It was an act of generosity—my father wanted to give us somewhere civilized to live while bringing our baby into the world. But in spite of my father's exquisite diplomacy, Tom knew it for what it was. His hand squeezed my shoulder. "Mr. Jefferson," he said, his tone just shy of indignant. "I don't—"

"I realize, of course, that I couldn't ask you to toil here on my account forever," Papa said quickly to soothe stung pride. "Not when you want a place of your own. But perhaps, in small repayment for your help, I could go to Tuckahoe and talk with your father about securing Edgehill for you. Perhaps his happy nuptials will put him in a mood to agree."

At that moment, the gratitude I felt for my father was sweeter than jelly on fresh bread, hot from the oven. For a long moment, Tom didn't reply, and I felt that I might burst in waiting for his answer.

Finally, Tom's hand relaxed again and he gave a small bow. "I'm your humble servant, Mr. Jefferson, as always."

Happiness welled in my chest. *Farewell Varina.*

I was to be, for the first time in my life, the mistress of Monticello.

ON A RIBBON WORN ROUND MY GROWING BELLY, I wore the keys to all the cabinets and storerooms at Monticello. And as a woman soon ready to birth a babe, I was in a frenzy to put the house right. I counted and polished my father's silver like my mother had done before me. I kept close records of everything coming in and out of the kitchen. I brined meat in a big wooden salting barrel. I went a thousand times a day from the storehouse, to the washhouse, to the orchard, to the garden, to the kiln, then back to the storeroom again, navigating my way among sacks of grain and loaves of sugar and boxes of supplies.

And, of course, I found myself in command of the house servants—doling out their rations of cornmeal, fish, and pork. In France, when Sally was our maid, I'd not hesitated to direct her, but now that she'd returned to Monticello in my father's absence, what was she? Fortunately, Sally took on mending and cleaning without having to be told, and so we settled into a silence all our own.

I'd lost a friend in her, without realizing that I'd had one. I tried never to show just how much I missed Paris and our friends there, great and small. Still, I did long for them. More than I would, or could, ever say. Which is why I nearly swooned when, as the Indian summer gave way to the first bite of winter, a letter from Marie de Botidoux came to the house.

The packet had taken some time to arrive because the post was in a shambles. Now, moving as fast as my belly would allow, I made for the parlor, my little sister trying to snatch the thick paper from me, crying, "I want to read Marie's letter!"

Fortunately, my height made it easy to keep it from her reach. "It's not for you, Polly."

"Well, then, fine," she fumed. "But I'm too grown-up to be called Polly—if you're going by *Martha*, I want to be *Mary*."

I lowered myself into an armchair. "If you're so grown-up, go see if Mammy Ursula needs you to read out a recipe, then study Spanish so I don't have to tell Papa how lazy you've been."

Once she'd skulked off, I held the letter close, realizing that I might never see my friend again in the flesh. I was careful with the wax seal and reverently unfolded the page, grateful for the news from France.

Mirabeau—who had worked with my father and Lafayette to draft the Declaration of the Rights of Man—was dead. The French tricolor flag was officially adopted. Hereditary titles had been abolished. Catholicism would no longer be the religion of the state. Finally, the king tried to escape and rouse Prussia and Austria to restore the monarchy by force of arms, but was captured by the revolutionaries before he could do so.

And I couldn't find it in myself to feel sorry.

Who but Papa would understand this news as I did? We'd returned to a country much transformed by six years of relative peace. America's war of independence was already, for some, a distant memory—the extraordinary sacrifices now an unpleasant recollection, easily buried under the business of rebuilding ordinary lives.

People forgot the fragility of our enterprise as a new nation, and sometimes forgot, too, how much we owed France for it. But it was different for my father and me. We'd gone from one revolution to another, leaving America flush with victory only to find ourselves ensnared in the same struggle for liberty on a distant shore.

For us, the revolution had never ended.

Papa's words had shaken the world, but if liberty failed in France, it could still fail in America, too. Then everything we'd sacrificed would be for naught. However, letting my eyes caress each cherished word of Marie's letter, it wasn't only the politics that pained me—there were also the lines she penned of William Short.

According to Marie, he had despaired my leaving France. So much so that when she asked after his feelings for me, William angrily renounced them. Marie didn't believe him; she wrote that she thought he still loved me. But this was long ago. It had been just over a year since I'd left him, and now I was great with another man's child.

It doesn't matter any longer, I told myself.

Nevertheless, my mind was still in a fog of regret when I

stumbled upon my husband in the greenhouse, some unrecognizably bloody animal hacked to pieces on a butcher block under his hands. "What *can* you be doing?" I asked, tugging my shawl around me.

"Dissecting a dead opossum," Tom replied, as if there were nothing odd about it at all. The kill was fresh, judging by the steam still rising off the remains of the carcass in the chilly air. "Your father has engaged in a debate with someone about the creature, and asked me to perform some experiments and observations to keep in a diary along with meteorological readings."

I pressed my hand to my mouth, unable to look away from the gore. Only my father would debate anyone about opossums! If Papa still did have a madness, it was in that he had to take a measure of everything under God's creation, obsessively recording the tiniest minutiae, as if it would all add up to an answer for what ailed us in this world. And now he'd dragged poor Tom into it. Poor Tom, who was here running another man's plantation—*my father's* plantation—instead of his own. And for my comfort.

I cleared my throat. "I regret my father has troubled you with this."

"It's no trouble," Tom said, wiping bloody hands on a gardener's apron.

He was being mannerly. My husband had been ripping out dead trees for my father and planting new ones at Monticello, working himself from dawn to dusk. And when he wasn't busy with that, he was kindly tutoring my little sister in arithmetic and botany. He wasn't as tired as he'd been at Varina, but he was restless, as if always finding new ways to prove himself.

"Papa will understand that you're too busy to indulge every little curiosity."

"Patsy," Tom said, with a sheepish shake of his head, "I'm happy to do whatever Mr. Jefferson asks because your father wants to learn everything, whereas mine thinks he's got nothing left to learn. And if my father ever *did* have a question, I'm the last person he'd ask for help."

Seemingly of its own accord, my body moved closer to him. My hand found Tom's cheek and stroked it tenderly. Bashfully, he turned his face to kiss my palm, careful not to touch me with his own bloodied hands. "Don't suppose you've a French recipe for opossum stew?" he asked.

I laughed. And in that moment, my life in Paris seemed as far away as the stars.

Part Two

Founding Mother

Chapter Nineteen

Monticello, 8 February 1791
To Thomas Jefferson from Thomas Mann Randolph Jr.

Patsy continues in very good health and would've written herself had I not prevented her from the fear of her being fatigued. The little one is perfectly well and increases in size very fast. We are desirous that you should honor her and us by conferring a name on her and have deferred the christening till we hear from you.

OUR DAUGHTER ARRIVED three weeks into the new year, a whole month early, leaving me fevered. But love cured me of that fever. Love for the little baby, bald and blue-eyed as she was, with a pink gurgling smile.

Because we were waiting on Papa for a name, the poor baby girl went without one for two whole months. But it was worth the wait. Papa chose *Ann,* after Tom's dead mother.

Nothing could've pleased my husband more—except maybe a son of his own. The night of Ann's christening, I rested in bed with Tom, the baby between us. My husband looked happy, and it made me want to find ways to make his happiness stick.

As the baby suckled, I whispered, "If it's in God's will to bless us, I'll yet give you a boy."

Planting a playful kiss on my bared shoulder, Tom's eyes smoldered. "When can we start on *that* business, Mrs. Randolph?"

Though I wasn't in any condition to entertain the notion, I smiled. "In due time, Mr. Randolph. In due time."

With an uncharacteristic grin, he nodded, gently brushing our baby's cheek. "For tonight then, I'll content myself to be truly pleased with our Ann."

He'll be a good father, I thought, softening to him as I hadn't allowed myself to before. We were a family now—a reality brought home to me more powerfully when my husband's four young sisters fled to us en masse one cold day.

"We can't stay at Tuckahoe anymore," said Nancy, at sixteen, the oldest of the four. "Our father's wife is a monster!" Nancy wept on Tom's shoulder while he patted her back. "She slaps the little ones. She says it'd be a happier home without them, so I took them with me . . . not that our father cares one way or the other."

The servants had ushered the younger girls into the kitchen for a spot of warm milk, and I was glad for them not to hear Nancy's words, true though I believed them to be. "I'm sure Colonel Randolph loves you all very much," I said, though I was sure of no such thing.

"No," Nancy sobbed. "He loves only that vile woman."

With baby Ann in the crook of my arm, I knelt before Nancy and grasped her hand. "Oh, he's just enamored of her youth. In time, when the ardor fades—" I stopped speaking then, because Sally came in, setting down a tray of tea for us.

"It'll be too late then," Nancy cried. "My father insists that I marry the man he chooses or leave his house. But it's *her* choice."

I could guess which kind of man Gabriella Harvie Randolph might choose for her stepdaughter. Someone old and wealthy, on a faraway farm. So I persisted in my silence until Nancy sniffled and said, "Well, I left her a farewell gift anyway. I scratched the date of our mother's death into a windowpane to remind Gabriella that no matter how many coats of white paint she puts in the parlor, she's only the mistress of Tuckahoe because our mother is dead."

"Oh, dear," I said, imagining the trouble that might cause. Did all the Randolphs show their emotions so openly—going so far, even, as to enshrine them in glass? "Well, now you'll have to stay with us until tempers cool."

Nancy sobbed her gratitude. "I won't be a burden to you. I won't stay long. I'm not sure what to do with the younger girls, but Judith says I can live with her family at Bizarre plantation."

At this, my husband stiffened. "No."

Tom's flat refusal surprised me. He must have surprised Nancy, too, because she whined, "Why ever not?"

Tom narrowed his dark eyes. "You know what I think of Richard Randolph."

Curious. He'd never said anything about his brother-in-law to me.

My husband continued, "The Matoax Randolphs are scoundrels, every last one of them. Richard, Theo, and John. No. To say they're *scoundrels* is too kind—and does a bit of injury to scoundrels."

Nancy gasped. "But I'm so fond of Theo!"

The tension in Tom's ticking jaw made it clear how hard he worked to keep his anger reined in. "All the more reason you can't stay at Bizarre unchaperoned."

Tom was being strangely unreasonable. If he couldn't trust his own brother-in-law to look after Nancy, who could he trust? But my husband's family had a knack for working him into a state.

He crossed his arms. "Richard Randolph isn't a fit guardian for you, Nancy."

Nancy blew on her tea. "He's *married* to our sister."

"Only because we had no choice but to let him marry her!" Tom's sudden shout was so unexpected that I jumped and baby Ann wailed in my arms. I rose to rock and console her. Meanwhile, Tom seethed. "Richard purposefully got Judy into a delicate condition—"

Tom's gaze cut to my face, and he swallowed his words, as if belatedly recalling my presence in the room. Or perhaps it was the sight of my mouth hanging agape that gave him pause. Richard and Judith's wedding had seemed a happy one, without a trace of distrust or discontent, and Judy had borne no child. So why did Tom think . . . ?

I didn't know. But I *did* know that appearances could be deceiving, and Virginians are better at hiding their troubles than just about any other people on earth. So, I snapped my mouth shut again.

"Oh, Tom," Nancy said, waving her handkerchief in dismissal. "Judy and Richard aren't the first country lovers to fall into bed before they said vows. Why, you and Patsy—"

"Did no such thing!" Tom roared, a vein throbbing at his temple. "I'll thank you to apologize."

Nancy paled. "Oh, Patsy, I'm sorry, I didn't mean—"

"It's quite all right," I said, though I was sure she meant exactly what Tom feared she did.

Nancy turned her eyes back to Tom. "Richard did marry Judy, and no child came about in the end, so what difference does it make?"

Tom's eyes bulged. "What *difference*? That you could ask is a demonstration of why you're not going to Bizarre. And that's the end of it."

That wasn't the end of it. When Tom stomped off to attend one of the many chores my father set for him, Nancy pleaded with me. "Patsy, won't you soften my brother to my situation? My prospects for love and marriage are better at Bizarre."

I saw her predicament. Without Colonel Randolph's protection, all Nancy had was youth and looks. I didn't blame her for being terrified of becoming either the wife of a man she loathed or a spinster, dependent on all her relatives.

That night, I asked Tom, "You won't send all your sisters back to your stepmother's care at Tuckahoe, will you?"

He rubbed at his face with both hands and blew out a sigh. "Gabriella Harvie is evil incarnate."

I nodded. "Your father must be blinded by her beauty."

"She's not beautiful," Tom grumbled. "There is nothing interesting about her face or manner whatsoever." Oh, but Gabriella *was* beautiful. So it warmed my heart that Tom couldn't see it. But then, he never even liked trees in all their showy foliage. "You cannot imagine how I want to keep my sisters from her, but how—"

"Let them stay here with us as long as they like," I said.

His head jerked up and he stared. "Patsy, your days and nights are already occupied with caring for a newborn baby. How will you manage all our sisters, a gaggle of motherless girls ranging from the ages of four to sixteen?"

"I'll manage it somehow," I said. "And meanwhile, we might as well let Nancy stay at Bizarre, where she'll have a better chance at finding a suitable husband than here, where we'll be caught up in caring for all the girls."

All at once, Tom kissed me. A kiss full of gratitude and urgency. And it reminded me of the kiss he'd given me when I'd first voiced my concern for his sisters. In the carriage. His love and concern for his sisters, whom no one else in the world cared for, made me love him yet a little more.

Tom understood the need to protect your family, something that had always been so important to me. As a new babe grew in my belly, I thought perhaps the thing for Tom I felt that was deeper than love might be *dedication.*

And it was because of that emotion that I changed his mind, and in the end, Nancy had her way.

A thing that gave us all much cause to regret.

⟶

"WHY, MY DEAREST DAUGHTER, you've brought forth a reformation here at Monticello," Papa said, approving of the way I'd organized the larder. He'd come home that autumn to dote upon me and my baby girl, but had kind words for Tom, too, and the way he'd managed things.

This paternal praise fell on Tom like rain on dry, drought-ridden fields; my husband swelled with such pride that I began to wonder if he'd ever heard a kind word in his life. But we weren't the only ones hanging upon my father's every kind word. . . .

Sally Hemings put on her best dress for Papa's homecoming, and I watched—while pretending not to watch—the reunion between my father and his lover, the first since the death of their child. But neither Papa, nor Sally, gave my prying eyes satisfaction. In fact, for some curious reason, my father kept a scrupulous distance from her.

There were no flirtatious glances and—as if by silent assent—Sally no longer tended my father's chambers. It was her older brother Martin who brought a daily bath of cold water for my father's feet. I wondered if perhaps they were just keeping their affair secret, given all the girls now living in our house. In Paris they'd kept it secret . . . until they couldn't. Papa had been shamed to be thought a seducer, but he was infatuated then. Maybe now the shame was stronger than the infatuation. Or maybe their sadness over the baby's death had extinguished the fire of ardor between them completely.

When Papa readied to leave again for Philadelphia—this time to take my little sister and our cousin Jack Eppes with him—Sally and I found ourselves standing on the front steps together to say farewell. Papa gave her a chaste hug good-bye and I heard her sigh. She'd given my father her freedom and a son. Now both were lost to her . . . and perhaps he was, too.

Understand that at eighteen years old, Sally Hemings was more beautiful than ever. Men flirted with her, but I never saw her encourage them, and I had the sense that even if we hadn't been watching, she never would. I believed that my father was the only man she wanted, and he'd just left her on the steps without so much as a kiss.

I would have sighed, too. And my sympathy for Sally overcame the pang of jealousy that my sister would be living in some tidy town-home in the nation's capital with Papa. Hopping up into the carriage, my sister reminded me, "You had Papa to yourself in Paris for a long time. Now it's my turn!"

Conceding, I kissed her nose. "Don't be too lazy to write, little Polly."

"Call me *Mary*, now. Or *Maria*, if you must." She wouldn't have suggested that name if she remembered Maria Cosway, but that woman was an ocean away now, rumored to have abandoned her husband and their newborn daughter to join a convent.

Inhaling the milk scent of my own daughter's cheek, I couldn't imagine life without her, much less becoming a nun. If love had shaken my faith in a convent vocation, *motherhood* had shattered it completely. So I banished all thoughts of Maria in the convent, and as my sister tucked herself into the carriage next to our father, I cried, "Adieu, Papa. Adieu, Maria."

Sally and I stood there together until the carriage rolled out of sight.

Then it was time to deal with Tom's sisters.

With the hickory smoke of November rising from smokestacks at every farm, we took Nancy, according to her wishes, to live at Bizarre plantation in Cumberland County. There was nothing especially *bizarre* about the modest two-story house that sat atop a giant slab of cut stone, though the *people* who lived there were a bit strange.

Theo Randolph was a thin, sickly young man whose nervous disorder required a dependence on laudanum. Or so he said. Then there was his flamboyant brother John, whose youthful appearance belied his years as a result of a childhood illness. An illness some said occasioned his high voice, dramatic manner, and impotence with women.

Richard and Judith—the master and mistress of the plantation—seemed ordinary enough, but there didn't seem to be much planting going on here, where they believed themselves far too genteel to embrace any other profession. Tom, grumbling that one of the Randolph brothers of Bizarre had been expelled from school, added, "I feel like I'm leaving her in a bawdy house!"

I tried to soothe him. "Why don't we take them up on their offer to winter over here?"

As Tom held our daughter's little arms, teaching her to walk, he grumbled again. "They didn't mean for us to take them up on it."

"Nevertheless, they can't refuse now that they've offered. We can help the girls settle in and ease your worries."

Tom eyed me, as if stunned by the devious turn of my mind, but agreed. And during those blustery cold months, I helped set up housekeeping, since Judith was heavy with her first child. We ended up staying for nearly three months in all, Tom watching—like a hawk—Theo's every move toward our virginal Nancy.

If only he'd been watching Richard.

I scarcely took notice of the way Nancy giggled whenever our host said something amusing. Or the way, when Richard hugged her, they embraced too long. Holding hands briefly before bed. Whispering in one another's ear. I suppose I *noticed* all these things but dismissed them as Nancy's gratitude to her brother-in-law for taking her in when her own father was so utterly indifferent to her.

"Tom, truly. Neither John nor Theo has an eye for Nancy. And Richard's watching out for her. You see how attentive he is," I said as we prepared for bed one night.

I should've been more suspicious. I should've wondered what those whispers and giggles meant, but by February I was distracted and bursting with happy news. "Mr. Randolph, I'm going to give you the son you so desire."

Tom lifted me up, clasping me against him, spinning me round, and in our joy, we left Bizarre plantation without suspecting a thing.

Monticello, 9 September 1792
From Thomas Jefferson to President George Washington

I was duped by the Secretary of the treasury and made a tool for forwarding his schemes, not then sufficiently understood by me; and of all the errors of my political life this has occasioned me the deepest regret. That I have utterly, in my private conversations, disapproved of the system of the Secretary of the treasury, I acknowledge. His system flows from principles adverse to liberty, and is calculated to undermine and demolish the republic.

The summer just before he wrote this letter, Papa returned to Monticello in a state of agitation, telling of all the indignities he'd suffered at the hands of the cunning and ambitious secretary of the treasury, Alexander Hamilton.

At dinner—a meal put together with the freshest vegetables from my new garden—my husband asked, "What kind of fool is this Mr. Hamilton?"

My father set down his spoon and mopped sweat off his brow with a napkin. The infernal heat of that summer had been so stifling that we hadn't been able to sleep comfortably even with every door and window open. But it wasn't the heat that vexed him. "The secretary of the treasury is no kind of fool at all. He is a colossus."

Never had I heard of my father speak of a man this way. Half in awe, half in mortal dread. And because there was a crowd at our table, including my Carr cousins, in thrall with his every word, my father continued. "We are daily pitted in the cabinet like two cocks." Papa shook his head and pushed away his plate. "I've confronted the president, who assures me there are merely *desires* but not *designs* for a monarchy."

A moment of appalled silence fell upon the table as we considered the president's most unsettling—and scarcely reassuring—reply. None of us wanted to believe our liberty to be in so much danger, but Papa's sense of betrayal at the way his compatriots had twisted the revolutionary spirit to which he'd best given voice was clear. And seemingly warranted.

"What will you do?" Tom asked, his brow furrowed and eyes serious.

"I'll resign." Before anyone could protest, Papa added, "No

man has ever had less desire of entering into public offices than me. Only the war induced me to undertake it. Twice before I've refused diplomatic appointments until a . . . domestic loss . . . made me fancy a change of scene. Now I want nothing so much as to be at home."

A domestic loss.

Papa still couldn't speak of it, I realized. Even in the privacy of his home, even so near to the anniversary of her death, he couldn't speak of my mother's passing except as a domestic loss.

I forced a smile and chirped, "We'll be so happy to have you home for good, Papa. We'll be together. Everything we always wanted." And, at long last, it would be everything Mama had always wanted, too.

Of course, I had no way of ensuring that would come to pass without my husband's consent. But Colonel Randolph had finally agreed to sell Edgehill to us, and I believed, deep in my heart, that Tom would be happier living nearer to my father than his own.

I became more sure of it in early August when we received news that Colonel Randolph's wife had given him a brand-new baby. A boy named *Thomas Mann Randolph*—same as my husband.

If I hadn't hated Colonel Randolph before that moment, I did then, because Tom took it hard, like a bullet to the heart.

It wasn't uncommon to name a baby after a sibling . . . if they'd *died*. From which Tom inferred that his father wished he'd never been born. "I've been erased," Tom said, staring bleakly out the open parlor window with a glass of liquor dangling precariously from one hand. Then he drained it, his throat working hard to swallow the poison down. "*Replaced.*"

With the imminent birth of our own new baby, I was too overcome by my belly and the stifling August heat to rise swiftly up from my chair to comfort him. It was Papa who put a hand on Tom's shoulder and said, "Nursing this wound can't remedy the evil, and may make it a great deal worse. Don't let it be a cankerworm corroding eternally on your mind. Forgive your father, because Colonel Randolph surely meant nothing but to indulge his new wife in this."

That was putting a shine on manure, and my husband surely knew it.

But then my father added, "You have your own family now, and a new baby to arrive any day. How can anything cloud the joy of that? If you have your wife and children, you have the keystone to the arch of happiness."

Tom looked down for a long moment. He gave a single nod, but I didn't miss the sadness that deadened his eyes. And despite my father's attempt to comfort Tom and make him see all the things he had around him, I feared it was a wound from which my husband might never recover.

I worried over it until my son was born a few weeks later, fearing even as I held him in my arms that Tom would name the child after Colonel Randolph, either from tradition or from provocation, and make his own wound even deeper. But taking our cherub into his own strong arms, Tom proudly named him, "Thomas Jefferson Randolph. We'll call him *Jeff* for short."

I gasped with delight, knowing how much it would please Papa. "Oh, Tom!"

"You'll be the only one with that name," Tom promised the boy as he hugged him close against his broad chest. Then little Ann came running into the room to hug Tom's knees. Chuckling, Tom settled his big hand on Ann's head and smiled down at her. "You're a big sister now, Miss Randolph."

She reached up her hands for her baby brother, and Tom knelt down to give her a closer introduction. In that moment, seeing the three of them together and happy, I felt suddenly overcome by a pang so deep in my heart that it undid me. Grasping at my chest and swallowing hard over my confused emotions, I realized what had happened.

Why, somehow, I'd fallen in love with my husband.

It wasn't a sweet, dreamy love that made my heart skip. It didn't make me want to shout and spin pirouettes on my toes.

It was some other kind of love, so quiet it snuck up on me in the shadows. Nevertheless, it was as *real* as any love I'd ever felt, and my eyes misted over to feel it.

Tom peered up at me. "What's wrong?"

"Nothing at all," I said, resolving to be so kind to him that he'd never need any other family but ours. And what a family it was. My son was a remarkably fine boy. Smaller than my daughter had been at his age, but healthier. So much so that, within a few weeks, we felt confident in taking little Jeff out into the world for a visit to Bizarre.

Given the news about Gabriella Harvie's baby boy, I expected to find the Randolph sisters in a state and braced for the gnashing of teeth. But we found our hosts quietly melancholic. Judith smiled to see us, but it was a brittle smile. And Richard was wound tight as a drum as he told us about the recent death of his younger brother, Theo. Tom and I had already heard it was the laudanum that did him in. That, in the end, the young man had been a skeleton, unable even to walk on his own. But as we sat around the parlor at Bizarre, Richard insisted, "It was tuberculosis."

My husband's gaze flicked to his sister Nancy, who hadn't found a husband yet and who wasn't likely to find one, looking as frail as she did now. Her skin was like paper and she was unable to muster even a brittle smile. Indeed, the back of the settee appeared to be all that held her upright. I knew Tom was imagining what sort of mischief she'd gotten herself into here at Bizarre.

Was she taking laudanum, too?

"Nancy hasn't been feeling well," Richard said, putting a comforting hand upon her knee. The gesture was so intimate that Tom went rigid, a shadow over his eyes. And in spite of my happily gurgling baby boy, and Ann's giggles as she ran about the house, the air went thick with tension.

So thick that I actually startled when someone banged on the front door.

None of the house servants went to answer it, but Judy got up and peered out a window at an angle from which she couldn't be seen. Going pale, she said, "It's our neighbors."

"Well, aren't you going to let them in?" I asked, anxious as any southern woman to the dictates of hospitality. Of course, if I'd known what the neighbors had come to say, I'd have barred the door myself!

The Harrisons hadn't come on a social visit. Indeed, while her husband glowered, Mrs. Harrison left her bonnet on, though she tugged nervously at the pink ribbon holding it to her head. Standing just inside the room, as if she intended an abrupt exit, she finally said, "The rumor is still being passed around, Miss Nancy. We thought you ought to know."

"What rumor?" my husband asked.

Mr. Harrison continued to glower, but to answer Tom, Mrs. Harrison chirped nervously, "The slaves are saying that the night your sisters and your brother-in-law stayed as guests in our home, Richard was seen taking a bundle out to the woodpile, and—" She glanced at Nancy's belly, fluttering a bit in her unease.

Before she could continue her thought, Mr. Harrison cut her off with a blunt, "They're saying Miss Nancy gave birth to Richard's bastard and that he chopped it to pieces."

Shooting to his feet, Richard cried, "Slander!"

Richard's outrage was so convincing that I put a hand on Tom's arm to still him. But my husband, too, shot to his feet. And he was plainly not convinced.

Richard insisted, "That's a damnable lie."

"Is it?" Mr. Harrison shot back. "You drag your whoring to my house and stain my name—"

"*Please*," his wife begged of him, as if she might swoon away at the unpleasantness. And when her husband quieted, she added, "Nevertheless, you should know it's being said. The servants claim they heard screams in the night and found bloody sheets in Miss Nancy's bed."

Nancy's pretty big eyes rounded with fear or outrage; I couldn't say which. "They were *groans*. Not screams. I was ailing from womanly troubles and pains in the abdomen. I've always suffered from colic. My sisters can tell you that's true. Isn't that right?"

"Of course it's true," I said, reflexively. "She's always had terrible colic." She'd never had colic in her life as far as I knew, but what else could I say as my husband went from red to purple?

The moment the Harrisons uttered some stilted courtesy and took their leave, Tom whirled on Nancy, grabbing her by the arms and pulling her to shaky feet. "Were you seduced, sister?"

Tears filled Nancy's eyes. "There was never any baby. Someone's telling lies!"

My husband didn't believe it. He shook her, that familiar angry vein pulsing in at his temple. I'd never seen him so angry before, but I understood the cause. Not just the fear that young Nancy had been exploited by the man to whom we'd entrusted her care, but also that if her honor had been sullied by a baby begot out of wedlock, it'd sully Tom's honor, too.

And that was to say nothing of a dead baby!

When Nancy looked to Richard for help, my husband's rage worsened, his knuckles going white. Tom turned to Richard, too, and I thought he might commit murder then and there.

But just then, Judith gave a bitter laugh. "It's just slave talk. This is what happens when we hold Negroes in bondage. I imagine this dreadful rumor is being spread by Mr. Harrison's slaves to embarrass him. Or to urge him to be a better, more benevolent father over them."

Judith's explanation had merit. Mr. Harrison *was* known as a cold and heartless slave master. His slaves very well might want to call his honor and authority into question. I glanced at Tom, hoping he'd calm himself. But my husband's jaw was so tight I thought he'd chip a tooth if he tried to speak.

He didn't speak. Not a word. Only later that night, on the pillow beside me, did he finally ask, "It's too preposterous a tale about Nancy to be believed, isn't it?"

"Entirely preposterous." Silently, I counted back the months.

"Why, in order for it to be true, she'd have got with child when last we visited here!"

Besides, I couldn't imagine how any woman could hide a pregnancy. Sally hadn't been able to hide it. When I was fat with my own two babies, there wasn't a person alive I could've fooled. And even if Nancy could hide such a thing, I couldn't imagine anyone killing a baby. Certainly not my own kin.

"Don't think on it another moment, Tom. We'll put it out of our heads," I said, stroking his arm.

That's precisely what I aimed to do. Especially since I was nursing the newborn and worrying for my daughter, whose tummy troubles brought her whimpering into our bed in the wee hours of the morning. Laying her against the warmth of her father's strong shoulder, I took a candle from the bedside and padded barefoot down the stairs to search out some peppermint for her to gnaw on.

The kitchen at Bizarre was much the same as I'd left it, but when I opened the canister where I expected to find peppermint, I found something else. With a mounting sense of dread, I recognized it as gum guaiacum—the very thing Judith once said could get rid of an unwanted child.

I stood there, staring into the depths of that shadowy canister, trying to deny the truth of what I was seeing. Then a question came out of the dark. "What are you looking for, Patsy?" Nancy's sharp profile emerged from the shadows, startling me. And the sight of her in her nightclothes, hair unkempt, as if she'd just tumbled from a man's bed, made my heart hard.

Rounding on her, I whispered, "Who was it? Who was the father?"

Nancy turned so that her face fell into the shadows. "I don't know what you're saying."

I brought the candle closer, wanting to see the truth in her eyes. "Was it Theo, God rest his soul?" It couldn't have been freakishly boyish John, whose impotence made it impossible.

That left Theo as the least horrifying possibility. If spirited young Nancy had fallen in love with sickly Theo . . . if he'd meant to marry her but died before he could . . .

"There was no baby," Nancy hissed, still turned away.

I wanted to believe her, truly I did. But if she was telling the truth, why couldn't she meet my eyes? "Then it was Richard?" I asked, appalled. Their union would be considered not merely adulterous but also *incestuous*.

Still, there was a worse possibility—one that might explain the determination of slaves to spread the gossip even under threat of their master's whip. I took another step closer, my own voice trembling. "Or was it a Negro slave?"

Nancy's jaw snapped shut, and she finally dared to meet my eyes, hers burning like coals. "I said there was no baby, Patsy. Do you hear me? *There was no baby!*"

I didn't know if she was lying to me or lying to herself.

I only knew she was lying.

Every hair lifted on the nape of my neck at her desperation, hoping it was only the kind of desperation that would drive a terrified, unmarried girl to abort her baby and not the kind that might allow her lover to chop up that baby once it was born. "Oh, Nancy," I said, nearing tears for the dead child and the pain this would cause her family—and how it would destroy my husband.

She grabbed my arm like a drowning woman. "Say you hear me. There never was a baby."

There never was a baby. Just like my father had never wanted to kill himself, never taken a married woman as his lover, and never conceived a child with Sally Hemings.

"I hear you, Nancy," I said, bitterly. "I hear you."

Chapter Twenty

Philadelphia, 12 November 1792
From Thomas Jefferson to Martha Jefferson Randolph

I have nothing to tell you but that I love you dearly, and your dear connections, that I am well, as is Maria. I hope your little one has felt no inconvenience from the journey, that Ann is quite recovered, and Mr. Randolph's health good. Yours is so firm, that I am less apt to apprehend for you: Still, however, take care of your good health, and of your affection to me, which is the solace of my life.

WANTING TO PROTECT MY *HUSBAND'S* GOOD HEALTH, I said nothing to him about the gum guaiacum or my confrontation with his sister. It wouldn't have done him any good, and may have done a great deal of harm.

If it became known that Nancy had been pregnant, the prospects of her entire life would be forever diminished. She'd find it nearly impossible to secure a husband. She'd become a spinster, forever a financial burden on the family without any place to call her own. So, I told myself to be kind to Nancy, that she'd been preyed upon by a man who ought to have known better. That she was a victim of error if not slander, and it'd be best to carry her away from here.

We'd take Nancy with us. Maybe to Charlottesville, where we could marry her quickly before the rumor spread. But Nancy would have none of it. "If I go, it'll only feed the gossip."

"Nonsense," I said, folding my own clothes for the trunk as my maid was nowhere to be found. "No one in Albemarle will have heard about this."

I was determined to drag Nancy away if necessary, but Judith surprised me by making herself the most formidable obstacle to my plans. She went directly to my husband and said, "If you take Nancy, it'll reflect poorly on Richard. It'll look as though you don't trust your own brother-in-law."

Knowing Richard had seduced Judith before their marriage, I guessed my husband wouldn't find this argument compelling. Tom snapped, "How can it be unmannerly to take my own sister home with me?"

Then Richard's brother John intervened. "Now *Toooom*," he drawled, smoothly stretching out his name. "If you take Nancy, it'll look as if you don't believe her innocence." If there was anyone at Bizarre we were certain hadn't seduced Nancy, it was John. Stunted but more effusive than a Frenchman, he was as persuasive as a serpent in the Garden of Eden, so we left Nancy there.

We were quiet on the way home, but for little Ann, whimpering at every bump in the road, unable to keep down her breakfast of milk-soaked biscuit. The journey should've only taken hours, but with our girl spitting up and our boy fussing at my breast, it seemed like days. I was already weary when we rolled up to the mountaintop and saw Sally on the front portico, her amber eyes intent on me.

"Miss Patsy," she said with an urgency that told me she'd been waiting. Though every other slave on the plantation now called me *Mistress Randolph*, Sally rarely did, either a sign of her intimacy with me or our complicated history. Waiting until Tom had gone in the house with the babies, she rushed up to me. "There's a rumor in Charlottesville about your Randolph kin—about Miss Nancy."

That the news had traveled so far, so fast, surprised me. But it shouldn't have. In slave society, families on one plantation almost always had kin on another. Slaves hired out, they traveled as messengers, worked as boatmen and coach drivers, and saw one another at church. If they wanted to get word to each other, they could. What should have surprised me was the insistence of the slaves telling this tale, even under threat of their master's whip.

With a weary sigh, I nodded. "We've heard it, Sally. It's just Mr. Harrison's people telling a malicious story and they'll be punished for spreading it."

Sally gave a quick shake of her head, her bronze fingers tightening into fists. "At least twelve of Mr. Harrison's people claim to know something of it personally. Maids saw Miss Nancy naked and big with child. Some heard her scream at night. Some saw Richard Randolph go into her room. And there's a bloodstained wood shingle."

So Richard had apparently taken no care to shield his sins from their eyes. Such indiscretion might be that of a man who wished to help his sister-in-law in need. Or in a man who was guilty.

Either way, it was the act of a fool.

Sally leaned in. "White folk are talking, too. Mr. Page says he's seen Richard Randolph's familiarity with Miss Nancy, kissing and hugging on her. Nancy's aunt says she saw her in a state of undress . . . that she *was* with child. And the white housekeeper saw bloody sheets the next day."

White witnesses. That changed absolutely everything. I glanced nervously at the house, hoping Tom was well out of earshot.

Sally lowered her voice to a whisper. "I heard it at Mr. Bell's store. My sister Mary thought it might touch on us, here at Monticello, given that Miss Nancy stayed here for a time. And given what people are saying about your father."

That stopped me cold. "What are people saying about Papa?"

Sally's pretty dark lashes swept low. "You haven't seen the gazettes?"

Most of the Hemingses could read and write, though how they'd learned, I'd never asked. Still, it surprised me a little that they'd been following matters in the papers. "Let me see them."

"We haven't any papers here," Sally said. "They're all down at Mr. Bell's store. But it's dreadful. In the press, Master Jefferson is being attacked for everything from intrigue to dishonor."

Fury washed through me. I was already road weary and worried for my husband's state. And now to learn Papa had been attacked! Despite my exhaustion, I got back in the carriage and summoned Sally to follow, telling the driver, "To Charlottesville, straightaway."

MR. BELL'S STORE stood on the corner of Main Street. Boxes and barrels crowded together in the middle of the wood plank floor while tins and glass bottles and blue-painted plates lined the shelves. The scent of lavender wafted down from baskets hanging on the eaves overhead so that, tall as I was, I had to stoop to get to the counter where Mary Hemings busied herself boxing up a pipe for a customer, who replied, "Thank you, Mrs. Bell."

Mary wasn't Mr. Bell's wife, but given the way Thomas Bell smiled at her from where he stacked goods on a high shelf, he was plainly smitten. Everyone in Charlottesville seemed willing to accept the arrangement, and I was happy to do the same.

Sally sorted through stacks of pamphlets and pulled free some copies of the *Gazette of the United States*. Handing them to me, she warned, "It'll sicken you."

Nevertheless, I began flipping through the pages of papers published this past summer and fall. My eyes landed on one passage right away.

Cautious and shy, wrapped up in impenetrable silence and mystery, seated on his pivot chair, Mr. Jefferson is involved in political deception. . . .

I'd seldom heard a word of censure against my father. He'd been, here in America and in France, idolized by nearly everyone. I suppose that's why my cheeks stung to read such pointed criticism. Rifling through pages so violently I might've torn them, I found another attack.

> Had an inquisitive mind sought evidence of Mr. Jefferson's abilities as a statesman, he'd have found the confusions in France. As a warrior, to his exploits at Monticello. As a mathematician, to his whirligig chair.

I frowned anew that anyone might blame the "confusions" in France upon Papa and not the royalists who bankrupted their country and left the peasants to starve. It embittered me, too, that we were to still suffer censure for our late-night flight from Monticello—where I suppose they believed we ought to have brandished pistols and pitchforks against the trained British dragoons, women and children, and all.

And what was their obsession with my father's chair?

> As a philosopher, his discovery of the inferiority of blacks to whites, because they're unsavory and secrete more by the kidneys.

There I stopped, remembering that Sally had brought this to my attention. Perhaps if I'd not come of age in France, I wouldn't have felt such an acute shame, but I couldn't look at either Sally or Mary. I could only whisper, "Who wrote this? Do we know these men?"

Mr. Bell stepped down off his ladder. "Some say it's the secretary of the treasury using different names." Given all my father had said of Mr. Hamilton, I believed it. "But plenty of others agree with him. Not just northerners either. John Marshall is leading the Federalists here in Virginia, and now Patrick Henry is going over to that side, too."

Patrick Henry. The very man who cried *give me liberty or give me death,* had spread the story of my father's supposed cowardice in the face of British soldiers. Though I had only childhood memories of the famous orator, I'd long disliked Patrick Henry as my father's political enemy. Now my anger was fueled anew.

"They're calling on your father to resign," Sally said, pulling me from my bitter thoughts. "They're digging for an excuse, and the gossip about your kin—"

"Nancy Randolph hasn't been under my father's roof in nearly two years!" Quickly, I brought my fingers to my lips, as if to recall what I'd said, for it was a tacit admission that I believed my sister-in-law guilty.

Fortunately, if the Hemingses knew anything, it was discretion. Clutching one of the screeds against my father, Sally replied, "It doesn't seem as if Federalist writers care much for facts or fairness."

No, they didn't. And if these men could work themselves up into such a furor over my father's *chair,* what would they make of kin who lived in incestuous and adulterous union, and murdered a baby? Still, I tried to persuade myself that the scandal wouldn't touch my family. "Surely, no one could think my father would tolerate the debauching. . . ."

There I trailed off. I couldn't pretend in front of the Hemingses—no matter how discreet they might be—that nothing improper ever took place under my father's roof.

For Sally Hemings was proof that, in fact, it did.

⁓

HONOR. IN VIRGINIA it wasn't merely a matter of masculine pride—it was a matter of survival. Every loan for the farm, every advance of credit for seeds and foodstuffs, every public office and proposal of marriage depended on honor.

Men would fight and die for it.

And women would lie for it.

Which is why, whenever asked about the rumors about Nancy and Richard—as I was, more and more often that spring—I dismissed it as an absurd story having no merit.

If only others had done the same.

When Tom learned there were white witnesses, he flew into a rage that had him slamming about the house, heaping undeserved abuse on every servant he passed. And whenever he heard Richard's name, he cursed in the most obscene manner possible. Egged on by his younger brother, Tom determined to ride out and rescue Nancy from the clutches of her seducer, who must be made to confess and suffer the loss of his honor.

Tom said it often, and to everyone who'd listen, which struck me as madness, for it fueled the gossip.

But then, the entire *world* had gone mad.

The new revolutionary government in France had charged Lafayette with treason. A galling notion—the very *idea* of Lafayette being a traitor to the revolution he helped start was an unjust, enraging indignity! More ridiculous and horrifying was that in attempting to escape arrest, Lafayette had been caught by counterrevolutionary forces, who *also* deemed him a traitor.

He was, as of the last news we had, in a dungeon awaiting execution.

Even consumed at Monticello with chores, child rearing, and family scandal, I couldn't seem to shake the violence this news did to my faith in the revolution. What knaves had come to power in France that they could turn on Lafayette?

Perhaps the same sort of knaves who hounded my father in the papers, savaging his ethics, and twisting every word that flowed from his pen . . .

That's why I wasn't surprised when Papa wrote to tell me that he couldn't resign for fear his enemies would say he was driven out of office or that Washington had no confidence in him. Or they'd say that he ran from public office like he ran from the British.

No, he couldn't be seen to leave under a cloud.

I was brooding about this while making bayberry wax candles,

Tom's favorite, because of its pleasant fragrance. It soothed him, he said, and he clearly needed soothing, given the way his boots banged heavily into the cellar kitchen where I prepared the wicks.

Arms crossed over his chest, as if he could scarcely contain his pounding heart, Tom growled out, "Richard dared to show his face at Tuckahoe, the shameless cur!"

Shameless indeed for the seducer to have visited the home of his victim's father and brothers, I thought. Reckless, even. It wouldn't have surprised me to hear Colonel Randolph had pulled a pistol on him. "What did he have to say for himself?"

Tom threw out his arms. "Richard asked—nay, *demanded*—that we stop accusing him of despoiling our sister's purity!"

Let it never be said that the Randolphs—any of them—lacked in boldness.

While I let out a surprised puff of air, Tom ranted on. "Richard first insisted it was all a malicious lie. He claimed Nancy's virtue is still intact and that if we wanted to preserve her reputation, we ought to all keep quiet and join a slander suit against anyone who'd spread the tale."

"Perhaps that's best," I ventured. "If the family doesn't rally around your sister and profess a belief in her innocence, Nancy will be ruined."

"She *is* ruined!" Tom exploded, his voice echoing off the ceiling. "When my father refused, Richard tried his next gambit. He has a letter written by Nancy confessing her pregnancy and naming a dead man as her seducer. Her letter allegedly says Theo was the father, the child was stillborn, and she absolves Richard of all culpability."

I gasped that Nancy should put such a confession to paper, then flushed to remember that I'd suggested Theo as her seducer in the first place. Poor deluded Nancy must have determined that if she couldn't save herself she'd save her lover instead. "You have the letter?"

Tom's hand flexed at his side, then balled in a tight fist. "Richard kept it and intends to vindicate himself on a field of honor. He's called out my brother."

Icy dread rushed through my veins. "Your brother will *duel* over this?"

"No. My brother won't give Richard the satisfaction of pretending he's an equal or a man of honor. But I swear, if Richard Randolph tries to transfer the stigma and evade blame, *I* will wash out the stain on my family honor with his blood."

Now the icy dread froze inside me, for I'd never heard such a sure promise of violence in my life. And it came from the man that I'd married. The man I'd come to love. Trying to reason with him, I murmured, "But Theo is dead. He's the one least likely to suffer for it. Maybe you should let him take the blame for the blot on your sister's reputation."

Tom slammed his hand to the tabletop. "Richard did it, Patsy! He did everything they're saying he did. That creature seduced my sister—*both* my sisters. Then he killed an innocent babe. It isn't gossip. I know it happened. I know it's all true."

Alarmed at the state he was working himself into, I put my hand on his cheek. "Tom, if it's going to destroy your family, what does it matter if it's true?"

At this question, my husband jerked away, his black eyes burning. "What sort of man do you take me for, Martha Jefferson Randolph?" He so seldom used my proper name that I stiffened. So did he. "If he pushes me to it, I'll put a bullet in his heart, because I'm a gentleman of Virginia and cannot countenance a lie."

To this day, I don't know why his words provoked me so. Perhaps it was that like my mother before me, I'd heard my fill of supposedly high-minded ideals that rocked nations, put unhappy women in their graves, and somehow ended with people I loved being chased or captured to await execution.

Which would be exactly the fate of Richard and Nancy if their own kin wouldn't come to their aid. Or it could end with a duel and my husband, the father of my babies, shot dead. I wouldn't have it. I simply wouldn't have it. "What sort of man do I take you for, Thomas Mann Randolph? Why, I suppose the sort of man who has enough sense to keep his mouth shut even if it costs him some pride."

In reply, Tom screamed in my face, "You dare speak to me about the cost of pride? We were *there* at Bizarre when my sister's bastard was conceived! There, where I took Nancy on your say-so. If Richard Randolph isn't to blame for my sister's disgrace, then *I* am. And everyone in Virginia seems to know it but you!"

I never saw the blow coming.

My husband's backhand caught me high on the cheek and pain exploded behind my eye in a burst of tiny fireworks. I don't remember falling, and for a second or two, I couldn't fathom how I came to be on the floor. My vision swam with tears and black fuzzy cobwebs of pain.

No one had ever put violent hands on me. Never in my whole life. Not even a nun had so much as laid a strap across my knuckles. I think it was the shock of it, more than the pain, that left me trembling so badly I couldn't rise to my knees. When I finally looked up, I saw that my husband looked just as shocked.

"Dear God," Tom whispered, hoarsely, sinking to the floor beside me. He brought his shaking hand to my hair, and I flinched, refusing to let him tilt my face to his view. "*Dear God, what have I done to you?*"

I'm not sure what I'd have said had the door not flown open. But open it did, and there stood Sally, her kerchief tight on her head, her brow furrowing as she took in the scene.

"What do you think you're doing, Sally?" Tom snapped. "No one called for you."

She ought to have fled, but when her majestic eyes found me sprawled on the floor, she stubbornly set her jaw. "Thought I heard something fall . . . you all right, Miss Patsy?"

I couldn't bear for Sally to know how I'd been disciplined by my husband. That he'd struck me, just as I'd once struck her. "Perfectly fine," I said over the lump in my throat. "These long and clumsy legs of mine get tangled up sometimes. Tripped over that basket."

If she knew I was lying, she gave nothing away. Pushing past my husband, she said, "I'll help you up."

But gently taking my forearms, Tom said, "No need. I have her now."

～⟩

I WAS ALMOST GLAD THAT HE'D HIT ME.

Glad because it absolved me of my guilt.

I'd fretted about my father's reputation, but I'd given too little thought to Tom's. I deserved to be slapped to my senses. Everyone would have thought so. Besides, the incident seemed to have shaken Tom to his foundations. The man who said his honor wouldn't countenance a lie hadn't contradicted the story I told Sally. He'd taken me to our bedroom and suffered no one else to tend me, bringing me a cold wet cloth for my face and my supper tray with a bouquet of springtime flowers from the gardens.

Now he sat at my bedside, kissing my hand again and again, wetting it with his tears. "Forgive me, Patsy, though I don't deserve it. Please, forgive me for lifting a hand against you. What a wretched man I am. Heartless, just like my father."

"You aren't wretched or heartless," I said softly, reminding myself that I'd no right to speak to him the way I did and that he had every right to correct me for it. "I'll gladly forgive your lifting a hand against me if you forgive me for having given such offense to have occasioned it."

His voice was still shaky, his thumb reaching to brush the rising bruise underneath my eye. "There's nothing you could say to justify my leaving such a mark on you. I've hurt you. My adored wife."

Though my cheek still throbbed, I said, "It'll heal and be forgotten."

His expression crumbled again, with anguish and self-loathing.

"No. I'll never forget it. And it'll never happen again. I'll never again betray the sacred charge your father put in me in giving you over into my authority. A husband ought to be kind and indulgent with his wife. To protect her from harm. It won't happen again, Patsy."

I believed him.

His tortured expression would have been enough to convince me, but his behavior after confirmed it. For Tom never again spoke of dueling with Richard Randolph and resolved to be the peacemaker in his family. He didn't even rise to the bait when Richard published a screed in the *General Advertiser* proclaiming his innocence and condemning his accusers without naming them. Everyone in Virginia knew he was slinging mud at my husband, but Tom kept his peace, determined not to give himself over to rage again.

And I loved him more for it. Watching him struggle against undeserved abuse from such a villain made me forgive him, truly. But then, I was prone to forgiveness in the aftermath of Richard Randolph's wretched newspaper notice. Especially since the very same issue announced the execution of the king of France.

In truth, this news was more of a blow than the one my husband had dealt me. I never thought the French would put King Louis to the guillotine. The revolutionary men in my father's parlor in Paris never even suggested it. Perhaps with France at war with its neighbors, the revolutionaries feared to hold the king captive when his very life encouraged enemies to attack them. And King Louis *was* guilty of all the crimes they accused him of.

But even believing that, the account in the paper made my fingers rise up to my own throat as I fought back the horror of imagining the blade slicing through it. Who were these *Jacobins* who had condemned Lafayette a traitor and killed the king? And would they come next for the friends I left behind in France, like Marie?

Until this news, Papa and I had held in contempt those who

complained of the revolution's excesses. They hadn't witnessed all we'd witnessed in France. But the men who had seized the reins there now, could they be the same men that Papa and I had known and admired? Surely not.

Papa could explain it, I was sure. And I was near desperate to have him home—especially when he wrote that the news of Richard and Nancy's disgrace had reached him all the way in Philadelphia.

The damned story would not die. The slaves wouldn't let it. And every white man in Virginia who ever resented the haughty Randolphs called for justice. By the time April wildflowers were in bloom at Monticello, Richard sat in a Cumberland County jail, accused of fathering a child on his wife's sister and murdering the babe.

And I was called to testify.

Chapter Twenty-one

THE CUMBERLAND COURTHOUSE WAS PACKED, cheek to jowl, between old wooden walls. "Jefferson's daughter," someone said as I entered, and the courtroom erupted, every gawker and gossip-monger in the county craning their necks to get a better look.

"Mrs. Randolph!" someone else cried, but beneath the white satin bow and broad rim of my fashionable hat, I kept my eyes on the magistrates—sixteen men in powdered wigs in whose hands the fate of my family's reputation now resided.

I made my way through the crowd with the gliding gait I had learned at the Court of Versailles, my skirts swishing, white lace upon blue-ruffled petticoat, while whispers flew from one row of wooden benches to the next.

Is her gown from Paris?

She's wearing a revolutionary cockade!

What will she say?

I knew the lawyers for the defense. The fire-breathing Patrick Henry and the grim-faced John Marshall. Federalists. Both men nodded to me respectfully, as if they thought I didn't know them to be my father's enemies. As if those glory-seeking creatures thought to convince me, for even one moment, that they wouldn't use whatever happened in the trial to tarnish my father in the papers if they could.

I smiled serenely as I was called to stand beneath the drape of red, white, and blue—the colors of both beloved flags I'd seen waved to champion the cause of freedom. Pushing artfully coiffed copper ringlets of hair from my face, I looked out into a crowd of old Virginia gentry in fine coats and breeches, frontier planters wearing hunting shirts and homespun, and housewives in mobcaps and bonnets.

Some were friendly. Others were eager to see the Randolphs fall.

Offered a leather-bound Bible on which to swear, I was informed that the charge was murder. A fact I knew all too well. Murder of an infant, punishable by death. As my hand hovered above the Bible, I glanced at the accused. My sister-in-law and her vile seducer. Richard looked smug, but Nancy trembled.

Beneath my gloved hand I felt the warmth of the leather. If ever there was a time to repair my breach with God, I thought, it was now. So I swore my sacred and solemn oath to tell the truth.

Then I thought of the promise I had made to my mother to care for my father always. I thought of the sacrifices I'd made toward that end. A stain on Tom would be a stain on my father's name, too. A stain on all of us.

"It was gum guaiacum," I said, when put to question, my hand still upon the leather Bible. "That's what Nancy Randolph had been taking in her tea."

At the table for the defense, John Marshall didn't look up; he merely continued to scribble notes of the proceedings. His co-counsel, Patrick Henry, however, threw me a look that blazed with surprise.

Coming closer, Mr. Henry asked, "How could you *possibly* know this, Miss Jefferson?"

"Mrs. Randolph," I corrected. "I'm a married woman now."

He hadn't called me to testify at this hearing, after all, because he suspected I knew anything material. I hadn't been anywhere near the Harrison place when the wicked deed was allegedly done. I'd already told him this before the hearing, but he'd insisted on calling me anyway. These two Federalist lawyers had called me to perform at this spectacle for one reason, and one reason only—to embarrass my father. To connect the Jefferson name to this scandal by whatever means necessary, even while arguing on behalf of my Randolph kin.

They thought they were so clever. They thought they knew my father's weak spots. Maybe they did. But they didn't know me or mine. "You're asking how I know Nancy Randolph took gum guaiacum?"

I let my eyes slide past the old firebrand to settle upon my pale and trembling sister-in-law and the devil that brought us all to this state. Not Richard—though he, too, was a villain—but Colonel Randolph, whose indifference to his children had sent them fleeing his house. There the old buzzard stood, gouty and in ill health, doing nothing whatsoever to save his own daughter's life. And standing next to him was Gabriella Harvie, with a sweet smile on her face, as if she weren't half to blame for driving her stepdaughter to such peril.

Richard stood accused, but Nancy's life was at stake, too. Popular sentiment ran so strongly against them that the prisoner had to be taken to the jail under heavy guard. If this hearing went badly, he'd face the gallows, because murder was a capital offense. Adultery, fornication, incest, and bastardy were crimes, too, but I doubted anyone could remember the last time someone was prosecuted for those, even here in Virginia. No, it was the death of the baby that'd put Richard in his grave, and Nancy thereafter—for *she'd* be charged with infanticide, the only crime for which women were legally presumed guilty, rather than innocent.

Knowing this, I steeled myself. I made sure not to look at my tall, beautiful, but temperamental husband. And though each false word bit at the edge of my tongue with the sharp conviction of the guillotine, I let the blade fly. "The reason I know Nancy Randolph took gum guaiacum . . . is because I gave it to her."

A collective intake of breath punctuated a chorus of shocked murmurs that echoed from one side of the courtroom to the other. All sixteen magistrates leaned in closer to hear my words, the curls of their powdered wigs bobbing as they stared. Even the unflappable John Marshall looked up from his scroll, one eye twitching.

Patrick Henry's jowls reddened. "You mean to say—do you mean to say—Miss Jefferson—"

"Mrs. Randolph."

The fire breather advanced. "Are you telling this court that you provided an *abortifacient* to your sister-in-law?"

Without lowering my gaze, I nodded. "Yes, I did."

The prosecutor was suddenly on his feet. "Do you know what you're saying, woman? It is your testimony that you knowingly aided and abetted Nancy Randolph in ridding herself of a bastard child by giving her a dangerous medicine to produce an abortion?"

Inside, I was all atremble, but I somehow kept my voice steady and calm. *You're a Jefferson,* I thought, as if to spite Colonel Randolph. *Sunny disposition, but ice water in your veins.* "No sir, I'm not confessing to a crime. In truth, I hadn't the slightest notion that Nancy could've been with child, though, obviously, I suspect it now."

At my words, Patrick Henry couldn't recover swiftly enough. It was John Marshall whose cool question cut through the crowded courtroom. "If you had no notion that Nancy Randolph might be with child, why did you supply her with the gum?"

That was the question I'd needed someone to ask, and I wanted to pat Mr. Marshall on the head like a good dog for asking it. "I gave her the gum because I know it is an excellent medicine for colic. So when my sister-in-law complained of colic—you know, Nancy has been afflicted with colic as long as I've known her—"

The judges looked impatient with my aside, but I saw hatted heads nod amongst the spectators. I'd laid my ground over a hundred teacups these past weeks, sighing of Nancy's delicate stomach. Was there a soul in Virginia who wouldn't swear she'd always had colic? Not after the seeds I'd sewn.

"She's delicate that way," I said. "It runs in the family. So when I visited a few weeks before the incident, I added some of the resin to her tea and encouraged her to avail herself of it whenever she felt her pains coming on."

Nancy went even paler at my story, shock and confusion warring in her expression. Meanwhile, Mr. Marshall was quick to seize upon my testimony. "Did the defendant, Richard Randolph, know that you provided such medicine to the women in his household?"

I gave a disdainful sniff. "Womanly troubles are hardly the sort of thing a gentlewoman of Virginia discusses with menfolk . . . unless, of course, she's dragged from hearth and home to talk about it before the whole county."

I heard a chuckle in the audience, followed by another. I'd been a little tart, but not *too* tart. They were charmed by me, I hoped.

Marshall leaned forward. "Is that why you didn't mention it before now?"

Acutely aware that my husband was in this courtroom, no doubt burning a hole in me with his dark eyes, I replied, "I hadn't thought of it before now. I came here believing the accusation was against *Richard* for some criminal mischief. But when I heard witnesses blaming Nancy for taking an elixir, that's when I remembered the gum."

I don't think I fooled the owlish Mr. Marshall, but he wasn't about to lose a case by contradicting me. I'd given him the bait. Now it was up to the illustrious lawyers for the defense. I'd provided all the evidence they should need to persuade the magistrates that even if Nancy had been delivered of a child, it was likely stillborn—its death an accident, not murder.

But would anyone believe me?

~~~

"*NOT GUILTY,*" CAME THE VERDICT.

Richard let out a triumphant cry, while Nancy's knees nearly buckled underneath her. Some people cried, "Shame, shame!"

Not at Richard, but at his accusers, many of whom were slaves, forbidden from testifying at all.

Given the glee with which Richard celebrated the verdict, hooting with no sense of decorum, he seemed to believe himself vindicated. His honor restored.

I knew better.

In the end, he'd been saved by women. By Nancy's willingness to sacrifice her own honor by writing that letter, by my willingness to lie, and even by his poor betrayed wife.

Judy had stayed by his side, insisting to the court that her husband and her sister were innocent. What other option did she have? She couldn't let him die. Neither could she leave him and go back to her father, even if Colonel Randolph would've had her back. She was Richard Randolph's wife and could never be separated from him. His fate was her fate. If he was ruined, so was she. So if she had to *pretend* her husband had no carnal knowledge of her sister, then that's what she'd do.

I felt so sorry for Judy, betrayed once already by her husband and her own sister. Sorrier, still, when Richard insisted that Nancy return with them to Bizarre. For a moment I feared that my husband would rush upon Nancy and tear her away from her lover. Or, much worse, that he'd descend upon Richard and dash his head open on the cobblestones. But in spite of all the rage brewing in him, my husband kept his silence, a thing more galling to him than perhaps any other indignity of his life.

And I was so unutterably proud of him, though I remained more than a little frightened of his reaction to what I'd done. Nancy never thanked me for it. Never spared me a glance. I supposed it was because she knew perfectly well the judgment she'd see in my eyes—for she'd already seen it, that night in the darkness of Bizarre's kitchen. For my husband's sake, I'd saved her life, but I knew they were guilty. I knew not only that they were guilty, but also that only a small part of the world would be influenced by the decision of the court.

Nevertheless, we watched Tom's disgraced sister climb into

Richard's phaeton and drive off with him, either too stupid, or too deluded, to realize that she ought to be chastened to her soul by the entire sordid debacle.

In our carriage back home, Tom quietly said, "They'd have strung my sister up."

"Yes," I replied, nervously wetting my lips.

His gaze burned into the side of my face. "They would've strung her up—if not for you."

"Yes," I said, again, swallowing hard.

This dark man of savage impulses stared so hard I felt on the precipice of something awful. But then his voice lowered to a whisper. "I suppose, then, it's good you remembered the gum."

I turned to him but wasn't able to meet his eyes. "I wish I'd remembered it sooner."

He tilted his dark head of hair against the cushion as we rattled down the road. He was tired, wrung out from the whole ordeal. But just when I thought he'd fallen asleep, he said, "I pray I never hear another word about it."

⁓

AT SUMMER'S END, Papa burst in the front door of Monticello, my little sister all but yipping at his heels with the dogs she'd left behind. After patting their ears and kissing their heads, Polly ran to me, threw her arms around my waist, and hugged me so tight I could scarcely breathe.

I couldn't get enough of looking at her. During her time with Papa in Philadelphia, she'd somehow transformed into a beautiful girl of fifteen with a heart-shaped face, bones like a bird, and a tiny waist that would be the envy of every woman in Virginia. My father shook Tom's hand, and Tom managed to smile—he'd been dreadfully ill that summer, as though the family scandal had sickened him to the core. But at his smile, my father's return, and Polly's embrace, I felt whole again.

Everything was right. Safe in the warm glow of my father's

love, I hadn't the faintest urge to tell him anything more than must be told about the recent unpleasantness.

Meanwhile Sally, who hung back in the hall, twisted her hands anxiously, as if it took a real effort not to run to Papa, too. Papa noticed her, I was sure, but turned away as he settled into his favorite chair in the parlor and said, "I have news. . . ."

President Washington had personally asked him not to resign as secretary of state, but he felt that his term would soon come to an end. First, however, he hoped to negotiate for the release of Lafayette from prison.

Polly piped up with, "Hopefully Mr. Short can help. He's been appointed minister to the Netherlands, but he's had contact with Lafayette."

The sudden pain William's name caused caught me entirely unawares. I'd forbidden myself to think of him. I was a wife and mother and I loved my little family. I *loved* Tom. But I'd never told my husband about William, and the unexpected mention of him now, with Tom sitting close beside me, holding my hand, made me acutely aware of the lie of omission. I nearly burned with it.

But my curiosity pricked at me even more sharply. Affecting nonchalance, I asked, "I thought Mr. Short was to be the minister of France."

"That post went to Gouverneur Morris," my father replied. "Some say it's for the best. Mr. Short has, after all, become disenchanted with Paris since the king and the Duke de la Rochefoucauld were executed."

The duke, much like Lafayette, had helped give birth to France's constitution. Why was the revolution now eating its fathers? I wondered if such a thing could happen here.

Polly said, "After the duke was executed, Mr. Short was quite frantic for the safety of the widowed duchess. He proposed marriage to her, to rescue her from the violence in France, but she refused him."

I doubted that William's motives in proposing marriage were

entirely altruistic, as I'd heard too many rumors of his love for Rosalie. But at this news, I was surprised to feel more sadness than jealousy. More pity than bitterness. I felt sorrow that William Short had twice tried to marry a woman, and twice been refused.

The conversation turned to the latest conflict between Papa and his nemesis, Mr. Hamilton, but my thoughts stayed with poor William. He'd wanted nothing more than a wife and children and to follow in my father's footsteps. He'd wanted it desperately. And yet, nearly four years had passed since I left him in Paris, and he still had no wife, no family, nor even my father's post in France, where he'd made his career.

But he *had* been made the minister to the Netherlands. That had to have pleased him. He'd wanted to be of both service and consequence to his country, and he was. I was glad for him, and I pushed down the treacherous, unworthy part of me that imagined myself the wife of an ambassador, strolling with my parasol through the streets of The Hague, wearing fine gowns, having my hair done at my toilette before going down to entertain at a dinner table set with the finest silver. . . .

That evening I strolled with Papa at Monticello. My arm looped through his, we made our way down the pebbled walkway along the vegetable garden as the sun went down. The vibrant hues of autumn stretched out for many miles in every direction, Papa's mountain providing an unmatched vista of the new country unfolding below. We walked for many long minutes in silence.

"How are you, dear Patsy?" he finally asked, peering down at me.

Because I worried he'd see in my expression my troubles— the scandals, the rift with Tom's family, Tom's long illness, our debts—I plastered on a smile. "I'm well, Papa. Even better now that you're home."

He leaned into me and winked. "Always my brave girl, aren't you?"

"I try." In truth, I felt ridiculously close to tears in that moment and had to look away. Perhaps it was how small I felt beside him, or the knowing look in his eyes, or the relief that we were all together again. "It will be nice when you can stay for good."

"I desire very much to exchange the labor, envy, and malice of public life for ease, domestic occupation, love, and society. Here, where I may once more be happy with you."

The words lifted an unseen burden from my shoulders. "Soon, Papa?"

"Soon," he said.

The conversation marked the beginning of a period of happiness at Monticello. We celebrated my twenty-second birthday in grand style, with a fine dinner, and a chorus sung round my harpsichord while I played. Papa lavished love on his little grandchildren; it wasn't unusual to find him on the floor of the parlor, telling stories and playing at games with Ann and cooing over Jeff. All of us reveled in the bounty of the season, everyone healthy and happy, until the cold of November struck with bad tidings.

Holding a letter, my husband said, "My father is dying."

He gave immediate orders to fetch his horse, then took my hand. "I must ride to Tuckahoe without delay. Follow as soon as you can with the children."

"Of course. As quickly as I can." Not knowing if I should feel grief or relief at the news that the main source of my husband's longtime suffering might soon leave us forevermore, I threw my arms around Tom's neck. "Ride safely."

He grasped my face, kissed me, and departed.

Tom wanted us to hurry, but my maid was so slow and sullen that I nearly shouted at her. Thankfully, Sally took the baby, shooing my maid away before I lost my temper. "Hush now," Sally said to my baby son. Then to me, she said, "If you like, I'll go on with you to Tuckahoe, Miss Patsy. Lay some flowers on my baby's grave before the snows come."

It would only be right, I thought, so I nodded. Besides, she'd keep out of the way at Tuckahoe, where the Randolphs were surely set to feud again. Oh, I never *really* worried that the old man was truly dying. I was sure he was entirely too mean to die. This latest crisis was almost assuredly another bit of Randolph theatrics.

So I was stunned when, after more than a day's travel, we rolled up the long tree-lined drive to Tuckahoe and my husband met us at the gate, overwrought. "He's dead, Patsy. He's dead!"

"Oh, Tom," I said, clutching his hand.

He lowered his head, tears welling in his eyes. "I was too late. Rode as hard as I could, but when I got here John Harvie was in the door, telling me I didn't get here in time."

Seeing my husband in such a state, Sally disappeared somewhere with my children, for which I was enormously grateful. I went into the house with Tom, into the very room where the Randolph book of ancestry resided, with its drawings and coats of arms. And the moment we were alone behind closed doors, Tom went to his knees, burying his face in my belly, letting me stroke his hair while he sobbed.

My heart broke for Tom, who had now lost both a mother and a father in only a handful of years. We'd known, of course, that one day it'd come to pass that we'd be master and mistress of Tuckahoe. But neither of us had desired it, nor expected it, so soon. Even as much as I loathed that old man, I hadn't wished death on him.

At only twenty-five years old, my husband had already taken on the role of patriarch—that's why he'd been so upset about his sister's scandal. As the eldest son, his younger siblings already looked to him for guidance, but now they'd look to Tom for everything. And I couldn't begrudge him his torrent of grief in light of the burdens that were now his to bear.

Once spent of his tears, Tom asked if I'd take on the education of the children. "My sisters look up to you, Patsy. Your learning in France will stand them in good stead. Maybe Nancy will come back to help so she can have a life with her family even if no decent man will have her now."

My throat swelled with emotion. "Of course I will, Tom. I'll do whatever you need me to. And with utter devotion." I meant it with all my heart, because I understood that with Colonel Randolph's death, our lives would never be the same. We'd have to move to Tuckahoe, lock, stock, and barrel. We'd have to make this bleak plantation, and all its slaves, support the whole family—all Colonel Randolph's children, and his widow, too. We'd have to mend the quarrels with Gabriella and reconcile Tom's unmarried sisters to living under one roof again, as family ought to.

I'd have to help him do that. I'd have to be more loving to my husband and his family than ever before. Which was why when I went down the next morning and discovered the widow presiding over the sitting room in fine black silks, I resolved to be kind to her. She'd driven my husband's sisters away—even the littlest ones, who had lived with us at Monticello ever since. But I was determined to forget that now.

Bleary-eyed after a night of troubled sleep, I sat beside Gabriella and said, "You have my sympathies in your loss, and—"

"Colonel Randolph is with God now," she interrupted, standing up and walking to the window.

I rose to follow her, imagining she must be frightened, widowed and with two babes, now at the mercy of my husband for her upkeep. "You mustn't worry about anything. Now is a time for family to come together. Please let me know what I can do to ease your time of mourning."

Very calmly, Gabriella traced a finger over the windowpane where Nancy had carved the date of her mother's death. "You think of me as family?"

I hadn't. Not truly. But I was resolved, henceforth, to do so. "From this day forward—"

She spun to face me. "Don't bother. It won't be long before I remarry. I have my looks, two babies to prove I'm fertile, a respected family name, and a fortune to bestow."

I supposed there were advantages to being the daughter of John Harvie, but to say such things while her husband was only a few hours dead . . . well, I excused it as the shock of her loss. "Just know that you'll always be welcome here at Tuckahoe. It's your home."

She gave an amused snort. "*I* will be welcome here, of course."

It was a strange remark, but I dismissed it. And I thought it was merely her father's natural aristocratic sense of command that made him strut about the place, giving commands to the slaves at Tuckahoe as if it were his own plantation. None of this went down easy with Tom or his brothers.

And, adding to the tension, the Randolphs of Bizarre arrived for the burial the next day. Judith, Nancy, and Richard all arrived in one carriage. For his safety, I suppose Richard counted upon the solemnity of the occasion, and the protection of his women-folk, as always. Having escaped justice—though not the censure of all right-thinking Virginians—he obviously felt free to go in public with his lover on one arm and his wife on the other.

But whereas Nancy and Richard were unrepentant, the scandal had obviously taken its toll on poor Judy and her baby son, who had been afflicted with deafness. Some said it was God's punishment for Richard's crimes. I myself sometimes worried about God's vengeance, having broken my promise to enter his nunnery and having sworn falsely upon a Bible at court. But would God really visit the crimes of the father onto his child? Judy must've thought so, because she wore her mourning clothes as if she might never wear any others, clinging to her Bible, praying more devoutly than a nun.

Draped in expensive black lace that made her an even prettier widow than she'd been a bride, Gabriella leaned in at the grave site and whispered to me, "He's thinking of divorcing her, you know."

"What?" I asked, sure that I'd misheard.

"Richard," Gabriella replied, impatiently. "He's been consulting a lawyer in Richmond about the possibility of divorce and showering his whore with little gifts. I suppose he means to switch sisters."

I'd never known anyone who'd been divorced. Not even at the convent in Paris, where I'd met women who had run away from their husband and wanted annulments, but never divorce. I didn't even think it was possible in Virginia. Especially not to divorce one sister and take the other as a wife! "Poor Judith," I breathed.

No wonder she was clinging to her Bible, thumbing the pages, murmuring a prayer by her father's grave site that seemed more desperate than devotional. And while we waited on the officiant, my husband stooped beside his mother's unkempt grave site and began to clear the weeds with his bare hands. "Couldn't someone be bothered to tend her grave?" he muttered, and I had to put a hand to his shoulder to silence him. But his sisters overheard and cast looks of blame at Gabriella.

I kept my silence because, even as I tried to remember this was my family now, I didn't understand the Randolphs. A short time later, listening to the officiant praise a man I'd never thought of as any sort of father, my eyes drifted to the edge of the woods where I saw Sally Hemings standing by a field of wildflowers, mourning for her dead son—a little boy who, like her, was my family in truth.

I was still thinking about her—worrying for her—after we'd returned to the house for tea while the men closeted themselves together to go over Colonel Randolph's will in the great hall.

All at once Tom burst out of the arched double-doors, looking as if he'd been struck with a hammer like a hog at the slaughter. Without a word, he walked right out of the back door of the house, staggering toward the river, like a man come unmoored from his senses.

"Tom!" I cried, hurrying after him. I had no idea where he was going as he then changed his path and circled the house. He never turned when I called his name. Holding my skirts in both hands, tromping through autumn leaves, I chased after him, realizing that we'd come again to the little white schoolhouse my grandfather built when he'd presided here at Tuckahoe.

All at once, Tom whirled and pulled me up the stairs and inside. "It's my fault. My fault for not staying at Varina."

"What's your fault?" I asked, looking into his bleak eyes.

"John Harvie says that if I'd stayed at Varina, the plantation my father gave me, I'd have been close by at the end."

"Oh, Tom, no," I said, thinking it extraordinarily cruel for someone to say such a thing to a grieving son. "You rode out the *moment* you heard your father was ill. You rode like a madman to get to his side. You can't think—"

"I was too far away," Tom broke in. "If I'd been at Varina, I'd have been at his bedside. And that's why . . ." He shuddered.

A sense of dread washed over me. "That's why *what*?"

"That's why he changed his will!"

My stomach clenched. "What can you mean?"

"I'm not the heir to Tuckahoe," Tom said, his eyes dropping from mine, as if he couldn't bear the shame. "He took from me my patrimony as eldest son and gave it to the new boy. He gave Gabriella's son everything. My name, my father, my ancestral home. As if in my twenty-five years on this earth, I was never anything to him. And now I'm *nothing*, Patsy. He's left me with nothing."

Chapter Twenty-two

THE MAGNITUDE OF THE DISASTER—both emotional and financial—was too much to take in. "That can't be true," I said, my head spinning as I grappled with all this would mean for us.

"It is true," Tom said, too weary to stand. Sinking down onto the schoolmaster's desk, he said, "My father rewrote his will in his last hours. He chose to spite me with his very last breaths."

Suddenly, Gabriella's strange remarks at breakfast took on a new light. No doubt Colonel Randolph's young widow and her father hovered like buzzards over the mean old bastard to the last. They'd stolen Tom's patrimony, but I'd have to put a more charitable spin on it, because Tom looked on the verge of shattering to pieces.

Regardless of the inheritance, my husband would be guardian over the children and steward of the estate. Much as my grandfather had been when he built this schoolhouse. That was the custom, and Tom could find some solace in that. "Tom, I'm sure your father was only worried the child would have nothing. That boy isn't even two years old and will need us to look after him and his mother. It'll be nearly twenty years before he comes into his inheritance, and with your stewardship at Tuckahoe—"

"You don't understand," Tom said, sharply. "I won't *have* a stewardship at Tuckahoe. I meant what I said. I've lost my ancestral home. Not just the profits and enjoyment of it. But everything. *John Harvie* was named guardian over the younger children."

I gasped in outrage and insult, my arms hugging my stomach

against the sudden burning ache that settled there. Never mind the money; how could Colonel Randolph have entrusted his children into the care of the Harvies? And I was suddenly struck with fear that little Jenny, who had been living with us for years now, might be ripped away. "That cannot be true."

Tom gripped the edge of the table so hard the wood creaked. "You think I'd make it up? Until the boy comes of age, Harvie will be master of Tuckahoe, not me. My mother's children have no place here any longer." My husband laughed bitterly. "But my brother and I *do* have the singular honor of executing my father's estate."

Which meant that Colonel Randolph had left my husband to settle his debts.

My throat tightened and my heart raced, sending my head into a spin. I pressed a hand to my forehead. That malevolent old rotter said my Jefferson blood ran cold. But nothing could have been colder than this. Colonel Randolph hadn't simply impoverished us, but aimed to rip Tom's sisters away from us and saddle us with costs and expenses besides.

He was as petty a tyrant as any king who'd ever lived, and the most un-Christian feelings welled up inside me such that I wanted to make the trip to the cemetery just to spit on Colonel Randolph's freshly dug grave.

But my fears, disappointment, and anger were nothing in the face of Tom's loss. "I—I tried to obey him," Tom murmured through bloodless lips. "Tried to please him when I could. You saw that. I tried to make of myself something he might be proud of, but I didn't *always* obey and I never could find a way to please him no matter how hard I tried. Even so, I never thought he could hate me. What did I do to make him hate me so?"

Reaching for my husband's face—which was somehow even more beautiful in its anguish—I cradled his cheeks in my hands. "Your father didn't hate you." It was a lie, but I'd told others and for lesser cause. To protect my husband from this pain, I'd tell this lie and a hundred others. "No father could ever hate his son, and especially not you. Not a learned, hardworking, loving, and lovable son like you."

"I'm not lovable, Patsy." Tom clutched at my arms. "Never have been."

"You *are*." I brought my lips to his brow, like I was soothing a babe.

But he drew back with a shudder. "You know better than anyone that I'm not worthy of love. You've always held yourself back because you see what's in me—this darkness. This melancholy and temper that slips its reins. I think my father must've seen it, too. Must've known that something was broken in me, like dogs know there's something wrong with a pup."

At the sight of tears in his reddened, swollen eyes, I brought my forehead to touch his, whispering, nose to nose. "There's nothing wrong with you, Tom Randolph."

A sob escaped him. "Then why would my father do such a thing to me?"

For spite, I thought. But it wouldn't help Tom to know his father was a spiteful worm, lower than dirt. When a man knows that he's come from nothing he may never aspire to better. So I said, "Your father was very ill. To do such a thing, in the end, he must've been quite out of his senses."

A spark of hope lit in Tom's eyes. "Do you think so?"

I nodded, firmly. Convincing myself as much as him. "I do. Why, any right-minded person might suspect your father's widow stood over the bed and held the pen in the dying man's hand."

I was sowing discord amongst the living when it was the dead who was to blame, yet, in my estimation, the Harvies had stolen my children's birthright, and I wasn't apt to be charitable.

Meanwhile, Tom choked back another sob. "I should've been here. I should've been here sooner."

I was to blame for that. I was the one who hated Varina. I'd hounded him to move to my father's mountain, thinking it was the best place for my children. Was I wrong to have done it? "You went to him the moment you heard," I reminded him, stroking his hair, still marveling at the thickness of it between my fingers.

Since the day Tom struck me, I hadn't felt the stirrings of arousal and desire, so I was surprised to feel them now, stronger than ever. Tom was so vulnerable that I remembered how sweet he could be. How much pleasure we'd found in one another. How he'd driven away my pain and heartbreak with the sheer force of his desire.

Now I wanted to do the same for him.

He'd accused me of holding myself back from him, and I had. There still seemed something too dangerous in admitting that I loved him, so I tried to show him, kissing him with a brazenness I'd never dared before.

At my kiss, Tom tugged me closer and pressed his mouth on mine with a mad, desperate urgency. The abandoned schoolhouse was hardly the place a gentleman ought to make love to his wife. But it'd been here in this very schoolhouse that he'd asked me to marry him, and the emotions of the moment ran so high that I cared nothing for propriety. I welcomed my husband's roaming hands and plundering mouth, wanting him to find in me some balm for his pain. And when my hands opened his shirt and my palms skidded down his chest, I took deep satisfaction in the way he groaned, as if my touch was a mercy.

"You're all I have, Patsy," he whispered. "All I have now . . ."

THAT WINTER, my father limped home from his battles with the secretary of the treasury, battered and bruised in spirit, desiring to give up the work of government forever. He had resigned and retired.

It was, of course, what my sister and I wanted most.

We wanted our father home. We didn't want to share him with the world anymore, and we both believed he'd be happier as the simple gentleman farmer he professed to be.

But when Papa returned to Monticello, it wasn't with the high spirits of a man finally freed from public duty. Oh, he nattered excitedly about the price of wheat and molasses, sheep and potatoes, and seemed to be eager for the spring thaw. But I knew him too well not to notice the tension leaking out the edges of his daily routine.

On his third day home, he and Polly came in from a ride, and Sally Hemings was there in an instant, eager to attend him. I suppose that after years of living under Tom's authority while steering clear of me, Sally was as grateful as I was for Papa's return as unquestioned master of the plantation.

Perhaps she was also eager to repair whatever had been ruptured between them, which had made her status on the plantation uncertain. But when Sally reached for my father's coat, he nearly jolted at the brush of her fingers at his neck. And when she stooped to take his muddy riding boots, Papa stopped her. "That's all right, Sally. I'll do it."

Her lower lip wobbled and she bolted away, disappearing somewhere into the recesses of the house.

"What the devil was that about?" The look of bewilderment on my father's face might've been comical were the cause for Sally's distress not so plainly obvious.

"She's a woman who wants to please you," Polly said, her cheeks pink with the cold. "Can't you see that, Papa?"

"She does please me," he protested, looking between us. "I found no fault in her. I said nothing harsh whatsoever."

My sister put a hand on her hip, addressing my father as no one else dared. "You didn't have to say it, Papa. You don't let her do anything for you. Not even pour your tea."

My father gave a little snort. Then, as if to make us forget the scene with Sally, he asked me, "Isn't Mr. Randolph coming down?"

"Tom's not hungry." Or at least, that's what he said whenever I tried to take something up to him. He'd taken ill after his father's death and was now unable, or unwilling, to rise from our bed. But it was an erratic illness.

One day, Tom would be so low in spirits he couldn't muster the energy to rise and shave his own cheek. The next day, he'd be up before dawn working on threshing machines at such a fevered pace he'd forget to come to bed entirely. It'd been that way for weeks.

I worried for him.

Since he wasn't hungry, I had some strong tea sent up with white sugar—some of the few goods that could still be bought with cash, for the smallpox outbreak and want of commerce had rendered the whole of Virginia a place of only barter and trade.

But when he refused it, I went up myself to coax him. "At least drink a little tea, Tom. Then maybe you'll want supper with us tonight. Asparagus has finally come to our table and pairs nicely with eggs."

The toll on him was evident; it hollowed out his beauty and made his eyes sink into his head. "I can't keep anything down," Tom insisted, bunching the quilt under his chin and turning away toward the wall. When he did, I saw his ribs beneath the broad expanse of his muscular back. He was wasting away while trying to make sense of who he was if he wasn't his father's heir.

Wasting away to the nothing he feared he'd become.

And I didn't know what I could say, or do, to help him.

When I went back down, my father asked, "Is he feeling any better?" I gave a quick, distressed shake of my head and Papa frowned. "You know that you're both welcome to stay here at Monticello as long as you like."

"We're so grateful," I replied, wishing that my husband could see that even if his own father had never valued him, mine did. But Monticello wasn't Tuckahoe. My husband had been hurt and humiliated by his father's last wishes. What Tom wanted now was to make his own lands profitable, because the longer he lived in another man's house and managed another man's farm, the more he doubted his worth as a man.

My father had his own solution for the problem. "There's an opening for justice of the peace; Tom should run. It'll be an honor and a distraction. He'll have more time for studying the law if he puts off leaving. Besides, it's been a great comfort having you both here to look after my farm, and now that I'm in a position to enjoy Monticello, who else can I share it with?"

My father had no sons to give it to, that's what he meant. Not by blood. Not even Sally's dead boy. And I was reminded again of just how much my father's promise never to remarry had cost him. My mother had extracted that from him to fend off women like Gabriella Harvie. And my father had given his word without hesitation, even though it now left him without an heir, and fearful of his legacy.

But I had given him a grandson. A namesake. Jeff. My thriving baby boy. And I hoped I was about to give him another. Touching the small swell of my belly, I said, "Perhaps my husband will be persuaded to stay when he learns that I may be in a delicate condition."

Papa's face lit up. "Why, that's wonderful, Patsy. A baby is just the thing to give a man a renewed sense of purpose." Then I watched the direction of Papa's eyes as they settled on Sally in the far room, where she was making noise by scrubbing the floor on her hands and knees like my mother used to do. He watched her with longing, his throat bobbing with every bounce of her earrings as she worked. "Do the floors really need scrubbing?"

"Sally must think so." When it came to the servants, I never had to ask Sally or Mammy Ursula to do anything. But whereas Mammy ruled over the other slaves like a queen who must be obeyed, Sally just quietly claimed dominion over whatever she felt needed to be done.

And in her unhappiness, I suppose she'd decided the floor needed scrubbing.

Papa murmured, "When we left Paris, I promised never to work her hard. That's why I don't ask her to tend me." It was, I thought, a startling dishonesty, for tending to him was the easiest work on the plantation. Then he added, "Your sister's right about women. Even while employed in drudgery, some bit of ribbon, ear bob, or necklace, or something of the kind will show that the desire of pleasing is never suspended in them . . . they're formed by nature for attentions, not for hard labor."

It was none of my affair. Truly, it wasn't. But at a loss as to how to fix everything else that had gone so wrong for the people I loved, I wanted to fix just this one thing. There was no undoing what had passed between my father and Sally, but I was convinced that no good could come of their continued estrangement.

"Why, Papa—you've just reminded me that I meant to buy some ribbon from Mr. Bell's store. He's been a good friend while you've been away. He treats Sally's sister kindly."

"Pleased to hear it," my father said, eyes still far away.

"People talk, of course, about how he can possibly keep a former slave as his lady, but since he holds no public office, society seems content to let him live as he pleases."

My father, who *no longer* held public office, slowly lifted his eyes to mine, seeking something in my gaze. Redemption, forgiveness, or permission. I wasn't sure which. But whatever he wanted, I was happy to give. I ought to have made my peace with his relationship with Sally long ago. Perhaps the moment Sally had chosen to return with him to Virginia. "Would you like me to bring back some papers?"

"What?" he asked, his voice thick with emotion.

"From Mr. Bell's store," I replied. "I'm sure there's news from the capital . . . then again, you're free from public business now, aren't you?"

"Indeed." A dim light grew behind his eyes. "I believe I'll stop taking newspapers altogether."

From that day forward, things changed at Monticello.

Instead of writing ten or twelve letters a day, as was Papa's habit for as long as I could remember, he now put his correspondence aside and replied only on rainy days. He told us—and anyone who would listen—that he was happy to have left the service of his country into abler hands. He styled himself a simple farmer, the master of his plantation and everyone on it.

Now, it's true that I never saw Papa and Sally strolling in the fields, hand in hand. Never saw them share a kiss. He certainly didn't squire her around town to shop for dresses, and if he gave her jewelry, she never flaunted it. But after that day, no one but Sally was ever allowed to tend his chambers. She had dominion over his most private places and possessions. And I was grateful my father found solace, comfort, and companionship in a woman so much better than Gabriella Harvie.

Sally would never steal my father's name, love, or fortune. I believed that she would never, and *could* never, be the cause of harm to my family. And so I raised no objection to the fact he left her spending money in a drawer, to do with as she liked. Nor did I mind that she was left to her own authority about the plantation. Within a year, she was again with child. A fact that seemed to satisfy—and even embolden—the brothers Hemings.

James still earned a wage as he'd become accustomed but considered himself free as soon as he trained up his replacement in our kitchens. And Bob Hemings pressed for his freedom, too. Like almost all the Hemingses, Bob was a bright mulatto who sometimes passed as white, making it easier for him to travel freely when he had the yen. For years now, Papa had let him come and go as he pleased, and maybe that's why Papa reacted to Bob's request for emancipation as a personal rebuke.

"He's already a free man in all but name," Papa groused.

I was a little vexed that my father, who had penned so many lines about liberty, might be surprised a man might not be content with freedom *in all but name*. When Papa grudgingly granted Bob's request, I resolved to make peace in that quarter if I could.

Because at long last, we had my father happy and contented at home. And we aimed to keep him there.

Chapter Twenty-three

Monticello, 27 April 1795
From Thomas Jefferson to James Madison

My retirement from office had been meant from all office high or low, without exception . . . the little spice of ambition, which I had in my younger days, has long since evaporated, and I set less store in a posthumous than present name.

TWO YEARS AFTER MY FATHER wrote these words, he lost the election for the presidency of the United States. My sister and I believed this to be an utter calamity, but not because he had lost the presidency. It was a calamity because, through a quirk in our system, having won the second highest number of votes, he would now be obliged to serve as vice president to John Adams—the very man he'd run against, and whose political sentiments he opposed.

We urged him to refuse the office for fear he'd again be the subject of scrutiny, censure, and newspaper attack. He'd again have to leave his plantation and his people and his family. And this time, he wouldn't even have James to look after him, for Sally's brother had since quit the plantation with his freedom to travel the world.

Sally didn't like the idea of my father returning to public office any better than we did. The three of us sulked, as if the combined weight of his womenfolk's displeasure might bring my strong father to his knees.

But in the end, Papa said he feared to weaken our fledgling system of government by refusing the office, and he wouldn't be moved on this point.

In all, my father's retirement had lasted only two eventful years during which it seemed every friend of liberty we'd known in France was either dead, jailed, or in exile. And we'd been consumed with tumult and tragedies closer to home. Polly fell through the rotting floorboards into the cellar of my father's half-demolished house, upon which he'd begun more ambitious renovations. Miraculously, there wasn't a scrape on her, but others didn't fare as well. At Bizarre, Richard Randolph died, quite suddenly, of some mysterious ailment, leaving Judith and Nancy in dire straits.

And I lost a child—a little angel named Ellen, not even a year old.

She had apple cheeks and the longest toes of any baby I ever saw. I held her in my arms as she struggled for her last little gasps through lips tinged with blue. And when she closed her eyes for the last time—the tiny veins beneath her porcelain skin pulsing once, twice, then no more—the grief was unfathomable. The pain was like a burr, the kind that only digs deeper when you try to pluck free of it. So I just let the pain dig into me deep, where I keep it to this day, since I couldn't keep my baby girl.

But after we buried her, the grief put Tom into a nearly hopeless state. My husband was struggling with what the doctors called a nervous condition. He took mineral water at the hot springs, but I knew it'd do no good. After all, no magic elixir was going to transform him into the master of Tuckahoe, and we could never be happy at Varina, where we'd moved to build up Tom's only inheritance.

And oh, how I hated Varina.

Not because it was filled with memories of that first miserable summer we spent as newlyweds. Not because there weren't enough rooms for the children and our servants. No, I hated Varina because whenever Tom came home from overseeing the fields, he'd stand on the porch with a glass too-full of whiskey, his eyes on the blue horizon, as if he could *see* his father's malevolent ghost hovering over the childhood home at which we'd never again be welcome.

As if he sensed Colonel Randolph looking down on us, standing in judgment.

And I hurt for my husband. Truly, I did.

Tom seldom spoke of the lawsuit he was fighting with his father's creditors, but it weighed on him. My husband was likely to lose, which would saddle us with even more of Colonel Randolph's debt. I would've sold bloody Varina and left everything having to do with Colonel Randolph behind, but Tom couldn't stomach it, which meant that my husband's only hope of paying the mortgage was to get in a few good crops, and sell them at a profit—a nearly impossible feat, given British tariffs on our goods.

That's why I was so alarmed when Tom announced, "I'm going to stand for the state legislature."

He was standing on the porch, deep in his cups, so I wasn't entirely sure he meant it. And I didn't like the idea at all. Tom was a better farmer than most, but inconstant with his attention to his own plantations—always distracted on some errand for my father. It was so much worse now with Papa away in the capital. Polly had come to live with us at Varina, which meant Tom and I were both struggling to make a functioning household with our sisters and our little children underfoot. I didn't know how we'd manage it if Tom took on public duties besides. "What of . . . what of the farmsteads?"

My husband squinted. "Patsy, I've always wanted to serve in public office. That's why I went to Edinburgh. It's why I admire Mr. Jefferson so much. My father never thought I could do it. He wanted me *here*, digging in the dirt . . . but it's these little specks of land which prevent mental effort and accomplishment in youth."

My family had already suffered enough for public ambitions, but because I thought the source of my husband's recurring illness might be that he'd so long denied himself a political career, I forced myself to say, "I suppose the country needs good Republicans." Tom was no great revolutionary thinker, like my father, but he was intelligent and honorable. Two things I thought might put him in good standing with the public.

Which shows you just how much I still had to learn about politics.

Tom declared his candidacy. Unfortunately, he did little more than that. Maybe he thought he didn't need to; he had the Randolph name, after all, and the support of Thomas Jefferson, Virginia's favorite son. Hadn't my father just been elected to the vice presidency without campaigning for it?

But when it came to the state legislature, a presence was expected. Candidates were to go to the town square to press flesh and charm country voters over barrels of whiskey. When Tom ought to have been putting on his finery and practicing speeches and witty barbs, he decided upon another course altogether.

"There's a doctor in Charlottesville who will be administrating smallpox inoculations," Tom said. "I'm taking the children to have it done."

It always moved me that he was so intent on the welfare of our children, but smallpox also struck terror in my heart. "But they're so young."

"Best to do it while they're young," Tom said.

That had been my father's thinking, too. Unfortunately, a mother's heart is, of all things in nature, the least subject to reason. The idea of exposing my children to such a disorder made me perfectly miserable. Polly and I and our dearly departed little Lucy had made it through. Sally, too. But sometimes the treatment killed the patient, and knowing that made me clutch my babies tight against my skirts. "It takes some time—we can't leave them without a nurse to tend them. I'll have to go with you."

"I need you here at Varina," Tom insisted. "Someone's got to look after the girls."

His little sisters, he meant, including little Jenny, who was still with us now, as if she'd been our daughter to start with. His father hadn't left him the estate, but Tom had still taken on the responsibility of the family.

"I can look after everything," Polly broke in. "I'm eighteen now, Patsy. You can go watch over your children and I'll play mistress of Varina for a time."

Tom and I looked at my delicate little sister where she was indolently reclining upon a sofa in nothing but a slip of a gown, with all her chores undone. And the decision was made in one glance. Tom would take the children, and I'd stay behind.

On the appointed day that first week of April, my eyes filled with tears at the thought that when I said good-bye to my little angels, it might be for the last time. I consoled myself with the certain knowledge that Tom would be a tender and attentive nurse; he could be gruff with Jeff, but he was always sweetness itself with Ann. What I didn't expect was that he would tarry there with the doctor, studying the science of the thing, sitting at the bedside of his children on election day itself.

Tom never showed up in the town square.

Never slapped any backs. Never cracked open a barrel of whiskey. Never gave a speech. Never thanked his supporters—not even the local militiamen who came out to rally in my father's name. By the time I realized it—when a neighbor came riding up to the house in a cloud of dust to ask if something terrible had befallen my husband—Tom had already lost the election and looked like a sore, brooding loser to boot.

Not knowing what else to do, I hurriedly sat down at the table to scribble a letter to be read out to interested parties, explaining that my husband was tending to sick children. But it arrived too late to do any good, and the humiliating rumors spread like wildfire, such that they reached even my father in the capital, who was obliged to apologize on my husband's behalf.

When I finally heard Tom's wagon roll up that warm day, I grabbed up my skirts and raced out into the yard to scoop up my children, kissing them all over their faces in relief to see them alive. But Ann pressed shyly against my bodice, whispering, "My papa isn't well."

Tom was drunk. It was the middle of the day and he was drunk—so red-faced and staggering I wondered how he'd driven the horses. "Go," he barked at the children. "Get on in the house."

When they ran off, my husband put his finger in my face and drew near enough that I could smell whiskey on his breath. "You think you're so much above me, don't you, Patsy? All that *convent learning . . .*" Scarcely knowing what I'd done to anger him, I was struck by his sudden resemblance to his father. And while I stood there in bewilderment, winding my hands in my apron, he shouted, "Don't you *ever* apologize for me."

So he'd seen the letter I'd written to excuse his absence on election day. "I only thought—"

"Who are you to apologize for me? You're Mrs. Thomas Mann Randolph. That's who you are. You're the wife of a man who has been erased by a younger brother, rejected by the voters of Virginia, and can do nothing whatsoever right. You're *that* man's wife and that's *all* you are."

With that he shoved past me, leaving me to stare off in the horizon, where I, too, fancied I could see the shadow of Colonel Randolph. But I decided then and there that old tyrant could only haunt my husband.

Not me.

I *wasn't* just Mrs. Thomas Mann Randolph. I was first, foremost, and above all, Thomas Jefferson's daughter. So while Tom slept off his hangover, I packed up my sister and my children, and returned to Monticello.

Philadelphia, 8 June 1797
To Martha Jefferson Randolph from Thomas Jefferson

> *I receive with inexpressible pleasure the news of Jack's proposal of marriage to your sister. After your own happy establishment, which has given me an inestimable friend to whom I can leave the care of everything I love, the only anxiety I had remaining was to ensure Maria's happiness. If she had the whole earth free to choose a partner, she could not have done so more to my wishes. I now see our fireside formed into a group, no one member of which has a fiber in their composition which can ever produce any jarring or jealousies among us.*

"I do believe you're faking," I said to my limping sister, helping her with her stomacher. "If you don't stay still and let me finish dressing you, I'm going to tell everyone that you turned your weak ankle on purpose to force Jack Eppes to carry you over the threshold of your wedding chamber."

"I'm not that clever," my sister protested, radiant in her best gown, and blushing. "Besides, why would any bride willingly forgo dancing at her own wedding? It's not my fault that Papa's house is in perpetual disarray. Silly me for expecting there to be a stair under the door to step down onto!"

I'd regretted the dangers of returning to Monticello's permanent chaos of construction as Papa's Italian-inspired architecture took shape into a domed manor house that would have three stories while appearing only to have one. And yet, we were still happier here amongst hammers and plaster dust and tarps than we'd been at Varina. When Tom discovered that I'd left, he'd been enraged. But I'd only meant to strike a little fear into his heart, not mount a rebellion, so I lied to him about the reasons why. I told him that in his shamefully drunken state, he'd commanded me to go so he could put all his attention on the harvest. And when Polly—who disapproved of men who drank—

confirmed my story, Tom was too embarrassed to admit that he couldn't remember what he'd said. I sensed there lingered in him a fear that he had a willful wife who might not always tolerate his outbursts, which suited me.

And I saw some of the same sincere regret he'd shown after he'd struck me. But more happily, our return to Monticello had coincided with a visit from Jack Eppes, our country cousin with whom Polly had spent many years. He'd proposed marriage, and she'd agreed straightaway.

Jack Eppes wasn't as handsome as my own husband, but then few men were. Still, Jack had a sunny disposition. He seemed amenable to my father's plan to have us all live close together when he retired from office. And so we were all very optimistic that autumn. We anticipated long sojourns here at Monticello, which would—Papa promised—be completely renovated and habitable by New Year's Day.

Sally herself was with child again, which seemed to give my father great pleasure, though he never said so. He guarded the privacy of his rooms, which must have been their lovers' sanctuary, but I wondered where Sally took herself on days like this one, when our country neighbors and relations gathered for Polly's wedding.

Kissing my sister's cheeks, I said, "*Mon Dieu,* Polly. You are a beautiful bride."

"It's Maria!" she cried, laughing in exasperation.

"Maria," I agreed, with a grin.

She beamed, taking up a bouquet of lavender, feverfew, and coneflowers. "You are my very best sister, and I promise, when we live apart, I'll write you every day."

At this, I snorted back a laugh. "That's what you said when you went off with Papa to Philadelphia, but I can scarcely count one letter you sent me. I'm afraid you deal much in promises, but very little in deeds performed with a pen, *Maria.*"

"I'll do better," she said solemnly, staring at her reflection in the mirror.

Though I doubted it, I kissed her again, for it was a day for joy.

Alas, after the vows were exchanged, I found my husband miserable, leaning against the rail of the gallery, a glass in hand, watching everyone else dance in the entrance hall below. "Martha," he said stiffly.

Since the day I'd left Varina, we'd scarcely spoken a word, so I simply answered, "Mr. Randolph."

"They make a handsome couple," my husband said, eyeing Jack, who whirled my sister around so that her petticoats swirled up under her skirt, heedless of her injured ankle. "Your father says Jack's a talented lawyer."

Truthfully, Jack wasn't terribly talented at anything in my opinion. Certainly, my sister's new husband didn't have Tom's intellect or scientific curiosity. And where my husband had a manly swagger, Jack still presented himself as a pudgy-cheeked boy. There wasn't anything better about Jack Eppes but his temper.

Yet, he had a patrimony and a father who loved him.

Two things Tom envied.

Two things Tom would never have.

And I hurt for him, but I couldn't let my husband's jealousy or fears put a damper on my sister's wedding. So I put my hand on his arm, where it rested upon the colorful buffalo robe on display over the rail, and said, "I think I forgot to tell you—my father is hoping to compare his meteorology book with yours. He doesn't trust anyone else's." Shaking my head with feigned bewilderment, I added, "You two and your record keeping. Two peas in a pod, you are. I can't imagine how your scientific minds work."

"Your father likes Jack," Tom said, an edge in his voice.

Frustrated, I said, "Everybody likes Jack. And Jack likes everybody."

"No, he doesn't. He's all pretense," Tom said, finishing his drink in one gulp. "He proposed to your sister because his parents wanted him to."

Which—even if true—was no bad reason for marriage.

"Don't spoil things, Tom."

Setting his glass down, he lowered his eyes. "Say what you will, Martha, but I wanted *you* . . . and I still do."

It softened me to hear it, and I smoothed my hands over the bodice of my gown, knowing that the striped silk taffeta in shades of gold brought out the fiery hues in my curled hair. "Then why don't you come downstairs and dance with me." Taking his hand, I drew it to my hip. "Look at our guests flapping about without any grace. They need our example."

"Patsy," Tom said, his fist balling within my grasp. "I'm trying to tell you something." His throat bobbed, as if he was mustering courage. "It pains me to be an embarrassment to you, but I don't know how to remedy my flaws. All I know is that whenever I feel strongly compelled to any act, a doubt always arises. And whereas the voice of reason is low and persuasive, passion is loud and imperious."

It was a kind of apology. And I was reminded again that there was no guile in my husband. What he thought, what he felt, was always there on his skin. He wasn't a diplomat; he wrestled every day with the necessary fictions of gentility that came so easily to me and my father, born politicians that we were. Sometimes Tom's directness was refreshing, intoxicating, even.

Tom finished by saying, "I wish I knew what part of my nature prevents me from being happy."

I knew exactly what part of his nature was to blame. It was *the Randolph* in him. And when I considered his miserable father, his shameless sisters, and all his selfish, hotheaded kin, I counted it a miracle that Tom was, at heart, a good man. That he wasn't a happy man couldn't be counted much against him.

So I pushed onto my toes and kissed him, very softly, at the corner of his mouth. "Ask me to dance, Mr. Randolph." And when he finally swept me onto the dance floor, I whispered, "I'll tell you a secret about being happy, Tom. Sometimes you just have to pretend at it until it becomes real."

Monticello, 11 October 1798
From Thomas Jefferson to Stevens Thomson Mason

These Alien & Sedition laws are merely an experiment on the American mind to see how far it will bear a violation of the constitution. If this goes down, we shall see another act of Congress declaring a hereditary President for life or the restoration of his most gracious majesty George the third. That these things are in contemplation I have no doubt after the dupery of which our countrymen have shown themselves susceptible.

My husband snapped open his paper at the breakfast table. "This damnable Jay Treaty is going to be our undoing."

I wish he hadn't said it, only because I didn't want Papa agitated about politics during his visit. It some ways, we all lived in a state of suspended animation until my father came home each autumn, and I didn't want to spoil our time together.

Unfortunately, Tom's words worked Papa into a rare state of heat. "For President Adams to side with Britain against France." Papa fumed, glancing at Tom's paper and adjusting the spectacles he'd purchased for his sore eyes. "Against our sister Republic, our lone ally in a world of monarchies!"

The treaty had gone down badly. Violence between political factions broke out in Philadelphia and had to be dispersed by light cavalry—much as in Paris on the eve of revolution. What's more, President Adams had authorized the prosecution of critics of the president's administration, which now included my father, his vice president.

Federalists claimed these measures were necessary to keep anarchy—and the guillotine—from American shores. But we saw in this the possibility for the very end of the American experiment with liberty. We were afraid to write political letters of any kind for fear of being jailed—especially since Papa was certain his were being intercepted and read.

He removed his spectacles and rested them upon the ledge of the small mahogany lap desk he once used to draft the Declaration of Independence itself, then gave a mournful sigh. "I know not which mortifies me most—that I should fear to write what I think or that my country bears such a state of things."

"Papa," I said, trying to soothe him. "Perhaps you should resign the vice presidency in protest. Retire early, because in a very short time, there will be another election and it shall all be someone else's worry."

Papa should've agreed with me. He might at least have pretended to think about it, especially considering the weight it would take off Tom. Instead, Papa snapped, "This reign of witches must end!"

That was the moment I realized my father was going to run for the presidency. Not be reluctantly volunteered. But actively campaign for the office.

He was ready for rebellion. Papa's powerful, implacable, political outrage reminded me that underneath his gentility, he would always be a revolutionary. He wouldn't retire. He'd run for the presidency of the United States, and this time, he wanted to win.

Like a soldier readying for battle, he'd returned to Monticello only to regroup in the bosom of his family. A thing made even plainer to me when he groused, "Where the devil is Maria? I gave Jack my chariot to make it easier to come, and assured them both the house and servants would be ready to receive them."

But Jack hadn't seen fit to bring my sister home. In fact, we'd scarcely seen Polly since her wedding the year before. In that time, Sally had lost poor little Harriet to some childhood illness and borne my father another child—a boy named Beverly. It must've been some consolation, but babies were fragile, and Papa had already lost so many children he was apt to guard his heart against loving the new ones too dearly. So, my father centered his anxieties on my sister. "Is she ill?"

"Just a newlywed," I said, because if it was an illness, it mysteriously reoccurred whenever it served to excuse a visit to Monticello, and I began to harbor a belief the Eppes family was keeping my sister from us once again.

My husband had cause to know how very much this upset me and as we prepared for bed one night, he attempted to raise my spirits against the specter of a holiday without my sister. "You ought to chaperone the Christmas Ball in Charlottesville, Patsy. It promises to be a gay season."

I didn't know about that. I knew Nancy intended to try to find a husband there, in spite of her blackened reputation. And Tom's littlest sister, Jenny, would come out into society for the first time. I myself hadn't been out in society in years and couldn't imagine that it'd make me feel any better about missing Polly or about losing my father to politics for another four years.

But then Tom added, "I'll go to the Christmas Ball with you. It occurs to me you need a chaperone. One never knows what kind of trouble you might get up to without me, young lady."

Lighthearted flirtation didn't come naturally to Tom, and it warmed me to know that in spite of all his own struggles, he was trying to help me with mine. In my nightdress, I sat on the edge of the bed, my fingers trailing along the neckline. "Mr. Randolph, it's your sisters you need worry about. I'm an old woman of twenty-six years and quite above reproach."

Tom tugged me against the strong muscles of his bare chest and playfully leaned his face close to mine. "But I might like to give you a stern reprimand or two anyway."

He wanted me. That hadn't changed. Not since the day he decided he *must* have me did his desire wane. Sometimes I thought it was because whenever he made love to me, he was reaching inside me for something more than the love I bore him, reaching for something I couldn't give. But as long as he kept reaching, I thought it would hold us together.

So that Christmas, we loaded up Jenny and everyone else we could stuff into the carriage. Tom and I danced and exhausted the youngsters, putting them to shame. We were still laughing when we returned, much to the consternation of our children at Monticello, where we'd left them in Sally's care.

When Tom smooched my cheek, our six-year-old son Jeff—a little heathen who refused to wear shoes even in coldest winter—made an ugly face. His older sister Ann complained bitterly of the unfairness that we hadn't allowed her to come with us, threatening to go to *Phildelphy* with her grandpapa who would surely spoil her with cake. And two-year-old Ellen—a child I named after the daughter I'd lost, promising myself to love her enough for *two* angels—babbled her complaints, clinging to my skirts.

Oh, how I loved my little cherubs, and by springtime, I was expecting another. At this news, my husband leapt from his chair to spin me around. Tom wanted another boy—of course he did. And the knowledge we had another baby coming set him off on a manic fit of activity, building us a new house at Edgehill.

Tobacco was in the ground, and everyone was predicting high prices. "This will be a good year, Patsy," Tom said. "We'll get a good harvest, sell at the peak of the market, pay off debts, and live easy the rest of our lives. Just you wait and see."

Chapter Twenty-four

Varina Plantation, 1 July 1799
To Thomas Jefferson from Thomas Mann Randolph Jr.

There is a story of an ancient king whose touch turned everything to gold. You will recognize in me the makings of Midas, except that everything I touch turns to dust.

NOTHING CAME UP out of the dirt that summer. What plants did grow were small and sickly things. Most farmers lost their entire crop; we lost most of ours. Tom worked desperately to salvage what he could. In the end, he had to rely on tobacco, which was his undoing.

That summer prices reached dizzying heights, but the odious Federalists had suspended commerce with France—the biggest market for Virginia tobacco. By autumn, prices crashed, and we couldn't give it away. My husband had gambled and lost, but he wasn't the only one—not the only one by far. Every man in Virginia suffered that year.

That's why I burn this old letter.

I thrust it into the flame and watch the edges curl, happy to protect my husband's too-earnest heart, as he was never able to do for himself. Tom's bitterness was a cause of much misery in my life, but he came by some of it so honestly that I can't bear to think of people reading this letter and mocking his pain.

And so I burn it, gladly, to ash.

At the time he *wrote* this letter, of course, Tom kept from me the magnitude of the financial disaster. It wasn't a wife's place to know the particulars. I was meant to concern myself with raising our children—four in all now, including baby Cornelia, who we'd named after the famous Roman matron, in keeping with the revolutionary spirits of the time. But in the midst of chasing after the little ones, I had guessed that he wouldn't be able to pay the mortgage on Varina and tried to comfort him, hushing baby Cornelia in my arms. "You couldn't know the right time to sell the tobacco, Tom. Nobody could. Besides, the trade embargo with France will expire in the new year and you can sell then."

"By which time it will all have rotted, with my luck!" Tom's shout reverberated throughout the house. Then he turned and smashed the wood window frame, sending a crash of icicles down from the impact. He kept punching and punching with his fist until I feared he might break his hand, or the window, or both.

"Tom!" I cried, and from somewhere in the house, I heard one of the older children whimper. My heart hurt to think they might live in fear of their father's temper. I thought it might do us some good to go somewhere. Get away from our troubles for the Christmas holiday, as we'd done the year before. We'd been happy dancing in Charlottesville. Maybe we could be happy somewhere Tom didn't feel the walls closing in on him.

When he finally stopped punching, I appraised his bleeding knuckles and said, "We should go to Eppington for the holiday. I want to be with Polly for her lying-in."

My sister was pregnant for the first time, and it was only natural that I'd want to be with her, but Tom gave me a baleful stare. "You're going *nowhere*, Martha. You're scarcely out of childbed yourself."

It wasn't true. Cornelia was nearly five months old. Old enough to travel. So I argued, "I'm worried for my sister. You know she's prone to illness. Always too sick to come to visit us or to have visitors."

Tom snorted. "So says Jack Eppes."

He had a point. Papa had gone from persuasion to pleading to bribery when it came to luring Jack to bring my sister for a visit, but we hadn't seen her in nearly two years. "She's all I can think about, Tom."

"All *I* can think about is tobacco."

"There's nothing you can do about the tobacco. Nothing but brood." Working myself up into a true lather, I said, "My mother died in childbirth, and Polly has her frame. I have a moral duty to be with my sister now."

"It's only your anxiety that makes it so," Tom said, pacing. Oh, the irony of Tom accusing *me* of being overly anxious! But before I could protest, he announced, "You're not going, Martha, and that's the end of it."

I wanted to argue, but there was something inside my husband that kept twisting and twisting in on itself, and it left him wound so tight I was afraid he might strike me if I dared to argue. Instead, I went downstairs with him and helped dress Jeff.

I got one shoe on my son just as he removed the other, which exasperated me, because he needed his shoes and a breakfast of bread and milk before he could make the two-mile walk to school. And while I tried to wrestle him into his shoes, my squirming son delivered an accidental kick to my belly. I cried out in surprise at the pain, which set my already-furious husband off like a powder keg.

Tom grabbed our boy and shook him, screaming in his face, "You ever kick your mother again and I'll beat you bloody! Do you hear? I'll beat you down until you can't ever get up again."

"Tom!" I struggled to pull a wailing Jeff from his father's grasp. "Stop! It was an accident!" But my husband's hold seemed to tighten the more I fought him. "Tom, please!"

The next thing I knew, Jeff was in my shaking arms, the unexpected shifting of his weight against me making me stumble back. Meanwhile, Tom paced, tugging at his hair with one hand. "He should learn proper respect for his mother!"

The time he'd struck me, maybe I'd deserved it, but I knew

from the depths of my soul that my sobbing little boy had done nothing to earn such rough treatment. As I cuddled him close, my heart ached in my chest, and my stomach soured and burned.

Because I knew that day that more than just our financial affairs were falling apart.

~

SEEKING TO ESCAPE THE TROUBLES UNFURLING AT VARINA, I unwittingly brought my children to a tragedy at Monticello. For the winter of 1799 was a reaper of souls in Albemarle.

Mammy Ursula's husband and son, affectionately known as *the Georges*, died of some mysterious ailment. Then my father's old personal servant, Jupiter, came down with it, too. He believed himself poisoned and, against all advice, went to the same black conjure doctor who had treated the Georges.

I learned of it after a commotion outside, where my daughter had been playing in the dusting of snow with the slave children, all of whom called for me in a panic. Sally and I both flew out of my father's house to witness a sight I'd never forget.

Jupiter had fallen to the cold and muddy road in front of the new carriage house on Mulberry Row, twitching in a convulsion fit so strong that it took three stout men to hold him. Catching Ann up by the arms, I tried to quiet her sobs. "What's happened?"

"He took a dram, Mama," she said, clinging to me.

"The conjure doctor gave him something that would kill or cure," Sally said, bitterly, for the doctor had done the same for the Georges, both dead now.

"Take the children away," I told Sally quietly, trying to keep my wits about me. Then, to the men holding Jupiter down as he writhed in pain, I commanded, "Take him to a bed. And tell me where this doctor can be found."

"He's long gone, mistress," Ursula answered. "Absconded two and a half hours ago, after giving Jupiter the potion."

I paced, my skirts dragging as the men lifted up Jupiter's twisted form, his eyes bulging so that we could see the whites, a bloody froth dripping from his lips down the black skin of his neck and into his woolly hair. My heart broke at the sight. I wanted to rail at the servants for trusting such a butcher, but more than that, I wanted Jupiter to be well.

I tended him myself. Nine days he languished and never recovered, not even to speak his last words to anybody. Horrified by my failure to protect our people, I was relieved to see Tom ride up to the house. Our troubles seemed suddenly quite small with death all around us. "I should think this doctor's murders sufficiently manifest to come under the cognizance of the law," I told Tom, wanting justice.

I wrote the same to my father.

But my rage all came to nothing. My menfolk raised no fuss. I suppose they were all hoping that winter's reaper of death had absconded away with the murderous doctor, and didn't want to call either back. Alas, nature demanded more payments that winter.

Sally's newborn daughter died.

Polly's baby died.

George Washington died, too.

Such was the bitter partisanship of the day that my father didn't feel he'd be welcome at the funeral for his friend, our first president, the great Virginian whose Federalist followers mourned him like the king they wished him to be.

And I cared nothing about it, because all I could think of was the poisoned slaves I hadn't been able to help, and my poor grieving sister, so far from me.

Thanks to Tom, I hadn't made it to her lying-in. And I learned about her baby's death back at Edgehill as winter gasped its last cold breaths. The house Tom built for us was no architectural marvel; it was just a box, no wider than forty feet and two stories high. But it was the first thing we had without the taint of Colonel Randolph on it.

Alas, the windows were done badly, and the insides had been spattered with rain and wind and mud come up from the cellar.

For days after we arrived, I cleaned from dawn 'til dusk, sweeping and scrubbing until my hands were raw and cracked, while Tom worked at repairing the windows.

"Martha," Tom said a few mornings into our stay. He caught me with the servants in the kitchen where I was setting up housekeeping. The months of loss had taken a toll on me, and an even worse toll on us, and so I kept my eyes on the piles of dirt I was sweeping and my mouth closed. "Patsy," he said when I didn't look up. "Might I trouble you for a word?"

My husband had spoken sweetly to me ever since learning that my sister's childbirth had come to grief. For my part, I'd scarcely answered him with a word more than was necessary. He'd kept me from my sister when she needed me. I wanted to fly to my sister now and comfort her, but having been disappointed before in doing what perhaps *my anxiety only* deemed a moral duty, I was afraid to indulge any hopes in the matter. "I'm listening, Mr. Randolph."

My broom swished, swished, swished against the rough-hewn planks of the floor, highlighting the stretch of silence between us.

"Your father has advanced me the money to save Varina," Tom said, sheepishly.

I swept harder, whacking the broom against the wall as I did it.

Tom heaved a great sigh. "How can I ever express my gratitude for his kindness? I was really on the point of ruin from my own neglect."

I slammed down a dustpan and collected up the debris with more force than was strictly necessary. Then I yanked open a window and emptied the pan with a clatter.

Tom cleared his throat. "I knew all along that I should've sold my tobacco in full time to meet my debts. But a great price for that crop would've rendered us perfectly easy for life." He stared at his feet. "I risked ruin with the hope of fortune but fear I've only procured embarrassments."

It was the kind of frank admission of fault that Tom was, alone amongst the men I knew, capable of giving. And I worried he had beggared us for the rest of our lives. How long would he really be able to keep Varina, even with my father's help? He should've sold that damned farm. Let it go. Started fresh. But that's not what I really blamed him for. "My sister is ailing. Her breasts have risen and broke."

And this is your fault because you wouldn't let me go to her, was my silent accusation.

He frowned, not needing me to say it. "I'll take you to Eppington, if you still want to go."

We left that very day, and when I saw my sister half-dead in a fetid bed, I thought I might swoon away at the shock of seeing her so thin and frail. But my resentment of Tom was utterly eclipsed by my anger at yet another quack physician. This one had Polly confined to bed taking so much castor oil that she'd wasted away. "My poor Polly!"

"*Maria,*" she whispered with a faint smile, unable to lift her head from the pillow, but fluttering her eyes at me as if grateful that I'd finally come. Childbirth had ravaged her. Even beyond the grief of losing her baby, the damage done to her delicate body was like nothing I'd ever seen. The doctor murmured that she wasn't the sort of woman God made for childbearing, to which my sister replied, "Patsy, rescue me. . . ."

I vowed I would—because I feared that under his regimen of mysterious elixirs she might never rise from her bed again. Fortunately, I wasn't the only one stricken by the state of her.

Tom was adamant. "She needs to be up and out of that sickbed and her breasts need to be drained of the swelling." Whether he was dissecting opossums, nursing our children through smallpox, or theorizing how to relieve a new mother's breasts when her baby had died, my husband's peculiar interest in science made me think he would've done better to pursue a career in medicine than farming. And I hoped that Jack Eppes would take my husband's advice.

Unfortunately, Jack and Tom mixed like oil and water. Maybe it was because Tom seldom laughed at Jack's jokes. Or maybe it was because Jack laughed too much at Tom, poking fun at his serious nature. Whatever the reason, Jack defended the physician as an old family friend. "We're perfectly happy with his ministrations to my wife."

"My apologies for intruding, then," Tom said stiffly, sensing he'd pressed the matter as far as he could in another man's house about another man's wife.

But Polly wasn't only the wife of Jack Eppes, she was also my sister. I wasn't about to leave it alone.

That night, after the fire burned low, I left Polly in the care of her maid Betsy—another Hemings girl—and went to find Jack, where he was shutting up for the night. "My sister wants to stretch her legs. Breathe in fresh air. Get a little food into her without castor oil purging it. Surely you don't want her confined forever, do you?"

"Oh, Patsy," Jack said, giving me a genial pat. "I want her alive and well!"

Jack was smiling that glib smile of his, and I had the most unladylike urge to punch it from his face. He was supposed to take care of my sister. To love her and take seriously her ailments. The fact that he could smile at me like that while she wasted away hardened me. "If you truly want her alive and well, Jack, then understand that she can't ever have more children."

A planter needed sons and it was a wife's duty to produce them. I considered it my duty, certainly, but my mother had considered it hers, too, and died trying. "My sister wasn't made for it, Jack. You take one honest look at her, and you'll know it's true—"

"What am I supposed to do about it if it is?" he asked, an edge of anger in his voice. And maybe he had a right to be angry with me. This was an interference of the highest order, but in the past months, I had not been vigilant enough.

"Stay off her," I said. "For the love of God, Jack. Stay off her."

He stared at me a moment, shocked, but then all the masks fell away and he hung his head, as if in shame. I put a hand on his shoulder, to soothe him, and was rewarded with Jack's teary nod.

PAPA WAS DEAD.

Or so it was reported that summer, when the presidential campaign for the election of 1800 was in full swing and the newspapers were hard at work with vile slanders. My father was said to be dead, an atheist, and a coward. President Adams was said to be a tyrant and a criminal. My father was said to be "a swindler begot by a mulatto upon a half-breed Indian squaw." President Adams was said to be a hermaphrodite.

It would've been laughable if the stakes weren't so high.

Indeed, I worried that my poor sister would hear the news of my father's passing before we could tell her the truth, and that it might stop her frail heart. It vexed me that she wasn't with us at Monticello, where Papa desired us all to join him. Jack Eppes had promised they'd come, but now he pled the excuse of the harvest, even though we all knew perfectly well my sister would be of no use to him on the farm. If Jack had let her come with us, I wouldn't have to fret for her like I did. Or, at the very least, I'd have someone other than Sally with whom to share my amazement at the circus in my father's house that summer. . . .

Though we lived in the same house, I scarcely saw Papa, for he was always in a crowd. Politicians, financiers, and newspapermen flocked to our mountaintop to pay court to the man they wanted for their next president. They behaved as if he belonged to them, and I suppose he must have. But at night, when he retired to his private chambers, he belonged to Sally. For even though we had a house full of guests, he'd recklessly got her with child again by autumn.

And while Sally tended to Papa, I was left to cater to my father's guests—men and their wives who hadn't waited on an invitation, but nevertheless, needed to be fed and offered every hospitality. They ran over us like locusts, and it reminded me of the weeks we were under siege by the British, and the legislators gathered together at Monticello to avoid capture. There were no dragoons hunting us now, but there may as well have been for all the chaos. As if, in campaigning for the presidency, they were bringing about a new revolution.

For my part, I wanted none of it.

If only Papa's candidacy had been the most troubling thing we faced.

In early September, alarming news reached us from our long-time friend and neighbor, Mr. Monroe, now the governor of Virginia.

"I've just received word," Papa said, indicating a letter he held in a shaking hand, and a crowd drew round him in the entryway. "The planned slave insurrection in Henrico has been clearly proved. Ten Negroes have already been condemned and executed, and there are upward of forty more to be tried."

While the crowd of men murmured at the news, I held my breath. News of a possible slave rebellion near Richmond had reached us days before, but the terrifying specifics of the plot were just now becoming clear.

Varina was in Henrico County. Had Tom's slaves been involved? And what if Tom had been at Varina when the violence began?

"As many as forty more you say?" one of the men asked, as if startled to learn so many slaves would be willing to take up against their masters in concerted effort. To imagine slaves killing whites and setting fire to the Virginia countryside—not in far-off Haiti, but actually *here*—was a thing of which not a few slaveholders' nightmares were made.

Though he usually hung back in a crowd, Tom frowned and shook his head, saying, "Were it not for a thunderstorm thwarting their plans, who knows how many more might have joined them?"

This comment caused an uproar with our guests, some of whom opined that these rebel slaves ought to be made terrible example of. But Papa wandered off while they ranted, and they didn't seem to notice his leaving.

Tom and I followed him into the solitude of his study, where the wavering candlelight cast Papa's big shadow upon the octagonal walls. I looked from my husband's face to the parchment in Papa's hand, and dared to ask, "What else does Mr. Monroe say?"

Papa sighed and rubbed his forehead. "He wishes to know my opinion on how to deal with the conspirators." This had been a frequent topic of conversation at our dinner table amongst Papa's guests, who also wished to know his thoughts, as it seemed everyone did on every topic these days.

After a long moment of silence, I asked, "What will you say?"

Laying the letter upon an open ledger, Papa sat in his red revolving chair. "This is unquestionably the most serious and formidable conspiracy we've ever known in these parts. But there's been hanging enough."

Tom nodded his agreement. "We open ourselves for condemnation if we indulge in a principle of revenge, or go one step beyond absolute necessity."

"Indeed," Papa said. "The problem is how to strike the balance between justice and public safety." Sally knocked as she came in from the greenhouse, interrupting the conversation with the news that more guests had arrived.

"I'll greet them," I said wearily, gathering my skirts. As I passed Sally, I wondered what she knew of this rebellion. What did any of the slaves at Monticello know of it? For, the instigators had reportedly gathered support from slaves as far away as Charlottesville. And I'd long ago seen proof of how quickly important news traveled amongst the slaves.

Out in the hall, I took a moment to gather myself before I greeted our visitors. My father had once said on the eve of the Constitutional Convention, with respect to the dangers of a failed rebellion in Massachusetts, that *the tree of liberty must be refreshed from time to time with the blood of patriots and tyrants.*

Only, here and now, with so much in turmoil in our young nation, I couldn't help but wonder who was who.

Chapter Twenty-five

Washington City, 16 January 1801
From Thomas Jefferson to Martha Jefferson Randolph

Here one feels in an enemy's country. It is an unpleasant circumstance, if I am destined to stay here, that the great proportion are Federalists, most of them of the violent kind. Some have been so personally bitter that they threaten a dissolution of the government if I'm elected.

WE WERE INFESTED. Not merely with the vermin and detritus of politics, but also with the dreaded itch at Edgehill. "Hold still," I told my son Jeff, shearing off as much of his hair as possible to rid him of the nits he'd caught running about with an apprentice boy. Though it was winter, I was covered in sweat from the nearby cauldron in our yard where I was boiling his clothes.

And I felt agitated and upset at every little thing.

Why, I was even cross with Ann because I'd told her to finish her Latin translation, but she'd abandoned her books to watch her brother's delousing.

In truth, since taking upon myself the education of the children, I was beginning to believe that both of my eldest were uncommonly backward. Jeff was a willful hooligan who couldn't read without moving his lips. Ann had a good memory but never applied it without prompting. Only four-year-old Ellen—who was smart enough for *two* little girls—showed any aptitude for learning. I knew I ought to have been satisfied if my children turned out well with regard to morals, but I could never sit quietly under the idea of my father's grandchildren being blockheads. Still, I told myself to be content with the idea of my son as a simple but industrious farmer because blockheads weren't likely to run for president.

That's what I was thinking when my stomach cramped so hard that I doubled over. I went down onto the cold ground to retch. Heaving into the grass, I was so very sick I had to crawl my way back into the house. The sickness came in waves, and I could tolerate neither meat, nor milk, nor coffee.

We thought I might be with child again.

I *was* with child, as it happened. But Tom thought it was more than that. "It isn't healthful the way you hold your feelings in, and push them down," he said, as if I'd somehow reached the limit of emotions my body would allow me to suppress.

Sitting on the edge of my bed, his big hand closing reassuringly on my knee, Tom said, "I know the election worries you, but nothing is going to happen to your father."

"You can't know that," I said, vexed that Tom had somehow guessed at exactly the fears that consumed me. "He's surrounded by violent men who will do anything to prevent him coming to power."

"He's beloved of the people—"

"Lafayette was beloved of the people, too. And they threw him in a dungeon anyway." Unlike Tom, I'd already lived through two revolutions, and I was certain we were in the paroxysms of a third. The Federalists bayed that if my father were allowed to take the presidency, murder, robbery, rape, adultery, and incest would be openly practiced, the soil soaked with blood, and the nation black with crimes. Which made me sure that they meant to kill him or usurp the government. I was equally sure there'd be chains, dungeons, and the gibbet for his supporters . . . to say nothing of his children and grandchildren.

I wasn't alone in my fears.

Everyone now talked of civil war, and militias were being mustered. I'd seen this before in France—shouts of violence turned into bloody mayhem. I couldn't count the revolutionaries I'd known who had, in the end, been eaten by the nation they birthed. As it was, the French Republic was still careening from constitution to directorship to the authority of General Bonaparte, and *still* the will of the people hadn't triumphed.

So even though my father's Republican Party had swept the election, taking both houses of Congress and the presidency besides, the Federalists weren't prepared to surrender the government. A constitutional defect had allowed a tie between my father and his running mate, Aaron Burr. And now, in a spirit of perpetual war, the vanquished monarchists threatened to make mischief by elevating Burr to the presidency instead of Papa.

But I knew there was a far easier way to keep my father from the presidency. They could, for example, send him the bullet I'd been shielding him from since I was a child. . . .

And I couldn't sleep, eat, or defeat the guilt consuming me for having secretly wished the Federalists would prevail. For having wished Papa would lose the election and come home to set things right, because it was all, *everything*, coming apart.

Even my silence.

"I'm so very worried, Tom. We have four children and another on the way. We've a house that's cold, and wet, and too small." I bit my lip. I knew wives weren't supposed to know anything about the business of planting, but I was expected to manage the economy of the household, and how could I do it without knowing how bad off we were? "How are we going to pay our debts? How will we survive?"

"We'll live on the profits from wheat this year," Tom said, rising to pace at the foot of my bed. "And give up on tobacco."

I peered up at him through bleary eyes. "I hope so, Tom."

Then a sudden clenching pain had me groaning and curling into a sweaty ball. Tom rushed back to swab my forehead with a cool cloth on the nightstand. Sitting on the edge of the bed, he rubbed my back and whispered soothingly until the cramps eased off.

Later, after I'd managed a few hours of fitful sleep, he came back with some tea, still warm from the kettle. "You're letting everything frighten you, Patsy. Trust in me to take care of you. Trust in your father to take care of himself. The Federalists don't have to kill Mr. Jefferson to keep him from claiming the presidency. They just have to resort to legal trickery, and they've shown a willingness to do it. Because of the tie vote, the House of Representatives says they may choose neither candidate and settle upon John Marshall instead."

John Marshall. I remembered that man from the trial of Richard Randolph—his cool eyes appraising me as I stood there with lies on my tongue and my hand on his Bible. It horrified me to think he might become president.

But my husband continued on with his thoughtful, and admittedly well-reasoned, assessment. "Either way, it won't come to a fight. In spite of all the saber rattling, your father won't lead us into war. He doesn't want the presidency *that* much. The Federalists won't go to war either, because above all, they cannot bear anarchy and disorder . . . that's the one thing they have in common with your father."

He was right. My father was a man of routines, civility, and particularity. In France, at the height of the danger, he'd encouraged Lafayette and the others to principled stands, but pragmatic compromise. He often told them to take what they could get in the hopes of pressing for more later. Papa could write fiery screeds, but he was, in fact, an even-tempered, rational actor.

And in the end we were all saved by it. By my father's temperament, his reputation, and the respect of his enemies. What else can explain the way Alexander Hamilton stepped into the breach to resolve the crisis? Yes, my father's bitterest foe threw his full weight behind my father's election to the presidency. Hamilton hated my father. But he hated Aaron Burr—and perhaps John Marshall—much more.

After the House of Representatives voted thirty-five times in a deadlock, on the thirty-sixth ballot my father was elected, peacefully and democratically, to the presidency of the United States.

~

PAPA AND HIS PARTISANS called it the Revolution of 1800.

Our countrymen delivered the nation into my father's hands—with much hue and outcry and paroxysms of bitter slander—but ultimately, without blood. Power passed from one faction to the other in accordance with the wishes of the people, and the rule of law was obeyed. It was the first time such a thing had ever happened in our country, or perhaps anywhere.

Papa wanted my sister and I to rejoice, insisting we make annual visits to the presidential mansion and promising that he'd return to Monticello so often we'd be together four or five months of the year. But it was a plan that ignored reality. With all our little children running afoot, Tom couldn't do without me. And Jack Eppes couldn't stay off my sister.

Polly gave birth to a little boy at the end of September, and somehow, it didn't kill her. But she was so ill that she fled to me, fearful of the physicians near Eppington.

When I felt how thin she was in my embrace, I cried, "Polly, you look so unwell." My nephew was a fragile creature who had still somehow robbed his mother of nearly all her life's blood. Her pallor was deathly, and as unreasonable as it was, I blamed Jack Eppes for that. "You're white as a ghost and thin as a scarecrow!"

Cradling her delicate new baby boy, she smiled softly. "Mr. Eppes is so happy to have a son that he says I've never looked prettier. Besides, we can't all breed so easily and often as you do, Patsy. Why look at you, set to give birth yourself any day now and you're trying to haul my baggage into your house!"

"I'll carry it," my son Jeff said, always a little helper even then. Though I couldn't get him to crack open a book without bribery or threat, he was a sweet boy. And I was grateful that he dragged my sister's trunk into the house so I could get her inside.

"I'm fine, Patsy," Polly insisted as my daughters crowded around. But she wasn't fine. She was so weak she needed to be helped up the stairs. At which point I realized how much nursing she required. And given how ill I had been during the election, and how ailing I still felt now, I determined that I'd have to have my baby at Monticello, where at least I could count on Sally's help.

Truly, I longed for my father's house, the attentions of his servants, windows that didn't leak, and a bed to birth my baby that was comfortable and clean. After all the terrors of the election, I wanted nothing more than sweet seclusion with my family now.

But in that simple desire, I was to be utterly thwarted. For when Papa came riding up his mountain that summer to fetch us home, he was accompanied by a multitude. Neighbors, relatives, well-wishers, sycophants, and every manner of hanger-on all ascended with him, calling, "President Jefferson! President Jefferson!" He rejected all trappings of monarchy, but our guests fluttered about him like courtiers attending a king.

Except royal courtiers—as I recalled from France—had duties and obligations to their sovereign. Royal courtiers were bound by strict rules of etiquette and social niceties. Royal courtiers didn't demand berths without invitation. Royal courtiers didn't lounge about in various states of dress, insolently ordering servants who were not theirs to command.

There was very little I could do about it, however, because my father insisted that as a man of the people, there must be no formality in our entertaining.

During the mornings, I planned the menu then waddled up and down the narrow staircase with my big pregnant belly to unlock the storerooms and cabinets so the servants could keep our guests fed. After meals, I played music to entertain or chased after the children, though my ankles had swollen up so much that my shoes were painful. And by evening, I tended to my sister, who was still too weak to leave her bed.

Perhaps realizing how weary I was, Papa promised, "Next time I visit, I'm resolved to do a flying visit by stealth, telling no one but you that I'm coming."

On the night my labor pains started, I surprised myself with the thought that I was happy for the pain, because it'd confine me to childbed, where I could rest. After a hard night of panting and pushing, I gave birth to a little girl. And Sally swaddled my baby with crisp efficiency. Later, she and Polly sat with me while I nursed my newborn child, the three of us reminiscing about Paris, a time when all options were open before us. Those memories were preserved forever in our minds like bubbles suspended eternally in glittering glass.

Sally liked to speak of them, though whenever she spoke in French, it annoyed the other slaves. It set her apart. Served as a reminder that she was my father's pretty, genteel, sophisticated mistress. Sometimes I worried about those resentments and jealousies . . . but on this night, I only enjoyed our reunion, all three of us with babies at the breast.

Sally was nursing little Harriet, named after her poor daughter who died. But *this* Harriet, who was as pale and rosy as any little white child, also had my father's piercing blue eyes. I think Sally loved her best, and how couldn't she? After all, Harriet, like my Ellen, must be treasured enough for two daughters.

But, of course, daughters were of little help to a planter. Sons were prized—even ones who foamed at the mouth in fits like my sister's baby, Francis. "Poor little thing," Sally said to me when my sister drifted to sleep. I thought she meant Francis, but her amber eyes settled on Polly with as much worry as I felt in my own heart. "Miss Polly won't survive another. She gave Mr. Eppes a son now. That ought to be enough for him."

No other slave would ever dare say such a thing, but I wouldn't scold Sally for it. She was only confiding in me what no one else had the courage to say.

"It ought to be enough," I said.

But I feared it wouldn't.

~—

"WE'LL CALL THE NEW BABY VIRGINIA—Ginny for short," Tom said, and I didn't gainsay him, because I felt his disappointment. A son could help in the fields, but a daughter was another mouth to feed and another bride to dower. He had four daughters, a plantation deeply in debt, and failed crops. And so, at a time when I ought to have been filled with joy for the beautiful new daughter in my arms, I was still sick with worry.

That is, until the day came that I realized I couldn't afford to be sick with worry.

It started with a cough. First Sally's children, then my sister's child, then mine. The illness spread so quickly that our flight from Monticello in the autumn came too late. "It's the whooping cough," Polly insisted, wringing her tiny hands. "I'd know that sound anywhere!" She'd been young when she'd taken the cough at Eppington, but she hadn't forgotten. She'd survived the illness, but our little sister Lucy hadn't. And at the memory, Polly's eyes filled with tears.

What could I say to comfort her or myself when our children fell ill, one by one? My clever five-year-old Ellen, after composing her very first letter to her grandfather, promptly fell into a fever and slowly began to strangle with the rest. The children were afflicted with coughing fits that made their eyes bulge, their ribs ache, and their throats so raw they sometimes vomited blood and sobbed. My newborn baby turned blue in the face and gasped for breath. My Ellen and Cornelia both cuddled together under the last clean, dry blanket I had. In her delirium, Cornelia laughed and sang to some unseen spirit above her. But Ellen had the good sense to be gloomy and terrified by her own hallucinations.

"My God, they are *dying*," Tom whispered when I passed him in the doorway to the nursery to fetch some honeyed water for the little ones to sip.

Unwilling to credit his whisper, I asked, "Would you do me

the favor of fetching my cloak? The blankets and linens I washed aren't dry yet. But I can keep the girls warm and covered with my cloak."

Tom took a deep, shuddering breath, then dropped his face into his hands. "We're going to lose them. Our precious baby girls."

"We can't think it," I said, almost as weary as I was terrified. Then, edging past him, I hurried down the stairs and into the kitchen to scrape the last of our honey from its jar.

Tom was right behind me, his big frame all atremble, and he spoke in a panicked whisper, "I can't think of anything else, Patsy. I dreamed it last night. Little coffins!"

How was I to hear such a thing and not sink to my knees? But I *couldn't* sink to my knees, because our precious children needed me. "Please, Tom. Please stop."

"It's my curse, Patsy. Everything I do goes wrong. Everything I make withers away. Now my daughters," he cried, grabbing hold of my shoulder and sobbing into my hair. "My *daughters*."

He was so strong, so hardened from horse riding and laboring in the fields, that I couldn't push him away if I tried. It wasn't as if I didn't want to cling to him. That I didn't want to offer him solace—and receive it in return. But in his state, I knew Tom couldn't help himself, or me.

Stroking his hair, I called to my son. "Jeff, fetch my cloak for the girls."

A moment later, Jeff came into the kitchen. "They'll only spit up on your cloak. Why not—" His eyes widened at the sight of his father weeping in my arms.

And Tom roared in a sudden rage that burned away all his tears like a brushfire. "Don't you backtalk your mother!" Then my husband's long arm snapped out, and a slap sent our boy reeling back, stumbling for balance.

"Tom!" I cried, half in disbelief as he tore himself away from me and grabbed up our boy by the shirt, pushing him against the wall. I couldn't guess what had turned his mood so swiftly, but my voice came sharp like the crack of a musket. "*Tom.*"

My husband never laid a violent hand on our daughters—never seemed to take anything but delight in Ann, who cowered in the doorway, at the edge of tears. But Jeff worked my husband's every last nerve. I suspected this time, it was simply that Tom couldn't bear the thought that his son had seen him weep. He stood there, his chest heaving as he glowered at the scared little boy, then let him go with a shove. "Go do as your mother told you."

With a hand to his stinging red cheek, Jeff ran off for my cloak. And I turned to Ann. "Your father is tired. Won't you take him into the other room and read him one of the little newspaper stories Grandpapa cut out of the paper for you?"

Pretty Ann bobbed her head in obedience with a little hiccup before leading Tom out. And I was glad he went with her, even if half in a daze. For I was half in a daze myself. I turned back to my pitcher of honeyed water and stirred the honey into it, catching a glimpse of myself in the surface of the water once it stilled.

Then I took a deep breath as something snapped inside me. I'd told myself that Tom would one day recover from the blow of his father's death and rejection. Just as my father had come through his madness. That given enough love and time, my husband would stand up like the man he wanted to be, and I could lean on him in times of trouble.

Now I knew better.

I could never, ever, lean on him or my sister or anyone else. I hadn't chosen a life in which I might be cared for and pampered. I'd chosen a different path. And I ought to be grateful to Tom, I told myself, for having obliged me to exert all the strength and energy I had at my disposal. Because in this exercise, the mind acquires strength to bear up against evils that would otherwise overcome it.

Realizing it, my aches and pains and ailments melted away, to leave me in more perfect health than I had enjoyed in years. For if I wanted to hold my family together, if I wanted my children to survive, I could neither be tired nor ill. If I wanted to carve out anything for myself or anyone I loved, I couldn't lean or waver.

I'd have to be the pillar to hold it all up . . . if *only* because I was Thomas Jefferson's daughter.

～

Washington, 18 April 1802
From Thomas Jefferson to Robert R. Livingston

The cession of Louisiana by Spain to France will form a new epoch in our political course. Of all nations France is our natural friend. Her growth we viewed as our own, her misfortunes ours. But it's impossible that France and the US can continue long friends when they meet in so irritable a position as they do now. The day France takes possession of New Orleans we must marry ourselves to the British fleet and nation.

My father was not, as the Federalists suggested, blind to the dangers of Napoleon. Rather, I believe it was his well-known sympathy for France that made possible—in a way it wouldn't have been possible for any other president—the successful purchase of Louisiana.

Even before it was completed in the third year of his presidency, it was plain that the Louisiana Purchase would be one of his greatest achievements, a staggering success of careful and opportunistic statecraft that doubled the size of the country. And the Federalists could scarcely mount up an opposition to it.

My father's political victory had been *a bloodless revolution,* we said . . . but there had been blood. Hamilton's blood. Spilled from the body of his eldest son in defense of his honor. One of my father's supporters had claimed Mr. Hamilton intended to overthrow the government to stop a Jeffersonian presidency. That claim now proven utterly untrue, Philip Hamilton confronted his father's accuser in a duel and was shot dead.

It was a reminder to me that public life could be fatal, exerting a toll on families that was difficult to underestimate. So my husband couldn't have astonished me more if he'd grown a horn in the middle of his head, when, before the purchase of Louisiana was negotiated, he said, "Jack Eppes is running for Congress. I'm going to do the same."

My sister's husband was running in a newly created district where his chances of victory were good. The seat Tom wanted was already occupied by one of my father's strongest supporters. If Tom lost, it'd not only alienate the man against my father, but would also crush my husband utterly. And even if Tom won, they'd say he hadn't earned his seat in Congress on his own merits, but on my father's name; for both of Jefferson's sons-in-laws to run together was to invite rumor of a Jeffersonian dynasty.

But when Tom told me, there was an earnest pride and eagerness in his expression, one I hadn't seen since he was a boy, gazing up at my father with admiration. I realized what it would mean to him to win a seat in Congress. What it would mean to him to *succeed*. Tom had never wanted to be a planter. His responsibilities as a father and a husband had probably put a legal career out of reach forever. But he didn't need that to serve in Congress.

I didn't know how we'd manage the plantations without Tom or my father, but I didn't have the heart to discourage my husband; I simply didn't have the heart. "Why, I think it's a wonderful idea, Tom."

He embraced me, planting a thousand kisses on my cheeks. "What a lucky man I am to have you for a wife," he said, holding my face in his hands. "Don't you worry about the farms. I have a plan."

I *was* worried. If Tom won, he'd be absent from home, just as my father was perpetually absent. Our already shaky fortunes would suffer. I wasn't worried about Monticello; in Papa's absence, the Hemings family ran everything there from the blacksmith shop to the dairy. We only needed to send an overseer there once a week to discipline the nail boys. But the outlying farms . . . slaves could do the planting, but the operations would need to be overseen every day, and I doubted we could recoup the expense of a more permanent overseer. Though I'd found more strength in me than I knew I had while nursing my entire family back to health through the whooping cough and managing a household besides, I feared that along with the children, and the house, and the outbuildings, the responsibility for the farms and the crops would now fall to me. And that I might not prove worthy of the challenge.

So I girded myself for his answer. "What plan?"

"*Cotton*," Tom said as he began to describe his scheme. "It's like printing money, it's so profitable."

This confused me utterly. "I hadn't thought cotton a profitable crop in Virginia."

He nodded. "That's why I'm going to Georgia. I thought, originally, to try the Mississippi territory, but every white man there is outnumbered by slaves and dangerous Indians. So I'm going to purchase land in Georgia."

The blood drained from my face. It was, of course, a husband's prerogative to decide where his family would go. But if Tom thought I'd submit to dragging our children into parts hitherto unknown, he'd misjudged me thoroughly. My voice actually quavered when I said, "You want to pack up and move to Georgia?"

He stroked my hair. "No, no. Of course not. I can't hold a congressional seat in Virginia if we make a home in Georgia, can I? No. I'll go to Georgia to prospect land, and when I find a good place, I'll establish all our Negroes there." My horrified expression must not have changed a whit, because he quickly added, "I know you're worried about our people, Patsy. I have nothing but the deepest concern for those whose happiness fortune has thrown upon our will. We won't break up any families—we'll send them all together. I promise you, the culture of cotton is the least laborious of any ever practiced. It's a gentle labor."

Maybe. But what about domestic servants? Even if I could part with them, I couldn't bear to see them sent away in fear. "They'll be terrified, Tom."

"We'll have to ease them into it," he agreed. "We'll have to tell them that we're all going. My slaves are willing to accompany me anywhere, but their attachment to you would make their departure very heavy unless they believed you were to follow soon."

No wonder my husband never liked deception. Even when he could muster up the stomach for a lie, he had no talent for it. There was no earthly way we could fool our domestic servants, who watched our every move and listened to our every word. And if our domestic servants knew we weren't going with them to Georgia, our field hands would soon learn it, too, at which point the entire thing would be completely unmanageable.

Which is why I agreed to it.

I knew it would never work. Like every other wild-eyed scheme of easy fortune I'd ever heard, this one would require a sharp focus that my husband could never bring to bear while campaigning for a seat in Congress. A campaign he'd decidedly lose, after which maybe we could get back to the sensible business of paying off the debts on farms he already owned.

In the end, I was half right.

Tom's interest in cotton came to nothing. He never even made the trip to Georgia. But he and Jack both won a seat in Congress. Jack by a landslide. My husband by thirteen votes.

And I was now the daughter of the president and the wife of a congressman.

Chapter Twenty-six

Monticello, 12 August 1802
From Thomas Jefferson to William Short

Will you not come and pass the months of August and September with us at Monticello? Make this place your home while I am here. You will find none more healthy, none so convenient for your affairs and certainly none where you will be so cordially welcome.

THIS ISN'T THE FIRST TIME I've found William's name while thumbing through my father's papers. Not even the first time I've traced the lettering of his name with a bittersweet ache. Since our break in Paris, William continued to exchange letters with my father, though Papa was always prudent enough not to speak of them to me beyond the occasional *Mr. Short sends his regards.*

At the time, it had seemed perfectly natural that William would—upon finally returning to America—call upon his mentor. But I never knew, until finding this letter, that it was my father's invitation that brought William back into my life.

And now that my father is dead, I'm left to wonder why.

That summer, my father came to Edgehill to fetch me in a fine carriage pulled by even finer horses. At the sound of wheels grinding up the road, I came flying out of the house, my daughters behind me, squealing with glee to see the kindly grandfather who sent them books and poems and other treats with every packet.

My children all loved him, and he loved each of them in return. And I nearly envied my children the sweet, playful side Papa always showed them. If I were to tell them that he'd once been a stony and remote father with exacting standards, they'd scarcely believe me. Why, watching him play the Royal Game of Goose with my children as we loaded up the carriage, I could scarcely believe it myself.

And I'd lived it!

"This visit is going to restore our spirits, Martha," Papa said, boldly placing a smooch on my cheek when we were ready to leave. How I basked in his love and affection.

Tom and Jeff would follow our caravan on horseback, but I climbed into the carriage with my father. As the wheels rattled on, I said, "I'm relieved to see you've somehow come home without your presidential entourage. I hope we won't have many visitors this summer."

"Just the Madisons." My father bounced little Ginny on his knee with genuine delight. "And one special visitor we've been waiting to see for a very long time: Mr. Short."

It'd been nearly thirteen years since I left William Short in Paris. *Thirteen years.*

In that time, I'd taught myself to forget him. But when Papa told me that he was to visit with us, my practiced indifference unraveled. And I couldn't decide if it was a blessing or a curse that my husband knew nothing about my anxieties at this reunion.

One evening, Tom asked, "So this Mr. Short, was he one of your suitors in Paris?"

I'd just finished playing the harpsichord for the Madisons and my fingers froze over the keys, unable to make my tongue move in answer. Fortunately, Papa rescued me by saying, "Oh, Patsy had a gaggle of suitors in Paris. Even the son of a duke, I seem to recall."

I smiled gratefully at my father, but Mr. Madison's face pinched in a sour disapproval far more affecting than it ought to have

been from such a tiny little man. "Mr. Short has had a very sto-
ried career."

Madison's wife—whom everyone was encouraged to call
Dolley—put her delicate hand on his arm and laughed until the
careless plume with which she'd ornamented her hair shook with
merriment. "They *do* say Mr. Short has a way with money, and
he's done the country a great service." Then her eyes twinkled
with the promise of juicy gossip. "But I've heard notorious stories
about him living in open congress with his lover . . . a French
harlot at that."

Tom's eyes widened.

My father winced.

I did not. "The Duchess Rosalie is no harlot."

"Oh, you knew her?" Dolley asked me, leaning forward with
rosy pink cheeks that matched the satin of her gown. "I suppose
you're quite right to hold her blameless. It's Mr. Short who hasn't
made an honest woman of her. He's allowed himself to be de-
bauched away from the morals of his countrymen. I daresay, in
returning to America, he's likely found himself in another world.
It's good that he isn't returning with the duchess on his arm or
the stain on his honor would be more difficult to wash out."

As painfully shy and withdrawn as my sister had become, this
prompted her to break in with, "Perhaps we ought not judge them
too harshly. I remember Mr. Short very kindly from our time in
Paris."

"Well, you *would*, you sweet dear," Dolley said. "You give us
all a good example to follow. We must be very kind to Mr. Short,
for I fear our neighbors won't be so forgiving."

What *I* feared was that William wouldn't be forgiving. Had
he ever forgiven me? I still had Marie's letter—the one that said
how angrily he'd denied loving me. I wondered if he was angry
still. And I wondered, too, how he might look now, at the age of
forty-three. I hoped he'd grown bald and portly. Certainly, he
wouldn't be as handsome as my own husband, whose beauty had
only sharpened with years.

I was to find out for myself at the start of August, when William arrived in a carriage even more splendid than the president's, with scarlet velvet curtains and gilt trim on the doors, driven by matching black horses with red plumes.

For a moment, watching William step down from the coach, I was transported in time and place. Paris, before the revolution, when such carriages went every day to and from Versailles. And when William flashed a grin, I could see, to my great disappointment, that he hadn't grown soft or bald or portly. Nor did he even look as if he'd aged—his facial features remained boyish, even if there was a hint of silver in his sandy hair. In an embroidered blue tailcoat, a dangling gold watch fob, a newly fashionable top hat, and breeches tucked into tall riding boots, he gave every impression of a dignified courtier and man of importance. It was suddenly easy to imagine people calling him *His Excellency, Mr. Short, the minister of the United States of America.*

All the more when he stepped forward to greet my father and executed a very correct bow. "Mr. President," William said, as if the words gave him delight and satisfaction to speak aloud.

At their long-awaited reunion, my father pulled into an embrace with the man he'd once considered his adoptive son, patting his back with so much vigor and affection that I thought I might weep. The two men who had been most important to me in my youth held each other by the arms, taking stock of one another after more than a decade, laughing at the joy of it.

William said, "President Jefferson, from the harbor all the way here, I've heard nothing but joyous thanksgiving. You're very much in the public favor, sir."

With his arms about William's shoulder, my father replied, "I fear more confidence has been placed in me than my qualifications merit. I dread the disappointment of my friends."

"Never that," William replied, even though, in his case, I knew it to be a polite lie. Though he tried to disguise it, his eyes swept uncomfortably to the servants who ran forward to fetch his bags and water the horses. There was no mistaking his loathing of slavery, but it wasn't in his nature to criticize his host. He was, after all, still a Virginian; diplomacy ruled him. And it's because I knew that he was a diplomat, well practiced with words, that I startled when he lifted his green eyes to mine and said in French, "*Vous êtes une vision angélique,* Madame Randolph!"

These were the first words we'd spoken to one another after thirteen years and an ocean of silence. I'd expected some tightness at the mouth that might hint of pain or regret. Instead, he'd made his eyes twinkle while comparing me to an *angel,* of all things.

Did he mean for his words to cut? Perhaps I'd been so eclipsed in his life, and in his heart, that he didn't even remember he'd once pointedly praised me not as an angel but an *Amazon.* And I was suddenly swamped by the memory of that day, when he confessed to having stolen a lock of my hair to keep as a token—a memory so bittersweet that it was hard to speak the words, "Welcome home, Mr. Short."

But I said it, and then it was done. The moment that had filled me with dread and anticipation was simply over, as if it were of no significance. Not even attended by the awkwardness that might have made it of some comforting consequence.

Instead, the awkwardness belonged to Sally Hemings. Seeing her on the portico with her two light-skinned, blue-eyed, freckled children clinging to her skirts, William made an elaborate and courtly bow. "What a delight to see you again, *madame.*"

We all froze in an awkward tableau, for William had acknowledged my father's slave-mistress with a courtesy title, one accorded ladies or women whose marital status was unknown, as one might do in France when openly acknowledging a man's mistress. At Monticello, my father kept quiet his relationship with Sally—such that even my children seemed unaware of it.

But, of course, William had been there when it started.

Thankfully, Sally was quick to bob an exaggerated curtsey like a French courtier, then adopted the strange sliding gait we'd all practiced at Versailles. "*Monsieur.*"

Her antics broke the tension and allowed everyone to laugh, but I was unsteadied enough to miss a step going into the house. Tom noticed, catching me by the elbow and hugging me against his side with the fit of good humor that had struck him since his election to Congress.

"It seems Mr. Short will be amiable company," Tom said, oblivious to the storm of emotions inside me. "The children certainly like him."

Ahead of us, my little cherubs all danced around William, who had a bag of half-melted chocolate drops for them. *Chocolate drops.* Another reminder for me, or simply a gift for the children? And why should it bother me that I didn't know?

I was overaware of William every single day he spent with us that hottest of summer months. I tried desperately to stay away, but the sound of his laughter carried to me through the house wherever I went. I seemed to sense him even before he passed by the doorway of the blue sitting room where I taught my children. I knew when he took his seat at the supper table beside my father, before even turning to see. And that is how, without even having to look up, I knew it was he who had come upon me in my father's garden that day.

"I think you're avoiding me, Mrs. Randolph," William said, bareheaded, shielding his eyes against the sun.

"I think I'm harvesting the garden, Mr. Short," I said, from beneath the shadow of my straw hat, fretting that he should come upon me in my housedress, my hands covered in dirt. A Virginia gentleman would've pretended not to see the lady of the house hard at work—even if the garden was her sweet escape from the demands of everyone inside the house; a Virginia gentleman would've passed by without a word and waited to address me in polite company.

But perhaps the code of Virginia gentlemen no longer applied to William Short. "Not growing Indian corn this year?" he asked.

I plucked a squash for my basket, too nervous to do more than glance at him. "Are you missing it?"

"I've missed many things from Virginia," he said, moving with gallantry to take the basket from me.

Feeling as if I must surrender it to him, I said, "You've been gone a very long time."

"Seventeen years. Partly in service to my country, partly for powerfully personal reasons."

I had no right whatsoever to ask about those powerfully personal reasons and I was determined to say nothing of his duchess. "You must find everything much changed."

His eyes fell upon our enslaved gardener, Wormley Hughes, working with spade and hoe at the far end of the rows, and he frowned. "Some things not enough changed." Then William turned his gaze to me. "And other things changed nearly beyond my comprehension. I daresay your friends in France won't believe me when I tell them the girl who ran through the convent with her petticoats in the dirt is now a reserved and nurturing mother of five."

He walked with me as I worked down a row. "Six if you count Tom's little sister Jenny—and I always do. Of course, she's of marriageable age now, and so very pretty I don't doubt she'll have her choice of suitors." I rambled, unable to stop myself. "I'll have to write more to my French friends." *Especially Marie,* I thought. Marie, whose letter from a year ago I still had not answered, finding it too painful to acknowledge that we would never see one another again. "I will write the ones who I still have a way of finding. We've been very afraid for them since the revolution."

His posture stiffened. "With good reason. I'm afraid your father was entirely too optimistic about the happenings in France. But I suppose it's difficult for anyone who wasn't there to imagine the horrors that have unfolded."

"I thank God Lafayette has finally been released. Papa says it was your doing."

"I wish that were true. Thank Monroe and Morris. I was merely a go-between, but I'm happy for Lafayette. And I wish others had been as fortunate."

Then I knew that I must say something about his duchess, if only because it was beyond the bounds of decency not to. "Please know that it pained us to learn what befell the Duke de La Roche-foucauld during the September Massacres. My heart suffered for Rosalie to become a widow in such a tragic way. When you see her next, please convey my deepest sympathies and my hopes for her happiness."

William stared, as if doubting my words. But there was no artifice in what I'd said. Though I harbored jealousy for Rosalie—I could never wish her unhappy. Or him.

At length, William must've seen the sincerity in my eyes, because he said, "If I see Rosalie again, I'll give her your message."

"*If* you see her again?" I asked, unwisely, rashly.

At my question, his gaze slid away. "She and I have come to a crossroads. Three times I asked her to marry me and three times she's refused. At first, in respect to her husband's memory. Then because she couldn't leave Madame D'Enville to the mercy of the Jacobins. And finally, because she'd rather be the dowager Duchess de La Rochefoucauld in blood-soaked France than simply Mrs. William Short anywhere else."

I sensed more bitterness than truth. "You can't mean that."

"I'm perhaps being unjust to Rosalie. It's simply been my misfortune to fall under the spell of women whose loyalties to family and country cannot be shaken by my love."

My mouth went dry at this very soft, but very earnest, remonstration. I thought to offer some apology, some explanation that might undo the pain I'd caused him in leaving France. "Oh, William—"

"Please don't," he said, cutting me off. By using his given name, I'd abandoned the propriety and formality without which our conversation might be a guilty thing. An offense to my husband and my father, both. And it seemed more than he could bear. "It's the fate of diplomats—a natural hazard of foreign service. But as

I said, Rosalie and I have come to a crossroads. Your father has made plain to me that we cannot go on as we have been."

"My father?" I couldn't imagine Papa in frank discussion about . . . well, almost anything. But certainly not matters such as illicit mistresses.

William nodded. "When your father was elected president, I hoped, at long last, to secure the position as minister to France that I've coveted. Your father, however, informed me that such an appointment is now quite impossible for I've been too long absent from our country to represent its sentiments. So I've come home."

He was wounded; I could see that. Nor could I blame him. Though I was certain my father had good reasons, the result struck me as profoundly unjust. William had spent the better part of nearly two decades toiling for his country overseas, sometimes in dangerous places, deftly securing our nation's credit, making endless intelligence reports to better our position and save us from war. For it to be implied to such a man that he was somehow not enough *American* to represent his country . . . William must've seen it as the grossest ingratitude.

I wished that I could think how to soothe his hurt feelings, but instead, I asked, "How long will you stay in America?"

He shifted the basket between his hands and looked again across the garden. "Until a solution presents itself. There are apparently those who disapprove of my conduct in France and will thwart my appointment to any diplomatic post."

William could win them over, I thought. He was as charming as he'd ever been. More charming, I thought, when he finally reached for a vine to help me with my forgotten harvest and said, "I've much mending of fences to do in Virginia, where it seems I've been replaced entirely."

Wary of his closeness, I wondered if he knew that there'd been a small secret place in my heart that I'd always kept for him. I loved my husband, but Tom had never taken William's place up entirely. "No one could replace you."

His eyes twinkled with amused outrage and he lowered his voice to an intimate whisper. "The young and heroic Meriwether Lewis certainly has. Your father dotes on his new secretary with a fatherly affection I once believed he reserved only for me."

I'd caused the breach between my father and William. Still, his jest snipped the tension. I began to laugh. Then we laughed together. "Meriwether Lewis is no William Short," I declared.

My father had always cultivated an endless stream of protégés, but William had been the first and best of them. For unlike the others, he had a most personal acquaintance with my father's faults and was devoted to him anyway.

Even having been snubbed for the appointment that would've crowned his career and maybe even won over his lady to marriage, still here he was, paying homage to my father at Monticello. "I don't believe you ever need worry of being replaced, William. Papa always says that those we loved first, are those we love best."

William smiled very softly then. In a way I hoped meant that we could still be friends. "Come, Patsy. You're getting pink. Let's take some shade in one of your father's porticoes."

"We're likely to trip over a workman's hammer and come away covered in plaster dust," I protested, since Monticello's renovations were endless.

"Here then," he said, guiding me under the sheltering leaves of a cherry tree at the far end of the garden and setting down the basket by my feet. He offered his forearm to help me lower to a seat against the trunk, which I took with as much elegance as my housedress and apron would allow.

"So what will you do until some foreign post is offered?" I asked.

He took a seat beside me but angled away, so that no one who might come upon us could think it an impropriety. With our backs to the tree, side by side, I couldn't see his face, but only his hands as he plucked a blade of grass and rolled it between his clean, elegant fingers. "I suppose I must find somewhere to live. Some years ago I prevailed upon your father to manage my investments while I was away. With that money he purchased for me some land called Indian Camp. Very fertile, he says. Very advantageous lands here in Albemarle County."

Here in Albemarle. Where we might be neighbors.

Yet I couldn't let myself hope for it, not even for a moment, because I saw his hands reach to pluck up more grass, this time violently. And I remembered what he'd said in the heat of anger when we argued in Paris. That Virginia is stained in the evil of slavery, impossible debts and a way of life that can't last. "But you don't care to make a home at Indian Camp."

He crossed his legs at the ankle, so that the steel buckle of his shoe glinted in the light. "I suggested to Mr. Jefferson an experiment of sorts. That he should rent out my Indian Camp property to tenant farmers. Part of the acreage to free white men. Part to free black men. As an experiment."

"An experiment?"

"I hoped to prove something to him about the potential for emancipation," he said, watching some of the slave children play with my own little ones on the lawn. Amongst those children was Sally's pretty Harriet. And William swallowed. "Consider, for example, the perfect mixture of the rose and the lily. I've suggested to your father, too, that the mixture of the races is our surest path to doing away with racial prejudice. But his unwillingness to pursue my experiment at Indian Camp, nor even acknowledge my argument, tells me that an honorable life cannot be made in Virginia. Because if a man in your father's singular situation cannot do it—if an icon of liberty cannot do it—I must conclude it cannot be done here at all."

I blinked into the sun. Then blinked again. William had always favored the abolition of slavery, but what he spoke of now went far beyond the sentiments of even the most adventurous thinker on the matter I had ever met. I could not think his mention of my father's *singular situation,* with regard to race mixing, was an accidental mention. But I wasn't a naive girl any longer who could muse on such matters with impunity, and he should've understood that our southern silence about the color line wasn't one I'd break even for him. "So you'll sell Indian Camp. Can you afford to?"

A breeze blew, and his hands let loose the grass, which floated away. "I can afford a great many things now, Patsy. Even excluding the value of Indian Camp and my lands in Kentucky, not to mention the sums still outstanding from the State Department, I estimate my fortune at nearly a hundred thousand dollars."

It was a very large sum. So large, in fact, that I went numb from the tip of my nose down to my tongue, and sat there stunned, like a felled ox.

At my silence, he continued, "It's ill-mannered to speak of money in the presence of ladies, but I bring it up to set your mind at ease about the loan I've made to your father. I don't want him to feel honor-bound to repay it when I can see plainly that his fortunes have fallen here."

I took instant umbrage, and would have objected that of course the state of reconstruction only made it *look* as if my father's fortunes had fallen, but I was too stunned by something else he'd said. "You made a loan to my father?" How had it come to pass that the man my father had once lectured about gold not falling from the sky had come to be our creditor?

In soft tones that somehow still assaulted my disbelieving ears, he explained, "I—I'm so sorry. I was sure you knew. Yes, I made a loan for his nail factory here at Monticello and a flour mill. But personal exigencies have prevented him from repaying the loan with what profits he has taken from those enterprises."

I could guess at the personal exigencies that occasioned my father's inability to pay. Papa had advanced money to my husband to pay the mortgage on Varina. Had divided up his properties to make another gift to keep us with a roof over our heads. All along I'd been so very grateful to my father for saving us from ruin, never suspecting Mr. Short was our savior. William Short, who had somehow accumulated a fortune without putting his shovel in the dirt.

Though it was unladylike for me to ask, improper in every way, William had been the only person to whom I'd ever spoken in frankness. And thirteen years of separation didn't change this. "How—how much does he owe you?"

Though I'd wager he knew the exact sum down to the cent, he said, "Somewhere in the order of fifteen thousand dollars. I've offered to forgive the debt entirely, but your father won't hear of it. So I must rely upon you to persuade him not to let pride be the cause of his impoverishment."

"I've no knowledge or involvement in my father's finances," I said, which was only the proper way of it, but somehow, in light of this man's expectations of me, felt like a shameful confession. "He never speaks of them to me."

William nodded. "Nevertheless, I have no other avenue of appeal because no one has more power or influence over the president than you do."

I wondered if I ought to feel flattered or terrified to believe it. It was a fact that my bond with my father was strong enough that even sometimes Polly complained of it, gently accusing Papa of loving me better. And though only Sally Hemings was allowed to freely roam his private chambers, whenever he returned from the capital, he didn't race back to Sally, he came straightaway to Edgehill to get me.

"You're too kind, William. Both to my father and to me."

"I would be kinder, if I could," was his reply. Then, after a few moments of silence, he added, "Your children are wonderful." William breathed in sharply, then snapped off his succinct evaluation. "Jeff seems a very robust little fellow. Ann and baby Ginny are sweet enough to rot teeth. Your Ellen is very clever. But I see the essence of you in Cornelia's eyes. That little girl isn't all she seems to be."

I smiled. "I'm afraid I've become exactly what I seem to be."

He gave a dubious laugh. "And I'm afraid that I have become an old bachelor, with nothing to show for my efforts but the adoration of other men's children. I suppose I'll have to take more of an interest in my nephews." With a comedic sigh that in no way disguised the seriousness, he added, "In the meantime, I suppose I must now leave you to your gardening and sow seeds of my own. We dine with Mr. Madison tonight, and, as your father has made plain to me, I must reacquaint myself with our countrymen."

I must reacquaint myself with our countrymen. . . .

William had said this lightly, but at supper that night, it became manifestly evident that my father wasn't wrong to have insisted upon it. The unique situation of my father's house being unfinished—the expense of the redesign project Papa had conceived upon our return from Paris combined with his frequent absences to make the rebuilding of a large portion of Monticello an unending affair—led to an informality that permitted women to remain in the dining room after the men began to drink, and I was present to witness an argument.

It began amiably enough, with the Virginia gentlemen all sipping wine and peppering William with questions about Europe. They wanted to know especially of Napoleon Bonaparte, the new *First Consul* of France, which now modeled itself even more closely after ancient Rome. William harbored some admiration for the sense of order restored by Bonaparte, but warned against embracing the brilliant revolutionary general, given his hunger for power.

This quickly turned into a disagreement about the nature of French diplomacy, pitting Mr. Short's cynicism about French revolutionaries against Mr. Madison's faith in their good intentions, leaving Madison to simmer like a teapot, growing more florid by the moment. The conversation went from bad to worse when the subject turned to finances. My father and Mr. Short agreed that the James River Canal Company was an opportunity for profitable investment. I confess I was distracted in that moment, scolding Jeff for running past the tables, so all I caught was Mr. Short making the wry remark, "No doubt the Virginia legislature will attack the canal company as soon as the dividends begin to excite envy."

A scandalized silence followed until Jack Eppes cried, "An outrageous accusation!"

My husband, thankfully, only set down his glass. "Why ever would you say such a thing, Mr. Short?"

Mr. Madison accused, "Because he's thrown in with the stock jobbers and paper men."

It was so chilly a remark, filled with such disdain, that it couldn't be dispelled by the thin smile that followed. Good southern Republicans were planters. Northern Federalists were stock jobbers and paper men. Virginians were suffering financially, suffering badly, but William had profited. I understood the unspoken assessment of the secretary of state, my father's closest political friend and ally. Madison was saying that William Short wasn't *one of us* anymore.

Though William ignored the insult and quickly steered the conversation to more pleasant topics, I worried for his reputation, not to mention his future as a diplomat at Mr. Madison's Department of State. And I worried for the disruption of our domestic tranquility when Tom was still brooding about the discussion that evening.

As we checked on the children in the nursery, he murmured, "This country is so divided."

"Yes," I said, though a part of me wondered if it was ever thus.

"Mr. Madison and Mr. Short . . . they're accomplished men. Lawyers. Jack fits with them better than I do. I feel like the proverbially silly bird who can't feel at ease amongst the swans."

Had I somehow betrayed my feelings for William in a way that brought Tom's insecurities about? Lacing my fingers with his, I said, "You really *are* a silly bird if you think Jack Eppes is better than you in any way at all. You're more thoughtful than he is, and the country needs men like you, Congressman Randolph. My father needs you."

I did mean that, even though the thought was eclipsed the next day when I came across the strangely nostalgic scene of William Short in the hallway, lurking near Papa's door like he used to in my father's times of trouble.

In his hand, he held folded pages, newsprint upon his fingers.

Another man—any other man—would've told me it wasn't fit for ladies to read. But William merely reddened, saying, "You need to see this, Patsy. Though you won't thank me for showing you."

Chapter Twenty-seven

THE RICHMOND RECORDER

I September 1802

It is well known that the man whom it delights the people to honor, keeps, and for many years past has kept, as his concubine, one of his own slaves. Her name is SALLY. The name of her eldest son is TOM. His features are said to bear a striking although sable resemblance to those of the president himself. The boy is ten or twelve years of age. His mother went to France in the same vessel with Mr. Jefferson and his two daughters. The delicacy of this arrangement must strike every person of common sensibility. What a sublime example for an American ambassador to place before the eyes of two young ladies!

PAPA KEPT THIS CLIPPING.

It's here in his wooden filing presses amidst his belongings, as if it were no more than a passing memorandum, or a recipe, or a scrap of poem, and not a devastating exposure that set the political world aflame.

It was also a betrayal, written by James Callender, one of my father's partisans turned odious blackmailer. So I burn this clipping, even knowing there are a thousand more like it in the world. And worse things were printed after it.

The newspapers brought me and my sister into the scandal directly, offering sympathies for the supposed humiliations my father had visited upon us by forcing us to see illegitimate mulatto sisters and brothers enjoying the same parental affection with ourselves. They asked why Papa hadn't married a worthy woman of his own complexion. They lampooned him as a bad father, a bad owner, a bad president.

But this first article—the one that William Short showed me—somehow did the most damage. "I'm sorry, Patsy," William had said. "This is going to be a very difficult time for all of you."

My hand came to my mouth as my eyes traced over the words a second time. Anger curled inside my belly. Would the entirety of my father's presidency find him under constant attack? "How could they print such a thing?"

He gave me a sad, sympathetic look. "Because partisanship has made anything fair, which honor and propriety might once have kept quiet."

Shaking my head, I stared at him. "I don't . . . how will we . . ."

William looked down for a moment, his brow furrowing as he gathered his thoughts, and then his eyes returned to mine. "Well, do you think it's possible that your father has been given a rare opportunity? He could simply acknowledge Sally. Bring her out from the shadows—"

"You've *no* idea what you're saying," I hissed. Did I not hold in my hands the evidence of exactly why he could never do such a thing? "It would bring down his presidency."

William lowered his voice, conciliatory. "Even in the short time I've been back in this country, I've heard about a certain Mr. Bell who recently died and left everything to his wife. Everyone in Charlottesville seems happy to treat Mary Hemings Bell as his widow, and a free white woman."

Did he think my father could take Sally as his *wife*? It was the kind of madness only William would advocate, and I tried to fan away my anger with the paper in my hands. "Mr. Bell was a store owner."

"And your father is the president of the United States. It isn't the same. I understand, but—"

"No, I don't think you do understand."

I don't think anyone did. Which is why I left William standing in the hall and took the newspaper to my father myself.

My father and I had never had an open discussion about Sally Hemings. It wasn't our way. But now we'd have to. I tapped only once upon the glass-paned door before unlocking and entering the sanctuary of his cabinet, where Papa sat enthroned upon his whirligig chair, his theodolite aimed at the window behind him like a scepter, a number of books open before him. As president he might be a man of the people, but at home, he was a king in his castle. And, glancing at the newspaper in my hands, he knew exactly why I'd come.

"I intend to say nothing about it, Patsy."

"But, Papa—"

He pressed his fingers to his temples, as if staving off one of his infamous headaches. "I've never allowed myself to be compelled to comment publicly on any private matter."

Certainly, that was the truth. I'd learned long ago that he would never be compelled to speak about anything he didn't want to. It was a source of great frustration to me as a girl, but a wonderment now that I was grown. I wished I could follow his example, but I didn't have the self-discipline. "The Federalists are trying to destroy you with this."

"They've been trying for years. They've said I'm a mixed breed, a swindler, a coward. Why, they've even said I was dead. This is no different."

"But this *is* different. This is—"

True, I thought. *Those were lies and this was true.*

Oh, the papers were wrong about many of the details. But Sally's children were living, breathing proof of the scandal. My father's reputation would suffer amongst those who had no understanding of how it was with our slaves. This had a salacious element to it.

I knew perfectly well how damaging scandals like that could be. William's affair had tarnished him and limited his career. A marital infidelity had damaged the once-formidable Alexander Hamilton's reputation beyond repair. And an incestuous liaison had nearly sent my sister-in-law and brother-in-law to the gallows.

But there was more to this than bedroom matters. This was about race. The papers emphasized how my father's relationship with Sally was long-standing. It was to be read as an insult to whites that my father could *prefer* Sally when he could have his choice of any white woman. Sally had been branded a *slut as common as the pavement* to imply my father must have a degraded character to have cared for her or enjoyed her for more than one night.

It was a calamity, and I couldn't imagine how my father remained so calm. "There must be some reply, Papa."

"No reply is owed. If I've stood for anything, it's that the essence of liberty is to be found in the sanctity of a man's home and private life."

My father always held back some part of himself. He didn't belong to the people wholly. Maybe he belonged to no one, wholly. Not even my mother or me. But I took his reluctance for a desire not to serve up Sally to a slobbering, condemning, Federalist party. "Deny it. Just deny it all."

Papa said nothing. He merely stared at me with shock and surprise.

"Papa, you *must* deny it! If you won't, then let Tom do it. He can publish a letter in the papers saying—"

"*Patsy.*" My father said my name with such a quiet agony that it silenced me. "I won't answer the charges. I won't deny it. The storm will pass, just as all the others do. I don't care what people think."

I did not believe *that* for one moment. My father was, like all Virginians, extraordinarily sensitive to censure. Neither could I agree that the storm would pass. For my father was still tarnished by the lie that he'd fled the British in cowardly fashion when they invaded our mountaintop, a story that had originated more than twenty years before. He was still pained by that, too.

Trying to protect him, I said, "If you won't deny it, at least send Sally and her children to live with me at Edgehill."

"Monticello is her home."

And that's all he had to say on the subject. He wouldn't send Sally away, not even long enough to quiet a scandal that threatened the reputation of his whole family. His presidency was meant to prove that we could live freely in a republic, but he was willing to endanger that, too.

He hadn't been able to let Sally go in Paris and he wasn't going to give her up now. He wouldn't send her away. He wouldn't speak of her or against her. And I didn't know whether to count him a stubborn, selfish old fool or to admire him for it.

Here we were, once again, in the little chamber where I once watched him pace, fighting with madness when my mother died. When he believed that every private happiness had been torn from him because of his commitment to the cause. But now he'd found some measure of contentment in a woman who ought to have posed no threat to anyone.

He was right, I decided. This part of him belonged to no one but Sally Hemings.

I had decided this even before he said, "I can bear the contempt of others, but the children. . . ."

My children, he meant. His adoring grandchildren.

"They'll never know," I said.

He wouldn't deny it, but I would. To my dying breath.

His shoulders rounded and his head drooped. "Patsy, I am heartsick to know how this must lessen your love for me—"

"Never," I said, tears brimming. "You must never think that, Papa. Whenever you come home, I look forward to it with raptures and palpitations not to be described. The heart swellings convince me of the folly of those who dare to think that any new ties can weaken the first and best of nature. The first sensations of my life were affection and respect for you and nothing has weakened or surpassed that."

Papa's eyes misted. "Please believe that my absence from you always teaches me how essential your society is to my happiness." Reaching for my hand and bringing it to his lips with more than courtly emotion, drawing the warm palm of it against his cheek, he said, "When it comes to my character, I offer you and your sister as my defense. Neither of you have ever by a word or deed given me one moment's uneasiness; on the contrary, I have felt perpetual gratitude to heaven for having given me, in you, a source of so much pure and unmixed happiness and pride. That is why I need you in Washington City. Your sister, too."

We'd been in a very long sulk over his return to public life, but I decided then and there that if he needed us in Washington City, that's where we would go.

I WAS SEVENTEEN the last time I ventured out into any kind of political society. Now, I was almost thirty.

The shimmering bronze gown from my debut in Paris was nothing but a faded memory. Every stylish gown had long since been moth-eaten or worn away to scraps for the quilts on my children's beds. And I was anxious for how I should go out into the new capital when long seclusion had rendered me unfit for public life.

Moreover, I could scarcely afford a new dress.

But Papa insisted on paying for every little thing, directing my sister and me to charge to his account all the fancy gowns and bonnets we could ever want. And he'd hear absolutely no excuse from my sister this time. When Polly tried to demur by saying that she was too unaccustomed to the attentions she might receive as the daughter of the president, my father sent her an essay on the dangers of withdrawing from society. When she said she couldn't meet us at Monticello to make preparations because Jack wouldn't spare the horses from his plow, my father said he'd hire a coach to fetch her. When she worried that little Francis might catch the measles, Papa vowed to clear the mountain of every child but mine within a mile and a half of the place.

There might be no bribe Papa could make that'd induce Jack Eppes to become our neighbor, but my father had finally decided that he was the president of the United States, and if he wanted both his daughters with him, he *would* have us.

Papa needed us, so we'd join him in Washington City in November, and that was all there was to it.

"Martha, don't fret!" Dolley said, adjusting the lace of my shawl. "All you need are some new dresses that flatter your bosom. Something distinctive and stylish. You're already a lovely and charming hostess, so it'll be no difficulty to transform you into what your father so desperately needs."

It pained me that my father should so desperately need anything. Dolley was too much of a southern lady to ask if the stories about Sally were true. She didn't even acknowledge them, but she knew. Everyone knew.

Dolley retrieved her bonnet from where it lay upon the alcove bed in the octagonal bedroom she and Mr. Madison always used when they visited Monticello. Trellis wallpaper in green and white covered the walls, a relic Papa brought home with him from France. "What your father needs right now is a . . . a *first lady*. And given that he's a widower, a *first daughter* will have to do. There needs to be a woman of grace and good sense at the presidential mansion, since there hasn't been one there before now. Mrs. Washington retreated, and her daughter flitted about at parties like a shameless princess, born to deference. And that's to say nothing of *Her Majesty, Mrs. President Adams*, who received visitors seated like royalty in Buckingham Palace."

Though I still harbored soft affections for Abigail Adams, I knew better than to say so to Dolley, despite the fact that this conversation reminded me of one I'd had long ago with Mrs. Adams as she guided me through what fashions I'd require in France.

"I shouldn't like to cause any sort of scandal by doing the wrong thing," I said, glancing out the window toward the corner terrace.

"Martha, your father's presidency is a new start," Dolley replied. "Our first real experience with a republic. That's why they're trying so hard to bring him down. President Jefferson needs a hostess to set the example, making no distinction between our people and theirs. Everyone will look to you for a model of what a virtuous daughter, wife, and mother of the republic should be. So don't you worry about gowns. I'll order everything for you and your sister. Hairpieces and every fashionable thing universally worn by ladies in society today. You must simply *play the part.*"

THE PUMPKINS WERE FINALLY RIPE, perfect for pies and breads. So I was grateful when Tom came upon me in the garden and instead of scolding me for not leaving the task to Wormley Hughes, he helped me lift the heavy pumpkins into the wheelbarrow. "Sally knows," Tom said, wiping sweat from his brow on his forearm.

I bit my lip. He didn't have to say more. He meant that Sally knew what was being printed about her in the papers, and also that I wanted her gone from my father's mountain. I sighed, shaking my head that my truce with Sally Hemings was now imperiled.

We'd long ago patched up our quarrel and reached accommodation. When I was away, Sally was mistress of Monticello, but when Papa returned with his entourage of guests, she made herself scarce, giving way to my sister and me, certain not to intrude on our time with Papa. In recent years, whenever Sally and I crossed paths, it was always a pleasant, cordial encounter. Sometimes even an affectionate one.

But in the days after the story broke, such a chill descended between us that I worried to touch her, lest I find myself bitten with frost. And at the precise moment Sally Hemings ought to have made herself invisible, she was at my father's side every moment of the day, serving his food, doing his mending, massaging at the damaged hands and wrists he needed for his writing.

And her mixed-race children were at his knee, alongside mine.

Sally was—by nature or practice, I could never tell which—amiable and eager to please, but she was never a simpering coward. She could, in a crisis, carry herself like an amber-eyed queen, wreathed in a mantle of golden dignity that left her quite beyond reach. And she'd let me know—with a tight-lipped stare as she removed her lace mobcap at the end of the day—that she resented my suggestion to put her out of the way.

"She must be terrified," Tom said as he turned to place two pumpkins into the barrow.

"What do you mean?" I asked, kneeling over a vine.

My husband glanced at me and narrowed his eyes. "She must be terrified your father is going to sell her and the children away. Pained, too, by the things they're saying in the newspapers."

And at that moment, I felt suddenly shamed. Whoever had been telling tales to the newspapers knew how many times Sally had been pregnant, but not how many of her children had survived. Knew that she was pregnant in France, but not that her son had died. To anger whites about the president's black son, the papers were saying that Sally's first boy grew up to be a man, and was now strutting about the plantation like a gentleman born to the manor. My heart seized at the thought of how much Sally must've wished her eldest son had lived to do just that. For Sally, these revelations must have been a torment.

And it was my husband who had to remind me of that simple fact. I'd worried for my father's reputation; William had worried about the principles of the matter. Only *Tom* had given any care to the pain of an enslaved woman. My husband understood fear and sadness and suffering, and because he did, my heart filled with love for him. It made it easier to content myself with being his wife when William Short was sleeping under the same roof.

Easier still, when William began his preparations to leave Monticello.

He didn't bother making pleasantries when I found him at the carriage house, placing his gentleman's grooming kit on the seat of his chariot. "He's not going to reply to the revelations in the papers, is he, Patsy?"

I knew—could see in his every gesture—that William was disappointed that my father would never serve as the champion of equality that he wanted him to be. But William's ideals were wild-eyed. It was a comfort to know he hadn't changed and that he wasn't afraid to challenge Papa, but it angered me to see how eagerly he wanted to be off.

"So you're going to abandon us again?"

William bristled at my question, spinning to face me. "*You* can ask *me* that?"

Let him say it, I thought. Let it all out into the open, then. He could say that I abandoned him and I could answer that he forced a seventeen-year-old girl to make an impossible choice. Yet, in the end, what did it matter? I'd married another man. A man not nearly so charming or successful. But a good man. A man I *loved*. A man who would never have let me go.

So I only said, "My father needs you now more than ever."

A horse nickered and stomped in the nearest stall, and William nodded. "I'll be in Washington City when he gets there and stay with him at the President's House. But I can't stay at Monticello another day."

He didn't say why, and perhaps he thought he didn't need to.

I cleared my throat. "You have my thanks. It comforts me to know that Papa will have you at his side with such infamy hanging over his head."

William straightened his waistcoat without acknowledging my thanks. "As I understand it, you and your sister will arrive in November. I'll be gone by then to take care of some business in New York. So I'm afraid I'll miss your debut into the political society of the capital, just as I missed your debut in Paris."

Why should he mention that? It sent a pang through my heart. "I remember nearly nothing of Paris except when you were with me."

I shouldn't have said it and he shouldn't have let his gaze drop to his feet, abashed. "I have regrets in life, Mrs. Randolph. One of them is the loss of a friendship between us."

"It was never snuffed out, Mr. Short, I assure you," I said, re-membering another conversation, a much different one we once had in a carriage house, a thousand miles away and at least as many years ago. Or so it seemed.

"It *was* snuffed out," he said. "I assure you it was. But now, I would prefer . . . or at least dare to hope that we might part in friendship, once so precious to me."

Then I realized, with a profound ache, what this was. "You're saying good-bye."

"Think of it as only *au revoir*. I'll be in Virginia next year. Per-haps we'll cross paths."

He didn't say it like a man who intended to cross paths with me. But he leaned forward to press two quick, chaste kisses upon my cheek in the French style. Then we stood awkwardly together while I reeled.

Our bitter parting in France had weighed upon me all these years. I couldn't bear to part bitterly again, so I was grateful that he'd asked for my friendship. I wanted to clasp his hands tightly and show him the full measure of my feelings, but our situation was already more irregular than I ought to allow. So I said, "Be well, Mr. Short. Be happy."

Then I turned to go.

"Mrs. Randolph?"

I turned to see him looking very wistful. "Your friend Mr. Madison once wrote that if men were angels there'd be no need for government. Remember, when you go to Washington City, that there's no place for an angel in the capital."

Chapter Twenty-eight

To Thomas Jefferson from "A Friend to the Constitution"

This comes from a stranger but a friend. Know there is a plot formed to murder you before the next election. A band of hardy fellows are to have ten thousand dollars if they succeed in the attempt. They are to carry daggers and pistols. I have been invited to join them but would rather suffer death. I advise you to take care and be cautious how you walk about as some of the assassins are already in Washington.

WE HEARD WHISPERS—sometimes dangerous whispers—even before our carriage rolled into Washington City, which was, at the time, neither a town nor a village, but more a cluster of brick and wooden houses connected by unpaved roads.

Dusky Sally. Black Sal. African Venus.

Salacious gossip about Papa's preference for dark wenches was just another line of attack . . . though an enduring one, because it aroused carnal curiosity. But not everyone gossiped about my father's mistress with malicious glee. The capital was still a southern place, built by slaves and filled with people who understood our ways. But it was also—at the moment—filled to the brim with Federalists eager to seize upon any reason to criticize my father.

Some of them were still threatening his life, which led Polly and me to fret that he slept alone upstairs in the presidential mansion. The solitude seemed unsafe, for the Federalists resented my father's presence in the largely unfurnished Georgian manor, which housed a mammoth and indecorous wheel of cheese—a gift from admirers for Papa's commitment to the separation of church and state. The Federalists didn't like the way Papa showed his defiance to the British crown by greeting their ambassador informally, in slippers. And they were appalled by my father's insistence upon pell-mell seating arrangements that eliminated the status of rank and privilege.

"We're going with Papa to a religious service," I told my sister before our bags were even unpacked. Dolley advised we do so to dispel the notion that Papa was a godless man who meant to overrun the capital with mixed-race bastard children. And I was happy to take her advice, because my skills in the public arena were rusty, and because Dolley was more naturally attuned to politics than any woman I'd ever met.

She dressed us in the right colors and most appropriate fashions, introduced us to the right people, and made certain we knew whom we should shun. In truth, with Dolley, I sometimes felt as if a canny and persistent sheepdog was herding us, nipping gently at our heels.

But I had my own political instincts. I was accustomed to royal courts, but my father's court wasn't a royal one. Dolley had clearly given great thought to what an American court should be . . . and I began to do the same. So I set out quite deliberately to befriend the wives of newspapermen. And at dinner parties amongst hostile Federalists, I always singled out the most belligerent man for my attentions and kept him so busy in conversation that he couldn't make mischief.

A thing that much impressed Dolley Madison. "How is it that you manage to sniff out malice before the troublemakers say a word?"

"I listen to what they do not say," I told her.

Papa used these dinners to enforce collegiality by never mixing

Federalists and Republicans, limiting the guest list to twelve at a round table, and by keeping ladies present at all times. "Your father is very sociable," a man said to me with a wry smile. *"For a Republican."*

It was John Quincy Adams, son of the former president. And though he was a Federalist, it wasn't hard to smile at him, given I still harbored affection for his family. To that point, he'd seemed very much ill at ease at my father's table, paying little attention to the chef's creations, but staring longingly at the tray of dried fruit just out of his reach. And because he was the son of Abigail Adams, I was determined to put him at ease. Taking the liberty of slipping an apricot to him, I said, "Mr. Adams, I'm afraid I'm old enough to remember a time when there weren't any Federalists or Republicans. A time when we were all simply Americans. Why it was your very own mother who helped choose my first real dress in Paris. You would've laughed to see the chaos of it!"

"Do tell," he said, and we laughed together the rest of the evening as I happily reminisced. I smoothed ruffled feathers when I could, most notably at a public function when my father gave accidental offense by overlooking an Irish poet.

No one else seemed to have noticed the reddening face of the little man, but I quickly stepped forward to say, "Why, Mr. Moore, I'm afraid you're so young and handsome that my father mistook you for a page boy!"

Of course, at the time, I had no idea that Thomas Moore was responsible for fanning the flames of the Sally Hemings scandal with depraved poetry; I doubt my father knew either.

But when it came to the English, Papa seemed to give offense quite *deliberately*.

First, he invited to dinner both the British emissary and diplomats from France, with whom Britain was at war. Then, when dinner was called, I quite nearly panicked when my father casually escorted Mrs. Madison to the table instead of Mrs. Merry. I knew it would be considered by her husband, the British ambassador, to be an utter breach of protocol. And I wasn't wrong. He was as outraged as if a treaty had been broken. But unlike the matter of the overlooked poet, my father's glance to me showed that he had done it with every intention.

It was in the highest pique that the ambassador's angry wife asked me, "How shall I address you, Mrs. Randolph? Do you prefer the distinction of being the president's daughter or the congressman's wife?"

Given her fury, I carefully considered my reply. "Why I claim no distinction whatever, but wish only for the same consideration extended to other strangers."

She huffed as if I'd spat in her soup.

But I couldn't find it in myself to be sorry. I hadn't forgotten that the British tried to capture and hang my father as a traitor. That they'd chased me and my family from our home, captured our slaves, and destroyed Elk Hill. That they'd taken the opportunity of the chaos in France to make such mischief that a power-mad Napoleon had risen. I might have to smile and pretend I didn't know about the vile attacks of my own countrymen on my father's presidency, but I didn't have to pretend to be a monarchist just to accommodate the pride of the ambassador's wife.

There's no place for an angel in the capital, William had said.

And I wasn't here to be my father's angel, but his Amazon.

~

"I CAN'T DO IT ANYMORE," Maria said, peeping out the wide, paneled door. "I can't go out there. The salon is filled with ladies and gentlemen!"

"My dear," Dolley chirped, fastening a green satin ribbon under my sister's bosom. "That's the point of a New Year's Eve gala. An open invitation to the President's House is meant to make everyone in Washington feel welcome."

But my sister's expression was one of undiluted panic. "I can't bear another party with these sophisticated strangers. They think me quite backward!"

"Nonsense," Dolley said, tugging the ribbon tight. "They think you're very beautiful."

My sister *was* a beauty—especially in a white neoclassical dress that bared her arms and stretched tight over her bosom with ornate gold pins at each shoulder. And she was still pale enough from her ordeals in childbirth to make her resemblance to a Roman statue complete. "People only praise me for beauty because they cannot praise me for anything better," Polly said. "Patsy is suited to this. Not me."

My sister had a distressing habit of comparing herself unfavorably to me—determined that my father mustn't love her as much. I harbored a suspicion that my Aunt Elizabeth had put this notion in her mind, and I was determined to stomp it out, but Dolley wasn't to be distracted by family jealousies. Clucking about us in her exotic silks, she said, "Nonsense. You and your sister are *both* beautiful and suited for society."

It was a lie, of course, with regard to my beauty. I'd always been more handsome than beautiful, but I looked dignified and elegant in my gown of deep blue with long white gloves. This was to be our first truly formal occasion at the President's House at which we'd be expected to stand in as hostesses. And I knew my sister's anxieties were not to be soothed with compliments. "Won't you give us a moment?" I asked, smiling at Dolley.

Dolley bobbed her head. "Just don't dally too long or the whole schedule might be thrown off. You don't want your father to have to serve melted ice cream, do you?"

With that, she ducked out the door, and I took my sister's hands in mine. They were cold. Shaking. "My sweet sister, you've done so well up until now."

"How can you bear it?" Polly asked, biting her lip. "Just this morning, I heard two women talking about Papa and Sally's imaginary son, *President Tom*, who intends to come live at the

President's House. Everyone is saying that you and I must weep to see a Negress take the place of our mother. Maybe you don't hear these whispers, but I do. While you're chatting with the ladies, I'm quiet in the corners, and I hear what they say."

"They can go on saying it like the rot-mouthed buzzards they are," I replied. "Because they're never going to get the satisfaction of seeing Papa run out of office. They're never going to see us with our heads bowed, do you hear?"

My sister nodded, swallowing with difficulty, as if the humiliation was choking her.

"Besides, we're not doing this only for Papa," I reminded her. "It's for our whole family. You're a congressman's wife now. We both are. Representative Jack Eppes is out there waiting for you. Waiting for you to take his arm so he can proudly show you off."

That revived her flagging spirits a bit, and so we went out together that New Year's Eve into the throngs of my father's party, a lavish entertainment given at his own expense. And I'd scarcely turned a corner before I saw the most handsome man I'd ever seen in my life.

My breath caught at his dark hair, touched only slightly by silver. His tall distinguished form, trim in a suit of fawn trousers and a black tailcoat with gold piping. My knees went a little weak at the familiar slope of his shoulders and the dark flashing eyes that I knew so well.

By God, Congressman Thomas Mann Randolph was a sight.

He was my husband of more than a decade, but I hadn't seen him like this since before his father died. Winning the election had changed something in him. Gave him a renewed sense of confidence, a straighter posture, clearer eyes. Watching people flock around my husband made me wonder what kind of man Tom might have become ten years sooner if his father hadn't discouraged his education. And I was ever so glad that I hadn't discouraged him from running for Congress, even though I'd been sorely tempted.

Doubly glad when he saw me in my beautiful gown and his eyes smoldered with hunger. "I do declare, Mrs. Randolph, you're going to make me the subject of envy tonight."

I was the daughter of a public man; I hadn't wanted to be the wife of one, too. But if politics was the arena in which my husband might finally come into his own, I was grateful for it.

For the first time in years, I harbored true hope for my husband's future. It was a new year, a new chapter, a new era. And when Tom settled upon me that night with kisses that tasted of champagne, I found myself unexpectedly eager for him.

~—

MY SISTER WAS PREGNANT AGAIN, AND SO WAS I.

"Patsy, I believe you could give birth accidentally if you sneezed," my sister teased, but there was an edge to it, because she was afraid. And while our husbands were in Congress, I was determined not to let my sister out of my sight, which was why we'd left our menfolk in Washington City and come home to Virginia, to Edgehill, together to have our babes.

Before the weather turned too cold, we went together into Charlottesville to shop for tumblers, wineglasses, and some groceries. Normally, we'd have taken our maids, but given the size of my belly I wanted more room in the carriage.

On the road, my sister asked, "Are you hoping it's a boy?"

"A son would be helpful to Tom, but I think in his secret heart, he prefers daughters."

"I hope mine is a boy. Then Francis will have a brother and maybe Jack won't feel as if he needs more children."

My jaw tightened at that, trying to bite back harsh words for my sister's husband. Why was it that women were expected to restrain our every passion for the sake of propriety, but men couldn't do it even for the sake of the women they loved? I knew that in getting another child on my sister, Jack had done only what a husband has every right to do. But the last two had almost killed her, and she was terribly afraid. Polly would never blame Jack; no one would.

But I was her sister—and I blamed him.

"I think Betsy Hemings might have him," my sister said.

I dragged my eyes from the chariot window to fix them on her. "Who?"

"Jack," she said, as if I were quite a dullard. "I think my maid would welcome him into her bed, but I don't think my husband would put a hand on her unless I was dead."

I stared in numb shock at what she was implying—no, what she was saying outright.

"Jack is the best beloved of my soul," she continued, furrowing her brow. "So it hurts to think of him with another woman. But if I should die in childbirth, Betsy might be a comfort to him. Better for my children, too."

"Maria!" I cried so savagely that the baby inside me kicked.

I didn't want my sister thinking this way. Not about dying and not about making another Hemings slave-mistress. But she was thinking of my mother's example when she said, "If I die in childbirth, I don't want a Gabriella Harvie over my children. Better that Jack should take a concubine. I'm not brave enough to broach it with him, but if I were a good mother, I'd at least plant the idea in Betsy's head. Maybe I should mention it to her mother."

Betsy's mother was, of course, Mary Hemings Bell, the proprietress of the store we were to shop in.

"Have you lost your wits?" I asked, having half a mind to tell the driver to turn the carriage back around. Fortunately, my sister seemed to have abandoned the idea by the time we reached Main Street.

Polly and I, both round as eggs, waddled our way into Mary Bell's store, just in time to hear a man at the counter say, "Chocolate drops."

I confess, even if I hadn't been flustered already, I was in no way prepared to see William. My hands went straightaway to my bonnet to make certain it wasn't askew, but my sister let out a girlish squeal. "Mr. Short! Whatever are you doing back in Virginia? Why last we heard, you'd gone off to New York, and then Kentucky to see your brother."

"Been there and back again," he replied with a tight smile, holding up three fingers to the proprietress to indicate how many bags of chocolate drops she should make for him. "Now I'm on my way to Richmond."

"Why didn't you send word?" my sister asked. "We're staying at Edgehill. You should winter with us there, like old times."

I knew perfectly well why he didn't send word. We'd said farewell at Monticello a year ago. He hadn't intended to see me again, I thought. Certainly, not so soon. And as much as I might welcome William's company, it'd be beyond inappropriate to have him stay with us while our menfolk were away.

So I protested, "You presume on the man, Polly!"

"It's Maria," she said, rolling her eyes at me in exasperation. "At least come for supper, Mr. Short."

He winced. "Please forgive me, but my business makes me quite unsociable. I hope you'll accept these confections as my apology. Or at least consider them an offering to two goddesses of motherhood."

Polly was delighted, digging into the bag of chocolates at once. But I was made entirely self-conscious; I never wanted him to see me so fat and swollen. "Thank you, but I shouldn't want to overindulge."

"Whereas I make a habit of it," Mr. Short said. "Is there a place we can take some coffee or tea together as we did in Paris?"

My sister laughed. "I'm afraid you'll find Charlottesville wanting if you're hoping for those tables that sink down into the ground and come back up with pastries on them . . . oh, I do miss strolling the galleries of the Palais-Royal. All of us, and Sally, too."

Mary Hemings Bell studiously did not look up from her counter at the mention of her sister and France.

William said, "Shall we take a walk then, ladies?"

"Oh, no," my sister said at once. "You two go ahead. I'm too tired for that. I'll stay and chat with Mary."

There was no way for William to know why the prospect of Polly having a private word with her maid's mother should give me pause. But he didn't give me even a moment to object. Instead, he laced his arm in mine and said, "Let's walk then, Mrs. Randolph. I'll go slow, so as not to tax you in your delicate condition."

"There is nothing delicate about my condition," I assured him. I fell into stride beside him on the main street, determined not to let him think I couldn't still match his steps on the cobblestones. "Nothing delicate at all. There's a reason our husbands are so happy to have an excuse to be absent until after the children are born."

Mr. Short laughed. "You plan to hole up the whole winter at Edgehill with only a houseful of women and girls?"

"And my son, of course. Jeff is the ten-year-old man of the house, now. He's been riding out each day to check on the property. He fancies himself quite a man grown."

"He seemed like a very earnest boy. Like his father."

It was strange to hear William's assessment of my husband, and a good one at that. "Yes, but he'd hate to hear it. Jeff aims to be just like his grandfather, one day."

"Don't we all?" William smiled, wryly.

It was a subject entirely too close to old pains. But still, I asked, "You've ambitions to be president?"

"Nothing so lofty. Just the minister to France."

"You'd go back to Paris? Given all the danger, given the state of the revolution, now with Napoleon—"

"What other American knows the whole of what has happened there, start to finish, better than me?"

No other American, I thought. Not even my father. "Then you're here in Virginia to mend those fences you spoke of?"

William cleared his throat. "Alas, I'm not sufficiently regretful for having kicked at Mr. Madison's delicate fences. I confess, I've seldom disliked a man more than I dislike Madison."

It was strange to hear; no one but Federalists disliked Madison. And most of them hated my father much more. "But—"

"Don't let it trouble you. I'm certain the feeling is mutual. And I'm sure you've had enough of conflict after your time in Washington City. I'm told you quietly conquered the place during your winter campaign."

I felt myself blush for his characterization of it. How was it that he always saw me as some sort of warrior? And how was it that I never minded? "I hope I did some small good."

"Margaret Bayard Smith sings your praises," he said. "You may count yourself a success when a newspaperman's wife says that you're one of the most lovely women she's ever met, with manners so frank and affectionate that you put her perfectly at ease."

Margaret's husband was a Republican, so she was apt to praise me, but still my cheeks burned with peculiar pleasure. "Given such a recommendation, Mr. Short, I'm confident enough to advise you. If you're seeking a diplomatic post, you must reach accord with our secretary of state."

William's gaze slid from mine and landed at our feet. "Your father is the president. If he wishes for me to serve as an ambassador, I'm pleased to serve in that capacity. Madison's approval shouldn't be required."

But it would be, I thought. Mr. Short ought to have known it. Surely he did know it. And I suddenly suspected his unwillingness to swallow his pride was a ruse. He was, for some reason, postponing a return to Europe. I traitorously wondered if it had to do with me.

It would be better if he left. Better for him. Better for Rosalie. And better for me.

Because I was unsettled every time we met. Unlike Jack Eppes, I would never risk all that I loved for fleeting desire. But it would be better never to be tempted in the first place.

Chapter Twenty-nine

Washington, 23 January 1804
To Martha Jefferson Randolph from Thomas Jefferson

The snow is still falling with unabated fury. I expect Mr. Eppes will leave in order to be with Maria at the knock of an elbow in February. On Friday Congress gave a dinner on the acquisition of Louisiana. As much as I wished to have yourself and sister with me, I rejoice you weren't here. The brunt of the battle falls on the Secretary's ladies, who are dragged into the dirt in every federal paper. You'd have been the victims had you been here, and butchered more bloodily. Pour into the bosom of my dear Maria all the comfort and courage which the affections of my heart can give her, and tell her to rise superior to fear for our sakes.

MY SISTER'S CHILDBIRTH was no knock of an elbow.

As the bloody child tore itself out of her, Polly's screams drowned out the howling winter wind. Though I was scarcely recovered of giving birth myself, I held my sister's hand, mopped sweat from her brow, and coaxed her to breathe when she was too tired to do even that. When the childbed fever ravished her, she had no milk for the child either, so I took my sister's newborn to my breast with my own. Two precious baby girls. Mine dark-haired, dark-eyed, and plump as a piglet. My sister's pale, ghostly, and fragile as a flower. I cradled them both in my arms until I was so tired and sore and weary I could no longer feel my arms at all.

But still I held the baby girls. Because it was the only thing I could do for my sister, who tossed and turned in pain that radiated from her empty womb, while she whispered, "Jack . . . where's Jack?"

I suppose he must've set out from Washington City as soon as he got my letter, but it wasn't until almost the end of February that Jack Eppes walked his half-frozen horse up the road. My son ran out to take the reins, and Jack took giant strides into the house. "Is she—"

"She's asking for you," I said, and watched him dash to her, leaving puddles of muddy snow on the wooden stairs in his wake. My sister loved him, and his kisses on her forehead brightened her mood. She seemed happier still to see him take his newborn daughter from my arms and cradle her in his own.

And I began to hope.

At least, until the morning she rasped, "Patsy, take me home." Perhaps she meant Eppington. I couldn't be sure. But a journey that far would certainly kill her. Monticello was closer. The air was healthier there. And we could dose her with my father's sherry. *Yes*, I decided. Now that the spring thaw had come, we'd take her home to Monticello.

She couldn't sit a horse, nor could I risk her in a bouncing carriage. So we put her down upon a litter, and slaves carried her the entire four-mile journey. Jack and I followed on foot with all the children, splashing across a muddy stream, and scrambling up a thorny and overgrown mountain path with a fierce determination to make my sister well.

Dear God, I prayed. *Make her well.*

But I'd prayed this prayer before and reneged upon my bargain with God, and I feared retribution was now at hand.

"Make your sisters keep up," I said to my eldest.

"Momma, they won't do as I say unless I holler," Ann said. "And you told me a lady should never holler."

Maria whispered from the stretcher upon which she was being carried. "Your momma never has to holler to get anyone to do her bidding. She just fixes you with that sensible gaze, speaks in dulcet tones, and you're simply overcome by the superiority of her rank."

I was so unbearably relieved to hear my sister in good humor that I didn't take umbrage. And more relieved to see Sally come running out into the dreary spring weather to greet our ragtag band of refugees. I'd sent word ahead, so she'd made up a bed for my sister on the main floor, complete with budding spring flowers in a vase on the side table. Wearing an old housedress with her dark hair braided straight down the back, Sally took the children from my arms, then helped me wash my sister of the sweat and grime of our journey before tucking her into bed.

"You're giving us a terrible fright," Sally scolded my sister.

"Papa," my sister said, softly. "Is he . . ."

"He's riding from Washington City right now," Sally said. "So we can have a happy reunion."

"Is Papa coming?" my sister asked, as if she hadn't heard.

Sally and I did everything for her, in silent conspiracy that no one else should. When my father finally arrived, Maria wanted to be dressed and upright. For twelve days, every morning she woke up and declared that she was on the mend. But on the twelfth night, her fever burned so hot and her pain was so great that she couldn't speak without her lips trembling on every word.

That's when she pleaded with Sally and me to dose her with double the laudanum. I knew then that she was dying, well and truly. So did Sally, who looked to me, those hard amber eyes finally softening with anguish. It was Sally who had seen my sister safely across an ocean. Sally who was, in some ways, a sister to her, too.

But I was the one who held the bottle of laudanum.

"Please," my sister begged, writhing in pain. And when I gave it to her, she sighed softly at my brimming tears. "Courage, Patsy.

We mustn't cry. We must be of good cheer. Our papa is burdened with such sorrows that we must never burden him with our own."

Those words broke my heart.

Snapped it in two.

For they were *my* words, spoken after my mother's death, when we were both still little girls. Words I hadn't thought she remembered. Heavy words that I had pressed on her delicate shoulders and made her carry all her life.

And they were also the last words I ever heard my sister say.

SALLY AND I WERE BOTH WITH MY SISTER in the early morning, when the nightmare scene of my mother's death played itself out again. The frail and delicate beauty, pale and gasping upon her pillow. The grieving husband, weeping against her hand. Hemings servants gathered round. And me—in my Aunt Elizabeth's place—holding my sister's newborn daughter at the precise moment she was made an orphan in my arms.

The nostalgic horror of it all sent my father stumbling back, fleeing into another room while weeping into his handkerchief. But I stood there, deaf and dumb as a stone while everyone else wept. I couldn't accept the loss of my sister—my beloved sister—who was my child before I had any others.

My little Polly.

The loss of her couldn't be borne. And I couldn't make myself let go of her baby when Jack reached for the child. Jack wanted his daughter. It was only natural. His wife was dead and this baby, her namesake, was a living connection to her. So I ought not to have hated him for tearing the infant away from me.

But I did. Oh, I *hated* Jack Eppes.

And when he took that child from me, I thought my knees might buckle. But Sally's hand slipped into mine, squeezing tight, as if to keep me upright. And we stood there by Polly's bed like two honor guards, determined that no one else but us would prepare my sister for burial.

I washed her hair, dried it, then combed it to the grim music of the carpenter's hammer outside, as he made her coffin. Sally found a pretty dress for my sister to wear. I gathered a bouquet of spring flowers and returned to find Sally mending my sister's garments in the places they'd been worn, swiping at her eyes so that she could see her own needle.

They were all crying. The servants. The menfolk. The children.

But I didn't cry. I didn't cry because my sister had bade me not to. I didn't cry when they put my sister in her coffin. I didn't cry when they lowered her into the ground near my mother. I didn't cry when they shoveled dirt on top of her.

Nor did I cry when my father clutched at me by the fireplace, murmuring, "I've lost the half of all I had! Now it all hangs on the slender thread of a single life. On you, Patsy. Only you."

He no longer had the strength, I think, to rage violently in his grief. There'd be no smashed glass, no overturned lamps, no splinters of tables left in his wake. And no pistols, so long as I was there. It was as it had been at the beginning. Papa and I were forged together in sadness, and were still forged, such that no other person in this world was so dear. My life, too, was suspended by the slender thread of his. So I understood the truth of what he was saying.

And yet, it was not the whole truth of it either.

I had a family and he had his mistress, and with her, they had children. And I was never so grateful for Sally as I was that night when she relieved me at my father's side.

I began to retch the moment I returned to my room. I heaved drily into a pail that my husband held under me, nothing coming up. Alarmed to see me in such a state, Tom said, "Let me get you into bed."

"No," I said, refusing to let him tend me. I couldn't lean on him. I was in too much pain. I could neither sit nor lie down anywhere without agony. Instead, I paced, panting like a horse that'd been run too hard, until I was struggling for every breath the way my sister had struggled for hers.

"My poor Patsy," Tom said. "You're having a fit of hysterics."

Dragging in a ragged, desperate breath, as I tried to escape the cage of his arms, I snapped, "It's nothing of the sort. I ate radishes and milk together for supper, both of which are unfriendly to my stomach."

"It can't be healthful to hold the pain the way you do. You're a woman. There's no shame in your tears. You need a good cry on my shoulder, Patsy."

"Would you mind terribly fetching me some peppermint?"

With a frown, he sighed, then went down the stairs. I shut the door behind him, gasping, suffocating in my own garments and struggling to tear them off. Something finally tore inside me, too, and I began to sob.

I sobbed as I'd never sobbed before, falling to my knees amidst the shreds of my garments, shattered by the knowledge that I'd never see my sister again. She'd been twenty-five years old, now gone from me forever. And it was a pain like nothing I'd ever felt before—one I scarcely knew how to survive.

⁓

"IT'S SO HARD TO LOSE A SISTER," Nancy Randolph was saying.

She'd come to Edgehill ostensibly to offer her help in my time of grief. Now she was trying to draw me out past the usual pleasantries because the Randolphs seemed to want to speak about *everything*.

But I was a Jefferson and I could scarcely hear my own infant daughter Mary's name spoken aloud without bleeding anew for the sister I'd named her after. Condolences came from all over the country. We even received one from Abigail Adams. But I didn't want to think about the loss, couldn't bear to think about it, so I just stood there, hanging laundry while my infamous sister-in-law nattered on, insensible to the fact that I was barely listening.

"I know it's not the same," Nancy said. "But I've lost my sister Judy, as sure as if she'd died. Truly, I have. She harbors nothing but bitterness against me now."

I imagine I might be bitter, too, if my sister had fornicated with my husband, then killed the bastard born of that incestuous union, and exposed us all to scandal and poverty. Nancy had no one left alive to blame but herself.

So I said nothing. Just hung a petticoat on the line.

Handing me another wet petticoat from the basket, Nancy said, "John's causing mischief between us."

John Randolph, she meant. The only surviving brother at Bizarre. John was a sharp-tongued dandy who'd lately taken to calling himself *Randolph of Roanoke*. I disliked him immensely because he'd also taken to criticizing my father's presidency. But I didn't see how he could be to blame for the estrangement of Nancy and Judith, and I said so.

"I'll tell you how," Nancy explained. "John falsely accused me of carrying on with slaves in my sister's house as if I lived in a tavern. He's saying I poisoned Richard, and he's giving Judith the excuse she needs to turn me out."

For years now, I'd held my tongue about the scandal at Bizarre, even though my blood still ran cold at the thought of a dead baby hidden under a woodpile. Now, with grief eating me alive, I couldn't hold my tongue one moment longer. "Does Judy need an excuse, Nancy? We all know the kind of desperate acts you're capable of!"

Nancy drew back, pale as the petticoat on the line. "I thought—I thought you knew the truth, Patsy. I thought that's why, at trial . . . that's why you said . . ." My blood ran even colder at the thought of her lying to me again after all these years. So I said nothing. But Nancy sputtered, "You think I'm guilty. You think I killed my baby. But if you believed I was guilty, then why—"

"I didn't want to see you hanged," I said, very quietly.

Nancy let out a cry, as disconsolate as if I'd turned against her before the entire tribunal. "You don't understand, Patsy. I wanted to confess from the start, but Richard wouldn't let me. He wanted to protect me. It's true that I surrendered my virtue to the man I loved. It's true. But I did nothing to harm the child, and neither did Richard. I swear it."

"Do you forget that I saw the herbs?"

Nancy blinked. "You can't think they were mine! It was always Judith who had my mother's way in the garden. I was never any good with herbs." That was true, and the whole world realigned under my feet as I remembered it. Tears spilled over Nancy's cheeks, her lips trembling. "Judith notices everything. Always has. She knew I was pregnant before I did. She put the gum in my tea. I didn't know what I was drinking, Patsy."

Had Judith noticed—from the start—her husband's attraction to her sister? Had she given her sister the herbs to be rid of her husband's bastard?

As I asked myself these questions, Nancy was near hysterical, more than a decade's worth of anguish bubbling to the surface. "When you testified that you gave me the gum for an upset stomach, I thought it was because you didn't want anyone to know what Judith had done."

In shock, the freshly laundered undergarment fell from my grasp into the dirt, but I didn't stoop to retrieve it. Instead, I shivered, wondering if I'd somehow saved the wrong sister from the gallows. "But she defended you, Nancy. She defended both of you."

"How else was she to cover up the crime of killing my baby?" Nancy asked. "Judy wanted both of us to pay. Me and Richard, both. You have no idea what it was like returning to that house. Richard finally told her he intended to divorce her. And lo and behold, two days later he was dead of cramps in his stomach. But John blames *me* for bringing disgrace on the family, and I think she has him convinced that if Richard was poisoned it was my doing."

Richard Randolph's death had been strange. But then, everything about the people of Bizarre plantation specifically, and Tom's family generally, was strange. Still, I couldn't wrap my mind around it. "What you're saying, Nancy! If you suspect these things of your own sister, why did you stay with her at Bizarre all this time?"

Nancy gave a bitter laugh. "I'm a spinster sister with a blackened name. I had nowhere else to go. The Harvies would never have me at Tuckahoe. I knew you'd never have me in your household. Besides, how was I to leave until one of my brothers came for me? Judith reads all my letters coming or going. No one visits Bizarre since the scandal. Even those willing to associate with me, Judith keeps away, claiming pecuniary embarrassment. Every night, Judith takes out her Bible and makes me pray forgiveness for every little gift or kindness Richard ever bestowed on me. She employs me with drudgery every day and locks me in my bedroom at night. I've been so guilt ridden, I could hardly complain. I felt . . . I felt as if I deserved it. Especially since now I'm nothing but an object of charity."

I didn't want to believe her. I didn't want to believe a word. Yet, it had the ring of truth to it. And tenderness for Nancy stole over me at the thought she'd been silently suffering. We'd been taking care of Tom's younger sisters for years and I didn't know how we'd afford another, or how our reputation would endure the scandal, but I said, "Stay here for a spell, Nancy."

Smearing tears with the back of her hands, Nancy said, "You can't mean it."

"I do."

It took her a moment to believe me. When she did, she threw her arms around my neck. "You're so kind. My brother is so fortunate to have you for a wife. Never did there exist a more excellent woman! And you won't be sorry. I'll be a helper for you. And a sister in truth. A new sister for the one you lost."

Chapter Thirty

Washington, 1 July 1805
From Thomas Jefferson to Robert Smith,
United States Secretary of the Navy

You will perceive that I plead guilty to one of their charges, that when young and single I offered love to a handsome lady. I acknowledge its incorrectness; it is the only truth among all their allegations against me.

THIS LETTER IS A DENIAL OF SALLY. Or at least, it will be read as one. Which is why I don't burn it, even though it contains an admission of dishonor.

The handsome lady my father attempted to seduce was Mrs. Walker. And I learned of the incident in the spring of 1805, when, after having been reelected to the presidency, my father sent to me at Edgehill a carefully sealed letter in the care of my husband, with instructions that it should be delivered directly into my hands, and shown to no other.

I'd never received such a mysterious letter, folded quite small, heavy with its wax seal. And it was a letter that struck terror into my heart, because it was a message of love and repentance . . . and farewell.

"Get me a horse," I said to the nearest servant, still clutching the letter as I left my babies in their beds and rushed out of the house. I was up and into a saddle without so much as a cloak before Tom could stop me.

"What the devil are you doing?" he shouted after me. "Patsy, you can't go riding off into the night. It's dusk. I'll take you to your father in the morning."

"Monticello is only a few miles," I said, kicking my heels into the horse's side. Tom shouted for his own horse as I galloped off, but I never looked back. Instead, I rode with the sureness of the trained horsewoman I'd nearly forgotten I had inside me, racing up Papa's mountain like Jack Jouett did in raising the alarm that the British were coming. Breathless by the time I swung down in front of my father's house and still stinging from the lash of tree branches, I hurried into the entryway. "Sally?" I called, but heard no answer. And in a place like Monticello, where it was never quiet, I found myself instantly alarmed.

I found Papa—secretly returned from Washington City—alone at his table with a glass of sherry, perusing a box of curiosities from Captains Meriwether Lewis and William Clark, whom he'd sent on a grand expedition. Inside the chest were the preserved skeletons of all manner of creatures. Wolves, weasels, and elk. And I had a sudden memory of my father in his much younger days, feverishly scribbling down the correct way to preserve dead birds.

"Patsy." He shook his head, as if he wished I hadn't come.

I fought for both breath and composure. "Papa. You can't just send me a letter like that and—"

"Spoken words fail me where my pen rarely does."

I held the back of a gilded chair for steadiness. "You cannot mean to fight a duel."

Just the summer before, my father's old nemesis had died in a duel. Alexander Hamilton was dead before the age of fifty, and it was my father's vice president who killed him.

Hamilton—whose reputation had also been sullied by the revelation of an affair with a married woman—had tangled with Aaron Burr, who demanded satisfaction upon a field of honor. And as if seeking an end to his life, Hamilton dueled upon the very same spot where his son had died, using the very same pistols. Blood for reputation. Blood for honor. And now my father intended to follow in his footsteps. "You're the president of the United States. Surely you don't intend to dignify—"

"It's true, Patsy," my father broke in. "I did try to seduce Mr. Walker's wife. It happened before you were born or conceived. Before your mother. I regret that you should have to know the truth of it."

After all the other truths to which I was privy, did he really think *this* truth would matter to me? He clearly condemned himself, because his posture was stiff, tortured, and guilty indeed. Guiltier, I think, than when I asked him to deny Sally Hemings. He believed he had a right to his relationship with Sally. In some ways, he'd become defiant about it—allowing her to name their new baby James Madison Hemings, after both her beloved brother and my father's closest political ally.

If Papa felt shame for Sally anymore, he never showed it. But this matter with Mrs. Walker was something else altogether because he had lied to me. He had told me that his quarrel with the Walkers had arisen over money matters, a thing I had repeated, unwittingly fanning the flames of the scandal. Now he stood shamed for that, and I could see, in the bleakness of his eyes, that he feared an irreparable breach between us.

Poor Papa. Didn't he know that a breach between us was not possible?

Taking a deep breath, I pulled the crinkled letter from the bosom of my dress where I'd tucked it away. "What matter can it possibly make that it's true? I'm happy to throw your confession on the fire and forget such an incident. As you should."

Papa gave a slight shake of his head. "For years, I've tried to suppress the stories. Alas, they're in the papers now, saying I made a cuckold of Mr. Walker. He's demanding satisfaction."

What a farce to imagine my elderly father taking up his pistols to duel with the elderly Mr. Walker over a matter nearly forty years in the past. "Let Mr. Walker demand satisfaction. You don't have to give it to him."

My father downed his sherry in one gulp—something I'd never seen him do before. "Mr. Madison has already attempted to negotiate a peaceful resolution. I'm afraid it cannot be escaped this time."

This was madness. We lived in a world where a sitting vice president had murdered the former secretary of the treasury. That my father should open himself up to die the same way, shot over some trivial matter—was tempting fate's sense of irony.

But I had judged Alexander Hamilton to be an intemperate man. My father was, in almost all matters, a man of cool reason. How could he let himself be goaded to such foolishness? Perhaps he didn't require much goading. Once, I'd put myself between him and his pistols. Perhaps now that my sister was dead, he was still, after all this time, trying to keep an appointment with them.

Dragging a chair close to my father, I collapsed into it, then took his aging hand in mine—the one that had been broken and disfigured for foolishness in France over a different married woman. "Papa, I'll never let you do this thing."

His chin bobbed up. He was the president. The most powerful man in the country, and a master of his own destiny. Who could stop him from doing anything? Certainly, it wasn't the place of a daughter to tell a father what he must or must not do. But it was my place. It had always been my place to pull him back from the abyss.

Perhaps he knew it, because his expression crumbled. "Oh, Patsy."

"You wrote to me because you knew I'd never let you duel Mr. Walker. So what does he want other than your blood?"

My father's shoulders rounded and drooped. "He wants me to publicly admit my fault and declare his wife innocent—which she was. She rebuffed my advances. The wrongdoing was entirely mine."

"Perhaps then, you ought to confess it." I'd advised him to deny Sally Hemings, but Mrs. Walker was a white woman, and the circumstances were not ongoing. An appeal to pragmatism was unlikely to move him, given his guilty heart, so I argued, "Admit it for Mrs. Walker's sake. If she's innocent, a gentleman would do no less than clear her name."

His gnarled fingers tightened on mine, but he didn't answer.

"That will have to be enough for Mr. Walker, Papa. Because dueling isn't for fathers or for those charged with other great moral concerns. Do you remember in Paris how you pleaded with me to choose you over a life in the nunnery, though I felt called by God?"

He nodded, made sheepish by the reminder.

"Well, you're only being called by Mr. Walker."

My father sputtered in soft laughter, and brought my hand to his lips to kiss. "He's one of a thousand hounds baying for my blood." He still felt besieged. He had virulent enemies in Congress, not least of whom was the pretentiously styled *Randolph of Roanoke*. "I need you there with me, Patsy. In Washington City. I hesitate to ask it of you, because I know you've long wished that I wouldn't seek public office . . . but I need you with me."

"You must never hesitate to ask anything of me, Papa," I said, making my mind up at once. *Your father needs a first lady,* Dolley Madison had once said to me. I hadn't wanted to hear it. I'd spent half my life resenting my father's political career. Why, I hadn't even congratulated him when he was elected to the presidency.

Some part of my resentment was worry for how public service had dwindled our family fortune. Another part was the sullen memory of a young girl in France whose father answered her every political inquiry with silence. But I was no longer a girl, and he'd never dream of discouraging my political curiosity now; if anything, he filled his letters to me with all the news of the day to ensure I was informed.

My father had changed, and so must I.

My mother, in her final breaths, had tried to make me understand that my father was a great man. But he might not be remembered as one if his presidency failed. I couldn't let it fail—

not if everything my family had suffered and sacrificed were to mean something in the end.

Papa and I were seated like that, close and affectionate, when Tom burst in the door. "Martha!" Tom cried, fixing me with a glower. Then, to my father, he said, "She rode out like a mad-woman before I could stop her."

"Just in time to pull me back from the edge," Papa murmured.

I'd always done it and I always would.

~~~

TOM DIDN'T WANT ME TO GO TO WASHINGTON CITY.

He had good reason, in that our financial situation was bleak. As a congressman, Tom only made six dollars a day, and saved on expenses only by living in the President's House with my father and Jack Eppes. Meanwhile, the Hessian fly had come to Virginia and laid waste to our wheat, leaving us nothing to sell, and scarcely enough to make bread or lay grain away to feed us for the year. Tom's sister Jenny found an upright man to marry, which meant my husband felt honor bound to pay an enormous dowry.

And because Tom wasn't willing to sell Varina, our creditors were at the door. Add the fact that I was pregnant again, and my husband had good reason to worry about the expense of bringing his growing family to Washington City.

By this time, baby Mary was talking. Six-year-old Cornelia was already an artist with her pencils. Whip-smart Ellen had moved on from Latin to debating with her grandpapa. Jeff was old enough to run errands but not yet strong enough to be a real help to his father. And my pretty Ann was now a lady of fourteen, of age to come out into society.

They were growing up fast—faster than we could keep them clothed, in truth. Certainly not in a style befitting their status as the president's grandchildren. But to have me near, my father insisted on taking upon himself the entire expense of our trip.

He sent half a dozen pairs of shoes for Ann. He had Dolley buy me hats and dresses and wigs for my hair. Tom didn't like it and took my father's every generous gesture as a comment on his own inability to provide for his family in wealth and luxury. But I was overjoyed when he finally consented. "Thank you, Tom. It's going to mean so much to my father."

"I'm sure it will," he said, digging his hands down into his pockets. "But that's not why I'm allowing it. I'm taking you with me to Washington City because when your sister died, I cursed myself a thousand times, knowing that it could've been you." He gave an emphatic, pained shudder, repeating, "It could've been *you*. Maybe Jack Eppes can smile and laugh again, now that his wife is more than a year in the ground. But that's not the man I am. If I should lose you, Patsy, it would destroy me. So I'll keep you with me in Washington City, and watch over you in your pregnancy, even if it's financially unwise. Even if it should bankrupt us."

He said all this with his head hanging down, as if it unmanned him shamefully to confess such tender sentiments, but I was deeply moved. I supposed the same thing in his nature that made him so temperamental and morose was what let him pour out his heart in such a way. So I kissed his cheeks, one side, then the other, finishing with a tender kiss to his lips that I hoped might tell him how my heart swelled to know his true feelings.

Then I set out that autumn, six months pregnant, with all my children crowded together in a carriage, making our way slowly over bumpy roads to Washington City.

"Look at the capitol building," Ellen said, wrestling Cornelia to see out the window.

"One day it will have a great dome atop it. Your grandfather designed this city, you know," I told my girls, and watched their eyes widen. Even now when I look at the great capital Washington has become, I see the bones of it as my father laid them. And I marvel. But Jeff wasn't as impressed as his sisters by his grandfather's handiwork—he was merely disappointed that the

Mammoth Cheese no longer occupied the downstairs of the President's House. Fortunately, my son gorged his curiosity on Papa's new camera obscura, which made silhouettes, and the collection of fossil bones my father had all in one room, displaying the artifacts of the America he was building and exploring.

The capital had grown since I last visited, but the more important change was the society in which Dolley Madison now reigned as queen, spearheading numerous charity events at which people fluttered about me, hanging unnaturally upon my every word.

"Your father's plans are ambitious," Dolley explained. "They won't be passed without the support of the congressmen's wives. We'll have to win them over."

I realized after only a single luncheon that these ladies were introducing a new version of the parlor politics I'd become so well acquainted with in France. When last I was here with my sister, I hadn't embraced the role Dolley had advised me to play. Not truly. That had been a mistake I intended to rectify.

I couldn't rival Dolley's bright sense of fashion—especially when I was so big and round with child. But I ornamented my darker, more sedate gowns with yellow sashes and red ribbons and white bonnets with gauzy trim. I quietly informed the chef and the secretaries and staff that I'd be hostess at all my father's events from the moment Congress convened until it adjourned. From seating arrangements to etiquette, from soup to dessert wine, to conversation and music—I took my place at my father's side, where he needed me. Where I was meant to be.

~

EARLY IN DECEMBER, my daughter excitedly pulled on long white gloves over her delicate arms and exclaimed, "I heard the guns from the frigate at the Navy Yard!"

It was to be Ann's first formal dinner in the President's House, one at which we'd greet the envoy from Tunisia. And though she could be a shy, tremulous thing, tonight Ann vibrated with excitement. "I've never met a Muslim."

"I've never met one either," I said.

She turned to me, astonished. "Not even in France?"

I was charmed that my children seemed to believe I'd seen and done and knew everything because I'd been to France. What I *did* know about the visiting Tunisian envoy, Sidi Suliman Mellimelli, was salacious. Dolley had whispered over tea that the ambassador was perfumed like a woman. And her husband had been obliged to provide concubines for the Tunisian delegation at a nearby hotel, which had set tongues wagging. Papa insisted that the cause of making peace with the Barbary pirates was too important for us to balk at the "irregular conduct" of their ministers. That's why I'd postponed dinner from late afternoon to after sunset in honor of the religious practice of Ramadan.

"We're to be the only ladies in attendance?" my daughter asked.

I nodded. "Ambassador Mellimelli is unaccustomed to the calming presence of women in political society, and we'll have to ease him into it."

There was much bowing and greeting when the ambassador and his two secretaries arrived, and upon seeing me and my daughter, he begged our pardon, through an interpreter, to retire to smoke his pipe.

"Feel free to smoke here," Papa said, and the gold-and-scarlet-clad ambassador stroked his long beard, thoughtfully. Looking first to his two secretaries, who wouldn't partake of wine, he nodded, then lit his wonderfully unusual four-foot pipe.

I was painfully worried of giving offense—especially considering the company. Amongst our American guests—John Quincy Adams and our own snarling kinsman, Congressman *Randolph of Roanoke*. After making snide quips implying that my husband and Jack Eppes held their congressional seats only through my father's influence, John finally leaned over to me at the table and whispered, "I'm so glad you didn't bring the vampire with you."

"I beg your pardon?"

"Nancy," he hissed. "She's sucked the best blood of my race."

Whether he was accusing her of murdering his brother or making some lewder accusation, I couldn't guess. "I'm sure I don't know what you mean."

"I'm sure you do. You and your husband are harboring her. Don't think I'll forget it."

He had *the Randolph*. He was irritable, jealous, suspicious, and habitually indulgent of the meanest little passions. But I was a Jefferson, so I merely announced, "Ann and I will retire now to leave you gentlemen to your business. Ambassador Mellimelli, I look forward to spending a lively winter with you." Having observed that even a perfumed man wished to be thought manly, I added, "I'm sure you'll be the lion of the season."

Lion. The ambassador liked that word. He liked the comparison. I could see the pleasure of it light in his eyes when the interpreter whispered it in his ear. And later, he joined me and Ann in the drawing room, leaving the other gentlemen behind.

Ann and I started to rise, but he waved us back into our chairs and surprised us with nearly perfect English. "We're not the only delegation here in Washington, no? I've seen bands of people, not so fair." For a moment, I thought he meant the slaves. But then he gestured to the feather in his turban. "Ornaments and buckskin. Long dark braids."

"Indians," I answered. And when he squinted, I added, "*Our* Indians. They've come from the western territories to speak with my father."

"Which prophet do they follow?" he asked, showing Ann a diamond snuffbox to charm her. "Moses, Jesus, or Mohammed?"

"None," my timid Ann offered, and I was so proud of her for finding courage to speak to the man. "The Indians worship . . . the great spirit, as I understand it."

The ambassador took a pinch of the snuff, which smelled like roses. "Then they're vile heretics. Another thing interests me,

Mrs. Randolph. In your Congress, where your husband serves, everyone has the right to speak?"

"The members do, yes," I replied.

He laughed. "Then it will take years to finish any business! In my country, all matters are decided swiftly and with final resolution. In fact, if I don't succeed in my mission here, they'll behead me."

I wasn't sure I believed him, but he was such a colorful character that everyone was eager to meet him. Invitations to every fashionable ball in Washington City were extended to the delegation, and curious onlookers gawked near the hotel to get a peek at turbans, long mustaches, and ceremonial garb. Given the fascination, I worried we wouldn't be able to admit all the guests who flocked to Papa's annual New Year's Eve gala.

"Will you dance?" Tom asked at the gala, dressed in his best blue tailcoat.

"I'm quite near my time now," I told my husband. "I'd feel like a stampeding buffalo."

Tom brought my fingertips to his lips for a brief but very earnest kiss. "Never."

Nearby, Jack Eppes was laughing with a flirtatious woman from Annapolis. He was courting again, and Papa said we must be happy for him. I agreed, because I feared we might never see my sister's children again if we didn't lavish approval on her widower.

But Jack's laughter—and the music—were interrupted dramatically by the ambassador of Tunisia, who stopped dancers midtwirl. With a flourish of his colorful cape that mesmerized the crowd, he let his interpreter speak for him. "The ambassador has heard that the Madisons desire children, but have been unable to conceive them!"

Rarely shy of attention, Dolley smiled and murmured something about how she'd welcome any blessing God were to bestow.

Striding to her, the bearded ambassador said, "If you want a child, I'll give you one." Then he wrapped the cape around her with such intimacy that her husband, the diminutive secretary of state, stiffened and went white.

Confused by the reaction, the ambassador explained, "It's a magic cape."

But his words didn't carry, accented as they were. And as the room went silent, men reached for their ceremonial swords in anticipation of violence. I swallowed, wondering which of the men would break the mounting tension in the room. And when I realized that none of them would, I knew that there was no choice but to take it upon myself. Clapping my hands, as if delighted in the way of a child, I cried, "Oh, a magic cape!"

My father—the man of science who had decried a reign of witches—looked entirely appalled. But upon seeing me smile and clap, all the other ladies quickly followed suit. Papa could scarcely keep the displeasure from his presidential expression, but he would simply have to endure it. It was a New Year's Eve party, a night for frivolity, and if offense could be avoided by laughter and merriment, why not?

Besides. I was the hostess here, so I pretended at great fascination when the ambassador murmured an incantation over Dolley, declaring, "I promise you, Mrs. Madison, you'll soon give your husband a son!"

Everyone applauded the spectacle. Dolley was very amused. When everyone else had gone home for the night, she grabbed at my elbow, grinning. "Why, I've never seen Mr. Madison go so white before. As exciting as it might've been to see men duel over my honor, I suppose I must thank you for averting an international incident. But, I must know one thing. . . ."

Still holding Tom's arm, I asked, "What's that?"

Dolley grinned mischievously. "Is *that* your secret? A magic cape? Given your brood of children, I suppose you must have a closet full of them!"

"There are no capes involved," Tom said, quite seriously.

Dolley and I found this so terribly funny that we exploded with laughter.

Which prompted him to accuse, "You've been drinking, both of you!"

For whatever reason, that seemed terribly funny, too. I hadn't laughed since my sister's death, and it felt disloyal to do so. But Dolley was irrepressible. "I'm afraid I don't put much stock in the ambassador's incantation."

"Well, you ought to give it a try anyway," I said, scandalizing my husband utterly. "With or without the capes."

Days later, I gave birth to the very first baby ever born in the president's mansion. A boy, at last. And Tom had no objection to the name that would give Dolley the most pleasure: James Madison Randolph.

"A son," my husband kept saying, as if astonished that it'd finally come to pass. At long last, Jeff had a little brother. And we were happy.

For a brief, enchanted winter in the spacious rooms of the President's House, we forgot our troubles in Virginia. I hosted nearly sixty-three dinners at my father's side, including one before the day I gave birth and one after. But when I couldn't be there to soothe partisan tempers, my daughter Ann was there in my place—more beautiful and less sarcastic than me in every way. And I made certain she was aware that every dinner and every lady's tea was a mission to beat back the calumny heaped upon Papa's head by his enemies.

"Have you seen this?" my father's new secretary asked, timidly offering me a clipping from some newspaper. "I apologize for bringing something so indelicate to your attention but—"

"You did quite right to show me," I said, burning to read the filthy poem.

> The patriot, fresh from Freedom's councils come,
> Now plea'd retires to lash his slaves at home;
> Or woo, perhaps, some black Aspasia's charms,
> And dreams of freedom in his bondmaid's arms.

There was a cartoon, too, called "A Philosophic Cock." A drawing of my father as a French rooster and Sally as his hen.

All part of a campaign to tarnish his image as a devoted father, doting grandfather, and father of this nation.

I went straight to Papa with it in a flash of temper, stunned to hear him laugh. "How can you laugh at this, Papa?"

"What else is there to be done? It's demeaning. It's petty. It has nothing whatsoever to do with the business of the country. And they're spilling their ink on it while Republicans trounce them in every election. Unless you think I should call them out onto a field of honor, there's nothing to do *but* laugh."

Soothed, I gave a soft smile. "We're done with pistols now, aren't we?"

He stood, still tall and straight, grasping my hand. "Yes, we're done with pistols now."

But in that, we couldn't have been more mistaken.

Chapter Thirty-one

Washington, 23 June 1806
From Thomas Jefferson to Thomas Mann Randolph Jr.

Should they lose you, seven children, all under the age of discretion and down to infancy would be left without guide or guardian but a poor broken-hearted woman, doomed herself to misery the rest of her life. And should her frail frame sink under it, what is to become of them? The laws of dueling are made for lives of no consequence; not for fathers of families. Let me entreat you then, my dear Sir, take no step in this business but on the soberest reflection.

A SHADOW OF DEATH hung over us that summer in Virginia. A neighbor was found dead in his carriage—he'd drunk himself to death. More devastating was the murder of Papa's law teacher, Judge Wythe, whose jealous nephew poisoned him, his manumitted black housekeeper, and her freeborn mulatto son—to whom Judge Wythe intended to leave his fortune.

The judge lived only long enough to tell physicians, "I am murdered." The nephew stood trial, but black witnesses weren't permitted to testify—not even the housekeeper who survived the poisoning. And the villain had been promptly acquitted.

Papa took it hard.

Not only, I think, because he'd lost a friend and justice was thwarted. But also because it was a repudiation of Judge Wythe and Mr. Short's idealistic dreams of racial coexistence in Virginia. A warning almost tailor-made to discourage my father from bringing Sally and their children out from the shadows.

And then, of course, there was *Randolph of Roanoke*. Was there ever a more deranged example of Virginia gentry in decay? The spiteful creature had singled out my family to torment. In protest of my father's programs for public education, canals, bridges, and roads, he broke with the Republicans to create a brand-new political party called the Quids. And when that didn't achieve his aims, he provoked a quarrel with my husband on the floor of Congress.

Admittedly, Tom had been rash, putting himself forth as a more true patriot, and when his apology was deemed insufficient, adding, "Lead and steel make more proper ingredients in serious quarrels."

Sensing an opportunity to provoke two very public men to duel, the papers took sides, spilling a barrel of ink on the subject. The *National Intelligencer* defended Tom while the Richmond *Enquirer* championed John Randolph. And the dangerous intensity of my husband's temper sent all the children fleeing whenever he entered a room. They knew to stay out of their father's way while he paced, fulminating at every new accusation.

I didn't blame my husband for his anger, truly I didn't. I felt certain John Randolph had been trying to goad my husband into a duel for a very long time. I only wished Tom wasn't so easy to goad.

"It's because of me," Nancy said, packing up her meager belongings. "If I'm not living here, John might leave my brother alone."

I think she hoped I'd stop her, reassure her that she was mistaken in leaving us, but she had the right of it. "Where will you go?"

"To Richmond," Nancy said. "We have other relations there. I'll go visiting for a time and see about seeking employment as a housekeeper there."

Tom was appalled by the very idea that any sister of his should seek employment, but given Nancy's ruined reputation, she had few options. Tom was a Randolph; he saw himself as wealthy landed gentry even if our house at Edgehill had fallen to pieces in our absence. It needed repairs and plaster if it was to prove good against any kind of weather. And with the new baby, Edgehill felt smaller and more cramped than ever.

That's to say nothing of the drought. The oats were lost. The peaches and cherries, too. We might only have another sickly wheat crop and apples. We weren't in any position to support his sister, so Tom gave Nancy money—more than we had to give— and let her go off to Richmond.

Before climbing into the carriage, Nancy gave me a quick hug and whispered, "Try not to worry about the duel. The Randolph temper burns hot, but sometimes burns itself out."

I hoped she was right, but when my husband returned from Richmond, he was in a worse state than before. He considered it his sacred duty to care for his sisters and felt unmanned by his inability to do so. And when I found my husband in the yard sighting his pistols and practicing his paces, I realized his temper wasn't going to burn out. He was going to kill or be killed, and I could no longer keep my peace. "So you're going to let him murder you and leave me a widow?"

Tom turned on me. "You think I'll fail at this like I've failed at everything. It's a wonder you don't *want* me dead."

Given how happy we'd been only months before, this caught me utterly by surprise. "Tom, how could you ever think that I wish such a thing? What would I do without you?"

Tom gave a bitter twist of his beautiful mouth. "Turn to your father like you always do. He can do no wrong in your eyes, whereas I. . . ."

"Well, my father found a way to avoid a senseless duel, didn't he?"

I shouldn't have said it. Should never have taken that tone. And the reward for my foolishness was a resounding slap to the face. It didn't knock me to the ground. It wouldn't bruise me. But because it made me feel like both a desperate wife and a chastened child I stood there gawping in shock, holding my face where it turned red.

My husband hadn't struck me since the last time he was in a fit of rage inspired by one of the Randolph brothers of Bizarre. And now *Tom* seemed just as shocked as I was, his eyes filling with shame at the sight of me holding my stinging cheek. With tears in his eyes, he shouted, "*God dammit*, Martha. Look what you've made me do! Look what you made me do."

He never dueled John Randolph.

But it wasn't because of my father's letter, or my pleas, or because good sense prevailed. It was because he'd struck me, in spite of his promise never to do so again. He'd dishonored himself in his own eyes and, in so doing, lost all appetite for a duel of honor. I knew this, deep down where we know such things about the men we marry, and counted it well worth the price. I would've provoked him to strike me a thousand times to keep him from dooming our family to utter ruin.

But the price I didn't understand was one exacted from Tom's soul. For he was never without his pistols ever after, and I feel certain he was keeping a bullet ready for himself.

He had inside him the kind of wound that left a man staring at pistols in the night. The kind of wound that left a man without a head, lying on the ground with a gun in his hand. The kind of wound the men in my life all seemed to suffer. And for the first time, I wondered if those wounds were put there by God or if it was something about me that brought them about.

Washington City, 2 July 1807
A Proclamation by Thomas Jefferson

During the wars among the powers of Europe, the United States of America have observed neutrality. At length a deed, transcending all we've hitherto seen or suffered, brings our forbearance to a necessary pause. A frigate of the United States, trusting a state of peace, has been attacked by a British vessel of war. This was not only without provocation, or justifiable cause, but committed with the avowed purpose of taking by force, a part of her crew.

An attack. An insult. An act of war.

Publicly, my father prepared for battle. Privately, he confided we weren't ready.

The fate of our nation was, as always, caught between England and France, and my father no longer harbored a preference for either, observing, "France is a conqueror, roaming over the earth with havoc. And Britain is a pirate, spreading misery and ruin over the ocean. Fortunately for us, the Mammoth cannot swim nor the Leviathan move on dry land. And if we keep out of their way, they cannot get at us."

Thus came about the Embargo Act of 1807.

Did Papa know he put the fate of the nation in the hands of its ladies? If we couldn't buy tea, clothes, or goods from overseas, then wives and daughters would have to make them at home. And if women weren't willing, the embargo would fail. After all, what did men know about making homespun?

I set about straightaway to oversee the production of cloth both at Edgehill and Monticello, where we transformed the stone workmen's house into a weaver's cottage. And in this endeavor, I found an ally in Sally Hemings, who'd always been a talented seamstress and whose six-year-old daughter, Harriet, was becoming one, too. I tried never to think that fair and freckled Harriet was my sister, but was pleased at how well the girl took to the spinning jennies and was so impressed by her deft use of the flying shuttle on the clattering loom that I could scarcely pull my attention away when Sally said, "With the help of the women who don't get put in the ground come harvest, we can make a thousand yards of cloth by springtime."

To that end, Sally and her children moved from a slave cabin into the weaver's cottage, using another room in the southern dependency by the dairy, too, and as naturally as that, she defined for herself on the plantation a home and office of her own.

After that, I decided my children could do no less for the effort than hers. I told Ann, "We're all going to learn to manufacture cloth. In the meantime, look through your dresses and put away anything that wasn't made at home."

My eldest had recently caught the eye of the young and dashing Charles Bankhead, who'd complimented her on the fashionable dresses she'd worn when we'd attended dinners at the President's House. And now that she had a suitor, Ann wanted nothing to do with my scheme. "*Slaves* wear homespun. How will we look wearing such things?"

"We'll look like patriots," I said, with a reassuring smile.

Ann pouted. "Charles won't like it. I don't see why I should have to."

I kissed the top of her head. "Because you're the president's granddaughter."

And that was that.

From tattered flags and uniforms to friendships strained to the brink, the women of my country had always been the menders to all the things torn asunder. But now we'd do more than patch with needle and thread. We'd have to weave together a whole tapestry of American life with nothing but our own hands, our own crops, and our own ingenuity. And I would prove myself able to the task.

There was no mistaking that my father's legacy was at stake, because the embargo was deeply unpopular. "You're the damnedest fool that god ever put life into," read an anonymous letter to my father. Another accused him of having starved children. Papa was burned in effigy in New York, whereupon he suffered the most violent and painful headache of his life. But a trade embargo had been our only alternative to war, so Papa couldn't relent.

Not even as we watched the financial calamity swallow up the landed gentry in Virginia. While we were bottling, pickling, and spinning, our neighbors lost their farms. Proud wearers of the Randolph name were reduced to running boardinghouses. My husband's brother lost every last thing he had. And, unable to find work in Richmond, Nancy had been forced to try her luck in one of the northern states where no one knew of her scandalous past.

Pleas for help came from all quarters, but there was little we could do to help. Tom felt churlish and small turning anyone away, but I did my utmost to convince him that if we avoided new debts, we might finally right our own ship. Neither Tom, nor my father, permitted me to check the ledgers, but at thirty-five years old, having overseen plantations in their absence for nearly six years, I had a suspicion of where matters stood. So I forced myself to be harder and more pragmatic than either man was willing to be—especially now that Sally and I were both pregnant again.

It was with the desperate concern for what sort of future my babies might have that I confronted Papa while showing him the textile mill, where the girls were busy at their spindles. "Papa, I assure you, sending Jeff to the University of Pennsylvania would be money wantonly squandered," I said, for much as I loved my eldest son, Jeff got by with the good looks he took from Tom, and the breezy southern charm he took from my father. He was a sweet boy, respectful and obedient, but unlike his sisters, he had no head for learning.

Papa ignored my warning. "Jeff must be given the opportunity. You know it's weighed on your husband all these years that Colo-

nel Randolph never approved of his education." I knew exactly
how it weighed on Tom, but my son wasn't anything like his
father. Papa misread my hesitation. "I'll incur all the expense for
Jeff's education. Your husband needn't worry."

It was a generous offer that'd bruise Tom's pride when it was
already battered—by the strain between us, by our financial
struggles, by Tom's belief that Papa still preferred Jack Eppes to
him. Consequently, I was more forceful than I might have otherwise been. "Papa, it's too great an expense for such uncertain
benefit!" Our family might go down in ruin with Tom's debts, but
I couldn't bear taking Papa with us. So when I saw that my father
was stubbornly set upon sending the boy to school, I called Jeff
inside from where he was standing in the yard outside the mill.
"Go on, tell your grandfather your wishes."

Alas, such was the quiet authority of the president that my boy
took one look at his grandfather and gulped. "I—I wish to make
you proud of me. If you think a university education is right, then
I'll go, but what about my sisters?"

My father removed his spectacles, leaning curiously forward.
"Your mother is more qualified to educate your sisters than any
other woman in America."

The compliment made me flush, but Jeff shook his head. "I
meant I'm worried to leave my sisters. When my father rages . . .
if I'm not there, he might go after Ann or Ellen or—"

"Your father is a Virginia gentleman," Papa broke in sharply,
even more appalled than I was by my son's fears. "He'd never
raise a hand to a woman or a girl."

That was mostly true—but not as true as my father hoped.
And when I looked into my son's gaze, I saw that Jeff knew it, too,
though I didn't know how. An anguished glance passed between
my son and me while I beseeched him with my eyes to keep that
secret.

Papa's hand traced around one of the big spinning wheels. "It
does you honor that you're thinking of your sisters, Jeff. Some-

day, they'll be in your care. Which is why you need to spend your youth well. So let's ride down to the store and get what sundries you need to take to school."

Jeff was my father's namesake—the first of his grandsons to reach majority. It wouldn't reflect well on Thomas Jefferson, or his legacy, to have a blockhead for a grandson. So we couldn't refuse, even when we knew better.

In the carriage, I warned Jeff, "Philadelphia is a bustling place."

"I've seen cities before," my son protested, bristling with manly pride.

But, of course, he hadn't seen cities. *Paris* was a city. Philadelphia was . . . less so. And I realized with a bittersweet pang that at Jeff's age, I'd seen more of the world than my children were likely to. "Philadelphia will be busier than Charlottesville or Washington City. It won't be anything you're used to. Perhaps we can ask Mr. Short to look after you in Philadelphia," I suggested, reassured to know William would be nearby. Turning to Papa, I said, "I'm sure he'll take Jeff under his guidance."

That's when Papa surprised me by saying, "That won't be possible. I'm sending Short to Europe on a diplomatic mission."

I didn't know if I should be delighted for William or unsettled at the thought of him leaving the country again—perhaps this time for good. We hadn't seen one another in years, but there was some comfort in knowing he wasn't an ocean away. "Where will you send Mr. Short?"

"First to France. Then to Russia," Papa said. "Short will treat with the tsar on behalf of America."

First to France, where William would, no doubt, be reunited with his duchess. He'd like that. This appointment would be the capstone on his career. And though it pained me to think I might never see him again, I smiled to imagine him charming the ladies of St. Petersburg.

It was, after all, a time for letting go. Letting go of Mr. Short, of my son Jeff, and of my daughter Ann, too, who had accepted a proposal of marriage from Charles Bankhead.

Papa insisted that the wedding be held at Monticello, where the airy design and eighteen-and-a-half-foot ceilings were sure to impress the guests. And on her wedding day, all dewy-eyed in anticipation, Ann asked, "Grandpapa's house is so beautiful now, isn't it?"

She was beautiful. Of all my daughters, Ann was the most delicately rendered, with soft doe eyes and an adorable nose. Ellen's face was sharper, but then everything about my nearly twelve-year-old second daughter was sharper.

Excited to serve as her sister's attendant, Ellen declared, "Monticello's new hall is the most beautiful room I was ever in, even including the drawing rooms in Washington City!"

Monticello had, indeed, come along grandly. The renovation had taken fourteen years; Papa would never be truly finished with it, for he was never finished improving anything. But there was now an excellent road up the mountain right to the house; the dining room grandly boasted Wedgwood ornamentation and dumbwaiters on either side of the fireplace; and while the landscaping was still dismal due to the mean little sheep who ate our orange trees, Monticello was otherwise quite a handsome place.

Before Ann's wedding, Sally and I both gave birth to boys. Her new son was named after my father's acquaintance Thomas Eston. Mine more grandly after Benjamin Franklin, my father's old admired friend.

Dolley visited shortly after the birth. Cooing jealously over my infant as she scooped him from my arms, she said, "Aren't we a pair? I can't have children, and you can't stop having them!"

"Are you saying the ambassador's cape wasn't really magical?" I teased.

Her eyes twinkled. "Apparently not, but I was quite taken with his turban. I've made it my trademark fashion."

Quite exhausted, I flopped back upon my pillow, morning sunshine spilling across the floor beneath my childbed. "I pray this babe is my last. I keep my babies at the breast as long as I can to fend off conception, but . . ."

With no apparent shame for the delicacy of the matter, Dolley frankly advised, "If you want no more children, you must discourage Mr. Randolph. Take a separate bed with the children if you must. Say you don't want to wake him, feeding the new baby. Say whatever you must."

"I—I don't see how I have the right." Besides, I couldn't fathom how to rebuff my husband's amorous advances without angering him. If there was anything Tom had a true talent for, it was making babies—and in his arms I felt womanly, desirable, and desired. But what came of that desire had worn me down to the nub. "I wouldn't know where to begin."

Very quietly, Dolley said, "Some women, in your position, put in the path of their husbands an agreeable Negress."

Dear God. That she could make such a suggestion. But hadn't the same thought occurred to my sister? I was certain Jack Eppes had taken up with Betsy Hemings, just as my father had done with Sally. Just as my grandfather Wayles had done with Sally's mother. It was the way things were done, and if I hoped to secure my children's future, it'd be an advantageous arrangement. But even if I could reconcile myself to the heartbreaking thought of my husband's hands on another woman, I recoiled to imagine my daughters struggling with the emotional turmoil I'd struggled with.

The thought of their confusion over sisters and brothers that were also their slaves was enough to decide me. And even if it hadn't been, the thought of choosing a girl . . .

My eyes drifted to my window, which overlooked Mulberry Row. Some of the Hemings girls would soon be of age, but the wickedness of the thought was so horrifying to me I immediately thrust it away with a violent shudder. "I couldn't encourage such a thing. I suppose I was just wishing for some secret way. . . ."

"There is only one secret to anything," Dolley asserted. "And that's the power we all have in forming our own destinies."

Washington, 27 February 1809
From Thomas Jefferson to
Martha Jefferson Randolph

In retiring to the condition of a private citizen, I have a single uneasiness. I'm afraid that the administration of the house will give you trouble. Perhaps, with a set of good and capable servants, as ours certainly are, the trouble will become less after their understanding the regulations which are to govern them. Ignorant too, as I am, in the management of a farm, I shall be obliged to ask the aid of Mr. Randolph's skill and attention.

On a marvelous spring day, my father commemorated forty years of service to his country by surrendering the reins of government—and a brewing war—to the new president. Celebratory cannons fired, ladies flirted with Papa, and a special farewell march was played for him at James Madison's inaugural ball. The latter was a touch only Dolley would've thought to include, and I loved her for it.

Then Papa loaded up wagons with all the belongings he'd acquired as president. Spoons and pudding dishes, coverlets and clocks and shoes. Boxes, books, and furniture strained at the six-mule team pulling the load.

In anticipation of his homecoming, my heart beat with inexpressible anxiety and impatience. I wanted nothing so much as to clasp Papa in the bosom of his family, for the evening of his life to pass in serene and unclouded tranquility in the home he'd spent twenty years rebuilding.

A home in which my entire family would now reside.

The proposal was put to Tom in ways to spare his feelings: What would people say if we left my sixty-five-year-old father to live alone with Sally as his housekeeper? Besides, Papa couldn't manage without us. He hadn't Tom's genius for preventing soil erosion. My husband, whatever else his faults, was a hardworking, inventive planter whose failures were due to bad luck and the rotting legacy his father left him.

My husband surprised me by listening to this entreaty in silence, finally nodding his head in assent. And I realize now that it was because he already knew he couldn't support our still growing family at Edgehill; the arrangement spared him more embarrassment than it gave him, lifting his family from certain poverty with the fig leaf of caring for my aging father. Even Ann and her new husband, Charles, would move in with us so that she could help work in Papa's gardens to make it just so, for they shared a special bond over flowers and herbs. We'd have the whole family together!

At last, after trials of blizzards and crowds demanding speeches of him in taverns and inns on the way, Papa was *ours* now, and I went running down the road to meet him, in rapture, in joy. We embraced one another, all the children gathered round, hopeful for the family idyll and ignoring the rumble of the coming war in the distance.

Part Three

Mistress of Monticello

Chapter Thirty-two

Monticello, 21 January 1812
From Thomas Jefferson to John Adams

A letter from you carries me back to the times when we were fellow laborers in the same cause, struggling for what is most valuable to man: his right of self-government. Sometimes I look back in remembrance of our old friends who have fallen before us. Of the signers of the Declaration of Independence I see now living not more than half a dozen on your side of the Potomac, and, on this side, myself alone.

IT IS DIFFICULT NOT TO SMILE with a bittersweet pang in reading the letters between my father and John Adams, exchanged in the twilight of their lives. My husband couldn't fathom how Papa could set aside political acrimony to resume the old friendship, but those were happy years at Monticello, and harmony was our pursuit and our reward.

My bed at Monticello was an alcove, and I slept snug and toasty between my husband's body and the wall. In the morning, the warm light of dawn spilled from the windows near the floor. They were double-paned; they never leaked. And everything in our sky-blue bedroom was neat and clean, which had a decidedly happy effect on my mood.

"Good morning," Tom said, his breath warm on the back of my neck, his hand gently cupping my belly under blankets that smelled of lavender.

I knew what he wanted, and his touch ignited something inside me, too, but I feared another child. "Tom, it's so early."

"The rooster's already crowed," he protested, nuzzling my shoulder. "Besides, I'm riding for Edgehill straightaway this morning. I've a long day ahead of me."

"Then you can't afford to lose daylight," I chirped. "Let me up and I'll see the servants get you a quick breakfast."

Reluctantly, Tom swung his long legs over to let me rise from the bed. "I'll take the boy. Hopefully we'll get the fields prepared for another good crop."

By "the boy," he meant Jeff, who had, after a single year's instruction, returned home from the University of Pennsylvania in near disgrace. Before he could be entrusted to help manage our plantations, Jeff would have to prove himself to his father—a thing he was doing by outworking Tom in the fields and at every other plantation chore.

Having quit Congress, my husband's luck had turned. We'd had two good harvests, and Tom's were the only fields in the county that survived the storms because of his new method of plowing. Between that and the fact Papa was housing, clothing, and feeding our children, we were finally making payments on our debts.

But I worried about my father's largesse, which extended itself to everybody. Papa was more popular now than when he was president, and people felt no shame in prevailing upon our hospitality. Unexpected visitors cluttered up our entrance hall beneath the quirky great clock, powered by cannonball weights on a rope, for which a hole had to be cut in the floor. They marveled at the inventions and curiosities my father collected—everything from maps and soil samples to Indian artifacts, mastodon bones, and classical statuary. And Papa took on the expense of a plentiful table with all the seasonal bounty our plantation had to offer, topped off with Italian and French wines.

Which is why, I think, we always had guests. We had persons from abroad, from all the states of the union, from every part of the state, men, women, and children. In short, almost every day for at least eight months of the year brought people of wealth, fashion, men in office, professional men military and civil, lawyers, doctors, protestant clergymen, Catholic priests, members of Congress, foreign ministers, missionaries, Indian agents, tourists, travelers, artists, strangers, and friends.

They'd line up in the passageways for a glimpse at Papa. One lady even punched a windowpane with her parasol trying to get a better view!

Neverthless, I scolded Ellen when she moped down the narrow staircase in the morning, eyes half-lidded. "Be more cheerful in the morning lest your grandfather's guests think you're a sullen girl."

"You know I hate mornings," Ellen said, unrepentantly sullen.

I did know. Indeed, since she was a child my father had made a game of catching her in bed long after sunrise. And I also knew her love for him would make her behave. "Your grandpapa relies upon us to leave a good impression."

Ellen plastered a sarcastic smile on her face as we took our places in Papa's chrome yellow dining room with its wispy white curtains. My daughters were all practiced hostesses at my father's breakfast, where we had fried eggs and meat, biscuits, tea, and honey. Then, while our guests amused themselves in my father's book room or by walking our gardens or horse riding in our woods, I made the girls help me tidy up and find places for the strange little trinkets people sent Papa from all over the country just because he might find them fascinating.

Mary and Cornelia bickered about the proper way to do everything from planning a menu to choosing cloth for the servants, and Ginny goaded them on to avoid doing any of the work herself. Meanwhile, I taught the children from early afternoon until our supper at four or five in the evening. The schoolroom was my sitting room at Monticello, painted a cheerful blue. It's where I did my sewing, and breastfeeding, too. And where the servants found me to ask for direction at least two dozen times a day.

All except Sally, of course.

Sally and I both worked in proximity to my father's private rooms, where he emerged each day like the glowing Jove to reign over Mount Olympus. The grand patriarch made all the rules for the house—including that the children were to keep out of the flower beds and that no one but Sally was to venture into his sanctum sanctorum.

Such was my children's adoration for him that he only had to say *do* or *do not,* and they'd all obey. And he adored them in return, playing games with them in the evening. In returning from overseeing cloth production at the textile mill, I'd see my father throw down his kerchief to set the children off on a race on the lawn—sometimes with hoops. And while Sally's children only ever looked on, the racers were sometimes joined by my sister's only surviving child, little Francis, whom Jack Eppes finally consented to let visit.

Jack hadn't been persuaded by my pleas nor my father's cajoling. There wasn't anything any of us could say to convince Jack that his son wouldn't be exposed to my husband's lingering ill will. No, it took someone in the Hemings family. My sister's maid promised that her aunt Sally would watch over the boy. And Jack trusted his concubine in a way he'd never trust me.

But I counted myself grateful for it, because I never tired of hearing my sister's laugh in her son's voice. And every night after Tom returned home and the children were all tucked into bed, we had the best fruits from the orchards with our tea and enjoyed the relative quiet.

The only blot on our happiness was our son-in-law. When Ann married Charles Bankhead, he'd been a student at the law with a promising future. He'd since quit the profession to better appreciate my father's stock of wine, leaving us to worry for Ann and my new grandson. But my father was fond of Charles and optimistic about his future.

Tom was less charitable. "We made a mistake with that one, Martha. He'll never go farther than a tavern."

At the time, I thought it an unkind thing to say, and hypocritical, too, considering my husband so often retreated to drink. I reconsidered my opinion, however, the night my twenty-year-old son came to the table after a day of backbreaking work, during which he nearly put his father into the ground.

Serving great portions of ham onto his plate, Jeff asked, "Grandpapa, do you think war with England is inevitable, now? We can make enough to eat and drink and clothe ourselves, but we can't have salt or iron without money. Without a market for our wheat, we just feed it to the horses. Tobacco isn't worth the pipe it's smoked in. And whiskey . . ." He paused, casting a sly glance at Ann's husband. "Well there aren't enough drunks in the world to drink it."

My son should've never given that sly, knowing glance to Charles Bankhead, who guzzled down my father's brandy as if in defiance of Jeff's remark. Charles and Tom were both good and drunk that night. So much so that my husband fell into a deep, exhausted slumber before I finished tucking my children into bed in their nursery.

I suppose that's why I was the first to hear the commotion downstairs.

Coming into the dining room in my bedclothes, I found Bankhead hurling abuses at one of the Hemings boys, my father's new butler, Burwell. The reason? Poor Burwell refused to serve him more brandy or give him the keys to the wine cellar.

I realize now that Ann must've been too afraid to intervene, but at the time, I only wondered where my daughter had got herself to while her husband screamed incoherently.

"Charles!" I hissed. "Everyone's gone to bed. Surely you don't mean to drink alone?"

"I do," Bankhead sneered. Then he picked up a silver candlestick. "And I'll smash this insolent boy's skull if he won't give over the keys."

Fearful of the certain violence in his voice, I stepped between them. "You've had enough to drink, Charles."

Bankhead brought his reddening face close to mine, then gave me such a shove that I fell against the table, sending a tureen crashing to the floor. Shocked and struggling to right myself, I caught a flash of Burwell's fierce brown eyes just as his fists clenched, as if he meant to come to my defense.

"Burwell!" I snapped the warning, because a black man attacking a white man in Virginia, even for good cause, would end in utter tragedy. "Go fetch Bacon."

Edmund Bacon was the overseer on our estate—a burly white man who could help me manage my drunk son-in-law. But Burwell glanced at Bankhead, then back at me, and shook his head, as if unwilling to leave me alone with the drunkard. I had to straighten to my full height. "You do as I say, Burwell. You get on!"

Only when Burwell was gone did I face my son-in-law, who was beyond reason. Charles shoved me again, and this time I knocked over a chair before catching my balance. He still had that candlestick in his hand, and he rounded on me, slamming me into the wall, his hand at my throat, nostrils flaring like a bull. Smelling the liquor on his breath, I stayed very still and breathed very shallowly, my pulse pounding in my ears. *He's going to strangle me*, I thought. And that thought seemed to stretch on for an eternity.

Footsteps finally sounded out from behind us, and my son-in-law cried, "Gimme that key, you lazy, good-for-nothing—"

That's when we saw Tom, his eyes bloodshot with exhaustion, alcohol, and rage. What happened next happened so swiftly, I heard it more than saw it. Tom grabbed up a fire iron and the air parted with the swoosh of its arc. A heavy thunk sounded as metal cracked on a human skull. A crash as Bankhead crumpled to the floor, leaving me gasping as I grasped my throat, standing over the body of our son-in-law as a pool of blood fanned out under my bare feet.

"Dear God!" I cried, horrified by the sight of flesh split from bone. The blow had peeled the skin off one side of my son-in-law's forehead and face. I dropped to my knees in terror. "You've killed him, Tom. You've killed him."

I was wrong about that.

Tom had swung that iron poker hard enough to kill, but it had glanced slightly off to the side, leaving Charles badly injured, but alive. Groaning and sobbing, Charles tried to get to his feet, slipping on his own blood just as Ann stumbled in. Seeing her husband dripping in gore, she let out a blood-curdling scream that drew the servants and even our children from their beds.

Sally scarcely took two steps into the room before she herded everyone away. Meanwhile, my husband was still in an unthinking and murderous fury, so I threw myself into Tom's arms before he used the poker to finish the job. "You saved me," I whispered, holding tight to his waist, using my body to force him back from the scene.

But even Tom's shock as he came more fully awake did not make him relinquish his desire to murder. "You think you can get away from me, Bankhead? Get back here, you dog."

"Don't kill my husband," Ann sobbed, trying to stop his bleeding.

I put my hand round Tom's to make him drop the fire iron, and he roared, "I want him out of this house!"

Had this been Edgehill, he'd have been well within his rights to be obeyed. Truthfully, I thought he was within his rights anyway. But Ann was hysterical now, with her husband's blood staining her nightdress and her hands. "This is my grandfather's house. He'd never send me out with a dying man into the dark. You've nearly killed him. You've nearly killed my husband!"

Ann didn't know—hadn't seen—how it had happened.

And by morning, Charles was so apologetic and ashamed that Ann felt nothing but pity for him. "He tries to stop drinking, Momma. He swears it off. But then he can't stop. I don't know why, but he can't stop."

At her words, I pulled the shawl tighter around my neck, hiding the red marks that had bloomed there just as my clothing covered the bruises Charles's rough handling had caused. I'd been careful as I'd dressed to ensure Tom hadn't seen them, either. If any of the men in my family saw *my* bruises, the violence would erupt all over again.

Meanwhile, my father suggested Bankhead might be suffering from some sort of illness, that perhaps a doctor could help him. Not knowing the full violence of Charles's actions, Papa was unfailingly kind to the young man, which infuriated Tom so much, he slammed out of the house and stayed gone for two days.

My son only made matters worse. Jeff had been away on his grandfather's errands during the altercation—the trust my father increasingly placed in him to conduct matters of business emboldened Jeff and chafed at my husband, who thought our boy wasn't ready for such responsibility.

When Jeff heard about the fight, he said, "Just two drunks having a row, then. I'm sure they'll patch it up straightaway."

I didn't tell him how it had really been. No one knew but me and Tom and, to some extent, Burwell. To tell my proud and devoted son a thing like that would've invited a duel. So I only said, "It breaks my heart to hear you speak of your father that way."

Truthfully, Tom had never been more justified in his rage, but there was no question that if the fire iron had hit Charles Bankhead squarely, he'd be dead. Dead on my father's floor, at Monticello, where the eyes of the whole country seemed to look for example, especially now.

Because that summer, the United States of America declared war on Great Britain.

If we'd waited a little longer, we would've discovered the British had finally cracked under the weight of my father's embargo. They'd decided against harassing our neutral merchant ships. They'd surrendered to my father's policies. But as in the Revolutionary War, the British had come to their senses too late.

Now there would be blood.

And both my husband and my son were called to fight.

LIKE MY FATHER, I'd begun to count things for comfort. *Twenty-three* was the number of years I'd been married to Tom Randolph. *Nine* was the number of children we had, with another on the way. *Forty-four* was my husband's age the day he declared that he must join the army because if he didn't fight to defend America, he'd be unhappy for the rest of his life.

Tom wanted and expected my father's blessing and encouragement, but Papa worried that my husband was beset with military fever. "His willingness to sacrifice for his country is admirable, but at his age, with all that depends on him—what can be driving him to it?"

I understood precisely what drove Tom. As my husband, he was doomed to live in the shadow of the country's greatest living patriot. But a patriot who had never been a soldier. Strip even that away, and Tom was still haunted by the shadow of *his* father, the colonel. So it didn't surprise me to see the pleasure Tom took in being commissioned by President Madison as a colonel, and given command of the Twentieth Regiment of the infantry.

Still, I couldn't shake the sense that Tom still felt the pull of the grave. I'd kept him from dueling Randolph of Roanoke, but deep down, I feared that my husband was still looking for the bullet that would give him an honorable exit. The night he received his commission, he perched at the edge of our bed, holding papers duly signed and sworn.

"Martha, I want you to look at this." I realized with a glance that it was a last will. Bringing both hands to my mouth, I pleaded with my eyes for him not to show me. But he persisted. "If I should die—"

"Please don't," I said, turning toward the wall. I knew Tom could die. Of course I knew. But I was my father's daughter, so I didn't wish to speak openly of such things. We didn't acknowledge them this way. I wasn't sure I could bear it.

"Martha." Tom took me by the shoulders and drew me to face him. "If I should die, I intend to give you everything."

Stunned, I asked, "What of the children?" It wasn't done that widows were left with unfettered power over their husband's property. It wasn't done because a widow's property would pass into the hands of a new husband the moment she remarried, and women weren't thought to be capable of managing it.

Tom swallowed. "I recommend you sell Varina to pay off the debts. You should probably give Jeff the better part of Edgehill and divide the rest amongst the younger boys. But I leave it to your judgment, and to your use, as you think fit."

I was dumbfounded, both by these spoken words, and the heartfelt ones he'd put to paper. *"I place my full confidence in the understanding, judgment, honor, and impartial maternal feeling of my beloved wife Martha."*

God as my witness, every offense Tom had ever given melted away to nothing. This man had worked himself to the bone for me. For my father. For our children. This man had nearly killed to defend me. And he had, with what might be his last official act, placed the trust of everything into my hands. My eyes misted at the well of tender love I felt for him—the depths of which I hadn't felt in some time. "Oh, Tom."

He sat taller, bracing himself. "I'd only like to know if you think you might, in the event of my death . . ." He shook his head, clearly uncomfortable. "Would you seek another husband?"

I didn't think. I only *felt*. Like my father before me, in that most vulnerable moment, when my spouse contemplated his death, I merely took my husband's hand and vowed, "Only you, Tom. I swear by God that I'll have no other husband."

That was all I said on the subject until it came time for him to leave for an assault on a British-held fortress near the Saint Lawrence River. President Madison said we couldn't forget the glory of our fathers in establishing independence, which must now be maintained by their sons.

The *fathers* he invoked were mine and John Adams. It was important to the cause—perhaps essential—that my husband and my son join the fight.

Jeff readily agreed. "God forbid that I should be last to come forward in defense of my country, for which I shall be proud to sacrifice my life."

But for every proud smile and farewell kiss and bland pleasantry about how short this war was sure to be, how we'd repelled the British once and could do it again, I nursed unworthy thoughts I dared not give voice to.

I'm going to lose them, as I lose everything, to the cause of this country.

I'd lost my mother, my siblings, my childhood. I'd lost my first love and my financial future. And, now, pregnant again and half out of my mind with fear, I couldn't bear to sacrifice another thing.

I'm not proud of it now. Nor was I then. But I went to my father and together we hatched a plot against my husband's military career.

~~~~~

DOLLEY FOLDED ME INTO HER ARMS to welcome me to Montpelier. "Why, Patsy, I didn't expect you in your condition. Then again, you'd never go anywhere if you waited until you weren't with child."

Papa chuckled. "At this rate, we ought to put her in a nunnery."

It was an entertaining jest in spite, or because, of the fact that I'd once desired to be a nun. But such was my fear for my husband that I couldn't find the heart to laugh. Papa gently squeezed my shoulder to reassure me of his intention to speak with Mr. Madison about my plight. It was left to me to prevail upon Madison's wife.

All my life, I'd gotten by with smiles and pleasantries. But the moment the gentlemen were out of hearing, I wept into my kerchief. Dolley was so startled by my uncharacteristic outburst that she teared up herself. "Oh, my dear, whatever can be the matter?"

"I'm so low-spirited," I wept, unbearably relieved to tell the truth. "I fear this baby is going to be the end of me and I'll never see my husband again. One of us is going to die before we're reunited."

"You mustn't think that way," Dolley said, stroking my hair. "Why, you have a perfect constitution. You're not due until the new year, and when the army retires to winter quarters, Tom will come home for the birth."

"At a time like this, every able-bodied man must be called upon, but my father thinks perhaps Tom could serve in the Virginia militia, closer to home." I held my breath in anticipation of her reaction, my stomach sick with worry and guilt.

For a long moment, Dolley was quiet. She should've told me that this was men's business. She should've pretended not to have any sway. But she simply tapped her fan against her cheek until an idea came to her. "What the president needs is tax collectors. Wars need to be paid for, and when we don't send men of prominence to collect, they're just run out of town on a rail. Your husband, with his name and connections and service, why, he'd make an ideal choice."

It was, in the end, my father's private word with Madison that led to the appointment. But I played my part. Which is why I took the blame when, after helping to lead a successful attack on Fort Matilda in New York, my husband returned in November from winter camp to learn the president had appointed him to collect revenue.

Tom went from puffed up and proud of his successful military campaign, to slack-jawed and bewildered as he'd read the appointment orders. I sat watching him, my stomach in knots.

He didn't talk to me for the rest of the day. But at bedtime, when his bewilderment gave way to fury, Tom entered our room and slammed the door. He paced and pulled at his hair, then turned to me and shouted, "What have you *done*, woman!"

Sitting on the bed's edge, I fisted my hands in my skirt. "I merely explained—"

"I'm offered a commission on application of my *wife*?"

I fell silent, because I knew it would anger him, and yet, I'd done it anyway. Still, with my father's encouragement, it'd seemed the right course.

Tom threw his sheathed sword across the room where it hit the cast iron stove with a clatter. "You and your father would have the president believing I want to hide behind a vile cloak of cowardice as a *tax* man?"

"Please don't blame Papa! It was my doing."

Tom squeezed his eyes shut with a shake of his head. "My confidence in myself has never been blind. I've scarcely in my life felt confident before. But on the battlefield, men looked to me. They trusted me. I didn't let them down. Which made me trust *myself*. Never did I suppose you might undermine me this way! The whole world might go against me, but never *you*."

"I'm not against you," I cried. I hadn't done it to undermine him, but to save him! Jeff was young and able-bodied, and if he didn't serve it would bring shame upon the family. *But no one expects Tom to fight,* Papa had said. And so, as my husband stared at me, demanding an explanation, all I could think to say was, "The appointment pays four thousand dollars."

I said it because I knew it grated on Tom that we lived in my father's house. I knew it made him doubt his worth. This salary would ease that—that's all I meant by it.

But he heard stark betrayal.

He grabbed me by the shoulders, and I yelped. Then he shook me. He shook me until my teeth rattled. He *hurt* me. Though I was heavily pregnant, he threw me to the floor, where I lay gasping as he stormed away.

It'd be years before the crack in our marriage became obvious to all, but I always knew it was that moment that shook our foundations. All our married lives, Tom had made a silent plea. *Need me. Need me the way a woman is meant to need her husband.* I'd finally allowed myself to realize how *much* I needed him, and look what it had unleashed. For desperate need of him, I'd stolen his pride. And now I feared he'd never forgive me.

Tom didn't sleep in our room that evening. I don't know where he went. And when our baby girl was born that winter, he wouldn't even suggest a name. *Seven,* I thought. Our seventh daughter. I named her Septimia.

Twenty-one. That was another important number. That's how old my tall, rock-steady son was on the summer day in 1814 that he was called into active duty in the militia to fend off invasion.

The last time the English attacked Virginia, my father had been pilloried for taking flight. Which meant that for my son, there was nothing to do *but* fight. And, in the end, all my schemes to keep Tom from the battlefield were for naught. As the summer days grew long, he prepared to command the Second Regiment of the Virginia Cavalry.

Before he departed Tom warned, "If the British win, it'll be an end to this nation. We'll likely be made colonies again. The English will consider your father a traitor and our entire family useful prisoners. So think of that before you say another word against my taking to the field."

Ashamed, I said nothing. For the defense of our country— and our family—my husband would drill troops on the muddy, mosquito-ridden banks of the York River while my son joined a company of artillerists to fend off the invasion. Still smarting and betrayed, Tom gave me the coldest of farewells, and I was too afraid to press him for more.

But before they marched off, I held my son's freckled face in my hands, memorizing every line. Jeff was as beautiful as his father had been at that age, but without the darkness. In temperament and strength, he was more like *my* father.

But where was I in that mix?

In his heart, I hoped. Where I'd *will* it to keep beating.

Chapter Thirty-three

Monticello, 28 August 1814
From Thomas Jefferson to Louis H. Girardin

Of the burning of Washington, I believe nothing. When Washington is in danger, we shall see Mrs. Madison and Mrs. Monroe, like the doves from the ark, first messengers of the news.

P.S. Since writing this I receive information undoubted that Washington is burnt.

T HE SHAME OF IT." Dolley wept, her pink lips quivering as she recalled her flight from the capital. Their escape was such a narrow miss that British officers actually dined on the meal that had been prepared for the Madisons before they put the President's House to the torch. The house where my father had served as president. Where I'd been his hostess. Where my son James had been born.

The English also burned the Naval Yard, the War Office, the Treasury, and the congressional buildings—including the Library of Congress and all the books therein. And Dolley sniffled, "My poor husband, when he saw the wreckage, was as shaken and woebegone as if someone had cleaved his heart in two."

My father looked every bit as heartbroken. "Barbarism," Papa said, pretending to dab at sweat with a kerchief, when I could see plainly there were tears in his eyes.

"I cannot do justice to the destruction with words," Dolley continued, having stopped at Monticello briefly on her way to Montpelier. "The country's monuments and architectural triumphs are all ash. The President's House burned to a charred shell. The capitol building without a roof and gutted to the marble like an ancient ruin. Priceless paintings slashed; their splintered frames nothing more than kindling now."

I'd hoped Dolley might bring some comforting word of my son and my husband, who would now face the British as they turned their guns south, but instead, I found myself comforting *her.* "At least you rescued some national treasures."

"Only trifles," she said with a dismissive wave. "A wagonload of papers, some silver and velvet curtains. There wasn't time to save more. I told the servants to cut down the painting of George Washington or destroy it if it couldn't be cut down, lest it fall into British hands. We hid it in a farmhouse—that's what we were reduced to. Mr. Madison sought shelter under armed guard while I spent the longest night of my life without him, hearing cannons booming. Explosions, too. I had to disguise myself in someone else's clothes to sneak back into Washington City."

I'd never admired her more.

"And the *Federalists.*" She uttered the word like a curse. "Never let them tell you they're true patriots. They cared for wounded British soldiers in preference to our own and crowed at the rout of *our* army and the destruction of *our* capital." She finished with a lament. "I wish I could've mounted the battle guns that our ill-trained and cowardly militia abandoned."

It was the most unladylike thing I'd ever heard her say, and it plucked not even a note of censure on the harp of my conscience. "I pray this war ends soon."

"Have you turned to your Bible, Patsy?" Dolley asked.

"No more than before," I said with a nervous glance to Papa. There was, of course, bad blood between God and me. I'd forsaken his nunnery and he'd forsaken my sister. I didn't wish to provoke the Almighty against my husband and son, too.

Papa excused himself on account of a growing headache, while I poured Dolley tea and readied my napkin in case she spilled it in her agitated state. But her hand was steady as she withdrew from her satchel a packet of papers. "I don't know on what terms you parted with your sister-in-law, but you'd better see this before your husband hears of it."

Curiously leafing through the pages, I recognized the handwriting of Nancy Randolph—though I supposed she was more properly thought of as Mrs. Morris, now. My infamous sister-in-law had found employment in the northern states as the housekeeper of Gouverneur Morris, whose strange sense of humor seems to have led him to marry Nancy in spite of her reputation, if not because of it. But just as she seemed poised for happiness, *Randolph of Roanoke* sent warning to Mr. Morris, saying that Nancy killed her bastard baby, killed Richard Randolph, and was likely to kill him, too, to steal his fortune.

"Poor Nancy," I said, reading that. "This goes back to an incident twenty years past now! I tell you truthfully, I believe Nancy was innocent."

"Not entirely," Dolley said, pointing to the passage in which Nancy admitted to having been seduced by Theo. "That might be enough to destroy her marriage. And *Randolph of Roanoke* is nothing if not a destroyer." Dolley put scorn behind the name, as if to mock his pretensions. "Nancy sent this letter, hoping I'd defend her reputation, but her husband is a Federalist, and as one first lady to another, I'll let her sink if you wish."

I smiled at Dolley giving me that title—a role she created herself—and I spoke from the heart. "In truth, I seethe for her. Nancy has finally found a respectable place for herself, and John can't leave her in peace."

Dolley watched me carefully. "So you take her side?"

"Whatever side John takes, I'm on the other." That made Dolley laugh. But then I added, "No matter where I stand with Nancy, it'd be a disgrace to let that villain harry her to death."

Dolley rose to stare out the parlor window to the gardens

beyond. "That does seem to be his aim. I hope he doesn't succeed."

I'd relied altogether too much on hope. Papa's stubborn faith in the goodness of humanity seemed to bear itself out less and less every day. And after seeing all the ills in the world, I no longer merely hoped justice would come to the wicked. "John Randolph is running in the upcoming election against my former brother-in-law, who'd be far more helpful to your husband in Congress."

John Randolph had miscalculated the damage ladies could do. We couldn't fight in the war, but reputations were won or lost on *our* fields of battle. And Dolley and I were prepared to set our cannons blasting. Tom wouldn't like my meddling in politics, would like even less my doing anything to help Jack Eppes. But he might approve for the sake of his sister. I'd saved her once before, and he'd been grateful. I was desperate to win back his affections now. So I sat down with Dolley to write some letters to influential ladies, taking up Nancy's banner and blackening John Randolph's name. If we'd been men, he'd have called us out. Unfortunately, the only advantage afforded a woman in Virginia was that we couldn't be challenged to a duel.

"Soldiers!" The cry came from Sally's thirteen-year-old daughter, Harriet, who came running in with her dark auburn hair streaming behind her, marshaling my younger children into the house. For a moment, I saw my sister in her. It was Polly that I saw in fright, and my heart stopped.

But Dolley had the presence of mind to ask, "Redcoats?"

"*Our* soldiers, I think," the girl said.

We crowded onto the portico steps, watching a ragtag group of boys marching up our mountain wreathed in gray mist. Even from a distance, they looked dirty, lean, half-starved. Some used their muskets like canes. One towered over his compatriots, and I caught a glimpse of auburn hair.

"Jeff!" I cried, wilting with relief. "It's my boy."

He broke away from the company, raced up the drive, and clomped up the stairs. He spoke in a rush as he swept me into his arms. "The British went north. We never saw a redcoat!"

That meant the British never met my husband's regiment, and the men in my life were safe. The British might've attacked Richmond and won, but instead they chose Baltimore, where Fort McHenry withstood a bombardment of more than twenty-four hours, leaving our flag, as immortalized by Francis Scott Key, *still there.*

"Where's your father?" I asked, overjoyed by the news.

Jeff only shrugged. I learned later that my son and husband had quarreled so violently that Jeff was nearly brought up on charges. My son wouldn't say why, but the details didn't seem important if the peace was won.

～

BY FEBRUARY OF 1815, everyone was giddy. Southern gentlemen swaggered about, confidence restored, honor defended, reputations built as a new generation of Americans defeated the British once again. Some called it a second American revolution.

"Get on your best dress, Mother," Jeff said, his spirits high since returning home. "I'm taking you and Ann to visit my lady love."

With his father's looks and his grandfather's charm, Jeff caught the eyes of beautiful women. But I'd heard the name of the governor's daughter bandied about more than once. And now that the war was at its end, Jeff was eager to see her. I was just as eager to lay eyes on the girl, so I dug through my closet.

Homespun wasn't in fashion anymore, but we hadn't had occasion to buy anything new, so Ann and I donned our decade-old dresses from when we played hostess at the president's table. Mine fit without alteration. But motherhood and marriage to a drunk had made my daughter so thin that her dress positively swallowed her up.

"I'll take it in," Sally said, going for her thread and needle. And when she was finished, we went off to meet the girl my son wanted to marry.

Jeff rode ahead on horseback, while Ann and I followed in the carriage, a blanket on our laps to guard against the cold. When we arrived at Mount Warren, Jane Nicholas bid us welcome. I was surprised to find her quite plain, but she had a warm smile.

Her mother, however, did nothing but scowl, apparently flummoxed to see us. As was the custom, Jeff went off to call on the gentlemen, whereas we were left to socialize over tea. And though Mount Warren was a prosperous house, we were offered *only* tea.

At some point during the surprisingly stiff and chilly conversation, I urged Jane and her mother to call upon us at Monticello, and Mrs. Nicholas asked, "Why ever would we do that?"

Sure that I'd heard her wrong, I only sipped at my tea. But Ann flushed to the tips of her ears.

The rude mistress of the plantation eyed me squarely and said, "My people were merchants. Merchants know that wealth is money. But planters prize land, no matter how useless. And I pray that none of my daughters will bury themselves in Virginia, married to boys who have nothing but an old name and a patch of dirt."

Jane cried, "Momma!"

Refusing to reveal my own shock, I patted the girl's hand. "Don't be upset, dear. Your mother is only speaking her mind, as we're free to do in the glorious nation my father helped to build."

Mortified, Jane rose, dragging her mother from the room. "Please excuse us. We must find some biscuits to go with our tea."

Ann fanned herself furiously against the stifling heat of the fire. "Why, I *never.*"

From the entryway beyond, where Mrs. Nicholas argued with her daughter, I heard her call me a *very vulgar-looking woman.* I seethed when I heard her say Ann was a *poor stick.* And I burned to hear her ask, "Don't you find it strange that Jeff Randolph, who owns nothing but a small tract of land and five Negroes, thinks he's ready for a wife? Of all the pretty girls who pant after him, you think he'd choose *you*?"

Having heard quite enough, I said, "Come along, Ann." We didn't wait for Jeff. While Jane and her mother argued, my daughter and I simply climbed into the carriage and rode off.

All the while, Ann kept saying, "I *never*! They think they're too good for us. They think Jeff's after her money!"

"If a girl may be judged by her mother, Jeff is better off without her."

We were still carrying on this way when we reached the top of my father's mountain, and someone wrenched open the carriage door. Ann shrieked in surprise to see that it was her husband, drunker than usual. And though the air was chilly, his face ran with sweat as he hauled her out. "Where were you?" Charles demanded.

Wide-eyed, Ann stammered, "We—we went to meet Jeff's girl. I told you—"

"Are you going to lie to me?" He threw her to the cold, hard ground. "Go on, lie to me."

"Charles!" I cried, scrambling out of the carriage. But I wasn't fast enough to stop him. He kicked her. He kicked my delicate daughter in the ribs, and when she tried to rise up, he kicked her in the face, sending a spray of blood from her mouth. "You lying little bitch."

People would say he had a right to do it. He had a right by law. But I was her mother, and there were other laws than the ones made by men. Seeing my baby girl's bloody mouth, I reached for the coachman's horsewhip and lashed at Charles. The whip caught him on the side of the face, where he was still scarred from the blow my husband had given him with a fire iron.

And Bankhead seemed so shocked to see that this time *I* was the one to lay open a stripe of blood on his cheek that he stood like a stunned ox.

"Run, Ann!" I cried, ducking a swing of his arm. I wasn't afraid for myself; it wasn't me he wanted to hurt. So I grabbed hold of him, making myself a dead weight. I might be a vulgar-looking woman, but I was sturdy, and my rampaging son-in-law couldn't easily throw me off. We grappled while Ann staggered to her feet, and while Burwell and Beverly Hemings went running to fetch the overseer.

"You leave her alone, Charles," I said, gripping his shirt tight. "You're mad with drink."

"You may rule your husband," Charles snarled. "But Ann's *my* wife and I'm going to beat her until she remembers it." With that, he tore himself from my grip, leaving a patch of his shirt in my hand, then took off after Ann at a run.

Monticello was in an uproar, servants shouting, Bankhead kicking everything and everyone in his way. Chickens went squawking. Dogs yelped and growled. And after a few moments, Sally rushed out of the house to help me up from the ground, whispering, "Charles passed her by. She's hiding in a potato hole."

The thought of my daughter, my first baby, hiding in the dirt from her husband made me wish that I'd let Tom kill him. As she helped me to my feet, Sally's long-ago words about the importance of the man a woman winds up with had never rung more true—because Ann was trapped with a cruel drunkard, and there wasn't a thing that we could do.

Sally was my father's mistress, not the mistress of the plantation, and yet it felt right to have her at my side. The drunken brute's shouts echoed from the house, and Sally and I took the stairs two at a time in the vain hope of getting to him before he got to my father.

Meanwhile, Jeff's horse came galloping up the road, in a cloud of dust. "What the *devil* is going on?"

We didn't stop to answer but burst into the house where the madman screamed, "Show yourself, Ann."

Jeff was on our heels, gripping his horsewhip. One look at his frothing, bloodied brother-in-law, and no one had to tell him what had happened. And my son went white to the tip of his nose.

"Did you do something to my sister, you rabid dog?" Jeff asked, advancing on Bankhead. "Someone ought to put you down. I think that someone is gonna be me."

Those were words that started duels. Words that demanded satisfaction. But Bankhead was so drunk I'm not sure he heard. Instead, he was transfixed by the sight of my father, who emerged from his rooms in stern disapproval.

"*Enough*," Papa said, very quietly, very severely. "We value domestic tranquility, here. Charles, I must ask you to reside under your father's roof for a time, not mine."

At my father's quiet show of thoroughly *presidential* authority, Bankhead seemed to suddenly shake free of his madness, and he sank to his knees and wept. Bankhead was being banished, and he knew it. He begged my father a thousand pardons, sobbing that he'd tried to stop drinking but never was able to. That it was something *in* him, like a demon.

I didn't care. I fetched Ann, took her upstairs, bandaged her ribs, and cleaned up her mouth and jaw, which were bruised and swollen. Then I put her in my bed, dosing her with some laudanum so she could rest. Bolting the door, I leaned back upon it like a guard.

That's when Jeff came up the narrow stairway with murder in his eyes. "You keep away from Bankhead," I said, keeping my voice low in case children might be eavesdropping from the nearby nursery or their bedrooms on the third floor. "And when your father returns, don't tell him what happened here today."

"Why not? Cracking that monster's skull is the finest thing my father ever did—too bad he botched the job, like always."

"Stop saying things like that, Jeff. Disrespect from a boy is one thing, but you're a man now."

He nodded grimly and leaned back on the door next to me. "Then you won't object to my taking Jane for a wife?"

"I'd think you'd rather marry someone who'll bring no more strife into this family."

"Jane isn't her mother," Jeff said, reasonably, staring at his feet. "I'm set on Jane. She's the prudent choice."

I stared, remembering my own seemingly *prudent* choice. "Oh, Jeff, be careful."

"I know what I'm about. My future prospects from my father I consider as blank. From my grandfather, not very cheering."

That my husband's fortunes were negligible, I knew. But since Papa retired from the presidency, Monticello had never seemed more fruitful or alive. "Why would you say that?"

Jeff crossed his freckled arms. "I've seen grandfather's books. Monticello is large but unprofitable and, unless judiciously managed, will probably consume itself."

My father was a sunny optimist, and I was neither entitled nor desirous to know the extent of his debts. But my son was pragmatic and clear-headed. And I believed him. "Even so, marrying a woman you don't love—"

"You won't tell my sisters to marry for love. You want to, but you won't. You don't want them to end up at the mercy of a penniless drunk like Bankhead. It'll be a miracle if they find husbands with their promised *thirty cents* per annum. Though, with Ellen's caustic tongue, no amount would be enough."

"Don't be sarcastic," I said, reaching for his hand.

Our shoulders touched in the doorway.

"My brothers are still boys," he said. "I'm going to have to provide for all of them. My sisters and brothers. So I can't marry anybody but a rich woman, and Jane's sweet. If I can make myself love her, you can do the same."

I glanced up at him, shamed that he should have such burdens. But I'd raised a man who could be relied upon, and that filled me with pride. So I never uttered another word against Jane, not realizing that she'd cost us everything.

THE NEXT MORNING, I rocked my grand-baby in his cradle as Ann continued to sleep fitfully in the nearby bed. The movement of the rocking was a comfort when so little else was. Everything seemed in a turmoil.

Ann awoke on a gasp. "Where is Charles? I have to go to him," she said, her words slurred because of the swelling around her mouth.

"He must've kicked the senses out of you if you're even considering going with him," I said, my heart hurting that *this* was the reality of my daughter's life.

She struggled to sit up against the pillows. "Where else can I go?"

"You needn't go anywhere," Papa replied from the doorway, surprising us both, for he so seldom mounted the steep stairs that the crowded upper floors in which my family lived must have seemed to him like another world completely.

Papa crossed the room and rested an age-spotted hand on her shoulder. "You're always welcome here at Monticello, dearest Ann."

Bravely wiping away the tears that flowed down her bruised face, Ann said, "But my place is with Charles. By law, he can take the children. You know he can."

"He'll soften, fearing the loss of you," Papa said. "His family will talk sense to him." All his life, I think my father believed, in principle, that a woman belonged to her husband. But now he tried every way possible to encourage Ann's separation from Charles. Every way but telling her she had a right to do it.

Maybe that would've made the difference.

"It was my fault," Ann insisted. "He worries when he can't find me."

My heart sank to my stomach, where it weighed like a stone when, later that day, Ann rode off with Charles, their children, and belongings. "Patsy, I had to send him away," Papa said from where we stood upon the south terrace, overlooking the garden, the vineyards, and the breathtakingly broad vista beyond.

"I know," was my truthful reply.

Papa squinted up at the clouds. "Dr. Bankhead will have more authority to deal with his son. And if I let Charles stay here, and Tom found out . . ."

I knew exactly what Tom would do if he found out that Bankhead beat our daughter. And I didn't know if I should be sorry or grateful that Tom was still too furious with me to come home.

Rounding his shoulders, Papa said, "In the meantime, I've sold my library to Congress to replace the one burned by the British. I'll use the profit to secure property for Ann alone, to make her independent if the worst should come to pass."

"Oh, Papa," I said, pressing a grateful kiss against his aging shoulder. It was startlingly generous and also startling because my father had never encouraged independence in any woman before.

"I'll save some for Ellen, who'll need to attract a husband of her own soon."

"Given the fate of her sister, I almost wish Ellen would never marry," I said. I deny loving any of my children more than the others. But you take more pleasure in some. Ann, Jeff, and Ellen were the children I knew best and to whom I'd formed the first tender attachments. Even amongst those three, Ellen was special. "She feels things too acutely for her own happiness. She's like her father, but without his temper, and such people aren't well suited for this selfish world."

My father smiled because Ellen was his favorite, too. "She's the jewel of my soul, but we mustn't be too selfish. We must allow her into society and hope she finds a perfect love."

"Perfect love?" Ellen asked, swishing her skirts as she came up behind us, not even pretending she hadn't eavesdropped. "Ann loves Charles, and look how that's turned out. There may be no such thing as perfect love."

My father smiled. "There will be for you, pretty girl."

Dark-haired, sloe-eyed Ellen wasn't as pretty as Ann, but at the age of nineteen, Ellen was slender and dashing, with supreme confidence. And she used it now to distract us from the sadness of Ann's departure. "I recently met a handsome gentleman who was so perfectly the victim of ennui that it destroyed every attraction I might've felt for him. Truly, I'd bore you to list the suitors

I became completely disgusted with visiting Richmond. I'd just as soon become a spinster and devote myself to the care of my beloved grandpapa."

She was teasing, I hoped, but the marriage prospects of our daughters were very much on my husband's mind when he finally returned for Jeff's wedding to Jane with the first hints of spring. Tom had never been a cheerful man, but he returned to me a dour one. He now styled himself Colonel Randolph, and it relieved me that though he'd taken his father's title and demeanor, he wasn't unfeeling toward his children. When he crawled into our bed after having been gone so long, he said, "Now that our son has taken a bride, it's time to think about the girls. Mrs. Madison extended an invitation to have Ellen in Washington City. She'll find a higher caliber of gentleman to court her there."

Quietly, I gasped at the expense this would entail. Ellen couldn't properly go to the capital without new dresses, new shawls, bonnets, and triflings of every sort. She'd be advised by Dolley, whose expensive tastes we could scarcely afford.

But when I confessed my worries, Tom exploded in temper. "What sort of man do you take me for? You think I'd help marry my sisters off but will deprive my own daughter of the few dresses and combs she needs to secure her happiness?"

Lowering my eyes, I said, "I know you'd never deny your daughters a thing if it were within your power. I'm only worried for the expense."

"Did your father spare any expense for your coming-out in Paris?" Tom asked, staring hard. "I've heard the stories, so many balls you had to limit yourself to not more than three a week. Stories your daughters have heard, too."

With that single, astute observation, Tom leveled me. I'd so often entertained my children with stories about my days in Paris that any one of the older girls could have named my friends at the convent and recounted their exploits. To buoy spirits in hard times, I'd fed my girls a steady diet of opulent tales. How could

I deny my vivacious Ellen the opportunities I'd enjoyed? "You're right, of course. I beg your pardon—"

"It's not your place to worry about expenses," Tom ranted, in a fever of anger that'd been brewing since I'd meddled in his military career. "That's always been the trouble with you, Martha. You don't know your place."

He then proceeded to show me my place, by roughly tugging my nightclothes and pinning me to the bed. I made no attempt to refuse him. I didn't dare. And, in truth, I hoped that our coming together—even in anger—might mend the wounds. After all, Tom's ardent kisses usually broke through my reserve, and his release usually unraveled the knots inside him.

But on that night, not even pleasure could untangle the trouble between us.

In the dark, I whispered, "Tom, I offer my sincerest apologies. I know I've hurt you and offended your sense of honor. But please know that what I did, I only did for fear of losing you. I erred in love."

To that, he had no reply whatsoever.

Chapter Thirty-four

Poplar Forest, 3 December 1816
From Thomas Jefferson to Martha Jefferson Randolph

We've been weather bound at this place. Johnny Hemings and company will set off on Thursday. Our only discomfort is not being with you. The girls have borne it wonderfully. They've been very close students and I'm never without enough to do to protect me from ennui.

M Y FATHER KNEW I'd go through his letters once he was dead. This letter is proof that he meant to spare me from having to burn more than I already have. The *company* my father mentions in reference to their Uncle Johnny were Sally's sons: Beverly, Eston, and Madison.

They were almost always with Papa in those days, engaged in a grand project to build a new octagonal house at Poplar Forest, where we once hid from the British. My father fled there now for the same reason: to escape. To escape *Monticello*, which had become, in some respects, a glorified museum and inn.

Though it was a great expense, my father wouldn't deny his hospitality to visitors. It seemed to him somehow undemocratic, or at the very least, un-*Virginian*. Strangers stopped without even a letter of introduction, expecting supper and a bed. Most of all, they desired to lay eyes on the former president, the sage of Monticello. And, of course, to satisfy their curiosity about *Dusky Sally*.

Under that scrutiny, Papa increasingly withdrew to Poplar Forest, where he could make plans for his new university and enjoy the sons Sally had given him.

But he never wrote their names down in any letter.

He knew better. And so did I.

Perhaps my father also absented himself to give Tom the illusion of being in command, hoping it might ease the strain on our marriage. And I made myself as obedient and accommodating as possible, even though Tom had scarcely a tender word for me. I missed the husband I'd known—temperamental and morose, but fiercely loving. And I despaired of having lost that love, possibly forever.

Meanwhile, from Washington came a steady report on Ellen's beaux:

> Mr. De Roth was "an insignificant little creature."
> Mr. Hughes was "a man of no family or connections."
> Mr. Forney was "aloof."
> Mr. Logan was "not at all clever."

Though my daughter had success pricing the *Scientific Dialogues* for her grandfather's library, she made no progress in finding a husband, and I couldn't find it within myself to encourage her to try harder, given how miserable my own marriage had become.

I tried to count myself content that the love Tom once lavished upon me he now gave to our daughters. But it left me lonely even in a crowded house. I missed Ann unbearably and worried every day what her husband might do to her. As for Ellen, I wanted her to come home straightaway from her husband-hunting trip, but Papa sent her the profit from his tobacco so she could visit Baltimore and then Philadelphia. Which put me in a near depressive state until she returned to regale us with tales of her adventure.

"Everything's so cheap and good in Philadelphia. And the

people were most hospitable. Mr. Short came to see me, too," Ellen said, working her polishing cloth over one of the silver goblets Papa bought our last summer in Paris.

Nearly the whole of Papa's silver inventory lay spread out before us on a dining room table, and I looked up from the silver tumbler I'd been polishing, one from a set of eight that Papa had commissioned a silversmith to make per his own design. It must've been because Tom and I were so unhappy that I felt wistful to hear William's name again. And surprised, too, that William had visited my daughter.

Papa had, indeed, given William an appointment that sent him to France and then Russia. But when Mr. Madison became president, he brought about an abrupt end to William's diplomatic career. For spite, I suppose. No matter the cause, William's return from Europe had been unheralded and shrouded in mystery. I only knew that he'd settled in Philadelphia—without his duchess—and I was painfully curious to know more.

"Mr. Short called upon you?" I asked, setting the tumbler aside.

"Twice, actually," Ellen replied. "He took me to see the house you lived in with Mrs. Hopkinson when you were a little girl. It's now occupied by trades people and has nothing to distinguish it. But I gazed on it with mixed feelings of pleasure and melancholy."

I, too, had mixed feelings of pleasure and melancholy to think of the man I once loved squiring my daughter about Philadelphia, walking cobblestone streets I once walked, and telling her stories from my youth.

Ellen continued, "We also visited the spot where my grandfather lived as secretary of state. And I strained my eyes to get a distant view of his lodgings while vice president. I was gratified by the sight of these now humble buildings which recall those in whom my fondest affections are placed."

The swell of my heart made it ache. William had done more than watch over my daughter. He'd taken her places that recalled me and my father. Places I was sure I'd never see again. But William gave these memories to my daughter, and it moved me beyond words to think he was still, after all these years, doing for me what I couldn't do for myself.

Ellen would do well to find a man like him in the northern states where everything was so cheap and so good. I'd never say it out loud, certainly never in my father's presence, but like Mrs. Nicholas, I, too, now prayed that none of my daughters would bury themselves in Virginia.

~⟶

"WHY DOES ELLEN HAVE ALL THE FUN?" Ginny asked at my old harpsichord. She'd been playing song after song to entertain our company. And once our guests had retired, leaving only family and near-relations, she complained, "First her travels, now Grandpapa intends to take her to Poplar Forest. Not just Ellen, but Cornelia, too!"

My father gave an indulgent chuckle. "Oh, it's a very monastic sort of existence at Poplar Forest. Ellen and Cornelia are the severest students. In daytime they never leave their room but to come to meals. About twilight of the evening, we go out with the owls and bats, and take our evening exercise. You wouldn't enjoy it."

Jeff added, "There'll be better bachelors at the governor's mansion than amongst owls and bats at Poplar Forest. I've asked Governor Nicholas to host a party for you girls to come out into society in Richmond next winter, when the legislature is in session."

There were advantages, it seemed, in his having married the governor's daughter. But I worried that Jeff arranged this for his sisters without asking Tom. Hoping to stave off an argument, that night as I got ready for bed, brushing my hair out in front of the mirror over my marbled dresser, I gently broached the subject with my husband.

He surprised me by saying, "The girls would like that."

I nodded, abandoning my brush to climb over Tom to get to

my side of the alcove bed—a ritual that had once been flirtatious but had now turned to annoyance.

He stopped me, hands on my hips. "What ails you, Martha?"

"What makes you think something ails me?" I was resolved to say nothing about my worries for the expense. My husband would tell me it wasn't my place, even though his generosity—the dresses, the ribbons, the fripperies—would come out of pockets that were already empty. It *wasn't* my place to question him; my meddling is what had brought us to this unhappiness, so I bit my tongue.

But Tom's eyes bored into mine in the candlelight. "I suppose Jeff told you I intend to sell slaves to bolster the family finances, running off to his mother like he always does. He's still tied up in your apron strings."

I'm not certain how he could've surprised or appalled me more. When Tom proposed marriage, he said he was against slavery. Since then, of course, we'd quietly reconciled ourselves to the evil, convinced that the poor slaves needed us, as children need parents. But selling slaves . . . how could we ever reconcile ourselves to that? "Tell me you'd never do such a thing."

"I'm only selling one sullen girl," Tom answered. "She's difficult to manage, but she could go for more than five hundred dollars. It'll be an investment in the happiness of our daughters, and maybe the slave will be happier with a new master, too."

I rolled off him. Turning to the wall, a scream echoed in my mind. I'd held back my news as long as I could, but upon hearing the evil thing my husband planned, I was too upset to dissemble. "We're having another baby, Tom."

I heard nothing but silence behind me. It'd been four years since our last child, and we'd assumed my child-bearing days were over. I'd been grateful for it. But now, at nearly forty-five years of age, I was pregnant again and near tears to think it.

I already had ten children—far more than I had the strength to care for. Much as I loved them, I was wrung out with little ones climbing on me night and day. Giving birth to my last had weakened my health. God forgive me, I didn't *want* another baby. But children were a source of manly pride. So, given a moment or so, maybe Tom would find his composure and tell me how happy he was. Then I'd force a smile and tell him what a joy it'd be.

Except it would all be a lie—all of it.

So I turned and said, "I don't know what to do about it."

At these words, Tom eyed me with a mixture of curiosity and horror. Perhaps he was remembering my testimony in which I claimed to have given his sister an abortifacient. I was remembering it, too. It seemed, at the moment, like an answer. We'd never stand trial for it. My father, if he knew, might not even object, for he'd commented almost admiringly on the practice amongst Indians. I'd hate myself, but I already hated myself for bringing another child into the world when we couldn't provide for the ones we already had.

And yet, I should never have implied such a solution to Tom. Not even as a desperate consideration that I'd talk myself out of. Not even to get my husband's reassurances. Tom's lips thinned into a mean line. "There isn't anything to be done about it, Martha."

Chastened, I lowered my eyes and murmured what I believed to be the truth. "It's likely to kill me, this time."

Then I turned back to the wall, where I lay trapped.

⁓

DURING THAT PREGNANCY, I was so sick and swollen and sad all the time that I couldn't stand myself. The birth left me so insensible that I had to be told I'd given birth to a living babe—a fragile little boy, tiny and blue, for whom my father would eventually choose the name George Wythe Randolph.

I was too weak to hold the baby or feed him, consumed with excruciating, debilitating pain and delirium. And though I was grateful to have lived through the ordeal, every time it seemed as if I might recover, I succumbed to a new cough or ailment.

Scarcely able to sit up, I was confined to bed and bedpan, and

Ellen moved into the room across from mine so that she could nurse me. In the months that followed, my daughters were forced to take turns at housekeeping in my stead. But the entire estate would have fallen to pieces if not for Sally Hemings watching over my girls and instructing them where I couldn't. And I simply *couldn't*. Neither smallpox nor typhus had rendered me so ill. Not even fears for my father's reputation could get me out of bed. Not even to converse or dine with our guests.

Papa's brilliant courtship with the public went on below stairs—but my world was suddenly and sharply confined to the warren of attic rooms at the top of the house. Oh, I saw and heard most everything, for Monticello was a noisy place, with creaky hinges and floorboards, and more than twenty family members in residence at any given time. My window overlooked the same expansive vista as my father's did—but my room was at a higher elevation. I saw more. I saw the reality. I saw, every day, Mulberry Row and all the little nail-shop boys who worked from sunup to sundown for our happiness—which only fueled my sickness and melancholy.

One night, when Cornelia brought my supper up, she burst into tears. "Oh, Mother, you're so very pale, and I'm such an unworthy daughter!"

"Why would you say such a thing?" I offered my arms, and when she came to me, I removed her cap and stroked her dark hair.

Cornelia cried, "How do you remember the numberless variety of orders and directions for the servants? I'm so tired of putting away the books and other things that seem to get everywhere all the time."

"It becomes routine," I assured her, knowing she longed to trade the keys and the cookbooks for her drawing paper and pencils. "You'll get better at it."

"Father doesn't think so," she said, wiping her eyes and reaching into her apron for a scrap of paper written in Tom's hand. I worried that he'd written a stern reprimand, but instead, it was a poem about her housekeeping.

While frugal Miss Mary kept the stores of the House,
Not a rat could be seen, never heard was a mouse,
Not a crumb was let fall,
In kitchen or Hall:
For no one could spare one crumb from his slice
The rations were issued by measure so nice
But when spring arrived to soften the air,
Cornelia succeeded to better the fare,
Oh! The boys were so glad,
And the Cooks were so sad,
Now puddings and pies every day will be made,
Not once in a month just to keep up the trade.

It was such gentle teasing from Tom—and so unusually good-humored—that I laughed. But Cornelia wept inconsolably until Tom came to comfort her. Speaking soft words before sending her off, Tom closed the door and pulled a chair up beside our bed. Taking my hand in his, he said, "Your hands are so cold."

"I'll feel better in the morning," I said, cheered by this unexpected husbandly affection.

"You've been saying that for some time." He clasped my hand tighter and lowered his head. "The physician says you won't survive another birth. And I've no intention of doing what my father did to my mother or what Jack Eppes did to your sister. It may be that we're better off sleeping apart."

Even as ill as I was, I didn't want to sleep apart from Tom. For twenty-eight years, we'd lain together, and as much as I'd come to resent him in my bed, it pained me more to think of him never there again. "Oh, Tom, can't we . . ." I trailed off, wondering what to suggest.

I hadn't been willing to find an "agreeable Negress" to sate my husband's needs when Dolley suggested it. That unwillingness had nearly cost me my life. But I heard from downstairs the violin of Beverly Hemings—now nineteen years old and a great favorite at Monticello—and it bolstered my resistance. Sally's oldest son had my father's freckles, his posture, and shared Papa's love of music, science, and hot air balloons. The time was coming, I knew, for Sally's son to be set free, and I dreaded explanations that would need to be made to friends, neighbors, and even my children. I'd found a way not to think of Sally's children as my siblings—not to think much of them at all beyond a bone-deep guilt and sadness. A guilt and sadness I never wanted my children to feel.

That's why I hadn't taken Dolley's advice, and nothing had changed. So I never found a suggestion. Now Tom made one of his own. "When Governor Nicholas vacates the office, I believe I'd be a good successor. I can be appointed to the post from the state legislature, and . . . the governorship comes with a salary. Money that can't be lost to droughts or tobacco rot or Hessian flies. Money that's certain."

It was as close as my husband could come to admitting that the planter's way of life that had sustained generations of Virginians in wealth and luxury was a lifestyle in utter decay. My father's idealistic visions of an agrarian Republic where men's wealth could be measured in land no longer reflected reality. At least not our reality.

Tom didn't need my permission, but he seemed to be asking for it. "Richmond's not so far that I can't be at your side within a few hours' hard ride. But I'd have my own bed there—in my own house."

That might be the most important part, I thought. Tom would no longer be living under his father-in-law's roof. No longer a man whose position was uncertain. He might no longer be thought of as Thomas Jefferson's underachieving political and intellectual heir—and dependent, but rather, master of a mansion in Richmond and the entire state of Virginia.

"Of course you'd be a good successor," I managed as I debated the wisdom of an even greater distance between us. Given the long tension between us, how could I do anything but support him?

Chapter Thirty-five

Monticello, 1 January 1819
From Thomas Jefferson to Francis Wayles Eppes

A school master is necessary only to those who require compulsion to get their lesson.

I SMILE TO READ THIS LETTER, filled with stern advice for my sister's son on how to perfect his Greek grammar. Papa never seemed to believe that his own brilliance was unique to him. Instead, he believed his grandchildren all inherited his intellectual capacity and that if they only applied themselves, they'd easily match his accomplishments in science, architecture, and statecraft.

But he was always overly optimistic about the generations that came after him.

Jeff was so burdened with his own growing family and managing my father's plantation that there'd never be any opportunity for him to become a man of letters, a thing for which he felt an acute lack. Perhaps one of my younger sons might attend the university my father was founding in Virginia, but until then, our hopes for the next generation of intellectuals rested upon Polly's son.

My daughters, meanwhile, were likely to end up spinsters. Nothing came of their season in Richmond during which the men allegedly considered them altogether too educated in the male arts and not enough in the womanly ones. In the end, only a single offer of marriage was made—and it was worse than none at all. The offer came from Nicholas Trist, a neighbor, the son of a friend, an idealistic but penniless boy of seventeen who wanted to marry my penniless daughter Virginia of the same age. Though I'd married at seventeen—or maybe because I did—I thought them both too young to be entangled by an engagement that would decide the happiness, or wretchedness, of their lives.

Inexplicably, the young suitor, who aspired to be a diplomat, addressed his request to me, rather than to Tom. And so from my sickbed, I composed a short note, entreating him to learn more of the world before judging whether Ginny was vital to his happiness. It'd buy time, I hoped, for my daughter to seek an older, more established man with whom to build an easier life—if such a thing could be had in Virginia, where the price of cotton had fallen nearly 25 percent in a single day. The irony wasn't lost on me that in warning away my daughter's suitor, I was doing exactly as my father had done to me and William, but I better understood my father's position now and felt a pang of sympathy.

It was February before I was able to get out of bed and go below stairs. And the first full day I spent upright was on account of a special occasion. There was to be a reunion at Monticello, as we were expecting Ann and her reportedly now-sober husband to dinner. So I summoned my girls down from the attic cuddy they had fashioned into a salon for themselves, where they were happier to contend with wasps and rafters than with Papa's guests. Then I had one of the servants carry down for me a comfortable but worn gilded chair from France to the kitchen, where I held my *Le Cuisinier Royal* cookbook open to my handwritten notes.

Amidst the shiny copper pots and sooty walls of the kitchen, Ginny moped in like a kicked puppy, having apparently surmised that I'd thwarted her nascent courtship. Nicholas Trist would never have been so bold as to declare his feelings to her without my blessing. But I remembered the artful games William and I had played and knew such matters could be understood without being spoken.

In any case, if Ginny was nursing a broken heart, she was too much a Jefferson and not enough a Randolph to say so. Instead, she sulked. "I don't see what the point of learning this is. A few months of housekeeping badly done aren't going to give me one useful acquirement, not even the industrious habits which would enable me to spend my future more profitably. I'd rather read than sew or keep house."

With a sharp look at her sister, Ellen said, "Which will profit you not at all. Taking turns means we can each learn what we need to be useful wives, then go with Grandpapa to study like men do, for gratification and because it's the most agreeable way of passing time." Then Ellen rounded on me. "And, Mother, your insistence on supervising is defeating the purpose of giving you rest."

"I've been resting for nearly a year. I'm quite weary of rest," I complained, as the cook and the servants who did the arduous work here all bustled about. "Besides, the less occupation we have, the less we're disposed to do."

That day, I rode the girls like an overseer, right up until the great clock reached the dinner hour according to the gong at the top of the house.

"Charles is coming along soon!" Ann chirped, having arrived ahead of him. "He had to stop first in Charlottesville at the store."

My daughter Ann had turned into a scarecrow since I'd seen her last. She and the grandchildren lived poorly; their threadbare clothes and worn shoes told the tale. And an hour later, Bankhead still hadn't arrived. Jeff was late, too. So late that Papa didn't want to hold supper any longer.

Finally, at evening, the dogs barked at a rider galloping madly up our road. Burwell went for the door, but Ellen also raced for the entryway with unladylike haste.

I tried to follow but was such an invalid that the blood drained from my head; I nearly toppled Ann when she tried to steady me. "Mother, careful! You're not well, yet."

"It's only a visitor," Papa said.

But I never remembered anyone riding a horse that violently to deliver good news. And Ellen returned to the dining room, ashen, overseer Bacon behind her, sweating and breathless from his ride.

"It's Jeff," Ellen cried, her eyes flitting with fury to her older sister. "Your worthless malignant husband stabbed our brother!"

As my heart leapt into my throat, the napkin fell from my father's hand. Papa rose to his feet at once. "Where?"

"Charlottesville," Bacon answered. "They came to blows in the courthouse square. I had them carry your grandson inside Leitch's store and put him upon a bale of blankets, but . . . he can't be moved. He's bleeding badly and the physician doesn't expect him to live until morning."

Those words ringing in my head in all their horror, my legs went out from under me. The next moment, I was on the floor staring up at the fireplace where fickle Fates carved in Wedgwood danced in blue mockery before my eyes.

"Loosen her stays," Ellen insisted while my other daughters crowded around me, fanning my face.

In my continued illness from childbirth, I'd swooned away like some delicate damsel when all I wanted was to get to my son. "*Jeff*," I gasped. Servants rushed in to help and all the while I kept saying, "Tom, please take me to Jeff." But Tom wasn't there. My husband, the new governor of Virginia, lived now in Richmond, a thing I'd somehow forgotten in the fog of my terror. "A carriage—someone get me a carriage. I must go to my son!"

"No, Martha." The long absent steely edge of fatherly command returned to Papa's voice. "If Charles is on a drunken rampage again, he'll come here next for Ann."

"He can't have done this," Ann sobbed. "Charles isn't drinking anymore. He wouldn't stab my brother for no reason!"

"He *is* drinking again, Mrs. Bankhead." Bacon accepted a glass of water and chugged it down. "He literally rode his horse into a tavern. Your brother confronted him. Jeff said something to him about abusing you, and Mr. Bankhead sprang on him with a knife. I had to pull your husband off your bleeding brother myself."

Ann backed away from the truth of Bacon's words. "Not for my sake. This can't have happened for my sake!"

As deeply as I felt her anguish, I could think of nothing but Jeff. I struggled into a sitting position and grasped at Ellen's shoulder. "Get the carriage." The elegant arched room spinning around me, I looked up at Papa, then to Bacon. "Get the carriage *now*. Please!"

"Patsy, you're not well enough," my father snapped, using my childhood name to command me. "Stay with the girls. Bolt the doors. Hide if Charles comes. I'll post Burwell, Beverly, and Bacon to stand guard over you."

Ellen rose and stepped in front of my father. "You're not riding out by yourself, are you?"

"Fetch my horse," he instructed the servants in a tone that brooked no opposition. "Eagle."

Eagle was a far more accommodating mount than the spirited Caractacus had been, but still we worried. The servants wouldn't oppose Papa, but Ellen did. "Grandpapa, it's cold and dark. You can't go galloping into the winter night!"

But that's exactly what my seventy-five-year-old father did, hurtling himself up into the saddle like a man half his age, applying the whip, and, with only the moon as his guide, disappearing in a clatter of hooves off into the snowy forest.

THEY BROUGHT MY SON HOME IN A WAGON, my heart breaking with each turn of its wheels on the icy road. The servants rushed to lift the makeshift stretcher upon which my boy lay covered in dried blood, one limp hand dragging in the snow.

Jeff was still alive, but barely. We had him carried into the bedroom opposite my sitting room, onto the alcove bed, which the girls stripped of its damask bedspread. He'd been stabbed in the hip and arm. He'd lost so much blood that he was as pale as a newborn babe, and I still remembered Jeff that way. My father's little namesake, the baby who made me realize for the first time that I loved my husband. The little boy who, from his first breath, embodied hope for my family.

If he died, so would everything hopeful or loving in me.

While the physician rebandaged Jeff's wounds, servants got a fire burning and warmed sherry for him. Meanwhile, my daughters crowded in the doorway. "I hope Charles swings for this," Cornelia said, her dark eyes flashing with *the Randolph*. "I hope he's tried and convicted and that I'm there to witness him at the end of a noose!"

Ann recoiled, sobbing into a handkerchief. "You don't mean that. He's the father of my children. Surely you don't mean that!"

"Of course she doesn't," I said, very calmly. My daughters were Randolphs; their tempers ran hot. But mine ran cold. "A trial would cause a sensation and bring shame down upon your grandfather's good name. Instead, we'll hire a keeper to prevent mischief, lock Charles in a room with all the whiskey he desires, and let him finish himself off."

My words made Ann shudder. She eyed me with scarcely disguised horror, backing away, as if she had apprehended a monster in me she'd never known dwelt there before.

But I meant every word. I'd done my daughters no favors hiding behind feminine virtues, allowing men to do as they pleased with little more than sarcasm and secrecy for protest. Seeing my son half-dead, something changed in me—my willingness to obey, my willingness to accept, to *let the men handle it* was gone.

When the doctor went out, I went in. On a moan, Jeff tried to rise up on the arm that *wasn't* nearly severed from his shoulder. And I snapped, "You lay back down! Jane will be here soon or we'll take you to her when you've recovered."

"My arm." Jeff groaned, falling back against the pillow. "The doctor says I'll never be able to use it again."

I held my breath, trying to imagine my boy maimed. My strong son with his broad back who prided himself on his ability to outwork his father . . . diminished forever in his abilities. And

I didn't care so long as he lived. Stroking his hair, I murmured, "My precious Jeff."

He gritted his teeth. "Where's Bankhead?"

"He's been arrested for attacking you."

"He didn't attack me." Jeff closed his eyes in an excess of emotion that might've been shame. "When grandfather found me lying in my own blood, he bent his head and wept. He wept for me, and I couldn't disappoint him. I couldn't tell him the truth." Jeff cried in anguish. "I struck the first blow. I swung down off my horse with my whip and advanced on Bankhead. We quarreled about some things he said about my wife, and I swore that if he did violence to my sister again I'd beat him down like a slave. He shouted that he could kill Ann dead and there wasn't anything I could do to stop him. So I hit him with my whip and I remember nothing else till Bacon was pulling us apart."

"Oh, Jeff," I said, one hand to my cheek.

"Charles isn't guilty. I am."

"You're guilty of *nothing*," I whispered. I didn't care what the law might say. I never felt prouder of my son and wasn't about to let him think he'd brought this misery upon himself. "Jeff, you're remembering it wrong. Your pain is bending your mind. Rest easy with a clear conscience. Overseer Bacon says Charles attacked you."

And I vowed that Bacon would keep on saying it.

When the laudanum did its work and Jeff drifted to sleep, I ought to have been too weary to stand. But anger is a kind of fuel, and I went in search of my father. I found him in the greenhouse, near a carelessly abandoned stack of clay pots and digging tools, feeding seeds to his newest mockingbirds, who serenaded him with a French tune.

"What are you doing out here, Papa?" I asked, rubbing my arms against the cold.

Looking over the dried-out stalks the gardener had yet to prune for next year's planting, he murmured, "It's winter. A time when everything we've planted withers and dies on the vine."

No. I would not hear it. I would *not*. Choking back tears, I said, "Jeff is strong. He'll live."

My father hung his head. "Ah, Patsy. What tragedy that two young men of my own family have come to this."

"They aren't both family," I snapped. "Vows were said, but if Charles were Ann's husband in truth, would he put hands on her the way he does?"

I waited for my father to utter some optimistic platitude, but his shoulders slumped. "I fear she'll meet her end at his hands unless we keep her here."

"She won't go back with him," I insisted. "Not after this. We won't let him take her."

But by morning, Ann was gone.

"DON'T TELL ME I CAN DO NOTHING!" my husband shouted, love for his son showing itself as pure, unadulterated fury. "I'm the governor of the goddamned state."

Charles had made bail and fled the county, taking Ann and our grandchildren with him. And having returned from Richmond to hear this, Tom was an inferno. "I wish I'd caved in his skull, even if it ended in my swinging from the gallows."

A savage part of me understood just how he felt, but I wouldn't trade my husband's life for Bankhead's blood. We were promised that if Charles set foot in Albemarle, he'd be jailed. Meanwhile, neighbors were feeding a steady stream of gossip and my poor son begged us to let the matter drop. It was because Jeff carried guilty secrets with less alacrity than I'd always done, but my daughters all believed it was a gallant gesture to protect Ann. And they privately blamed her for taking Charles's part with a ferocity only sisters can. Cornelia confided that if justice wasn't served, she hoped never to see Mr. *or* Mrs. Bankhead ever again.

Though I had a babe still in diapers to care for, little children who ran about like wild things, and a plantation full of servants to manage, I spent that spring and early summer dedicated entirely to helping Jeff use his arm again. Jeff tried riding, but couldn't do it without assistance. Each night, he'd collapse in my sitting room, suffering, inside and out. "It's no use." He stared with withering scorn at the offending limb. "I'm maimed." And when his wife pressed a cloth to his forehead he shouted, "Leave it alone, Jane! I'm good for nothing."

When she scurried from the room, Jeff sulked in my chair.

A boy might rightly expect coddling from his mother—to be taken against her soft bosom to weep at cruel fate. But it was a soft heart that brought my family to this place. "How would you feel if you heard your father speak to me that way?"

Jeff's eyes blazed. "I *have* heard him speak to you that way."

There was no use denying it. "Well, I suppose you have, but the way you hollered at Jane just now . . . that's how your sister's husband behaves. Except that you're sober and don't have the excuse of Charles's madness."

Jeff lowered his eyes. "I feel so useless, Mother."

I rubbed at his sore shoulder. "You can't afford to be useless. Too much relies on you. Don't you know how important you are? There's a reason you're named Jefferson, you know. Your grandfather hurt his wrist twice. It was never the same after, but he never let it leave him maimed. Use your arm until it heals, every day, even if you feel weak as a newborn pup."

Jeff's head jerked up. "You don't know what I've done."

"The blame is on Charles," I insisted.

"I'm talking about Jane. I brought her into this family, and now, because of it, I've led us all to disaster."

Had the laudanum dulled his wits? "Your wife is lovely!"

Jeff seemed unable to swallow over the emotion. "Grandfather keeps these things from you, but—"

My hands stilled on his shoulder. "You're scaring me, Jeff."

"You know about the panic in the banks. Well, Jane's father has become indebted."

"What's that to do with us?"

"Grandfather signed as a guarantor on one of his loans."

Virginia gentlemen did this sort of courtesy for one another—especially when there were family ties between them. It didn't surprise me that the former governor would take a loan or that my father would help him do it. Only that a man of his means would *need* my father's surety. "Are you saying Mr. Nicholas can't make the payments?"

Jeff nodded. "Because of the panic, they're calling in the loan in total. Hamilton is dead, but his banking system is still ruining the country."

My stomach twisted. "Jane's father has property . . . surely he can pay his own debt."

Jeff actually trembled. "I fear the burden is going to fall entirely upon my grandfather. It could be a crippling blow to his finances."

It seemed impossible that Papa would suffer for another man's debt. "How much?"

"Twenty thousand dollars."

I nearly swooned away again. Twenty thousand dollars was so much money, I couldn't fathom what might be done to raise it.

Chapter Thirty-six

Monticello, 22 April 1820
From Thomas Jefferson to John Holmes

There's not a man on earth who'd sacrifice more than I would, to relieve us from slavery, in any practicable way. But, as it is, we have the wolf by the ear, and we can neither hold him, nor safely let him go. Justice is in one scale, and self-preservation in the other.

EVERYONE'S SO SAD," Ginny cried, swishing into my sitting room. "We're estranged from Ann. Jeff's afraid to look Grandpapa in the eye. And Ellen's so dispirited she's thinking of teaching school."

Ann, Jeff, and Ellen. My oldest three understood harsh life. While Papa put stock in the assurances that Mr. Nicholas wouldn't leave us on the hook for even a dollar, Ellen and Jeff refused to pretend that all was well. If Ann was with us she'd have done the same.

But the rest of the children—their memories were here at Monticello where they'd always lived in luxurious comfort and their grandfather's cheer. "All this sadness and strife can't be borne," Ginny chirped. "For Grandpapa's sake, we should be happy and gay! So I'm inviting you to a dance."

I allowed frustration into my tone. "A dance?"

"Yes, a dance," she replied. "On Saturday next, the youngsters of Monticello will adjourn to the south pavilion and dance to Beverly's music. I'd like to invite Jeff's wife, who must be morti-fied that her relations put ours in jeopardy. After the stabbing and now this, we're in need of cheer. And so is Grandfather. All this gloom can't be good for his health."

That I couldn't argue. I wondered if Papa could weather such distress at his age. "Well, if your grandfather has no objection—"

"He doesn't!" Ginny clapped her hands. "He's going to invite scholars from the university to form up like soldiers and have Ellen make a speech for him. Perhaps in Greek. But he said if *you* object, we must give up the idea."

I'd never deny my father anything that would add to his hap-piness. If he wanted a dance, he'd have a dance. So we gathered on the terrace with a mountaintop view of the countryside below so clear that it was as if we could see the whole nation my father helped build. A nation as beautiful, imperfect, and unfinished as every other project my father ever undertook.

And it was there we gathered to listen to Beverly Hemings play his violin. While Beverly worked his bow and filled the air with music, from the corner of my eye, I caught Papa staring at Beverly with fatherly pride. Sally watched with pride, too—and it broke my heart, because the servants didn't know what was coming.

If Papa was forced to pay even half of the twenty-thousand-dollar debt, slaves would have to be sold. Jeff would have to un-dertake it on Papa's behalf; he'd start with the field hands, but what about the families on Mulberry Row? Not the Hemingses, of course. Papa would never agree to sell them if it weren't by their own choice. But what of those who worked in the textile mills or Papa's nailery? Those slaves we knew, we saw their faces every day. The idea of selling them was barbarous.

Yet, we fiddled and danced and laughed because it would have done no good whatsoever to cry.

～

WHEN EVENING FELL, I followed my father into the house, leaving the young people to their festivities. We stopped together in the empty book room, alone together for the first time in a good while.

"He's twenty-one," Papa said. Beverly, he meant. The boy's birthday had come and gone in the chaos of stabbings and debt. I hadn't remembered it. My father obviously had. Papa was kind to Sally's children, but he wasn't in the habit of showing them fatherly affection. At least not in front of me. So I was surprised to hear him say, "He can read and write and play music. He takes as much joy in science as I do. And if he's pressed, he knows carpentry, and how to make nails and how to be useful on a farm. Beverly's grown to be a fine man, hasn't he?"

"I believe so," I said, cautiously, wondering if I'd feel the pull of jealousy at my father's pride in his son. But all I felt was the truth of the sentiment. Beverly *was* a fine young man. "The overseer complained about him not going to the carpenter's shop for about a week or so, but I've never heard another word spoken against him by anyone."

My father's expression betrayed great anxiety. "Beverly knows his freedom has been promised. It's time, but I worry. . . ."

I refused to let myself calculate Beverly's monetary worth and the loss it would mean to my father's estate. "What worries you?"

Papa looked stricken. "I'm worried about the explanations that'll be demanded of me when I petition the legislature to grant Beverly permission to live and work in the state of Virginia as a free man."

That's when his anxiety infected me. Since the last slave revolt years ago, freed Negroes couldn't live in Virginia without special dispensation. And the moment my father asked for that dispensation, there'd be a thousand questions. Beneath my sheer linen cap, a cold sweat broke across my brow. "You mean to acknowledge him?"

My father's lips tightened into a grim line. He knew—surely a man of his political genius knew—that to ask for dispensation would be to acknowledge Beverly as his son. And every old story about his *Congo harem* would be splashed again on the front page of every paper in the country. Had pleas from men like William Short finally reached into my father's guilty heart and shaken something loose that he would want to admit to his relationship with Sally after all these years?

"Papa, after all the denials . . ." He'd left his friends and family to deny it. I'd have denied it and defended him anyway, but a great many people were likely to feel deceived. They'd never forgive any of us. It'd taint his legacy and our whole family. "You chose to keep this secret long ago."

He lifted his tired blue eyes to mine. "I also made a promise to Sally."

Did he think me so heartless that I'd want him to break it? Somewhere inside me was still the naive girl in Paris who so ardently wished for all the poor slaves to go free. But my concern was my father. He'd promised to let Sally's children go free, but he hadn't promised to sacrifice himself on the altar of public opinion. If Beverly wanted his freedom, there were other ways to get it. "Can't you just . . . let him walk off this mountain?"

"I've considered that," Papa said, quietly. "I could call him a runaway and never send anyone looking for him. But then he could never return and this is the only home he's ever known. Where else could he go and make his way?"

Beverly was a capable young man, I thought. He could make his way anywhere. Washington, maybe. He might enjoy living as a free man in a city that our father brought into being. "The capital isn't so very far away."

"Far enough we'll likely never see him again," Papa snapped.

Was he angry with me, with Beverly, or himself? Papa had always been possessive; he'd never forgiven Sally's brothers for insisting upon the formality of their freedom, when he'd allowed them to live as free men in practice. Did he resent Beverly for insisting upon the same?

But when Papa turned his head to hide a sudden welling

of tears, I realized it wasn't resentment of Beverly's freedom that upset him. It was love. Beverly shared his looks, his temperament, his taste in music, and his interest in science. Beverly was a young man who was always aware—much as I was—that our father had penned the lines that began: *All men are created equal.*

My father would've been a monster not to feel a prick of pride that his son wanted liberty. But the price of that liberty was steep. "Papa, Beverly can live as a freed black man here in Virginia, with your reputation in tatters, or he can forge a new identity as a white man anywhere else. It seems to me that you ought to ask Beverly his preference. It's his future, after all."

That had seemingly not occurred to Papa, so I left him pondering, congratulating myself that I'd handled the situation with as much grace as might be expected of me and done right by Beverly besides.

So it was with alarm that I awakened the next morning to find Sally Hemings inside my bedroom, her back stiff against the door, her hands behind her on the handle, as if to steel her nerve, and her eyes filled with fury.

"Mistress Randolph," she said, instead of *Miss Patsy,* as was her habit since our childhood. "I realize the sight of me offends you, but I beg you not to take it out on my son."

I rose from my bed, bewildered. "Whatever can you mean?"

Sally met my gaze levelly, but her lower lip was atremble. "I loved your sister. I loved Miss Polly all her life, and she loved me, too, but I could never win your affection." I started to tell her that she did have my affection, but she ran over my words. "That's why I've always kept out of your way and made myself of use to you so that someday you might feel some small bit of love for me—"

"I do feel it," I protested. "Of course I do."

"Then why are you trying to take my son from me?" Her anguished question echoed through the room, and I was speechless in its aftermath. She pointed with an accusing finger. "I know it was you. Your father wouldn't speak to anyone else about such a thing. And whatever you said to him—"

"I advised him to ask Beverly what he wanted!" I cried, in defense of myself.

But this appeased her not a bit.

"*Beverly*? My son is too young to know what he wants."

Older than you were when you had to decide, I thought. "He's a grown man, Sally."

She shook her head, nostrils flaring. "He thinks he knows what's out there for him in the world. Thinks he can leave this mountain behind without regret and make his own way. But it's a decision he can't take back. I want him free—but I'm not ready to let him go."

How could I blame her? Especially after so nearly losing my own son? But from the edge of my bed I said what I believed to be true. "Wouldn't it be kinder to let him go, Sally? His Negro blood . . . it's only one-eighth. He's legally white. If Papa petitions to keep Beverly here in Virginia, everyone will know your boy as a former slave. He'll live with the taint and the shame of it all his life. But if Beverly leaves . . . he can *pass,* Sally. Beverly can marry into white society. Isn't that the best future you can give him?"

She blanched, wiping tears with the backs of her hands. "That's what you'd want, if he was your son?"

I thought hard about her question. I'd been afraid for my son when he marched off to war. Terrified when they brought him back to me in a wagon, bloodied and maimed. Each time, the thought of parting with him forever nearly unraveled me.

But if I had to give my son up to save him, I would. I was sure Sally would, too. I'd always known her to be a protective mother. And it'd taken the courage of a mother lioness to confront me this way. "Yes, I would, Sally. God as my witness."

And this time, it was no lie.

She narrowed her eyes, hugging herself, bronze arms against a bright white apron. "What happens when your father dies and his estate passes into the hands of a man who hunts Beverly down as a runaway slave?"

Though I couldn't bear to think of my father's death, his health and vigor wasn't what it once was. When we lost him, his estate would pass to my husband and my sons. "I'll never let anyone hunt down Beverly. I vow, I'll never let that happen."

When she was sixteen, she'd relied upon my father's promise. Staked her whole life upon it. I couldn't say she'd been wrong to, but she was less trusting now.

And my vow mustn't have persuaded her, because she kept Beverly at Monticello and sent him back to work as a slave in the carpentry shop.

~~~

JEFF'S FATHER-IN-LAW DIED in the autumn of 1820, leaving everything and everyone ruined: his people, his plantation, his once-haughty widow, and quite likely my father, too.

The only good news was that Jeff was moving his arm. It still pained him, but he had the use of it, which improved my spirits and Tom's, too. Returning from Richmond for Sunday dinner, my husband set down a carefully folded piece of paper onto the writing table beside me. "A letter from Nancy for you."

I smiled, blandly, not wanting to tell him all the letters we'd exchanged since I took her part against *Randolph of Roanoke*.

"Nancy sent crayons for Cornelia," Tom continued, rubbing the back of his neck. "And the girls tell me she sent you an extraordinary cup and saucer." He turned, his muscles knotting tightly beneath his white shirt. "Martha, I know what you and your lady friends did for Jack Eppes during his campaign against John Randolph."

My stomach clenched because I couldn't be sure who my husband hated more. Jack or John . . . or me? "We did it for your sister. But it didn't work."

"Oh, it worked," Tom said, turning to face me, again. "Mr.

Morris took my sister's side in the matter before he died, didn't he?" Thankfully, that death couldn't be blamed on Nancy—having come about due to Mr. Morris's botched self-surgery with a whalebone to remove a blockage from his urinary tract. "My sister is a wealthy widow now, and she has you to thank. You kept the villain from doing real mischief."

"But John Randolph won the election anyway," I said, bitterly.

"Doesn't matter. He'll think twice before going after Nancy again. Besides, anyone could've beat Jack Eppes in that election. With the war over and Virginians so angry, Jolly Jack would never make a proper representation for popular rage."

He didn't use the word *jolly* in any complimentary way. Nevertheless, it was, I thought, a correct assessment. "I'm glad to have been any help."

"You're adept at influencing people, Martha," he said, staring out the window at the mountain's turning leaves, as if contemplating the bleak winter to come. "You're clever at social discourse. You'd be an asset to me in the Governor's Mansion."

By that point, we'd lived apart for nearly two years, during which I'd learned to prefer loneliness to my husband's hostility. I'd assumed he was happier without me. That's what gave me pause. But Tom took my hesitation for something else, and snapped, "Martha, without you, I'll lose this upcoming election and the salary that goes with it. You ought to do at least one of your duties by me, since I'm not holding you to the others."

Our marriage bed, he meant, which irritated me enough to resist. "My father needs me here—"

"Are you his wife or mine? Sometimes, I wonder!"

I didn't dignify the question with an answer. Instead, I fumed, no longer able to soothe my temper by reminding myself that ladies were never angry. "Are you so very unpopular a governor, Tom?"

He crossed his arms. "If I'm not now, I soon will be. Because I intend to introduce a bill for the emancipation and deportation of slaves in Virginia once they reach the age of puberty. I want to abolish slavery in Virginia." The import of these words crashed down upon me like a house in collapse. Congress had just wrangled its way through an unhappy compromise to admit the new state of Missouri to the union while prohibiting slavery north of it. There was no cause of greater controversy, and now my husband wanted to take up the antislavery banner. "Martha, I decry the new morality which tolerates slavery in perpetuity."

"As do I," I said, swiftly, because I felt accused. "Of course."

"Your father says the same, but he won't lend his support to my proposition. His voice would carry enormous weight, but he says he must leave the accomplishment of ending slavery to the work of another generation."

That startled me, though it oughtn't have. For years, Papa had been asked to advocate more actively against slavery. William Short had all but begged him. Friends like the Coles who had sheltered us in our flight from the British all those years ago had tried to shame him into it. And now my father was old, tired, and often in ill health. Sometimes I believed the love of Virginians— the love of the nation—was all that sustained him. To throw his weight against the slaveholders of the South would surely be a struggle for him beyond his strength.

But as his daughter . . . I might serve as a symbol of his authority. And I realized with some astonishment that Tom was asking me to be just that. He was looking to me to help him tackle the moral problem of our time. And if he deserved my obedience in anything, it was in this.

But it would be more than obedience. For Tom's request rekindled in me an old flame of Parisian idealism that I thought long snuffed out. I *wanted* to play a part in dismantling the system of pain and degradation that undermined our union. My father said that the work of ending slavery belonged to another generation. Maybe he was right.

Maybe it belonged to me and mine.

THE GOVERNOR'S MANSION WAS A MESS. My husband had been living like a lonely bachelor. Everything was in disorder, windows unwashed, carpets unshaken. I couldn't find a square inch of the place not coated in a layer of dust. That was the first thing I set right that Christmas season. Then, of course, was the matter of sociability.

Tom was thought to be an irascible hermit by Virginia legislators, so I determined we'd make the rounds of parties and dinners and holidays balls. I acquired for these functions a beautiful white crepe robe, a lace turban and ruff, and looked fashionable for the first time in more than a decade.

I'd played the part of first lady for my father. Now I played that role for Tom. I went with him to academic lectures, to see an exhibit of jaguars and elephants, and together we strolled the cobblestone streets where we might be noticed by newspapermen. On his arm, I smiled so persuasively I almost convinced myself that we were happy.

But that illusion came unraveled after a supper at the Governor's Mansion one evening in early December. "Your turban is very becoming," said a courtly gentleman, David Campbell, a dashing man of great political future, who knew my husband from their service during the war. "It's as though you mean to become the incarnation of Dolley Madison."

I smiled, flattered. "I can think of no better lady to emulate."

"Can't you? I suppose you hope to be as popular."

I sensed in him some hostility, and wondered at his angle. "I hope to be anything that will do honor to my husband."

Mr. Campbell sipped coolly from his glass. "You're going to get him reelected."

I smiled more brightly. "Oh, Governor Randolph's own conduct will secure his reelection for him, not mine. His ideas are right-thinking, courageous, and worthy of the greatest consideration."

Mr. Campbell raised a brow. "You're going to stand loyally beside him? I suppose you owe him that much."

My head tilted as I tried to form a genial reply. "As do all his friends."

"It wasn't his friends who destroyed his military career."

My smile froze upon my face, so shocked was I to be confronted on such a matter. "I beg your pardon, sir."

Mr. Campbell's eyes were cold, though he spoke with a chuckle. "You ought to beg your husband's pardon."

I *had* begged my husband's pardon. I'd begged it a hundred times. But never did I think Tom would confide our troubles to an outsider, especially when no one need ever have known that I took part in his reassignment. Tom might have spared himself the greater part of the humiliation he felt if only he'd kept quiet about it!

But alas, self-command was never one of Tom's virtues. And in that moment, I feared it wasn't going to be mine. "Mr. Campbell, during my visit I've become acquainted with a number of rare creatures. They're my favorite curiosities. So I'm afraid you must excuse me, as I'm in search of that rare creature still left in Richmond called a gentleman."

With that, I left him.

Mr. Campbell later wrote that I was cold, vain, and sarcastic.

But I was satisfied, there in the crowded gallery on the cold winter day when my husband was reelected to the governorship, feeling within myself a stoic satisfaction in my duty well done.

Would that I could've been as effective when it came to my husband's policies. Papa had worked the levers of power with geniality and personal charm, but he'd always properly gauged the public mood. I remembered a time no gentleman of Virginia would ever *advocate* for slavery, even if none of them took steps to change it. But that was all changed now within a generation. My husband's proposal to emancipate the slaves was met with fierce and bitter opposition, even though it promised to compensate slave owners for the loss of their property. No matter what Tom said to the legislators and no matter what I said to their wives, our efforts to cleanse Virginia of slavery fell upon deaf ears.

For Virginians now argued that slavery was a moral good, encouraged by the Bible. I thought it had more to do with the fact they were discovering that slaves were more than an asset in and of themselves; they could be *bred*. They could be bred for sale to barbarous plantations in Georgia and South Carolina. Though Tom was ready to empty the state's treasury to bring about an end to the evil, the gentry resisted the antislavery movement as nothing but northerners bent on consolidating power by taking advantage of the virtuous feelings of the people.

I was ashamed of Virginia that year.

Tom's proposal would've failed even if my father had supported it. But because it failed *without* Papa's support it further embittered Tom.

It also revealed my father's paralysis on the matter of slavery, a paralysis brought about by his true intimacy with it. For there was one "wolf" Papa could neither safely hold nor safely let go.

The last time I saw Beverly Hemings was at Christmas the next year, just before he took his violin outside into the snow to play holiday songs for the slaves on Mulberry Row. Shortly thereafter, he left Monticello and didn't return.

I was there when my father grimly took up his pen and listed Beverly as a runaway in his record book. "I'll send his sister to him on a stagecoach with enough money to establish herself." Papa said, eyeing me, as if anticipating some objection to the money he meant to give his illegitimate children.

I put my hand atop his withered one. "You're a kind and generous father."

He looked away, and my heart broke for him. Because I could imagine the pain I'd feel to send my children away, knowing I'd never see them again. But I believed it *was* a generosity to part with Beverly and Harriet this way. Beverly might never be known as a gentleman, but Harriet had a good chance of becoming a gentleman's wife. She'd come of age in a genteel household and could both read and write. She'd been trained in the womanly arts of spinning and sewing and keeping house. She was more beautiful than her mother had been, which meant that so long as Harriet disavowed all connection to the Hemingses of Monticello, she might do better than my own daughters in securing her future.

And in the end, I was right about Sally. Her fierce determination that her children should be free overcame all other instincts. I saw her on the terrace, her arms round her only surviving daughter's neck. When they finally parted, Sally stood there, staring after her daughter's carriage, knowing it was likely to be the last time she ever laid eyes on her. Then Sally quietly walked to her room by the dairy and shut herself inside.

For weeks, Sally didn't take meals nor did she answer the door when her youngest two sons knocked, nor even when my father sent for her. She pled illness, and my father pretended to believe her. For with the departure of Beverly and Harriet, our gentler way of life was more fiction than it had ever been before.

Chapter Thirty-seven

Monticello, 26 January 1822
From Thomas Jefferson to Alexander Keech

It's not in my power to give you a definite idea of when our University may be expected to open. We shall be truly gratified should it become an instrument of nourishing those brotherly affections with our neighboring states which it is so much our interest and wish to strengthen.

WHAT A PAIR of schoolmasters we've become," my father said when my youngest boys dragged their school desks from my sitting room into a circle round his stuffed leather chair for a Latin lesson. Having recently taken a fall that put his arm in a sling, and with the winter weather harder on his bones than it used to be, Papa was housebound.

The weather kept visitors away, so during our quiet winter respite, we made a little university out of Monticello. And because Sally was less and less at my father's side since her eldest children left Monticello, Papa looked increasingly to me for his happiness.

I enjoyed every moment of our harmonious idyll, but when spring thawed our mountain, Papa was restless and called to Burwell. "I want my horse."

We'd always relied upon Sally to quietly and sweetly dissuade Papa from folly, but the competent and devoted Burwell was too pliant, leaving only me to protest my elderly father's insistence upon riding. "At least take a servant with you!"

"I've been roaming this country since I was a boy. No one knows these lands better than me." Soon after, he was up and into the saddle, riding off with the air of power he still carried with him even at his age.

That busy day saw me chasing after my recalcitrant boys, who insisted on pelting one another with chinaberries from their grandfather's ornamental trees. Ranging in age from five to seventeen, my four rowdies were as noisy and dirty as the half-alligator, half-horse men that infested our western country. They kept me so busy that the great clock chimed the dinner hour before I realized my father wasn't home.

In the parlor, Cornelia looked up from the architectural rendering of my father's university and dusted her fingers. "I'll ride out and look for him."

"Let your brothers go." But before I could call them, we heard a commotion near the terrace where my father, frail, soaking wet, and muddy, was being helped up the stairs by Sally's sons. Papa's good arm was draped over an adolescent Eston, who in the light of that early spring evening looked much like my father in his youth. Supporting my father on the other side was eighteen-year-old Madison.

My tongue let loose before I could measure myself. "What the devil happened?"

"Fell in the river," Papa said, and nothing more than that. He was shaken, but he didn't seem injured. Though when we finally sat down together at the table for a meal that had gone cold, he explained, "The horse fell upon me and pinned me under the water. I'm mortified that if I'd drowned on that shallow spot, everyone would think I'd committed suicide."

I gasped. *"That's* what mortifies you?"

Papa's raised his now bushy white eyebrows. "What's Hamilton remembered for? That he died in a senseless duel with a traitorous madman. My days are waning, and it would mortify me to perish in an unbefitting way."

His mind was on legacy . . . and the family he'd leave behind.

That evening he said, "Patsy, arrangements must be made in the case of my death. I must know you'll be taken care of. I fear Tom won't be able to provide for you, and whatever I leave will be swallowed up by his creditors."

I didn't want to speak of it—could scarcely bear the thought of life without him. "Give what you like to the children and don't worry for me."

"You are my primary worry. Ann has already been provided for monetarily if she should get free of her husband, and I've made provisions for Jeff in part . . . the remainder of my holdings will be divided amongst the other children, but you'll have a life estate in Monticello so that you may always have a home here." My heart hollowed at the thought of living at Monticello without Papa. And into the space of my mournful breath, he added, "We'll have to see the younger boys into professions. Medicine and the law."

He was more of a father to the boys than my husband had been. We all basked in Papa's unfailing kindness. My father could be an exacting man, but he was predictable and steady. I knew how to make him contented. Would that I knew how to do the same for Tom, because in the winter of that year, after three increasingly contentious terms as governor, Tom was finally coming home.

We hadn't shared a bed in years, and though there was no longer danger of children, I greeted the prospect of his return with acute anxiety. Alcove beds were one of my father's favorite space-saving innovations, and Papa didn't understand why I wanted to be rid of mine. I couldn't tell him that I didn't want to be trapped between Tom's body and the wall. Instead, I prevailed upon Papa, night and day on the subject of converting my alcove to a much-needed closet, until he finally lapsed into a dignified but resigned silence that I decided to take as consent to do as I pleased.

Upon setting down his satchel in my renovated bedroom, Tom said, "You've changed it."

These were the first words he spoke upon his return. His spine was stiff as he took in the closet filled with floral hatboxes where our bed used to be. He noticed the lace valances, too, which I'd fashioned from the scraps of an old dress long ruined, and how they now framed the view I enjoyed each day upon waking, in all its bittersweet majesty.

"Do you like it?" I asked of the feminine touches I'd put on this room to make it mine.

"My writing table is gone," Tom said, quite peevishly. "I see everyone has gotten along here quite well without me. I shall now feel even more the intruder."

Having predicted this very glum prognostication, I said, "Nonsense. I have a surprise for you that I hope will make you feel as if you have a place of your own."

We walked together to the north pavilion, where I'd had the slaves move my husband's writing table. "What's this?" he asked, genuinely surprised at the neat rows of books upon the shelves, where I'd carefully ordered his science and agricultural journals.

"It's a study for you. A place for you to read and write in solitude when the noise of the children grows too much. A place to escape Papa's guests. Your very own sanctuary."

A sanctuary as far away from my own bedroom as it was possible to get on this plantation. It was a fact not lost on him as he eyed the chaise. "Where you should like me to sleep, I gather."

I think he meant to shame me, to make me feel as if I were refusing his love, when, for years now, he'd been refusing mine. "I'd like you to stay wherever you can be made happy, Tom. It would mend much between us if you could be happy beside me, but if you can't, then you should sleep here."

Tom's chin jerked up. I thought he might upbraid me, but instead a flash of anguish crossed his face. "Dear God, Martha. Don't you know that beside you is the only place I've *ever* been happy?"

OUR RECONCILIATION, TENTATIVE AND FRAGILE, bolstered my health. I still suffered the aches that'd plagued me since giving birth to George. But I resorted to a charcoal remedy and rebelled completely against the household management of my daughters. My spirits were also brightened by my friendship with Dolley, who brought with her into every room a constant sunshine of the mind.

In short, that first year after Tom's retirement from the governorship was a happy one.

I think that's why its end was so devastating.

On the morning of her birthday in January of 1824, Septimia raced down the narrow staircase—certain her father had brought something special back for her from a recent business trip to Richmond. "What do you think it is, Mama? Could it be a new pet? Maybe a songbird of my own, like Grandpapa's?"

As the family gathered round, Tom was near manic in his merriment. He had gifts for Septimia and stories of new curiosities in Richmond, including an Egyptian mummy. "It's wrapped in dusty old bandages, preserved eternally, the insides having been scooped out." Tom's description set the children mad upon the subject of the mummy, hoping they could see it for themselves. Then Tom reported, "There's a new Unitarian minister, too."

The children wanted to hear him speak, which exasperated me. "Haven't we done enough already to scandalize the neighbors? We already stand suspected in religious matters for shunning their revivals. To do so in favor of a Unitarian . . ."

But my concerns had no place amongst the frivolity of a birthday party, and Ellen rightfully twitted me for it. "Mama wants to go to a revival!"

Laughing, I said, "Heaven forbid. I cannot bear the ranting."

"But think of the amusement," Ellen smirked, taking a bite of gingerbread.

Throughout our little celebration in the bright parlor, my husband maintained great cheer and humor—virtues not amongst his chief traits. I didn't take it as an ominous sign until he overlooked the misbehavior of our sons at the table. You see, Tom indulged our daughters to the point of criminality, but never our sons, so I found myself wary. When the cakes were eaten and the children put to bed, I found Tom in the solitude of his study, hunched over in his chair, head in his hands.

"Tom?" I asked.

He never looked up. Perhaps he could not.

"Martha, there's something I must tell you." And with those ominous words, he explained, in halting words, the derangement of his financial affairs.

"How much is owed?" I asked, sure that if I knew the number, it'd make it more solid and less frightening.

"Thirty thousand," he murmured.

I barely suppressed a gasp.

How wrong I was. Knowing the number made it worse.

A debt of twenty thousand had ensured that my father would never know true security again—but *he* had resources in his possession. What did Tom have? Only Edgehill and Varina, the latter of which he'd been unable to sell.

Though he was a Randolph, a former congressman, a three-term governor, and the inventor of the furrowing style that had been adopted in nearly every farm in Virginia—he was fifty-five years old. He could never pay back that debt in his lifetime; he'd end up leaving it to our sons . . . and only if the creditors didn't call in the loans first.

The truth was, my husband was ruined.

Finally and utterly ruined.

After years of struggle and loss, of financial instability, Colonel Randolph's long shadow had finally swallowed Tom up. I went to him where he sat bent and miserable, and stroked his hair as he buried his face against my belly. "You mustn't reproach yourself, Tom. You've rarely spent even the fourth of your income, nor ever the half of it in any year. Our expenses are small and your profits would've maintained our whole family in affluence were it not for . . ."

I trailed off, wondering what it was. Bad luck? His father's spite? I didn't know, but Tom wept in my arms as he'd done all those years ago when we were first married, when he'd loved me so fervently . . . and so blindly. His financial ruin was a profound humiliation to him, I knew. But we were more fortunate than most. My father would provide for the children; they'd always have a roof over their heads and food on their table.

"I had to go to Jeff," Tom blubbered. "The shame of going to my own son for help. But he's going to take on my debts because they won't foreclose on him. Creditors are more apt to be lenient with Jeff. He still has his youth, and he's the grandson of Thomas Jefferson."

It was a sensible argument, and yet, I was horrified. How could we expect Jeff to risk it? I argued against it. I *railed* against it. But in the end, the men in my family negotiated together in private the instrument that put the burden of the whole family upon Jeff's shoulders.

"WHY WON'T ANYONE let us do something to support ourselves?" Cornelia sniped, sighing over the figures in my account book. "I suppose not until we sink entirely will it do for the granddaughters of Thomas Jefferson to take work in or keep a school!"

Ellen stared gloomily out the window from a stealthy place behind the curtains. It was Sunday—the day of the week I distributed rations and heard the concerns of the slaves, but it wasn't our people that made my daughter frown. "There's a carriage. I suppose it's another visitor trying to avoid paying an innkeeper at our grandpapa's expense."

I shared Ellen's hostility toward the leeches and hangers, so I didn't scold her even when, overhearing the visitor's Bostonian accent, she rolled her eyes. "It wasn't enough that we had to wine and dine that strange wandering dullard who walked the length of the country with nothing but one change of clothes to his name? In the face of so many other indignities, must we receive *Yankees,* too?"

Our visitor was Joseph Coolidge, a Harvard graduate who had just returned from a recent tour of Europe. "I've now come to see the greatest wonder in our own country," he said. "The sage of Monticello."

We'd heard it all before, albeit perhaps not from such a well-formed mouth. Mr. Coolidge was a handsome man, and it seemed to me that rather than charming my Ellen, the man's beauty irritated her beyond reason. Snorting at him indelicately, she said, "You do realize, of course, that my grandfather isn't a monument, but a man. One who cannot be prevailed upon by every stranger to—"

"You're welcome here, Mr. Coolidge," I broke in. "And while I can't say my father is well enough today to receive you, I'll be sure to give him your warmest regards."

I'd become something of a palace chamberlain, a keeper of the gate. My father couldn't possibly pass time with every stranger who came to the mountain, so I made excuses. To my surprise, however, Papa was eager to meet this stranger because he was from Boston. "Maybe he'll have some news of Adams!"

In spite of the damage politics had done to their friendship, the two survivors of the Revolution reminisced and lived on each other's memories. In truth, I sometimes feared that when John Adams died, my father would not be long in following.

At supper, which we took at several drop-leaf tables, arranged to accommodate everyone in a style half-French, half-Virginian, the conversation turned to poetry. And while my daughters engaged in every subject upon which their grandfather opined, Ellen was subdued.

"I fear my knowledge of poetry isn't expansive enough to impress Miss Ellen," Mr. Coolidge teased.

"Forgive me, sir," my daughter said. "But you seem impressed enough with yourself for the both of us."

"Ellen!" I cried. Her capacity to drive away suitors was now legendary but seemed hardly sufficient excuse for rude manners.

"It's quite all right, Mrs. Randolph," our visitor said. "I've done too much speaking tonight and not enough learning. Perhaps Miss Ellen would allow me to make up for this lack of gallantry by taking me on a tour through the gardens? If so, I promise to hold my tongue."

"I'm a poor tour guide for the garden," Ellen replied indifferently, and I remembered how I tried to put off her father in much the same way. "The garden was my sister Ann's domain."

She said her sister's name with such sadness that Mr. Coolidge sobered. "Oh, dear. I'm afraid I didn't know of her loss—"

"Oh, Ann isn't dead," Ellen replied. "Though she might as well be."

A sharp look from me silenced her. The tensions in our family weren't to be shared with outsiders. Not ever. And she knew it.

Mr. Coolidge cleared his throat. "Perhaps some music?"

Ellen frowned. "Music is my sister Ginny's domain. Art is Cornelia's—"

"And *your* domain, Miss Ellen?" He surprised us both, I think, with his persistence.

"My grandpapa's book room," she finally said.

"I'd very much like to see it," he replied with a triumphant smile.

"I'm afraid you can't," Ellen said, with a triumphant smile of her own. "It's part of my grandfather's private suite of rooms. Strangers aren't allowed beyond a peek through the glass panes, but if you'd like to borrow a book during your stay, I'm sure it can be arranged."

It seemed that the crueler Ellen was, the better he liked her. Days later, at the end of his visit, he declared himself smitten. "That's wonderful to hear," I told the lovelorn young man. "But certainly yours has been a very short acquaintance for such a depth of feeling."

With a smile, Mr. Coolidge replied, "Long enough to know my heart. Now I need merely win hers . . . then Ellen and I shall live our lives together, happily ever after."

How simple he made it seem. The winning of hearts. Living together. Eternal happiness.

But after thirty-four years of marriage, I now saw union between man and woman was the same as union among the states—as a series of debates and compromises that might hold it all together for a few more years, or end in a painful separation.

My husband, you see, had gone mad.

Both our defenders and our enemies will say his madness was always lurking in the savage wildness of his Randolph blood. I let them say it because it absolves me. Tom was always a man of temper, that much is true. But he was *driven* to madness. His callous father, his bad luck, his choice to marry the daughter of a great man. His sense of himself was always fragile, his spirit easily broken—but in the end, I think I'm the one who snapped it to pieces.

I'd argued against allowing our son to assume all our debts, but it seemed never to have occurred to Tom that our boy would take one look at the books and decide there was no hope for it but to sell everything, lock, stock, and barrel.

"So he means to sacrifice me!" My husband had come to confront me in my sitting room where I'd retired to write a letter to his sister Nancy, and where silhouettes of our children adorned the blue-painted wall. Holding a near-empty glass of liquor in his hand, the length of Tom's body filled the doorway. His voice was low and dangerous. "Jeff says you support this decision."

I laid my quill aside, tasting bitter indignation on my tongue. Why did it always come to this? To be forbidden from making decisions, asked for my advice only after the fact, and then blamed for it as if I'd made the trouble in the first instance? Sally had blamed me when my father took my advice about her son. Now Tom blamed me for agreeing with Jeff—and yet neither dilemma had been my making.

But my heart filled with agony for my husband, for I understood why he hated Jeff's decision. I hated it, too, even as I advocated it. "I see no advantage in putting off the evil day to sell everything, Tom, for come it must, and with accumulating interest for every day that it's delayed."

Tom's glass went hurtling across the room, where it shattered against the fireplace and fell into the fire. I cried out, but not before Tom was across the room and upon me, shaking me in his steely grip. "After all these years, in this one critical moment, you desert me. You want to see me unmanned, is that it? To witness the final humiliation of my losing my land?"

"Tom, land isn't everything. There are many ways a man of your experience—"

"Land is everything! Without it, you'll see me stripped of not only my honor and pride, but even my citizenship."

Only men who owned fifty acres could vote or hold political office. Without property, Tom would lose even the fig leaf of status, and I felt his impotent rage burning through his skin into mine. He was still strong, so strong that I couldn't squirm away. "Tom, we're irretrievably ruined. But Jeff needn't be. I'm thinking of our children's future."

"Just one child. Jeff. Your favorite. Our son has swindled me and yet, you're choosing him over me."

It was Ellen—always Ellen—who was my favorite, if a favorite must be named. But Jeff was no swindler. If anything, my son's efforts to save something for the family were heroic. The creditors had given him a year to wind up the affairs of the estate and sell for the most profit possible. Our support was the least he deserved. The men in my family had conspired all my life to keep me from thinking in the language of money, but I knew enough to argue now. "Mortgages and deeds of trust embrace the whole of your property, and if the banks foreclose, they'll sweep it all away and leave our son as burdened as your father left you."

"That boy's malice and greed will see him always secure. He's trying to steal Edgehill from me."

My lips thinned at such an unjust insult hurled at the son who could've easily abandoned us all. "Jeff has submitted so affectionately and cheerfully to the privations which we've cost him that he's due nothing but gratitude. For when not distressed with our problems, he's been distracted with managing his grandfather's affairs."

"*Now* we come to it," my husband said, his words fumed with liquor, as he gave a baleful glance at the locked door between my sitting room and my father's chambers. "Your father is your true worry. No one can ever shine so brightly in your eyes. He's always your first concern. First and foremost. And you've been artfully persuaded that if I'm completely sacrificed, your father can be saved."

I could make no sense of this. "My father's plantations aren't tied to your troubles—"

"I'm entitled to Monticello!" Tom shouted, his fingers digging so hard into my arms I was sure they'd bruise me. "For thirty years, I've worked his plantation, sat patiently at his table, indulged him in every way, asking no recompense, merely waiting my turn to one day be the master of my own family. But you'll never have that, will you? You only serve one man—even if it means my ruin."

The only way to shield Monticello upon my father's death was to leave it to trustees—a plan to which I'd given my consent, without realizing my husband would believe himself disinherited. "Tom, so long as the property is vested in me, you'll always have a home. Papa is only using the law to protect me and the children—"

"*My* children! They aren't the center of your life. Your father is."

I might've denied it—it was my duty as a wife and mother to deny it. But in that moment, looking into the bloodshot eyes of a husband come utterly unhinged, a defiance rose up in me. I didn't deny it. I only whispered, "You're hurting me."

That made him shake me harder. "How could I ever hurt you? You never feel a thing! You're unmoved. You're like *him*. Unbending as marble. A statue. What man of flesh and blood can live with that?"

What man, indeed? By any other measure, Tom would be counted a great man. By any other measure than my father's.

"You're *hurting* me," I repeated.

Tom let me go all at once before making his retreat, his boots crunching on broken glass. He slammed the door, the sound exploding through the house. I remember that sound and the way it shook me to the marrow of my bones. I remember, too, that Tom slammed the door with such force that the frame cracked and the door bounced back open again.

Weeks later, it was still broken, and through that open door walked a man I'd longed to see for years.

Chapter Thirty-eight

Boston, 29 August 1824
To Thomas Jefferson from Lafayette

Here I am, on American ground. I will hasten to Monti-
cello. How happy I will be to embrace you, my dear friend.
And I know the pleasure will be reciprocated.

LAFAYETTE HAD SURVIVED IT ALL.

Two wars, the Reign of Terror, imprisonment, and even
Napoleon. He was the last surviving general of the American Revolution, and President Monroe had invited Lafayette to
celebrate the forty-seventh anniversary of the Battle of Brandy-
wine, where he had been wounded in our cause.

During Lafayette's triumphal tour, he paid a call upon John
Adams, accompanied by John Quincy, the secretary of state.
Lafayette also traveled with the widow of Alexander Hamilton,
whom he still called his brother. And in anticipation of Lafayette's reunion with my father, people were already flocking to our
mountaintop.

Given my state of distress and the rage the mere sight of me
evoked in my husband, I closeted myself up with the servants in
my sitting room, planning menus and making lists of supplies
that must be purchased, while my daughters tended to the locust
swarm of visitors. I startled when a knock came at my door and
instead of a servant—in walked a hallucination, or apparition, or
miracle—I couldn't decide which.

Not Lafayette, but William Short in the flesh.

"*Mon Dieu!*" I cried.

"*Cher Jeffy*," he said, his green eyes twinkling with mischief at my convent nickname. "It's been too long, Mrs. Randolph."

Indeed, it had, I thought, rising to take his hands. A glance out the window at his fancy hired carriage and heavy baggage told me that William hadn't come all the way from Philadelphia on mere impulse. So how did he take me so unawares? My father hadn't warned me to expect him. Was Papa's memory failing him or did he hope Mr. Short's visit would be a happy surprise?

Suddenly, I clutched at my cap, overaware of my curls, which had, with age, gone from copper-red to reddish-brown. "Mr. Short, you've caught me in quite a state of dishabille!"

He drew my hand to his lips for a kiss. "Not as great a state of dishabille as a man with my proclivities desires."

It was a highly inappropriate remark to direct to a lady, married or otherwise. The kind of remark only a Frenchman would make. I blushed like a schoolgirl, but we were surely both of an age to render harmless such flirtation. He studied me while I studied him, taking in the changes. I knew I was thicker about the middle, my face rounder. His hair had silvered, and laugh lines crinkled at the corners of his eyes. I found his presence more reassuring than I could admit.

"What happened here?" Mr. Short asked, motioning with his chin to the broken doorframe. "Don't tell me your father is tearing all this down to start over again."

"I would not discount the possibility when it comes to Papa and his projects, but Monticello is nearly perfected," I replied, deciding upon evasion. "Johnny Hemings will send one of his apprentices to fix the door shortly."

By *one of his apprentices,* of course, I meant Madison and Eston. But there felt to me something deeply disloyal in mentioning Sally's sons to William, who knew their father was also mine. "We're all being kept very busy in the preparations for Lafayette's visit."

Glancing at the array of little papers and notes stored in all the cubbies on my overflowing desk, not to mention the line of servants waiting with baskets outside my open window, he said, "So I see."

"I'll make sure a room is readied for you—"

"Oh, no. I've already picked one out. I'm staying in the room with the trellis wallpaper," he said with a little incorrigible smirk. "I hear Madison favors it, and it amuses me to think of leaving my nail clippings there for him to find when he stays here. So don't let me interrupt whatever you're doing. . . ."

Fighting a smile that would only encourage him, I said, "I'm buying up all the eggs and vegetables the servants can provide me with from their own gardens."

"Aren't your father's own gardens productive here?"

"Certainly! It's only that Papa is a scientist who insists upon growing fifty different varieties of peas, and we must have some variety on our plates for the arrival of Lafayette."

Mr. Short laughed. "Well, I hope I can be a help rather than a burden in the preparations."

"Oh, William, you could never be a burden."

But by evening, I knew that to be a lie. For it taxed me to hide our family troubles from him. Since the night Tom slammed out of my sitting room, my husband spoke not two willing words, sour and taciturn at any question addressed to him. Not even by the power of my father's authority and conciliatory nature could my husband be compelled to stay sober. And that first night of Mr. Short's visit, by the time the girls and I returned with the tea tray at seven o'clock, Tom was drunk.

Papa retired at ten o'clock every evening, and kept to this routine as religiously as he did his morning footbaths. But to discourage Tom's drinking at the table, my father called an early evening. "I must meet the welcoming committee in the morning, so I'm afraid it's time to retire." Then, smiling at Mr. Short, he said, "Still, I'll sleep easier tonight than in many years having set eyes upon you again, my friend."

William smiled, rising to his feet to take his own leave, but my husband didn't follow suit. Instead, taking another bottle of wine from the dumbwaiter, Tom asked, "Still a bachelor, Short?"

William was so famously a bachelor that we'd have assuredly heard if his status had changed. But he merely gave a rueful smile. "Alas, I'm still without a wife."

"Lucky," Tom murmured, pouring more wine.

My girls froze, their teacups half aloft. My boys stiffened in their seats at the far table, their biscuits left without a nibble—all looking to their older brother Jeff, whose eyes told them to keep their peace.

Meanwhile, my shame at Tom's indictment was so acute that I couldn't move from my place. The open insult to me, fallen so casually from the lips of my husband, came to me like a knife in the dark. I dared not look up from my tea, but merely set the cup back down so no one would see my hand tremble.

"*Unlucky*, yes," Mr. Short replied at length, pretending to have misheard. "As you say, Randolph. Very unlucky. But perhaps that's to put too much upon luck. I'm to blame by declaring myself for women who were too wise to marry me."

My gaze locked on my teacup with the cornflower garland pattern, my stomach churning with upset. Mr. Short's self-deprecating remark was to be understood as chagrin about his wayward duchess. But I understood it to include me.

And that was salt in the wound my husband had just opened.

Into the awkward silence, Septimia blurted, "Mr. Coolidge declared himself for Ellen. She says she can't be persuaded to marry him, but I don't believe her."

"Tim! I can't possibly marry Mr. Coolidge," Ellen explained, as if to distract from the undercurrents. "Firstly, I'm an avowed spinster and will make an unreservedly excellent old maid. More importantly, Joseph Coolidge lives in Boston. I couldn't possibly leave Mother and Grandpapa and the rest of you!"

In that moment, I let myself understand—really understand—why Ellen rejected all her suitors. Ellen was my companion, and my father's nurse when I couldn't be. Did she feel so bound to us that she'd turn away love, as I once did?

Into the wound went more salt.

Septimia chewed her bottom lip. "But if you truly love Mr. Coolidge, you have to marry him. Even if it takes you from us. Don't you think so, Mr. Short?"

I dared not look at William during his excruciating hesitation. Finally, he said, "I'm the wrong man to ask. In my experience the heart is always torn between competing attachments. I once considered my fate a great tragedy, but now I think it a blessing. After all, I've known extraordinary love and have nephews to whom I look upon as sons."

"Sons," Tom snorted. "Everyone counts sons a blessing, but I assure you . . . daughters are a man's only comfort in the end."

The veins on Jeff's good arm swelled as he clenched his fist. For months now, my eldest son had endured his father's hostility. But his honor could finally stand no more. He glared at Tom. "Do you want to say what you mean, sir?"

Under the table, I put a hand on my son's knee, silently pleading with him to swallow his bile. He could do it, I knew. But Tom's dark eyes flashed savagely. "If you were any kind of son, you'd leave me a few acres on Edgehill for a vineyard or a sawmill."

I gasped that Tom would broach our financial troubles in front of a guest—even William. Perhaps especially him.

"I'm the kind of son who won't lie to you," Jeff shot back, shoving from the edge of the table. "I can't leave you even an acre. If we somehow manage to keep Edgehill in the family, I'd need the whole of it to produce tobacco—"

"And to produce Negroes," Tom accused.

Jeff winced. "Do you want to leave your wife and children with nothing for their survival but the charity of my grandfather? Is that what you want?"

Tom stumbled to his feet as if ready to beat my boy, and my daughters let out terrified cries. "*Gentlemen*," our guest interrupted, white-faced with anger, and with an authority few men but my father possessed. "It's unseasonably warm in here," William said with calculation, like the diplomat he'd once been. "I'll escort the ladies outside where the cool mountain air may calm and soothe."

It ought to have shamed them. Both of them. If a quarrel was inevitable, it ought to be taken outside. Instead, my children and I were forced to flee our tables while the argument raged on. And somehow, I found myself on the winding flower walk in the glow of the setting sun, staring at showy scarlet plumes of cockscomb and golden marigolds, fighting back the tears that burned behind my eyes.

Ann, my beautiful eldest daughter whom I sometimes despaired of ever seeing again, had planted those flowers. And now the rest of my family was splintering apart, with my oldest and dearest friend as a witness.

"How much is the debt?" William asked.

I couldn't tell him. Not even as furious with Tom as I was. It would've been a disloyalty. "It doesn't matter. It's no excuse for what you were forced to witness. I apologize—"

"Don't *you* apologize," William broke in, with a sharp edge of anger. "Mr. Randolph is shockingly disrespectful to you. I cannot imagine your father would countenance it."

"He wouldn't. He doesn't," I insisted, trying to find the words to explain. "It's simply that Tom feels abandoned. As I recall, you were once just as angry with me and for the same reason."

William must've known that Marie reported back his long-ago furious renunciation of our love. He couldn't deny it. Instead, he asked, "Is it true that your son intends to use his father's property as a slave breeding farm?"

I swallowed, shaking my head. I might've lied to him, as we lied to visitors and to ourselves all the time. We pretended that our slaves were treated like family. That they were never abused. That whips were wielded justly. That violence—true violence— was not done to them at our whim. I had deceived myself about this for years. But it wasn't in me to deceive him. "I don't know what Jeff intends in that regard."

It was a mortifying admission, one that revealed the ugliness beneath the glow of all the pretty flowers. An admission far uglier than I'd allowed myself to accept before. William paused beside spires of lavender and pinched the bridge of his nose, a gesture that filled me with overwhelming shame.

No one else could've made me feel shame for it. I'd never, *could* never, condemn the men in my life who relied upon slavery, especially when my lion of a father believed himself impotent against the evil and my idealistic husband had been politically ruined for his efforts to stop it. But I was now standing beside the man who had offered me a different reality, a different life, from which I had turned away. And I felt some shame and regret for that, too.

~)

ON THE ELEVENTH OF SEPTEMBER, in her best dress, Virginia made her bridal procession—not at her father's home of Edgehill, but at Monticello. And awaiting her upon the grass-green floor of the entry hall was her happy groom, Mr. Trist.

My new son-in-law beamed with joy as he spoke his vows, and we all sighed happily when my sweet Virginia spoke hers. Everyone but Tom, that is. He stood stiffly at my side, as if he were merely a guest and not the father of the bride. He delegated all those responsibilities to her grandfather, saying that he didn't wish to ruin the wedding with his malaise. I think he recognized in himself the malignant spirit that had broken free and meant only to shield Ginny from it.

But our poor daughter kept searching out her sullen father's eyes in the crowd, pleading a smile from him. And it seemed to take all the strength Tom had just to lift the corners of his mouth. He didn't laugh or mingle in conversation. He didn't dance. And he didn't offer toasts—though he drank deeply whenever they were offered. So, for the bride's sake, I tried to be happy enough for both of us.

It wasn't difficult. For nearly six years, Mr. Trist had been constant in his attachment to Ginny. They'd resisted all our attempts to discourage their love until we were simply forced to acquiesce to its power. Theirs was not a marriage for money or advantage, but born of long friendship, shared troubles, and a true meeting of hearts. They might live poor as church mice all their lives, but their romance was perfectly obvious to everyone. And when the bride and groom pledged themselves to one another, their voices trembling with emotion, it wasn't Tom who gazed at me with wistful remembrance of our wedding day.

Instead, I felt William's gaze upon me, as if imagining the wedding we'd never had.

Glancing furtively at him over the punch bowl and floral arrangements, I found myself snared by his wistful smile. I remembered that, like my new son-in-law, he, too, was once an aspiring diplomat that everyone feared would be penniless. My eldest daughter had married a man more like her father than I wished to contemplate, but Ginny was taking the risk I never took.

Later, William sat beside me to listen when Papa gifted Ginny with a gilded cittern guitar with which she serenaded her new groom. *Love endures,* I thought, then tried to shake the thought away. But it was a thought that stayed with me well into the night.

~~~~~~

THEREAFTER, TOM ABSENTED HIMSELF FROM MONTICELLO. He didn't come for dinner, nor take tea in the early evening. It was only after the music was played and our guests had retired that he returned—hiding away in the north pavilion, refusing my company.

I knew my husband was in pain, shattered to atoms in body and spirit. I hurt for him. I wanted to reassure him of my love, of my father's love, of his family's love—even Jeff's love. But the only thing Tom wanted from me was to persuade Jeff to leave the creditors unpaid. And, for the sake of our children, that was the one thing I wouldn't do.

"Where do you think he goes during the day?" Ellen murmured as the younger children ran inside the house ahead of us, their feet pitter-pattering across the cherry and beech wood parquet floor.

I suspected Tom actually went to Charlottesville to drink in the taverns, but couldn't bear to tell even Ellen as much. "I'm sure I don't know."

Ellen leaned against one of the columns of the west portico. "I can bring my father a tray tonight. He's made a recluse of himself in the north pavilion, but he might open the door for me. If not me, then Septimia."

Yes, he might open the door for Septimia because she was a child, but I didn't intend to use her in such a way. "Your father has always suffered dark moods. Then he comes out of them. He always comes out of them. So we must give him privacy."

From the parlor, where he'd been setting up a chessboard, my father called, "Ah, Ellen, come play!" Papa was inordinately proud of both his granddaughter and his chess set—a gift from the French court. "I've been telling Mr. Short that if you'd been born a man, you'd have been a great one. So show him how you've learned to use my chessmen."

William had been examining Papa's "magic" double doors, which, by some ingenious innovation, opened of their own accord. But he looked up when Ellen pulled a crimson damask chair to the board by the window and challenged him to a game. "You won't go easy on account of my sex, will you, Mr. Short?"

William smirked. "To the contrary, I'm contemplating asking special dispensation on account of my age."

Ellen threw her head back in laughter, a dark tendril of hair escaping the bun at her nape . . . and proceeded to a ruthless victory.

Smiling in easy defeat, William turned to me. "Your daughters have inherited your talents, Mrs. Randolph. Ellen's wit. Virginia's music. Cornelia's artistry . . . why her architectural drawings rival those of professional draftsmen. I've advised your father to hire her for the University."

My girls were delighted by this praise, and I was, too. Even so,

I felt compelled to say, "You forget I was an abysmal artist in my youth—to this day, I can scarcely sketch a pea."

"I remember perfectly well," William countered. "It's only that paints and pencils were never the tools of your trade. You were a different kind of artist. The craft you mastered was spycraft!"

"*Spycraft*?" Ellen asked, eyes round at the mention of the disreputable business.

My children were fascinated, and William looked very satisfied. "Shall I tell your children how you rooted out an English spy?"

I gave my assent with an indifferent shrug and a secret smirk, deciding that so many years had passed there could hardly be scandal in it.

The story of how I'd stolen papers from the rooms of Charles Williamos was one my father had never heard before. And in hearing it, poor Papa looked as if he didn't know whether to scold or congratulate us. "The secrets come out only when your children think you're too old and feeble to discipline them!"

We laughed together beneath the rows of paintings that my father prized. All of us had needed to laugh. Which left me even more grateful for William's visit. He paid court to my father with the affection and comfort of an old friend, bolstering his spirits. He played games with my children and told them stories about Lafayette, which put them in even more excited anticipation of setting eyes upon our beloved Marquis.

William made us forget our troubles; he made it easy to pretend that my husband wasn't lurking on the grounds each night . . . or even that I wasn't married at all.

After winning another game, Ellen announced, "Mr. Short, you're paying too much homage to your queen. But I'll allow you to avenge yourself with one last game."

"I'm content to leave the field in ignominious defeat," William said.

She clasped her hands together. "I fear your years in Philadelphia have turned you into a Yankee! No Virginia gentleman, born and bred, would bow so easily."

A *Yankee*. It no longer had the same bite on her tongue as it did the day Joseph Coolidge came to our door. That's how I knew that my Ellen was in love. In love with a man she wouldn't marry because she feared to abandon me.

That night, I took her chin and made her look into my eyes. "If you can be happy with Mr. Coolidge, then marry him. You must go and be happy."

Her long dark lashes fluttered with surprise. "But I'm accustomed to spinsterhood. And my duty—"

"Don't let duty chain you," I said, though it would break my heart to lose her. "Not to me, not to your father, not even to your grandfather."

Ellen blinked, her brow furrowed. "But I wish to do as you've always done, Mama."

My heart sank at the sentiment, sweet as it was. There had been sacrifice enough for duty. Ellen deserved to make the choice I hadn't been able to. I grasped her hands. "No, Ellen. You've done your duty. It's time to consider your own happiness." For I was determined that my precious daughter, the one I clung to the way my father clung to me, would well and truly find it.

~~~~~

I AWAKENED TO THE SILHOUETTE of a man in my bedroom doorway. It was my husband, drunk and ornery. He stumbled into my closet—where he must've still expected to find a bed. Smashing instead into trunks and hatboxes, he uttered a dark curse.

"Tom?" I asked, not fully awake.

He never answered. Instead, he followed my voice in the dark, then hefted his body onto the bed, climbing atop me. "You're my wife," he snarled, yanking down the blankets.

"You're drunk," I accused, pushing him away.

"So you're the wife of a drunk," he said, forcing upon me a rough, wet kiss.

I didn't want him. Not like this. Not angry and rough and stinking of wine. "No, Tom. We decided—"

My words were cut off by a blow to the face.

I tasted blood and anger, even as my head swam with terror and shock and pain.

"*You* decided," Tom said, pinning my arm and getting his knee between mine.

I might've cried or pleaded or used feminine wiles to prevail upon him to let me go. But I did none of those things. Instead, when he tugged at his trousers to free himself, I freed myself with an upward jerk of my knee.

Unsteady from drink, he toppled from me, howling in pain. I rolled out of the bed, my bare feet pounding on the floor as I ran. He gave chase, knocking pictures from the wall, tripping over a small table in the hall, sending knickknacks clattering to the floor.

Hearing the commotion, Ellen flung open the door to her room while children stumbled down the stairs from their rooms above. Crowding around me, the children whimpered in confusion, and George began to cry. Tom glared at me where I stood within the refuge of my children's arms. There was something akin to pure hatred in his eyes. By Tom's accounting, he'd been rejected by everyone in his life. His father, my father, the legislators and voters of Virginia . . . and me.

This refusal of him was another betrayal. But he didn't pry me away from our children to force himself upon me. Instead, without a word, he lumbered back down the stairs. And I didn't follow or even call after him.

Instead, I found myself grateful that William's lodging on the first floor had kept him from being witness to yet another humiliation.

Chapter Thirty-nine

I FELL OUT OF BED," I said to explain my bruises.

Sipping chocolate, Papa sighed. "You wouldn't have fallen from an alcove bed."

I nodded absently, grateful that my children said nothing of their father's rampage. They all joined into the conspiracy of silence. But William Short wasn't fooled for a moment. He was unusually subdued as we took our chocolate from my father's favorite urn. His face as serious and stoic as the plaster busts hovering over us of Washington, Franklin, and Lafayette.

And later, once my increasingly frail and elderly father found his ease in his campeachy chair, William followed me on my rounds beneath the mulberry trees, delivering rations to slave cabins. "Your husband mistreats you."

I could say nothing. I could only hurry along the road, hoping our people would swarm around me for their parcels and force William to some other subject.

But he was, as always, a dogged man. "Did he strike you?"

"William, leave it be," I said, picking up my pace, suddenly desperate to flee. To escape his infernal prying into facts.

William darted in front of me, blocking my path. "I thought you loved him."

One look into William's eyes and I came undone. All the emotions—the anger, the bitterness, the fear—everything I'd so carefully wound tight into my pleasant and placid smile now unraveled.

And I fled.

Dropping the basket in the road, I took hold of my skirts and hurried away from him down the hill into the vegetable garden, for it seemed the most likely avenue of escape, past rows of artichokes and beans and brown Dutch lettuces.

I didn't think he'd follow me, because it meant sinking his well-made shoes into the autumn muck. But he more than followed. He *chased.* "Patsy," he cried, taking the liberty of using my childhood name. And when we reached the garden pavilion, he took the further liberty of grasping my wrist before I could close the glass-paned door in his face. Again, he insisted, "I thought that you loved him."

"And I thought you loved Rosalie," I shot back. "So love has carried neither one of us to the destination we wished."

Startled, he let go of me, and I retreated inside the square little fortress lit by tall windows on every side. My father had built it so that he might peacefully survey the whole of his world in any direction, but I tucked myself into a corner, feeling vulnerable and exposed.

At length, William mustered the courage to step inside, rubbing his face in his hands. "Rosalie said she wouldn't marry—she feared for her husband's reputation, she feared to leave her elderly relations, she feared to leave her country. But the truth was, she simply wouldn't marry *me.* When last in France, I learned that she'd married the Marquis de Castellane, an aging nobleman of some prestige. So trust me when I say that I understand perfectly what it is to love someone who can never give you what you want or deserve."

I withdrew farther into the corner, wrestling the sob that threatened to overtake me. He stood beside me, our hands brushing where they dangled. We touched, skin to skin, an unmistakable intimacy as his finger linked, softly, tenderly, with my own.

And a longing I'd buried so long ago coiled within me anew, very much alive. We breathed in perfect harmony, bound again, finger to finger, even as we ached for more. And I felt the strength and comfort which I'd not experienced this way in more than thirty years.

His voice was a whisper. "I loved Rosalie, yes. But I loved you first, Patsy. Always have loved you. Always will." He turned to me, touching my bruised lip very gently, right where it hurt, a very tender gesture.

Then he moved in, lowering his head as if he meant to kiss me.

And it took every bit of strength in me to turn away.

~

"WHO IS HE TO YOU?"

The growled words startled me, coming from behind me in the washhouse where I'd come in the cool of the evening to search out some missing stockings. Sally was there, having set soiled clothing to boil in a copper cauldron outside. Sally disliked when my daughters and I visited the dependencies, where the slaves did their work, for my father's concubine ruled here, in her quiet and competent way. Perhaps that's why she turned her head with scarcely disguised imperiousness to see who was stooped in the low doorway.

But I knew before I looked.

It was Tom, having lumbered down from the nearby north pavilion where he was sleeping these days, his face red from cheek to jowl, with rage or liquor, or both. "Get out," he barked at the laundry girls, and they darted past him in the doorway. Sally was slower to obey, her glance flicking to me. Only when I nodded did she tug at the bodice of her gown to make it straight, then gracefully ducked under my husband's outstretched arms to make her exit.

We stood there then, my husband and I, the sound of the laundry bubbling and hissing in the cauldron behind him. Then Tom roared, "*Who is he to you?* William Short. That sanctimonious stock jobber. That morally bankrupt lecher. I saw you. I saw both of you."

My heart leapt to my throat like a shot from a pistol and I could do nothing but brazen it out. "I can't imagine what you mean."

"You left your basket in the road," Tom said, his teeth clenched together like an animal trap that had taken so long to spring it was now rusted shut. "Couldn't fathom where you'd got to until I looked up at the garden pavilion. I saw you there, with him. In his arms. I saw it!"

Sweat broke across my brow and the nape of my neck, not only from the big fire under the cauldron nor even the heat of this stifling little room, but because guilt seared its way through me until I worried I might faint dead away. Haltingly, I began to say, "I wasn't in his arms, Tom. You know he's an old friend. A dear one. He offered me comfort and solace in a moment of need. That's all."

That was a lie. That wasn't all William Short had offered me in my father's garden pavilion. He told me he loved me. He'd tried to kiss me, too, but I'd turned away.

"Nothing carnal took place," I insisted. "He was my suitor once. In France. But I spurned Mr. Short, then married you."

I hoped it'd soothe his wounded pride.

It didn't.

"William Short makes whores of other men's wives." These words carried such quiet fury that they frightened me more than if he'd shouted them. Tom came toward me, very slowly, very quietly, wrapping his big hand around my throat like Charles Bankhead had once done. Tom didn't squeeze but merely held me there against the wall, slightly suspended, like a rag doll hanging from his string. "Short is infamous. His exploits are so well known he was too ashamed to make his home in Virginia. But you're giving him what you won't give me, isn't that right?"

How absurd it was. Beggaring belief, even. At our age, for two men to be vying for a mother of eleven children. "Tom, you're letting jealousy poison your mind! Don't you realize the absurdity—"

"Tell me you haven't bedded him. Go on. Lie to me, you convent-trained *whore*."

My husband's chest heaved with anger so deep and divisive that it seemed to open the very earth between us. It seemed to make strangers of us. And perhaps we *were* strangers now. For I was no longer the young wife who believed that her husband's violence was her own fault.

And slowly, pulling from some reserve inside myself I didn't know I had, I stood taller on my side of that chasm. "Whatever I am, Thomas Mann Randolph, you're not worthy of."

On that last, I broke free of him. But I didn't run. I'd run from him when he'd tried to force himself upon me—run from him like Ann ran from her maniac of a husband.

But I was done running from Tom.

I *walked* out of that washhouse, even as my husband called after me. "I'll have satisfaction, Martha. I'll call him out!"

I snorted with bitter laughter, grateful to be certain of one thing. "William will never fight a duel with you."

"If he won't, it's because he's no Virginia gentleman."

"No, Tom. He won't duel you because *you* aren't. Not anymore."

⁓

WILLIAM AND I MET IN THE GROVE, a canopy of autumn leaves overhead, strangely reminiscent of that long-ago day he found me on the ground, having fallen from my father's high horse.

"Patsy, say something." Those words, too, were an echo of the past, but I was hearing them again now as he pleaded, "Your silence cuts me deeper than the sharpest rebuke."

He was wrong. My words would cut him deeper, I knew. And I wished I could say anything other than what I'd come to tell him. But we weren't young comrades amongst a tangle of saplings at the start of our journey any longer; we were grizzled veterans standing atop the rotting fruit of our long struggle. And so, with the stink from the leaves of my father's chinaberry trees in my nostrils, I forced myself to speak, even as the words themselves left a painful sting on my lips. "I must ask you to leave Monticello."

William reeled, as if he'd taken a blow. "I meant to comfort you and have made a fool of myself with unwanted attentions. I'll leave, of course, if that's your desire, but I promise I'll never allow myself such a lapse. It will never happen again."

I wanted it to happen again. I wanted that desperately. "You're no fool, William, and your attentions are not unwanted. To the contrary, they're temptations that my virtue is no proof against." He startled, his expression lighting upon some hope that I was soon to dash. "But Tom saw us. He saw us in the garden pavilion. So you must go and never come back."

"God," William said, though the word carried with the sound of a profane curse. Color came to his cheeks, and he put a hand to the back of his neck. "I'll speak to him. I'll assure him of your blamelessness."

"But I'm not blameless." My heart cried out that I never wanted to part with him. That now, more than ever, I wanted to keep him near. "And you must go, because he means to call you out."

An unexpected bloodlust filled William's eyes. "*Does* he?"

"He thinks himself betrayed. Here under his own roof."

"Your father's roof," William corrected, then blanched at his own words.

I didn't have to explain to him the scandal of gentlemen with pistols meeting on my father's lawn, only weeks before the arrival of Lafayette. And that was to say nothing of the fact that such a duel might very well end in blood and tragedy. I had no doubt whatsoever that my husband would try to put a bullet in William's brain. Even if he missed—even if it was William whose aim was true—it'd make a widow of me and an orphan of my children.

"Please forgive me, Patsy. I should have never—"

"Loved me?" I asked, tears welling in my eyes. I'd made of myself the model Republican wife and daughter, reputed for virtue and spotless reputation. Tom would try to take that from me now; he was angry enough to tarnish me and my father's legacy—the only thing of value my children might ever inherit. And I'd been reckless enough to give him the means with which to do it. I had no excuse but one. "Don't regret loving me, I beg you, because I return your love, a thousandfold."

William blinked, and when he finally found his voice, it quavered. "I worry that you're saying it because this is a trying time, one of overwrought emotion, and here I am, conveniently—"

"I *love* you," I insisted, certain to the marrow of my bones. "Do I need to carve it in one of these trees? I loved you first, I loved you always, and will never stop loving you. Which is why I'm begging you to go. We must never see one another again. This must be good-bye."

He stared, his throat bobbing with emotion. "How can you ask me to leave you at the mercy of that man? Not after you tell me what I've waited thirty years to hear. If I leave Monticello, Patsy, leave with me."

He wanted me to leave with him. To leave Monticello behind. The beauty and grandeur, the violence and slavery . . . and my father. It was more impossible now than it'd been in France all those years ago. Then, I had only my father and my sister. Now, I had children.

My hand to his cheek, I whispered, "My dear, beloved man, I'm married to another."

"I don't care," he said hoarsely. "Divorce him or leave him, I don't care which. I'll live with you as husband or lover, in discretion or open scandal. I've been the subject of notoriety before. I don't care about reputation. I don't care!"

It was a wild and reckless dream—one that I would cherish—but one that could only ever be a dream. *I* cared about reputation and always had. I'd sacrificed for it again and again. Reputation had toppled governments and lost people their heads. Taking a lover as Frenchwomen did would shame my father and hurt my children, but more than that . . .

"It would destroy me, William."

"Why should it?"

"Because I'm my father's daughter. And you're his adoptive son. That is why you must go before we both bring down disgrace on him. This must be good-bye. This *must* be good-bye."

I didn't need to say more than this. Twice, he'd offered me a life with him, and twice I'd turned him away. With a white-faced grimace, he nodded, then pulled from the inside of his jacket a very old and worn piece of paper, folded many times. He slipped it into my hand and before I could ask what it was, he explained, "This is something I have held onto for too long. I meant to give this to you in farewell when you left France, but I could not bring myself to do it then. In my youth, I thought it was because I was too angry. But perhaps, throughout everything, even through my love for Rosalie, I held out hope for us." His eyes dropped away. "At least, until this moment."

With that, he brushed a soft kiss to my cheek, leaving me to open the paper in which a curl of my hair was still enclosed. But the page was no longer blank. In elegant script, it read:

> *I let myself be sacrificed*
> *For what you hold most dear*
> *Could I love you more?*
> *Do not shed bitter tears*
> *Over my destiny*
> *As you look at the object who knew so well how to please you.*
> *You will soon be consoled of its loss.*

The poem was French, the words as painful now as they would have been to read in 1789. And I stared at them in agony, as William Short walked away.

Within the hour, William called for a carriage. He made an emotional farewell to my father, excusing himself on some urgent business up north. He requested that we express his regret to Lafayette, pleading forgiveness for any distress his visit may have caused.

As I watched his carriage roll away from Monticello, I believed that I'd never see him again. And a part of me died, leaving a cold and hollow spot inside my heart where he used to be.

~~~~~

"HE'S GONE," SALLY INFORMED ME while I scattered feed for the chickens—a job that wasn't mine, but useful work was the only defense against profound misery.

"I know," I said, without looking up from the flock of birds pecking in the dirt. "I wish Mr. Short could've stayed longer, but his early departure leaves us with another bed for Lafayette's entourage."

"Your *husband* is gone," Sally said, sharply. "Master Randolph packed up his things from the north pavilion and took his leave, asking me to deliver you this message."

Sending the chickens scurrying with a swish of her skirt, Sally pressed into my hand a letter, and in her eyes I saw a shade of disapproval. She'd been witness to Tom's rage at the washhouse. No doubt, she'd overheard his accusations.

Perhaps she even believed them.

I didn't think it was an accident that he'd chosen Sally to deliver his note.

Though numerous men sought her charms—even my cousins the Carr brothers, a thing I always hinted at when any stranger raised the subject of the scandal—Sally never allowed my father to fear that she shared her body, or her heart, with any other man. Not for a moment. Not even when she burned with grief at losing Beverly and Harriet. And if there was a haughtiness in her, it was in that.

I suddenly understood why my father's enduring attraction ran much deeper than her beauty. Though she was a servant and a concubine, Sally had nearly perfect self-command. She'd borne a lifetime of slavery without allowing anyone to know her beyond what she was willing to be known. She seldom let pass an unguarded word, she kept a near iron rein over her passions—a virtue my father prized and admired more than any other.

It was my strength, too, but in this, Sally believed she'd finally bested me. I could read it in those amber eyes when she said, "I fear it'll embarrass your father to have to explain why Master Randolph has absented himself for the ceremonies in honor of Lafayette."

What she feared was that it was Tom's *intention* to cause embarrassment and that I'd allowed matters to come to this dreadful crossroads with a lapse in virtue, or at least in judgment. I didn't defend myself, but broke open the seal and read my husband's note.

I don't recall the exact words of Tom's note now. I burned it straightaway, for it was both obscene and demented, promising vengeance upon me for my betrayals. And it hardened me against Tom, because I'd just sent away the man I loved and admired to honor vows to the husband I no longer respected.

So instead of feeling compassion for a husband in the grip of madness, I felt only relief that Tom was gone. And fear that he'd return.

In the soft golden veil of that Indian summer, my poor father was nearly eight-two years old, and though he never celebrated his birthday—only the birthday of the country—there was no denying anymore the slow and steady degeneration of his body. Thankfully his mind and spirits remained intact, but it pained me to think anything in connection to me might disturb the latter.

"Don't fret," Jeff said, chewing uncouthly upon a stalk he'd plucked from the edge of the lawn while the groundskeepers scurried to clip every stray sprig from a bush. "Lafayette will have an escort of a hundred and twenty armed and mounted men. Not even my father is foolish enough to attempt violence with them present."

The number of this horde astonished me. "A hundred and twenty men?"

Jeff nodded. "At least two hundred more on the east lawn.

There isn't a gentleman in Virginia who doesn't want to witness this reunion."

When that glorious and golden November day came, the first thing we saw were the banners of the horsemen in red, white, and blue. A bugler blew his horn in small mimicry of the grand French ceremonies to announce the arrival of the prancing smoky white horses and Lafayette's elegant calash.

All this delighted my young sons, who were arrayed in their finest clothes, standing next to their sisters, whom I'd dressed in white robes for the occasion.

Until the bugle blew, I'd allowed myself to feel nothing but anxiety that everything should go well. But seeing the cavalry with their pikes and the train of carriages roll to a stop at the edge of the lawn, I found myself longing to see our old friend. And my father, standing at my side amongst the Doric columns of the portico, slipped his aged and shaking hand in mine and squeezed with all his strength.

The footman set down a stair for Lafayette, and the Guest of the Nation emerged gingerly—bulkier than in his youth and without the powdered wig that covered his now cropped graying hair. But it was him. He limped from the wound he'd taken in our war or from whatever they'd done to him when he rotted away in the dungeon at Olmütz.

But at the sight of me helping my father to slowly and painfully make his way down the steps, Lafayette hurried toward him, crying, "Ah, my dear Jefferson!"

At this, my father let go of my hand and his decrepit shuffle somehow became a run. "Ah, my dear Lafayette!"

They fell into each other's embrace, both of them bursting into tears. By my accounting, no two men in the world had done more for the cause of liberty. Together, they'd changed the world. And I loved them both. These two giants of my childhood now come together in the evening of their lives.

And emotion swelled in my throat, forcing from me a little sob. I wasn't the only one caught up in the storm. There wasn't a dry eye in the crowd as the two men kissed each other's cheeks in the European fashion and sobbed on each other's shoulders with abandon.

We watched in respectful, sniffling silence. Even the slaves choked back cries of their own.

When at last the two heroes broke apart, my father led Lafayette up the stairs. "This is my daughter Randolph—you knew her slightly in France."

"Slightly?" Lafayette looked at me with red and watery eyes. *"Mon Dieu!* I remember very well tall Patsy, the schoolgirl from the convent, the indomitable young mistress of her father's house."

Lafayette kissed both my cheeks, then captured my hands and brought them to his lips, pressing tearful kisses into them with great affection. "Madam, the sight of you makes my heart sing with pride and joy."

My vision blurred with tears. "My heart sings in echo."

Four hundred people waited for introductions, but Lafayette lingered with *me,* drawing my hand to his stout chest, placing it over his heart. "My dear, you won't remember this, but there's a moment in time as real for me still as if it were happening now. I was leading the royal procession into Paris—facing down thousands of angry citizens with pistols, swords, and pitchforks. . . ."

Oh, but I remembered that day perfectly well. It was the first time I refused William. The first time—but not the last time—my head conquered my heart. And the scars of that victory throbbed with such renewed vigor that I said, "How could I forget, General? It is emblazoned on my soul."

Our eyes met again, and he shook his head very slowly. "You cannot remember it as I do. For you cannot have guessed your part. I was still a brash young man then, a soldier who thinks more of glory than fears the loss of his life. What I feared that day was to lose a king, a queen, a whole nation . . . and be blamed for it. In truth, even as the people chanted my name, I'd never been more afraid. Then, in my terror, I looked up at a window and saw a flash of red hair, like the very fire of liberty itself. There you were, my lady liberty, looking down at me, a reminder of your father and his words. You gave me courage, for I couldn't bear to disappoint him . . . or you."

These words obliterated me to dust, then lifted me toward the heavens on a breeze. I had been Lafayette's lady of liberty? Made timid by the reverence in his eyes, and the stares of onlookers from whom I couldn't hide my tears, I tried to shrink away, but he still held my hand against his lion's heart. "You were my touchstone, sweet lady."

And he had been mine.

I felt somehow that we were two veterans of the same wars. Perhaps we were. . . .

Looking into his eyes, his courage became mine, once again.

The debts, my husband's madness, the loss of my love—like Lafayette, I knew I'd somehow survive them all. And I whispered, "I remember you bowed to me, General. And never before or since have I received a bow of which I was so proud." I showed him then the old, faded tricolored cockade pinned to my hat. "I've kept mine all these years since."

Lafayette inhaled deeply, filling his chest until it puffed out with pride. "How blessed my friend Jefferson is to have such a lady at his side. Are these your children?"

I nodded, introducing each and every one of them as they crowded around, eager to touch the hand that had wielded a sword in our great Revolution. With this and other introductions, we were treated to addresses. Then, at last, we retired into the entryway with its Indian trophies and antlers and animal bones, a fireplace burning a cheery wood fire, leaving the crowd to wave handkerchiefs in farewell, cheering *Vive Lafayette! Vive Jefferson!*

Inside the house, we retired to the crowded dining room where tables had been squeezed to accommodate nearly fifty people, with not an inch to spare. There, the two aging patriots presided at the main table, recalling stories of the Revolution in the heavenly glow of the skylight overhead. And so animated did they become, with such eloquence did they speak, that, carried away by the enthusiasm of the moment, we found ourselves abandoning all decorum, rising from our own chairs to surround the two old sages.

Even the servants drew near so as not to miss a word that fell from their lips, as the golden glory of the setting sun shone through the many tinted mountains behind which it was sinking. Seeing them sit together, their heads bent in the occasional quiet remark, I could imagine us in Paris, all of us young again. For this visit had restored Papa's vigor to the point that he wished to stay awake past ten o'clock.

The next day, Lafayette was to be feted at the University of Virginia, with Presidents Jefferson, Madison, and Monroe. What a sight the four patriots made in their carriage. When Papa returned, he said, "The government is voting Lafayette a pension, you know. He deserves it."

I didn't doubt that for a moment. "As do you, Papa. You built this country."

My father's dry lips pulled to a thin line. "In truth, I merely held the nail; Lafayette drove it."

But, of course, even two such old and loving friends cannot be at ease in all things. . . .

The general wasn't shy to confront my father in the presence of our servants. Their faces strained to show indifference, but I wasn't blind to the way their bodies leaned in, how they made themselves busy in such a way as to best hear every word when Lafayette said, "I gave my best services to, and spent my fortune on behalf of Americans because I felt you were fighting for a great and noble principle—the freedom of mankind. But instead of all being free, a portion were held in bondage. My old friend, surely you must concur that it would be mutually beneficial to masters and slaves if the latter were educated and emancipated."

"Indeed," Papa replied easily. "I believe there'll come a time when the slaves will all be free, but I leave its accomplishment to the work of another generation. At the age of eighty-two, with one foot in the grave and the other uplifted to follow it, I do not permit myself to take part in any new enterprises." Of course, Tom's experiences as governor taught us the difficulty of the enterprise. But my father was ever an optimist, and spoke those words with confidence and conviction. "I do favor teaching slaves to read . . . but to teach them to write will enable them to forge papers."

"For the better!" Lafayette had insisted. "I've heard it argued that black faces cannot make their way in white society," he said, his eyes flicking briefly upon Madison and Eston Hemings where they readied to entertain us with their violins. "But I put this to you. Whatever be the complexion of the enslaved, it does not, in my opinion, alter the complexion of the crime the enslaver commits. A crime much blacker than any African face. It's a matter of great anxiety and concern to find that this trade is sometimes carried on under the flag of liberty, our dear and noble stripes, to which virtue and glory have been constant standard-bearers."

My father was unaccustomed to anyone speaking so baldly to him on the matter. But Lafayette was more than a guest. He'd saved our lives and our Revolution and enabled us to live in this beautiful house atop the mountain in Virginia. He had the right, more than any man alive, to harangue us.

My father endured it gracefully and I could never bring myself to be angry at Lafayette. Not only because of all I owed him, and all he'd inspired in me, but also because he was the only guest present who never asked me to account for the absence of my husband.

Tom had left himself, and us, without a fig leaf. We couldn't say that he was ill, because he was seen in taverns by our neighbors. We couldn't say he was about urgent business, since everyone seemed to know he was ruined. So we employed artful dodges when possible and inartful ones the rest of the time.

In spite of this, I was enormously relieved not to have him

there. He left no lonely gap in our society, no awkward place at the dinner table. His absence left us strangely comfortable as a family. And as I hosted the greatest patriots of our age, I was as content as I'd never been before in my place as the mistress of Monticello.

Chapter Forty

Monticello, 5 June 1825
From Thomas Jefferson to Thomas Mann Randolph

You can never want a necessary or comfort of life while I possess anything. All I have is devoted to the comfortable maintenance of yourself and the family. I have no other use for property. Restore yourself to the bosom of your family and friends. They will cherish your happiness as warmly as they ever did.

I SHOULD BURN THIS LETTER for what it reveals about my husband's abandonment of me—and perhaps mine of him. But these words are a testament to my father's character. Proof of how warmly he reached out to my husband, when I could scarcely find it within myself to do the same.

That spring, I found Tom brooding in a little white house in Milton he said he was using as an office, alone, drunk, unshaven, and in squalor. In the dark recesses of the entryway—for he'd shut the curtains against the sunlight—Tom heard my plea, then said, "I'll never go back to Monticello with you."

"I'm not asking for myself," I said, trying to quell my rising anger. "I'm asking for Ellen. She wants you at her wedding."

"Of course you're not asking for *you*. You'd have been happier if I died in the war."

"That's not true," I said, knowing that most of the bitterness between us had arisen precisely because I was desperate to keep him from dying in that war!

Tom snorted. "I won't subject myself to the supercilious stares of your father's guests. So get out, Martha. Go."

I stood there, wringing my hands, wishing I knew the words that might help matters—but it occurred to me that everything we'd ever had to say to one another of import we'd said skin to skin. And though he was still, even at his age, rugged and well made, my desire for him had died completely.

"I said get out!" Tom shouted, launching his boot at me. Fortunately, his drunken aim was so poor that the boot sailed harmlessly by my head and crashed with a clatter into the wooden door behind me. "Just go and be grateful that I haven't taken the children from their whore of a mother."

A chill swept over me—not for the insult, but for the threat. Tom couldn't take the older boys because they wouldn't go. But Lewis, Septimia, and little George . . . my husband *could* take them. I'd simply never believed he'd be so monstrous as to try. Why, he was more cruel, barbarous, and fiend-like than ever!

Ignoring the stench of an unclean plate upon his table in the room beyond, I wrapped my shawl around me. "However much you blame me, surely you wouldn't make the children suffer."

"Oh, I do blame you, Martha. But I blame my ungrateful son even more. Understand that if my children step one toe over Jeff's threshold, you'll never see them again. Don't think I can't do it, for it's the only thing still in my legal power, and by God, not even your father can stop me."

I didn't stay to argue with him.

When I told Ellen, she straightened before the mirror and smoothed her wedding gown. "My father ought not be made to suffer embarrassment because he has no dowry to give me. His pride has already endured too many blows. How could I be happy today knowing I'd brought him low?"

She was devoted to her father, in spite of his weaknesses, and I wouldn't have it any other way. My dear daughter, still as precious as two angels in one . . .

And so Ellen married Joseph Coolidge in the drawing room of

Monticello, without her father, her hands shaking so badly she could scarcely hold a prayer book. Her sisters sent her to Boston with gifts they made themselves. Cornelia fashioned for her a painted screen to shade her from the sun, Mary packed a basket of cakes and wine, and Septimia presented her with a bracelet of chinaberries she'd strung like beads. Then our dear, witty Ellen was gone, leaving her grandfather lonely.

My other daughters took turns sitting with him, but Papa confided, "I didn't know what a void Ellen would leave in our family."

I didn't despair at losing Ellen. To the contrary, I *gloried* in her escape from the sinking ship upon which the rest of us now sailed.

In December of that year, Edgehill went up for auction with all its slaves and livestock. I worried that the notice would attract traffickers in human blood, Negro buyers who'd take my husband's slaves deep into the South to grow cotton or rice, putting them to such hard use it'd leave them in the ground. And I couldn't stomach the sorrow of seeing our house servants and their children sold out of the family.

"There's nothing you can do for them," Jeff said, trying to reassure me. "I can try to arrange for buyers for them amongst our friends and neighbors, and failing that, I can bid myself on your household favorites, but there's nothing *you* can do to spare the slaves from sale at all. You mustn't blame yourself, Mother."

Then why did I feel to blame?

In the face of such a system of injustice, I determined a course of action. Having learned bitter lessons from the unhappy fate of so many ruined friends and relatives, I said, "There is something I can do. If I give up my dower rights in my husband's holdings, I'm entitled to one-ninth of his estate before the creditors are satisfied. And if I take that value in slaves . . ."

My son's eyes bulged. "You'd be better off to take—"

"No," I said, twisting a kerchief in my fists, understanding the import of what I was saying. "I'll take the slaves."

And with those desperate words, I agreed to become a slave-holder.

For the first time in my life, I'd own human beings whose entire fate would rest in my hands. It shattered me to do it, but would've shattered me more to do nothing. Better that they were mine than given over to some breeding farm or a field in the Deep South.

I spared from the block Sally's relations—the wives of her brothers. But I did so over Jeff's objections. "They're aged, Mother. They wouldn't have sold for much. If slaves are all you're taking from the estate, you need strong young men."

But I went on sparing the women. I took eleven in all, including Burwell's daughters, though my son thought my choices emotional and without good sense.

What I'd done was all that kept me sane on the bitter winter day of the auction. First on the block was Susan, so bad a servant, so negligent, so heartless, and of a family of such bad disposition generally that we ought to have been glad to be rid of her. But I was overcome with nausea when the auctioneer cried out into the biting winter wind. "Five hundred, five hundred! This nubile girl, strong arms, wide hips. Five hundred, do I hear six?"

The discomfort of slavery I had borne all my life, but its sorrows in all their bitterness I'd never before conceived. Tears slid down Susan's black cheeks when a man offered a higher bid. And feeling a fracturing in my soul, I lost all sense of decorum.

Rushing to her, I begged that she be allowed to choose for herself amongst the buyers—a thing that embarrassed my son as he pulled me away, mumbling apologies to the bidders. "You aren't planning to do something even more foolish, are you? You cannot rely now on my father for anything anymore. What you've taken in human property is now all you have of your own to provide for the six children you still have in your care, all under the age of seventeen."

He was afraid that I'd free them. And I might've. But just because I couldn't bear to see these slaves naked on a wooden block for rich men to inspect, didn't mean I'd cast them out into the world without any way to support themselves. That's what I was thinking when the auctioneers cried out the price for Edgehill's parcels, hour after hour. "Sixteen an acre! Do I hear seventeen?"

Standing there as everything Tom and I built was sold away—earth, animal, and human—I felt my husband's accusing eyes on me. But however much he hated me that day, I hated myself more. I hated myself, and slavery, and Virginia, and everything.

Everything.

For four hours the auctioneers cried out, extolling the virtues of Edgehill, a plantation with the healthiest climate of the whole earth, sheltered from cold winds, well watered with pure springs, nestled amongst woods of oak, hickory, walnut, and ash . . . until finally, at the end of the fourth hour, with bidders beginning to go off, my son offered seventeen and took the whole of Edgehill.

"You *swindler*," Tom sneered, drawing so near to my son I thought they might come to blows. "You took advantage of a father's distress to get possession of his property and turn him adrift in his old age, penniless. You didn't even raise enough to satisfy my creditors and now they'll consume my earnings for the rest of my life. You've even taken from me a roof over my head—"

He reached for our son's bad arm, as if to wrench it, and I stepped between them. "Tom, you can never want for a home while my father possesses one. And our son won't leave you—"

"I'll take nothing from a thief." Tom trembled like a man swept up in a storm, clutching at his chest, all the color gone from him. Then he limped away.

To escape the prying eyes of onlookers, I hastened to the carriage, murmuring, "He's ill." For I knew no other name for it. "His health's failing from excessive anxiety of mind."

Handing me into the carriage, Jeff said, "I cannot have yours doing the same, so I've made arrangements with a common friend to assist him. He won't accept help from me, but he'll take it from a friend, and I'll reimburse that man for his pains."

I grasped his hand, grateful beyond measure. This'd been no

easier on Jeff than on any of us, but he'd borne it. "Your father won't appreciate it, but I do."

The tapestry of my life was unraveling, one strand at a time.

Once the grandeur and radiance of Lafayette's visit was gone, I looked around me and saw everything at Monticello in disrepair. The paint flaked off the walls and railings and molding. The roof let in melting snow and rain. My father, so proud of his house, so fastidious and attentive to its appearance, didn't seem to notice, and I told myself that Jeff had been too busy with the calamity of my husband's bankruptcy to give my father's estate his attention.

But that winter one of my father's loans had come due . . . and Papa couldn't pay.

"What can you mean that he can't pay?" I asked Jeff as the carriage jostled us along, having relied upon my father's promises to look after me and the children, no matter what befell my husband's fortunes.

"Grandfather overestimated the value of his holdings," Jeff told me, gravely. "Monticello is difficult to make profitable. Water and supplies must be hauled up. The house itself requires an enormous amount of firewood to heat it. There's the expense of supporting the Negroes. We'll have to move the family to Poplar Forest."

I didn't understand what he was saying.

And he braced himself, continuing on. "We'll take with us only the necessary furniture and a small household of servants. Then we'll sell or rent the whole of Monticello and auction as many Negroes as we can to pay the debts."

The blood drained from me so suddenly I sank into the cushions of the carriage in a near swoon. This had already been the ugliest day of a life filled with its share of ugly days, and this blow nearly stopped a heart that was already broken.

Leave Monticello? It'd been the constant star, the steady anchor in all our troubles. Surely Jeff was overstating the financial situation in which we found ourselves. "But the price of crops will go up. They do. Up and down."

"Mother," Jeff said, covered in a sweat in spite of the cold.

"You've no notion of the debts Grandpapa has acquired. More than my father's debts. More by far. And the crisis is at hand. To delay it will be complete ruin only a few years down the road, without a home to shelter you or the children."

I couldn't fathom selling Monticello. It'd be a bitter sacrifice to leave its comforts, but nothing compared to the anguish of seeing my father turned out of his house and deprived in his old age of the few pleasures he was still capable of enjoying. "Have you told your grandfather this plan? It'll kill him!"

And it nearly did.

I was there, holding my father's hand, when Jeff delivered the news, and the shock was as dreadful as we foresaw. My father—my strong, giant of a father—began to weep. "I've lived too long. My death can only be an advantage to my family now."

"You're very wrong!" I cried, for his death was the thing I most feared all my life.

My son, always pragmatic, echoed my horror but explained the financial reality, too. "Grandpapa, even independent of our love for you, your death under existing circumstances would be a calamity of frightful magnitude. Your life isn't only precious to our hearts, but necessary to the interests of your daughter and grandchildren."

What he meant was that just by living, my legendary father cast a shield over us all. While he was alive, the most ruthless of our creditors wouldn't dare to strip us bare.

They say tragedies come in threes. There was first the auction of Edgehill. Next the blow that we might lose Monticello. And then my daughter Ann came to us in the dead of winter, battered, bleeding, and bruised.

⟨⟩

ANN STAGGERED INTO MONTICELLO clutching a threadbare shawl too small to cover her swollen stomach. She'd been badly beaten—her eye half-shut with swelling, bleeding scrapes on her elbows and knees. Ann wasn't very heavy, even with her rounded pregnant belly; she was nothing but shivering skin and bones. "I can't stay with Charles," she said, weeping, as if we were in any doubt. And when we got her in front of a fire, she said, "He'll kill me. I fear he's already killed the baby in my womb. Please don't tell Jeff I'm here. He'll convince Grandpapa to turn me out, and I'd deserve it. I'd *deserve* it."

"Never," I said, rocking her as if she were still a small child. "Jeff's in Richmond on your grandfather's business, but even if he were here, he wouldn't turn you out. Nor would your Grandpapa ever hear of it. You're safe here, my precious Ann."

"How will I face my sisters? The last time Cornelia saw me, she nearly turned me to stone with those gorgon eyes."

"Your sisters will be as delighted to see you as I am." And if they weren't, I'd make them pretend. Because Ann had never been taught to do anything but honor and obey a husband, and none of this was her fault.

Ann was too weak to go up the steep stairs to the family bedrooms, so we put her into the same bed Jeff had used to recover from his stabbing. And for the same reason. Both my children were victims of that vile wretch Charles Bankhead!

Would he come after her? Would he dare? My husband had abandoned us, my father was frail, and none of the slaves, or even the overseers, were brave enough to confront Bankhead with the force required. So I made my own plans to defend us.

My sons James, Ben, and Lewis were all young men now, between the ages of sixteen and twenty. While closing every paneled shutter over the windows of the house, I told them to arm themselves—not with a horsewhip or a fire iron, but with pistols. Because if the moment came, I didn't want them to injure Bankhead, but to see him to his grave.

Instead, we saw Ann to hers.

In scream-inducing pain, she gave birth to a little boy. Seeing the bruises on her body and the bleeding that wouldn't stop, the physician dosed her heavily with laudanum. Ann didn't want it, and I protested the physician's prescription. But the doctor said my daughter had internal wounds that couldn't be repaired. Then he gave her a dose that left her speechless and insensible.

Slipping into much the same condition, I lingered with Ann, holding her hand. Such was the state of my own distress that, for a moment, I saw not only my beloved daughter dying in childbed, but also my dear, sweet sister, who'd lost her life in childbed. I'd blink at Ann's brown hair, and for a moment see my sister, then my mother, then my daughter again.

I was so lost in time and place, I scarcely heard the words of the doctor, who finally said, "Mrs. Bankhead is past hope."

I suppose I heard these words. They were simply too shattering to accept. Inside my head, I screamed a glass-shattering scream, but in truth I made not a sound. I sat there with my dying child—the grief swirling like fury in my skull—blind and deaf to the whole world.

I couldn't rise until afternoon, after Ann breathed her last. Even then, it was only because, like a sudden dam that must be built to fend off the flood of anguish, I was frantic to do for my child the very last thing that I could do for her in this world.

I couldn't cry. I couldn't swoon away. I couldn't lock myself in my room and pace the floor howling and smashing and breaking things. I couldn't ride through the woods in madness, though I wanted to. How desperately I wanted to!

Instead, I went to my father and said, "We must arrange for her burial."

"Our poor, dear Ann." My father wept. "My little garden fairy. I'll never see flowers again but with her in heaven. Though now, heaven seems to be overwhelming us with every form of misfortune, and I expect the next will give me the coup de grâce."

I couldn't hear it, couldn't accept how frail and dispirited and heartbroken my father was, because I needed him now as I'd perhaps never needed him before. "Send for Bankhead."

My father cried, indignant, "Charles?"

"Yes." My mind was quite made up. "Send for Bankhead and ask him to bring the children and Ann's best dress."

"Surely a servant—"

"We must send for *Bankhead*," I insisted again, speaking to my father with a commanding tone I'd never employed before, and scarcely recognized within myself. "We must welcome him home to bury his wife. We must offer hope at reconciliation after so many bitter years. We must elicit from him a warm glow of gratitude in his grief and guilt. And in the moment he's most vulnerable, we must ask him to leave the children with us."

I said this with perfect clarity of mind and terrible resolve. I wouldn't lose Ann's children as I'd lost Polly's. And not to a man like Charles. I believed, sincerely and utterly, that even if we were fated to abject poverty, my grandchildren would still be better off with me than at the mercy of that drunk, violent monster.

I'd swallow down any poison to wrest Ann's babies from her murderer. And so I felt no compunction in demanding cooperation from the family. "The natural consequence of our having the children will be a reconciliation with their father. When Bankhead arrives, there'll be no accusations, no recriminations, no coolness to him in any respect. We'll smile at him and make up our quarrel—even you, Jeff."

Something in my voice, something in my dry eyes, seemed to frighten the family into perfect obedience. And when the slaves shoveled dirt over my daughter's grave, Charles sank to his knees by Ann's grave, trembling, and retching in guilt and grief. There was no hope for Ann and there was no hope for him. The only hope was that my grandchildren might be saved, so I did the most difficult thing I'd ever had to do in my life.

I forced myself to put a hand upon Bankhead's accursed shoulder and offered him the solace and forgiveness that would bend him to my will. Then I whispered sweetly in the ear of my daughter's murderer how her babies would be best left with me . . .

. . . until, at length, he agreed.

And I am not sorry for it to this day.

Chapter Forty-one

Monticello, 17 February 1826
From Thomas Jefferson to James Madison

If a lottery is permitted, my lands will pay everything. If refused I must sell every thing here and move with my family where I have not even a log-hut to put my head into. The friendship which has subsisted between us, now half a century, and the harmony of our political principles and pursuits, have been sources of constant happiness. To myself you have been a pillar of support through life. Take care of me when I'm dead and be assured that I shall leave with you my last affections.

I LEARNED THAT MY FATHER had concocted a lottery scheme from the newspaper. When I confronted him, holding Ann's orphaned infant in my arms, Papa explained that one night, awake with painful thoughts, a solution to our financial problems came to him like an inspiration from the realms of bliss. "If the state legislature approves the plan, we'll sell tickets all across the country for a chance to win some of my lands—the most beautiful and valuable property in Virginia. And the profits will save Monticello."

My father was optimistic that the legislature would approve the scheme. The people had voted Lafayette a pension, he reasoned—they wouldn't possibly deny a former *president* the chance to live out his days in comfort.

"Why, there's every chance that in patriotic fervor, the government will burn all the tickets and simply make a gift to me of Monticello."

I was too encouraged by my father's revived spirits to tell him that his faith in his fellow citizens was misplaced. There'd be no bonfire of lottery tickets to honor my father's service. Virginians would genuflect before my father the *monument*, but they wouldn't pay one penny in taxes to support the *man*. It was against their creed, and so were lotteries. Now, more than ever, the state legislature was filled with ranters and evangelists who thought games of chance were a sin. And even if they approved a lottery, the one thing no one needed in Virginia was land.

We could hope patriots in other parts of the nation were hungrier for it, but I was afraid to hope. My life had become such a tissue of privations and disappointments that it was impossible to believe any of my wishes would be gratified, or if they were, not to fear some hidden mischief flowing from their success.

And on the day Jeff delivered the news we hoped would be our salvation, he was as ashen as the day Bankhead stabbed him. He came in from the drizzly cold, tracking mud on the floor from his riding boots, and we went together to knock on my father's door. Where Sally was, I couldn't guess, but Burwell let us in, leading us to Papa, seated at his desk, his legs raised up to keep the blood in them, squinting through his spectacles as he tried to write with his own withered hand.

Jeff cleared his throat. "The lottery has been approved with a condition that Monticello must be the prize."

Papa went white from his snowy white hair to the tips of his fingers. So white I feared he'd become a statue before my eyes. His lottery scheme had been meant to save our home, but might prove to be no better than if we'd auctioned it off. When Papa finally spoke, he asked, "That's the only way?"

Jeff nodded, scarcely able to meet his grandfather's eyes. "You'd be able to live here until your death, and my mother until hers. But after that, Monticello will pass out of the family. I need to know what answer to carry back to Richmond."

My father swallowed. Removed his spectacles. Set down his pen.

"I need some time to think and consult with your mother," he said.

Jeff pulled a chair for me then found one for himself.

My father stopped him. "Only your mother."

There was a moment—a heartbeat of confusion—before Jeff nodded, and went out. Then Papa and I were alone together. We sat together in silence for a time.

Papa finally said, "I never believed it could come to this."

It's only a house, I wanted to say. But I knew better. "We'll manage somehow—"

He stopped me midthought, bringing my hand to his lips. "I've been in agony watching you sink every day under the suffering you endure, literally dying before my eyes. Do you remember, Patsy, when we first started playing music together?"

I smiled a bittersweet smile, remembering Paris, where I had learned to play the harpsichord. Where we'd made music together. And where I played for him when he could no longer play, due to his enfeebled hand. "Oh, yes. I remember all our duets."

"I have been hearing them, lately. In my sleep. Realizing that my whole life has been, in some sense, a song that could never be sung without you. There is almost nothing I've ever been that I could've been without my dear and beloved daughter, the cherished companion of my early life, and nurse of my old age. And your children as dear to me as if my own from having lived with me from their cradle . . . that's why I leave it all to you."

Unless the lottery wildly surpassed our expectations, there'd be nothing to leave, I thought. And worse, anything he gave to me would be taken by Tom's creditors. "Papa, Tom's debt's—"

"I'll settle the remains of my estate upon Jeff to hold in trust for your sole and separate use, until your husband's death, in which case the property should go to you as if you were a *femme sole*."

This would shield everything from Tom's creditors, but was also an acknowledgment, at long last, that I needed no man to rule over me. And as if to underline his trust, he said, "I'll need you to look after Sally."

"Dear God, Papa." I brushed back welling tears.

He took both my hands. "Burwell, Joe Fosset, and Johnny Hemings . . . I intend to free them with a stipend and tools and a log house for each of them. And the boys, Madison and Eston—they'll go free on their twenty-first birthdays. I'll petition the legislature for them to be allowed to remain in the state as if it were a favor to Johnny Hemings, naming them as his apprentices so that he can start a carpentry business."

It was, I supposed, the only option. My father couldn't do for Sally's younger boys what he'd done with Beverly and Harriet without depriving their mother of all her children. But I believed anyone might be able to see right through emancipation of Madison and Eston unless . . .

The ruse, of course, depended upon Sally's enslavement. Papa wouldn't free her, *couldn't* free her without exposing everything. Which is why he was leaving it to me.

In the end he left everything—all of it—to me.

～

"TELL THEM TO MAKE MY COFFIN NOW," Papa said from the confines of his sickbed, where I fanned the flies away from him in the still heat of summer.

He'd come home from some business in Charlottesville, slumped in the saddle, scarcely able to hold the reins in his crippled hands. Old Eagle clopped slowly along, careful and somber, as if he knew just how feeble Papa was. And once we got Papa down from the horse, it became manifest that his powers were failing him.

His plan was to fight old age off by never admitting the approach of helplessness. Not even in the approach of his death, which he intended to arrange to his satisfaction.

My father used his life, his talent, and his fortune to secure the rights of men to control their own destinies, and he still intended to command his. He'd decided to die, and nothing could discourage him, not even my cry of pure anguish when he ordered his coffin be made.

After that, my whole world reduced to the intervals of wakefulness and consciousness between my father's slumber. I shuddered when he said, "Take heart, Patsy. Jeff has promised to never abandon you. And when I'm gone, you'll find within that drawer," he said, spending his precious strength to point to it, "a little casket of gifts for you."

The pain that swept through me in anticipation of the end was nothing I'd ever experienced before, even for all the other losses. Nothing I thought I could survive. Even the thought of losing my father was a crushing, grinding agony of the spirit that left me not just shuddering, but quaking in its wake. "No, Papa. Not yet . . ."

"Not yet," he agreed, taking shallow, rasping breaths upon his pillow. "I want to breathe my last on that great day, the birthday of my country."

July the fourth, he meant. The fiftieth anniversary of our Independence. The day he became the most profound voice of his age. Of *any* age.

"Mother, let us relieve your vigil," Jeff insisted, his comforting hand upon my shoulder. "We'll stay with him all night. We'll drag in pallets so that he's never alone for a moment, if only you'll get some rest."

I couldn't consent to it—especially not when Sally sat so resolutely, her spine straight upon a wooden chair nearby. I don't know what words of farewell she exchanged with Papa.

What they'd shielded from the world all their lives they still kept, with possessive silence, to themselves. And I had to be coaxed away from my father's sickbed like a lamed animal to water. So violent was my own pain at the expectation of him being torn from me, I had to be pried away . . . until, at long last, on the third of July, my father's suffering seemed to demand a wish for the end.

Struggling for breath, Papa would ask, "Is it the Fourth?"

Because we couldn't bear for him to perish with even one more disappointment, we told him it was. An expression came over his countenance that my children naively believed to mean: *just as I wished*.

But I don't believe my father was deceived. Even after his limbs took on the clamminess of death and his pulse was so faint only the doctor could feel it, Papa stirred again to ask, "Is it the Fourth?"

This time the doctor said, "It soon shall be."

I stared at the clock, willing the hands to move. Wishing I had my father's indomitable will to shape the world and make the laws of the universe bend. Gladly would I give up a day of my own life, a day from the lives of everyone living, to deliver my father into the morning of his glorious Fourth.

But the physician said softly, "He has no more than fifteen minutes now. . . ."

An hour later my father was still alive and refused his laudanum. He then fell back into a disturbed sleep, and in a vivid dream, he roused himself, anxiously gesturing with his hands, as if to write upon a tablet. "The Committee of Safety ought to be warned!"

My children wondered what he could be dreaming about. I didn't have to wonder. I knew. He was, in his final breaths, readying for the British invasion, readying to fight the war for Independence all over again.

We'd later learn that in Quincy, Massachusetts, John Adams was also on his deathbed, equally determined to see the morning of the Fourth. He'd die on the cherished day, my father's name on his lips, but all we knew was that in Virginia, the struggle went on, and on.

My Papa's frail chest rose and fell under the obelisk clock that ticked the interminable stretch. Mr. Short had that clock made for Papa; and in remembering that, it seemed as if William, too, was hovering over Papa in vigil. Burwell helped to arrange Papa's head upon his pillow. Jeff swept his lips with a wet sponge, which my father sucked and appeared to relish.

Just a few more hours, I thought, until the Fourth. And I turned to see Sally, too, straining to see the hands of that same clock move.

When the clock finally struck midnight with a sweet silvery ring, sighs of relief exploded around us. And upon seeing the faint breath of my papa upon a glass held to his lips, I felt a grim satisfaction, like a commander upon a battlefield who has seen a victory.

But Papa didn't leave this victory to chance. He soldiered on until noon when, with eyes wide in apprehension of his triumph, he ceased to breathe.

That moment, for me, was an eclipse of the sun. A blackening of the whole earth. An unfathomable grief in which I no longer knew myself, or the world, or my place in it. But my father—who had always known his place in that world—passed like the hero he was from life into legend.

～

ON MULBERRY ROW a white sheet draped over a thornbush, flapping ghostly in a light summer breeze to signal to neighboring farms that my father was dead. In the carpentry shop, Madison and Eston helped their uncle sand the rough edges of Papa's wooden coffin. On the western side of the mountain, slaves dug the grave.

And I . . . I did nothing.

Numb with grief, overwhelmed by loss, I couldn't seem to

catch my breath. "Take some fresh air," one of my children said; I don't know which one. I was blind and deaf to everything. I couldn't feel my limbs. All I felt was the slow calcification inside me, spreading so that I couldn't move. Someone grasped me at the elbows to prompt me outside onto the terrace; someone else called for the doctor to tend me. And it was there, on the terrace, in the most acute distress, that I heard the pounding of horse hooves.

Papa, I thought. Was he riding hard upon Caractacus, as he loved to do in his youth? Then the vision swam before my eyes, not of my father, but of my husband. Tom in his youth. A young and handsome horseman, riding up the road toward our house.

I blinked and the vision came clear. It *was* Tom. No longer young or beautiful, but still riding like a demon. Where he'd gotten the horse, I didn't know. Nevertheless my husband swung down from the saddle of a frothing, pawing animal. "Is he dead?"

At my elbow, the doctor nodded. "Mr. Jefferson expired a quarter after noon."

To hear it said again, I nearly stumbled. Behind me, the children must've gathered, because I heard little George blubber while Septimia choked out tiny, delicate sobs. "Grandpapa is gone."

"You poor children," Tom said, a light in his eyes strangely fueled by the sight of our misery. "Look how grieved you are to lose him . . . but not your mother. Her eyes are dry as always. Can't you shed a tear, Martha? Not even for your father?"

The physician stiffened at my side. "Colonel Randolph!"

Colonel Randolph? He was entitled to be called that, of course, but I could only think of his father. That's who Tom had become. A miserable old rotter like the one who begat him.

Tom advanced upon me in a scatter of flies. "Don't you think it's unnatural for such a devoted daughter to lose her father without even a tear? And Thomas Jefferson, no less. A great man that the whole of the country will mourn, but not his own daughter."

The doctor barked again, "Colonel Randolph!"

All that escaped me was a tiny keening sound. And my husband's face twisted in feigned concern. "Don't you see, doctor? She can't cry. My wife must be suffering from a morbid condition. Won't you prescribe some medicine to cure her?"

The outraged physician said, "The medicine she needs is *quiet*, sir."

The admonishment did nothing to dissuade Tom. In fact, a maniacal grin broke over his face. "*Quiet*? Oh, yes, by all means, give her quiet. All the country will be firing cannons, tolling bells, and wailing in grief, but Martha will quietly go on. She'll quietly persevere. She has ice water for blood—"

"*Enough*, Tom," I finally said, all the emptiness my father had left filling up with a terrible rage. That my husband had descended into madness was without question. But I was sure to follow him there if I let this go on today, of all days.

"You don't tell me what's enough." Then he began working the muscles of his face, spasming and contracting them, as if to manufacture the sudden tears that swept down his cheeks. "I know you won't mourn me when I'm dead, but I thought you might be able to muster a tear for the only man you really loved." Tom sobbed, howling as if to mock me. "And I loved him. He was my father, too, and I loved him."

"You hated him," Jeff snarled, having come out of the house with a bang of the door to encounter this scene. "You hated my grandfather in life and you neglected him in death. You're only here to harangue my mother like some scavenging beast over the corpse. You're more ferocious than a wolf and more fell than a hyena!"

Jeff put himself between his father and me. The other boys drove my husband off, but I knew he'd be back again for the funeral. It was open to the public, so we couldn't keep him away. I knew there'd be talk, whether because my lunatic husband was absent or because he was there. There was nothing for it. And I was scarcely sensible enough to care. My world was shattered. The loss I felt unfathomable. And it wasn't just my own loss, for my father belonged to the people, perhaps now more than ever.

The bells had tolled for my father's death, and the towns-people closed the city. Donning black armbands, they formed a processional up the mountain that was delayed by the rain. While we waited for people to arrive on the dismal and dreary day, Sally and I stood on either side of the open grave, Papa's coffin between us, held up on planks.

Huddling with her enslaved family against the rain, Sally wore a plain black dress with the locket my father had given her long ago, her eyes trained not on the coffin but on me. She must've known her fate now rested in my hands, but there was nothing servile in her expression. Only an expectation of justice.

She seemed to believe herself a free woman and didn't lower her eyes in deference. Not even for Tom when he appeared to taunt us. "Here are his two widows . . . and neither of them shed-ding a tear."

In that moment, I wished Tom straight to hell and believe Sally did the same.

"Let's start," Jeff finally said, fearing my husband wanted wit-nesses to cause a scene. He wasn't wrong. Tom quarreled with him that we ought to delay on account of the rain, then held him-self over Papa's coffin, wailing in affected grief while I looked on like a statue in the driving rain.

"You've got a heart of stone," Tom shouted at me.

But his words didn't pierce me. He was right. Until that moment, I believed my heart was flesh and blood like any other. But my heart *had* turned to stone.

The sky itself might cry, but I wouldn't. My tears, when they came—if they came—wouldn't be for Tom. All my life I'd held back my tears. For my father's sanity, for his reputation, and now for his legacy. However much I wished for release, for a moment to feel the loss, no one would ever see me fall to pieces. No one would ever see that.

Certainly not Tom Randolph.

So I endured his taunts.

I endured the shoveling of dirt over my father's grave.

And I endured the silence that followed.

Our silence. Our special silence.

Others would suffer, truly suffer, for what my father hadn't said in his lifetime. But I'd always divined his wishes in that silence, and could hear his words echoing in it even now. And those words were:

Take care of me when I'm dead.

Chapter Forty-two

Farewell my dear, my loved daughter, Adieu!
The last pang of life is in parting from you!
Two Seraphs await me, long shrouded in death:
I will bear them your love on my last parting breath.

THIS IS HIS LAST LETTER.

I read it often, wondering sometimes if he left one like it for Sally. If there are letters, tokens, evidence . . . well, she has good reason to keep them quiet.

Along with the linens, the artwork, the furniture, and the rest of the slaves at Monticello, she's been priced for auction. Her value has been set at fifty dollars. But she won't be sold with everything else.

On the night we buried my father, we faced one another in Papa's chambers and she gave me the keys she'd claimed as her own for decades. She surrendered to me her dominion over my father's private sanctuary . . . and her place in his life.

She hadn't bargained for her freedom in France, only for the freedom of her children.

But she *will* have her freedom. I'll see to that. I'll let her walk off this mountain like Harriet and Beverly did. She'll be given her time.

And her silence is the price.

I make Jeff swear upon God and country and his honor as a Virginia gentleman and upon his grandfather's honor, too, that Sally will not be sold. He doesn't ask me why; my son knows better than to ask. I wouldn't tell him the truth, anyway. If it comes to it, I will lie about Sally to my deathbed.

But in exchange for Jeff's vow, he demands that I make one of my own. I must agree not to witness the rest of the slaves being auctioned off at Monticello.

I feel as if I should be there. As if I must witness the final destruction of everything. As if I need to see every tear as my father's people are ripped away from their mountain, from the only home they've ever known. I ought to hear their sobbing as the auctioneer calls out their worth. . . .

But Jeff says, "It's making you sick."

"I am sick now, but shall be well again." Because I have to be. My work—my father's work—remains undone. And as with Ann's death, I must hold myself together until I've finished doing for my father the very last thing that I can do for him in this world.

Jeff puts a hand on my shoulder. "Spare yourself the bitter anguish of seeing his abode rendered desolate, the walls dismantled, and his bedroom violated by the auctioneer. And take the children before my father snatches them from you."

Perhaps he fears that in my grief, I'll become as unhinged as his father. Whereas what I fear is his father. I am uniquely vulnerable to Tom as I never was before in our marriage. I am his wife, and he has dominion over me, without having to answer to Thomas Jefferson. His conduct at the funeral is proof enough of his intentions. He will come for me now, either to claim me or tear the children away.

The law would say I must submit to him. The scriptures command it. But I do not wait to lower my head meekly and do what is expected of me. Not after all I've seen and lived through. No. I do not stay to see the slave auction and wait for the whirlwind of Tom's wrath to come down on my head.

Instead, I pack up the children swiftly, and take them to Boston. There are no slaves in Boston.

"There's more housewifery to do because the servants are unreliable," Ellen complains, showing me about her luxurious new home on Beacon Hill. "They're lazy because they know they can leave any time for better wages or any reason at all. Why, I've gone through three cooks in the past six months. But I cannot wish to ever return to a slave state."

"You should *never*." I catch myself by surprise with my vehemence. "Land and Negroes in Virginia are to nine persons out of ten certain ruin and a vexation of the spirit that wearies one of life itself."

And I *am* weary of life. I've really suffered so much that I cannot comprehend the possibility of better days. Consumed by despair, every morning is a struggle to get out of bed. I do it for the people yet depending on me, while I depend upon Ellen.

She does everything in her power to cheer me. She shows me the city, which has grown enormously since I was here with my father as a little girl. Everywhere I look now is perfect luxury and wealth. The stately homes, though all squeezed together, are unimaginably well furnished. In Ellen's house, I wash my feet each morning in a plain basin that cost at least thirty dollars, and the water's deep enough I might take a swim. The dining table glitters with cut glass and silver. And surrounded by such wealth, I'm consumed with guilt for the discomfort in which I left the rest of my family at Monticello.

We celebrate Christmas with trips to the theater and visits. Ellen arranges a party in an oval drawing room with paintings, silk damask curtains, and carved mahogany chairs. We dine on oysters and lobsters and other bounties of the sea. There's ice cream and every variety of cake in silver baskets. And people keep asking how it is that my father, remembered for his responsible management of the nation's finances, could have died in penury and embarrassment.

And I always reply, "His public virtue was the cause, if you should call that an embarrassment. I never shall be ashamed of an honorable poverty. It's the price we've paid for a long and useful life devoted to the service of this country."

Ellen owlishly watches my every move, so I smile for her sake. Until my father's debts are extinguished, I have no income but the monies earned by my servants, who have all hired themselves out in Virginia. Their wages won't be enough. Until a sale of my father's papers can be arranged, I'm now, like Nancy Randolph once was, utterly at the mercy of my relations and their goodwill. So I don't dare object when Ellen's husband enrolls Septimia and George in school. The children behave well enough there; it's only when they return home that they give themselves over to *the Randolph*, bickering like children who have no reason to know how precarious our circumstances are.

My older children know.

When it becomes clear that the lottery will be canceled, Cornelia writes bitterly, "It's over, then. After sixty years of devoted services, his children are left in beggary by the country to whom he had bequeathed them."

Ellen impresses upon me that I have no choice but to stay in Boston. "Live with us. You and the children together. My husband rented a place for you in Cambridge so as not to crowd this house. We'll send for Mary and Cornelia and see them married off well."

It's a generous offer, but it makes me uneasy to be a burden to Ellen's husband, who is already worrying about overcrowding the house. Ellen mistakes my hesitation, holding tight to my hand: "I know it pains you to leave Virginia, but I fear there are no ties which should bind any descendants of Thomas Jefferson to the state any longer."

She's echoing the sentiments of my sister's son Francis. Polly's precious boy wrote with bitterness over our plight, arguing that the liberality and generosity and patriotism of the Old Dominion has vanished under the influence of *Yankee* notions and practices.

But I don't blame the Yankees.

The lottery, grudgingly approved, was the only thing Virginia offered my father in his waning days. But the northern states raised money. Donations came from New York, Baltimore, and Philadelphia . . . where William still lives.

William sent money—tried to, anyway. But these and all donations Papa refused, out of pride or fear that it'd undermine the lottery.

I burned William's letter of condolence, filled as it was with tender sentiments and an unwise insistence that I visit him. I don't trust myself to see him. I'm so unmoored of everything but grief, I don't trust myself or my virtue. And my virtue must be pristine. For my father's reputation—and what is imputed to it by mine—is an asset I use shamelessly.

In the outpouring of national grief over my father's death, I see that Tom is given a public employment. Hopefully an income will restore my husband to his right mind.

More importantly, it will keep him away.

~

Milton, 6 August 1827
From Thomas Mann Randolph to Septimia Randolph

I have loved your mother, and only her, with all my faculties for thirty-five years next December. I wish to spend some happy years yet, in the decline of life, with her.

I am always reading letters now. My father's to me. Mine to him. His to everyone else. Letters from his friends. Condolences. Tributes. Poems. And now I'm reading another letter, having nothing to do with my father at all.

A letter from Tom expressing his wishes to reconcile.

I linger over the part where he writes he has loved me and *only me*. On its surface, a tender sentiment. But I know it's also an accusation. I loved Tom, but not only Tom. Not ever. And I feel no regret for that. Especially because Tom's declaration is to guard himself against divorce.

My son-in-law Mr. Coolidge explains, "I'm sorry to inform you that even in Boston the only grounds for divorce are consanguinity, bigamy, impotence, and adultery. None of which apply, I assume." I flush, shamed to even be discussing it, but he continues, "On the other hand, you may obtain a legal separation for cruelty or desertion."

Tom has certainly been cruel. And I'd argue that he deserted me—that he always deserted me—in times of need. But it's equally true that I've deserted him. I fled to Boston in the darkest hours of my grief, and now, there must be an accounting for it. "Tom will want to see his children and I can't keep them from him forever."

He would take them from me forever, if I tried.

Ellen's husband replies in his cool, flat Boston accent. "You can keep the children from Mr. Randolph for a few years at least. Then they'll be too old for him to force to his will. Unless there are grounds for legal separation, there must simply be a separation of miles. Even if Mr. Randolph comes for the children, I can see to it that they're hidden away at some distance where he can't get them into his hands."

There seems something immoral about this scheme. As well as impractical. I married the man and gave him children. The law puts me completely in his power even though he's destitute.

As if sensing my hesitation, my son-in-law says, gruffly, "You needn't fear him. From what I hear, Mr. Randolph is holed up miserably in a little house with much liquor and without a second blanket for his bed. Nicholas Trist will keep him from Monticello, and I'll keep him from here."

Far from alleviating my fears, this strikes me as profoundly unjust. Tom barred from Monticello, as unwelcome there as he was at Tuckahoe? Monticello is, until we can find a buyer for it, my home. And if it's mine, it must also be my husband's. That was always my father's intention. It was our vow to Tom, implicit and explicit.

"I cannot countenance abandoning Mr. Randolph to poverty," I finally say.

"Then he'll take your money," is my son-in-law's harsh reply.

In honor of Papa, the states of Louisiana and South Carolina have voted me $20,000 in bank stocks for my upkeep—not enough to save Monticello, but perhaps enough to support those who depend upon me. It's a generosity I hadn't solicited but which makes me the target of opponents who think me unworthy, as my father wasn't a soldier and I wasn't his widow.

I suppose they believe I've done nothing, and meant nothing, to this country.

It's a sentiment that has made me redouble my efforts to edit my father's papers. And it's made me think hard upon my own character. "So long as property is vested in me, and Tom is destitute, I must make some effort for his support."

"Surely you aren't thinking of returning to live as his wife," my son-in-law replies. "He can make no mischief for you or the children in Boston, but I can't keep that animal away from you in Virginia."

Ellen winces, carefully turning her head so her husband doesn't see how calling her father an *animal* causes her distress. Whether it's for love or shame, I cannot say.

I suppose I must now be beyond both love and shame. What matters now are my children, my grandchildren, and my slaves.

There's an option that my son-in-law hasn't considered.

One I learned from my father.

Negotiation.

And I'm my own best ambassador.

So in the spring of 1828, I return to Virginia and step into the now dilapidated white house in Milton to find my husband drunk and unkempt in the middle of the day. "Patsy?" Tom asks, squinting at my appearance in the doorway, as if I were a hallucination.

I want to be angry. I want to remember that this is the man who destroyed himself with resentments. The man who struck me and beat my children. The man who tormented me at my father's funeral. But when he tries to get up from a threadbare chair and his knees nearly buckle under him, I'm nearly undone with sorrow to see the ruin of him.

I'm shocked by the sight of him, so pale and haggard. Truly shocked. He's so emaciated I cannot think he's had a meal in weeks. Why hasn't anyone told me how very ill he is?

"Don't stand," I say, helping him back to his chair before he falls.

Clutching my arm, Tom barks, "Why have you come?"

"I've come to have a frank discussion." I hurry forth with the rest, taking advantage of his astonished speechlessness. "I can see that you're cold and hungry and suffering. You haven't a proper bath. And though you've come to this sorry state through your own stubbornness, understand that I'd never willingly leave you in poverty so long as I have a shilling in the world."

"*My* stubbornness?" Tom says, eyes bulging. "What of your son—"

"You must give up this hatred of your own flesh and blood," I insist, strangely unafraid. Then again, what can Tom do to me? He's as weak as a newborn babe. "Or do you want us to remember you the way we remember your father?"

Tom's once-beautiful mouth thins. "That's all you want?"

"That's where it must start, Tom. If we come to an agreement, we may all reside together at Monticello until such time as it's sold away. It's an unfurnished place now, but it's better than keeping rats for friends, as you must be here."

"What are you saying, Martha?"

"I'm saying that I want you to come home to your family. Of

course, given your unsocial habits and hatred for the necessary restraints of civilized life, I assume you'd prefer a little establishment of your own on some sequestered spot of Monticello."

He takes the opportunity I've given him to save face, but a bit too far, as always. "I'd live entirely in my own room, making no part of the family and receiving nothing from it in any way whatever."

"As you like." Though I'll insist he take food.

Tom's eyes narrow. "What about Short?"

No. I will not discuss William. "It's better for both of us to drop a curtain over the past. There's enough warmth of heart between us to live in harmony, Tom. But upon such subjects as we cannot agree, we must be silent."

He nods. And it's enough.

Truthfully, seeing him in such a state, he could've refused all my terms, and it would still have been enough. Because I realize even before my daughters and I get him settled into the north pavilion, that he's afflicted by more than hunger. He complains of stomach pains and gout, and is so meek and softened of temper that I think he must be dying.

My daughter Ginny is a disapproving sentinel at the door. "Mother, your children shall have a right to interfere if things between you return to their former state. He won't be allowed to disturb your rest."

"I'm not tired or in need of rest," I say, because after two years of grieving for my father I'm finally awakening. I said that I was sick but would be well again, and now it's come to pass.

Would that Tom were as fortunate.

I see to it that my husband has food and blankets and healthful teas and medicines to ease his pain. I sit by his bedside hour upon hour, day after day, reminiscing about the good times, of which we can both recount surprisingly many.

One morning Tom's eyes, bleak and teary, meet mine. "Did you love me, Patsy? Did you ever?"

"Oh, I did." I'm heartbroken by how easily the admission falls from my lips now. "The young man who told me he preferred trees stripped bare of their leaves and kissed me so passionately in a schoolhouse; the young husband who tried to coax a slave girl's infant to suck at a cloth soaked in milk; the man who rode so hard, worked himself sick in the fields, fought for his country, and wrote poems to his daughters. Yes, I loved you, Tom Randolph." My throat tightens and tears—real tears—roll down my cheeks. "I loved you truly and deeply."

As if he's been waiting for my tears his whole life, Tom reaches out and touches the wetness, smooths it with the pad of his thumb. "Oh, Patsy. My adored wife."

He weeps.

We weep together.

And when we're done, he says, "Send for Jeff. I cannot die without making friends with him, cannot leave him in anguish as my father left me."

My heart fills at that. Jeff comes straightaway. My husband asks for my son's forgiveness, and my tall, upright boy has the heart to give it. Tom has kind words for me and the children and the grandchildren. We nurse him, stroke his hair, hold his hands. His daughters surround the bed, fanning him of his fever during the day and his sons through the night.

Tom gives some strange directions about his shrouding and burial, then takes them back, fearing they'll confirm the idea that he's insane. And he looks to me, a bit fearfully, as he asks to be buried not at Tuckahoe with his kin and his own father but with *my* father at the head of his tombstone.

"It's only fitting," I tell him, moved by this final request, even though I know it will put Tom eternally in the shadow of my father's monument, as he was all his life.

Then Tom begs for Jeff to stay with him in his dying hours.

All I want is for his suffering to end and for him to die in peace with everybody. Which is just what he does, on the twentieth of June, without a struggle or a moan.

My sons must dig the grave because my father's people have been sold off. I'm told the auction at Monticello was no less heartrending than the sacking of an ancient city with children wailing and women rending their garments. And I feel as if I hear the echo of their anguish here.

They're all long gone except for Burwell, who continues from habit to tidy the empty house. Sally and her sons live in Charlottesville now, so I know better than to look for her at the grave site. But once we bury Tom and make the slow walk home past Mulberry Row, my eyes drift to her old cabin, as if I expect to see her standing in the doorway in her apron, those amber eyes saying: "*Now it's done. We've both buried our husbands now.*"

And so we have.

Every unkind feeling has been buried, too.

No longer an object of terror or apprehension, Tom became one of deep sympathy. But the bonds of affection were so much weakened by the events of the last years of his life, that after the first burst of grief is over, we cannot but acknowledge that all is for the best.

Returning health would've brought with it the same passions and jealousies. *The Randolph* was quite beyond his control. It would've poisoned our family and our memory of him. His peace and good end is Tom's legacy. I'm afraid he has no other.

The whole of his possessions amount to some six hundred dollars' worth of books and a twenty-dollar horse. And it's left to Ellen to write an epitaph for him:

THOMAS MANN RANDOLPH, OF TUCKAHOE VIRGINIA.
BORN 1768. DIED JUNE 20, 1828.
HE WAS A MAN OF TALENT AND OF LEARNING.
CHARITABLE TO THE POOR.
A GOOD SON TO HIS MOTHER, AND A
KIND FATHER TO HIS DAUGHTERS.
"NO FARTHER SEEK HIS MERITS TO DISCLOSE,
OR DRAW HIS FRAILTIES FROM THEIR DREAD ABODE."

A fair and fitting tribute.

I know of only one way to do him the basic justice Papa and I always wished him to have. Tom will be remembered, almost entirely I think, through his letters to my father, and my father's letters to him.

Of which I will shape every word.

Chapter Forty-three

Monticello, 1829
From Martha Jefferson Randolph
to Ellen Randolph Coolidge

We are at present engaged in a business that precludes
work, writing and reading of every kind but the one: revis-
ing and correcting the copies of the manuscripts.

THIS IS THE LAST LETTER I'll write from Monticello.
It's now a house of ghosts, dark and dilapidated with
age and neglect. Bare trees loom like skeletal fingers in the
yard, all pointing toward the heavens, where my father and his
angels surely now reside. The hall, once filled with statues and
natural curiosities, is empty but for a single bust of my father.
Bare walls once covered with paintings and a defaced floor no
longer polished to a high sheen open into the once gay and splendid drawing room, now comfortless.

And yet, Monticello is still an attraction for tourists. A vulgar
herd of strangers has stomped over the gardens, taking away my
choicest flower roots, my yellow jasmines, fig bushes, grapevines,
and everything and anything they fancy.

I feel like a spirit of the place that has survived the death of its
body, now deprived of even its purpose in going on because my
father's papers are ready to publish.

On the day the work is done, I somehow rouse myself from a
cold bed to watch the last wagonload of books and papers packed

into crates to be shipped away for sale. There will be no ground-breaking, no bugles blowing, no commemoration dinners for this patriotic monument. But I perceive in it an achievement.

More than an achievement. A triumph. A secret triumph.

For years now—sometimes for eight to ten hours a day—I've scoured every letter, every record book, every receipt and scrap of paper in my father's possession. I've burned some. In other instances, I took a razor to cut words away, just as my father once cut away what he believed to be untrue in the Bible. Eventually I entrusted the political letters to my daughters, whose eyes were better suited to such work, and kept the personal letters for myself. In the end, the collection will bear my son's name as editor, but the work is mine.

And I feel both gratified and damned by it.

I must leave Monticello now, and I feel an unbearable sadness, such that I might be better off to lie down and die. After all, I cannot feel at home or happy anywhere else. And when I think of what might be done with the place—that it might be transformed into an inn or a boardinghouse—it seems like profaning a temple. I'd rather the weeds and wild animals that are fast taking possession of the grounds should grow and live in the house itself than see my father's home turned into a tavern.

Indeed, there's a part of me that might be gladdened by the sight of the house wrapped in flames, every vestige of it swept from the top of the mountain.

I'm there on the terrace, watching the men load up the wagon, wondering where I might get a torch to set Monticello ablaze, when I hear the jingle of a carriage coming up the road. More marauders, no doubt, come to chip off a piece of red brick from the house or snatch away a broken rail as a keepsake.

I don't turn to greet them. My eyes are for the men who lift each crate of my father's papers, as I warn them with crossed arms and an unfeminine scowl that their cargo is precious.

"Patsy, you're going to catch your death, standing here in the cold."

The voice pulls me from my dark thoughts. I know it intimately. And I turn to see a face at once familiar, beloved, and impossible. *"William?"*

"I didn't mean to startle you." He tucks a top hat under his arm, taking in a deep breath of cold mountain air. "Did you really think you'd never see me again?"

In truth, I was sure I'd never see him again, and now I half wonder if he is only the conjuring of a mind bent with secrets and sadness.

"You're shivering." He removes his long dark coat with its high shawl collar and wraps it around my shoulders. The warm brush of his hands against my neck nearly convinces me he's here.

"I—I cannot invite you in to sit, Mr. Short, for there are no chairs. We close up today. Why have you come all the way from Philadelphia?" He cannot want a memento, though I'd find something to give him if he does, for he has as much right to a token of Thomas Jefferson as any man alive. "You cannot still have business in the area."

"Urgent business," he says, with a meaningful stare. "I'm told there's an effort afoot to purchase Monticello for you, Patsy."

After all our struggles, there's some chance to keep Monticello? I'm afraid to believe it. There've been too many false hopes. "But who—"

"It isn't important who. What's important is that I've come to put a stop to it."

I can make no sense of this whatsoever. It's hard enough to credit that I have an anonymous benefactor, but nearly impossible to believe William would stand in the way of anyone helping me. Have I finally turned him so thoroughly against me?

It's been years since, in tearful confessions of love and longing, we said our good-byes. But now he's here again, to witness my violent parting from this place. Has he come to take some pleasure in it?

No, I cannot think it of him. "But you were behind the donations from Philadelphia," I murmur, remembering the receipts I found in my father's papers. "Money in your own name and more than that, too."

His eyes fall to his feet. "Not enough, it would seem."

"Much more than was expected of you . . . or Philadelphia for that matter. I'm sometimes left to wonder why my father's own Virginia, which has most benefited by his talents and virtues, has given him a grave, and left others to give bread to his children. And now all he built here will crumble to dust."

"So what if it does?" William asks.

I startle, thinking I've misheard. But the grim line of his mouth tells me that I haven't. And I'm appalled. "You cannot mean that. I cannot believe that you, of all people—"

"This house isn't your father's greatest work. This is a *plantation*. And it ought to be abandoned, for it was, even at its height of beauty, built on ugliness—"

"How *dare* you," I say, wanting to slap him.

Am I fated to have the men I've loved torment me in my weakest moments? Tears sting the corners of my eyes, my heart hammering painfully beneath my breast. Much as it did all those years ago when he confronted my father in the woods.

And William is no less relentless now.

His words run over mine. "This is a place impractical and cruel—"

"And you, who were a guest here and enjoyed its benefits!"

He doesn't dignify my accusation with an answer.

"He isn't here, Patsy," William says, taking my arms.

"How can you say that?" Emotion nearly strangles me. "He's here, all around, his hand in everything—"

"He's gone. This isn't his home anymore. And it's not your home, either. It's a set of chains."

His words reach me in places I have never let anyone reach. In places inside me that I don't even let myself touch. They recall to me a vivid memory of my childhood and a rider who came up this mountain to warn: *Leave Monticello now or find yourself in chains.*

And William was there. He was there from the start. And so was I.

I want to strike him, pound my fists upon his chest. And I do raise my fists to strike him, but my agony of spirit leaves me only the strength to lay them on his chest as I howl with anguish. And for the first time since my father's death, or perhaps even longer than that, I fall to pieces. In truth, I fall forward, into William's arms, crying tears I dared not shed until the day I finished editing my father's letters.

And now that I've done it, I have not even duty to hold me up.

Lowering me to the stairs before I collapse, William whispers, "Abandon this place. I beg of you."

My tears burst forth like a broken dam, first a trickle, then a pouring, and I scarcely recognize the sounds that come from me. I weep for the loss of my husband. For my children. For my sister and her babies. For Sally's children, too. And I finally weep for my mother, whom I was too frightened to cry for when she died.

I cry the unshed tears of a lifetime until I am quaking and limp and so frail I don't think I can rise ever again.

"Let me take you from here," William whispers, his forehead pressed to mine. "It will be better for you. I promise you, it will be better for you to get free of it. It's the only way you can be happy."

Be happy. That's what I want for you.

My mother spoke those words to me when she asked me to watch over my father. But somehow I forgot them. That command was swallowed up in the enormity of my dedication to my father. But now Papa is gone and my vow has been discharged . . . all except for that.

Be happy.

Remembering my mother's words, the ache somehow eases, in the contemplation of leaving Monticello. "Where will I go?"

"Anywhere you please."

I don't know where I would go. I don't know what would please me . . . because I've never before asked. *This* is the first time I can, the first time I've ever allowed myself to even consider it. And I can't help but marvel at embracing my father's beloved ideal of self-determination for the first time . . . at the age of fifty-six.

And as a woman at that.

For now, all I know is that I wish to leave with William Short. Somehow I find within myself the strength to rise. We walk together from the terrace. At first, my steps are bent and painful. But the farther I walk, the less I feel the pull. Mindful of the cold muck on my feet, I straighten like the Amazon William always said I was.

Like the Amazon I am.

William hooks his little finger into mine, guiding me toward his carriage—but I pass it by. I look back once, then not again. I want to walk from this place.

I want to run.

Epilogue

Washington, 7 February 1830
From Andrew Jackson to Martha Jefferson Randolph

The President of the United States thanks Mrs. Randolph for the cane she had the goodness to present him with feelings of deep sensibility, as a testimonial of her esteem, derived from the venerated hands of her father.

I LIVE NOW IN WASHINGTON CITY with my daughter Ginny and her husband, who has taken a clerkship in the Jackson administration. We live in a rented two-story house with an excellent kitchen, beautiful fireplaces, and a large cheerful room for me where I keep my dressing table, a sewing table, portraits of Papa, and the coverlet under which he slept, which now warms me at night.

We live only two blocks from the President's House, which has been rebuilt since the war. It's now inhabited by Andrew Jackson, whose riotous inauguration has scandalized my lady friends. They've all warned of the new administration's vulgarity.

Nevertheless, I'm thunderstruck when I am summoned down the stairs one morning to find the president of the United States in the parlor.

"Madam," he says, with a courtly bow.

Though I've known personally five of the six presidents before him, I'm somewhat awed by the craggy-faced war hero turned populist politician. "Mr. President," I say, curtseying before I think better of it. "You must be here for my son-in-law."

"To the contrary, I've come to call upon the sole surviving daughter of Thomas Jefferson," Andrew Jackson says, as if *he* were in some awe of *me*. "Would you do me the honor of sitting for a spell, Mrs. Randolph?"

We find a sunny spot at the front of the house, overlooking the streets of the now bustling capital, filled as it is with shops and the comforts of a thriving city.

And no sooner have I congratulated him upon his election than does he say, "I need you, Mrs. Randolph."

"I can't imagine what you might need from an old woman."

He throws his head back and laughs. "Next to me, you're a young lady!"

Though he can't be much older, it becomes a small joke. He encourages me to call him an old gentleman. And finally at ease, I say, "Whatever you need, I'll be happy to give it if it's in my power."

"What I need is a woman more worthy than my niece, who has failed me utterly as first lady. I need a woman of tender sentiment who will prevent the harpies in this town from shunning the wives of my cabinet members."

He must be speaking of the notorious Peggy Eaton, wife of his secretary of war, John Henry Eaton, whom the ladies of Washington will not receive because they believe she was a tavern whore. "Nasty bit of slander," Jackson says. "The kind of thing that killed my dear wife. I'd rather have vermin on my back than the tongue of one of these Washington women on my reputation. There's nothing I can do to stop their pettiness. But you're one of the worthiest women in America, deserving of honors long overdue. I'd like to have you at the White House at the seat of honor beside me."

"Why, sir, I'm beyond flattered." With that, I cheerfully agree.

My swift assent sends his eyebrows up, his eyes wrinkling with happy surprise. "You've no scruples against Mrs. Eaton's attendance?"

There isn't a speck of anything but sympathy inside me for the women of public men. "I look very much forward to meeting her." And I look forward to blasting anyone who takes pleasure from the pain of such women.

A feral glint comes to his smile, and he takes a small pouch from his pocket, digging out some tobacco to chew, as if he means to stay a while. I think he'll ask me to tell him stories of my father—but he asks my opinions. He becomes my friend and ally, from that moment on. *I* am his standard-bearer of Jeffersonian democracy. He has my unwavering support for the primacy of the union over the rights of the states, and I don't mind that he wields me like a silk-clad sword against the ladies of Washington.

I am, after all, now the Grand Dame of the place.

The ladies will find it difficult to shun anyone I embrace, as I'm now regarded as a paragon of virtue. So formidable is my reputation that even John Randolph of Roanoke must praise me as the *sweetest woman in Virginia.*

I'm not in Virginia anymore, of course. And I am grateful for it. Virginia is stained now in the blood of Nat Turner's slave rebellion and consumed with terror that whites will be murdered in their beds. My son Jeff is an unflinching advocate of abolition. In the tradition of his father and grandfather, he's introduced legislation to remove the evil by emancipating slaves. But I'm sure this will destroy his future in politics, just as it destroyed his father's. The mean spirit of jealousy will win out and, in anticipation of that day, I've concluded that Virginia is no place for the family of Thomas Jefferson. Virginia's glory is gone. But *our* glory, I think, is returned. Here in the capital, the seat of liberty my father built, his family thrives.

"Do you have a smile for me, Mother?" It's my son Lewis, bedecked in green coat and cap, complete with bow and arrow. He has a government clerkship, but tonight he's Robin Hood at a costume ball at the rebuilt White House, where everything is a cherished reminder to me.

There is my dear father's cabinet . . . his favorite sitting room . . .

My unmarried daughters swirl past in gay colors as varied as nature; they are popular in the capital. Ginny's husband, whom William Short has taken under his wing, is to become the new American consul to Cuba. My son Ben is to graduate from his grandfather's university as a doctor. George has become a naval officer. I'm a very proud mother.

At the costume ball, near the dance floor, I spy the notorious Mrs. Eaton, at whom I'm sure to smile. Not far from the embattled woman is a senator who has sought my support for his legislation, and I escape him by turning to the punch bowl.

It is by this happenstance, as I reach for the refreshment, that I come face-to-face with a beautiful woman whose piercing blue eyes stop me where I stand.

My father's eyes.

I see through her mask. Through the palest amber sheen of her freckled hand, bejeweled as it is with a wedding ring, I know her at once, and she knows me, too.

We stand there, a breath apart, until Harriet Hemings begins to tremble.

Strolling to my side, the president asks unwittingly, "Are you ladies acquainted?"

Then he introduces Harriet to me by another name.

In terror of discovery, Sally's daughter cannot seem to speak, and on an impulse, I reach for her hand, squeezing it in soft reassurance and encouragement, bound as we are by a singular secret. "Mr. President," I say. "You're so attentive, someone may think you're courting me!"

"What if I were?" Jackson asks, loud enough that everyone may hear. "After all, I'm the president and you're America's First Daughter."

The guests all laugh at his wordplay, and I flush with triumph at this acknowledgment. It's a victory as complete as I could ever ask for, tainted only by the bittersweet stare of my secret sister behind her mask.

For if I'm America's daughter, *so is she.* . . .

⁓

WILLIAM AND I CANNOT MARRY because I promised Tom I'd never take another husband. Nor can we live in scandal. But at our age, who could censure our private visits?

Especially when I travel so often as to never rouse suspicion. I've been to Washington, New York, Boston. Why not Philadelphia?

When I go there, William and I stroll together the cobblestone streets I've not seen since I was a girl, and my heart fills to brimming at the constancy of his heart. But in other matters, he has changed. "I thought you believed that the races should commingle?" I ask.

"I do. But I fear that whites will never allow freed slaves to achieve equality here," he says, explaining his latest philanthropic efforts for the colonization of an African nation called Liberia. He's still struggling with the sin that taints our founding, and I still struggle, too. Though I know I have no right to sacrifice the happiness of a fellow creature, black or white, and I try to do right by all the people in my care, the truth remains that I am a slaveholder, even still, and will probably be until the day I die. It must tarnish me in his eyes, but I feel as if our sparring helps me do better.

When we're alone, he presses a fond kiss to my brow. "You must have your portrait made before you leave to visit your daughter in Boston. I'd like for everyone to see you so clear-eyed, so pragmatic, your father's traits in the planes of your face."

"Who would want such a portrait? And think of the expense," I complain.

But he won't hear of it, and before the visit is over, I'm painted for posterity. William observes the final portrait with approval.

"Your eyes are sparkling, your color heightened, and your whole countenance lit up!"

Ginny agrees. "Mama, I had no idea the attentions of an artist would do you such good."

It is not the attentions of the artist, but of William Short, that have invigorated me. The touch of his hand when we dine alone, the candlelight so soft I could almost mistake him for the young son of liberty in France . . . and the darkness of another, kinder alcove bed, where two sweethearts from an imaginary painting long ago finally find their happiness.

But further recollections of this kind are not to be written or spoken of or mused about while my daughter looks on, oblivious. Like my father, I, too, have a secret passion in my old age. Stolen kisses. Clandestine assignations. Love letters that are burnt after they are read.

For our love belongs to William and me alone.

And it is a love that endures.

William reads my mind, a smile of complicit mischief upon his aging face, his eyes still twinkling. "You must be looking forward to your adventure, Mrs. Randolph."

Indeed I am. For I'm to travel, for the first time, upon a railway train. It is a marvelous invention. A machine of such power and potential my father would've wanted to know the workings of it from the engine to the smallest gear. And on his behalf, I'm more excited to see it than I was to see air balloons as a child.

William goes with us as far as Providence, where my children and I crowd together in a little car by the train engine. As the fire is fed and the roar of the machine begins, I wave to William on the platform, which is draped in flags of red, white, and blue.

Then sparks fly through the air and burn little holes in my dress where they land. And I don't care, because they look to me like fireworks bursting in celebration of our American Independence, and I'm exhilarated with the possibility and promise of our extraordinary journey.

Note from the Authors

MARTHA "PATSY" JEFFERSON RANDOLPH'S relationship with her father, the third president of the United States, not only defined her life but also shaped the identity of our nation. For nearly everything we know of the author of our independence is what she let pass to us in posterity.

She came of age in a time of war. Colonial girls of her age and social station scarcely left the plantation, but she accompanied her father across the country and to foreign shores. At a time when women were dissuaded from involvement in politics, her father made her witness to two revolutions and the secret torments of the men who fought them.

Intelligent, highly educated, and fiercely loyal, she lived an extraordinary life of her own, while defending her father's legacy. And in his shadow, she became one of the most quietly influential women in American history. We wanted to write that history through her eyes, ever mindful that it would be biased in favor of her father and his politics. Knowing, too, that her perspective would be as flawed as she was. For what Patsy likely believed to be acts of family loyalty or even patriotism can be seen now in a much more troubling light.

At the time of this writing, the Thomas Jefferson Foundation and most historians believe that given the weight of the historical evidence—including DNA testing—Jefferson fathered the children of Sally Hemings. If true, it's all but impossible that Jefferson's daughter didn't know about it.

And if she knew, a very different picture emerges.

A picture painted in this book.

A picture only hinted at in her famous portrait by Thomas Sully—the one she posed for at the end of this story.

In her time, Patsy was known as a conventional woman of perfect temper, but our research revealed her to be as complicated a heroine as any writer could wish for. She was a privileged, passive-aggressive, morally conflicted, gritty survivor with a facile relationship with the truth. She was also heroically devoted and capable of both enormous compassion and sacrifice. Her contradictions captivated us, and we hope you enjoyed reading the story she inspired.

Now, to the explanation of the choices we made.

~

WE COULDN'T HAVE INVENTED William Short if he didn't exist. A political acolyte who was present at the most crucial junctures in the president's life, and also carried on a doomed romance with Jefferson's daughter? A man of radically progressive ideals for his time who challenged his mentor on matters of race and equality?

No one would have believed it.

But the romantic relationship has a basis in history, as explained by Patsy's biographer, Cynthia Kierner. We did not have to invent William's gallantry in procuring a miniature of Jefferson for Patsy, nor even William's request to keep his involvement secret. Nor did we have to invent William's indecorously frequent visits to Patsy at the convent in her father's absence. Marie Botidoux believed that William was still in love with Patsy even after she left France, and we adopted that view.

Though the seriousness and duration of this romance is not known, nor even if Jefferson was aware of it, the remarkable frequency with which William Short's life intersected Patsy's at crucial junctions is astonishing. Short was reportedly there when her family fled Monticello. He was there in Paris, where their flirtation began. He was present when the Sally Hemings scandal broke. He visited Monticello just prior to the final destruction of Patsy's marriage. And he was apparently involved in discouraging anyone from buying Monticello for her once it was put up for sale. Consequently, we've romanticized him for dramatic purposes and assumed that theirs was a very long love story.

Of course, when it comes to the personal lives of the Jefferson family, much *must* be assumed.

The Jefferson family papers were edited for posterity—a laborious family project. The letters they chose to share with the public are fascinating. But from what they held back or destroyed, much can also be discerned. With predictable regularity, letters missing in the historical record coincide with events that might prove embarrassing. One such example is Thomas Mann Randolph Jr.'s first election loss, where Jefferson's letters hint at a troubling episode, but Tom's letters from this period— the existence of which are recorded in Jefferson's notes—are missing.

There is also the mysterious case of Jefferson's letter index for the crucial year of 1788—the *only* volume missing from a forty-three-year record of correspondence. Even letters have disappeared to and from Jefferson's daughters during this year, which is when the relationship with Sally Hemings is thought to have begun. Additionally, the very letters most likely to shed light on Sally's pregnancy and whereabouts during the spring of 1790 are gone. All of which, of course, fits a very specific pattern supporting the charge of obfuscation by Jefferson's heirs.

No note to or from Sally has ever been found. That may be because Sally wasn't literate, or because Jefferson never wrote her, or because someone made sure such letters vanished—and if so, that someone was assuredly his daughter Patsy. If Sally Hemings was with child upon her return from France, no evidence of that child remains—which left us to incorporate the contemporary rumors that the child was a boy and named after the president. And the Jefferson family would have had *many* reasons to keep all of this quiet, including a little-known fact that sexual congress between a man and his wife's sister held the taint of incest until the nineteenth century.

As with most works of historical fiction, the most outlandish bits are the true ones. Patsy did, indeed, want to be a nun—an ambition frustrated by her father. Newly released private letters shared with the Thomas Jefferson Foundation reveal that she was also highly sought after by the eligible bachelors of Paris, including the Duke of Dorset who offered a diamond ring. The unsigned love poem we attributed to William Short is real but may have come from any one of her suitors, or possibly one of her convent friends, who, like Marie, expressed utter despair at her departure.

Patsy did give suspicious testimony after the scandal at Bizarre plantation. The colorful characters in that strange case are all drawn from history. The duels and threatened duels are all a matter of public record. Bankhead did beat his wife, Ann, at Monticello. He was set upon by Tom with a fire poker. He did stab Jefferson Randolph and live as a fugitive, even as the family sought to quiet matters, and Patsy mused on ways to let him finish himself off. Harriet and Beverly Hemings were permitted to "run away" from Monticello. Lafayette did, in fact, bow to Patsy Jefferson on that fateful day he escorted the king to Paris. And did also praise her publicly upon his return to America.

Tom tormenting Patsy in her time of grief and instigating grave site drama is a matter of record. And while we cannot know what Jefferson's daughter saw when she came upon her father the night of her mother's death—for she wrote that she dared not describe it—Jefferson's letters reveal that he was suicidal at this time.

Pistols didn't seem a far stretch and dovetailed nicely into the equally strange-but-true encounter he'd later have with a man who'd just blown off his head.

As for Patsy's estrangement from her husband, it's impossible to know whether Tom beat her, but we know that he beat her children. And those same children said that *she* suffered from his sullen moods and angry fancies. It is our belief that his documented behavior fits the pattern of a classic abuser, so we adopted that interpretation and faithfully followed the chronological deterioration of their marriage, stemming largely from financial problems, alcohol, resentments, and possible mental illness.

But we couldn't help but notice that Patsy's daughter Ellen mysteriously blamed the marital trouble—in part—upon Tom's hatred for Patsy's best friends.

William Short might've been one of them.

We confess to a reckless disregard for the almanac and a certain ruthlessness in condensing our heroine's story. Patsy's life was a long and full one, shared with one of the most iconic men of all time, a man who wrote so many letters that we know where he was, and what he was doing, almost every day of his adult life. In fact, some of his biographers required several volumes to tell the tale. Entire books are dedicated to the flight from Monticello and the Paris years alone. And because Patsy's life was so tied up in her father's, it was a challenge to tell her story in the space of a novel.

Extremely painful omissions had to be made. There simply wasn't enough room to explore all the fascinating people in Patsy's life, like the colorful Aunt Marks and the omnipresent Priscilla Hemings. Nor was there space for all the details of Patsy's political and family circumstances, or even all the important contemporary events she witnessed.

Instead we've combined or simplified events for maximum dramatic punch, and the astute reader might notice subtle changes in the time line. For example, Jefferson's famous headache in Paris occurred in September before his departure. However, we posited it slightly earlier, in our desire to consolidate the maelstrom of emotional and revolutionary events in Paris during the summer of 1789. The Merry Affair actually erupted in late 1803, but we moved it to accompany our heroine's documented comeback. The secret trip Jefferson made to Monticello to deal with the Walker scandal coincided with a secret letter he sent to his daughter in 1803, but because the possibility of a duel dragged out for another few years, we portrayed the whole thing at once in 1805.

In short, where a shift in the chronology didn't fundamentally change the choices faced by the people involved, we erred on the side of brevity. And to give the reader a front-row seat, we've sparingly placed our protagonist and other characters where they might not have been. For example, Patsy seems not to have been at her mother's deathbed though she describes the immediate aftermath in great detail. She and her sisters were inoculated from smallpox away from Monticello. And there's no documented evidence of Patsy attending a ball at Versailles. But during her sixteenth year her father described himself as being at Versailles "almost daily" and she was known to have danced with a member of the Polignac family—then in residence at Versailles—so it seemed a reasonable conclusion to draw. Another example is Susan, the slave that we describe as being sold on the block, who actually arranged for her own sale with the help of the Randolphs. However, since it prompted Patsy's embittered rant against the horrors of the auction she never actually described, we thought it proper to shift the date of the sale by a few months. Moreover, where a witness appears to have been in error, such as overseer Bacon's account of how many children Jefferson's wife had, when she held up her fingers on her deathbed, we've simply corrected it.

And what of the villains? Did Charles Bankhead beat his wife to the point it hastened her death? We don't know, but Jefferson feared for his granddaughter and took "for granted that she would fall by his hands." What really happened at Bizarre? Again, we can't know, so we named a culprit that best fit our story.

As for Monticello itself, we made a good-faith attempt to portray the architectural evolution, with occasional diversions, such as painting the dining room chrome yellow slightly earlier than is likely. We were aided in these endeavors by our visits to Monticello, where we were struck by the fact that Patsy is buried not beside her husband, but at her father's feet.

Jefferson is between them in death, as he was in life.

In closing, there is no child, or nation, that is ever born without leaving scars. We have done our best to be forthright and fair about the injustices and hypocrisies of our Founding Fathers. We hope the balance struck is one that furthers understanding and creates more interest.

For a more detailed explanation of our sources, choices, and changes, visit AmericasFirstDaughter.com.

Acknowledgments

O
UR DEEPEST APPRECIATION goes to the skilled and devoted staff at the Thomas Jefferson Foundation, Inc. Tour guides at Monticello were patient with our sometimes outlandish questions, and Tom Nash gave us Patsy's quip about her father and his peas. Monticello historian Christa Dierksheide was particularly generous with her time, expertise, and insights, and not least of all included the suggestion that Ann Bankhead may have "married what she knew."

We'd have been lost without the amazing resources at Monti cello.org and the cache of digitized letters the National Archives makes available at founders.archives.gov.

We'd also like to thank our families for their cheerleading and support. Our thanks, too, to Megan Brett for helping us to research things like judicial wigs, and for retrieving photographs of original letters for us from the University of Virginia. Additionally, we'd like to thank Jean Slattery for buying Stephanie that first Jefferson book all those years ago and inspiring an obsession; our editor, Amanda Bergeron, for being as excited about this story as we were; our agent, Kevan Lyon, for being our lioness on this project; Leslie Carrol for details about prerevolutionary France; and Kate Quinn for critiquing the manuscript.

Our bibliography is too extensive to list here, but we wanted to acknowledge especially our reliance on the letters of Jefferson, his family, friends, colleagues, contemporaries, and biographers in providing period-appropriate language, descriptions, and viewpoints. Additionally, we must cite the authoritative *Martha*

Jefferson Randolph, Daughter of Monticello and *Scandal at Bizarre: Rumor and Reputation in Jefferson's America* by Cynthia Kierner, from whom we adopted many theories and characterizations; also, *The Hemingses of Monticello: An American Family* by Annette Gordon-Reed, by which we were heavily influenced; *Thomas Jefferson: An Intimate Portrait* by Fawn Brodie, whose groundbreaking work helped inspire this book; *Flight from Monticello: Jefferson at War* by Michael Kranish; *Sally Hemings*, the beautiful novel written by Barbara Chase-Riboud, whose iconic portrayal of Sally inspired our own; *Jefferson's Adoptive Son* by George Green Shackelford; *The Diary and Letters of Gouverneur Morris* and *The French Revolution of 1789 as viewed in light of republican institutions* by John Stevens Cabot Abbott, whose descriptions of France and the chronology of the revolution we adopted; *The Plantation Mistress* by Catherine Clinton, whose exploration of the complaints of women on plantations our heroine echoes; *Master of the Mountain: Thomas Jefferson and His Slaves* by Henry Wiencek whose controversial book gave us a much needed counterweight to our heroine's too-cheery assessment of her father; *Twilight at Monticello* by Alan Pell Crawford; the memoirs of Casanova, for inspiring period-appropriate romantic gestures; *The Paris Years of Thomas Jefferson* by William Howard Adams; *The Women Jefferson Loved* by Virginia Scharff; and *Parlor Politics* by Catherine Allgor. More sources and resources can be found at AmericasFirstDaughter.com.

P.S.

Insights,
Interviews
& More...

Meet Stephanie Dray and Laura Kamoie

STEPHANIE DRAY is an award-winning, bestselling, and two time RITA Award–nominated author of historical women's fiction. Her critically acclaimed series about Cleopatra's daughter has been translated into eight different languages and won NJRW's Golden Leaf. As Stephanie Draven, she is a national bestselling author of genre fiction and American-set historical women's fiction. She is a frequent panelist and presenter at national writing conventions and lives near the nation's capital. Before she became a novelist, Stephanie was a lawyer, a game designer, and a teacher. Now she uses the stories of women in history to inspire the young women of today.

LAURA KAMOIE has always been fascinated by the people, stories, and physical presence of the past, which led her to a lifetime of historical and archaeological study and training. She holds a doctoral degree in early American history from the College of William and Mary, has published two nonfiction books on early America, and most recently held the position of Associate Professor of History at the U.S. Naval Academy before transitioning to a full-time career writing genre fiction as Laura Kaye, the *New York Times* bestselling author of more than twenty books. Her debut historical novel, *America's First Daughter*, coauthored with Stephanie Dray, allowed her the exciting opportunity to combine her love of history with her passion for storytelling. Laura lives amid the colonial charm of Annapolis, Maryland, with her husband and two daughters. ᔐ

The Paris Letters
New Details About the Life of Our "Cher Jeffy"

AMERICA'S FIRST DAUGHTER was many years in the making. From the dinner at a writers' conference where we conceived of the idea to the crazy night we stayed up past 3 A.M. outlining the plot, to the many months of research and writing, it was always a labor of love. One that we were proud to finish in July 2015, when we handed in the corrected galleys for this novel and toasted our accomplishment.

As multi-published authors, we both know the sense of relief and pride that comes with finishing a book, but also the sadness at leaving beloved characters and their world behind. In this case, though, we felt confident that we'd uncovered everything that we could about Martha "Patsy" Randolph Jefferson.

So imagine our surprise when, on August 12, 2015, we saw an announcement from the Thomas Jefferson Foundation that a family of descendants had made publicly available a cache of new and previously unknown letters, most of which were addressed to the heroine of this novel during the years in which she lived in Paris.

Our excitement at learning there were, indeed, new things to discover about our heroine was matched only by our anxiety that we might not get the chance to include them in this novel. We knew that we wouldn't have the opportunity to write in entirely new storylines—which Patsy's previously unknown relationship with the Duke of Dorset might have justified because of what it reveals both about our heroine's life choices and the political ramifications of the attention she received, not to mention her father's state of mind. But we hoped that by adding many new details into the existing story—such as our heroine's popularity with the men in Paris, the anonymous love notes she received, her closeness with her convent friends, and the artificial flowers she made to give as gifts— our book would offer the most current study of Martha Jefferson Randolph, including information not revealed in any of her biographies to date.

A particular favorite among the new letters was this one, from Maria Ball to Patsy, dated June 23, 1789: "I make you my compliments Dear Jefferson, as you took the prize. I heard of your party at the Palais Royale with the Duke of Dorset and his two nieces. A gentleman told me he had seen you and that you remained there till it was quite duskish and that the duke seemed to care very much about you, which I am not surprised, my dear Jef. His choice can only honor him and make many, many people jealous."* Letters like this bring Patsy's younger years to life in a way that rarely happens in the eighteenth century, and absolutely enchanted us, especially when we learned that on August 7, 1789, the duke sent Patsy a "simple ring" as a token of his affection after she'd refused to accept a diamond ring—and, possibly, a proposal—he'd given her. In the eighteenth century, a diamond ring need not have signified an intent of marriage, but the context of Patsy's refusal led us to think that she could've been a duchess!

Thankfully, the team at William Morrow was as excited about this development as we were and made special allowances for us to dig through the treasure trove of new letters to bring the heroine of this book even more fully alive. We hope you enjoy reading these details as much as we enjoyed discovering them.

—SD & LK ◠

*Translated here into contemporary English.
To see the original, visit http://tjrs.monticello.org /letter/2052.

Walking in Patsy Jefferson's Footsteps
A Conversation with the Authors

BEFORE UNDERTAKING this project, the authors separately visited Monticello and other historical sites in Virginia and France. However, in writing together, they thought a joint field trip to some of the Virginia settings in *America's First Daughter* was called for. And, oh, the adventure they had.

Laura: There were a couple of reasons I wanted to take this joint field trip to Virginia. First, since I was a girl walking the Antietam Battlefield, I've always felt that past events and people leave a mark on places. To me, a site's past often feels tangibly present. So I wanted to see what Monticello and Tuckahoe *felt* like. As a historian, I've always believed there is a lot to be gained from walking in a historical person's footsteps—learning what you can see from her room or how long it will take to walk between places or how sound travels through a house all give you a deeper understanding that you can't always get from documents, especially for a novel where you want the evocative details. Even more than writing nonfiction, writing fiction requires you to get inside the head and heart of a historical figure, and putting yourself in their physical spaces helps with that in so many unexpected ways. Field trips were always a big part of my teaching, and they certainly inform how I learn about the past, too.

Steph: I agree that if people leave some essence of themselves behind in this world, the work of a historical novelist is to channel it. Trying to understand the good and bad decisions of an important historical figure is an effort to make sense of the present world they bequeathed to us. But trying to get inside that historical figure's *head and heart* is a way of touching the past. Both are exercises in empathy that gave us goosebumps. Especially when walking the same paths that our characters walked. There were many times that our theories were borne out by evidence we found on this field trip. It was important to do it *together* and not just because we enjoy each other's company so much. We'd both been to some of these places before, but the *aha* moments we experienced because we had two sets of eyes on it were amazing.

Laura: Absolutely. One of the most memorable *aha* moments occurred when we were standing outside the black fence around the Jefferson family graveyard at Monticello. Next to Jefferson's tall obelisk monument, I noticed a plaque detailing who was buried in the cemetery and where. And the plat of the burials showed something so surprising that we had a total writerly freak-out as we absorbed all its implications—Patsy isn't buried next to her husband. Instead, Jefferson is buried *between* Patsy and Tom Randolph, and Patsy lays next to her father. If that isn't emblematic of so much about the relationships of these three people, we don't know what is. That moment wouldn't have meant as much if we hadn't been there together.

Steph: Yes, but of course, *because* we were there together, I'm afraid we made a bit of a menace of ourselves at Monticello! While all the other people in our group tour stood gazing admiringly at far more famous relics, we nearly tripped over each other to get a closer look at William Short's green and gold embossed grooming kit, which included, to our delight, a chocolate pot. (No one else seemed to find it nearly as amusing that Short's belongings are on display in the Madison Room, given the animosity between the two men.) Then, after asking a litany of strange questions, we tried to reconstruct ▶

Walking in Patsy Jefferson's Footsteps
(continued)

the violent altercation between Thomas Mann Randolph and Charles Bankhead in the dining room. I'm fairly certain they put a security guard on us after that incident . . . at least until we explained what we were about!

Laura: Oh, William's shaving kit was such a find! And exactly the kind of thing that made the visit to Monticello so valuable. We learned details not often remarked upon or recorded in the documentary record. Like how Patsy's daughters made necklaces out of berries from the stinky chinaberry trees, how small the dining room is despite them somehow fitting in fifty guests during Lafayette's reunion visit, and how Patsy's bedroom overlooked Mulberry Row—which seemed so fitting and even symbolic given both her ambivalence about slavery and tendency to see things about the world that her father preferred to block out.

Steph: Yes, I remember staring out Patsy's window, trying to see with her eyes. And I'm so glad that you brought up Patsy's daughters, because we had another great find involving them. We really got a feel for their personalities in exploring the attic cuddy office that they fashioned for themselves in the eaves behind the dome room. There wasn't a lot of privacy in that noisy house where children shared beds under sloped ceilings on the third floor, and where Jefferson's unending stream of guests made demands on the family below. That Jefferson's granddaughters wanted a place to themselves at the top of the house—even if they had to share it with the wasps—so that they could *study* instead of manage a household tells us a lot about them. And speaking of the top of the house, it was from this vantage point that we first realized just how far Tom Randolph's own secluded study in the North Pavilion was. Patsy put him about as far away from her bedroom as she could get him when their marriage deteriorated, and we thought there was some significance in that.

Laura: We learned a lot about Tom from this trip, too, especially on our visit to Tuckahoe Plantation, the Randolph family seat near Richmond. From the moment we made the *very* long drive up the shadowy tree-lined driveway, Tuckahoe had a dark, heavy feeling that neither of us could shake. It was like *the Randolph* survived there despite the fact that four other families have lived in the house since. And, then, as if Tom was acknowledging our presence, right after we parked, a dust devil whipped up and slammed into the side of the car. We looked at each other and both offered Tom some acknowledgment right back!

Steph: We already knew, of course, that some very unhappy people had lived at Tuckahoe, and that dark and heavy mood was reflected in both the restored black walnut paneling in the house's foyer and the false windows on the brick sides. But nothing illustrated the oddness of Tuckahoe more than the date etched into a pane of glass in what may have once been a sitting room. Our tour guide told us it was part of a family tradition where the Randolph girls would carve into the glass to prove their engagement rings were made of diamond. But there was only one date in the glass— March 16, 1789, the day Tom's mother died. Back outside, Laura was all but scaling the facade to get a decent picture of that pane, because we came up with an alternate explanation pretty much on the spot: It was Nancy Randolph's vindictive departing gesture to Gabriella Harvey.

Laura: That house left such a strong impression on us! And, as if all of that wasn't ▶

Walking in Patsy Jefferson's Footsteps
(continued)

strange enough—the Randolph cemetery lies within a totally enclosed brick wall with no gate or door and not a single Randolph burial is marked with a headstone, only a shared plaque on one of the walls. It's possible the original cemetery was destroyed by natural elements long ago, but it gave us the impression that the Randolphs took no more care of one another in death than they had in life. So in spite of its beauty, Tuckahoe gave us a sad, heavy, troubled feeling that seemed to fit Tom so well—and maybe all the trauma and anger that existed within those walls helps explain the troubles Tom had. Tuckahoe definitely had a "feeling" that informed our writing.

Steph: And the difference at Monticello was noticeable. It's important to remember that Jefferson spent a part of his childhood at Tuckahoe, which must have informed *his* ideas about what a great house should be. Though it sits on a bluff above the James River, Tuckahoe's face is on a flat plain, everything about it exhibiting a bleak, near-militant control over the landscape. And yet, Monticello, by contrast, sits at the top of a mountain, where Jefferson's fields, orchards, and roads are carved gracefully into the slopes, as if he were in a continuous negotiation with nature. From zigzag rooftop gutters that collected water in the cistern, to the fifty-mile view of the countryside, everything about Monticello seems to have sprung from a vision. It was a reminder that Jefferson strove to find a balance between his idealism and his sense of ruthless reality, not just on his plantation but in the vast nation unfolding below it. Sometimes he succeeded in that, and sometimes he didn't.

Laura: Which brings us to one thing both sites had in common: the presence of spaces related to the history of slavery. Tuckahoe has one of the oldest remaining plantation streets in Virginia, complete with slave quarters, kitchen, smokehouse, storehouse, and stable. Archaeologists at Monticello have found the remains of numerous workshops and quarters, which are now marked, interpreted, and in some cases rebuilt for visitors to see. One cannot visit either plantation and forget that enslaved labor made the social life, economy, and business of these places possible. Mulberry Row was the heart of the enslaved community at Monticello. It was where countless boys began their labor in the nailery and where numerous women manufactured cloth in the textile factory. It was where the Hemings family had their cabins, and where Sally Hemings lived and raised her children—Jefferson's children. Just imagining how Sally made her way each day to Jefferson's chambers—either through the private spaces of his greenhouse or past the kitchen, under the south terrace, into the basement, and up the stairs that came to the first floor right outside his rooms—reinforced to us how slavery was both ubiquitous and hidden in plain sight, how some of the people who were most important to not only Patsy's life but to the founding of this nation were hidden.

Steph: Erased even. And I will never forget the particularly emotional tour we took focusing on slavery at Monticello. Our fellow tourists were a mix of all ages and backgrounds. At one point, a nine-year-old African American boy, wearing wire-rim spectacles much like Jefferson's, asked what life would have been like for him if he had been a slave at Monticello. Our tour guide, Tom Nash, did not shy away from the question and his powerful explanation about the injustice ▶

Walking in Patsy Jefferson's Footsteps
(continued)

of slavery prompted a white boy around the same age to ask how a man like Jefferson could have written *all men are created equal* while continuing to own slaves. It was a poignant moment for many reasons, not least of which was the clear demonstration that hundreds of years after the Declaration of Independence was signed, citizens of all ages and from across the country still gather on Jefferson's mountaintop to wrestle with the painful contradictions of our nation's founding. ᔓ

Reading Group Guide

1. If Thomas Jefferson's wife hadn't died, how might he and his daughter have lived different lives? Historically, Jefferson is said to have made a deathbed promise to his wife, and in the novel his daughter makes one as well. How might their lives have differed if they hadn't made those deathbed promises?

2. As portrayed in the novel and in their letters to each other, how would you describe Jefferson and Patsy's relationship with each other? Was Jefferson a good father? Did he change as a father over the course of the novel? Was Patsy a good daughter?

3. Does seeing Jefferson through his daughter's eyes make him more relatable as a Founding Father? How so or why not?

4. The limited choices women had available to them in the Revolutionary era is one theme explored in this book. What were the most important choices Patsy made throughout her life? Do you agree with why she made them? Could or should she have chosen differently?

5. What did you think of Sally's choice to return to Virginia with Jefferson? Why did she make that decision? What were her alternatives and how viable were they?

6. Another theme explored in this book is sacrifice. What does Patsy sacrifice in her effort to protect her father? What did Jefferson sacrifice? What did Sally sacrifice? What did William Short sacrifice?

7. Why does Patsy think her father needs to be protected? Why does she think she is the only one to do it? In what ways does she protect him? What do you think of ▶

Patsy's effort to protect Jefferson? Would you have done the same thing?

8. How are Patsy's views on slavery portrayed in this novel? What factors influence her thinking? How do her views differ from her father's or from William Short's?

9. Why did Patsy decide to marry Thomas Mann Randolph Jr.? How would you describe their relationship and how did their relationship change over time?

10. Why can't or won't Patsy cry? Why does she finally cry in the final scene at Monticello?

11. Do you agree with William that Monticello was "a set of chains"? Why not or how so? Were you on William's or Patsy's side during their fight in the final scene at Monticello?

12. In what ways did Patsy shape her father's legacy? In what ways did she shape our own? In what ways is she America's First Daughter? ⟿

For Further Reading

Fiction

Flight of the Sparrow: A Novel of Early America
    by Amy Belding Brown
Jack Absolute by C. C. Humphreys
The Jefferson Key by Steve Berry
*Jefferson's Sons: A Founding Father's Secret
    Children* by Kimberly Brubaker Bradley
The Midwife's Revolt by Jody Daynard
The President's Daughter by Barbara Chase-
    Riboud
Redcoat by Bernard Cornwell
Sally Hemings by Barbara Chase-Riboud
Thieftaker by D. B. Jackson
The Traitor's Wife by Allison Pataki
Turncoat by Donna Thorlund

Nonfiction

American Slavery, American Freedom
    by Edmund S. Morgan
*The Hemingses of Monticello: An American
    Family* by Annette Gordon-Reed
*Jefferson's Adoptive Son: The Life of
    William Short, 1759–1848*
    by George Green Shackelford
*Jefferson's Secrets: Death and Desire at
    Monticello* by Andrew Burstein
Jeffersonian Legacies by Peter S. Onuf
*Liberty's Daughters: The Revolutionary
    Experience of American Women, 1750–1800*
    by Mary Beth Norton
*Martha Jefferson Randolph, Daughter of
    Monticello: Her Life and Times*
    by Cynthia Kierner
*Master of the Mountain: Thomas Jefferson and
    His Slaves* by Henry Wiencek
The Mind of Thomas Jefferson by Peter S. Onuf
*Parlor Politics: In Which the Ladies of
    Washington Help Build a City and a
    Government* by Catherine Allgor
*Sally Hemings and Thomas Jefferson:
    History, Memory, and Civic Culture*
    by Jan Lewis and Peter S. Onuf ▶

For Further Reading *(continued)*

*Scandal at Bizarre: Rumor and Reputation in
    Jefferson's America* by Cynthia Kierner
*Slavery and the Founders: Race and Liberty in
    the Age of Jefferson* by Paul Finkelman
Thomas Jefferson: An Intimate Portrait
    by Fawn Brodie
*Thomas Jefferson and Sally Hemings:
    An American Controversy*
    by Annette Gordon-Reed
*"Those Who Labor for My Happiness":
    Slavery at Thomas Jefferson's Monticello*
    by Lucia Stanton
*Twilight at Monticello: The Final Years of
    Thomas Jefferson* by Alan Pell Crawford
The Women Jefferson Loved by Virginia Scharff
*Women of the Republic: Intellect and Ideology
    in Revolutionary America*
    by Linda Kerber ∿